A Warrior's Fate

MELISSA KIERAN

A Warrior's Fate
Copyright © 2022 by Melissa Kieran

All rights reserved. No part of this publication may be reproduced or transmitted in any form or by any means, electronic or mechanical, including photocopying, recording, or any information storage or retrieval system, without prior permission in writing from the publisher.

This novel is entirely a work of fiction. The names, characters, and incidents portrayed in it are the work of the author's imagination or used fictitiously. Any resemblance to actual persons, living or dead, events or localities is entirely coincidental.

Cover Design: Cover Dungeon, Franziska Stern
Editing and Proofreading: Let's Get Proofed, Kirsty McQuarrie
Map Design: Etheric Tales

Identifiers
979-8-9865229-2-0 (eBook)
979-8-9865229-0-6 (paperback)
979-8-9865229-1-3 (hardcover)

www.melissakieranauthor.com

To my readers from Inkitt and the TAATW family for being the best community a writer could ask for. I could have never done this without you. Thank you for everything.

CATAEA
THE LAND OF WITCHES

GREAT OCEAN

← TO THE FAE RUINS

WITCH TERRITORY
VALKERIC MOUNTAINS
IO
GANYMEDE
IMPERIAL CITY
BARIT SEA
OBERON
CALLISTO
THE GATE
RHEA
MAVEC
THE WILDS (PHOBOS)
DEIMOS
CHARON
THE WALL OF NIESLE
IAPETUS
MIMAS
TETHYS
MORAI
THE LAND OF WOLVES
SOUTHERN WATERS

A Warrior's Fate

PART I
THE TROUBLE WITH FATE

CHAPTER 1

As Isla listened to the man standing beside her droning on about the natural dangers that lay on the outskirts of their homeland, the only thought running through her mind was how in the world, Goddess forgive her, could she *possibly* have almost let this imbecile become her mate?

One could claim the citizens of their home, the Pack Kingdom of Io, had a superiority complex. Callan, however, took the notion to a whole other level.

The humanoid form of egocentrism had come out of nowhere, butting his way into Isla's conversation with a fellow trainee from the Pack of Tethys. The trainee, whose name she hadn't gotten to, was decently attractive and as their conversation flowed, showed promise of being intriguing as he could talk about things *other* than fighting. And the bonus—besides the fact he'd gazed down at her breasts *just once*—he was also unmated as she was.

Though she may have given up seeking her forever, that did not mean she was opposed to the temporary.

Isla knew Callan's interruption was for no reason other than to make her aware of his presence at this exclusive Hunter's Feast. That and so she could bear witness to his newly acquired mark: a symbol of his recent bond with his chosen mate.

As if that would make her regret ending things with him.

Callan, the master story-stringer, kept the trainee hanging on his every word, discussing Io's "City of Fallen Embers", otherwise known formally as the Imperial City. What was surely one of their continent's most glorious landmarks, the city had taken on the moniker following the momentous volcanic eruption—that Callan was nowhere *near* involved in—centuries ago.

While he continued with his grandstanding, Isla let her narrowed ice-blue eyes scan his features from his coppery hair to his amber eyes and his nose tweaked from battle. Over his lips that had long ago caressed her skin and the stubble that had accompanied it.

When one caught him at the right moment, Callan *was* easy-on-the-eyes, though a little generic and plain, and aside from a few selfish rendezvous, he wasn't too bad when the *season* rolled around. But what he had in mediocre looks and being the occasional decent lover, he destroyed with his undeservedly garish personality.

"May I step in?"

Isla jolted when she felt a hand on the bare skin of her back that was exposed by her low, sweeping, crimson gown. Instinctually, she swung her arm in the assailant's direction before she came to her senses and realized she recognized the voice. She stiffened her limb and dropped it to her side, for this was not the ideal time to be descended upon by the Imperial Guard. Not on the eve of one of the biggest nights of her life.

"I hate when you do that," she muttered, just loud enough for Adrien to hear, and with a glower, she turned to meet the golden-green stare of her longest friend. Whether the bond was formed by default or choice, it was too hard to judge now.

As Callan, to Isla's bliss, fell silent, Adrien took another step, his detectable scent and aura of power no longer masked as an element of surprise. His hands were behind his back as he stood at Isla's side, and though his posture was tall and regal, his grin held a reckless charm.

Callisto, the region where the Gate to the Wilds lay, had a tempered climate. Nothing compared to the heat Io had been experiencing following the recent summer solstice. So, instead of his customary home attire, the Heir donned more modest cloths, crafted richly and finely, cut in a way that made it hard to miss the magnificence of his form beneath the fabric. The sash across the front of his intricately stitched tunic bared the blood-red jewels and gold mined long before his time from the land of the ancient packs. It was the appearance expected of royalty, despite Adrien's occasional indifference to it.

"Goddess…"

Isla spun to find the trainee's eyes blown wider than they had been while tuned into the stories of catastrophic death and molten rock. He nearly snapped his neck, bowing his head to the ground. "Alpha…Heir…Your Imperialness…Highness…sir."

With every fumbled word, any attraction Isla had previously felt to the man dwindled, likely visible in the gradual frowning of her face.

Adrien's eyes flashed with amusement as he nodded in recognition of the paid respect. "At ease."

The trainee lifted his head, still in awe, like a child meeting their hero, though Adrien was not much his senior.

And although he claimed he wasn't always for the grandeur of being at the top of the wolves' hierarchy, being the future *Alpha of all Alphas*, the *King of Kings*, Isla knew the Heir relished the fanfare. His hubris—which typically drove her mad—was enough to quell even the biggest of egos; even one as big as Callan's.

Isla watched, the inside of her cheek between her teeth, as Adrien turned his head slowly and expectantly to the grimacing man beside him. She knew she wasn't the only one amused by this.

Despite lacking a notable bloodline, Callan was a formidable fighter, deemed a warrior through a victory in the Hunt a few years ago, and was a worthy sparring partner for Adrien in their early days, training and learning the strength they possessed as shifters. That was until the alpha-blooded wolf rocketed to his own seemingly limitless potential.

"Warrior," Adrien greeted his former training mate, unable to mask the smug grin on his face.

Callan begrudged a bow of his head, envy laced with defeat in his eyes. "Your Highness."

"I never had a chance to formally extend my congratulations." Adrien, still in the business of being cordial as a leader, gestured to the mark visible on Callan's neck beneath his collar.

Callan stiffened, as did they all, and his eyes flicked briefly to Isla. But it wasn't to gloat. No, it was a cry for help. It was the most unsure she'd seen him in a while, maybe ever.

Would he say just the right "wrong" thing to piss off one of the most powerful wolves in the continent? Would an incorrect slip of his tongue serve as a reminder to his future Alpha of the sacrifice he'd made at his own expense for the she-wolf he'd once loved? That Isla wondered sometimes if Adrien still loved.

The Heir's tribulations of the mate variety had been the hottest pack news and gossip for the past year. Even this gathering was one of the earliest events Adrien had been to since the unbinding and his own personal hell that followed. It was one of the rare times Isla had seen him as of late.

Callan coughed. "Thank you, Your Highness."

There was the smallest downturn of Adrien's lips. A flicker of words that would remain unspoken in his eyes. "Well, may the Goddess bless you both with a bountiful future," he said with sincerity but also a finality in his tone.

And following the words, he turned his attention to Isla.

The air of moroseness was no more as he put his uniform grin back on and cleared his throat, knowing what had to come next. Isla glared at him but having been drilled in etiquette since she was a pup, knew her place. She dipped her head.

Adrien was all too happy about it. "Milady."

Isla wrinkled her nose. What the ever-loving-fuck was that address?

Adrien, with his own look of distaste, spun back to Callan and the trainee. "May I steal her a moment?"

Isla grabbed Adrien's arm with a huff, sick of his act and being amongst this group of males. "Yes, you may."

She could hear her friend chuckling as she dragged him away, likely the only person in the room who'd get away with the manhandling of high royalty.

As the two dove into the depths of the gathering, past the attendees and the bustling staff setting the grand table up in the middle of the room for the feast, Adrien's laughter quieted. "Do I sound like as much of a pompous ass as I think I do?"

Isla dropped his arm. "More so than usual."

Adrien scoffed. "I never want to address you—or anyone—as *Milady* again. I'm burning Winsy's Pack Relations Code Encyclopedia and leaving the ashes in his front yard. I don't need to sound like I have a stick up my ass to be a good Alpha." He veered in a different direction, and Isla followed. "You're welcome, by the way. You looked like you were ready to kill him."

"No, not murder. Maim him, maybe. I'm surprised you both fit in this hall with your giant heads," she jeered, trailing her gaze around the party's patrons. "And speaking of a disproportionate number of inflated egos, where's my brother?"

Adrien left her in suspense as they approached the open bar. He called the tender for a spiced gin while Isla ordered herself a glass of wine before situating himself behind the counter's decorative willow, shielding himself from the eyes of the room.

"I don't think I even need to answer that," he finally said.

Isla retched, regretting the inquiry, very aware of her sibling's lack of self-control and favor with women. "We haven't even eaten yet."

A mischievous look lit up Adrien's face, an innuendo most likely on the tip of his tongue.

"Don't," she chided, leaning back against the bar and looking out at the floor.

There weren't many unmated wolves at this gathering, from what she could see and sense, but enough for a few to pair off, had the desire risen. She wasn't *that* desperate tonight, though it had been quite a while, thanks to training…

"I'm surprised you're not off screwing someone," she said to Adrien. "That waitress seems just your type."

The Heir peered around his plant-formed shelter to follow Isla's gaze to the woman setting up the centerpieces on the table. Long legs, caramel skin, chestnut hair—probably not the best comment for Isla to offer, given how much she looked like Corinne.

Adrien's eyes drew lengths up and down the waitress's lithe body, considering, and thankfully, not frowning. Instead, he settled back in his spot. "If it was easy for me to sneak away, I'd consider it, but my father would rescind my title and probably have my head if I do *anything* off the book to make the Imperial Council question me. Even baseless rumors by pack gossips are enough for Winslow to pop by my house to 'have a chat'."

The last of his words came out mockingly, a perfect impersonation of Io's *Head of Pack Relations* and *Interpack Liaison*. The poor official had been the butt of all their jokes and receiving end of their mischief since they were kids.

Isla sighed. "Have to keep the hierarchy looking polished."

Adrien grunted. "Goddess, help me."

As they lost themselves in another conversation, Adrien giving Isla more crucial tips for finding the safest routes through the Wilds and achieving the fastest kill in the Hunt, the bartender brought over their drinks. They were gone quickly, both realizing they were just about ready for the night to end—or at least blur—before it had truly started.

"I think they've had me placed next to the new Alpha of Deimos," Adrien said after Isla had asked him about the feast's seating arrangements.

"Deimos?" Her voice went high. The kingdom's name was enough to send a shudder down her spine.

She glanced around, the discussion feeling taboo this soon. The next person at the bar was a few feet away, although for wolves, that barely meant inches. But as they weren't mates, it wasn't possible for Isla and Adrien to share thoughts or exchange unspoken communication. Not unless they shifted and conversed as only their wolves could.

Not in the mood to tear up her dress, Isla kept her voice quiet. "He really came?"

Adrien matched her volume. "He is an alpha, and this is the Hunt."

"But his father and brother just died like a month ago. An—and his mother, she…"

"Probably doesn't have much time either. Not that she'd want it."

Horrible. Isla looked towards the ground, reminded of the realities and weaknesses of their kind. Having a soulmate, one's perfect "other half" or as some felt, an extension of themselves was considered one of the greatest gifts from the goddesses. A bond so sacred, so special, and yet—fragile.

It made *them* fragile.

The soul-splitting, crushing pain that came with losing a mate was one Isla never wished upon anyone—or ever wanted to deal with herself. At least, not any time in the near future.

The bartender brought over their next round, and she and Adrien fell silent, mulling over the recent tragedy with alcohol on their tongues.

Isla tried to picture the Alpha of Deimos, the *new* alpha. The boy, or man, who'd just lost everything and gained a throne. She'd never met him before, she realized. She couldn't even remember ever learning his name. All she knew was of his existence; that he was the former alpha's *second* son.

Second.

He was never meant to take control. The *eldest* child inherited alpha.

Isla thought back to all the training, all the lessons, lectures, and talks Adrien had endured in their youth. Goddess, that Adrien continued to endure *now* after they'd grown. Prepped to become the Imperial Alpha since he was a child, so young that he barely knew how to shift. Every move he made, every step he took was down the path of what everyone knew was his future. Or thought it was—because, apparently, Fate was a fickle bitch.

The new Alpha of Deimos likely had none of that.

Isla scoffed. How could it have even happened? People, wolves, they didn't just…die.

"Has your father heard anything about it? Any reports?" she asked Adrien who had his gin to his mouth.

"No." Adrien finished the drink, put his empty glass on the counter, and waved for another in what seemed like one fluid motion. "No one's claiming a kill. No one's come to the Council requesting a challenge. No one's trying to take over that pack. It doesn't make sense."

"So, he's just alpha now? His father and brother die, and he's alpha." Isla couldn't wrap her mind around it either.

"That's the Code. It's a birthright until someone steals it for their own bloodline."

"But it wasn't *his* birthright." Isla echoed her previous thought and chose her next words carefully. A million questions with the same notion bore heavily on her mind. "Do you think he's dangerous?"

"Do I think he's responsible?" Adrien asked plainly, receiving his third glass. Isla's silence was enough of an affirmation. "We don't have the grounds to think so. I hope not." He drained the drink once again and rose with a whispered curse. The Beta of Charon, the pack's second in command, had spotted him and was calling him over.

"Deimos has already had enough to deal with being next to the Wall," he offered, taking a few steps away. "They don't need a family-slaying alpha as their leader, too."

And with those inspiring words, her dear friend was off.

Isla followed his confident stride with a deadpan stare. Maybe Winslow needed to give him some more lectures on sensitivity.

With a purse of her lips, Isla swirled the wine in her glass and settled against the bar. Her mind, the curious spirit and unyielding inquisitor that it was, ran wild with possibilities. Trying to find an answer *no one* had…except maybe the Alpha of Deimos.

Now alone, Isla's gaze swept the room from left to right, scoping the crowd. She spotted the trainee and Callan who'd returned to their state of being complete strangers, but she didn't necessarily want to converse with either of them again. No one really looked interesting enough to talk to.

She definitely needed more companions that weren't Adrien and her brother.

Sighing, she lifted her glass to sip on her wine and let her mind wander. A carnal desire reared its head in her tedium seemingly out of nowhere. Warmth spread through her body, and there was a tugging at her gut. A stirring that made it a bit harder to breathe, impossible to stand still. Like a strange kind of drunkenness. She inspected her wine with furrowed brows.

Though the sense had eventually faded and her mind cleared, she felt the strong urge to just…get away.

Isla set her glass down on the counter with a hollow clank, and against the grain of the party, she traveled away from the congregating bodies until she found a dimly lit, empty hallway with a long stretch of statues and art pieces showcasing Callisto's history and the *three sisters* they worshipped—the Goddess, Fate, and Eternity. The corridor ended at a glass door leading to a terrace. She pushed it open, the old metal of it creaking as it gave way.

Her steps echoed off the platform's stones as she walked out into the tepid night air. The only source of light was the full moon; it was all she needed.

Isla approached the terrace's stone railing and placed her hands on it as she drank in the lunar aura, breathing deeply and absorbing its glow. The *lumerosi* markings etched into the skin of her shoulder throbbed. The intricate swirls and symbols of black ink, bestowed upon her once she'd mastered her shift, took on their signature iridescence as she teetered on the edge of the mundane and mythical. For a moment, she considered ripping off her gown, shifting, and hauling through the trees.

No one would know she was gone, right?

"Beautiful."

Isla's markings flared, her eyes following in their glow as she spun around to face who had snuck up on her.

But then the furious light dwindled to nothing as she froze, disarmed by one of the most striking men she'd ever seen.

CHAPTER 2

When first confronted by something—or someone—she knew nothing about, Isla, historically, was a "claw first, ask questions later" kind of she-wolf. An automatic *fight* in the fight-or-flight dichotomy. The reaction had both saved her life and gotten her in deep trouble in the past. The latter more so than the former.

That called for training and with it, she eventually learned to hold off on the snap actions, and instead, use her senses first to quickly and efficiently run down the mental checklist, evaluate the threat, then strike if needed.

She tried to call upon the teachings now, but the only sense that was working was her sight.

And then…there was also something deeper.

Isla felt a tug at what seemed like the core of her being in a way she'd only experienced once—just a few moments ago at the bar. Was this it? The day she'd once dreamed of and now dreaded?

No. This wasn't quite how that mystical, magical fated attraction felt, at least, in the way she imagined it would from the descriptions she'd heard.

"It's like a light just shines and the heavens open and…"

"It's a…ping!"

"Suddenly, the world just made sense."

"I saw her, and I just knew."

No. This definitely wasn't any of that. That sounded romantic, wistful, and dreamy, even. This was just…carnal.

It consumed her like wildfire, spreading through her branches of veins and torching the hills and valleys of her skin. It budded fantasies like roses, each one unique, but the one most intoxicating was the vision of him reaching for her, pressing her against the banister, and lifting her dress to take her right then and there under the lunar glow. No words. No time for pleasantries.

She blinked as she descended back to some form of reality, trying to figure out, by the Goddess, what had just come over her. Had it really been *that long* since she'd been taken to bed?

"Excuse me?"

"The moon?" The stranger stepped closer, gesturing upwards, and Isla took him in. Handsome. Very handsome. With his dark hair pushed back from his face and his eyes visions of storm clouds, reflecting in the moonlight. "Beautiful."

Her tongue felt heavy as she spared the goddess a glance. "Yes, it is."

The stranger moved forward until he was beside her at the railing and leaned against the stone. He turned to face her. "I'm assuming you're here for the Warrior's Feast? For the Hunt?"

Isla wouldn't bother pointing out his incorrect labeling of the night's gathering. "Yes."

He looked out at the silent forest before them. "Are you from Callisto?"

"No…" Isla breathed, trying to regain her sense. There was no reason to feel flustered. He was just a very attractive man who came upon her on a night when her libido was at a peak. "Io."

The stranger smiled, and even though she didn't know him, the grin seemed out of place on his face.

Her brows furrowed. "What?"

"That was my original assumption," he said, his features shifting into a faint smirk. "Immediately ready to fight at the slightest sound. Probably try to rip my head off with your teeth." He nodded his head to the side. "But then…"

"But…then?"

He glanced up at her again, thunder meeting ice. "Nothing. The whole doe-eyed thing threw me off. My fault, really." He gazed back up at the cloudless sky. "I mesmerized you."

Isla jerked back. "Mesmerized?"

It was a strong word—the right word—but too powerful for her liking. It felt worse *hearing* that she lacked control and composure than just feeling it herself. She hated that she'd been so transparent. And she *despised* that he didn't seem flattered or surprised. Like he knew exactly where her mind had fallen the second she looked at him.

She narrowed her eyes. "You did not *mesmerize* me."

"The pounding of your heart says otherwise," he said.

Isla placed a hand over her chest where the organ was surely thrumming wildly beneath her skin.

Mesmerized.

She bit down on her tongue and folded her arms. "Can I help you with something?"

"I was out here first, you know." He gestured behind them.

Isla followed his movement, turning to take in the actual expanse of the terrace. She'd been so hypnotized by the moon in front of her, she hadn't noticed how much it extended towards the sides with curved staircases matching those in the hall down to green and blue sprouted gardens. She noted the spots a predator could've surely lurked in the shadows.

She glowered into the darkness.

Zero for two tonight in terms of awareness, then.

In the Hunt, distracted could mean as good as dead.

Isla turned back and sized him up. Underneath his black, well-tailored, long coat stitched in intricate patterns of silver, he seemed solidly built, but considering she'd spent the past two years training tirelessly to throw herself into a forest laden with feral beasts, equipped with nothing but her wolf, she probably could've taken him if she wanted to. A hard battle without a doubt, but she'd hold her own.

"Why are you out here?" she asked him.

Her annoyance and attempts at being intimidating seemed to amuse him more than anything. "For the same reason you are, I'm guessing."

"And that is?"

"Looking for something worthwhile amidst the tedium of the night —and I found you."

The words escaped his mouth in a way that made Isla's breath catch, for some reason wooing her into an illusion a bit more innocent than before. Until...

"You win some, you lose some, I suppose."

Back with the patronizing.

"And there's that heart again."

Arrogant prick.

Isla snarled, her lumerosi and eyes glowing as she clenched her fists. The stranger was facing her not even a foot away.

Isla looked up to meet his eyes, still the same hue. She was a decent height, typical for a she-wolf, but he was a considerable amount above her. Breathing became difficult as that feeling returned. The rush, the attraction, the hunger—all more intense than before. She struggled to tear her eyes from his but eventually traced the lines of his face, his neck, along his broad chest and shoulders, down his arms to his hands. She bit down so hard on her cheek that she tasted blood.

All she wanted was for him to *touch her*.

But just as she moved the slightest fraction to put her on the path to her desire, the creaky glass door from inside flew open. The spell dimmed but not dissolved, the two wolves turned in its direction.

And then the intoxication faded to nothing, at least, for Isla because powering towards them was Winslow.

"There you are," the gangly official called, his waving hand high in the air. He was donning Io's classic maroons and golds, his signature notepad—because there was *always* work that needed to be done to sustain the prestige of Io and their continent of Morai—tucked under his arm.

"Yes?" Isla took a step back from the stranger, not one to enjoy involving her family, both by blood and those she considered herself closest to in the pack, in any of her personal affairs.

Winslow dropped his hand. "Oh, Isla, what are you doing out here?"

Isla scrunched her brows. He wasn't looking for her?

Winslow, a man of courtesy until one impeded his objectives, bumped her out of the way and slid an arm behind the stranger's back. "Please, Alpha Kai, the meal's about to begin. We have a seat for you above with the other leaders."

Alpha?

The stranger, Kai—*Alpha* Kai—cleared his throat and nodded, expression flat. He only spared a glance at the bewildered Isla before the two men headed off. She noted the shift in his demeanor. Gone was the cool arrogance, the man who apparently enjoyed pushing her buttons. Now all he felt was…cold.

Kai.

Isla knew the name of every alpha. She felt like she had to—given that her father was the Imperial Beta, Io's second-in-command—but for the life of her, she couldn't recall where Kai belonged.

Going to her failsafe method, she began reciting the packs alphabetically followed by their leaders to the tune of *Will You Find It,* a nursery rhyme her mother would coo to her as a child.

In Callisto, you find Alpha Kane.
And in Charon, Alpha Locke.

In Deimos…in Deimos.

Isla clenched her teeth, troubled and perplexed.

The Alpha of Deimos is dead.

But then it hit her, sharp and fast, like a punch in the gut. With wild eyes, she looked up just in time to catch the two figures crossing over the threshold, letting the door groan behind them.

The Alpha of Deimos *wasn't* dead…he'd just been inches away.

CHAPTER 3

Wedging shaking hands into her tawny hair, Isla paced the terrace.
Alpha...he's an alpha.
She couldn't decide if she was more confused or pissed off—at the alpha or herself.

It had been a few minutes since Winslow had escorted him back inside, and Isla just couldn't get herself to follow. Not yet. She needed to wrap her mind around what had just happened, what she'd done.

Looking past the lust she'd worn like a patch on her sleeve and the abandon of her poise that she prided herself on, Isla had broken so much of the Code, it would make the Elders of past and present roll in their graves. Even if she was from the Imperial Pack and her father was in high standing, she was still rungs below an alpha in the hierarchy. So far down, it surprised her *Alpha Kai* had spared her as much conversation as he had. That he'd tolerated her snapping and attempts at daunting him as much as he did.

In another situation, maybe with a different, quicker-to-enrage, crueler alpha who viewed himself as a god and had no tolerance for disrespect—a dreadfully common variety—she wouldn't still be standing.

But he never said anything, Isla told herself, shaking her head. If he'd said something, she would've acted accordingly.

Adrien and Sebastian would surely get a kick out of this.

Isla—the good one of the trio who was viewed as an official's dream because of the facade she could put on in front of those in the highest of places—trying to intimidate an *alpha*. It was laughable.

Though she'd likely leave out the part where she desperately wanted to jump his bones.

"Whatever," she muttered, though this was far from a moment she'd forget.

Gathering herself, she made her way back to the ballroom. With every step towards its opening, Isla felt the strength of Kai's presence grow. She could *really* sense it now, his power. Alphas had an undeniable aura to them, and she realized she'd only got the faintest taste of it in that bitter moment just before he walked away. He must've been masking it before. But now, amidst his high-ranking peers…

Isla's eyes went to the raised part of the room where the alphas sat with their betas and selected officials. None of them had brought their lunas, the queens instead remained in their territories, ruling their kingdoms. Kai was where she'd expected, where she'd been told, next to Adrien. They were talking about something, and she couldn't help but wonder what it was.

As if he could feel her staring, the Alpha of Deimos peered beyond her friend. The second their eyes met, that fire returned to the pit of her belly. One of Isla's swinging arms paused at her side to take a light hold of her dress, bunching it up in her hand as she came to a standstill. She doused the flames as quickly as she could, looking away, though her cheeks still burned in fury.

This feeling wasn't normal, and her traitorous mind thought the worst.

But no, it couldn't be. It didn't fit the descriptions.

Along with the alphas and their councils, the feast brought together warriors of Hunt's passed. Isla took her assigned seat at the long table across from two of them she knew. Both Alina and Orson were native to different packs, but after reigning victorious in the Hunt and serving their time as warriors, they had taken the current relative peace the packs were having to settle in Io. Not an uncommon practice.

Both had the specialties, wisdom, and experience trainees were nipping to get their hands on, that Isla could use, but she couldn't get herself to focus on their advice for tomorrow's events.

No—because Kai's stare was on her back. She felt it, bearing, *burning* into her. And Goddess be damned if she turned to meet it.

She clenched her fork tighter in her hand.

This cannot *be what's happening.*

Isla snapped her head up from her plate. Someone had to have an answer for her.

"You two are mated, right?" she asked the warriors once they'd trailed off from their topic, respectfully. "Not to each other, obviously."

They both looked at one another, taken aback by the random line of questioning. Alina seemed far more amused than Orson did.

"Yes, we are." She glanced at him in case she'd remembered the fact incorrectly. Unsure of Isla's goal of the query, she lobbied back some small talk. "And you aren't, correct?"

"*No.*" The word fell out of Isla's mouth like the alternative was the worst prospect in the world, which *was* pretty much her opinion on the matter. At least, at this point in her life. But she wasn't going to tell them that and potentially get locked in some debate on whether finding a mate was worth it.

She had to make sure that a few minutes ago, she hadn't.

She cleared her throat and pushed around the vegetables on her plate. "Did you choose or was it a fated deal, if you don't mind me asking?"

Alina narrowed her eyes suspiciously but still donned her entertained smile. "Fated."

"Fate," Orson echoed.

Isla's eyebrows shot up.

It wasn't common to come across one's destined mate. In fact, the increasing rarity had become a concern for some. The continent was so expansive, the packs so large and spread out, unless your mate by some happenstance also lived within your region, unless you had means for consistent travel or attended the events meant to bring unmated wolves together, there was a low chance you'd find each other. Most ended up settling with another wolf of their choosing. Still strong bonds—loyal, loving bonds—but not a connection woven by a deity's hand.

If Isla were being honest, she thought that was the better option of the two—the *choice*—even with the risks and consequences that she'd witnessed firsthand.

She took a bite of food, and it felt like ash in her mouth, then lead in her stomach. "How did you know?"

"You want me to give you the play-by-play?" Orson seemed more tickled now, innuendo in his tone.

"You don't have to get *that* detailed." Isla smiled to mask the queasiness. "I just want to know how you knew. You saw your mates and what? The seas parted, starlight rained from the heavens..."

"I don't know what fairytale you're living in, but Fate's not that innocuous." Orson laughed. "If it's actually her doing, she'll let you know."

"It's like the feeling of *sealing* the bond with your chosen mate, but amplified by a thousand, it's crazy." Alina was beaming and her eyes looked distant, as if reminiscing. "And that's just the initial attraction. Everything else that follows is…intense." The warrior leaned in, half-covering her mouth as she whispered, "And *really* good."

Orson scoffed. "Until it isn't."

Isla could see on his face, reading between the lines, one of the unfortunate aftereffects of a fated attraction.

No one knew for sure how Fate decided who belonged together. Some speculated it was a matter of matched strength. Others, who would bear the best offspring. Others, opposites who would fill in what the other lacked.

The common theme, though, was the lack of autonomy. Most of the time, fated mates were complete strangers who had the decision to either take on life together from the moment they met or reject Fate's wishes and face horrible, hellish pain in her retaliation. That retribution, sometimes, was even fatal.

Most went with option A—*avoiding* the feeling of being torn apart from the inside—and not all of them were in the happiest of relationships.

Isla bit into a piece of steak, chewing slowly. "So, it's a feeling?"

Alina nodded. "And after that, it's all in the touch." She wiggled around her fingers. "Then you're basically locked in. A goner."

"Touch?"

Alina tilted her head. "Your mother never gave you 'the talk' before you turned eighteen, or told you any of this? The feeling, the touch, everything after?"

An acrid taste filled Isla's mouth.

Maybe now wouldn't be the best time for her to mention that her mother had been gone for nearly ten years. Given that she was so young the last time she'd seen her, merely eleven, going through the rundown on what would happen if Isla found her destined mate wasn't really part of the bedtime story repertoire.

"Yes, she did," Isla lied. "Thank you both. I was just curious."

After that, she changed the subject. Back to strategies for the Hunt, how to lure the Wilds' beasts closer to the Gate to make the kill and run back to civilization easier. But once again, as she was counseled, her mind wandered.

She risked a glance up in Kai's direction and saw him talking with some others now, alphas of Ganymede and Rhea. No look at her at all this time.

Maybe he isn't feeling the same thing, she thought, bringing her eyes back down.

Maybe this *was* just extreme lust. He was an alpha, after all, an *unmated* alpha, one could conclude by the absence of a mark on his neck. Exuding sensual grace and drawing in the available she-wolf population was like an unwritten part of the Code.

I'm just overthinking it.

Despite being unpredictable, Fate couldn't be so cruel as to put something like this—something so all-consuming, something so distracting, something she'd been *dreading*—in her path on the night before the biggest moment of her life. The moment she'd dreamed of since she was a child. Forget that if all of it *was* true, if he was her *destined* mate, then that meant the person Fate found to be her perfect other half, that the goddess felt completed her soul, was an alpha.

No.

That wasn't her fate. She was sure of it.

She just needed to get through the rest of the night, avoid Alpha Kai and his temptations, and then tomorrow, she would compete in the Hunt and become a warrior.

That was the extent of her story. No fate. No mates.

It had to be.

∽

As the night wound down and the dinner ended, following an awe-inspiring speech by Imperial Alpha Cassius, the mingling recommenced before everyone was to go their separate ways. Isla found herself up near the platform speaking with a new person of intrigue, a trainee native to Callisto, when she heard, "Isla!"

She spun around to find Winslow standing with a tall, rugged-looking man a little way away with his hand up. Considering what had happened earlier, she pointed to herself and mouthed *"me"*. The liaison, looking unamused, waved her over again.

She excused herself from the trainee and strode up to them, noting how the man's eyes tracked each of her movements.

A sudden tremor rocked her system and she took in a sharp breath. It was as if the room had become smaller, her sense of direction narrowed. A dark cloud hovered overhead.

And all she could sense was the alpha. Only one alpha.

Biting her lip, she turned and spotted him—Kai, standing across the room amidst a group of officials. A look of murder was in his eyes, directed at the man she was walking towards. His stare made her shiver, both in fear of its ferocity and...something else.

It felt like an invisible tether had been cast in her direction, tightening around her and trying to pull her towards him.

Avoid the alpha.

Isla looked away, determined to stick to her plan.

When she reached the men, Winslow made a broad gesture in presentation. "Isla, this is Eli, Beta Sampson's son. He's one of the warrior generals."

Isla smiled and nodded to him in greeting. "It's a pleasure."

She was surprised as Eli bent to her and reached for her hand. Lifting it to his lips, he placed a gentle kiss on her knuckles. The greeting wasn't *that* unusual but felt odd from him. He was soon to be her superior; had he not realized?

"I've heard much about you, Isla of Io," he said, brushing his thumb over her skin.

Isla laughed with the perfect air of lightness and pulled a piece of loose hair behind her ear. "Good things, I hope."

Eli grinned, and Isla caught his not-so-sly once over of her body. He hadn't dropped her hand yet. "The best."

Winslow left their exchange early without a word, apparently having something better to be doing.

As Isla and the general stood alone, she could feel that tether tugging at her harder and harder, squeezing tighter and tighter, the room becoming smaller and smaller. Her senses honed on one thing and one thing only.

The alpha's rage was growing, his essence leaking over and infecting pieces of her she didn't know she had. Like his soul was calling out to her, either intentionally or not.

Mine.

No.

"Come."

Isla snapped her attention back to the general who'd since taken a spot by her side. He wrapped an arm loosely around her back, hooking onto the dip of her waist. "I'll introduce you to some more of the ranks."

At Eli's touch, Isla steeled herself against the pull, the call, the ache of whatever Kai was doing.

"Sure," she answered a bit breathless and wriggled from the general's grasp.

Isla could still feel Kai watching her as they proceeded through the guests. See it, too, when she risked another glance—and maybe a *glare*—his way. Even from his distance, he muddled her mind, her senses. It was intoxicating and downright aggravating. She wanted to yell across the room for him to *stop it*, if only so she could focus on what she was doing. She was with a warrior general. How she acted here with him and whoever he introduced her to would affect her warrior career.

When a phantom pull from him had her stumbling again, she nearly had scaled the room, but she and Eli came to stop before two men Isla vaguely recognized.

"Father," Eli said to one of them. "This is Isla. Isla, this is my father. Beta Sampson of Iapetus."

Isla bowed to the beta, but not as deeply as she did the man beside him, Alpha Locke of Charon. The alpha of one of the eastern coast packs was large and crudely built, donning a rather simple suit but boasting large pieces of jewelry, flaunting his great wealth. It was a thick gold ring on his index finger of the many he wore that caught her eye most, reminding her much of Io.

Isla had learned her lesson and wouldn't make the same mistakes as she had with Kai, so she kept her gaze down and demure as the alpha brought up her father, apparently knowing the Imperial Beta well.

As they spoke, she fought for every scrap of proper etiquette, which at this point meant simply paying attention. Because there was Kai and that call to her. The tightening tether, the building ache, the pure need to be near him.

This. Isn't. Happening.

It was as if she could hear the goddesses laughing at her from above.

Relief washed over her as they bid Alpha Locke and Beta Sampson farewell, but it was short-lived. When Eli's hand brushed her back and his breath caressed her ear as he leaned down to say something, the rush reached a crescendo…Isla half expected it all to suffocate her.

But then her sense of Kai faded…and faded…and faded until it was eventually nothing.

With her breath heavy and feeling like a piece was missing, she spun to search the crowd for the alpha, but he was nowhere in sight.

CHAPTER 4

Avoid the alpha.
This should've been a good thing.

It was much easier to follow a plan when the biggest wrench in it had disappeared. But Isla's curious heart would not rest. As much as she didn't want the answer, she needed confirmation.

She had to know if Fate—that fickle, fickle bitch—had *really* brought her mate to her at the absolute worst possible time.

She had to find Kai, speak to him, and decipher whatever the hell was going on, and then she could move on from there.

"Can you give me a moment?" She stepped back from Eli and jerked her thumb behind her. "Ladies' room."

The general put his hands behind his back, the muscle in his jaw tensing. "Of course."

"Great," Isla said, hoping she hadn't weaseled into the poor graces of her future commander before spinning on her heels and descending into the crowd.

In the middle of the room, she paused and tried to pull on her keener senses. They were much better when she shifted, but her going full wolf in the middle of a dance floor would likely be concerning. So instead, she closed her eyes and sought out that tether again.

Come on, where the hell are you?

She couldn't feel him at all. Of course, when she wanted to.

Isla opened her eyes and weaved her way through the bodies, trying to keep her pace and heartbeat even. This room was full of the most powerful wolves on the continent—influential leaders, fearsome warriors, steadfast guards—if she presented any remote threat, the whole room would erupt in chaos and there would be no hesitation to neutralize her.

But her steady steps transformed into a run as she turned to head down the hallway she'd walked just hours before, her dress billowing behind her. She threw herself against the heavy door to the terrace, the glass rattling and creaking as it flew open, her heels clicking against the patio as she crossed outside. She was keen on the shadows, but the darkness was barren.

"Where are you?" she whispered into the wind through gritted teeth, taking a few more steps along the stones before coming to a stop.

She felt him now.

Isla rushed to the furthest side of the banister and found Kai down below in the gardens, pacing. He'd taken off his coat and left it thrown on one of the stairs. Now he was only in his fitted tunic, sleeves rolled up high to reveal the muscles of his arms, the black ink of tattoos snaking along one of them. She could see him tense, shadows dancing with the moonlight on his amber skin as he ran a hand agitatedly over his hair. Some of the pieces now curled towards his forehead.

She gulped, gathering her gall before calling out to him, "Alpha Kai."

It was the first time she'd said his name. It felt strange coming from her mouth.

Kai didn't answer. Didn't even flinch or look in her direction. Either he'd known she was there from the beginning, gone deaf, or was so lost in his mind that he'd missed it. She moved from her spot and took to the stairs, going down them so quickly that she nearly fell over.

When her feet hit the grass, he glanced at her and then away again. Up at the sky, then forward. There had been a mix of emotions in his eyes—anger and some type of bitterness laced with that coolness that he'd had when they'd first met.

Isla stayed silent, taking him in before she dug herself into a hole. The thought of turning around and forgetting her mission crept into her mind, but she pushed it away. She couldn't hold back. Not anymore.

"What are you doing out here?" A simple start. Easier than just jumping in and blurting, *I think you're my mate.*

She choked on her inhale when Kai stopped and turned to her fully. He was so…focused, his eyes drinking in every drop of her. Like he was stripping her down where she stood.

Isla struggled to temper the spark that his stare ignited, threatening to raise wildfire again.

Before she'd reached the point of impatience to repeat her question, Kai went back to his pacing. His fists clenched at his sides. "If I was in that ballroom for one more second, I was going to lose my mind, kill that general and every man who has so much as looked at you tonight."

Isla felt that throbbing deep at her core again. It was something about the unbridled emotions that fueled a power within him serving as a beacon to her. That forged and reinforced the tether to her soul meant to bring her closer.

Mine.

Maybe.

She was caught between being inexplicably aroused, terrified, and overwhelmed.

Isla hesitated before asking, "So…you feel it, too?"

Kai laughed but it didn't sound happy, more one of disbelief and aggravation. "It's burning me alive."

Isla took that as her confirmation, and it nearly took the wind out of her. He'd experienced the fire, the hunger, the draw. It was mutual. They were…

"So, this is it?" Isla's voice had gone high in surprise, her composure dwindling. "Us. We're…mates? You and me."

It was as if everything made sense, but absolutely nothing at the same time.

Just yesterday, she and the other members of her pack had made the long journey from Io to Callisto. Through the hours of driving—there were too many of them to attempt to fly, and they were too important to risk a tragedy with the newly developed transportation—her mind had danced with visions of the Hunt, the celebrations after her victory, receiving the crescent lumerosi tattoo and her blessing from the Goddess, and her future journeys through the continent with her fellow warriors. She had it all figured out. But now, this man, this *alpha* who had come into her life out of nowhere, could easily destroy all of it.

With one bite, one mark, one laid claim, her mind would be lost and for the rest of time, including tomorrow, she'd be fighting for two lives. Have her own in someone else's hands. A complete *stranger.*

She had to hold back her own laugh at the absurdity of it all. What were the goddesses thinking?

Now, Isla herself began to pace agitated circles on the greenery.

"My mate. I actually found my *destined mate*, and it's an alpha." Isla threw her arms out in exasperation. "You're my mate, and you—you don't even know my *name*, forget knowing *me*, and I know barely anything about you. How—how does this…"

In her peripheral, she realized Kai had stopped moving, so she slowed herself to a halt. She turned to find that same lazy smirk of his that she hadn't been sure if she wanted to slap off his face or kiss earlier. He seemed less annoyed now, but more amused by her franticness.

She was thrilled to provide some entertainment.

"What?" Isla snapped, all rules of proper engagement out the window.

His half-smile became a full-on grin. "You should know your family and pack members speak very highly of you, *Isla*. Especially the Imperial Heir."

Isla blinked, ignoring how hearing her name off his lips sent a shiver down her spine. "You spoke to my family about me?"

"As you said, I don't know you, and I wanted to learn something about the woman who was meant to become my mate," he explained. "They're very proud of you and what you're about to accomplish."

She didn't have the capacity to absorb the inspiring words. "You didn't tell them, did you?"

Kai shook his head.

She let out a sigh of relief, but as she replayed what he'd said, she caught onto the past tense. The woman who *was meant* to become his mate.

Looking from her feet to his, hers then his, it dawned that he was equally keeping his distance as she was.

What the hell?

She'd heard all the stories of alphas who'd laid their claims on their mates, chosen or by fate, without a second thought, bestowing that fateful bite without any consent. A mark that deterred all other wolves and potential suitors because no one would dare challenge them. The chauvinistic action made her want to punch them in the throat.

But still, here she was—and there she had been earlier—right in front of Kai, neck open and exposed, his *legitimate* destiny, yet he made no reach. Not an attempt.

As hypocritical as it may have been, she was pissed.

"Why haven't you done anything yet?" she asked before she could stop herself. "Is that why you didn't tell me you were an alpha when we met? Were you vetting me somehow? I know you don't know me *well*, but…am I not good enough for you or something? Because certainly, *Alpha*, I can assure you—"

Kai had been building up to a chuckle as she went on her rant but eventually cut her off.

"You're going in the Hunt tomorrow," he said. A statement, not a question, but an answer was expected.

"Yes?"

"You want to be a warrior."

"Yes, but what does that—"

"Tell me." Kai took a few steps forward. "How can you be a warrior and a queen?"

The question lingered in the air as Kai began pacing a languid circle around her, arms behind his back. Regal but also almost predatory. The movement was even; he didn't dare inch any closer. His voice was low, and his speech smooth. It reverberated deep into those untapped parts of her being.

"You and I both know the second I touch you, we're not going to make it back to our rooms or even back inside that building. We're going to seal our fate right here on this grass, on those stairs, probably even amongst those orchids—again and again and again—until we don't know where one of us ends and the other begins. And then we're entwined, we're *bound*. No others. No *choices*. You leave your family, become my luna, bound to my pack, to *me*, forever. Is that what you want?"

It took a second for Isla to register his question, her mind drunk on his words, on the picture he'd painted. On the thought of her naked body against his, his lips on every inch of her skin as he ravaged her and had her crying out under the moonlight. It would be more than just mind-blowing sex with a man she barely knew. There would be something else lurking there. A connection, an intensity, a burn so deep and divine despite being completely loveless.

She would never know the wonders of that bond with any other person. Never. *This* was her other half.

She could take him, she naively thought for a moment, blinded by the lust. Maybe after she'd gotten to know him, in time, at his simplest...

But there was no "simple" when it came to an alpha.

He'd said it himself, she would be not only bound to him but bound to his kingdom, his people. She'd have to leave her home and family forever. And she would be a queen.

A *queen*.

She may have had the poise of a lady—under normal circumstances when she *wasn't* confronted by her destined mate the night before she was to face potential death—and the spirit of a warrior, but not the true grace of a luna. She'd seen what the role demanded, and that wasn't even what lurked behind closed doors. She didn't fit the mold. She didn't want to be tied down and confined within walls and strict rules. Not like that.

Kai stopped in her eye-line and stared down at her, still wearing his sly smile. She wondered if he could sense what he'd aroused. "You're allowed to say no."

Isla took a deep breath and shook her head to clear it. Was he giving her an option to reject him? Was that even allowed with an alpha? Or was he rejecting her?

"Why…why give me an option?" she asked, narrowing her eyes in suspicion. "There's a reason we're destined. Having a mate, *me* as your mate will make you a stronger alpha, and your legacy…"

Our legacy…

"Why would I give her *any* satisfaction?"

It took Isla a little while to figure out who he was referring to.

"You're spiting Fate?" She nearly laughed. All of this was some grand scheme against a goddess? "I'm some kind of pawn in your vendetta against a deity?"

Isla regretted her question as Kai's face became dark, his smile faltering.

"She's taken nearly everything from me," he said, venom lacing his words. "And if I have any duty to you as your mate, I'm not going to let her do the same to you. Consider it my gift."

"So, you're rejecting me to save me?"

Kai's grin returned, though more faint. "There's no rejection. There's been no acknowledgment." He put out his hands, presenting, "We're free."

Isla's eyebrows shot up.

If they did not touch, she could not touch them. They were rid of the pain that came with turning away Fate's will. It made sense, in theory.

Kai continued while moving to grab his coat to go back inside, "When this Hunt ends, you will go back to your territory, and I will lead mine."

"And we forget," Isla finished for him despite feeling like there was a punchline here that she was missing. It all felt too easy.

"And we forget," Kai repeated, approaching her again, daring to move so he was only a foot away. "Hopefully, your warrior travels never take you to me in Deimos. I don't know if I'll have as much self-control a second time." His eyes drew long lines over her body as they had earlier. "You should thank that liaison of yours. If it weren't for him, we wouldn't be having this conversation."

Isla squirmed, fighting temptation under his close gaze. "Did he say something?"

"If he hadn't shown up out here when he did," Kai leaned down until he was just inches away as if taunting Fate—and testing Isla's willpower—as he whispered, "you and I weren't making it to dinner."

With that, he turned on a heel to walk back up the stairs to the party. He stopped part way up and spun back around, shoving a hand in his pants pocket. "If I can make one request. A favor."

Isla, who was working to regain her composure, cocked her head to the side. "Yes?"

"Turn in for the night. If I have to watch that general put his hands on you one more time, I may no longer be able to guarantee that I won't kill him."

Isla laughed, a true laugh that had been difficult for her to find lately. Considering whenever that passion of his shone through, she felt the nearly irrepressible urge to jump him; it was easy to heed. "Consider it a gift."

Kai snickered at her mocking and nodded in what was likely a thank you then continued his way up the stairs.

Isla watched him disappear, slightly mesmerized by the way his body moved, while an amalgamation of thoughts ran through her head. Within the span of a few hours, she'd found her destined mate, learned that he was an alpha—an alpha, need she not forget, she'd speculated was a murderer not too much earlier in the night—and conspired with him to work a loophole into a sacred wolf tradition to continue unhindered with their lives.

Maybe they *were* perfect for each other, equally insane enough to believe this would work. They were trying to make Fate their bitch, and Isla couldn't shake the gnawing feeling that the goddess wouldn't go down without a fight.

This was only the beginning.

CHAPTER 5

The Wall of Niesle—named after the Imperial Alpha under whose command it was raised—loomed menacingly above the mass of shifters as they moved along its base. The feat of stone stretched so high that it disappeared into the low-hanging fog, a consequence of the small bout of rain that had ceased just before the group set out to their destination.

Isla lifted her head to it and squinted despite the shadow that cast gray upon her face. Her narrowed eyes took in the barrier's surface, all the crevices and, thankfully, shallow cracks it had gathered over its centuries-old existence. Behind the border lay some of the more horrendous things she'd likely see in her lifetime—beasts known as the embodiment of fear itself. If all held up as it had, she'd never have to face them again but would be ready for another encounter.

Her body tingled with nerves and excitement. This was it. Today was the day.

"You know what to do, right?"

Isla snapped her attention away from the Wall to Adrien who was walking at her side. Sebastian had been on the opposite side at one point—offering his own warrior and big brother guidance—but then bounded off, jabbering something about a bet.

"Stay low," she recited.

"And?"

"Keep it in front of me and go for the legs."

"Good." Adrien's expression was serious, though, still at ease. "They're massive and dumb as shit, but that's what makes them dangerous. They can only think of one thing, and it's killing you. It won't stop fighting until it's dead or you are."

Isla swallowed and looked over at the Wall. She reached out and ran her hand along it, stone dust accumulating on her fingertips and flecks of rubble falling to the earth.

She knew all the details. She'd heard them countless times in the scary stories told to her in her youth and the endless hours of instruction barked in training. But hearing them now, so close to the grand barrier that shielded her people's greatest nightmares, the warnings held new weight.

"Got it."

She dropped her hand back to her side and opened her mouth to add on but was cut off by a heavy thud on her back. It was accompanied by warmth around her shoulders. There was no need for her to turn to know who it was, but she did anyway.

Sebastian had wedged himself between them, his hair, which held a more golden hue than his sister's, a wild mess atop his head. The curls poked at Isla's face as he leaned down to speak lowly between them, bearing most of his weight on her side.

"Alright, Pudge, I really need you to lock in here."

Pudge, a nickname given to her by her *doting* brother during her rounder days as a child. Despite the fact she'd grown since then, slimmed down, and gained muscle from all her training, the name, albeit fitting less and less, still carried through to their older years.

Recalling Sebastian's utterances before he'd gone off earlier, and knowing her sibling all too well, Isla gave him a dead stare. "What did you do?"

Sebastian flashed a snake-oil grin. "I have *a lot* of money on you being second in this thing, so you have to—"

Second?

Isla shrugged him off. "You think I'll be *second*?"

"You think you'll be *first*?" Sebastian scoffed. "And you say *I* 'have a complex'. You're hunting with an alpha."

"So?" Isla snapped, but then she processed.

An alpha?

She assumed Sebastian meant a *future* alpha, an heir. Actual *in-power* alphas never went into the Hunt, save a select few but those had long passed.

It wasn't a requirement to go through the warrior rite to rule a kingdom, though, it did help prove an alpha's strength to his people, which in the end only boosted morale, solidified trust, and instilled just enough fear to never cross them. But the immense dangers of the trial which made a victory so exulted were what made the participation by those in the highest of places avert it.

To compensate, heirs were trained and ran in the Hunt *before* they came to power. Same show of strength, same effect, but with less hierarchical risk. As horrible as it sounded, there could be another offspring waiting in the wings to take the fallen's former place, or there would be enough time for the alpha and luna to produce another.

There hadn't been any talk of an heir in this year's running. Though they typically trained separately, the news would've spread.

"What are you talking about? There are no heirs this year," Isla said.

"No, there isn't," her brother confirmed, then realization took over his face. "No one's told you?"

Isla didn't like how jubilant his features were becoming. "Told me what?"

Sebastian couldn't keep his smile at bay. She wasn't sure if it was a universal trait of siblings, but he found such joy in delivering news that would make her angry. "The new Alpha of Deimos is in the Hunt."

"I'm sorry?" Isla almost stopped moving from the shock. She thought she'd heard him wrong.

"Goddess, help me."

The words were uttered in a breath beside her, and Isla snapped her head, fury in her gaze, from Sebastian to Adrien. The Heir's face was laden with guilt.

"Did you know about this?" she asked.

Adrien hesitated. Not fear but wariness was in his eyes. He knew her wrath well. "He told me yesterday at the dinner. He hadn't told anyone else but my father and his own beta and asked me to keep it in confidence."

Isla resisted the urge to knock Adrien upside the head, Imperial Guard be damned.

"Why didn't you tell me?" she said, even though he'd already stated his case. Her fingers wedged into the tresses of her hair that she'd twisted into a high bun, surely messing it after she'd spent all too much time getting it perfectly smoothed. "I can't believe this."

Participating in the Hunt wasn't just a split-second decision. It required contemplation and planning, approval by the Imperial Alpha. To get anything to his attention took time, even if one was another leader, so this had to have been weeks in the making.

Which meant Kai knew last night when they spoke in the garden that they'd both be descending into the earth-bound hell at the same time.

I'm going to kill him.

"I did it," Adrien offered, pulling Isla from her thoughts with the wrong notion of her upset. "Other alphas have. It's a rite of passage for everyone. If you're second to an alpha, that's still pretty damn—"

"I don't care about being second," Isla breathed, shaking her head and looking towards the ground like it would offer some solace.

I care about staying alive.

She'd finally managed to get the alpha *off* her mind, scrubbed him enough from her senses so that she could think straight. It may have required a late-night shifted run through the woods, and addressing her pent-up frustrations by her own hand when she made it back to her room, but it was done. As she wrapped the customary hunter's cloths around her wrists and ankles and draped herself in the traditional silks when the sun rose that morning, her focus was on herself and her objectives as they were supposed to be and had been before she'd met her mate.

But who knew if her mental fortitude would hold?

When she lifted her head, she realized Adrien and Sebastian were looking on for some elaboration. Not in the mood to divulge, she conjured a lie.

"The Hunt isn't a requirement to be an alpha, and only two *actual* alphas have competed in it. The rest were just heirs, and he doesn't even *have* one of those." Isla found herself becoming increasingly irate as epiphanies hit. "If he dies in there, there's no leader of that pack. His bloodline ends. It's…it's reckless and stupid and—"

"Do I hear Isla questioning an alpha?" Sebastian heckled, maybe saving her from saying something that could be misconstrued as treasonous.

Isla threw him a scowl.

"You care a lot about the Alpha of Deimos," Adrien quipped, though she glared at him too, not forgetting he'd known what was happening without telling her.

"I don't," Isla snipped. "It's just going to be an absolute disaster for the hierarchy if he dies in there."

"Well, alpha was never his to take," Adrien said. "He's proving to everyone that he's worthy of it."

As angry as she was, Isla understood.

Forged and welded with labyrinthine patterns, protected by the wards and blood-runes of witches, the Gate into the Wilds didn't extend as tall as the stone in which it was set. Isla had her eyes fixated on it as she sat alone on the grass, stretching and trying to put herself in the right headspace again.

As the strength of its mystical reinforcements waned with time, it had long been debated whether to remove the passage entirely, bringing down the wrought iron and filling it with rock. But those who proposed the notion had been shot down. Despite the fact it had been centuries since its glory, people still clung to the fact that before the Wilds became the accursed region that it had, it was another kingdom full of their brothers and sisters that had been leveled, destroyed, and hexed by the most powerful witch their world had ever encountered. No other spellcasters from the witches' continent across the ocean had been skilled enough to break it. At least, not the ones willing to do dealings with wolves. Which wasn't many, if *any* of them.

Isla had learned the world hadn't always been so divided. That there was a time when wolves and witches, the dwellers of the night and the sea, and even the immortal fae lived amongst each other through the five regions of the mortal plane. But that history was so ancient, thousands of years in the past, that they barely taught it anymore. All that mattered now was the wolves had settled and flourished on their own continent, and the veil between the four realms—the mortal, immortal, divine, and damned—had been entirely sealed, the fae banished along with it.

As Isla looked away from the Wall, trying to ease her mind of images she'd envisioned of what horror she'd be stalking into, she spotted him.

Kai, walking past in his hunter's silks. Midnight-black—one of Deimos's signature colors.

She scowled.

He was surrounded by a horde of people—councilmen, guards, other warriors, the respected reporters who'd gained entry to cover the revered event. Isla couldn't imagine having so much commotion hovering around her just before she was to look death in the eye.

She continued to watch from afar as the group began to disband. Kai broke off even further with a man she vaguely recognized but couldn't put a name to. The two stopped a good distance away from the crowd, so far that they were almost specks. Maybe the alpha had wanted a break from the craziness.

Isla bit her lip as her annoyance mingled with the presence of opportunity. The Hunt would not begin until sundown, and she knew she could not descend into the Wilds with unspoken grievances on her chest. So, before she could second-guess herself, she jumped to her feet and made the trek over, keeping her steps soft and scent masked. But as she neared them, she slowed and then stopped. The men were locked in a heated discussion. About what exactly, she couldn't tell.

"If this is true then it will require immediate action. I can relay your thoughts to the council while you're behind the Wall for what should be done, or I can devise a plan until you better settle into the position."

"No, this is my call now." Although his back was to her, Isla saw Kai's hand raise to rub his forehead as he let out an aggravated sigh. "Disperse the covert guard into pockets of the city. Have them investigate if the threats are legitimate. I don't want to raise unnecessary alarm. And just in case, put a heightened detail on my mother. If this is really what killed..."

Killed?

Kai had trailed off as the familiar man he was speaking with lifted his hand to silence him as respectfully as one could cut off an alpha. Whatever they were saying, he didn't want Isla to hear. His eyes narrowed as he probably wondered who would be bold—or stupid—enough to linger in their vicinity.

Isla, however, didn't cower. She pulled her shoulders back to exude the confidence—or lunacy—a commoner would need to disturb an alpha in conference.

Noting that they were no longer alone, Kai spun to face who'd intruded. Isla was surprised to see the scowl he was wearing soften. Not to a full smile, but enough to instill her with the smallest amount of irritation and signal her to do what she was about to.

She stepped forward. "Alpha Kai, may I speak with you?"

One would think she'd smacked the older man across the face. He strode up to her, making sure to stand where he blocked Kai from her view. "Alpha Kai is preparing for the Hunt."

His tone held an air of condescension that made her blood boil.

"As am I." Isla gestured down to her own maroon garb. "I'd like to speak with him."

"Many *dames* would like an audience with the alpha. However, the Hunt is not the—"

"I'm not *'some dame'*," Isla sneered.

The man bit back with equal harshness, "Then *who are you*?"

"Isla of Io."

They turned to find Kai, having answered for Isla, advancing towards them, his small smile now a full grin. He met the eyes of his destined mate and co-conspirator against Fate, amusement tangling with her aggression and breeding smugness. "Daughter of Imperial Beta Malakai." He halted a couple of feet away, then glanced at his confidant. "Can we have a minute, Ezekiel?"

The man—Ezekiel—looked stunned. His eyes darted between the two of them before raking over Isla as if sizing her up. He turned to Kai. "With all due respect, Alpha, but Imperial Beta's daughter or not, this isn't—"

"*Beta*," Kai commanded. "We need a few minutes. Relay my message to the council."

With a clench of his jaw, the beta bowed his head. "Yes, Alpha." The words sounded almost out of place in his mouth, seemingly decades Kai's senior. He shot another dagger-filled stare at Isla before leaving, which she reflexively returned.

There was a pensive frown on Kai's face as he saw him off before he scanned the length of the Wall. When he lifted his gaze to follow the overcast clouds in the sky, Isla fought the nagging urge to ask if everything was okay, especially after what she'd overheard. But she knew it wasn't her place, so she refrained.

Though, speaking of *her place*…

"You let me speak to a beta like that?" she seethed, drawing Kai's attention down to her. "I was so out of line; you should've said something!"

"I was distracted," Kai said, his smile returning. "You're very attractive when you're angry."

Isla ran her tongue along her teeth. *Not this shit again.*

She refused to be swayed by the beguilement. "Were you too distracted last night to tell me you'd *also* be in the Hunt?"

"Honestly?" Her glower in return elicited a soft chuckle. "I didn't tell anyone."

"So, I'm just anyone?"

"So we've chosen."

"You don't think I deserved to know?"

"Are you now entitled to all of my secrets?"

"Just the ones that put my life at risk." Isla squeezed her eyes shut and shook her head. "Goddess, I can barely *think* when I'm near you. What's going to happen in there?"

"You seem to be mouthing off pretty well right now."

She looked at him hopelessly. "This isn't a joke."

"I never said that it was." Kai let out a long exhale. "You were dealing with a lot last night; I didn't see a need to add to it."

"You don't know what I can handle," she reminded him. "You don't know me."

Kai folded his arms, and Isla tried to ignore how his muscles looked beneath the silks. "Do you want to back out?"

"What?" The question took her aback. "Of course not. I can't."

"And neither can I," he echoed. "The Wilds are expansive, and the beasts are plenty. You stay on your side of the wood; I'll stay on mine. It'll all be fine." He began to swing and stretch his arms. "I shouldn't be long anyway. I hear there's a wager going around in my favor."

Isla's face went flat.

So, Sebastian's betting was really going around. Only he could make such a hallowed tradition into a gamble.

Indignant to counter his arrogance, Isla crossed her own arms across her chest and lifted her head. "Yes, well, I guess everyone will be in for a surprise when I'm the one who ends up on top."

Kai laughed as he began fixing the wrappings along his forearms. "I've admittedly dreamt of a few situations where that happens," he met her gaze, "and this isn't one of them."

She'd walked straight into that one.

Isla clenched her teeth as she fought away the images his insinuation had conjured. Images that had flashed in *her* mind while she'd been splayed across her bed last night. As much as she'd tried to banish his presence from her fantasies, his touch, though unknown to her, had been the one she craved and the only one her body would submit to, tangible or not.

She'd never tell him it was his phantom fingers digging into her hips and his name that had unintentionally escaped her mouth once she'd finally reached her blissful release.

At the reminder, her body thrummed, and she could tell from the mirth in his eyes that Kai could sense it.

Isla glared, quashing the feelings with a quickness that she impressed herself with. "You have the power of a deity on your side. You're not nearly as charming as you think you are."

With those as her parting words, she turned to walk away, but after a few feet between them, she heard, "Isla."

Isla spun back, expression stone. "Yes?"

Kai's own face was somber. "Be careful out there."

Isla swallowed and nodded as a form of returning the sentiment. She twisted to continue back, but before she moved, she threw over her shoulder, not to be rude but because it was necessary for her survival, "Stay out of my way."

As the sun finally set and the goddesses raised from their slumber, the moment they all had been anticipating was imminent. The hunters said their final goodbyes to those they knew in attendance, and Isla was lucky that the small group of people she was closest to were all able to be with her. Adrien and the Imperial Alpha had been the first to wish her well before seeing off the others.

Isla remained with her father who stood in front of her with his hands on her shoulders. His green eyes, which only Sebastian had inherited, were glassy. That was enough for Isla to clue in on his emotions. The hulking Beta wasn't about to break down in tears in front of his subordinates, even if he was sending his only daughter sailing off into perilous waters.

"Your mother would be so proud of you," he said, voice gruff.

Isla smiled softly, becoming very aware of that hollow place in her heart that had lingered since they'd lost her. She could only imagine how her father felt. All he had now was her, Sebastian, and the unsettling aura of a mate departed.

She placed her hand over his. "I know."

Sebastian came over and slung an arm around her, completing the family union. He gave her a shake. "Come on, big money, Pudge."

Their father eyed him skeptically, to which his eldest child responded with a pseudo-angelic grin.

As the moon reached its peak, the temporary farewells ended, and the hunters lined up facing the Gate. Isla could hear her blood rushing in her ears, her body buzzing as the call came to shift.

Silks billowed to the ground, and the shifters began their transformations all in one motion, the faintest glow of eyes and ink among raising fur, drawn claws, elongating teeth, and bending spines. Isla embraced her tawny wolf in full: feeling its power surging as she molded into an apex predator. Stronger, faster. Her senses heightened. Instincts sharpened.

When Isla turned her head, she found Kai further down the line. He was much bigger than everyone else as expected, and his coat was a shadowy black laced with the blood-red sheen where his lumerosi once lay. That, in combination with the intimidating hue in his eyes, was the true sign of an alpha.

As she looked at him now, gone were her human desires. Instead, there was a sense of solidarity. Not possessiveness, but…protectiveness. Like, even if a terrible fate befell him behind the Wall and her soul and physical body remained intact due to their rebellion, she'd still want to tear apart the world in retribution. She didn't feel lust. She felt a duty. Like she was meant to do right by him in all senses. She wondered if he felt the same.

The sound of clanging metal took Isla out of her contemplations. She followed the noise, turning to find everyone had shifted, except for one. The trainee from Tethys that she'd been talking to at the feast hadn't changed. Under the silks that he'd stripped, he'd worn battle leathers. A warrior brought him a helmet and a sword, and Isla realized to her horror that the man was unable to shift, or at least, unable to complete one. He was one of the few who attempted to go into the Wilds without a wolf.

Most of them never made it out.

A loud howl rung in the air, bellowed from the maw of the Imperial Alpha, who along with Isla's father, had shifted. The Imperial Beta followed it with his own call, and the hunters echoed in response.

With the signal, the Gate's heavy lock was wrenched open, breaking its ward of protection. It took several warriors to pry it open, the metal groaning, almost as a warning not to enter—but this was the Hunt.

And so, the pack of wolves descended into darkness.

CHAPTER 6

The bak were solitary predators—Isla had that in mind as her paws padded along the murky terrain of the Wilds. They did not dwell near the Gate or drift close to the Wall. They resided deep in their forest, blending in with the dead thickets and ever-present fog, their scent shrouded by a pungent vapor that seemed to emit from the ground in wheezes everywhere she turned.

No amount of training, not a single novel-length tale, could've prepared her for what the Hunt was truly made of. Not for the time, the effort, or the sheer force of willpower she'd need just to keep her head on straight. Her senses were so overtaken by the new world around her—besieged by foreign sights and sounds and smells, by the heaviness of the atmosphere and the unfamiliar texture of the earth—that she'd felt blind the second she entered. Like a newborn unable to walk, think, or exist without assistance or guidance, she had to learn if she was to survive.

In time, she adjusted to the sinking earth, dizzying odor, and piercing shrieks of some bird-like creature that taunted her with its incessantness, but how much time, she couldn't tell exactly. Maybe a few days, but it was hard to judge as mornings and nights shared the same absent sky, eternal grayness, driven by the heavy hang of overgrown forest. Or some may have argued, a lingering essence of dark, destructive magic.

Isla didn't know when she'd last seen true sunlight, let alone her family, friends, civilization, or any of her fellow hunters, including her mate. Kai had stayed out of her way as she'd asked, or maybe just by happenstance.

As he'd said in his reassurance before they parted, the Wilds was expansive, and as a result, all the wolves seemed to have spread far across the treacherous wood. She'd been alone with nothing but a lingering sense of doom and her thoughts for Goddess knew how long. And though the beasts were plenty, they weren't the easiest to track, so it seemed the spinning wheel would never end. She'd be cursed to either face the dishonor and shame of returning without a kill or to die here when the ravages of starvation claimed her. There was very little suitable to eat in this region, and much fewer safe sources to drink, and even those, cursed as they were, would eventually kill her if she consumed enough.

But maybe there was hope.

Isla's ears pricked at a rustle in the nearby trees: the first sound that wasn't birds or hissing soil.

This had to be it.

Isla turned in the noise's direction, her adrenaline surging, and crouched with teeth bared in a silent snarl. As she stalked along the forest floor, repeating the mantras of how to deal with the beast quickly and efficiently in her head, she tried to catch a scent. Need this one somehow evade her, she'd, at least, have a better chance to track another. But the odor she caught—though nearly indiscernible, so incredibly faint and mixed with the ground's almost-sulfuric odor—was familiar.

Very familiar.

She rose from her bend, snout high in the air, and sniffed again. Her eyes were wide as she deftly pressed through the decomposing shrubbery, stopping just before reaching a clearing. She had to rein in her excitement as her eyes fell upon a man—but not just any man.

A man with auburn hair beneath a helmet that mirrored his leathers and a face coated with grime. A man with a blade gripped tight in his hand and a look of intensity in his tired chestnut eyes.

The trainee from Tethys. Or just "the Trainee" as she'd now dubbed him.

He fully turned his back to her as he crept forward, his steps heavy yet delicate across the forest floor. His gaze was focused in front of him as his thick boots sunk into the muck.

Isla couldn't decide what emotion to feel—disbelief, elation, confusion. He was alive, that's what mattered. One of the few who'd attempted this tribulation unable to shift completely, and he'd survived this long.

She may have only known him through the pieces she'd gathered at the feast—and she'd have to remember to catch his name—but he suddenly felt like her greatest friend. So, there was a life outside of what felt like eternal damnation.

The Trainee came to a halt in his path, something on the ground seeming to catch his attention. As he bent to it, resting his arm on his knee and stabbing his blade into the dirt to stabilize himself, Isla took the chance to inch closer. She watched as he dipped his fingers into the mud and pulled out a sphere. The orb was coated in dirt and appeared to be rotting from its crater-like edges. He let go of his sword's hilt and tried to clean it with his fingers.

Isla dared move in closer, any sense of a hunting ability gone out the window as she carelessly stirred the foliage.

The Trainee jolted and whooshed around, his eyes bright as he took his sword in his hand. He'd spun directly to Isla's location and lifted the weapon in front of him, firm and ready to strike. "Come out, bastard!"

Isla wasn't sure if it was a sign of her declining mental state that she'd found his threats amusing. She laughed to herself before slipping out of the bushes.

At the sight of her, shock flashed across the Trainee's face, and his grip loosened. He was silent, eyes darting over her wolf's features frantically. She waited on edge for him to say something, eager to finally engage in some form of interaction.

Though she wasn't expecting the first words she'd heard in likely days to be, "Who are you?"

"You don't remember me?" Isla projected with a little levity.

But as he continued to stare at her hard yet blank, she realized the communication wasn't landing. His inability to finish his shift may have been the reason.

Against what some would declare good judgment, Isla, desperate for some camaraderie, called back her wolf. In a dimming of light and pain she was accustomed to, bones straightened, muscles tightened, claws, hair, and teeth retracted until she'd returned to her human form. Her limbs felt weak and wobbly, almost unfamiliar: typical when one remained in a shift for whatever extended length of time that she had.

"Oh, wow." The Trainee twisted his head away from her and looked up into the canopies. "It's you."

So, he did remember *her*.

Taken back by his surprise, fearing something had happened, she glanced down at her bare body. Though slightly worse for wear, covered in filth and some faint, healing scratches from battling through thorny thickets, there wasn't anything horribly alarming.

She gazed back at him, brushing her wild, dirtied blonde hair from her face. "Something wrong?"

"No." The Trainee cleared his throat, eyes daring one more glance before shooting up again. "This, uh, this just isn't how I imagined seeing you naked."

Immediately after the sentence had left his mouth, regret mixed with the redness peeking through the mud on his face.

Isla pursed her lips to hold back too big a grin.

With most of those in Io able to complete their shifts, nudity was inevitable and quite common. Clothing didn't linger after transformations—her own shredded undergarments from beneath her robe probably still sat in the field in front of the Gate, waiting for her to return—so it wasn't a big deal. But for other packs, other wolves, where partial shifts or no shifting at all was most prevalent, that wouldn't be the case. She understood how it could be…startling.

Isla smirked at the man who'd seemed like such a gentleman when they'd met. "You've imagined seeing me naked?"

His response was a garbled mess, an action that quickly reminded her of his fumbling with Adrien during his wonderment at the Heir. Back then, it had dwindled her attraction to him, but now, she found it endearing.

But as much as she would've loved to continue toying with him, they *were* in the middle of a wood full of monsters whose only driving force was to slaughter.

She took a few steps back into the bushes where she'd emerged, hiding everything but her head and shoulders behind them. "Better?"

The Trainee spared another look over, and his shoulders relaxed. "You don't have to—but if you want to, it's really…I didn't mean—" He sure had a knack for getting tongue-tied.

"It's nice to see you, too," she called with a laugh, pausing, for a moment, to tease out any foreign clamor to ensure they were safe before she ushered in a conversation. "Have you crossed any others?"

The Trainee coughed. "No, you're the first I've seen."

"Lucky you." She couldn't resist the teasing again. "And I'm assuming you haven't encountered a beast."

"Not one."

"Neither have I." Another pause. She lifted her head for a quick sniff. No changes; they were still alone. "What were you looking at before I showed up? That thing you pulled out of the ground."

"Oh, the marker?" he said, his features brightening. He paced backwards to pick it up again.

"A what?"

The Trainee held the ball up close to his face and examined it from all angles. "A sign that we have an incredibly long way back to the Gate." Upon Isla's crestfallen look followed by a perplexed stare, he elaborated, "We're on the Ares Pass."

It wasn't nearly explanation enough. "I've never heard of it."

"Because you're not supposed to." He tossed the ball up and down in his hand, proud of himself and eager to share. "It's the only road in the continent directly connecting two packs—or it was. I can't believe we found it."

Elusive roads she wasn't supposed to know about…that was one way to catch her attention. This really wasn't the best time to play inquisitor, but she was drawn in now and all-too enamored with having company.

"I still have no idea what you're talking about," she said.

"Phobos." The Trainee gestured left to right along the decimated ground on which they stood before waving further out into the clearing. "And Deimos. Every pack has its borders heavily guarded, but this pass had no barrier. It could be used freely. A straight shot into Mavec. So, we're beyond Deimos's borders with Callisto and are, at least, far enough to walk right into its royal city if it weren't for the Wall."

At the mention of his pack, Isla couldn't stop her tired mind from traveling to her mate.

She wondered if Kai had already conquered his beast and exited the Wilds. If he was safe. Ready to return to that *royal city*. So she'd heard, Mavec rivaled Io's famed capital in its beauty. If it weren't for many factors—the biggest now being that it was home of the man she intended to avoid for the rest of her life—she would've loved to see it one day.

Isla brought her attention back to the Trainee. The pass seemed innocent enough. "If it's just a road, why can't I know about it?"

"It's not just you. It's something the hierarchy wants buried from everyone."

"Then how do *you* know about it?"

"I read the right books and know the right people," he said before adding lowly, "or the wrong people, depending on who you ask."

Her eyebrows shot up.

She knew the hierarchy had its mysteries, far above her jurisdiction. Many secrets that would never pass her eyes or ears. Although, within an Imperial family, she was entitled to absolutely nothing. But what could this random Trainee—from Tethys of all places—have been privy to that she wasn't?

Seeing she was still lost, he explained, "Back before the decimation, the alphas of Phobos and Deimos were brothers."

"They were?" One bloodline ruling over two separate packs—it was unheard of.

The Trainee nodded. "They secretly made this pass to connect their people and bring their lands together, while *already being* two of the more powerful regions on the continent by themselves. You can imagine how that went over with the reigning Imperial Alpha. A sudden budding empire. *Challengers* to his highest rule."

"Not well?"

"No, definitely not well." The Trainee shifted on his feet, fear and uncertainty flashing across his face for the first time. As if he finally realized what he was doing. The secrets he was divulging. He hesitated, mouth opening and closing. "I—I saw you talking to the new Alpha of Deimos before the Hunt."

Isla stiffened. She hadn't really been covert about it. "Oh."

"I'd be careful if I were you," the Trainee said.

"Why?"

"You're of Io *and* the Imperial Beta's daughter," he said as if it were obvious. "He's the Alpha of Deimos."

"Why does that matter?"

The Trainee went quiet. It felt as if hours had gone by before he finished mulling something over and spoke again. "There's a lot of… darkness in the pasts of Deimos and Io. A lot of bad blood. It runs deep."

Isla found it difficult to swallow as the forest seemed to take on a new eeriness as if responding to his claims. She paused, listening again to make sure they were safe. Not just from bak but from other listening ears.

She'd heard of some disagreements and difficulties between their packs—not much different than any other internal strife—but nothing along the imposing lines of *darkness* and *bad blood*.

"But the decimation and this supposed pass were centuries ago," she argued for her own reassurance. "Surely any deep-rooted animosity has long diminished."

"I'm not so sure about that." The Trainee's voice was low. "Especially after everything that just happened."

Everything that just happened? "You mean with the alpha and heir?"

Rustling in the trees had them both tensing, the Trainee raising his sword and Isla drawing her claws in response. But it was merely a small cursedly-deformed, squirrel-like creature that skittered across the forest floor. It would've been smart to kill it for food, but Isla was still too wrapped in everything the Trainee had shared.

"I should go." The Trainee pocketed the marker and adjusted his hold on his weapon with a sigh.

He was right, but—

"Wait," Isla protested. "You have to explain."

His features fell, and he shook his head as if he regretted telling her all of this at all. "We'll…we can talk when we're out of here." He turned to head off in another direction. "See you on the other side."

Isla huffed, and as she prepared herself to shift again, an idea struck.

She stopped and threw up a hand. "Wait!" The Trainee spun back around, and she waved him over. "Come on, we'll work together and get out of this hell faster."

"I don't need help." His tone took on a sourness, assuming she was offering her aid due to his supposed "incapacities".

How could she explain she was just sick of wandering without company, their conversation had put her even more on edge, and part of her *needed* to make sure he made it out alive?

"I don't doubt it, but nothing says that the Hunt must be done alone as long as we each draw our kill. We're wolves. We work best as a pack."

The Trainee narrowed his eyes, though in good spirit, and moved closer. "I'm going to hold fast in my belief that you aren't patronizing me."

"Wouldn't dream of it." Isla smiled, her eyes glowing as she began to shift.

But then everything was *agony.*

She cried out as daggers swiped at her side, breaking the skin and drawing blood as something sent her soaring across the clearing. Her body thrashed into a tree, head slamming, bones screaming, teeth rattling, and the drying bark splintering beneath her on impact. For a moment, her mind went dark.

"Isla!"

She came to in a heap on the dirt, ears ringing as she slowly peeled open her eyes. Through the slits, her vision cleared enough to find the Trainee across from the most horrifying being she'd ever seen.

The creature seemed as though it was molded from the ground it stood on, murky and dark with what seemed like a shadow-like vapor emanating from its pores. Its sparse hair sprouted from skin taut over thick muscle, so dry that it looked like it could crack open with any movement. Two powerful haunches mirrored solid arms in their size, the beast's two bulky halves hunched at its narrower middle. Its black claws were so long that they dragged in the dirt. So sharp, they could've cut her insides out if it had taken a better shot at her.

But the most unsettling thing about the beast wasn't its ginormous build, its dark aura, or the weapons at its fingertips. It was how, in her gradual return to sense, with its features so akin to one of their own, she'd thought it was just a large wolf. It appeared as if it were someone demonized halfway through a shift.

She couldn't gather how she hadn't even felt it approaching.

The Trainee glanced over at her awakening with a heaved sigh of relief. He swung his sword at the bak as it tried to lunge for him. "Are you o—behind you!"

Isla barely had time to roll out of the way from another massive scythe-like paw heading straight for her neck, the very tip leaving a thin slash on her collarbone.

Her eyes flashed as she got to her knees and met the bright-red glower of a second beast.

CHAPTER 7

It didn't make any sense.
The bak are solitary.
The bak dwell alone.
Isla's heart pounded so hard, she thought it would break straight through her rib cage. So loud that she could barely hear herself think.
Bak are solitary.
Bak dwell alone.
The beast's roar was so powerful that it had her falling back, dirt embedding underneath her fingernails as she braced herself upright.
They are solitary.
They dwell alone.
It flashed its jagged razors for teeth. Not of a wolf, but something more menacing entirely. Crafted expertly to rip to shreds. To devour.
Solitary.
Alone.
It was primed to kill.
Soli—
Wrong. Completely wrong.
But she didn't have time to ponder how implausible it was. She was looking her death in the eye.
Isla rolled behind the tree at her side to cover her through her shift, the painful repetitions of transformation after transformation within minutes proving their worth as she gripped her wolf in seconds. She pushed away the nagging pain of the beast's first attack. She had to. The

moment she came down on all fours, daggers pierced the bark just above her head, inches away from ending her life.

The hit rocketed up the rickety husk, raining a cascade of dead branches. Isla jumped away from them and careened around the timber to meet the beast on the opposite side.

And then she squared herself off against her opponent.

Oh, Goddess...

Even with the larger build of her shifted form, the bak was still, at least, twice her size.

Massive. Dumb as shit.

Isla had to hope that fact still rang true.

Keep it in front of you.

She crouched low to the ground with a snarl, brandishing her own canines and poising herself to strike with the slightest motion.

The bak would move first. She knew it.

She *knew* it.

It had to.

With another ear-shattering roar, the beast hurdled forward.

Isla lurched out of the way, paws sliding in the mud as she twisted to sink her teeth into the nearly impenetrable flesh of its leg. With an acrid taste flooding her mouth, she bit harder and pulled. A gash was left in the wake of her attack. The piece stolen from the horror of a being fell from her maw as blood, black as night, oozed from its injury. The beast reared with a howl.

She shouldn't have celebrated the minor victory.

The creature whipped around, swinging its arm. A yip escaped Isla's mouth at the heavy contact, and a searing pain ricocheted through her spine when she became reacquainted with the tree. Now experiencing its third knock, it came down with a loud crack and a crash. Another close call as it narrowly missed crushing her leg.

She had to think fast.

Hours of training had gone into this moment—days, months, years —all to get this done quickly and efficiently. The longer she fought, the more injuries she sustained, and the more difficult it would become to maintain her greatest asset and defense. In a battle of endurance, the hulking monster would win.

Go for the legs.

She had to undercut it.

Seeing an opportunity and devising a, what could be shoddy, plan, she bounded to the opposite side of the tree and dipped. She hoped her dirtied fur did enough to mask her within the crusted brown entanglements. The monster released a breath through its snout, its eyes darting as it sought her form.

A little closer.

The beast took a few steps forward, slashing its claws over the branches, just missing Isla with yet another hit. She had to move now.

With a silent prayer, Isla vaulted herself out of the thickets and slammed her body into the bak's lower half. As it teetered off-balance, its howl almost a wail, she launched herself at its upper half. They went down with a thud that shook the earth around them.

As she forced her paws into its meaty upper arms, keeping its claws as much at bay as she could, it thrashed. Neck lurching, teeth gnashing; it was rabid. It wanted her face. It wanted her death.

She yelped as it landed a hit, cutting deep into her hind leg. The warmth of blood trickled into her fur, staining the dirty yellow a deep crimson. But she pushed beyond the pain.

It won't stop fighting until you're dead…

Just as it had almost got free from her grip, she slammed her paw to its face and jarred it away. Her teeth sank deep into its thick neck, taking away its howls as she ripped out its throat. Liquid flooded from the space, the darkness bathing the earth.

Or it is.

Isla remained atop the beast until all its fight had gone. Until she saw the light leave its eyes. Until it stared blankly into the abyss it called home.

When that rapturous moment came, she let its bitter flesh drop from her jaws. Her breath came out in pants as she stumbled from her perch.

For a moment, all she could do was stare. And wait. And wait. And wait for that fire to reignite. For the claw to swipe. For that roar to pierce her soul.

But none of it came.

It was dead. It was *really* dead.

She'd done it.

But before she could get too enthusiastic, her adrenaline began its decrescendo and her ailments made themselves well-known. Her body ached, and the gash in her leg hurt like a bitch. She lapped at it, hoping to relieve some of the sting. Time would heal it, but for now, it would be a pain in the ass getting back to the Gate.

The Gate.

She wasn't done yet…and neither was—

Isla whipped around and scoured her surroundings for the Trainee. The woods were silent, and he was nowhere in sight.

No, no, no, she agonized as she trotted forward. Her eyes continued their pursuit, preparing to come upon the worst—the monster hovering over the corpse of her ally. Its face dug into his chest.

Air escaped from her lungs in a whoosh when she saw him.

The Trainee had his sword positioned above his bak's remains, prepared to remove one of its claws. That, along with a tooth, would serve as their proof, and be joined with their hunter's robes in the Warrior Galley of their respective Pack Halls for all to see.

She'd never been so happy to be wrong.

The Trainee had lost his helmet and was cradling his shoulder. Blood leaked between his fingers, and he was favoring his right leg. So, it seemed he'd also sustained his fair share of injuries. This was going to be a nightmare journey for them both.

It had to have all just been an unfortunate coincidence—the two bak—or maybe a gift from the Goddess to allow them both to get through the task together.

Whatever it was, the hard part was over.

The Trainee felt her presence and turned his head. Seeing her snout coated in blood must've been a glorious sight as he beamed and lifted his sword. He let out a howl, not as deep and resounding as an actual wolf, but perfect either way. Isla called back out to him, giving a little lift of her front legs.

As Isla jogged back to her prize, the paranoid part of her brain was half-expecting the beast to be missing. Somewhere upright and ready to attack. Thankfully, that wasn't the case. It was by the fallen tree, right where she'd left it. Very dead and very ready for her to extract her trophies.

But as she dipped her head to its long claw, teeth ready to grab hold, she froze and cocked her head to examine its face.

Its skull was shifted at a different angle than she'd left it. Or maybe not, she wasn't sure. Maybe she was recalling it wrong or hadn't realized she'd hit it as she stumbled off. Maybe there had just been a rumble of the ground.

Cautiously, she tapped a paw against its cheek. Nothing. Still very dead.

Nevertheless, her stomach went watery.

Slowly, Isla retracted back and twisted her head to scan the woods.

Her blood ran cold.

Amongst the trees. Watching her. Waiting…

Red eyes. *Four* of them.

Two bak, side by side. Working together.

They're solitary. Dwell alone.

Isla had no idea what the fuck was happening, but she knew her odds against two of the creatures in her current state. She needed to *run*…and if her instincts were correct, so did the Trainee.

Her next moves went by in a blur as she twisted to the sky and ripped a howl so loud that she hoped to the Goddess that they could hear it in Callisto. Then she was gone, so fast she didn't even know if the bak had started to pursue her.

With the wolfish sense he did have, the Trainee picked up on her call and was already up on his feet. Little did he know, a couple of feet behind him, Isla's suspicions were confirmed. Another set of red eyes.

There were no more coincidences. They were being ambushed. Hunters hunted.

They both darted in a flash, Isla's injured leg hampering her enough to even their speeds. As they powered through the dead forest, hearing the roars and heavy steps of the bak behind them, Isla howled. She howled and howled and howled until she felt dizzy.

Someone had to hear her. Someone had to call back. Someone. Anyone. If they had any hope of getting out of this alive, not only did they need to sprint, they needed any backup they could get.

No response.

Another howl.

Nothing.

The Trainee hissed as he began to lose steam. Decisions had to be made. Quickly.

Isla could let him drop off and keep running, likely saving herself as the bak had their fill. The guilt would gnaw at her stomach until the end of time, but she'd be alive. What an existence.

Or she could turn and fight, hope to the Goddess that she could go three-on-one successfully. The Trainee would get more distance, maybe find some help, and then she'd take off too. If she was still standing.

For the smallest moment, she thought beyond herself, beyond him. The Trainee had a family. No mate, but a mother and father that loved him. A sister who'd just had her own child that he'd told her about at the feast. He was a son, an uncle, a brother, and a friend. He wanted to be a warrior, despite all the odds against him.

And if she had any say, he was going to be.

In a split second, she threw herself into a stop that hurt like hell.

The Trainee noticed and followed suit. "What are you doing? We have to go!"

Isla growled at him in response, and his face fell in shock as he understood. She turned, a snarl ready on her face for the predators to come barging through the brush at any moment.

If Fate let her get through this, she'd do exactly as the goddess pleased. Take Kai as her mate, upend her life, leave her family, move to Deimos, and even become its luna. Locked in a life she never wanted with a man she didn't love. She'd do it all.

Just let us get through this.

She jumped when she felt a presence beside her and turned to find the Trainee standing with his sword at the ready.

There wasn't even time for her to protest. Hell came down upon them quickly.

It was all a melee of teeth and claws and metal. Isla and the Trainee were back to tail, making sure to keep the beasts in front of them until Isla began using the environment to her advantage. She ducked through trees, agilely maneuvered under hits, camouflaged within cracked limbs.

Eventually, she was able to pick one of them off—a smaller, weaker one, miraculously—clamping down on its neck and tearing it apart, but the triumph had taken a toll on her body. She was becoming so exhausted; she wasn't sure she could maintain her shift much longer.

More decisions.

If she went down, this was all for nothing. The two remaining beasts would team up and take the Trainee out in seconds. They'd *both* be dead.

She had to draw them apart. Give him, at least, a small chance.

Making sure she had one of the creature's attention, she mad dashed further into the forest.

Inches, feet, yards—she wasn't sure how far she'd gotten before the beast got her legs out from under her and had her pinned to the ground, hovering over her body, its putrid breath flooding her senses, and its ravenous eyes all she could see.

It was going to devour her right there on the dirt. Leave her a shell or rid her from this world completely. Her heart felt like it had stopped beating in anticipation of its erasure. The will of her wolf faded as her systems felt their collapse.

Isla squeezed her eyes closed as the beast inched closer and lifted its paw. She thanked the Goddess for the life she'd lived and hoped her goodbye would carry on the air to her family.

But the coldness she felt was not death. It was a talon tracing along her ear, over her markings.

It was...toying with her. The beasts weren't known to play with their food.

As a last-ditch effort, she mustered whatever energy she could to break free to no avail. She recoiled as the bak gave one more roar, and then descended. She snapped her eyes closed again.

But then all she felt was air. A rush of air and a lightness as the beast's body was knocked from her.

Isla struggled to get to her paws and then to stay upright as she caught a swipe of crimson-laced shadow attached to the bak's back, dug into its neck. The monster flailed, ramming itself into the trees and through the bushes, anything to free itself before collapsing to the ground.

Then she watched in awe as Kai locked his jaws around the beast's neck again and tore it to ruin. Only when he was sure that the bak was dead, did he look up at Isla. His coat was matted with blood and dirt, she wasn't sure which part of the former was his own. She didn't think she'd ever been—or would ever be—so happy to see him.

"Are you hurt?" he asked, leftover aggression from his battle mingling with the concern in his tone. He ran over and stalked around her, searching, almost reminding Isla of how he'd been in the gardens when they'd made their deal. She'd known his wolf was bigger than hers when they'd been so far away in front of the Gate, but hadn't realized how much.

Isla stood tall. *"Not badly."*

"Isla." Kai stopped in front of her and held her stare. To most, the look of an alpha would've been intimidating, especially when he was in his greatest form, but to Isla, there was only...comfort.

"Our rules apply when we're like this. Don't get too close," she told him before something dawned on her. She turned and darted through the woods, saying, *"We need to get back and help him!"*

"Isla! Fucking hell, you're hurt!" Kai sprinted after her and easily caught up. *"Who are you talking about?"*

Isla willed through her injuries and pushed harder. *"The hunter from Tethys."*

"The one who can't shift? He's alive?"

"I really hope so."

When the two wolves arrived at the most recent battleground where Isla's second dead bak lay, the Trainee was nowhere to be found.

Kai bent and sniffed the carcass. *"This was your kill?"*

"Yes," Isla answered, trying to ignore the panic gripping her heart. He wasn't dead. He *couldn't* be dead.

She closed her eyes and focused on her senses, then heard it. The faintest sound of metal slicing through the air. As she took off again, Kai grumbled behind her. When she finally came upon the Trainee in another clearing, she nearly went faint. He wasn't just trying to fend off one bak, but two.

What the hell was happening?

Kai was equally stunned. *"There's two of them?"*

You have no idea, Isla thought to herself while trying to determine her next move of attack.

But before she could even move a step, the Trainee's eyes fell upon her. His face lit up, even amidst the battle, but his features dropped when his gaze shifted to Kai. Shock overtook him at the sight of the alpha. It stilled him just for the smallest moment.

And that time was all the bak needed to take him in its jaws.

The Trainee let out a blood-curdling scream as razors buried deep into his flesh. But it didn't deliver a final blow. It didn't kill him. It clamped down on the Trainee tighter and ran away, leaving the second with nothing to do but turn to its new prey.

Isla's eyes darted around the woods, going through her options as quickly as her mind could still function.

"Get him!" she called to Kai as she advanced a few steps towards the approaching beast. Kai was faster. He could catch them. *"Go help him! I have this!"*

But then Isla saw it in the second she risked a glance. It was obvious in Kai's glower and the menace of his snarl at the creature that was viewing *her* as its next meal.

Fate had snaked her way in. She'd intercepted their communication; instead, relaying her own whisper. A reminder of a promise never made, and thus one to never be broken. Of where their loyalties lay.

Kai made his decision in a few heartbeats, lunging for the beast in front of her and unleashing hell upon the creature who dare threaten his mate.

Isla didn't stay to hear its pathetic wails as it was torn to bits. The second she was free, she took off in the direction the Trainee had been taken.

She ran as hard as she could, joints groaning, paws aching as she treaded the earth at a speed she'd never known herself capable of, even uninjured. Blood was running along the soil, a mix of the Trainee's and the beast who'd apprehended him.

He still had his sword in his hand. There was a chance.

But then she heard a piercing howl. Loud and pained. Then that tug, that pull. That sense of duty.

Kai.

Her mate needed her.

Isla slowed to a stop as she looked between her two paths. If it were any other person, any other alpha, she wouldn't have paused. She would've had faith that Kai could hold his own. That it was just an unfortunate strike from which he would recover. But he—

Isla let out a cry as daggers sank into her side.

And then everything was cold.

CHAPTER 8

Cold and dark—everything was cold and dark and numb. Isla felt disconnected, detached like she was floating. On air. On nothing. Between it all, the world went by in flashes.
"This looks bad."
"Is she even still alive?"
"I hope so."
"Tell the alpha we found her."
Cold.
"What do we do with her?"
"Get her back...pick her up. Move quick but be careful of her arm."
Kai?
Dark.
"How much further to the Gate?"
"Almost there—how is she?"
"It's getting harder to sense her heartbeat."
"Move faster."
Numb.
"Oh, bless the Goddess, more are back! Wait—"
"Someone call the Imperial Beta!"
"Is she alive?"
"Isla...Isla!"
Disconnected.

It felt like someone had gone at Isla's body with a sledgehammer. Like she'd been broken apart, shattered, and put back together piece by piece but the wrong way. Everything was heavy. Her head, her legs, her arms.

Her *arm*. Goddess, her arm hurt.

Isla's eyelids, like all else, felt like lead as she peeled them open. A light overhead greeted her promptly, piercingly bright and making her wince. Her mouth felt like sandpaper. She groaned, a dull ache rising in her chest.

Where the hell was she?

This wasn't the Wilds. It couldn't have been.

The scent of sulfur, though lingering, had diminished. Breathing felt too easy—so much so that she had to check herself to keep from gasping down too much of the fresher air. And the earth didn't sink beneath her feet.

Actually, her feet weren't on the ground at all.

She chanced another glance upwards, squinting against the glare.

White—everything above was white, but she wasn't dead. Death shouldn't have felt like this. Heavy and painful.

Isla turned her head sluggishly to the side, only able to process bare minimum information; the observable details.

No, she wasn't dead but was in a room as monochrome as the ceiling. The walls, similar to the rest of the area, were barren, save one dull gray-cast portrait of what looked to be a lake. There was a single cabinet and a sink, both white. And then, what held her attention the longest, a window, the panes painted an eggshell that seemed to overlook miles and miles of forest. But she was sick of seeing trees, even if these ones were teeming with life. She was more evoked by the sunlight spilling through the glass, casting sunflower beams across the plain tile floor.

This *definitely* wasn't the Wilds.

Isla drew her eyes over the ivory gown she donned, following the cloth down to her blanket-covered legs and then over to something that startled her.

She wasn't alone. A man was at her bedside, sitting in one of the few items of some vibrancy. The cobalt chair was pulled up against the mattress, enough so that he was able to rest his forearms and head beside her. His face was turned away, but Isla could recognize his silhouette from anywhere.

Dragging over a shaky hand, she whacked Adrien across the head, maybe a little retribution for the multiple times he'd pissed her off recently. The hit was frustratingly weak, barely enough to displace his dark tresses. She followed it with a hoarse and painful, "Hey."

Thankfully, it didn't take much to jostle the Heir.

Adrien snapped up, though still half-asleep. Lids narrow, he let out a grumble and stretched as if he'd forgotten this wasn't his bed back in the grand estates of Io, and just...wherever they were.

As he scanned the subdued décor for an assailant, he skipped directly over her still frame.

"Good morning."

At the rasp, Adrien's gaze darted over, his eyes wide as if he were seeing a ghost. "Holy shit, you're awake!"

Isla cringed at the volume.

"Not so loud. Goddess," she chided, but the corners of her mouth still slid up.

"How do you feel?" Adrien didn't miss a beat in his urgency.

How did she feel...what a loaded question. Though in every sense, she could sum it up the same way. "Like hell."

"You look it."

Isla snorted, bringing about more nagging pain with the jolt of her ribs. "Asshole."

His intentions were not lost, judging by his smile, and she welcomed the small sense of normalcy. She wanted—needed—to relish in whatever ignorant bliss she could.

With every moment her eyes were open, every second she spent back in the realm of consciousness, her sense of reality rematerialized.

The trauma of all she'd encountered was hanging over, looming like a dark cloud ready to rain down psychological hell, but she kept the memories locked behind her own personal gate. And as their beastly forms fought hard to break free, all she could do was try to detach herself. Pretend that those experiences in her mind had been conjured by her imagination after hearing some horror story.

It wasn't *her* who'd spent days within a nightmare, in an unending state of terror. Not her who'd stared her death in the face, not once but twice. Not her who'd felt the empty pit of imminent oblivion. Not her who'd heard the screams of a man before he—

"Where are we?" Isla asked, jarring herself from the thoughts. The demons continued their fight.

Adrien leaned back and adjusted to sit comfortably in his seat. "One of Callisto's infirmaries."

It had been an unnecessary question. Besides being obvious from her observations, it was where the Hunt always led. It was rare that those who entered left the Wilds unscathed. While some hunters only needed a quick look over after they'd emerged—with injuries that would heal quickly on their own—others required a little intervention, a push in the recovery direction.

Be careful of her arm.

Isla suddenly became very aware of her left side, her arm in particular. The heaviness, the ache so persistent she'd adjusted to its existence. She found it wrapped in a plethora of bandages, propped up and immobilized at her side. When she tried to wrench it from its holding, a twinge of pain rocketed through to her fingers.

"Shit," she muttered. "What happened?"

"The bak did a number on you. We weren't sure if they'd be able to save it, but you're healing now." Adrien didn't bother going into the gory details, and Isla was fine with it. In hindsight, she was thankful she'd blacked out.

Gritting her teeth, never one to enjoy being tied down—physically and, arguably, emotionally—she repeated the action, trying to free herself from the platform. She knew her body would protest again as she bit her cheek to keep from whimpering.

"They said it would be a slower process than usual."

"I don't do slow." Most of the time, she found using her body helped it heal faster, or at least, that was the excuse she fed to those who tried to make her rest when she was injured. "How are the others?"

Adrien sighed, knowing that any protest he'd make would fall on deaf ears. "A few are pretty bad, but they'll make it. Everyone else is good."

A few are pretty bad.

A loud breath, a mixture of agony and relief, fell from her lips when she was finally able to get herself loose, though it rapidly devolved into shallow pants of worry. It was a type of deep, soul-squeezing unease she'd only experienced once before, and it was when she'd heard Kai's pained howl before everything went dark.

"The alpha was with me." She brought her arm back to her side and turned to Adrien. "Did he make it out? Is he okay? Is he hurt?"

Adrien's eyebrows raised, a hint of surprise at her distress. "He's fine. He'll heal quickly. If he wanted to prove his strength in there, he did, and then some. He took down four bak, more than his brother ever did…and he saved your life."

He spoke delicately as if trying to ease her into the reminder of what could've been.

Isla's mind flashed to Kai, standing before her covered in the blood of the beast who'd drawn hers, concern lacing his words, his hard gaze a bestower of comfort. There were so many questions that she'd wanted to ask him in that moment—how he'd found her, why he hadn't howled back if he'd heard her call—but they got lost in the subsequent chaos.

The chaos...

"Is the Hunt over?" She ran her tongue over her chapped lips before biting one until she tasted iron. In her heart, she knew the answer she was about to get was one she dreaded.

"There're two others that haven't come out yet, but you know the protocol. There's still time." Adrien's voice remained quiet, like he knew exactly why she was asking.

Even if she'd been prepared for it, the confirmation felt like a punch in the gut. "A bak took the man from Tethys."

"I know, but no one's seen his body. There's a chance."

"No."

Isla squeezed her eyes closed, clenching her teeth so hard that she thought they'd shatter. There was no more blissful illusion. The images, the sounds, the atmosphere—they all came down in a torrent. She felt the phantom tinge of the sulfuric air on her tongue. The uneven mud beneath her feet. Smelled the bak's breath as it descended to end her life. Heard the Trainee's screams. The loop of it all was relentless.

She heard Adrien shift in his chair and then felt his hand on hers. "Hey."

Her gaze was hopeless as she turned to her friend, squeezing back with whatever strength she had. "Do you still feel like you're in there?"

"The nightmares stopped after a few weeks, but everyone's different."

A few weeks. She could handle a few weeks.

"Pudge!"

The two wolves jumped back from each other and snapped their heads towards the doorway where the third member of their trio strode into the room with open arms. If Isla really needed a distraction from the darkness, Sebastian was surely the epitome of one.

"Have I ever told you how much I love you?" her brother asked, leaning against the pearly cabinet and folding his arms. His smile stretched as wide as his face. "My favorite baby sister."

"I'm your only sister," she replied plainly, with her own small but tired grin. "Why are you so happy?"

"You came in second," he bellowed as if it were obvious. Upon the flat look he received from his compatriot, he added, "And you're awake."

Isla's jaw went slack. "I was second? How?"

There was no way she was in any early position out of that forest. It had been too much time, and she hadn't even gotten out on her own accord.

"You killed two bak, the alpha killed four, everyone else only got one of those suckers. You were one of the last ones out, sure—and barely, you know, alive—but they ranked you second." He adjusted the collar of his coat. "And I just made a thousand bucks."

She couldn't hold in her laugh, both in disbelief at the fact she'd *accomplished* all she'd wanted and the fact that her sibling somehow always got his way.

"You have no shame."

"What's the point of being a brother if you can't profit off your sister being a badass? And I'm not a monster, it'll go straight towards your gift after you get your lumerosi."

"Your generosity knows no bounds," she deadpanned, but it was hard to keep a straight face.

New lumerosi, her ranking putting her in a prime position to be considered to lead a team in the coming years—it was all exactly as she hoped and envisioned. Although there was a small twinge of guilt in her heart, she tried to focus on the elation. "Where's Dad? Does he know?"

"Emergency meeting in Callisto's Hall—Imperial Alpha, the other alphas. They're trying to figure out if we should really be worried about whatever the hell happened out there."

The light dimmed from Isla's face. "Emergency meeting?" She turned to Adrien. "Aren't you usually there for things like that?"

Adrien shrugged. "I didn't have to, and I wanted to make sure you were okay. I'll get briefed on it later anyway." Isla gave him a look. "And then, of course, I'll tell you."

She grinned as a "thank you" but did not refrain from a narrow of her eyes, a reminder that she hadn't forgotten him keeping Kai's secret from her.

Sebastian paced over to look out the window, his eyes squinted as if searching for something. "Could those bastards really be evolving to be smart enough to work together?"

Isla bit the inside of her cheek. There were more issues than the fact they'd ambushed in groups, that they'd gotten within feet of each other without first battling over who would get the chance to have her as a meal. Their killer instinct wasn't just reserved for intruders—at least, it hadn't been.

"It didn't kill me." Isla swallowed, trying to dispel the detail without the barrage of mental baggage. "Two times I should've been dead, yet I'm here. It took its time. It...taunted me." She heard Adrien move, ready to jump up, wary she was about to fall down a rabbit hole. She almost had but steeled herself. "It didn't make sense, and it still doesn't."

Her words hung thick in the air, even for Sebastian who didn't have an immediate quip. They all went quiet, mulling it over. It bubbled into a tension that they typically didn't find themselves in. A tension that was soon broken by a figure crossing the threshold into the room.

Isla didn't even need to look to know who it was. She hadn't expected her body's reaction to be so...intense.

Kai was dressed in plain dark clothes with bandages peeking out beneath the neckline of his shirt. When Isla met his eyes, she was washed by an overwhelming sense of ease, comfort, and peace. Like she had been in the Wilds but amplified ten-thousand times. He didn't send her pulse skyrocketing, he didn't make her catch her breath, didn't send her burning with desire this time—at least, not in a lustful way. She just wanted him close. Not ravaging her body, but caring for it, for her.

"Hi." The word fell from her mouth simply before she cleared her throat, recalling their company. "Alpha."

"Hi." Kai looked between the three of them, making sure to lower his head to Adrien who just edged him out in the hierarchy. "I heard you were awake; I thought I'd come check on you."

There was a flash of perplexity on the boys' faces, likely wondering how he knew she'd awoken and why he'd gone through the trouble to come see her in the first place. Even with the act of heroism, there was no other *known* attachment between them. Most alphas would take the glory and disappear to continue with their leader duties, not visit the common girl they'd rescued.

"I'll be departing for Mavec in the morning," Kai added, feeding Isla's understanding of why he'd visited and not so much theirs, "so, I wanted to see how you were doing before I left."

So, this was it. The last time they'd speak. She tried to ignore the small pit forming in her stomach.

"I'm okay. Recovering." Isla winced as she held up her arm for proof. "Thank you." There was no need for the clarification that her gratitude was two-fold.

Kai nodded in response. "Good to hear." He looked between the boys before meeting Isla's eyes again. She wished she could decipher the words in his. "I'll leave you to it, then."

"You can stay if you want to," she blurted as he turned to leave.

The boys looked at her like she'd lost it. Maybe she had. But if no one was going to call out her apparent discourtesy, she was just going to roll with it.

She gestured between Kai and Adrien before pointing to Sebastian. "I know you two have met, but this is—"

"Sebastian of Io, older brother of Warrior Princess," Sebastian cut her off, so it seemed, mercifully. Likely in his eyes, if she was delusional enough to think the alpha required a familial introduction, who knew what else could come out of her mouth. He stepped forward to grab Kai's forearm in the traditional warrior greeting. "We met at the feast."

Isla's face curdled at the nickname, and she hated that it brought a lightness to Kai's eye.

"The man with the wager." The alpha chuckled before glancing her way with a knowing smirk. So, it seemed, that her "on top" was still just a vision of their fantasies.

Thankfully, no one understood the unspoken communication. Judging by how the boys had reacted to her relationship with Callan long ago, Kai would've been in for quite the treatment that his title may not have been able to negate—whether they'd capitulated their bond or not.

Sebastian beamed. "Both of you earned me some good money. A couple of bak-killing machines."

"We're a good team," Kai said, glancing at her again.

Isla let out an exasperated breath as she felt the beginning of butterflies in her stomach. Seeing him so natural with her family made those naive, simple thoughts crop up again.

"Thanks for saving Pudge, by the way," Sebastian added on, snapping her from her delusions.

"Pudge?"

Isla groaned, tossing a glare at her brother. "Please ignore him."

"Is the meeting over?" Adrien asked, sitting up in his chair, breaking his observational silence.

Kai's eyebrows furrowed. "What meeting?"

"The one in the Pack Hall about the Wilds?" Adrien's equally confused look also reflected on Sebastian and Isla's faces. "All of the alphas still here should've been invited."

The muscle of Kai's jaw lined his cheek as he looked off to the side, his rising agitation palpable. When he turned his head, he said, overly dignified as if to maintain his composure, "Excuse me."

And then he left the room.

The three members of Io all looked between each other awkwardly before Sebastian pointed to where the alpha had just disappeared. "Who told him you were awake?"

Knowing that divulging he'd probably sensed it would be a dead giveaway, Isla settled back in her bed, working hard to adjust to the annoying and bizarre feeling of "lacking" while smothering the fluttering that persisted in her stomach. She snickered. "Maybe he heard *you* screaming."

∼

By the afternoon, Isla found herself very alone.

Both Adrien and Sebastian had been beckoned to other obligations; her father was still locked in his meeting. There were nurses and healers' apprentices that had made their rounds occasionally but other than that, Isla had been solitary with her dour thoughts. She couldn't even get herself to sleep. Every time she closed her eyes, all she felt was suffocated by the atmosphere, by the ghost of a bak hovering above, by the inescapable screams of the Trainee. So, she just lay there, awake and staring at the ceiling, conjuring up anything to distract herself.

At first, it had been Kai and those damn butterflies, but then her mind meandered to Fate. And from there, her anger festered. She wasn't supposed to get out of bed until the physician came around to approve it, but she needed to move.

After fighting to her feet, she had to give her body a second to catch up. The unsteadiness after a long time in a shift was nothing compared to this. Something felt so…disconnected. Still, she gathered her bearings, hoping she wasn't too weak to mask her scent, and was off. To where, she wasn't sure.

The hallways of the infirmary were relatively deserted as she traveled them. Every empty room she passed was as barren in its décor and vacancy as hers had been. Occasionally, she'd spot someone or hear footsteps, forcing her to dip into one to evade discovery.

Typically, she didn't know the person or wouldn't bother turning to see who the stride belonged to, but this time, she had. It made her jerk in surprise. She hadn't been sure who she'd end up crossing paths with, but it definitely wasn't the Beta of Deimos.

Isla watched as he powered down the corridor, his heavy steps echoing. He stopped at a door that led to a stairwell, glancing around before pulling it open. Isla's eyebrow arched; there was a seed of distrust in her heart. She gnawed on her lip as she pondered whether the next move she wanted to make was as dumb as it sounded.

She did it anyway.

When she broke into the stairwell after carefully prying its entrance, she heard the slamming of a door reverberate from the floor above. The cavern air was frigid as she scaled the steps, her patters a soft chorus. Every so often, she'd stop in case he doubled back, but he never did. Upon reaching the next landing, she peered into the entryway's small window. The hall was pitch-black, abandoned.

Isla sucked in a deep breath before tugging on the handle, pulling slowly and controlled to lessen its groaning. The chilled air persisted when she closed it softly behind her. For a moment, her breathing hampered, the darkness taking her deep into her remembrances. Her pulse skyrocketed, the sudden panic brewing into something so unbearable that she almost turned around.

But then came the voices.

She turned her head and noted the smallest glow of light at the end of the corridor. Feeling an unearthly draw, she braced herself and went to it. As she neared, the voices increased in volume, enough to figure out to whom they belonged.

One of them was the Beta of Deimos's, and the other was Kai's.

Isla froze, their tones taking on new aggression. As she had in the fields before crossing through the Gate, she picked up pieces of their conversation. They were talking about the meeting. Something about the beta going in Kai's place while he recovered. Something the alpha *hadn't* agreed to.

In a lull, which she figured was a signal the exchange was coming to an end, Isla turned to dart away. But then—

"You're aware that trust is an alpha's biggest strength, that belief in their leader is what holds a pack together…you risked your life to save that girl."

Isla's steps ceased.

The last words had left the beta's mouth with such malice. Even though there were very, very few people he could be alluding to, she refused to believe he was speaking about her.

"I'm not going through this with you again, Ezekiel. I wasn't going to leave her in there to die." There was a coldness in Kai's tone she'd never heard before; it chilled her more than the air.

It was as if Ezekiel hadn't heard him. "Not only did you jeopardize your own hide, but the hierarchy within Deimos, the bloodline of your forefathers. And for what? A woman insolent and dim-witted enough to—"

"Watch your tongue," Kai growled.

Isla glared, even though the beta couldn't see it. Her un-bandaged hand clenched into a fist at her side. Protocols be damned if she had him face to face.

"*Who is* she?"

"Just someone I met at the dinner."

"And yet she was bold enough to approach you without invitation? In your graces enough for you to allow her to?"

Kai was silent.

"Need I stress how your personal affairs are no longer your own."

A pause. More silence.

"You are not just one of the alpha's sons anymore. The former antics of a second-born prince are over. They *cannot* happen." The beta's words were pointed, sharp. "Any dame you bring to your bed is one your people will cast as a future luna, the bearer of their next leader, a bloodline entangled and buried deep in our soil for the rest of time. It goes without saying the questions that would arise, the unrest that would ensue if rumblings emerged that a potential queen was not only of Io but the daughter of its *Beta*."

Isla wasn't sure which part of his spiel had made her more furious—his casting of her as some hapless girl sleeping with the alpha or his notion that it would be so abhorrent because of who she was.

There was another hesitation, but then came a shallow gasp. Isla could've sworn she heard a mumbled *no* before Kai answered, "She's nothing to me."

Upon his reassurance, said so absolute, she had to remind herself that it had been their deal. No one could know about their bond, as they'd decided. It was *their* choice to save her future. To allow her to do as she wanted, to become a warrior and not be trapped in the life of a queen. But Ezekiel was Kai's beta, his second-in-command besides whoever became his luna. *That* bond was also considered sacred, in a different kind of way. It required trust, honesty, and understanding. The function of a pack depended on it.

It hadn't been lost on her that Kai never refuted his beta's claims. No protest to the questions, the unrest, the threat to his stance as a leader if he dared take her as his mate. It was as if he understood the implications all along…and was actively avoiding them.

If one thought logically and pitted them together, who was *really* getting the truth from the alpha's mouth—the woman he'd known for just over a week whose only tie was something beyond their comprehension or his highest-honored officer with whom he entrusted his pack?

"It's imperative you keep it that way," Ezekiel said, his words terse. "It can't happen." He spoke as if he knew, as if he'd figured it all out.

Kai's response was low. "I've handled it."

CHAPTER 9

Isla had been holding her breath for so long, she could feel a singe in her cheeks, so hard that she could hear her blood rush in her ears, so strained that her pounding heart rattled her entire body.

But it wasn't because of shock. No—she'd surpassed that emotion a while ago. Now, it was rage: pure unadulterated rage, and she feared the furious sound would give away her location. Though, she didn't care for the consequences of being caught eavesdropping. She was more concerned with those which would occur if she were unable to hold back her desire to tear the alpha apart the second he met her gaze.

She felt like the floor had dropped out from under her, that the past week had been a ruse.

"You leave your family, become my luna, bound to my pack, to me forever. Is that what you want?"

What complete and utter bullshit.

None of this had been about what *she* wanted. None of this was about doing "right by her". None of this was a rebellion against Fate for all the goddess had taken from him.

"There's a lot of...darkness in the pasts of Deimos and Io. A lot of bad blood. It runs deep."

Bastard. Bastard. *Bastard.*

Kai had to have known all along what was likely to occur if their bond came to fruition—a luna born of Io by his side at the head of his beloved Deimos. He knew how horribly it would be received, how much doubt it would cast on him. When he'd met her that night on the terrace, figured out who she was and where she hailed from, he'd laid out his plan, smooth-talked her right into the palm of his hand, and played her like a fiddle. She ate it all up—the chivalry, the notion that she had any say in what was going on, the delusion that he was different from any other alpha who took what they wanted without abandon and dispelled what they didn't just as carelessly.

She almost wished she'd still been the girl she'd renounced years ago. The one who attended those sometimes overly pretentious and sometimes hideously sleazy events, clinging to hope in her heart that she'd find her mate. The one who almost settled for Callan. The one who'd say yes to anything, do everything—even things she wasn't proud of—so she could feel valued, noticed. Who would've jumped at the chance for a change, to move on to a new life, even if it meant leaving her family and her pack behind.

Then it wouldn't have been so easy for him. He'd *have* to reject her and go through hell.

"You've been in my life for a long time, Ezekiel." At Kai's voice, even Isla's bandaged fingers managed to curl in her fury. "And I've left you as beta to aid me in this transition for that reason and out of respect for my father, but this is your last warning. Don't go behind my back to go beyond my authority again." There was the echo of footsteps and his voice darkened, becoming so quiet that Isla nearly couldn't detect it. "And this is the last time you speak of her to me or anyone else, are we clear?"

His secret. She was to remain his dirty little secret.

Isla didn't linger to hear if anything else was said, if the beta had agreed to negate her existence for the rest of time. She was out of that shadowy hall and down the stairwell before she even needed to gulp air in a gasp. Her mind was buzzing as she powered through the lower floor's corridors with no qualms about who she crossed as she stormed her previous path.

"She's nothing to me."

Said with conviction. The words rattled in her brain, leveling her, taunting her with all she'd been blinded to.

"I've handled it."

Handled.

She wasn't something that needed to be *"handled"*, not some bother or nuisance in his life to be cast aside. She was supposed to be his mate, for the love of the Goddess, and even if she didn't want him, he, at least, owed her the damn respect to let her know the whole truth about what was going on, how *he* really felt.

That son of a bitch.

A dull ache pervaded her body, her muscles, her bones, and was completely welcomed. The frustration was manifesting into a familiar burn in her belly, calling deep into one of its greatest releases. She needed to break out from the confines of these walls, the confines of her forsaken bond, the horrible images that still dwelled in the back of her subconscious. She needed power, certitude. The one thing, if nothing else, that she had complete knowledge and control over.

But as she called upon that piece of her, not wanting to fully shift, but to feel just a brush, a reassuring touch of her gifts, the only response was pain. Searing, consuming pain that took the air from her lungs and had her stumbling. The wall became her savior as she braced herself against it, breath grating along her throat as she tried to even it out.

That certainly wasn't the splintering sensation of a shift that she'd grown accustomed to.

She crawled her hands up the cold structure until she was ramrod straight against it, then she remained there, clammy palms sticking to the plaster, clutching onto nothing until she found some relief. Her eyes darted around the hallway as if the answer lingered amongst its emptiness, but before she could reason it out, a figure appeared at the end of it.

"Isla?"

The voice rang in her fog, and she shook her head to jolt herself back to reality. As she blinked at the man who'd approached, the vaguest sense of who he was in her head, his eyebrows drew in concern.

"What?" It fell from her mouth in a breath.

"Are you…okay?"

She swallowed. Saying yes felt like a complete lie as it seemed there was *no* right answer. She couldn't remember the last time she'd felt so… off. Still, she nodded slowly and continued training her gaze over the man's face. He was so familiar, yet her mind kept sputtering.

"Who are you?" she asked before wincing. "Sorry, that was rude."

The man smiled, flashing crooked teeth with understanding in his eyes. "I get it—long week." He reached a hand to her. "Declan of Rhea."

Isla's body was so tense that she was surprised she didn't snap when she mirrored his action, stretching her arm to grasp his hand. But there was a stutter in her movement when he extended beyond her palm, instead, grabbing her forearm—a warrior's greeting.

Finally, something clicked. His face had floated around the feast. It had been down the line that beheld the Gate.

"You were in the Hunt." She returned his tempered squeeze with one of her own, thankful to have, at least, one of the many burdens off her mind. Judging by the fact he was here and offering the gesture, she'd take it he was successful in his endeavor. "Congratulations."

Declan beamed as he nodded in thanks. "You as well. Two bak and second-best in the run to an alpha: that's impressive. Though, I shouldn't expect any less from Io."

Isla returned the grin, though, a sourness lingered behind it that she hoped he couldn't detect.

Yes, the reminder of her accomplishment was wonderful, *needed* as a small reprieve from the chaos in her mind, as a reminder that all of this —the physical and the mental strife—had been worth it. But one little thing, one tiny string of words tarnished the statement.

Yes, Isla was of Io. Her entire life had been spent in those metallic, gold-covered streets shrouded in its rich, deep reds and warm colors. Watching the famed sunsets and sunrises from craggy hilltops. Training with some of the best fighters on the continent. But if she had to hear one more person speak beyond who *she* was, relegating her existence, her accomplishments, dismissing her due to the pack she happened to be a member of, she'd scream. For now, she thanked him.

"It's nice to see you upright," Declan said as the two pulled away. "You were in pretty bad shape when I carried you out."

"*You* carried me out?" Her mouth was so dry that she could barely swallow.

There was another reason she'd recognized Declan. His voice. It had been one plaguing her waking nightmares, taunting her as she hovered just above sleep.

"Is she even still alive?"

"After we found you in that house, we weren't sure what to do with you. You were pretty messed up," Declan said.

"A house?"

That hadn't been where Isla remembered being before she'd blacked out. She'd heard stories of how figurative ghosts lingered from a life once lived among the Wilds—the foundations of old cottages, the rotting fabric of old robes, the rusted metal of children's toys—but she never crossed any of it herself. Something she was grateful to be free from the haunting memory of.

"I think that's what it was before…you know." Declan shook his hands as if casting a spell. "A roof and four walls. Decrepit, creepy. You were left on the floor of it, unshifted, and…" He looked her over as she stood completely whole and shook his head. "We thought you were dead."

"We?"

"Me and another hunter. Alpha's orders to track you down."

At the mention of Kai, Isla's fingers twitched at her sides. Anger boiled. First, at him, but then at herself. For the fact that, just for a moment, she thought he'd actually cared.

"I wasn't going to leave her in there to die."

A courtesy. It was just a courtesy.

"No offense to the alpha," Declan began, "but we thought he'd lost it. He was facing a bak, and there was no guarantee you were even alive. But if we jumped in to help him, I'm afraid both him *and* the beast would've turned on us." His eyes scanned her again before throwing out a light-hearted, "I don't know what makes you so special."

Isla resisted a roll of her eyes.

There wasn't much, apparently.

Before she could draw a conclusion herself, Declan offered, "Imperial Beta's daughter, maybe Deimos is planning to make a run for resources or something."

"Yeah, that must be it," she said, battling to keep impassive.

Imperial Beta's daughter could join *from* or *of Io* in the list of phrases she didn't want to hear in her vicinity for at least a month.

"You weren't the only one in there either."

Her irritation subsided quickly. "I wasn't?"

"It's hard to scent anything in those woods, but there was blood in that house, fresh blood and definitely not yours." Declan went quiet before he pulled something from his back pocket. "And then there was this."

Isla's breath caught as she rubbed at her eyes to make sure she wasn't seeing things.

Lopsidedly perched on its decayed edges in the palm of Declan's hand was the marker from the Ares Pass.

"Where was that?" Desperation leaked into Isla's voice, and she struggled to keep her optimism at bay. So she'd learned, not everything was as it seemed, and the possibility that this shoddy ball of wood presented was so grand, so miraculous, it seemed too good for it to be Fate's will.

"On the floor next to you." Declan brought the sphere up to his face. He examined it as the Trainee had, though indifferent, clearly not realizing what he was holding. Not only a hope that their comrade may still be *alive* if the room had been barren of armor or weapons—something bak, unless all had gone mad, surely didn't consume—but a relic from one of the hierarchy's greatest secrets.

A new kind of unease gripped Isla's heart as she cast quick looks around to confirm the hall was still deserted. She wondered if anybody else would know what the marker was if they saw it. If anyone else knew the "right" or "wrong" people as the Trainee had.

"It's some old kids' toy or something," Declan said. "I was thinking it would be a good souvenir that wasn't scraps of bark or dead leaves, but the longer I have it, the creepier it gets." He grimaced, scratching hard at the surface. "For all I know, that hag's curse carries on in it. Maybe I should go slip it back through the Gate."

Isla jumped forward. "Wait, no, I'll keep it."

Declan's eyebrows knitted together. "What?"

She had to rein in her enthusiasm or else he may have thought it was something of value. Which it probably was, but he didn't need to know that.

"If you don't want it, I'll keep it." She shrugged, playing aloof.

"After I just said it might be cursed?"

"I like to live on the edge."

Declan peered between her—subtly jutting out her bottom lip in the slightest pout—and the sphere in his hand considerably before outstretching it. "If you start bleeding from your eyes or grow a second head, no blaming me. I'm not dealing with the Imperial Guard."

Isla took the ball from his hand, not even bothering to tell him her falling victim to a curse was the last thing the guard would ever be dispersed for.

She was startled by the amount of weight it had to it, how the worn edges didn't feel like the wear of curse-induced decay, just of served purpose. She wondered how it had looked back then as it lined the Ares Pass, who the people were who traveled by it. Just holding it felt like she was breaking so many rules, like she was ransacking the vaults of Io's Pack Hall, poring through the hidden archives.

"Declan, right?"

Isla stiffened and spun, hiding the marker behind her back as she pressed herself against the wall again.

She'd been so entranced that she hadn't even noticed Declan straightening as someone approached, hadn't heard the intruder's footsteps, hadn't sensed his presence around her. She didn't think it was possible for anger to come on so quickly, not in the rush that it had.

Kai stood tall over them both. Meanwhile, Ezekiel watched like a hawk a few feet away. His eyes were narrowed on his alpha's every movement, on hers, like he was searching for their connection, testing Kai's insistence of her nothingness to him, his handling it. Isla held back her glare, biting her tongue to keep from saying everything she wanted to. Every disrespectful curse that floated in her mind.

She needed to get away from here, from him, or be unable to guarantee she wouldn't cause a scene.

Isla squeezed the marker tighter in her hand, trying to envelop it entirely with her fingers, shielding it from view. Would they know what it was if they saw it? The pass had once gone straight through to their royal city. Did Deimos still have remnants of that former life or had that been wiped, too?

Isla remained tall as Kai's gaze flickered to her. His eyes weren't cold, not how she'd pictured them looking while he spoke of her to Ezekiel. It was the same dance of emotions she was accustomed to, the ones she'd spent time trying to break down to have some idea of what was going on in his head. But those days were over.

"Alpha," she said, face flat. No inflection, no emotion, mirroring it in her voice.

One of Kai's eyebrows went up, thrown off by her disposition.

Good.

"Warrior."

The address didn't fill her with any of the mirth that it would have if from another's lips.

"If you'll excuse me." Isla pushed herself off the wall, maneuvering so the marker would remain hidden.

She could feel Kai's stare on her back as she walked away, every fiber of her being trying to get her to turn and go back to him. But she fought it; harder than she would've wished she needed to.

It was time for the plan they'd laid out. The Hunt was over.

Kai was going back to lead Deimos.

She was going back to Io.

And though she was beginning to fear it impossible, they would forget.

CHAPTER 10

Isla needed alcohol. *A lot* of alcohol.
    Or sex. A lot of sex would work, too.
    From her spot atop the infirmary's roof with her skin kissed by the moonlight that slipped through the cast of clouds and the plume of smoke sent up by the glowing bonfire down below, she trained her eyes across the Wall stretched long behind the treetops in the distance. She now understood why newly minted warriors spent so much time in bars and what were essentially glorified brothels throughout the Imperial City upon their return home from the Hunt. Lulling one's brain to rest with booze or distracting it with physical pleasures seemed like it would be the only way to turn off the thoughts and memories of that horrid other world that lurked behind the Wall.
    She had yet to try either distraction, but no other diversions had yielded any success. Not talking with friends or family, not endless pacing, not reading, not card games. But she wasn't about to ask someone to smuggle her in a bottle of wine or find a stranger to drag into a supply closet for an escape, she had more class than that—she'd wait for the drinking and a casual tryst until she got back to Io—but with her discharge not until noon tomorrow, she needed something to leech some comfort.
    And that's when she sought out the moon.
    She sighed as she let the lunar glow work its magic, allowing its aura to seep deep into her pores. Beneath it, she finally felt some sense of empowerment. Her lumerosi thrummed along her body, but their iridescence was faint. It had to be related to her difficulty shifting

which, according to the healer—more practiced in the natural and spiritual and keen on her wolf's side—would take a while to come back. She'd had a brush with death, and as *Adrien* had relayed, the all-around healing would be a slow process.

That news, along with her lingering displeasure from having to see Kai and his beta again, almost had her flipping the bed. Thankfully, as a positive, she could get some of the wraps taken off her hand and forearm, and due to her self-approved escapade not resulting in any deterioration, she was free to move where she pleased as long as she stayed on the premises.

The roof counted, at least, in her mind.

So, with the marker in her pocket, she trekked up the several flights of stairs alone and broke into the chilled night air, greeted by the moon, the soothing hum of wind, a chorus of prattling insects nearby, and the faint smell of woodsmoke. She found her perfect corner, close to some shadows where she could look on at the people surrounding the fire at a distance and the trees while keeping herself hidden along the railing. And then she just closed her eyes and tried to relax.

To move on. To forget. Just for a second.

"Beautiful."

Or not.

Isla huffed at the voice. She didn't need to turn to know who it was. She didn't need to ask how he'd found her. Instead, she remained silent and glowered up at the night sky.

Of course, parting with Kai couldn't have been easy. Not a simple "excuse me" and walk away. Fate liked games. She had a sense of humor. She liked spinning stories, and what better way to have theirs end than the way it began, underneath the radiance of her sister.

Beautiful.

The word had been said in a chuckle, a soft rumbling laugh that stirred a few passion-driven emotions inside Isla despite herself. One of them, a derivative of what she'd felt when they'd first met, would be *far more* enjoyable for Kai than the other. But the more potent of the two was her rage.

Still quiet, she brought her hand to the rail.

"What, no smartass remark?" Kai taunted good-naturedly, taking a few steps closer until she could see the outline of him in her periphery. He kept to the shadows. "I'll admit, the brooding is nearly as arousing as the anger, but you silent is also quite unnerving."

So, he was really going to take this act of his to the end.

"What do you want me to say?" Her tone was even, but the rest of her body betrayed her, nostrils flaring and grip tightening ever so slightly.

Kai wasn't blind to the actions but apparently blind to the reasons for them. "It's nice you got those wrappings off," he said, softer than his earlier heckling. "Are you feeling okay? Does it still hurt?"

Isla's lips twitched downwards, but she wasn't sure for what. Anger? Sadness? He sounded like he actually cared.

She could continue her attempt to act cold—something she doubted she could keep up much longer—and hope he'd get bored and disappear, or she could do what she *really* wanted.

"I heard what you said about me to your beta."

Even just saying it felt like a weight off her chest. She had refused to turn and look at him as she spoke.

"When I introduced you at the Gate?" Kai asked, understandably confused.

"No."

The word hung heavy, and the air went still. No whir of wind. No distant crackling of fire. Even the chittering bugs seemed to fall mute.

It didn't take very long for Kai to put the pieces together. "You—" He stopped himself, apparently finding no need to waste his breath finishing a question. No need to ask how she'd heard or even berate her for the eavesdropping. That was all trivial at this point.

Instead, he sighed and began in a way one would to a friend—or lover—they'd done wrong, "Isla…"

"*No*," she repeated, this time sharp, dagger-like. "Don't *Isla* me. You don't get to *Isla* me."

"How…" Now Kai went quiet as if picking over his words carefully. "How much did you hear?"

"Enough."

Another hush followed her snapped response. Amidst the silence, Kai's long and careful deliberation, Isla fought to keep her temper in check. She'd let him know how pissed off she was, but she wouldn't let him take her poise.

"I'm trying to protect you."

"Protect me?"

Isla whipped her head around, her breath catching slightly at the sight of him. But she buried that feeling of connection deep down, hid it away in some corner of herself to shrivel and rot.

Her fingers constricted around the railing until the metal pulled the skin of her palms taut. Until it burned. Until it hurt. "None of this has been about 'protecting me'. Just yourself and your stupid title and bloodline. What you told Ezekiel is the truth, right? You can't have me —no, you don't *want me*—as your mate because if I became your luna, it would be a disaster."

"I didn't say that." A technicality.

"I must've missed you disagree." She scoffed. "*Questions, unrest...* how unstable is your pack if I could screw it up so easily just by *existing*?"

"*Enough.*"

Isla had winced even before Kai growled at her through gritted teeth. She knew she'd gone too far the second she finished the sentence.

With his eyes narrowed and a sharp line appearing on his cheek, Kai stepped closer, dangerously close. Close enough that a strong gust of wind could throw all their efforts of the past week out the window. Enough that Isla could see the bright flecks in his eyes, like stars managing to peek through a horde of stormy chaos. Enough that his breath was warm on her face, tickled at her nose, her cheeks, her lips.

Her skin prickled, and her heart pounded with ire and that maddening "something else" that only he could draw out.

"I know it might be difficult for you, but you're going to listen to me."

The stern, guttural words full of assertion and power, mixed with his proximity, proved to be something cruel.

Isla couldn't stop herself from becoming locked in place, hanging onto whatever left his mouth, focusing on the way it moved. That essence of their bond she'd tucked away was reviving and leaking back through her invisible armor. Kai had to have known what he was doing, or he wouldn't have risked the distance.

"I don't know exactly what you heard or what conclusion that mind of yours is running to, but everything I said in there was for a reason and in your best interest," he told her slowly, so she could absorb every part of it.

"But he's your *beta*, and he figured it out. Why not just tell him the truth?" As she stated her inquiry, Isla scanned his face, going back on her vow to never scour for his emotions or thoughts again.

When she reached his eyes again, the windows to that piece of him that she innately recognized, that had supposedly been split from her before their time, she concentrated. Followed the dark clouds and starlight until, much to her surprise, for the first time, she felt she found success.

Nerves.

He was nervous about something.

She would've thought that it was due to the fact she'd figured out his true intentions. Fear that, out of spite, she'd touch him just to reject him—because it had, admittedly, crossed her mind at the peak of her fury.

But that wasn't the answer because she also found honesty, truth. The same conviction she'd seen during the most certain fact spoken between them—that they were destined for each other.

Everything Kai had said to his beta *was* purposeful, and it had all been with her well-being in mind. Which made everything so much worse.

"Why do I have to be nothing, and why do I have to be 'handled' for you to feel I'm protected? This isn't just about what I want, and it's not just about that public unrest either. You're keeping the truth from your *beta*. There's something else—bigger. What am I missing?"

Kai's jaw clenched again, a signal she was on the right path.

"It's not your concern."

Isla blinked, dumbstruck. "Not my *concern*? Are you—no." She shook her head furiously. "No. Not acceptable."

"Not acceptable?"

"You can't tell me that you're trying to protect me, that I'm unsafe somehow, and then not tell me why. That's not how things work."

"It's pack business."

"And *mine* if I'm in trouble."

"I'm handling it."

"Is that your favorite phrase?"

Kai gave her a flat look at the retort and then hesitated. He opened his mouth to speak, like the explanation was on the tip of his tongue, but then closed it. "It's not your place, Isla."

"My place?" Isla's laugh came out in an astonished breath. "What even *is* my place? I mean, *really*. One touch is literally the only thing that keeps this from being my place. That keeps us from just *making it* my place."

It had been a simple complaint, a simple message, one well-established. The only thing stopping her from reigning at Kai's side was the fact they hadn't touched...or slept together, but one had to come before the other.

Such a simple gripe she'd proposed, yet, after watching Kai break his stance and shift on his feet at the mention, one she realized had been the key that she needed.

Isla knew nothing about the intricacies of mates or their bonds. She knew of the technical aspects—the being together for the rest of time, broken apart only by death, and the ability to share thoughts without being shifted. But all the emotions and deeper meanings, the intensity of the feelings, she was learning and discovering as she went along.

Kai never seemed to balk. He was always in complete control during those times he'd sent her mind spinning with his words and with his presence, all the while with a cocky grin on his face. *Except* for the night of the feast while he watched as she was touched and bestowed a kiss by another man. Gone was his grin and composure when she'd found him completely unraveled out in the garden. A break that stemmed from the deeply ingrained notion that her body was his and his alone.

Their bond was his weakness too, though manifested differently. A more physical way. And if she wanted to disarm him as he did her, if she wanted to bend him to her will, lock him down to get her point across, *she* had to take control and pull on that innate desire for her. For her touch, her body, for only him to feel.

"How do you think it would go?" she posed the question, feigning some innocence. Though, the air seemed to take a new charge.

"What?"

Isla swallowed and trained her eyes across the surroundings. "I personally don't think we'd make it off this roof or even waste time taking off all our clothes."

She flicked her eyes back to Kai whose gaze had turned suspicious, though danger lurked beneath. "What are you doing?"

Isla shrugged. "Just thinking out loud." She knew there was only so far she could toe the line before something manifested they may not have been able to come back from. "I think one touch and you'd have me up in the air and pressed against that wall."

Kai released a loud breath through his nose, not breaking their eye contact. He would know the game she was playing—he was likely a master at it—and yet, he seemed defenseless. She could feel it building already. That same possessive pull. That tether.

Isla kept her voice soft like the caress of silk—or her fingertips—languid to allow *him* to absorb every word, allowing him the time to paint the picture. "I think just one touch, and I'd be *begging* you to take me…I wonder if I'll have a hard time keeping quiet. How hard you'll have to kiss me to muffle the sound. Or if everyone down at the fire will just have to hear me screaming your name while you fuck me and make me yours." She broke her next words down to syllables, craning her neck to say in a hush as close to his ear as she could. "Again…and again…and again."

She had to stop, not just for his sake but for hers too, judging by the fluttering of her stomach and heat building between her legs.

Kai's gaze had gone completely dark as he ran his tongue lightly over his bottom lip. He brought it between his teeth, and his eyes flickered down to Isla's mouth, followed the line of her neck down to that little spot at the crook of her collarbone where he was meant to mark her. His chest rose and fell, deeper, faster, his breath mingling with hers.

Isla caught his hand moving forward in her periphery, almost grabbing at her hip before it stopped. She hadn't flinched at the action, she'd waited for it, almost leaned into it.

"What do you want, Isla?"

She shivered at her name said roughly, achingly.

If she was honest, right now—him. She wanted him. All of him. Everywhere. She wanted everything she'd just described. The toe-curling, back-arching, mind-numbing, forget-her-own-name sex that she needed. But she couldn't have it—*never* with him—so she stowed away the lust and stood tall, pushed her shoulders back, and took control.

"I'm your mate, *talk to me* like one. Because even without sealing this bond, you know, you *feel* that it means something. That I have my own place of exception." She took a step back from him to keep her mind unclouded. "You don't have to speak to me as an alpha. I understand pack protocol and that there are rules, I don't need all the official details. But I, at least, deserve to know enough so I can think about protecting *myself*. If you, as my mate, want me to be safe, *truly* safe from whatever it is, I need something. Give me *something*, Kai."

It was the first time she'd ever addressed him by his name, no formalities. At it, Kai's eyebrows shot up, but he didn't comment on it. He just looked off, past her, into the forest, and then paced a few steps away. As he took the moment to gather himself, Isla did too.

Her plan had been risky, but it worked.

"Ezekiel is very by the letter," Kai explained, finally. "And if there was even the slightest chance of this—of us—happening because I don't *resent* you, he'd batten down the hatches to prepare for the potential storm. Your name would be thrown up and down the hierarchy of Deimos like no tomorrow."

"Okay?"

"I…I don't believe I'm seeing the true face of everyone in my council. I don't believe everyone has the best…*intentions* for me, so the further away from Deimos and an association with me I can keep you, the better. For my sake and yours."

Isla fought the urge to ask for more information about who Kai felt distrustful of and why. Her skin crawled at what he was alluding to. It was one of the most heinous methods before regulations were imposed on challenges for an alpha title—go first for their mate.

Though they hadn't completed any type of bond or hadn't really initiated anything without touching, they didn't truly know, now that they'd met and recognized each other for what they were, what effect the death of the other would have. If someone went after her after learning that she was the alpha's mate, who was to say it wouldn't weaken Kai enough to lose a challenge, his title, and his life.

Isla couldn't stop herself from trying to dive further into it, piecing together what she could. The former alpha and the heir had just mysteriously died. And now Kai didn't trust members of his council?

"Don't ask me any more questions," Kai said as if he could see the gears in her mind turning. "Right now, you have to just stop being you for a few seconds and trust me."

"Are *you* safe?"

Kai let out a chuckle, a light air of disbelief, either for her complete disregard of what he'd said or that she cared. Or both. "I can protect myself."

Isla sighed and gazed off. She had so many questions…

"*Fine.*" Isla looked back up and noted how Kai's face had fallen into a grimace. "That wasn't that hard, was it?"

"*That* wasn't…isn't."

She caught the innuendo and felt another rise of heat. She had to stop her wide eyes from wandering down his body. She wasn't getting all twisted in that again.

"What did you expect talking like that?" Kai mused, noting her bewilderment.

Isla bristled. "I wouldn't have had to do it if you didn't make me."

"Oh, you enjoyed every second of it," he jeered. "Never thought such wicked things could come from such a pretty mouth."

She folded her arms across her chest. "That's because you don't know me very well."

"A regret I'll carry, apparently."

Back to square one again.

Isla rolled her eyes and spun to face the field, moving forward until she was back at the railing. The people down below were still at the fire, none the wiser to what was occurring up above. She felt slightly shameful, considering they were down there at the flames sending prayers up to the Goddess for the safe return of the remaining hunters. She was never necessarily fond of the tradition, meant to mirror the pyres burned for deceased alphas, lunas, heirs, leaders, and warriors. Wolves lost in wars and battles. The fallen.

No one was dead. Not yet. There was no need for the flames.

Isla felt Kai's presence as he joined her at her side, though he kept his distance. She gave him a sideways glance, feeling the marker of the pass still burning a hole in her pocket.

Bad blood…

"Why is it so horrible for me to become luna?" she asked, surprised by an inkling of hurt that crept into her voice. "*Why* the questions and unrest?"

"Politics." There was disdain in his tone. "Lunas have come from other packs, but you're the daughter of Io's Beta and have strong ties to its current and future leaders. There would be questions if you could ever fully renounce that pack membership and shift your full interests to Deimos."

Politics, though ruthless, didn't sound like deep-seated ancient grudges. But the Trainee had been so confident in his words, in his warning for her to be careful. She touched the marker in her pocket, felt along its ridges.

"So, nothing else? You have no problem with me being from Io?"

"I was two seconds away from claiming you on that terrace before your liaison came out, and while he went on about seating arrangements, all I could think about was if taking you in the restroom after dinner was a horrible way to remember locking our bond. Though, in hindsight, maybe not as horrible as the roof of an infirmary." He smirked to which she gave a dead stare. "But then I met your friends, your family, and I learned about who you were, what you stood for, what you wanted. I meant everything I said in that garden. I want to do right by you. I want you to have everything you want, that you've just earned for yourself."

That didn't sound like much of an ancient grudge either. Not someone to be wary of. It sounded—decent.

Isla chewed on her bottom lip. "And what if what I had wanted was you?"

"No matter what we decide to do with this bond, it's ours, not an issue to be dealt with by my council. If you wanted me, Deimos, then we'd make it work."

Something else that she hadn't been expecting. That innocent fluttering began brewing in her stomach again, that warmth, that comfort.

What if she *had* said yes? How different would things have been right now?

As a thought popped in her head, she couldn't hold back a sharp laugh.

Kai furrowed his eyebrows. "Are you coming up with another way to seduce information out of me?"

"*No*—I just wish I could've seen your beta's face when you told him that the *insolent, dim-witted* woman is one screw away from being his superior."

Kai broke out in a grin, tilting his head, signaling that it was just as amusing as she'd imagined it would be. "He means well."

"I'm sure he does."

"He's protective of our pack and of me, and sometimes he oversteps because of it," he said. "He was my father's best friend. He's known me since I was a pup."

That made sense. An alpha's beta was their choice. Typically, it ended up being the alpha's closest friend, their greatest confidant. Like her father and the Imperial Alpha. And what would likely be Adrien and Sebastian—frightening.

"And that's why you haven't replaced him?"

"My father was alpha for almost twenty years with him as beta. He has experience and connections with the council I can only hope to maintain as well as my brother would have...I'm starting to regret spending more time avoiding Mavec growing up than being at home in it."

Isla arched an eyebrow, both at his aversion to the city and at the fact he was so freely speaking with her about something that felt so personal. "I heard Mavec's beautiful?"

"Beautiful, yes, and incredibly suffocating. If your warrior travels eventually bring you our way—and I'm sure they will—I'd say don't waste too much time there. Stay at the Starlight in Ifera and spend the rest of the time out in Abalys—not alone, though, definitely not alone. Probably have a weapon on hand, and don't wear anything expensive." He listed the rules with mirth, a reminiscence. Like he'd done it all before. "And if you end up drinking and playing cards at Talha, stay away from Charley's table. He's a cheating bastard, but great if you want a decent war story or need a good laugh. He's won the tavern's limerick contest the past ten years...I'd warn you that the rhymes are quite dirty, but you don't seem to have much of a problem with that."

Isla hadn't realized that as he'd gone on his tangent, the grin on her face grew and grew. His joy was infectious. She'd never seen him speak so highly of something, seen such a spark in his eye. And from what he was describing, she also became exceedingly curious. Abalys didn't sound like much of a fit for an alpha, though Kai spoke of it like home. A reminder that there was so much about him that she didn't know… and would never know.

"I'll keep it in mind," Isla said, and Kai looked at her, his smile softening. She felt so exposed under his gaze. "What?"

"I wasn't sure what to expect when I realized my mate was at that dinner, but you definitely weren't it."

Isla's smile faltered, but she recovered quickly, masking it with a snicker. "Sorry to disappoint you."

"You didn't."

He said it so sincerely that it scared her.

Her breath hitched, and those damn butterflies multiplied. If this were any other man, this would typically be the part she'd kiss him, sweet and soft, an urge she surprisingly hadn't felt yet with him until now.

Kai looked away from her and back out at the field, saying nothing more. He just rested his forearms on the railing and alternated his focus between the fire and the sky. For a moment, Isla felt obligated to cut into the silence, to ask him what he was still doing there, but then stopped herself.

She didn't want him to go.

So instead, she turned and rested in her spot, her perfect spot, letting her eyes slide closed, listening to the soft sounds of wind and bugs and fire and Kai's soft breathing. And then finally—not just for one second, but several—under the glow of the moon and with the comfort of her mate beside her, Isla's mind found peace.

PART II
THE BUSINESS OF SHADOWS

CHAPTER 11

The mate bond of wolves was something revered.

It was sacred. It was special. It was a foundation of their kind, a fabric in their hallowed Code, and what made them unique from the beings of the other continents, other realms. But the ethereal connection was also an onus. It made them weak. It made them vulnerable. One could say it held so much power that it almost negated any notion of free will.

And for that reason, among some others, Isla had decided years ago that it wasn't worth it. She didn't want it. *Especially* not after she finally felt like she had some control over her life.

This led to the thing she hated *most* about the annoyingly handsome and infuriating Alpha of Deimos—for the smallest of moments, he made her question that.

Seconds became minutes, minutes not quite hours, as they remained standing in silence on the roof of Callisto's infirmary. While Isla was lulled by the murmurs of wind through trees and the hush of breaths, she could feel the tension release from her muscles, webs unweaving from her mind. Occasionally, she'd peek over to watch how the moonlight and faint fire glow danced on Kai's face, and then she'd hold in her sigh.

Goddess, did she hate Fate.

The peace, their bond was a parasite, latching onto her thoughts and leeching her sense. She was so…tired. Tired of fighting—for now. Tired of the answers that only spurred more questions. If only he was *completely* irredeemable, enough that she couldn't even tolerate the sight of him, that would make things easier.

On another scan in his direction, Kai turned, too, like he'd been aware the whole time of her roaming eyes. The corner of his mouth was up in a smirk, and Isla snapped her head forward again, silently cursing. Maybe she should've been thankful for it because whatever he was about to say would *surely* break whatever enchantment of ease she'd been feeling.

"You know," Kai began. "I'm sure there's a reporter skulking around somewhere that we can grab a camera from. You can take a picture and leave it by your bed for those lonely nights back in Io when you're having those dreams of me. Help get you there."

And she was right.

"You make it so hard to enjoy your company," Isla sighed. "I've surely had my fill and had *enough* of men like you. Thinking you're the Goddess's gift to women. You're all the same."

Kai chuckled and turned around, leaning back against the railing with folded arms, that cocksure grin on his face. "According to the Great Book, I'm specifically the Goddess's gift to *you*."

"Open to interpretation."

"I'm not too sure it is."

He was right—the language of the Book was explicit when it came to mates—but she wouldn't endorse it.

There was a sudden flash of puzzlement across his features as he shifted on his feet. Clearing his throat, he trained his eyes around them, saying offhandedly, "Exactly how many *men like me* have there been?"

Isla's eyebrows rose at his interest. "Jealous?"

"No." Kai sustained the air of indifference, shrugging. "Curious. That mouth came from somewhere."

She couldn't hold back a wicked grin, ready to go toe-to-toe with him again.

"I think I got it from Levi," she said, pulling her own facade, once more, of innocence. "He wasn't my *first time*, but he *was* the first guy who ever took me outside of a bedroom. And the first to *get me there* a couple of times. There was this thing that he did with his—"

"Alright, alright." Kai's face was a mix of amusement and slight perturbation. "We're not doing this again."

"You started it," she cooed mockingly, secretly happy he'd stopped her. After Levi, there was only Callan, and there wasn't much to rattle about in that regard. "I can write down how it went for you if you want. You can leave it by your bed for a read during those *lonely nights* in your palace when you're dreaming of me. On top, right? That was it? Just put yourself in his place. Should help *get you there.*"

Kai's grin, bright and full, his laugh genuine, made her heart skip.

"I don't live in a palace," he said before the air seemed to change. His joyous demeanor dissolved gradually.

He drew his eyes over her—in long, slow lines—from her feet to the top of her head, back down, back up. Not with impish intention that could've been spurred by her words, it seemed, but just taking her in. For a moment, Isla swore that he frowned, but it was hard to judge as he'd recovered quickly.

He lifted himself from his spot. "It's getting late. We're departing early, and you should get some rest."

Isla's stomach twisted and she straightened.

Kai took a couple of steps forward, stopping between her and a path to the stairwell door. "Goodnight."

She looked up at him and blinked. It felt so jarring, like the floor was dropping out from under her—but this was the plan all along.

"Goodbye," Isla affirmed gently despite the piece of her clawing its way out attempting to cry "stay". "Hunt's over."

"It is," Kai agreed before a flicker of mischief, of defiance, shone in his eyes. He closed in on her again, slowly, and bent so his breath was warm on her ear as he whispered, hot on her cheek, a phantom kiss to her skin. "*Goodnight, Isla.*"

Antagonistic until the end.

Isla inhaled sharply, eyes closing for just a moment, embracing as her heart tightened, as the tether went taut. As if it were a last-ditch effort by that part of them to bring them close, like it knew. It took all her willpower not to lean into it, into him.

She shivered. "You really like to test limits, huh?" Her whisper caught in the breeze.

"Only with you, *my gift.*" His tease caressed the shell of her ear again before he pulled back. "This little game of ours has proven to be a joy that's been hard to come by lately. I might actually miss it."

Miss *it.* Not her. Just their dance around destiny, their defiance of a deity. Their game. That was it.

Thankfully, before any type of sting could settle upon being relegated to entertainment, a loud howl rang through the air, urgent and alarming. They broke away from each other, turning in the direction in which it came. It seemed as if the entire world had arrested again—the wind, bugs, fire—even for those down below.

Isla's blood rushed, and her heart began thrumming wildly. Her hand went straight into her pocket, feeling the marker's edges. If it weren't for the mutual reactions, she would've thought she'd hallucinated. "Is that—"

The howl came again, cutting her off. A confirmation. Everyone down below began running.

Her mouth fell open as she stepped back, and Kai, her opposite, moved forward, placing his hands on the railing as his eyes narrowed on the top of the Wall in the distance. "The Gate—someone's coming through it."

Isla had taken off for the stairwell before he even finished his sentence.

"Who do you—Isla!" She heard Kai shout from behind her. "What are you doing?"

"What do you think?" She nearly ripped the door off its hinges getting it open.

Mind and body buzzing, she took the steps as fast as she could, focusing on her feet so she didn't fall over, occasionally jumping to a landing when she could manage the distance and impact.

The door above never had a chance to close. Kai's voice echoed through the chamber down to her. "Are you supposed to leave?"

"No!"

Kai grumbled something under his breath, reverberated by the cavern, about how she didn't listen to anything before his steps thundered down her same path, the exit slamming behind him with a bang that made her flinch and nearly stumble. She didn't care enough to protest him following her. Her mind was focused on the Gate, the marker, the Trainee, and those things alone.

When she broke out of the side door, Isla wasn't sure exactly where she was going. The world on the ground felt different. The atmosphere felt charged, overwhelming. In the distance, thanks to the moonlight, she caught the specks of those from the fire. They had to have some sense of direction.

Just as Kai made it to her, opening his mouth to speak, she was off again. "Un-fucking-believable." She heard him curse.

"Thank you!" She threw the words haphazardly over her shoulder.

The dry grass crunched beneath her shoes as she sprinted across the open field, pushing herself so hard that the crisp air and smoke burned her lungs. What she'd give to have a handle on her wolf again. But there wasn't time to try working out a shift. She didn't have the patience or fortitude to recover from the pain, to deal with the disappointment of not being ready or fully healed.

The Wall loomed as Isla drew closer—for the first time since she'd gone behind it. Her breath hampered but not in exhaustion. She fought back the paranoia, the demons, the darkness, the fear, pressing forward despite it, unsure of how long it could be kept at bay.

Her battered body was nearly depleted by the time she could sense a crowd—hear them, smell them, finally see the faint glow of lights and torches. The top of the Gate's wrought iron blended into the night, only the bottom illuminated. The shadows of the spectators danced large and menacing on the stone around it.

She slowed to a stop, observing the scene from a distance. People were pocketed all along the field, some daring to stand close and others maintaining a separation from the wretched land. Everyone here had not come from the infirmary, judging by the various types of dress. The call from an emerging hunter, followed by the signal from the Gate's surveyor, could be heard for miles.

She'd never witnessed a re-emergence—unconscious for her own and not present for Adrien's or Sebastian's. What she expected was excitement, celebration…but everyone just seemed distraught. Taking a couple of steps closer, mingling into the horde of those deciding to keep some space from the Wilds, she began picking up on some of the words spoken. Her heart gradually filled with foreboding.

Something was wrong.

The Gate should've already been opened, waiting for the hunters to come through.

She perked up when she spotted a silhouette, one she could find in any crowd.

"Adrien!"

The Heir spun, face laden with confusion at her nearing form. "Isla? What the hell? Where've you been?" He looked her over as if searching for injuries. "We went to your room, and you weren't there."

We, she assumed, were him and her brother, wherever he'd gone off to as he was nowhere in sight.

Isla opened and closed her mouth, unsure how to answer—certainly not with that she was in a battle of wanton wits with her mate—so she didn't. Instead, she faced the Gate. "What's happening?"

"It's stuck."

Isla jumped as Kai's voice came from behind her, even if she knew he'd been tailing. She would've thought he'd been closer, but he must've stopped to ask questions.

He silently nodded in respect and greeting to Adrien before his eyes were drawn upwards, taking in what was before them. His nose twitched as he sniffed the air.

Isla's eyebrows nearly met her hairline, replaying his words and ignoring the perplexity on Adrien's face at the alpha's sudden appearance and her *lack of* surprise towards it. "Stuck?"

"You can smell that, right?" Kai's unsettled feelings were so strong, she swore they ricocheted down the tether and infected her.

Isla lifted her head and took a whiff of the air. The aroma was different, tangy. Not putrid and rotten, but off-putting, sharp. Too much eventually had tears pricking her eyes.

"It's been getting stronger," Adrien said before following their lead and inhaling deeply. He had to clear his throat from a cough. Uneasiness took his own features. "It's magic."

"Faulty magic," Kai clarified before his jaw tightened. "Something's wrong with the wards."

Isla's eyes went wide as she trained them along the welded patterns of the Gate, chosen and directed by the witches of the past who'd assisted the Imperial Alpha of ages ago in its construction.

She didn't know much about magic—only of its ability to be wielded by witches and fae, and that its only existence on *their* continent was localized to this very spot where it served as both a blessing and a curse. The heavy latch was what locked a ward of protection, completing a symbol that she'd never quite understood the true meaning and power behind. When opened and rendered incomplete, the protection was broken. The Gate became just a gate. An entryway, an exit.

But that wasn't happening.

The latch was lifted, the ward void, yet the metal frame wouldn't budge. Something else had to be at play, another rune misfiring. It wasn't protecting them from the Wilds, not keeping the horrors in—

"It's keeping us out." The realization fell from her lips in a murmur of disbelief.

A howl came again, this time certainly from behind the Wall. Now with time to process, Isla was filled with dread. The Trainee couldn't howl. Not like that. She listened for his attempt, not perfect but enough. It never came.

Though what did was far, *far* worse.

The roar was ear-shattering, *close*. It made everyone, including Isla, jolt and stumble back.

It was a bak…tailing the hunters, approaching the Wall.

Yet another behavior that didn't match any part of the legend. They were supposed to be repulsed by the borders, by the enchantment.

Isla's insides turned watery, fingers twitched at her sides, features screwed into a grimace. The fear threatened to overpower and suffocate her. She was back there again, *experiencing it* again in hasty, relentless waves—alone, terrified, fighting for daily survival, battling for her life, hearing the Trainee's horrid screams, spending semi-conscious moments just out of death's grasp.

She kept falling down, down, down into that endless, destructive pit until the warmth of comforting hands fell upon her shoulders. Her body recoiled but then settled as they pressed down firmer. Her forlorn gaze met that of the source—Adrien.

"You're okay," he eased, leaning closer, squeezing where he touched her. A reassurance, a grounding. "You're safe."

She took a deep breath and nodded, then felt it; a sharp phantom tug and release.

Isla snapped from Adrien and focused forward—only forward—not wanting him to see her look at Kai and not wanting her mate to gaze upon the torment in her eyes.

Kai couldn't see her vulnerable. Not like this. A victim to her own mind, to memories, to the past. Helpless and weak and pathetic, as she'd always been imbued she was before she'd found her purpose, before she became a warrior. She couldn't break. Not again. Not anymore. *That* hell was left behind years ago. That lonely, shattered girl was forgotten.

But that pull came again, harder this time, and reluctantly, she turned.

Kai's eyes weren't narrowed in disapproval of the physical contact as she'd been expecting. Instead, as usual, they housed a mix of emotions, nearly indecipherable without her immense focus, but all wrapped in that discernable protective fire. The same one as in the Wilds and on the roof.

He couldn't touch her, but he wanted her to know that he was there. For her, for what he could be, for what she needed. Their bond, incomplete, but still a promise. A deeper relationship, non-existent, but still, they meant something.

Though she knew very well it could bite her in the ass later, she accepted it. Smiled weakly and reached back, mentally digging for a piece of him that didn't need to be drawn out by lust. She tried to let him feel that she understood, some gratitude, though she wasn't sure if it ever landed.

Another howl resounded from the hunter on the other side. *Panicked.* He was close, so close that Isla could hear his paws padding the mud.

And then came a faint iridescent glow—his eyes, the lumerosi snaking through his fur—and next, the sound of a slam against metal. There was a thud as something fell off him, and he whimpered, pawing at the Gate.

"It's both of them!" someone nearby the iron shouted.

Goddess, the Trainee was alive!

The roar of the bak rumbled again, and horrified gasps descended upon the crowd. Commotion built. Some turned away from the Gate, retreating, anticipating a slaughter.

"Help us get this open!"

A mass of people rushed forward, Adrien and Kai included. Isla had taken a step, but the panic kept her rooted. She couldn't will herself any further.

Her fists clenched at her sides as aggravation with herself melded with the apprehension. All she was able to do was stand, bouncing on the balls of her feet, searching desperately for anything she could do to help, watching as her closest friend and her mate encroached on the Wilds' barrier.

The hunter pushed, and the mass of the brave pulled, metal screaming and rattling. All of it created a brutal symphony. The screech of iron, the gasps and wails of spectators, the whimpers and shouting and groans. The bak made no contribution to the chorus, which meant, following all she'd learned from her time in its home, it was nearby. Stalking…waiting.

There was a loud snap like a break somewhere, and the Gate creaked, an opening forming. But not by much, and it quickly ricocheted closed.

"Again!"

The orchestra came to a crescendo, peaked by the howl and thundering steps of the bak. The hunter clambered to the gap when it reappeared, tumbling through, and dragging what Isla now saw as the limp body of the Trainee with his teeth by the collar of his armor behind him.

Any light in her soul had dimmed as his body fell from the hunter's maw, motionless.

Dead. He was dead.

"Watch out!"

There wasn't any time for her to process it—the Gate slamming closed and the sound of tearing cloth, scraping flesh, and a scream made it impossible.

The man who'd been hit, from the looks of it, didn't get cut too deep, remaining upright though hunched over. Lights and torches illuminated the bak, in all its horrendous glory, pressed against the Gate's surface. Its protracted claws hooked through the metal labyrinth, its spittle flying as its teeth gnashed. It roared and roared. The Gate shook under its weight, threatening to give way, to let it through. The beast could've broken out if it wanted to, Isla knew, but it didn't.

The intention wasn't to fight them, to kill whatever it could until it was eventually slain itself. It was to warn them.

The Wilds was *their* territory. A fact known, but not one they'd ever been evolved enough to embrace. Not like this. Not to guard.

Her fingers ran over the fabric of her jacket where she knew the black ink of her lumerosi snaked in intricate swirls and symbols over the skin of her shoulder, over the top of her arm, tracing as the bak did when she'd been shifted, as it toyed and taunted.

Nothing made sense.

The beast trained its red feral stare over the crowd…and Isla went rigid when it looked at her, only her, she swore, dead in the eye.

Her blood ran cold as it bent. Acknowledging her, *knowing* her. A searing, splintering pain rippled through her body, and she grimaced, hand going to her head that felt like it was splitting. Her wolf. Her defense. Her greatest power. Pleading, desperate. Trapped.

"Murderer."

Isla's breath caught, and her eyes darted around for the source of the projection. The voice was unfamiliar, raspy, so broken that she almost couldn't decode it, and no one else seemed to have heard.

Murderer?

An unease rumbled in her stomach, and she looked back at the bak, no longer staring at her. It roared at the crowd once more before disappearing back into the forest.

Everyone remained still, terrified to move, to breathe until the false security of the latch was put back in place.

"Is he dead?" someone wailed as others rushed to give the hunter, now back to his human form, some aid and assistance.

"No," he answered as a cloth was placed over his shoulders. "I had to knock him out just to get him out here. He completely lost it."

Isla felt like she was getting whiplash, unable to keep up with the rollercoaster of the night, still feeling faint and now dealing with a pounding headache.

There was the sudden sound of a smack, an inhale, and then some sputtering coughs. "He's waking up!"

If she wasn't so exhausted, Isla may have jumped for joy as the Trainee roused, his eyes cracking open as he moved and groaned.

His voice was like sandpaper as he asked whoever the woman was nearby, "Where am I?"

Isla didn't know who she was exactly but could see the peeking of a warrior lumerosi on her back. "Back to civilization, Lukas," she said endearingly like she knew him.

Lukas—that was his name.

He fought himself into a sitting position. "Who are you?"

The woman jerked, taken aback. "What?"

Lukas's eyes trailed along the mob of onlookers, looking terribly confused before they blew wide. He pointed to the hunter and recoiled back, low on one hand and his feet. "Get away from him!"

"What? Lukas—"

"No!" Lukas, completely unaware of what it represented, all that it was, used the Gate to clamber to his feet. "He's a monster! I watched him!" His chest heaved as he panted, struggling to stay upright. "He—he's a wolf."

The declaration was met by gasps. One even fell from Isla's lips.

He didn't remember...anything.

CHAPTER 12

Isla's breathing was too loud in her ears. Ragged and rattling in her skull in a way that made it impossible to focus, to think.

The Trainee—no, *Lukas*, his name was Lukas—clutched onto the Gate like his life depended on it, one arm hooked through a glyph, while the other was speared by a finger in the hunter's direction. His accusation hung in the air, keeping everyone, including her, mute and still.

Get away from him…he's a wolf.

She had to have heard him wrong. The stench of magic had just… gotten to her head. Because he was *fine* when she'd last seen him. At least, mentally. He was himself. He *knew* who he was. What he was. What they *were*. But now…

Isla turned his words over and over like a stone as if somehow, she'd discover some hidden message. Some secret laced in every breath, every syllable. Like the mystery of the pass or the supposed ancient strife between her homeland and her fate. He'd enjoyed things like that— riddles and games, the ominous, the foreboding.

But the light in his eyes, the one that had been there during the initial time they'd spoken, was gone. The spark he'd possessed that first made her approach him at the feast—that he carried in every conversation, even when he was a bumbling mess—was missing. It felt as if someone else were wearing his face.

Like the man before her was a stranger.

"You see what I'm talking about?" Fury painted the hunter's blood-smeared features as he cradled his side. "He's lost his damn mind."

Isla's foot collided with something hard in the grass, pain shooting up her leg. As she stumbled forward, running into the back of the person in front of her, she glanced down, finding a rock jutting in her path.

Her path—she hadn't even realized she'd been moving.

The terror that had once kept her rooted had given way to alarm and concern, her mind releasing its hold on her body. Even the hellish repetition of that scratchy, accusatory voice—*murderer*—had faded to a nagging in the back of her subconscious.

The person she'd hit didn't respond to her muttered apology or gripe when she absentmindedly pushed against them for leverage to get upright again. They were just as dazed and dumbfounded as she was.

Two nurses beckoned from the infirmary tried to pry the hunter away. He needed help, like the man attacked by the bak who was already being guided up the field to some aid. No one approached Lukas, likely feeling exactly what she did. The gnawing in their guts that this was another trick, another brewing disaster.

The Wilds may have taken pieces of those who dared enter, forever changing them from who they once were. Sometimes it took them whole—their lives. Bodies left in the bellies of beasts. But it never took everything and nothing. No one emerged a shell. Not like this.

The hunter grunted in frustration, resistant to their assistance and vehement in his avoidance. She understood that well, at least. He'd tasted death only moments ago and who knew what he'd dealt with behind the Wall. The transition to safety and normalcy wasn't simple.

"Maybe I lost my mind, too," the hunter said, tone gravelly with ire. He rose to his feet and put some distance between himself and the caretakers. "I should've left your ass in there, you piece of shit. You almost cost me my life—*twice*."

"What do you mean twice?"

Isla's thought had been spoken aloud by another—the warrior who'd known Lukas. The woman wore a similar look of disbelief and confusion as she spun to the hunter. "What are you talking about?"

"This bastard tried to kill me."

Isla's heart stopped. "*What?*" Her whisper blended into the murmurs and sharp breaths of others.

Her eyes darted to Lukas. The auburn-haired man remained upright in his spot, though faltered now due to whatever injuries were hidden beneath his damaged armor. His shoulder, she was sure. His leg, she remembered.

The budding ruckus made him blistered, and his wide, cautious eyes flittered over the crowd. He reminded her of a doe, the ones that dwelled in the few lush forests on Io's landscape. Skittish and easily spooked, a persistent flight in the dichotomy, used constantly by Warrior Alina in training as an example of what the trainees *couldn't* be.

Isla snapped her mouth closed, teeth crashing together as it dawned.

"Why—why would you say something like that? Do you understand what you're accusing him of?" The warrior woman spoke sharply, a tinge of panic in her voice.

Isla understood, and she was sure that's where everyone else's minds had gone.

Treason.

Murdering a fellow hunter, a fellow wolf, in the Wilds—while they were utterly vulnerable and during one of their people's most sacred rites—could be viewed as treason. Being one with the monsters who wanted them dead. An enemy to their kind.

Punishable by death if you were lucky.

But Lukas *wasn't* an enemy. If anything, an attempt to kill the hunter after he'd felt threatened proved exactly how much he was still one of them. *With* them.

Lukas wasn't a fawn. He didn't cower. He didn't run. Even if he couldn't remember it, even if he couldn't fully embody that spirit inside of him through a complete shift, he was a wolf. His instincts, his nature, down to the deepest well of his bones, was to fight. There was no malice in his intentions. He was protecting himself. Which meant he was in there. Somewhere. Not a stranger—though definitely strange—just lost.

If only she'd had a clearer head. It may have occurred to her sooner.

And maybe then she could've stopped him from making a horrible mistake.

Isla barely had a moment to yell *"wait"* before Lukas reached for his boot, those instincts kicking in and helping him put the pieces together.

The hunter—the "monster" in his eyes—had brought him *here*. Here, where the monster was cared for. Here, where the spectators observed *him* like he had five heads. Looked on with apprehension, with disdain.

The blade he drew glinted in a mix of lights as he wielded it against whoever was closest. He tried to bury it in the chest of a member of Callisto's Guard, but off-balance and hopelessly outmatched, he was brought down in one swift movement. Lukas hit the ground with a thud, a wheeze escaping his lips at the impact. The guard slammed his foot down onto Lukas's hand hard enough that Isla heard the gruesome snap of his fingers. His cry was one she was all too familiar with as he lost his grip on his weapon. There was a metallic, taunting ring when it was kicked away and collided with the Gate.

The guard pressed his foot to Lukas's throat and bared his canines, brandishing his claws. "Wrong move," he growled, eyes becoming iridescent.

Lukas screamed and thrashed beneath him. The sound roared down Isla's spine.

No.

The crowd divided further than they already had been. Those who'd been pulling at the Gate who would've been the first line of defense against the bak, pressed closer. The weary, simple spectators, who'd been robbed of a look at triumphant history, pulled away. Some practically sprinted up the grass, likely wanting to forget the horror they saw and find a way to get the scent of magic out of their noses. The hunter had been pulled away, too.

Isla stood in the middle, lingering in empty space. The air became charged with power—their true power. Raw and untamed. Feral. Deadly.

No.

The horde surrounded Lukas in a way that nearly shielded him from her view. In a way that reminded her of the bak who'd taken him away. When she'd *let them* take him away.

She couldn't let it happen again. Couldn't. Wouldn't.

She sucked in a breath and balled her fists before taking another step forward.

Something pulled her back. Strong and intangible. Distinct. Wordless, but the message was clear.

She turned and like a moonlit path had been drawn, teased Kai from the bodies. He wasn't a part of the brutes she was prepared to confront. Instead, he stood by a farther section of the Wall, keeping his distance. Unlike everyone else, he didn't seem concerned with Lukas at all. Instead, his eyes were on her, *only* her, like she was all that mattered.

Just like the Hunt.

It was all just like the Hunt.

She winced as guilt gripped her heart, remembering the moment clearer now than she ever had in her nightmares. Not only had they been so distracted by each other that they let Lukas get so far out of reach, but they'd been a distraction themselves. Lukas had warned her to stay away from the alpha— why, she still wasn't clear—but then there they had appeared side by side, catching him off-guard.

Just a *split* second, and he was gone. Dragged like a ragdoll across the dank forest and left a bloody mess in a decrepit house.

The marker felt like an inferno in her pocket.

He'd had enough sense then to leave it for her, though she was broken and unconscious. He *knew her* at that moment.

So, what had happened? Where had he gone after he left it? She'd emerged only yesterday and had been found maybe a day or two's walk before. Not *that* much time for him to lose all sense.

Isla shook away the questions. She couldn't worry about that. Not now. Right now, she had to help him. Now, while she could. Then they'd worry about his memories.

Then they'd have their *talk*.

"Stop!"

Isla jumped to attention at the familiar voice. Adrien pushed his way to the center of the fray, and relief washed over her. If she knew anything about her friend, he'd be the last to support whatever vigilante-esque brutality was about to occur. The pack relations nightmare would be the least of his problems.

"Imperial Heir." The guard sketched a shallow bow but kept his foot firmly on Lukas's neck. Beneath him, Lukas grew more sluggish, losing his fight for air. For consciousness.

Bastard.

Isla snarled and moved a few more steps.

The tug came again, harder this time.

For the love of the Goddess. Leave me alone.

She whipped around to Kai just as he leaned back against the Wall and folded his arms across his chest. Almost like he was about to run out to stop her, but for some reason, elected not to bother.

He was the picture of confidence, of coolness, and never broke eye contact as he shook his head as if telling her no, to stay back, to not get involved. Isla initially ignored the way her mind began to feel fuzzy—itchy, if that were any way to describe it. Instead, she narrowed her eyes, ready to slice him with them…but then she stopped, and her features softened in realization. In shock.

She looked away, but not before noting their lack of proximity.

It wasn't possible.

At least twenty paces lay between them, only their wolfish senses allowing them to see each other from the distance in the waning lights. She noted the lack of high-scale emotion—no burning lust, no all-consuming, shuddering fear, at least for her, and if he feared anything, he didn't show it. He rarely did.

Both of those things had seemed necessary when their bond had connected them and allowed them to communicate in the most primitive ways. A pull here, a tug there. *Unintentionally.* Without much control over intensity or true knowledge of the repercussions.

But this…

Kai had wanted her attention, called to her for it, through a link, their bond, whatever it was, and had *got* it. Once. Now twice.

Isla's hand went to her head, her fingers wedging in her hair, scratching at her scalp to no avail. The itch wasn't physical. Not tangible.

But they hadn't touched. They weren't completely bound. Communicating like this, it wasn't…it shouldn't…

She looked at Kai again, who returned her gaze with raised eyebrows. She glowered. *Get out of my head.* She hoped he could hear it. That he could sense how angry she was for whatever he was doing, how ever he was doing it. *You get the hell out of my head, or so help me.*

She wasn't sure if it was her outcry's doing, but the sensation faded to nothing. Her chest rose and fell with every sharp breath as she brought her hand to her side. She ground her teeth so hard that she waited for them to break.

Too close. For keeping things separated, for keeping their bond broken, that was *too close.*

"Bring him up to the infirmary."

At Adrien's demand, she drew her attention back to the mob, to Lukas.

Any formality and respect the guard had shown earlier faltered. "Are you insane?"

Nearly everyone tensed at the out-of-line proclamation.

Adrien's eyes flashed, a deep, smoldering fire that was not quite the blood-red of an alpha, but not the bluish luminescence of a common wolf. A reminder. In this crowd, he was the hierarchy. A conduit of his father's highest power. His decisions were law until deemed otherwise.

"*Bring him* to the infirmary," he repeated. "He's one in a list of anomalies this week, and lucky for us, unlike everything else, he can speak. He may be able to give us some idea of what's going on out there."

The guard didn't have an immediate response. Neither did anyone else. But it was only moments before the glow left the burly man's eyes, and he lifted his foot off Lukas's neck.

Lukas choked down air in gasps, clawing for his throat.

Isla hesitated rather than run for him, a keen eye on Kai in her periphery.

The group retreated from Adrien, stepping further away from Lukas and lowering their heads. Then, they obeyed. Two of them hauled Lukas to his feet, his head limp and armor rattling before they trudged him up the field. Isla watched as they went, flinching every time they wrenched Lukas's body the wrong way—on purpose, of course—making him whimper. She scowled but stayed in her place.

Later. She'd get to him later.

Spinning back to face the Wall, she scanned who remained, preparing to ask Adrien what the plan was. She wasn't sure what she'd been expecting, but it certainly wasn't that her friend had gone straight to Kai.

They were locked in discussion, and like he felt her staring, Kai looked over. Quick but enough to show he was aware.

She narrowed her eyes, remembering, feeling the ghostly caresses of whatever he'd done to her mind.

Now, the smart thing would've been to walk away. To leave him and the connection and whatever he'd just pulled forgotten within the darkness of this horrible, *horrible* night and never look back.

But she couldn't.

Because there was a part of her, somewhere buried deep, deep down, that enjoyed the phantoms. That *liked* that he'd been there, pulling her back. That wished she'd heard him say something.

She growled under her breath and folded her arms, her fingers constricting and tugging at the fabric of her sleeves.

And here she thought he couldn't aggravate her more.

CHAPTER 13

A small piece of Isla couldn't help but thrum with pride as she stood, maintaining her distance, and observed Adrien and Kai while they carried on with their conference. Their voices were so quiet, she couldn't pick up a single word, and she knew exactly why.

Her best friend and her mate, essentially strangers—one more privy to those titles they bore to her personally than the other—and yet they both had been burned enough by her eavesdropping in the past that they knew to keep things to the faintest of whispers in her presence. That, and to angle in a way that she couldn't glimpse even their faces, take note of any expressions, leaving her view simply of Adrien's back and the dark waves of Kai's hair over the top of the Imperial Heir's head.

Her lips jutted in a pout.

What the hell could they have been talking about?

Minutes had passed—minutes that ticked along like *hours*—and they remained, jabbering like the sunrise frequenters of the Imperial City's Market Square. On and on like they had all the time in the world. It was all she could do to keep her foot from tapping impatiently. To seem relaxed and eased.

She knew if Kai peered over again and saw the action, her perturbation, he'd enjoy it all too much, and the last thing she wanted was to give him *any* type of satisfaction.

With a heaved sigh, she turned away, forcing herself not to care, not to question, not to speculate, even if it fought against every inkling of her nature. She needed to be done with him. She *had* to be done with him. So, she pushed down that piece of her that hoped they'd use her wandering eye as a false sense of safety to let their guards down, and instead, used the moments of limbo to scan the terrain, view the few spectators that had begun to fall away, pick some dust off her coat, check the ends of her hair, and then plot.

She couldn't wallow in guilt anymore. She needed to act. Lukas would likely be kept away from everyone, possibly brought up to one of the upper floors of the infirmary that had been abandoned. She wasn't sure if she could find a way to jog his memories, but she'd be damned if she didn't try. All she had to do was get herself inside his room.

"I'll let you know."

For the first time, Kai's voice sounded heavenly.

Snapping back to attention, Isla found, to her bliss, that the two men had broken away from each other. She'd picked up on the timbre of Kai's voice, the assertion of it. It tipped her off enough that whatever they'd been speaking of was serious.

But she didn't care. Nope. She wasn't curious at all.

"Finally," she'd muttered involuntarily, folding her arms.

Like they'd heard it, they both turned her way.

She stiffened, and as if she hadn't already been caught, cocked her head, deciding to inspect the flecks glittering in the midnight ink above.

"The queen of subtlety," she heard Adrien jeer as he encroached on her.

She brought her gaze back down to meet his, ignoring the comment and cutting to the main objective. "What now?"

"I have no fucking idea."

Her eyebrows shot up in surprise. He'd sounded so sure in his demands to bring Lukas to some aid.

The Heir rubbed his forehead. "I either did the right thing or I'm about to return home to another Winslow packet and lecture about how I'm supposed to handle myself in the subjacent packs." He eyed the space behind her as if he could see the former trainee across it. "He wasn't like that the last time you saw him?"

"No, not at all. We worked together when we were in there, fought together. He was himself. Perfectly fine until—"

Kai and I distracted him...

Kai and I let him get taken...

Kai and I—

Isla bit down hard on her cheek, the pain pulling her from the thoughts. "He was fine," she forced out.

Adrien nodded, thankfully not catching onto the spiral she'd gone down, too lost, likely, in his own. "I know my father departed after the alphas' meeting today, but your dad should still be here. I'll meet with him and then find Seb. We'll meet you in your room in an hour. *Be there* this time."

"Of course," she said, more eager and defensive than she'd meant to, not forgetting she hadn't offered him an answer as to where she'd been before. "Don't let them hurt him."

She received another nod, more like an *"I'll try"*, before Adrien stalked away. She spun and followed his form until he was nothing but a speck, then empty air. Along the way, she caught the last few stragglers departing too, which meant…

It was then that a gust of wind blew by, shockingly strong, casting her hair into her face and rustling her jacket. She tightened her grip around her body, blaming the chill she felt on that breeze, and *not* the sound of the grass shuffling behind her as someone moved through it. *Not* on the scent that wafted to her nose, overtaking the enduring bite of magic, and instilling a comfort in its essence of something warm and woodsy, with a hint of spice and something else she couldn't quite place.

And just like that, the world suddenly felt so, *so* small.

Even with the monstrous feat of architecture hovering above. Even with the vast and endless gem-freckled sky. Even with the oblivion the field seemed to fade into at either side…

It was just the moon, the stars, the dark velvet they adorned—and them.

Kai came to a halt what sounded like a few feet behind her.

Just walk away, she told herself, practically *begging* her feet. *Just walk away and be done with him. You already said your goodbyes. Just end this here. Right now. Go to your room. Meet Adrien and Sebastian in an hour. See Lukas. Fix him. Go back to Io. Move on. Forget. Forget, forget, forget—*

"What was that about?" Her traitorous tongue or her exhausted mind—she wasn't sure which to curse.

"Nothing," Kai answered plainly. "Pack business."

Isla held back a roll of her eyes and kept her tone unwavering. She'd gathered that much. "Of course."

"You're safe."

"Right." The response was quick and followed by the bite of her tongue. His reassurance was like salt in a wound, using her own words against her. If her life didn't hang in the balance, he owed her nothing.

More footsteps whispered through the grass before she felt the warmth of him radiating as he stood at her side.

"Are you okay?" His voice was laced with a disarming gentleness she wasn't expecting.

"I don't know." Once again, she damned her mouth and cringed at how weak the words sounded off her lips.

When she'd started to fall apart during the chaos with the Gate was the last and only time he'd ever witness her like that. She'd battle tooth and nail with herself to ensure it.

"You were in my head," she said sharply, adding a little extra bite, using whatever anger she'd felt at that moment to fuel the fire needed to weld her shattering mask back together. "You tell me."

"I wasn't *in your head*."

She wasn't keen on his aloofness. "You did *something*. How?"

"You know how," he said easily.

"Fine, then *why*?" Following the question, she craned her neck to briefly meet his eyes. The sight made her constrict her fingers so tightly that her nails dug into her arm.

Mate.

The word rung and rung and rung in her head like it never had before. It ebbed and bowed through every vein of her body, every patch of her soul. *My mate. My mate. My—*

"We're doing what we're supposed to." She looked away hurriedly and cut the train of thought off. "We haven't touched."

"You know we've been playing with fire. It's been fun, yes, but I suppose it comes at a cost," he explained, voice kissed by that softness again. He shoved his hands into his pockets. "You and I—" He paused as if searching for words. "You and I are two ends of the same broken road. Two pieces of a cloth stitched and torn by Fate's own hand. We see each other, and we know that, innately. We feel it. Every time. It's not a chosen bond. We don't have to wait for threads to form with time together to have any type of connection." There was the slightest catch in his voice as if the struggles she'd been having truly were mutual, like that repetition was running through his mind the same way. "I'm here. You're there. I'm *here*." He reached out, and his hand ghosted over her cheek. She didn't flinch. "You're still there, but you feel it, right? You have been. The threads winding, pulling—connecting."

She should've vexed her own instinct and curiosity as she allowed her eyes to slide closed. As she dug deep and allowed herself to give life and image to what she'd been experiencing.

In her center, her essence was a spool of rich, golden light, and from it spawned webs and webs of strings, inner connections of her soul, creating the fabric of who she was. But that wasn't it. There was also darkness leaking through, caressing the threads. Some pieces even twined with the shadow.

Kai?

"Why is it dark?" she asked, practically seeing how the inner machinations worked with the proximity.

"I can't help how you perceive me."

Her eyes snapped open, and with a small smile, Kai dropped his hand to his side, leaving her cold again.

She blinked, unsure what to say. Darkness and shadow infecting her soul…*that's* how she saw this?

Shaking her head, she fought the images away and fought the urge to ask what he saw when he closed his eyes. Instead, she focused on that winding. "So, what's the point then? All this dancing around each other if we're already more or less connected."

"The threads can try to tie together all they want, but they won't hold in the end. The bastards have gotten stronger because we're masochists, but they're not permanent. They'll break with time, with distance. Hell, even touch isn't *permanent*, but it would be damn near impossible to fight against what happens next." She caught the way he looked her over head to toe before adding, "And trying to hold off the inevitable after that, long enough for the ties to fray, would have us wishing it would kill us." He shrugged. "I'd say the waters get a bit muddier when the choices are losing your mind or the best sex of your life with your supposed 'soulmate'."

She couldn't help but snort. "Best sex of my life, huh?"

"Lewis would be a *distant* memory," he said with a taunting grin.

"*Levi* already is a distant memory, believe me." She battled to contain a smile.

Now that he'd finished his elucidation, she couldn't deny that she was not only stunned but mildly impressed. Where she lacked understanding, he'd filled in most of the gaps, and somehow, also managed to overwhelm her. When she'd wanted a mate all those years ago, obsessed over it, she hadn't truly known the depth of what it meant. When all that pressure came down the minute she came of age, she'd accepted it and done everything she'd felt she needed to. The idea hadn't sounded *too* bad. Having that one person to turn to, that shared a piece of her, that couldn't abandon her.

But it was more. It was so much more.

"You'll understand when you find your mate."

A female voice she hadn't heard in over a year clawed into her consciousness. It turned everything in her stomach sour. Made her nauseous. She fought that away too.

"How do you know all of this stuff?" she asked. "About the threads and connections."

"A friend of mine used to work those pathetic, money-hungry, mate-search events. The ones that leech off the sad and lonely. She told me all this stuff they'd tell people to mystify them and get them excited to finally find 'the one'—*with* their help, exclusively. I thought it was all bullshit until now."

She did her best to keep herself from frowning. She'd been to one of those gatherings—or several.

"So, was that a good enough explanation for you, or do you need more? Will I have to prepare myself for a striptease next?" he heckled. "As enjoyable as that would be, I'm afraid it'll likely be counterproductive."

And just like that, the illusion was broken by his knack for pushing her buttons at the absolute worst moments.

"You insufferable ass," she grumbled before turning and stalking away. Heading back to her room, back to planning how she'd find a way to get to Lukas, how she'd hopefully help him get his memories back, and wondering who she'd have to cross along the way.

His laugh from behind her was loud and bright before she heard his footsteps follow her own. She didn't turn but tallied them, tracked them. He could've kept up with her easily but had chosen to lag. It was like she could feel his eyes boring into her back, studying every movement. There was the smallest rush through her veins, and she denied the urge to use the opportunity to get him back. To move smoother, to exaggerate the sway to her hips. See how long she could tease and taunt him before he—

No. Not again.

About halfway up the field, he could have veered for a quick shot to the lodging areas where he, no longer a patient, stayed. But he remained at her tail.

"I believe *our* business is done, Alpha," she called to him.

"Back to 'Alpha' now, I see."

"That's what you are, is it not?"

"I think we're at the point where you can call me whatever you want."

"How about asshole?"

"I think you can do better."

She growled. There were plenty of things she'd like to say but refrained. "Stop following me."

Kai let out a breath. "I need to make sure you're okay."

Isla stuttered in her movements. *Make sure I'm okay?* He'd sounded so honest.

She recalled the look he'd given her as the Gate held tight, as the bak roared, and she began to crumble and descend into that *place*. When those connections wrapped around her and held for dear life. It was so easy to forget in the moments when he drove her mad, when the world kept buzzing around at a pace she could barely keep up with, but he looked out for her, even if it was for his own sake as much as her own.

Still, with that in mind, she said, "I'm fine. Don't worry about me."

A lie but he didn't need to know that.

Kai snickered. "Easier said than done when your favorite pastime seems to be sprinting towards danger whenever the opportunity arises."

Her jaw slacked. "I do not."

"You've proven otherwise."

"You've barely known me a week."

"And yet, you've stressed me enough for a lifetime," he said with a tinge of exasperation. "Every chance you've had to get yourself in trouble or nearly killed, you've taken it. And I've come to know that look in those *dazzling* eyes of yours."

She held in her groan as she fought her heart and mind to make sure neither took the beguilement for anything other than what it was.

She knew her mate's tendencies well, already. How he used charm to disarm and distract her, and surely others. How he calculated things. How he was always one step ahead of her, and by the time she realized, another. They'd said their goodbyes. They'd parted. No love or emotions to bind them. Just figments and fragments of fading stars, fraying threads. They had nothing necessary to offer each other at this point. So, there was a reason he hadn't left her alone yet. Another play at hand.

He'd since sped up to join at her side.

"What look?" she asked carelessly, barely peering over.

He pointed. "That one." She went cross-eyed for a moment as she stared at the digit, inches away from her nose. "You're about to do something you shouldn't, and you know it too."

"I don't know what you're talking about." She shot her narrowed gaze up to him. "And get your hand out of my face."

She hated the mirth her aggravation seemed to bring to his features

—and even greater than that, she despised that joy looked good on him. She hadn't noticed the slightest dimples bracketing his smile before.

He dropped his arm. "What's your thing with this guy anyway?"

"What guy?"

"The hunter from Tethys that you're running off to see." When her eyes widened and then promptly narrowed, he added, "I didn't *read your mind*, you're just horribly predictable. So, what is it? You seem to care a lot. Here—back in the Wilds. You were ready to jump into that mess to help him, and though I'd still hedge my bets on you and that temper, that guard looked—"

"Nothing like *that* if that's what you're worried about," she cut him off, sick of hearing how smug and correct he was.

"I wasn't."

She shook her head as the scene ripped through her mind again. Lukas lunging for the guard, being brought down to the ground, his screaming, the group descending. All the while, Kai was off to the side.

She met his eyes. "Why didn't you get involved?"

His brows drew together as if it were obvious. "He's of Tethys, and we're in Callisto. My thoughts and opinions don't matter here. If I inserted myself, it would've just led to a headache and more paperwork than I can afford attention to. And frankly, I have much more to worry about. A pack to return to and a mate who's ready to risk herself and take on the world at any minor transgression."

I suppose the Goddess has blessed you, would have been her retort. The snide remark sat just on the tip of her tongue, but that bit, *the words*...

Minor transgression.

Lukas losing all memory and sense wasn't a "minor transgression". His life hanging in some balance wasn't a "minor transgression". His family that was waiting back in Tethys for him to return triumphant, a warrior, wouldn't see it as a "minor transgression".

Her lips quivered and her nose twitched with unspoken words. All she wanted was to lash out at him. Her tongue ran over her teeth, but as she opened her mouth to speak, she felt wetness on her cheek.

Her gaze directed upwards, and another drop of rain fell directly into her eye. She winced, squinting, before wiping it away.

A stronger current of wind rocketed through the field, nearly forceful enough to move her as one drop became two then three, four, five. The crack of lightning came next, then the roar of thunder and a low whir before the steady stream of watery bullets. The chilly rain made quick work soaking her clothes, her hair.

Maybe it had been a gift from the Goddess to snap her out of it. For the smallest of moments, the corners of her mouth threatened to twitch upwards, and she resisted the urge to throw her arms out as it washed over her. She'd always loved rain and thunderstorms, so rare to come by in Io. On the times they did, she'd immediately go to her window perch in her small city apartment and sit, listening to the patter and watching the lights of the city glitter in the dew.

She could almost do that again. Be home, at least. Almost.

A gasp slipped from her mouth when a sudden rush of unease rocked her system—but the feeling…wasn't her own.

Kai, equally drenched—with his clothes clinging to his body, leaving outlines of the taut muscle beneath and his dark tresses straightening and bending in ways she'd never seen—wasn't looking up at the mist-like gathering storm clouds or even at her, but instead, beside them. His eyes were slits, and a sharp line, bolstered by shadow, cut through his cheek. Isla followed his gaze. It took a while for her to register the silhouettes of trees bucking in the whistling, brewing torrent. The feelings of unease grew stronger, morphed into anger and—fear?

"Alpha?" she voiced cautiously, breaking the title down into its syllables.

Kai didn't answer. Instead, he snarled at what seemed like emptiness before he ran to it, leaving Isla alone in the middle of the field where pools and puddles quickly formed at her feet, blinking and stunned.

"What the hell?" she mumbled as he disappeared into the blackness.

Technically, this was her opening. To walk away. To leave him behind and leave him, leave *them*, be—forever. But that connection fought, those strings and threads and tethers tugged and twisted and did everything they could to keep them together. And there was something else. Something worse. Something stemming from a similar place as her earlier peace with him on the roof that she didn't want to acknowledge.

She could leave him now. She *should*.

"Shit," she breathed, shaking her head before bounding toward the trees.

When Isla broke over the woodland's edge, it was as if she'd entered another world. The shrouded area possessed an odd and eerie stillness as both the wind and moonlight battled to break through the dense brush and heavy canopy. It was almost disturbingly familiar, like all it was missing was a simple curse before it became the twin to its bastardized and caged brother yards away. For that, Isla was even more grateful for the rain, the downpour like a lifeline, a rope to cling onto while she dangled over the abyss of her memories from beyond the

Wall. It was one of the few differences her brain could latch onto as a reminder that she was safe and out of death's grasp.

"Where the hell did you go?" She paused to look to either side of her.

Nothing. Absolutely nothing.

Though she hadn't been too far behind, Kai was nowhere in sight.

Her eyes slid closed as she honed her hearing, her smell, trying to pick up any type of hint as to where he was but she couldn't. Kai didn't want to be found—by her or whatever he'd run after, she wasn't sure.

Any annoyance she felt was usurped by worry, the unease she'd been infected with still crawling beneath her skin. She'd never felt or seen him afraid of anything. Nervous, yes, but not scared.

Reluctantly, she latched onto the emotion, clawing through it to find that tether again, hoping she could use the damn thing to her advantage. But it was weak, the tie fraying. Of course.

Still, she did what she could, continuing her trek and following an instinct she hoped had been guided by the webs weaved through them. Her path grew dangerous over terrain a mess of dips, valleys, and swamps she hadn't been expecting as she called out his name—through a link, out into the wind. Pockets of the moon's glow peeked to greet her.

She'd nearly reached her wit's end, her own terror icing her soul the way the rain was her body, at the notion of the complete unknown, when finally, she spotted him. A warming rush of relief took to her veins, but it didn't last nearly as long as she would've liked.

Skidding to a halt so fast she nearly fell over, Isla cocked her head. Kai was postured tall, head held high as if he were trying to catch a scent in the air. He had to have known she was there, even if she'd been masking herself, judging by the way his clenched fists had tensed, relaxed, and tensed again. Maybe he'd wanted her to find him out in the open like this.

She approached him slowly. "Is this you trying to be funny?"

The query was met by silence. Kai hadn't even bothered to turn around.

As she got closer, Isla could sense the faintest pull again, but she didn't need it to feel the simmering rage and bitter worry that emanated from him.

But—there was nothing. Nothing obvious here that should've sent him running, that should've elicited such a vehement reaction.

The chill up her spine was a potent concoction, brewed by the weather and the ominous silence. Her teeth chattered, and she wrapped her arms around herself. "What is—"

"Quiet."

Isla jutted her head back, the word holding like a block between them as Kai returned to his observation. A sense of quiet urgency seemed to power every breath of his, the twinge of each solid muscle as he remained on high alert.

"Stay here." Kai finally spoke, taking a step forward. "Be ready to shift."

The contents of Isla's stomach turned to lead. "Shift?"

"Yes." Kai's voice was unwavering like a general commanding a soldier, an alpha over his armies. "Have your wolf ready."

Isla blinked, finding it suddenly difficult to swallow. The statement had hit her two-fold.

No one besides her own father and physicians knew of her inability to tap into that all-important piece of herself—not even Adrien and Sebastian—but the realization that this was yet another way she could be viewed as broken wasn't the worst.

Shifting itself required a great deal of strength, and to maintain the state, an ample amount of energy. It was the pinnacle of all they could be and why so much training went into preparing for the often days-long Hunt. For that reason, taking on one's wolf for any type of fight or battle was typically reserved for the greatest of threats, and for lesser cases, warriors had learned other forms of combat to fall back on—hand-to-hand, weaponry. But for whatever was out here…that wasn't enough.

Finally, she confessed, "I—I can't."

Kai raked a hand over his hair, slicking it out of his face, though some stubborn pieces curled back to his forehead. He turned to glance at her sideways. Though it shouldn't have, given his tone, the darkness and seriousness of his eyes startled her. "What do you mean?"

Isla frowned, the words like cement in her throat. "I can't shift. I haven't been able to since I was hurt."

Kai's face flashed, not with anger but with concern, and Isla felt not a tug, but a twist. He spun fully, moving quickly in a way that had his body looming over her, blocking her view of the forest…or blocking the forest's vantage of her.

His eyes traveled over her features in earnest as if searching for some levity over a twisted joke she'd been playing.

"Why didn't you say something?" That aura of urgency and desperation had seeped into his voice. Before she even had a chance to answer, he pinched the bridge of his nose, shaking his head. "Why do you do this?"

"Me?" She stood her ground, pointing a finger, though she felt like a fraud. "*You're* the one that ran this time."

"You shouldn't have followed me."

Isla slowly dropped her hand. "Well, I didn't have much of a choice." Kai's features softened in understanding, but the moment was brief. She countered his displeased look with one of her own, while inside, she battled to feel confident and in control. "What's going on? And if you say 'pack business', Goddess help you."

Kai growled, but it almost didn't feel like it was directed at her, before looking off to the side. A slew of emotions ran over his face so fast she couldn't clock them, but it was enough to give her hope that he may open up. It was a dance they'd found themselves engaging in a few times already, and she wondered if there would ever be a point when he'd be ready to throw caution to the wind and completely give in.

Thunder rumbled again. The boom and its accompaniment of crashing lightning were so loud that it seemed to shake the earth around them.

At the rush of noise, Kai stepped back with an aggravated sigh and angled his head. He scanned the trees closest to them before nodding upwards. "Can you climb?" Isla's face twisted in confusion, but once again, before she had a chance to question, Kai added, "Go up into that tree and don't move until I come back."

"Excuse me?" Was he insane? "Come back from where? *Why*? What is going on?"

"I need you to trust me." Kai met her eyes again, and she swore she almost found some sympathy in them. "If this is what I think, I don't want you anywhere near it, especially when you can't defend yourself."

Trust him?

"I've been trained just as long to be able to fight without my wolf as with it." The counter was unsteady off her lips, not assured in the statement herself.

"It's not enough," Kai echoed the sentiments.

Isla took note of the rippling timber around them. What was she supposed to do? Just go up into a tree and—wait? "I'll just go back to the infirmary."

"No. You can't go back through here alone. It's not safe." Kai stepped closer again, though the warmth of his body couldn't quite melt the ice buried within her. "I *need you* to trust me, Isla."

There were those words again, conveyed with a sincerity that almost felt manipulative.

Isla straightened, not knowing what to do with the overwhelming emotion that seemed to be pooling up from her ankles. It grated every part of her to trust him, simply for the fact that the only reason she would was this bond she never wanted to acknowledge again.

Damnit.

Wordlessly, Isla turned and scouted the branches, then pressed her fingers firmly along the cold, slippery bark of the one she'd determined easiest to reach. The limb groaned as she hoisted herself up, but proved sturdy, barely trembling from her weight as she spun on it and sat. As much as she hated the idea—and judging by Kai's expression, he'd been second-guessing too as another gust of wind shot by and the threat of lightning loomed—she couldn't shake the gnawing feeling this was also the best option. It took scaling up one more limb for her to be nearly masked in the brush, protected from the view of whatever was lurking out in the shadows.

Kai approached the trunk's base, resting his hand on the branch just below her. One inch and he'd just brush her skin. "Stay quiet and stay hidden," he said, features hard as stone. "Don't move. Hopefully, I won't be long."

Isla bit down on her cheek. She hated this. With every piece of her, she hated this. How could she just stay up here, useless, while he was out there dealing with whatever this was?

"If you're not back in ten minutes, I'm going after you," she told him quickly, digging her nails into the bark beneath her. "I'm serious."

Kai's face remained unchanged. "I know you are."

And with that, he disappeared.

CHAPTER 14

Puffing out air that clouded in a mist, Isla threw her head back and looked up through the jutting branches. Her eyes slid closed as she embraced the dripping rain that peppered her skin.

Three minutes.

She'd only counted out *three minutes* so far, and she was sick of it. *This*. Sitting and doing nothing, locked in a cage of branches like a simple house bird.

She should've been out there, helping Kai with whatever the hell this was. A threat supposedly so great that she was useless without her wolf. That made it unsafe for her to roam the forest alone again.

As her narrowed gaze lowered to track beyond the trees he'd descended behind—a hope in her chest that maybe he'd appear—another long, steady stream of wind cut through. A choir of howls from the foliage followed in its wake, comforting if the tree hadn't bucked in response, her perch becoming rickety. She braced one hand on the rough bark of the trunk and the other on the branch above her head. The storm was getting worse. The wind stronger and the rain pelting harder. If the mysterious dwellers of the shadows didn't get her, the weather surely could.

When the surge finally calmed, she righted herself again and wiped her palms on her coat. It didn't do much for drying. Her clothes were still so drenched and heavy that she wondered if she'd be better off discarding what was failing to do its duty in keeping her warm. Upon bringing her hands up to inspect them, she noted flecks of the husk dotting her skin and a purplish tinge that colored the tip of her fingers —but that wasn't all she saw.

Isla flipped one of them over. Once. Twice.

Golden intangible light looped around each of her fingers, the delicate strands wrapping her wrist, traveling down the veins of her forearm to her heart, to her soul, down to the wolf wounded deep within her. She traced the same path back up to her fingertips, where it mingled with tendrils of shadow before the mirage faded completely.

Her eyes had been wide with awe before they narrowed. What a damn joke it all was—a *horrible*, mesmerizing joke.

How could something so lethal, something that destroyed—that she'd *seen* destroy, shredding the people she was closest to apart piece by piece—be so wonderful and mystifying?

You and I are two ends of the same broken road. Two pieces of a cloth stitched and torn by Fate's own hand.

Her other half, hand-picked by a deity herself.

It sounded so beautiful. So much larger than anything she could wrap her mind around.

We don't have to wait for threads to form with time together to have any type of connection.

For her entire life, her soul had been waiting to be reunited with his. Those threads, her, *made* for him. And him for her.

She looked out into the forest again before back to her hand, trying to will back the visual but nothing came.

It was all foolish…she was foolish. And she was also tired and scared and angry and—

In a tree.

She was in a tree.

What am I doing?

For the love of the Goddess, she was a warrior now—killed not one of their continent's most feared creatures, but two—and here she was, doing nothing but counting down seconds and having an unnecessary existential crisis while Kai could be in *actual* trouble. Ten minutes, be damned. He could give her all the shit that he wanted.

Isla looked out into the forest only to be greeted by something moving so swiftly over the floor, it was a smoke-like blur. Too large to be an animal that lived in these woods. The creatures she hadn't realized were housed in the areas around her grew restless from its presence, it seemed. Their caws, squeaks, and mewls joined the storm's symphony.

Isla's heart leaped into her throat as she braced herself against the trunk and leaned back to glance through the leaves in the direction it had gone.

Kai?

She moved further, twisting and turning to get another decent look. Maybe he'd forgotten what tree she'd gone up into.

The shadow doubled back again so close and fast that it spooked her. Spooked everything. In a horde, a mess of black-feathered birds soared down from the treetop, disregarding her presence, their wings skidding her jacket and catching her face.

She couldn't stop herself from losing her balance, and everything that followed moved in slow motion. Her body screamed in pain again as she descended from her perch, meeting other branches on the way. There was a flash of light and air fled her lungs in a whoosh the moment Isla hit the ground with a splash. A groan, that sounded more like a wheeze, fell from her lips. She was lucky she hadn't been higher up. A sharpness shot through her arm, her side. The same one that had been done a number on by the bak. She forced herself to roll onto her stomach in order to push herself up. The cold mud seeped into her clothes and coated the skin of her hands, her neck, her face.

Whatever that was, whoever—it wasn't Kai.

And whatever or whoever it was, she could feel it close by. Could feel it watching.

Breaths escaped her mouth in rapid clouds of white, and Isla shot to her feet. She swayed on her weak legs and stumbled back to her tree, bracing herself against its base. Using it for protection, she pressed her back against it to cover her flank.

She kept her gaze upwards as she lowered herself to the ground. Her fingers wrapped tightly around a thick, fallen tree limb. She held it firmly in both hands, constricting so much to counter the slippery mud, splinters embedded her palms.

Her eyes darted around her surroundings, and soon came the sound of fast, heavy footsteps at her back. Heart thundering and a scream trapped in her throat, Isla whirled around, swinging the branch as hard as she could.

The Beta of Deimos stopped it with his forearm, barely even flinching at the impact. Either he was incredibly strong or her hit was pathetic.

Isla's eyes were wide as she dropped the branch to her side. "*You.*"

For a moment, Ezekiel's expression mirrored hers, face fallen in shock. It didn't last very long, however. As his eyes traced over her, taking in her disheveled appearance, a look of distaste took over his face. "You look wretched."

She would be ridiculous to disagree with him—she was certain that she did—but as always, his tone held a condescending air to it that grated her nerves.

"I fell out of a tree," Isla said pointedly, harshly wiping the mud from her cheeks, a difficult task when every other inch of her was coated in it. "What's your excuse?" The last part had come out on reflex, and that piece of her that had been drilled in etiquette cringed. Technically, not crowned a luna, she still ranked far below him in the hierarchy, but she couldn't get herself to apologize. "What are you doing here?"

"I'm looking for my alpha," he said, crossing his arms over the slick sleeves of his overcoat where raindrops flecked off easily. She was surprised that he hadn't reprimanded her for the outburst or returned with his own retort. "I was told he'd last been seen down by the Gate with a woman. I'd been hoping it wasn't you, but I had my doubts." His eyes trailed the area around them, narrowed as he sought out what she assumed was Kai. "I was young and unmated once, and when I saw the woods…"

It wasn't hard for her to figure out what he was alluding to. *If only* that had been why they'd come in here.

Clenching her branch tighter in her hand, she did her own survey of the area again. Nothing seemed amiss. No blurs. No shadows. *Could it* have been Ezekiel moving that quickly?

"Of all the wolves on this continent, the daughter of the Imperial Beta," Ezekiel said, drawing Isla's attention back to him. "I have to say, I'm not surprised. On paper, you hail from an exceptional bloodline. Compatible strength with an alpha, I'd say."

So, he wanted to talk about this.

Pursing her lips, Isla recalled Kai's words to her. Why he hadn't wanted Ezekiel to know they didn't necessarily despise each other.

"You don't have to worry about me, you know," she told him, more eager than she'd intended. "The last thing I desire is to be his mate or become your luna, and be assured, the alpha wants me just as little as I want him. We have an agreement, and we're sticking to it."

Ezekiel raised a dark eyebrow as if challenged by her words. "Quite bold of you to assume you can conquer a goddess."

"You should be grateful," she countered. "Once I'm back in Io, I'm out of your hair forever."

At her words, another laugh passed his mouth, but aside from cavalier, it also sounded bitter. Ezekiel looked off into the forest again, and as silence descended between them and tension rose with each passing second, Isla prepared to walk away to find Kai.

That was until the beta began, "Our people have been through much in these past years, months—the last especially. What they need is stability and hope." He met her eyes again. "I could never imagine delivering unto them the news that their true queen wants no part of their existence."

Isla's breath caught. His words were sharp as blades, and they hit their mark, the last especially, cutting deep. But before she had time to *really* process what he was saying, Ezekiel continued, "I *am* grateful, Isla. I'm grateful for every brazen, stubborn, and proud bone in your body. Now Kai can find the perfect luna. The one our pack needs. The one it deserves."

It felt as if he'd stabbed her in the gut and twisted. Her jaw had unhinged as she blinked, staring blankly at him.

The one they need, and the one they deserve.
The one they need, and the one they deserve.
Now Kai can find the perfect luna…

She shook her head to get the sentences to stop playing over and over and over again. Taunting her. Reminding her. But there was no right for her to feel agitated. He was…right about what they deserved. About what her choice meant. And this *was* her choice, but—

Isla suddenly felt like she'd been slammed by a mountain of sheer force. She sensed an aura like a beacon. Not a reaction through the bond, but the simple reach of an alpha to any surrounding wolves. Pure power. Rage.

Kai.

Ezekiel had felt it too, she could tell, and it was only a split second before they both took off. She buzzed through the trees and thickets and swamps as quickly as she could, feelings through their bond now ebbing and flowing. They were all over the place. Anger and fear and sadness and back to enraged again. She gripped the limb tighter in her hand as a new wave of panic overtook her. Even her wolf grew restless, and that nagging feeling of being watched returned. But she brushed it away and pressed forward, following the beacon and the bond until she finally found—

"Kai." She let his name out in a relieved sigh when she came upon him. As before, his back was to her, only this time, instead of scoping a clearing, he was facing a tree with a base twice the width of the one she'd climbed up. Once again, he didn't bother turning as she approached him, her steps were small and slow as she used the time to compose herself, her wolf.

She could relax. He was here. He was alive. He was—

Isla's eyebrows shot up when she noticed the tears in his shirt, the black ink of lumerosi on the muscles of his back, his arms, his shoulders, a low, simmering red. He'd nearly shifted, but—stopped himself?

"Oh, Goddess." She hadn't realized Ezekiel had continued to follow her path, even up to Kai himself. The older man's face was pale when she looked upon it, and she followed his gaze.

"What the hell?" she muttered, examining the tree's bark. Freshly carved, it seemed, were symbols, markings, and—words? She didn't understand a single bit of it. The only thing that she could recognize were claw marks slashed right through them.

"What is this?" she asked and was met by silence. She tried again. "What does it say?"

Silence.

Isla bit her lip, stomach turning as she moved to get a better look at Kai's face. She held in her gasp as she took in the hard lines, the faint glow of his eyes, and once she dropped her gaze down, the drops of blood leaking from his clenched fists. His chest was heaving as he battled what seemed like himself, his wolf. And she could feel it—his pain. From what, she wasn't certain. But instinct kicked in, and she stepped forward, getting as close as she could, not caring about Ezekiel watching a few feet away.

She couldn't touch him, but she didn't need to.

Isla reached out and hovered a hand around his, hoping to pull whatever cord or thread she needed to. Kai's grip loosened, if only slightly, and crimson dripped from his hands, muddying the soaked earth. But his features remained hard, his lumerosi and his eyes still alight.

Isla swallowed. "Kai," she said his name gently before raising her arm, sending the same absent touch over his cheek, the cut of his jaw. "Kai, look at me."

He did, and the power radiating from him was suffocating. So intense that it would've made any other wolf bow in respect, in fear. But not her; she wasn't afraid.

Another deep breath. Isla mustered a small smile. "That was your ten minutes, asshole."

Somehow, that had done it. Kai's eyes softened until she was staring into the storm she'd grown accustomed to. The one she didn't mind getting stuck in sometimes. But something was different, off. In a way she'd never seen. There was pain. Not physical but emotional, and deep and buried. All-consuming and unrefined.

His features twitched as he was unable to fight off a frown, and Isla realized he'd had his own mask on this entire time she'd known him. A beautiful one made of iron and steel and everything damn near unbreakable. Nothing had gotten through it. Not completely. Not like this.

But whatever was written here—that's what did him in.

Part of her didn't want to know what it meant, but she kept her hand steady, close to his cheek, fingertips so close to running through his hair that curled at the nape of his neck. "What's going on? What is this?"

"Alpha."

Isla's eyes darted back to Ezekiel whose tone was heavy with warning. He *knew* what this was and didn't want her to.

Biting her lip and holding back a glare—because it wasn't the time—she looked back at Kai. His eyes had never left her face, not at all as she'd looked away. As if he'd needed her as an anchor, needed whatever lay between them to keep himself together.

"Kai." The name was so faint, it nearly got lost in a crash of thunder. She sent the next words out through their link. *"Tell me."*

Kai swallowed before drawing his eyes back to the etchings in the bark. She didn't know if he'd heard her, or if he'd decided on his own, but his voice was gravelly and Isla's blood ran cold as he said, "Whoever murdered my brother and father—they're here."

CHAPTER 15

"Murdered?"

Kai's words tolled Isla like a bell, clanging through every part of her mind, her body. The sentence running rounds as if on the seventh repetition, it would be less jarring. It would make more sense.

Her arm had gone stiff at the side of his face, her fingers trembling a mere inch from his cheek. So close that one wrong move, one spasmed muscle, one particularly strong gust of wind, and she'd touch him. Finally know what had eluded her—what would *forever* elude her—in the true feel of his skin against her own.

Still possessing some coherence—even though she *craved* feeling something warm and real to tell her this wasn't all some other waking nightmare—she lowered it shakily to her side. Fear played menacingly at her feet like a feral cat circling its prey.

There was a killer here.

There was a killer *here* in these woods.

One who'd taken down not just an alpha but also his heir and had gotten away with it. Unseen, unscathed.

"H—how do you know?" Isla choked out the question. "What is this?"

And, Goddess, *why* were they still standing out here?

Kai's eyes returned to her face. He took in her stunned silence, her surely aghast expression, and for it, his own features shifted. Steel and iron reforged as if him masking the rage and grief from the surface would do anything when she so freely felt it through what linked them. What had been twining with every second they spent in proximity.

"It's a message," he said. There was a strain in his voice. A hesitance. Isla whirled to take in the tree's surface again. She clocked every curve and symbol etched into the bark, doing what she could to see beyond the claw marks made, she was sure, by her mate's hand. But she couldn't discern a thing. Not one bend or loop or—were these even *supposed* to be letters?

Her hand lifted to graze the timber, but she halted. "What does it say?"

"I don't know."

"You don't *know*?"

"You're certain, Alpha?" Ezekiel's question was spoken so evenly, it nearly rang as a statement. The beta hadn't moved from his spot. His face, like Kai's, was set in stone, and Isla wondered if all who hailed from Deimos were specialized at wearing this mask when chaos was upon them.

"Yes," Kai said.

"Did you see them?"

"No. I just—I heard—I felt...I knew."

Kai's jaw tensed and his lips threatened to rise in a snarl as anger shone in his eyes. It was as if the moment was about to consume him again, the realization of who and what this was. Isla could feel it bubbling, burning through her in a way that almost made her want to keel over, but she weathered it and wouldn't let it show that it was having any effect.

"Kai."

At her voice, Kai met her gaze again, and his eyes scoured her face for what felt like forever before, thankfully, he relaxed. Isla could've sworn there was a flash of guilt across his features.

The words "are you okay" sat on the tip of her tongue, but they felt trivial at this point. Instead, she asked, "Should we still be out here?"

Kai dragged his hands over his face before moving to push his hair back to no avail. "They're gone."

Relief and doubt collided in a way that made her dizzy. "How do you know that?"

Kai lowered his arms. "Because I do."

Isla kept her features from twisting into a scowl.

Here he was being vague again, but before she could be annoyed by it, she saw his reasons. Kai had been right in his assumptions earlier. If she'd known who he was going after, there wasn't a *chance* she'd have left his side, and she probably wasn't equipped in her state to take on one capable of killing an alpha. But why was he being so ominous now? What was it about *how* he knew that still put her at risk?

As if he could see the inner workings of her mind, Kai's eyes hardened in the same way they had before as if saying yet again, *I need you to trust me.*

"Do you think they know about her?" Ezekiel cut into their silent staring.

Kai turned back to him, body tensing as he thought. He released a breath, shaking his head. "I don't know."

Foreign tendrils of fear kissed Isla's bones again as Kai absently moved another inch closer, in such a way that shielded her once more.

The beta's eyes narrowed between them, and his tone dripped with suspicion. "And you're certain you aren't bound in any way?"

"Not permanently," Kai said.

"The ties will fray in time," Isla chimed, almost in reassurance to herself. Kai glanced at her, donning a look of what seemed like stunned pride. She offered a small uptick of her lips before saying, "What? I listen."

Again, the exchange was watched with a keen eye, and again, Ezekiel fell into that tense quiet. He cocked his head away from them, briefly scouting the forest. Isla did the same. Kai too. Until—

"We should take her with us."

"Excuse me?" Isla felt a twinge in her neck from how fast she'd snapped her head back.

"What?" Kai echoed her confusion.

"If what I just saw is any indication, you're vulnerable like this, Alpha." Ezekiel kept his voice low. "Only days ago, you could sense her torment during the Hunt, and it made you turn back and risk everything. Now, it seems in your 'nothingness', you've grown even closer."

Isla had barely heard the tailing end of his statement—the unfortunate observation that she may have been able to argue a truth, though they remained very much in the dark about each other—and instead, focused on what came before it.

She looked to Kai, her eyebrows drawn. "You could...*feel* me during the Hunt?"

How could that have even been possible? They'd barely interacted but three times before then and certainly hadn't been as close as they had recently.

Kai let out an exasperated sigh as if he'd never wanted her to be aware of it. "Vaguely." The quick glower he sent his beta's way only supported the notion. "I knew when you started fighting the first one, so I waited and tracked you. I stayed out of your way and only interfered when needed."

"She is a weakness."

Ezekiel spoke before she could entertain Kai's words. He earned mirrored scowls from them both.

"*Your* weakness," he clarified, "as long as you are bound in a way that she offers no strength at your side. Fraying or not, in the scheme of an enemy trying to cripple you, you're nearly as good as mated right now. If we bring her to Deimos, we can keep an eye on her until your bond is truly nothing but a memory."

"Are you insane?" Isla gritted out.

"I'm looking out for my alpha and his mate," Ezekiel said pointedly, not doing well to mask his resentment in his typical air of arrogance. "Although, you've eddied some of the responsibilities per your 'agreement', there are some that must be upheld."

"Where would you 'keep an eye' on me in Deimos? You don't even want anyone to know I *exist*."

"There are some safe houses throughout the region. You'll be kept there until it's determined things are sorted."

"So, I'd be a prisoner."

"Those houses are far from a prison. You'd be given everything you need—food, water, and someone would come through every few—"

"Enough."

Kai, likely sensing how irate she was becoming, took a step forward, placing himself between them—the two people meant, in a way, to be his right and left hand. The two meant to advise and mediate *him*—not be mediated themselves.

"I think we've progressed beyond the times of kidnapping maidens."

Isla folded her arms and tilted her head. That was…debatable…but she'd let Kai go on.

"So, what do you suggest, Alpha?" Ezekiel asked.

"We move forward with what our plan always was." She couldn't help but notice the easy emphasis he'd put on those two words—*we… ours*. Kai pointed to himself and then to Isla. "Deimos, Io."

In the pause he'd left, she finished, "Forget."

Kai nodded, that satisfied look passing over again. "And we need to start now. There's a chance whoever this is has no idea who you are, and we have to capitalize on it. I don't know if they're coming back, or how or why they're here at all. I'll be around until morning in case anything—happens."

"You won't," Ezekiel said, earning raised eyebrows from both of them. "We must return to the pack immediately. It's why I came to find you."

Terror flickered in Kai's eyes. "What happened?"

"Emergent word from the council—matters that can't wait for us until the late afternoon," Ezekiel explained. "We must be back by dawn. They've already sent transport that should be here within the hour."

"What happened?" Kai repeated, a bit more forcefully.

Ezekiel didn't answer, instead, he looked towards Isla, and she knew.

"Pack business," she answered for him, wishing she could wipe the small upturn of his mouth that followed off his face.

"Zahra's alright, I've been assured," he told Kai. "The guards are with her twenty-four-seven."

Isla could practically feel the relief that washed over her mate, then realized, Zahra was the name of his mother. Another fact she could add to the list of the few she'd gathered of him.

At the thought of the former luna, Isla's insides felt heavy, and as she raked her eyes over Kai, the sunken feeling only got worse. How could she have let it so easily slip her mind the sheer *weight* of everything Kai, his mother, and even Deimos as a pack had been dealt? A family destroyed, an entire community's foundations shaken…she couldn't even imagine.

She was overwrought with the urge to apologize, to do—something —but before she could, Kai told Ezekiel, "Walk her back. I'll meet you at the Pack Hall."

"No," Isla said immediately as it dawned what that meant. "You're not going to be alone."

At her concern, Kai smiled in an almost endearing way, at odds with what he was presenting. "They could've tried to kill me already, but they didn't. It's something else I don't know the reason for, but they don't want me dead." He laughed. "Not yet, at least."

"That's not funny," Isla said, an uncharacteristic woefulness in her voice. "I don't like this. It's not…safe."

"Do you actually *care* about me?" he jested.

"Don't be a dick."

"Ah, but you make it so fun," Kai said, squaring himself off in front of her, blocking her and their mouths from Ezekiel's view.

Isla grumbled in response, though she wished she could wrap herself in the gentleness with which he spoke.

Though they weren't far, and the beta would surely hear everything they said, it still felt like they were the only two people out here.

Kai had turned serious. "I'm *really* going to need you to cool it with the warrior princess act for a few hours, though." Upon her even further flattening eyebrows, another smile threatened his mouth. "Are you going to be alone?"

Isla shook her head. "Adrien and my brother are meeting me in my room."

Kai took in a deep breath at the mention, jaw tensing before he said, "You trust no one but your family until you're back home, safe and away from this place. Away from me. Promise me."

Isla bit her lip as she fought off the protests roaring in her skull, fought off her instinct, her wolf's, to protect him. "Fine."

He leaned a little closer, unwittingly or intentionally pulling those threads. "*Promise* me, Isla."

She didn't know why he needed to hear her say it, but she obliged. "I promise."

She could see in his eyes that it wasn't enough—*nothing* would be enough to convince him everything would be okay—but still, he backed away and turned to his beta. "Ezekiel."

"As I would defend you, Alpha," the older man said, and Isla was sure the words grated his tongue.

As Kai turned to begin walking away, Isla realized what was happening—what was *finally* happening—and her stomach bottomed out.

"Goodnight," she said in a rush, the word falling from her lips without thought. She couldn't get herself to say the alternative, what she'd stood by so vehemently earlier—*goodbye*.

Kai halted, and as he had before, trailed his eyes over her long and slow, taking her in one last time. Her—drenched and covered in mud and twigs and blood, probably cut and bruised.

This would be the final image of her in his head—wretched, absolutely wretched. Not a queen needed or a queen deserved.

But Kai still smiled, genuine and soft, in a way that warmed her cold bones, a way that gave that tether one last tug. "Goodnight."

And that was it.

∼

Isla and Ezekiel had moved in stealthy silence through most of their trip back to the infirmary. The storm had died down by the time they broke the barrier of the forest, finding themselves in the open field just before the establishment's walls. An easy patter of droplets fell onto Isla's skin, and she used it to scrub away some of the dirt on her face with her free hand. The other was wrapped around the fallen limb she'd acquired which hung in her grip just as heavily as her sopping clothes that made it feel like she was moving through quicksand. The night was their cloak as they trekked, the moon, maybe blissfully, masked by the remaining dark storm clouds to keep them unseen amidst the barren area.

When she'd rubbed her cheek so much that she felt the burn of skin on skin and the grit of sand, Isla brought her hand back to her side, forcing herself not to look upon it—not to attempt picturing those golden strings—but even as she glanced at the Beta of Deimos for a distraction from her mate, Kai's voice was the one she heard in her head.

"He's protective of our pack and of me, and sometimes he oversteps because of it. He was my father's best friend. He's known me since I was a pup."

Ezekiel was yet another person that she hadn't thought much of, who'd been caught in the wake of the tragedy. For as horrible and obnoxious as she felt the beta was, she couldn't help but feel a pang of sympathy.

"I'm sorry for your loss," she spoke softly, out of courtesy and to also lessen some of the tension that always held between them.

Ezekiel gave her a sideways glance, his eyes widening. The thanks that followed was muffled and low but present.

Then everything was quiet and rigid again.

In the silence, Isla's mind became a mess, questions of every sort swirling, wave after wave crashing so hard against her that she could barely keep herself afloat.

Before, Lukas was the problem. The bak was the problem. Finding her mate was the problem. But now, everything had circled back to the query that had haunted her mind and baffled not just her, but the entire continent before she'd even stepped foot on Callisto's territory—

What the hell had happened in Deimos?

"Does the Imperial Alpha know?" she asked Ezekiel, a foolish action she was sure, but she was too tired to care, too overwhelmed. "About Kai's father and brother being...murdered?" The word made her gut twist.

Ezekiel went stiff and pressed his lips into a thin line before seething, "The former *alpha* and *heir*."

She would give him that, the titles. It was a matter of respect.

She clambered to find her way back to that lady-like poise she once portrayed so well, but even still, a rasp slipped through with her annoyance as she corrected, "The former alpha and heir."

If the beta had been pleased or displeased, he didn't show it. "Yes."

Isla started, thrown off by the response to a question that she'd already had a vague idea of the answer to—and she'd been wrong.

She recalled what she'd last heard from Adrien. According to him, the Imperial Alpha hadn't heard any reports of what had happened at all. Just that they'd—died. His father usually kept Adrien in the loop about everything, so he could see and understand the true scope of what it meant to be a leader, especially one as high-ranking as he would have to be. The unforeseen *murder* of an alpha *and* an heir was unprecedented. Why keep that from him?

Isla gnawed on the inside of her cheek, pushing the thought away. "Are they looking into it?"

"You really are a presumptuous girl." Despite his dig, Ezekiel went on, most likely to humor her. "The Imperial Alpha is meant to keep order with all of us, but first and foremost, he leads Io. This means to keep your pack on the pedestal it rests, the lesser packs must remain just that—*lesser*. Chaos and strife in our kingdoms are only addressed if it threatens your land or the continent's hierarchy. Even the warriors, our land's strongest and most elite fighters and strategists are weapons at *his* command to be dispersed where and when *he* sees fit."

Isla regretted asking because every word out of his mouth, every word spoken with that *tone*, roiled her. Set her blood on fire, made her wolf shudder.

The way he'd framed it...

She understood well the scheme of the packs—how Io rested at the top of the hierarchy, how decisions and sacrifices she wasn't entirely privy to had been made in the past—the far, far past—to maintain it. But now...things weren't like that anymore.

"Our duty is to protect *all wolves*," she battled one of his points, the one that had felt the most personal. "We serve *the continent*, not the Imperial Alpha."

"The fact you cannot see that there is no difference proves to me that you are doing us a favor in forgoing your role as luna."

At that moment, she swore her wolf howled. Grinding her teeth, Isla forced herself to move a little faster to get ahead of him, then swung the limb out, parallel to the ground, using it as a bar to block Ezekiel's path. Now halted, she slowly moved so she was in front of him and pressed the branch to his chest, making sure there wasn't enough force to hurt, but enough that he'd remember it was there.

That she was.

"It would do you well not to forget that fact. That I'm *choosing* to forgo my role," she seethed, pushing slightly to emphasize her words. "Because maybe one day, I'll change my mind. Maybe I'll come to your precious pack to claim what's *rightfully* mine, and you won't be able to do a damn thing about it while you're down on your knees, bowing to me." She threw the branch down at his feet and turned on her heel. "I can go the rest of the way myself—Beta."

As she began her walk, Ezekiel's laugh rumbled behind her. "Maybe they don't teach this in the *Imperial Pack*." The name was filled with pure, unbridled malice that made her pause. "But it would do *you* well to remember, Luna, everything *given* can just as easily be taken away."

And though his words sent a chill down her spine, possessing the faintest air of a threat, Isla continued forward.

CHAPTER 16

Isla groaned as she pressed the side of her forehead to the cool tile of the shower wall, letting the water fall onto her back in a near-scalding stream that flushed the skin leeched of its tan from being shrouded so long in the Wilds' darkness. Droplets from her lashes sprinkled onto her cheeks as she snapped her eyes shut. As she breathed… breathed…*breathed.*

The world was whirling, the universe teetering behind her closed lids, and she wanted to shut it all out. She wanted it to stop. Needed it to. Just for a few seconds. But her mind was still working at a furious pace. Her body, though horribly and thoroughly exhausted, was on high alert.

Lukas. The Gate. The Hunt. The bak. A killer. Her mate.

Her mate, her mate, her—

Isla gritted her teeth, opening her eyes to watch the grime washed from her skin circle the drain, keen on the mud, flecked foliage, and dried blood flowing away and disappearing the way she wished her memories would.

Like she wished the spindly, kneading fingers of paranoia would.

The feeling had nagged her from the moment she'd entered her empty room, so dark when she closed her door behind her that it made her heart drop into her already turning stomach.

She'd pressed her back hard against the entrance, clammy fingers imprinting the wood, as she scoured to confirm she was alone. To be sure whoever had murdered the Alpha and Heir of Deimos hadn't somehow figured out who she was and had been waiting here for her. If she'd even be on their radar at all.

She wasn't sure how long she'd remained like that—her chest heaving at the prospect, her eyes flittering back and forth, up and down, back and forth, one time, three times, five times before she'd gotten a handle on herself. Remembered who she was. What she was.

Isla had realized not long after that it had been *well* over the hour that Adrien had promised to arrive in, almost nearing hour two. And upon that time's passing, with the thick muck coating what felt like every nook of her starting to irritate her skin, she'd decided she could at least try to do something productive. So, now she sat under the fiery current, standing abandoned after the exhaustion and dizziness had got to her.

"Goodnight."

Isla grimaced at the voice in her head, the pang in her chest—a stain on her mind, heart, bones, on her Goddess-forsaken soul—as it was followed by one of a different nature.

"*Everything* given *can just as easily be taken away.*"

She dragged her knees up to hold them tighter to her body and lifted her face to the water again, allowing it to flood her senses as she scratched hard at her scalp. As she tried to claw out the thoughts.

Kai had been taken.

Her mate bestowed upon her and stolen away by the same divine hand. The one that had pushed him into a role that had never been his, that he'd never expected to have to take, that had put him on a path that she could never walk alongside him on…and she *hated* that she felt that way.

Hated that she was angry about it. That it mattered to her. That *he* mattered to her.

What *right* did she have to be mad? To allow the thought that she would never see his face or hear his voice again—that she would struggle to know if he'd even made it to Deimos safely—to make her want to rid her stomach of the very little she'd been able to keep down since she'd emerged from the Hunt?

A sudden bang echoed into the washroom. One time. Two.

Isla sputtered, bracing herself against the tub's edge.

It was the door. Soon, the thuds were replaced by the sharp rattling of its handle.

Even though she couldn't see it, Isla knew that the long metal was being halted by the fabric of the heavy cobalt chair she'd pushed in front of it, fitted perfectly beneath the handle's curve. A necessary measure as the rooms bore no locks.

Her breath caught in her throat. It could've easily, *finally,* been the boys trying to get in...but what if it wasn't?

Cautiously, Isla worked her way to her feet, leaving the water running to cover her sound as she peeled back the curtain and wrapped a towel loosely around her body. Stepping over the basin's lip, her fingers constricted around the scalpel, sitting on the sink's edge, that she'd stolen from the supply room. The dripping of her hair and the patter of her feet through the puddles forming on the floor still seemed too loud in her ears as she crept forward. Kicking further open her ajar washroom door, the steam billowed behind her.

The blade was up and at the ready in front of her face, her dark shadow stretching tall along the white-washed wall in the dim lighting as she moved. Inch by inch by inch. Step, step, step. The door continued to tremble at the assault on it.

"What the hell are you doing? *Relax.*"

"What is *she* doing? This is her room, right?"

Isla froze and stood tall at the voices. "Sebastian?"

The chatter stopped.

"Pudge?"

Adrien's voice came next. He'd been the milder of the two. "How did you lock the door?"

She didn't answer him. Instead, she moved to wrench the chair from its spot, pushing it back as close to its previous home a few feet from her bedside as she could. The legs made a low, rumbling *scrape* along the floor, prompting more inquisitive noises from her visitors.

Hiding the blade in her hand where they shouldn't have been able to see it, Isla reached for the handle and gradually pulled open the low-whining entrance. Her settled scowl was met by equally cautious and dubious looks.

"Where the hell were you?" she seethed, the gnarled grip of her fear edging into her voice. "You said an hour. It's been nearly three."

Both Adrien and Sebastian remained in their places on the other side of the threshold, and Isla caught the way Adrien looked her over while Sebastian immediately surveyed the room.

His forest eyes narrowed. "Who are you hiding in here?"

Isla countered it with a heightened glare of her own. "What?"

"I'm having war flashbacks," Sebastian said, brushing by her and Adrien, taking a few steps inside. "What was all that noise?"

She rested her hand on the doorframe. "You *do realize* I'm twenty-one and don't need to have suitors run through you for approval."

Sebastian's features curled at the words. "Then find some that aren't pretentious assholes."

"Says the pretentious asshole."

"I've earned it." He pointed to the bathroom, still suspicious. "Why's the shower still on?"

"Because you scared me, you ass."

"Obviously." Adrien's eyes were on the makeshift weapon in her hand, glinting against the brown stain of the door. "Where did you get that?"

"I borrowed it," she said plainly.

"Why?"

"Warrior Princess never sleeps," Sebastian mused before she could answer, flopping onto the chair with a small glance under the bed as he kicked his legs over the arms of it.

The name resounded through her head through another voice, and though she was mildly pleased by *that* being the taunting moniker Kai had stolen from her brother to utilize, she frowned. Adrien had caught onto it, flashing her an inquisitive and concerned look. It wasn't enough to force her into the effort of even faking a smile.

"I'm going to change," she announced and then turned on her heel before he could say anything.

When she'd emerged a few minutes later, again trailed by the residual cloud of steam lingering from the previous flow of water, Isla was donning a nurse's uniform about two sizes too big, shirt and pants a near-identical shade of blue as the chair her brother was lounging in. Adrien had moved from his previous spot and perched against the storage closet. Their idle chatter—which had either been so quiet purposely or just indiscernible by her in her wavering focus—had died away.

The Heir nodded towards her attire. "I didn't know you worked here."

"I had no other clothes," Isla deadpanned, working to gather her hair loosely atop her head.

Her brother snickered. "I don't remember thievery being a part of the Warrior Creed."

Isla rolled her eyes, electing to simply flip him off before taking a seat on her bed. As aggravated as she was, she was happy to have their company. To have some semblance of normal—even if their conversation would be far from it.

"You're over two hours late," she addressed them, "so I hope you have something."

They exchanged a look.

"They put him in one of the upper wings," Adrien said. "It's pretty abandoned and isn't holding any other patients."

She'd figured that much.

"Is he okay?"

Sebastian scoffed. "That's a loaded question."

She narrowed her eyes at him in suspicion. "Where were you when this was all happening anyway?"

"Taking care of something for Dad."

"Like what?"

"You know I can't tell you."

Isla pursed her lips. She *did know*—of course.

As had always been the case and would likely always be—no matter what she achieved in her lifetime—Sebastian would be issued respects she never would be, able to access information she never could. The Imperial Beta's firstborn, the only true candidate to take the mantle once Adrien took leadership—she couldn't argue that he hadn't earned it as he'd claimed earlier. For as conniving and obnoxious as he could be, her brother had completed the Hunt and knew how to use his snake-oil charisma to his—and whoever's bidding he'd been set on—advantage. And she knew it was used frequently.

"I know that he's restrained and tranquilized," Adrien broke in between them. "But his wounds are being taken care of."

"He's still restrained?" Isla asked with wide eyes.

"He pulled a knife, Isla."

"He didn't hurt anyone." Her response earned dual doubtful looks, and she sighed, directing back at her friend, "*You're* the one who thought he could help us figure out whatever's going on. Has he said anything at all that gives us an idea about what happened? Or shown any signs that he remembers who he is or why we're here?"

"I don't think anyone's been able to get to him. The order from my father's been to steer clear."

At the mention of the Imperial Alpha, Isla blinked and then held back the snarl as Ezekiel's malice-laced words about her pack's leader, her best friend's father, her best friend's *future*, rammed into her mind. "Your father knows now?" she asked, and Adrien nodded. "What does he think?"

"That there's a problem that we don't understand and that it needs to be taken care of—quickly," he said. "And he doesn't want any of it leaving Callisto."

Perplexity fluttered across Isla's features. "What does that mean?"

"No one's to speak of it outside of these pack borders."

"That sounds…how is that possible? People from all over came to see them re-emerge." Isla shook her head. "And don't people know what happened to me in there, to us?"

"*We* do. Some of Io's Council do," Adrien rattled. "The Alpha and Beta of Deimos, and whoever got you out, vaguely, but other than that, no."

"But I thought there was that alphas' meeting? To figure out what to do?"

"Apparently, they didn't talk about the Wilds at all. It just kept the alphas busy while they canvased."

Isla dropped her gaze down to the blankets beneath her and trailed her eyes along the embroidery as she thought. "They're trying to cover this up." The realization hit her in a particular way she didn't like. "I almost died in there. K—the Alpha of Deimos. Lukas." His name went through like a shot, and she darted her gaze back up. "What are they going to do with him?" The boys exchanged more wary glances. Isla pressed again, "*What* are they going to do with him?"

"Valkeric," Sebastian said, a grimness to his tone.

"You better be talking about a cabin in the mountains and not the prison." The silence that followed, confirmation of the worst sort, roiled through Isla's veins. "He's a victim, *not* a criminal."

"It wasn't an actual plan, just a possibility we heard tossed around," Adrien attempted to mollify her.

It wasn't enough to quell the frustration, the ire.

"He has a *family*," Isla snapped. "He has a mom, dad, sister, and new nephew who love him and want him to come home. He went into the Wilds, and he killed a bak. He earned what's his. He deserves to go home and to be a warrior." A thought that had been simmering since Lukas had emerged, finally boiled to the surface. "And—I—I was *with him*. That could just as easily be *me* up there in that room, *restrained* and *tranquilized*. Would you let *me* get thrown into Valkeric?" They both responded with similar answers of vehement disagreement. She settled back, feeling a sense of relief, release, and hope she'd gotten her point across. "So, let's not let it happen to him. There must be something we can do."

Sebastian was beaming as he said with mirth and no detectable taunting, "Alright, General, what's your plan?"

Isla, Adrien, and Sebastian had spent a solid hour constructing their plan, plotting in a way that almost rung back to their times as pups. Only now, instead of devising ways to skip lessons or sneak out of their homes, it was inadvertently to save a man's life. Isla wished there had been a better play than her simply getting in to talk to him under the guise of a nurse as the boys kept the key players who'd be aware of who she was at bay—but they had to work with what they had.

Even as her lids felt heavy, as the urgency of all of this hovered, Isla relished in the moment. Strategizing, taking action, with the prospect of Lukas making it back home safely in her view on the horizon—this was what she loved. What she wanted to do forever. For the continent. For her family.

She could never *leave* this. Never give it all up.

Even if the hollowness in her chest seemed to grow with each passing second. Even if the whole time they'd schemed, Kai's voice had lingered in the back of her head, teasing whenever she'd felt any sense of pride. In that way of his that annoyed her yet endeared him to her in a way she couldn't quite describe and would never, *ever* admit to him—if she ever even could.

"Is something wrong with your hand?"

Isla snapped her head up at Adrien who was hovering near the door that Sebastian had just disappeared from moments earlier, stating a desire to get a drink at the bar not too far from the infirmary to hit on its tender one last time before they'd departed for Io.

Isla glanced down, realizing she'd been tracing one of her fingers absently over her opposite palm as if lining the threads of light that weren't there. She quickly separated the two, shoving her hands beneath her crossed legs. "Uh, no."

That look of concern flashed across Adrien's face again as he quirked a brow. He was silent for a few seconds, unspoken words dancing in his eyes before—

"The Alpha of Deimos left."

Isla's own brows shot up. Why would he bring this up?

"Oh?" she said, trying to sound a mix of nonchalant and surprised.

Adrien hummed in confirmation, leaning back against the doorframe, arms crossed. "Some emergency in Deimos, I heard. I couldn't get a clear answer on what it was, but it was so dire they had to go in the dead of night."

To be back by dawn, she wanted to say but kept it to herself.

Upon her quiet, Adrien was standing tall again, making his way slowly to the bed. "Did he say anything to you?"

Isla forced herself to look him dead in the eye. "About what?"

He stopped a mere foot away. "About anything."

"No. Why would he?"

A long pause.

With a loud breath, Adrien sat down at the foot of the bed, resting his elbows on his knees, focusing not on her but their shadows on the wall in front of him. "I could scent him on you at the Gate once I parsed it out of the magic. You were with *him* when we couldn't find you, weren't you?"

The slightest hitch of Isla's breath had been picked up on instantly, and she silently cursed herself as Adrien turned to study her face.

She swallowed. Lying felt pointless. "Yes."

Adrien's jaw tightened. "Why?"

Steel.

She had to be steel.

They'd promised each other. She and Kai had sworn no one would know about their bond but them.

But—this was Adrien. Her *best friend*, Adrien.

Her best friend, Adrien, who'd been with her since they were babies. Who she trusted with her life.

Who…had found himself burned by a fated mate bond only a little over a year ago. Who she'd nearly *lost* because of that damned fated mate bond.

"He was around," she said before she could second-guess the fabrication. "We bumped into each other, and just—talked."

"Talked?" he echoed, sounding unconvinced.

"*Talked.*"

Another pause. Another breath. The answer had been accepted, but something was bothering him. Thankfully, it wasn't long before he said, "He asked a lot about you at the feast, you know. Who you were, why you were there. I think he's interested in you."

The final part was said with an uncertainty she would've been offended by if she weren't so grateful for his disbelief at the notion.

She capitalized on it.

"An actual in-power alpha interested in me? *Me?*" She forced a laugh. "I may be able to woo an official or two, but an alpha is far beyond my reach."

"You're the daughter of the Imperial Beta?"

That was getting old fast.

"And yet, I went to countless mate gatherings and some balls and galas, and not a single heir—not even an alpha's *scion*—spared me a glance."

Adrien looked her over, contemplative. "You're different now."

"How?"

"You just—are." He shrugged before going pensive again. "You asked me at the feast if I thought he was dangerous."

Back on Kai again.

Isla took a breath, remembering her words well. "That was a long time ago."

A line appeared on Adrien's cheek. "Alpha isn't handed down by strength. It's a birthright, only a birthright." He let the words hang for a bit. "I don't have any siblings. The title's mine as soon as my father passes it down. But I know how much my aunt and uncle resented him for the fact that Imperial Alpha was his, despite being just as much my grandfather's children and as alpha-blooded as he was. The Alpha of Deimos—the current alpha—is...a lot stronger than his brother was. He just proved it."

"Stop," Isla told him, and Adrien turned to face her. "Kai wouldn't do that."

"Kai."

Adrien had echoed the name without question, just deadpan observation, but Isla still corrected herself.

"*The alpha,*" she said before shaking her head. "Where is this coming from? You both seemed fine talking at the Gate." She wasn't even going to bother trying to pry from him what Kai had deemed "pack business". Not tonight, anyway.

Another rise and fall of Adrien's shoulders. "He's alright, especially for a guy who got a shitty deal, but...something's off with that pack. Something's *been* off for years, even before the alpha and heir just died." She noted the way he hadn't cited a killer, one other than Kai who he'd suspected. Like his father really *hadn't* told him. "I don't know what it is, but I don't want you getting tangled up in it somehow."

"I'm not," she replied quickly. Too quickly, maybe. She mustered a soft smile. "Believe me, I'm not."

"Okay." Adrien mirrored the expression before falling back onto the bed and rubbing his hands over his face, groaning.

She laughed. "Are you good?"

The Heir sighed before placing his hands on his stomach. "Tired." He closed his eyes, heaving another breath, one that she could really feel the weight behind. She couldn't help but wonder if it was due to recent events or if he still suffered effects from the severed bond. "Really fucking tired."

Now wasn't the time to ask.

"Join the club," she chimed.

He smirked before closing his eyes. "Wake me up in an hour."

Isla snorted, though she wouldn't fight him on it. Maybe she'd be able to get some sleep too.

"Fine," she said, chucking one of her pillows down for him to use. "But move down, fat ass. I need room for my legs."

Adrien obliged, sliding down the mattress, not bothering to crack open his eyes. "Alright, *Pudge.*"

She rolled her eyes, but a genuine smile graced Isla's mouth as she lay down on her pillow, not bothering to wriggle under the constricting blankets. It wasn't long after she'd settled that the gentle, deep sounds of Adrien's breathing filled the room. He really had been exhausted.

Isla, on the other hand…

She turned in her spot, laying on her side so she could face the window. With the shades drawn open enough, beams of moonlight spilled onto the floor. Isla trailed them out as much as she could to their source, to the world outside. One that held monsters and murderers and…Kai.

She brought her hand up to her face, so dark with the faint glowing backdrop behind it.

Everything given can just as easily be taken away.

She scowled, directing her gaze upwards, lingering as her fingers curled but one digit. She flipped off Fate, holding it until she felt the deity had received her message, and tucked her hand beneath her pillow. And though it may have been contradictory, she'd sent a prayer too, thanking the goddess for what could've been…for Kai to be safe and okay.

And then, finally, she closed her eyes and slept.

∾

Somehow, Isla felt worse when she woke up than when she'd gone to bed; her limbs were stiff and heavy as she peeled open eyes that took too long to focus. Oranges, reds, and purple-ish blue hues greeted her through the window, a calling to the sun's arrival on the horizon. Still, the sky held a lingering blackness to it, meaning it had to be an hour or so before dawn.

She grumbled as she stretched, wincing at the sharp pain in her arm and side. Her injury from the Hunt had clearly been aggravated somehow, and she'd place her bets on her *entirely graceful* descent from the heights of her hiding place amidst the branches. Adrenaline had kept it all at bay throughout the madness of the night—the movement that she had stood by firmly when it came to aiding recovery—but after being stagnant for so long as she lay curled on her mattress, her body was ready to make her pay. Taunt her for her hubris against nature's timing.

With a quick look at the clock, Isla realized that she'd only been asleep for a few hours if she could even call it that. It wasn't a deep sleep, just the in-and-out illusion of one. A back and forth into the murky depths of her subconscious. She had a gnawing feeling that the closest she'd ever get to sleep in these coming weeks would have been the day before yesterday—when she was unconscious.

She wavered as she rose to her feet, her knees buckling and almost sending her back to the bed. Something was…off. Again. In a way she'd never felt or experienced before, shocking as this trip had been *full* of foreign sensations. But this—this was truly unique. Like a fog clouded her head, thick and impossible to clear away entirely. Like pieces of her mind—of *her*—had been scattered, gone away, rendering her at a loss of how to retrieve them.

The reasoning for it hit her hard and fast, but she didn't want to acknowledge it. Didn't want to believe it. Even if it was painfully obvious.

"Forget," she said, the word seeming to echo in her empty room. Reverberate in her mind as she moved to the bathroom to freshen up and look at herself in the mirror. As she pressed along the dark circles under her eyes. As she took in her sallow skin and slightly chapped lips.

Isla forced herself to smile.

This was a new day. The start of a new life. The life she wanted. The life she *chose*.

A warrior—not a queen.

On her way out, Isla caught a piece of paper on the chair—a note that read:

Meet you back here at 9.

From both the handwriting and the very small pool of people that it could've been, it was easy for Isla to figure out it was from Adrien. She'd been faintly aware of when he left her room last night, though, after one hour or two, she wasn't sure. All she remembered was hearing him go in a hurry.

She looked at the clock again, tracking the hands as they sluggishly made their rounds. Nine AM meant that there was still quite a bit of time left until they put their plan into action. Until they made their last-ditch effort to get to Lukas, to glean some information about what had gone on behind the Wall. The timing just right, every diversion conducted to perfection.

One shot. They had one shot.

Because at noon, they'd be bound for Io.

But until then, Isla had some hours to kill, and so she figured, where better to go—where *else* to go around here—than the roof.

As Isla pushed open the heavy door and stepped onto it, she was met by the luster of metal bars and vents and chimneys in the rising beams of sunlight. The platform was surely different in the daytime. It seemed more functional now—and a lot dirtier too.

The observation drew a breathy laugh from her mouth and had the faintest smirk crossing her lips as she turned to look at the wall behind her. A structure that had almost led to an irreversible mistake.

For a moment, she let herself relive the rush, relish in the flashback to the sweet, painful tension. She'd surely never know what sleeping with Kai would entail, but if it was anything like the damn game they'd played—that push and pull, grip and release…

Any inkling of her amusement faltered when she trained her eyes to the empty space along the railing, feeling a tug, not from a bond but her heart. But before she could allow herself to fall into those nauseating depths as she had last night, that had lapped at her toes since waking like a rising tide, she forced herself to focus anew.

A glimpse down had her eyes locked on the now extinguished bonfire, reduced to a giant pile of ash surrounded by charred rock. Gone were those who'd sent prayers up to the Goddess. Those who'd received their wishes for the final hunters' return, though likely not in the way anyone had hoped or expected.

Isla gritted her teeth, picturing Lukas floors below her. Thinking of the horrendous prison carved into the mountainside of the tallest peak in Io's Valkeric Ranges. Home to the continent's worst criminals, those who would've been thrown into the Wilds for their transgressions if rules still held as those barbaric times of a past that she wished were a bit more distant.

They were going to help him. They *had* to help him. Even if bringing back his memories was unsuccessful, if they could find a way to prove him not a threat, to prove him helpful.

But if they were going to try covering all of this up…

Once again, Isla stopped herself from thinking down that route. Stopped her anger from festering.

A new distraction.

With a sigh, she pulled the marker out of her pocket, not keen on leaving it anywhere out of her sight. The wood had the slightest give under her touch as she held it between her fingers, the relic having spent so long in the soaking wet pockets of her coat. It was by some miracle that she hadn't dropped it last night.

She noted how pieces of the dirt, once embedded so thickly in the ridges, had begun to loosen. Isla used her nail to dig it away, realizing too late she may have been compromising the integrity of a timeless artifact.

Her eyes narrowed on it as she excavated a prominent ridge cast upon perfectly by a beam of sunlight, as if whatever deity was calling down from above was validating her attention.

"No way," she breathed, a fire stoked in her eyes as more grime gave way.

Isla continued furiously, brushing and picking and digging until under her nails were stained with dirt, and as she looked down upon what she'd unearthed, she choked on her breath and nearly dropped the ball off the ledge.

Her stare shifted slowly to the forest in the distance, where the trees danced with the softest sway in the early morning breeze. Their faint rustle like the song of something wicked beckoning her to pass its thicket-laden gates yet again.

Isla held the marker up to the light, turning it over several times, poking and prodding at it to ensure she was seeing what she believed she was. Her stomach twisted as she brought it so close to her face to examine it that she could almost smell the rotting earth it had risen from.

Symbols.

There were so many symbols.

Etchings of foreign letters that she didn't understand, but some she'd seen…dwelling in a mix of many other curves and claw marks.

Carved in a message left for her mate.

CHAPTER 17

Isla traced her finger along the marker's edges—six consecutive symbols at the top, three below that, and one big mark beneath those, three tick marks cut between by a bisecting line. That large singular marking was the one she recognized most. That she swore she'd seen sketched into the tree's bark last night.

Which meant…well, she didn't know what it meant.

She also wasn't positive that it was true.

In the grand scheme of things, after all she'd gone through and all she'd seen, Isla didn't necessarily trust her own judgment. She was so desperate for a resolution, for any type of sense, that easily she could've been creating something grand and revolutionary out of absolutely nothing.

Her eyes darted between the forest, what she could make of the top of the Wall, and back to the relic resting in her palm.

First of all, what *was* this?

Of the several known dialects in their ancient history—native to each original pack before the Common was developed with the rise of Io to centralize the continent, then the realm, to aid in the relations of the world—none used an alphabet like this. That creation was over a millennium ago. But the Ares Pass wasn't so old that it predated those primeval records…was it?

No.

No, Lukas had mentioned Io. That the in-power Imperial Alpha held issue with the pass's existence. With the alphas—the brothers—of Deimos and Phobos budding their own empire. Challenging him.

But exactly how long ago was that?

Isla tangled her fingers in her hair.

What was she supposed to do with this? What if she was *wrong*?

She shot another dejected look at the woodland in the distance.

Kai had asked her to keep herself contained for a few hours. It had been over that now, the pastels of dawn giving way to the clear blue of morning. He had to be beyond Deimos's borders by now. In Mavec, in his "not-a-palace". But the murderer of his father and brother...

She shouldn't do it. Shouldn't risk herself when she could still feel the glimmer of the bond between them, though it waned. Shouldn't go back into those woods.

Not alone, at least.

Her eyes traveled back to the marker.

She could tell Adrien and Sebastian—but then they'd ask about the message when they came upon it. What it was, why it mattered. And she could lie, she supposed, but...

"Goddess." Isla grimaced and rubbed her forehead.

The world was spinning again, and she didn't know what to do. Who to talk to. The best option—the person clued in on most of her secrets now because he was arguably the largest of them—was hundreds of miles away now.

But he was also someone she shouldn't trust.

At least, according to Lukas, and according to this piece of timber in her hand.

One step at a time, she told herself. One at a time.

First, she'd get Lukas, and then finally, she'd learn about the pass.

⁓

"Seb should be at the other stairwell soon. You have maybe ten or fifteen minutes at the most. That's the longest we can keep them occupied."

Isla didn't look up at Adrien as he spoke, instead, focusing on herself in the mirror of the bathroom as she finished twisting her hair into a proper low bun. Smooth and put together, so at odds with how she actually felt inside. "That's all I'll need."

"You know what you're going to say?"

"I'll ease him into it." She tucked any flyaways behind her ears. "Introduce myself. Find out what he remembers."

"Don't say your name," Adrien told her, leaning back against the wall. "No one can know we went to see him. I shouldn't even be letting you go." When she shot him a look, he added, "But I know better than to tell you that you can't do something." He snickered. "I mean, people told you that you shouldn't, that you *couldn't*, become a warrior, and now look at you. Second in the run to an alpha, killer of two bak."

Although the words had been meant as praise, Isla felt a wrench in her gut, an iron grip on her lungs. She scowled, glancing at herself in the mirror, catching the curve of her lumerosi creeping towards her collarbone as the too-large uniform was askew on her shoulders. She shuddered at the ghost of a sharp claw tracing her skin. One belonging to the beast seconds away from ending her life. Swallowing thickly, she reached up to do the same.

"Isla."

At the sound of her name, she dropped her hand, turning to Adrien. To divert his attention, she asked the first thing on her mind which probably wasn't the best. "Did you—uh—did you ever get a clearer answer about why the alpha had to return to Deimos?"

The Heir's eyebrows quirked at her interest. "Rogues," he said simply, shocking her as she wasn't expecting an answer. "A band of them from the barren lands between Rhea, Charon, and Deimos. They've been a problem for months on all three borders, but with the death of Alpha Kyran, they're trying to take advantage of the power shift and move in on Deimos."

Isla's body tensed at the mention of the former alpha, Kai's father, and a tinge of fear took to her heart.

Not all rogues—but most—were dangerous. Lawless. Cast out by their packs or choosing to leave themselves. While those who ventured out to those lands—so bleak and not worth being claimed by a pack—typically kept to their solitude, those who had been exiled formed their own coalitions. Never would they garner enough strength to take down a pack, but they could definitely cause problems.

She did her best to shove the fear away, to keep it from being evident. "To do what?"

Adrien's shoulders rose and fell. "Anarchy? What else do rogues do?" Isla must've been doing a horrible job of masking her concern because his voice became soft. "It's just some gangs stirring up trouble. We've had them too, on the western borders. I would think Deimos has a strong guard."

A guard that allowed the alpha and heir to be killed.

A guard that could let Kai get killed.

The last thought was nauseating.

Isla ran her tongue over her teeth, burying it deep and away with the bond and bak. "I know." She noticed how Adrien's eyes narrowed, how they carried over her with suspicion. "We should go," she said, heading for the door, not allowing any opening for him to question; only follow.

The path they took was the same one Isla had meandered when she'd managed to come upon Ezekiel, with a few extra turns down some quieter hallways. Though the corridors were a bit more bustling with the earlier rounds of nurses, they kept their heads down, but not in a way that would draw any attention.

When they finally reached the stairwell door, they gave the area around a quick once-over before heading up not one floor but three. Lukas was being kept as far away from everyone as possible while in reach of care.

The fifth-floor hall was as dark as Isla remembered of the third. But here, there was no light spilling from the hallway, no distant voices of her mate and his beta.

"After you're in, I'll get the guard away from the door," Adrien said. "You need to go fast. Seb can only distract the real nurse for so long."

Isla gave a hum of confirmation, and not wasting time with words, took off on her mission.

Two turns down two different barren hallways separated her from the eventual source of light, near a man guarding a door. She didn't recognize him which was good and all part of the plan. From what the boys had found out, this was the one guard put on duty with no affiliation to their pack, and he'd be switched out as soon as decisions were made on Lukas's fate. If he'd be brought to Io as a prisoner or have a chance to recover here or home.

As she made her way down the hall, Isla didn't try to mask her presence. The goal wasn't to sneak up on him. It was, in fact, for him to act exactly as he had. Bracing at the sudden appearance and relaxing upon seeing it was simply her...a nurse.

After a brief exchange that was almost *too* easy with the man asking if she wanted him to remain with her inside Lukas's room as protection —which she declined—Isla reached for the door's handle.

And she hesitated.

The marker was heavy in her pocket. Her scalpel, with the blade capped by a makeshift sheath, tucked into her waistband. Not to be used, but just in case.

Isla didn't know what to expect, but she knew what to hope for. What she wanted. By some miracle, they would both walk out of that room with answers. He with who he was, and she with what it all meant.

Her eyes briefly drifted upwards. *Don't let me lose him again.*

After one more subtle deep breath, Isla pushed the door and stepped inside to find Lukas reading. That alone almost sent her stumbling back. He was supposed to be tranquilized, restrained, stripped of everything. And she couldn't imagine, with all hostility towards him, a novel would've been offered for his enjoyment.

Either way, one of those things was certainly true, white binds were visible on his wrists, latching him to the bed. But he was well-awake and so entranced by the pages of his book, which barely spanned taller or wider than his own hands, that he hadn't even bothered looking up until the door closed behind her. Her stomach turned when the sight made him flinch. She knew it wasn't anything specific towards her, especially when she caught sight of the bruising on his body that she *wished* she could blame on the darkness of last night for not noticing.

His chestnut eyes became focused on her face, and as when he had emerged, she couldn't find that spark there anymore, that light. Nothing of the man who she'd caught studying a painting off to the side of the feast, who'd known a surprising amount of Callisto's art history. Nothing of the man who'd been rendered into a stuttering mess upon seeing her bare body, who'd apparently pictured it beforehand.

He just felt cold. Empty. A stranger.

But just lost, she reminded herself. *Lost and scared.*

"Hi." Her voice was as syrupy as it had been on the guard outside. The one she could very faintly hear talking until it faded as Adrien drew his prying ears away.

Step one—complete.

Isla noticed a file sitting on a table set at the foot of his bed. Maybe a bit too eagerly, she reached for it and flipped it open, only to be disappointed to find the notes brief.

Lukas had just been called *Patient*, noted as being traumatized and an amnesiac with no trace of him having been in the Hunt at all. Only one other nurse had cycled through since he was brought in, Isla sneaking in before the second meant to replace her. He was due for his tranquilizers soon, which may have explained why he was so awake.

"You're not a nurse."

Isla's eyes snapped up to meet his. His voice had been even and cool, the easiest he'd ever spoken to her. Even more so than when he'd so confidently boasted his knowledge to her of the marker.

She made sure to keep her face impassive, not fearful of being caught. "What makes you say that?"

"Because the other two have had someone come in beforehand to threaten me," he bemused, and the smirk he wore, so unlike him, almost made her skin crawl.

But maybe she'd been so distracted by what he'd said that she couldn't focus on it.

"Other *two*?"

"You *nurses* don't talk out there?"

Isla blinked but recovered quickly. "Apparently not." She feigned amusement, storing that fact about the second nurse away for later. She held up the folder. "They didn't write anything."

"They brought their own. *You* came unprepared," Lukas jeered. "Strike two—*nurse*."

Isla kept her eyes from narrowing, both in focused thought and slight annoyance with his heckling. "What time did they come in? They weren't on the schedule."

He shrugged. "Not long after the first, I don't think. But then again, I was out of it. The storm was over."

"What did they look like? Maybe I can—"

"No, my turn," Lukas said with a raised finger. "All I've gotten is questions and beatings, and no one will give me answers."

Isla pursed her lips, trying not to break under the weight of any guilt she felt. "What makes you think I'll give you them?"

He smiled. "Because you're desperate enough to lie to be here."

He certainly still had his wits about him. Even if he had mastered the art of fumbling over his own words, he was never a stupid man. Maybe there *was* hope he was still there, simply with those quirky parts of his personality stripped away in the absence of the memories that made him who he was.

Riddles and secrets and games.

She could use those old interests to her advantage.

"An even trade then," she proposed. "A question and answer for one in return."

That seemed to spark something as he flashed her the most genuine grin she'd seen since he'd smiled at her before the bak he'd killed in the Wilds.

"I'll go first," he said. "Who are you?"

No names.

"A friend," she told him.

He narrowed his eyes. "Be more specific."

"Ask in the next question." Her smile had his lips twitching up again. Was that progress? "What do you remember from behind the Wall?"

He rolled his eyes. "How original," he deadpanned. "I remember woods and a wolf." His answer was simple and to the point, as hers had been. But that small gleam of joy in his face made it okay. She was surprised when his next question wasn't for her name. "Where am I?"

Isla bit down on her bottom lip. They'd started easy, but now, she could try digging into whatever was lost. And if he held true to form, the more specific she got, the more detailed, he may mirror and clue her further into what happened.

Still, she chose her words carefully.

"An infirmary in Callisto. It's one of the ten territories on this continent—or I suppose, one of eleven," she paused, gauging his reaction before she continued. "Tethys is one of the southernmost—I've heard it gets pretty cold there. It's one of the smallest regions, I think. A little bigger than Rhea."

"Are you going to ask your question?" he asked, and it seemed the information barely fazed him.

Isla sighed. "Do you remember anything from before the woods and wolf?"

"Dark," he said. "I remember darkness. Everything being dark, and I don't know anything but the darkness before the darkness." He began drumming his fingers over the leather binding of the book he'd been reading. "How could he do that?"

From the grit of disdain in his tone, Isla knew what he meant.

She wrung her hands together and crossed her arms over her chest as she paced a bit. "It's called shifting," she eased, bracing herself and him in pause before she continued, "not everyone can do it completely. Some just claws and fangs, some unfortunate people only the hair, and others not at all. The Goddess gave us our abilities, our power, to protect the land we stand on, to protect each other as she'd been protected when she walked the world before us."

At her paraphrased citings from the Great Book, Lukas's nostrils flared. "You're one of them?"

Now or never.

Isla wasn't sure how much time she had left, but she could feel an end looming. An ethereal sensation that whatever she did and said next was *crucial*.

"You are," she said, tone firm. "Your name is Lukas. You're *from* the Pack of Tethys. Your parents live there too, and your sister who just had a baby. A boy. You're an uncle." Lukas's face was stone. Isla gritted her teeth and carried forward, heart thudding in her ears. "You've spent the past six years training to become a warrior. I met you a little over a week ago at a dinner. We talked about a painting that you were looking at, and then I saw you again when we were *both* behind the Wall." She reached into her pocket and slowly pulled out the marker, letting it rest in her palm before him as she stepped closer. "You found this on the ground, and you told me about it. What it was. What it meant for me—and someone else in my life."

Isla waited with bated breath as his eyes honed in on the marker, tracked across its ridges and carvings as she had countless times. There was a flash in his eyes, and a nag of hope blossomed in her chest.

"Isla." Her name tumbled from his lips.

With it, her own mouth had opened to beam, to say *yes*...but then she noticed the severed straps of his restraints, tucked beneath his pillows so one could barely see the detachment.

And she had no time to move out of the way as he rocketed to his feet and slammed her to the wall, pinning her beneath his body.

Any immediate thought to jerk and fight him away needed to be re-evaluated as something pointed and sharp pressed to her side. Not small like the scalpel she couldn't reach in her waistband—but a dagger. She caught the glint of it out of the corner of her eye. There was no time to ponder where he'd gotten it, how.

"Don't scream," he demanded, eyes so dark with rage that they were nearly black. "This is your fault. You're why I'm like this. Why I'm stuck here."

Isla's heart was in her throat. She didn't know what to say, what to do. Not yet. She would. She just needed to think. Focus. Calm. He was angry with her. Maybe she could talk him down.

"I'm sorry," she panted. "I'm sorry. I shouldn't have left you."

She swore something in his eyes changed, though quickly, they became endless depths of fury again.

"He said if I killed you, he'd let me out, and then I'm on my own. But if I bring you back—they'll let me stay." The blade was pressed further into her side, and Isla held in a scream as it pierced her skin and burned in a way that it shouldn't have. Her insides had gone watery.

Kill her. *Kill* her?

It was with the slightest jerk of his elbow that Isla knew she had to act fast, and it was with it that her wolf took over.

Claws breaking through, she swiped them across his body, wherever she could reach, meeting flesh deeper than she'd intended. His cry out mixed with her own as he keeled over, dragging his blade through her shirt, across her skin as he went down. She followed suit as pain took hold, falling a few feet away.

Isla hissed as she shakily reached for her side, the warm stickiness of his blood coating her fingers while her own leaked through the torn fabric of her shirt. The wound left in the wake of his weapon was shallow but still lit her insides on fire. Like a venom had seeped in and was coursing through her veins.

Breathing so hard and so fast that she was becoming light-headed, she darted her eyes to Lukas who was curled in a ball, putting pressure on the large gash she'd drawn from his back to his stomach. Crimson leaked from between his fingers, pooling beneath him. His eyes were shut tight while his teeth were bared as he sneered at the pain.

Isla noticed the book he'd been reading, fallen to the floor, smeared in blood as with the marker and the dagger, and she saw *red* when she realized the scribblings in it weren't in the Common, not in an alphabet she recognized.

There was no way.

But she didn't have time to question, not like this. She only had the facts in front of her.

Someone had given that book to him, someone had given him this dagger, and allowed him to get free. Told him to *kill her*.

Temper flaring, she reached for the knife, hilt dipped in his blood and blade slicked with hers, and fought to her knees, one arm wrapped around to hold her burning side.

She brought the blade to his throat. "Who gave you this?"

He didn't answer.

She pressed it to his skin, forcing out again, "*Who* gave you this?"

As she had at the metal's contact, Lukas recoiled like it burned, and Isla balked with it.

He became pale, and as his eyes opened to look up at her, Isla saw they were clear. Clearer than they ever had been since he came back from the Wilds. He blinked, as if seeing her for the first time before they fluttered closed, and he went limp.

Isla fell back, jaw unhinged as a wave of clarity washed over her. "No," she muttered, her eyes darting across his body. His breathing was slow, his heartbeat fading. "No, no, no, no. Lukas!" She dropped the knife to her side and crawled over to him, struggling as whatever the knife had been made of, whatever laced its surface, wreaked havoc on her.

As she pressed firmly against his wounds to slow the bleeding, the room's doors burst open. It was Adrien, the guard, and a nurse. Everything that happened next seemed to move in slow motion, yet so fast that all she could do was run on autopilot. She gathered everything. The marker, the book, and the dagger.

And left Lukas bleeding on the floor as Adrien carried her away.

CHAPTER 18

Whatever had been on that blade had to be some kind of liquid fire. It seared through every bend and curve of Isla's being and had her cursing anything and everything in the universe.

At how she was jostled with every step Adrien dragged her down through the stairwell. At the glow of the lights they passed on their descent. At how loud it all seemed around her—his footsteps, her heartbeat, his breathing, the echoes, the opening door. Her wolf was fighting —against what, she wished she knew—but the battle was leaving her body oversensitive and on high alert. And not only that, but she could've sworn that with the trauma, those lost pieces of herself reformed. Recaptured in a tether desperate to keep her rooted to this earth.

Or maybe she was going crazy. Whatever was on that knife was working through her. Poisoning her mind, driving her mad.

Either way, all of it was good—the pain, the odd sensations— because they distracted her from what lay above.

What she'd done.

The hallway Adrien had brought them to was just as dark as the one they'd left. Either the third or fourth floor, she assumed. Not her room.

He pushed open one of the doors and brought them inside, clicking on the light on the wall. Isla cringed at the sudden brightness and groaned as he placed her on the cold surface of an examination table. She dropped all she'd taken on the metallic tray sitting at its side, the items clanging as they met it. The ring of the blade hit her hardest, making her wince.

"How bad is it?" Adrien asked, ignoring the lot, sounding more panicked than she'd thought he'd be. He'd seen her much, *much* worse very recently.

"I'm fine," she tried to abate him, though she wasn't entirely confident in the statement. She inched up the table on her own accord, saying off-handedly, "It just hurts."

"Because you were stabbed, Isla," Adrien said. "He attacked you. I should've never let you—"

She let out a strained sigh, cutting him off. "He just nicked me."

"How did he even get to you? I thought he was restrained."

"I thought so too, but they were—cut." Her eyes went to the dagger, and right at that moment, the door flew open. Her heart leaped into her throat, expecting guards or her father.

But it was only Sebastian, who was somehow able to find them.

His eyes widened when they fell upon his sister, shirt bottom torn with blood smeared over her stomach and hands. "What the hell? What happened?" The door slammed behind him.

Isla made a movement and sound for him to quiet down while Adrien answered, "He stabbed her."

A look of murder took to her brother's face.

"He didn't *stab* me," Isla said, fighting to sit upright and failing. "It's a graze. There's just something on that blade." At her words, Sebastian brought his eyes down to the glinting metal. Isla painfully threw a hand up as he reached for it. "Be careful!"

Her brother took hold of the weapon and held it up to his face. Malice still shone in his eyes, and the same lividity flashed in Adrien's at the sight of it. Now Isla could really see what it was. Beneath its coating of blood, the hilt was ivory, entirely, from the guard to the pommel. The grip was made up of studs and corded patterns, but they were so steeped in crimson, she couldn't make much of them from afar.

As Sebastian examined it, he turned it in his hands, catching every angle, balancing it to test its weight. "How the fuck did he get this?" He brought it back to the table, and his eyes flitted over the book and the marker carelessly. He didn't even bother reaching for them. There wasn't pause for her to answer before he appended, "And why the fuck did you take it?"

Isla wished she could've grabbed all the items and hid them away, wished she had some method of washing their existence from the boys' memories. At least, until she knew exactly what she was looking at. Until she could gather her bearings and have a handle on the situation.

The writing in the book was the same kind as on the marker—that was simply her theory until she could confirm it. And if that happened…well, she didn't know what she'd do. But confirmation had to come first.

"I wasn't going to leave it there with him," she said before her mouth snapped shut.

With him—Lukas—who she'd left unconscious and bleeding out on the floor.

Whose body she'd clawed into.

Whose blood was on her hands. *Her hands.*

Chest heaving, Isla looked down at the stained palm not holding her side. A crimson concoction of them both. "Oh, Goddess," she breathed in panic before looking up at the boys. "Did I kill him?"

Sebastian's eyebrows shot up, not having been clued in on the entire story yet. He looked to Adrien who wouldn't look back, but the shift in their friend's facial expression was enough to tell her brother not to interrogate.

Neither had asked her to rehash the entire situation yet, she realized. Adrien had seen what he'd seen and dragged her out. Sebastian just accepted what he saw, ready to do whatever had to be done with as little information as he'd been given.

"He's probably fine," Adrien said.

"He survived over a week in the Hunt and the bak," Sebastian offered blindly. "*You*, of all people, aren't going to be the one to do him in."

Now Adrien turned his way, flashing a look that said, *are you kidding?*

Isla would've matched it if she wasn't so horrified by it all. If the image wasn't re-materializing in her mind. If she couldn't feel the weight of him on her chest, the tip of a blade on her side. She shook her head to rid herself of it. To compartmentalize as she'd been taught in training.

Focused and calm. She had to be focused and calm. Maybe not for the rest of the day, but a few hours, at least.

With determination written across her face, Isla finally got herself into a sitting position.

Adrien moved a step closer. "Let me see it."

Reluctantly, Isla slowly removed her hand, subtly cocking her head away to solely focus on her friend and not whatever lay beneath. She hissed at the removal of pressure and watched as his eyebrows shot up. Horror flooded her heart. "What is it?"

Adrien blinked, and Sebastian joined him in observation. She winced as Adrien's fingers brushed over her skin while her brother said, astonished, "You're healed."

"What?" Isla snapped her attention to her side, gazing a few inches below her ribs where the pain was worst. Just as Sebastian had said, the area was smooth, free of any injuries. But she still felt it. Her body battling. Her—

"It still hurts," she said, brushing her hand over the planes of the skin. "My wolf—it's—something's wrong."

Sebastian was examining the knife again, his jaw tight. "Is it wolfsbane?"

Terror coursed through Isla again.

It would take copious amounts of the poisonous root to kill her, but it could severely hurt her wolf. In archaic practices, it was used to aid those who couldn't control their shifting, but now, it was outlawed throughout the continent.

Adrien shook his head. "You could smell wolfsbane if it was on something like that. It would mess with her healing too. There would be a scar."

Sebastian looked away from the weapon. "Then what is it?"

"Maybe you re-aggravated something from the Hunt."

That wasn't the answer. Isla *knew* what that felt like. This was entirely different.

She recalled how Lukas had also recoiled at the blade's touch, but she wouldn't speak on it. She wanted them to drop the subject. For now. Just for now.

Sebastian went to sit in the chair meant for a physician, letting out a frustrated sigh. "Did he say anything worthwhile at least? Before he attacked you."

Isla swallowed. The most meaningful words had come *while* he was attacking her.

"He said if I killed you, he'd let me out..."

Isla replayed everything that he'd said to her. Everything she'd said to him. Looped over her name said with grit and—disdain.

Had he actually *remembered* her...or had he just been told who she was? The girl with wheat-gold hair who'd spoken with him at the feast, who'd been with him behind the Wall, who would, without a doubt, try to visit him.

Her blood hummed with a mix of rage and fear.

Whoever had given Lukas these things *knew her*. Had told him to *kill her*.

But she found a twisted comfort—she had to, to maintain any even keelness—in the notion that whoever wanted her dead was too much of a coward to do it themselves.

He. Who was *he*?

The only person who knew—who knew *many* things she'd been seeking—was Lukas.

It would be horribly idiotic of her to try getting back to him. Hands down, the worst, least thought-out idea she'd ever had—and she'd had many of those. But there was that clearness in his eyes before he'd gone limp. Something had been...different.

"Isla?"

Isla snapped her head up to find Adrien and Sebastian eyeing her expectantly.

"He just said a whole lot of nothing," she explained. "He doesn't remember a thing from before the hunter shifted and woods that emerged from the darkness. Not me, not the bak, not the m—" Isla cut herself off before mentioning the marker. "It's all nothing."

∽

Isla had told the boys that the marker and the book were hers. Not exactly what they *were*, but simply describing them as her "things", saying she'd dropped them when Lukas had jumped her.

They'd accepted the explanation, though with some suspicion—most of all from Adrien—but weren't as agreeable with her aversion to their plans of turning over the dagger. The proposal had come with the realization that they may have been screwed anyway, with Isla's scent flooding the room and her blood on the floor. At least something decent could come of their attempt at helping him, and they could figure out what had been on that blade. But Isla wasn't ready to hand it over. It felt important—all these things did—and she had to keep hold of them.

So, she'd convinced them that she had been able to keep her scent masked and that her blood hadn't gotten anywhere but on her own person. Never mentioned that Lukas had known her name. And that was enough chance for them.

But she didn't dispose of the weapon as she'd told them she would.

No, instead, she'd gone back to her room. She'd compartmentalized. Told herself that everything was fine—that Lukas was fine, even though she had no idea what was going on—and washed the blood from the dagger with a rag, careful not to touch the blade's surface. Then she shoved it, wrapped in one of her shirts, along with the marker and the book to the bottom of her travel bag that had already been packed with her things from her hotel room by Adrien.

And then she was discharged, and life went on as normal.

Nurses made their rounds through the halls. The occasional visitors to see patients. No extra security or guard.

It was as if nothing had happened at all.

Isla wasn't sure if she should've been unnerved or grateful for it.

She *did know* that it took everything in her not to turn back. Not to scale those stairs until she reached the fifth floor to behold the aftermath. To repent for—

No.

No, Lukas was fine. He was fine.

She repeated those words over and over until she reached Callisto's Hall because it was noon and time for her to leave this pack and as many memories of it as she could behind.

Many of those from Io who'd come for the feast and to witness the descent of the hunters only had already returned to the pack and their duties. The only few that Isla knew remained within the territory were she, Adrien, Sebastian, her father, and a few other members and officials. All of them were supposed to depart today, but as Isla boarded the scarcely populated transport vehicle parked in the hall's long driveway, she realized her father was nowhere in sight.

"Where's Dad?" she asked Sebastian who'd made a home lounging in the back, spread across two seats, prepared to sleep for as much of the journey as possible.

"He still has things to take care of here," he told her.

"What kind of things?" she asked, knowing the answer she'd receive.

"Things he won't even tell me about."

Isla ran her gaze over her brother's face. A skilled liar through and through—but she could tell he was being honest. A selfish part of her liked that they were both clueless, but the rest had gone rigid as her mind ran wild. She glanced out of the windows and in the direction of the infirmary in the distance.

Maybe they *were* screwed.

"I'll see you in prison."

She whipped around to glare at her brother and his ill-timed quip just as he closed his eyes and leaned further back in his seat.

Adrien boarded about ten minutes later, taking the spot a row behind Isla, but in her eye-line. He hadn't heard anything about Lukas either. But unlike her brother, she clocked something unspoken in his stare. She didn't press on it, though. Not here with others. Not here when the vehicle had already revved to life and set them off on their journey home.

Isla could tell how close they were getting to Io by the feel of the heat and the increasing humidity. Summertime in their homeland could be damn near insufferable sometimes, and the weather was not bound by borders. Even if they hadn't crossed into their territory yet, the cabin of the car was starting to become uncomfortable. The only form of cooling within the confines was the open windows and the air rushing through them. Isla had taken off her shirt, leaving her in the tight camisole she'd been wearing underneath that cut just above her midriff. The boys had stripped off their tops too, Sebastian dousing his fabric in water and putting it on his head.

Overdramatic, she'd thought at first until she became dizzy from the heat. But she had too much sisterly pettiness to copy his approach.

The ride was full of bumps and rocky patches, making it hard for Isla to find any type of rest as her leaning head ricocheted off the window more times than she'd like to admit. So much so, she swore she had a bruise on her scalp beneath her hair. Her entire body ached from the rumbling, including that nagging in her side.

At a stop they'd made at one of Callisto's outer posts to fuel, and while most were either sleeping or hadn't bothered to move, Isla had taken the opportunity to get out and stretch her legs, not drifting too far.

The moon had been half-full tonight. As she gazed upon it, a mix of light and darkness, she absentmindedly traced a finger over the creases of her opposite palm. Drawing out strings…*fraying* strings. The threads stretching and falling apart with every mile.

When Adrien had packed her bag, he'd also packed away her gown from the night of the feast—horribly, she'd noted, but that wasn't what got to her.

The fabric still held the scent of that night. The lingering smell of the flowers from the garden, and the faintest essence of warmth, woods, spice, and everything entirely Kai, who even then knew how to get close enough to test their limits.

She'd breathed it in deep—too deep—and blossomed that dull ache in her chest again. And now, being outside under the moon, as they'd found themselves frequently, it had gotten worse.

A little bit of desperation clouding her judgment, she closed her eyes and dug for that tether. One last time, she told herself, one *last* time. Sought that connection. That lapse. Some peace. A comfort.

But she couldn't find anything at the other end. No one. Just emptiness.

Just alone.

∼

Io's borders were under constant surveillance, the acknowledged lines stalked along by the wolves of the Imperial Guard. As the caravan was cleared and crossed into the territory, the soldiers howled, announcing the incoming travelers to the other units further inland...but also for her. The newly minted warrior.

Isla bit the inside of her cheek to keep from beaming. That was what she needed to focus on—reigning triumphant. She had to hold onto that for as long as possible for a reprieve before she lost her mind.

Even though they'd passed the borders, there were still a few more hours until they reached Io's Pack Hall. The route they'd taken went around the bustling Imperial City, through the roads with clear views of the towering mountains of the Valkeric ranges where one would find the High Ground, the prison.

As they curved into the outskirts of the city, Isla caught sight of the iconic golden gates that surrounded the Pack Hall, stretching high into the air, near-blinding in the brutal sunlight. A beautiful, behemoth of a structure—the building was at least three times the size than that of Callisto's. Pack members were buzzing outside of the gates as they approached, reporters and gossips too. As usual.

The boys had since woken up and found themselves looking out the windows at the gathered crowd who wanted to catch sight of the Imperial Heir, mostly. Adrien lifted his hand to wave to them, drawing more of a commotion and sending those reporters and gossips scribbling in their notepads. They'd take anything to record, Isla figured. Even the most professional of journalists were itching to get the inside scoop about what had truly happened between their prince and the woman who was set to be their future queen.

Some parts of the story were even still a mystery to Isla despite having been so close to Adrien and Corinne.

The gates of the hall were nothing like that of the Wilds. They drew open easily, and the vehicle rumbled up the extensive drive and by the long pool of water, sprouted with golden fountains and glittering with sunlight that Isla wished it would be acceptable to jump into.

She leaped to her feet before the van had even come to a stop, her body releasing groans and cracks in celebration of finally being stretched out again. Her head spun from the exhaustion, but despite it, she practically raced down the row of seats, eager to feel the earth beneath her feet, to maybe find a breeze in the open air.

She'd gotten one of the two.

"Shit, it's hot," Sebastian cursed, wiping the sweat off his brow as he joined at her side. His shirt, soaked again, was slung around his neck.

"It's home," Isla said with a smile, tying her shirt around her waist. But the words also felt…wrong out of her mouth. Out of place. She wouldn't dawdle on it.

As Adrien came to stand at her other side, Isla's eyes directed up the many stairs to the opening of the hall's grand doors. Out of it strode a familiar gangly man, a clipboard tucked under his arm. Of course. Isla's grin grew as she observed their pack's liaison walking down the stairs towards them.

Bags under Winslow's eyes were typical, as was the slight jitteriness he exhibited from drinking too much brew, but the veins spider-webbing his temples told her he'd been more stressed than usual. It didn't take much thought to figure out why.

"Welcome back," he greeted the three, a tiredness in his voice saved just for them, residual from the years he'd dealt with them as they grew up *"complete animals"*.

"Good to be back, Winsy," Sebastian replied, beaming in a way that made the liaison arch an eyebrow in suspicion. He'd given up trying to deter them from using the nickname.

Before any other comments could be made, the hall's doors opened again, and Isla's breath caught as the Imperial Luna came down the stairs. She donned a beautiful maroon dress, cut in a way that was both modest yet left enough skin exposed to keep temperate in the heat. The sudden wind caught perfectly in her long flowing hair.

Despite her closeness to their son and being their closest confidant's daughter, Isla had never been as friendly with the leaders of their pack, but she'd always been in awe of Imperial Luna Marlane. The easy, powerful grace she exuded. How beloved she was. How kind.

Growing up, through every rigorous lesson in etiquette she'd endured at the helm of the Elders, she'd been taught that the luna was the prime example of everything a she-wolf should be. Been taught about how the role she played at the alpha's side, the role she played for Io's people—a foundation of strength, a mother, a caretaker—would be one Isla would need to carry herself to a smaller scale in her *own* domestic life.

When Isla had a mate and children and was bound to those things and her home as she took care of them, she would try to emulate it... when she was ready for that. To be a mother and...*someone's* mate.

Grimacing, she brought her hands together, rubbing her thumb over her palm.

The Imperial Luna greeted Adrien with outstretched arms, pulling her son into a tight, tight hug as if he'd fade away if she loosened her grip. After everything, Isla understood, although, she knew the recent coddling had been driving her friend mad.

Once she pulled away, but not until she could bestow a kiss on his cheek, the Luna turned to the Beta's children, greeting them both before she focused on Isla.

"Congratulations, Warrior," she said, her smile as dazzling as her golden-green eyes. As bright as the sun above them.

Isla bowed her head, stomach twisting in nervous knots. *How* could she be expected to be someone like this?

"Thank you," she answered, and then noticed Winslow had drifted a few feet away, his hand up and gesturing her over. Praying she didn't come off as rude, Isla excused herself from the others and went to him. "Yes?"

Winslow kept his voice quiet. "The high general is here and would like to speak with you in the hall."

Isla's heart skipped. "The *Warrior* High General?"

"That is the only high general in Morai, I believe."

Isla pursed her lips at the sarcasm. "What about?"

"That's for you two to discuss," the liaison said, and then, wasting no time, turned on his heel to head up the stairs.

Isla took a deep breath, almost choking on the thickness of the air.

This was...sudden. But it had to be good news, right? Why else would the high general go out of his way to travel to Io from Ganymede?

Her insides bubbled with a mix of nerves and anticipation as she followed, the numerous steps to the door working the muscles in her tired legs.

She almost sighed in relief at the coolness that greeted her once inside the foyer, the establishment having as opulent an interior, drenched in burgundies and golds, as outside. Isla wished she'd been wearing something that seemed more put together than the outfit she'd donned after ditching her bloody nurse's uniform, a wrinkled shirt she untied from her waist and haphazardly threw back on and her, simply coated head to toe in sweat.

As she contemplated if there was anything else she had to change into—trying to remember where the bathrooms were in this place to freshen up—her blood iced over.

She still had her bag. She was still holding her damn bag.

She had the marker, the book, and the dagger *here* in Io's Pack Hall— a place ridden with the highest officials and, likely lingering somewhere, the Imperial Alpha himself.

One of the hierarchy's tightest kept secrets, and two items that she just knew, in her gut, meant bad news, simply dangling off her shoulder.

She balked at the thought, steps faltering, and nearly fell over when Winslow came to a sudden stop.

He turned to her, explaining something Isla could only half-listen to because she needed an excuse to leave. She needed to get out of here, couldn't risk letting anyone find what she had.

But this was the Warrior High General. It would be a blatant show of disrespect if she skipped the conference. It could cost her in her career, any position she wanted to hold.

Her grip on the strap of the bag tightened as Ravona, Winslow's assistant, appeared on one of the two staircases leading up to the second floor where the high general was waiting.

Isla gulped. *Focused and calm,* she repeated her mantras. *Focused and calm. It'll all be fine.*

And she followed.

There were three levels to the Pack Hall. The bottom was reserved for public use, holding functions, galas, balls, and some lodging for travelers. The second for more official business. But at the highest level, the level not many were permitted up to, were the offices of the Imperial Alpha, Beta, and highest-ranking Council members. Isla had been up there very few times in her life. Back when she was too young to know what she was looking at.

"Please wait here," Ravona said, stopping once they'd opened into a new hallway. "Let me make sure he's ready for you."

Isla muttered her thanks as the petite woman went a few paces down the corridor to one of many large mahogany doors and disappeared behind it.

Once alone, Isla released a long breath. "Shit." Her bag felt so heavy on her shoulder. "Shit, shit, shit."

But it was all going to be fine. It would all. Be. Fine.

This was just a quick talk, and then she'd go home. Walk back to her apartment near Market Square. Maybe stop for a drink on the way.

Maybe find someone to keep her company for the night. That *had* been her plan a couple of nights ago.

After a few more moments that felt like centuries, Ravona finally reappeared in the hallway. "He's ready," she said softly.

Isla nodded and then went to her, finding the butterflies were back, of anticipation this time. She embraced them, fed off them as the secretary pushed open the entrance and gestured inside.

Quick talk, get out, all will be fine.

Isla smoothed out her shirt the best she could, turned, and stepped forward, breaking the threshold of the room.

And then, she was ready for the ground to swallow her whole because she wasn't faced with the high general—but with Imperial Alpha Cassius.

•

CHAPTER 19

S hit. Adrien was the spitting image of his father—the only difference was, instead of the eyes her friend had inherited from the Imperial Luna, Cassius's were endless depths of dark brown, nearly black, especially when swathed in the dim lighting of the corner of the sitting room. The darkness accentuated the hard lines of his face and made the grin he flashed seem more feral. Isla wondered if he could sense her heartbeat, if he could hear it. If he could hear her cursing so vilely in her mind that it would make her ancestors roll in their graves.

Alpha Cassius tipped his head to the secretary. "Thank you, Ravona. We won't be long." He strode into the center of the room. Into some light. It didn't do much to soften his features or make him any less intimidating. "Ten minutes, and you can escort her out."

Ravona bowed in response, and Isla, shaking out of her terrified stupor, followed suit, eyes lingering on the ground a second longer than necessary while she continued the internal tirade. But there had also been something that struck her as curious.

It was more than likely that Isla was being guided out of the premises due to the several halls they'd taken to get here. Halls that she'd need a map to track again. But she couldn't fight the gnawing feeling that the Alpha didn't *want* her freely moving about this floor.

She wrenched up at the feeling of a hand on her arm and the jostling of her bag strap.

Whipping around, she found Ravona with an arm outstretched. "Would you like me to take this for you?"

Isla blinked.

She *could* let her take it. Get it out of this room, as far away from here as possible. But where would it end up? With Winslow or with some nosy guards who'd pry through it? She couldn't risk letting it out of her sight.

Fighting to keep her tone even, she said, "No, that's fine. Thank you though."

Ravona nodded before giving one more bow to them both and backing out of the room. The hard sound of the door closing behind her couldn't help but make her jump, and the high click of the latch may as well have been the snapping of a trap made for a mouse. Her body went stiff under the Imperial Alpha's stare—slightly narrowed, always calculating. And though it shouldn't have been her instinct before her leader, for a moment, all Isla wanted to do was match it—but that air of defiance was squashed before it could manifest into anything she'd regret. She shifted her gaze to meet his before quickly diverting it, remembering well the lessons of her childhood.

Never look an alpha—especially *the* Alpha—directly in the eye.

She was careful adjusting her bag on her arm, hoping there was no scrape of metal against wood or ruffling of papers. "I apologize, Alpha, for my appearance. It was a long ride back, and it's quite hot outside."

At her tone, Alpha Cassius chuckled, and Isla risked a glance again.

"Please, Isla, you're like family," he said, taking a few steps closer, resting his hands on the back of the long leather couch facing her. "We don't need the formality." He gestured to the dry bar against the wall beside them, a generous spread of liquors and spirits and wines. "Can I offer you anything?"

Isla sized up the array, mouth almost salivating at the idea of the burn of wine down her throat. At the thought of the blissful fog it would bring her into. But it was far too early to be drinking in front of the Alpha. Though it was *also* rude to refuse his offer. "I'll take some water if you have it."

The slightest look of amusement took to the Alpha's face as he walked to the table and grabbed a pitcher filled with clear liquid to pour. He placed her filled glass on one of the coasters atop the small table set in the middle of the seating area, both pieces etched with the Imperial crest.

Isla caught the hint and battled away the panic that rose in her chest.

The Imperial Alpha had taken time out of his day to sit and share a drink with her? To *talk* with her? She could count the number of one-on-one conversations they'd had in her twenty-one years of life on one hand, and most of those had been at times of convenience for no longer than a minute or two when her father or Adrien had stepped away. Never like this. Never direct and intentional.

She swallowed before slowly dropping her bag to the floor at a distance from where she stood. *Focused and calm.* She walked to the chair and sat, the soft leather caving slightly at her weight. *Focus.* She took hold of her glass. *Calm.* "Thank you."

Alpha Cassius nodded in response before preparing himself a small glass of whiskey. "If you don't mind...long day."

It was only a little past noon.

As Isla chanced a small laugh, the Alpha lowered himself to the couch across from her and lifted his glass. "Cheers to you, Warrior."

Isla stilled, blinking at the praise. At the unease that had come with it, rather than pride.

She raised hers too. "Thank you, Alpha."

At the formality, Cassius chuckled again before lifting his beverage a bit higher and tipping it back. Isla mirrored the action, more grateful for the clean, cool liquid on her tongue than she'd expected she'd be.

Cassius sighed against the burn of his liquor. "You're the only member of our pack I cleared for this year's running, and you didn't disappoint. You did us all very proud. I'm looking forward to having you in my ranks."

The words weren't missed on Isla. *His* ranks.

Ezekiel's voice crept into her head against the backdrop of their argument as they'd walked out of Callisto's forest and back to the infirmary. It was as if she could feel his wicked, haughty grin circling her thoughts. She'd been so vehement in her argument of where the warriors stood, who they served. They worked for the continent, to protect its people. They didn't act as agents to maintain the Imperial Alpha's position at the top of the hierarchy.

But Alpha Cassius knows that, she told herself. It was just odd phrasing. Though, still, she wanted to make a point. So, she grinned, putting on the charm she'd worked on mastering for years to finagle officials, and said with ease, "I'm eager to do my part in helping the continent."

The corner of Cassius's lips twitched up as if he'd clocked the precision she'd chosen, but he didn't comment. Instead, he sat back. "There may be action sooner than you think. I'm afraid our times of peace may be coming to an end. Rogues have been a problem on some subjacent borders recently—Rhea, Charon, Deimos. They're overwhelming the guard, getting into villages and towns, stealing supplies, terrorizing the citizens. I'll likely be deploying some warrior units to assist in the eradication efforts." Cassius downed the rest of his drink, then went quiet, staring down at his empty glass. "It's hard when people forget their place." He met Isla's eyes again, and she straightened. He'd been talking about the rogues, yet still, the words stirred something in her. "It's important to deal with the issue quickly and efficiently before too much damage is done or panic is incited."

Isla's grip on her glass constricted.

Quickly and efficiently. As he'd wanted everything with Lukas to be dealt with. The fewer people in the know about the divergence from order, the better.

There was so much that she wanted to say—to counter, to question—but knew their "informality" had its limits. She didn't have a death wish.

"It will likely be a while before I'm allowed out in the field, I believe." She settled for instead, hating the gnawing of something like cowardice in her gut. "I haven't even received my lumerosi yet."

"That'll be in a few weeks. And you're one of the most promising new recruits we have—slaying two beasts—I'm sure you'll be out there before you know it."

Isla's jaw tightened, missing the opportunity to extend gratitude for the compliment, too busy reliving the most terrifying moment of her life. And too angry.

Don't, she warned herself, biting down on her tongue. But she couldn't pretend it didn't bother her that the Imperial Alpha didn't want anyone to know *why* she'd killed two bak. How she would've rather *not* have had to.

"It's awful what happened out there."

Isla's features faltered.

Was he actually...*acknowledging* what had happened?

The Alpha's eyes flashed with a slight challenge, and Isla paused.

This was a test.

One to see if she'd speak freely about the incident or if she'd obey, keeping it all under wraps as he wished. But was that the *only* reason he'd wanted to meet with her? Why he'd gone through the trouble, taken time out of his day...*lied* to Winslow about it? Or had the liaison been clued in the entire time, and the whole point was to ambush her?

Isla held in her groan.

Too many questions.

Too many questions and she had enough to deal with already.

She could just give him what he wanted, all of them, this hierarchy. Lie and tell them she'd leave everything forgotten. That, or she could *actually* do it. Toss her bag with the marker, the dagger, the book, even her gown that still smelled of Kai into the Barit Sea. Let *all of it* sink to the depths of nothing and move on with her life. That would be the smart thing to do.

She looked down at her water as she swirled it around her glass and braced herself for the line she was about to toe. "They came out of nowhere. We're lucky we got out alive."

The Alpha nodded as if accepting her position. He threw an arm out to the side to drum his fingers along the back of the couch and rested his ankle on his knee. "Yes. It's a good thing Alpha Kai was out there with you."

Hearing Kai's name made her stomach flip, and hearing it from the *Imperial Alpha's* mouth, spoken as if her mate were a peer, not a lowly subject, had Isla becoming hyper-aware of the exact high-standing Kai held. As if she'd never truly gauged it all before.

Her eyes shifted briefly to the map at her side, a clear view of the masses of Io and Deimos with Oberon's territory set between them.

She tracked over the sketches of Deimos's own mountain ranges, over the long stretch of river that led out to the ocean, cutting between Mimas and Tethys. The land was broken up into four main regions—Surles, Abalys, Ifera, and then in its heart, denoted with a large black eight-pointed star and a sketch of a palace that she assumed was the Pack Hall, was Mavec.

Her lips threatened to twitch downwards, as she briefly wondered if Kai still thought of her too. If *he'd* sought something in their wilting bond—just randomly, just to see—and found nothing. If he'd been disappointed by that. If he'd ever felt that comfort from it, from her, at all.

Goddess, now's not the time.

Biting down on the inside of her cheek, her gaze went back to her glass.

Focus.

"He saved my life," she said, voice low.

The Alpha was quiet long enough to make Isla look up to meet his eyes again. "Saved your life and killed four bak," he boasted. "One of the highest counts in our history. The *'hero of the Hunt'*." Isla's grip tightened. There was something about the tone the Alpha had used that she wasn't keen on. "Your father and all of us are very grateful."

Her father.

Still back in Callisto.

"Taking care" of things.

She ran her tongue over her teeth. "I haven't been able to see my father much since I emerged. With all the meetings and whatnot." There was a bite to her tone that she hadn't intended. "I had thought he'd be returning with us, but it seems he stayed back."

The Alpha's eyes narrowed for only a moment before they softened, and he threw on a grin to match. It was more unnerving than anything. He rose to his feet and walked back over to the dry bar to pour himself more whiskey, letting the silence gather in a way that was almost suffocating. "That's my fault, I apologize. Reporting fatalities from the Hunt is typically my responsibility, but I have too much to tend to here."

The words clattered around Isla's skull as she watched the translucent brown liquid splash and pool into the glass. It felt like a lead ball had been dropped in her stomach.

Fatalities.

Fatalities.

"What do you mean?" Isla felt like her heart was in her throat again, and her tongue was sandpaper.

The Alpha gave a solemn shake of his head. "Unfortunately, the hunter from Tethys succumbed to his injuries."

She couldn't swallow. Couldn't breathe.

Lies.

He had to be lying.

Calm.

She battled to keep the bile rising in her throat at bay. She couldn't sound like it had affected her. "When?"

Cassius put the bottle down and picked up his glass. "I received the report early this morning. It's a shame. I really thought he'd pull through."

The room had started spinning.

She was going to vomit.

He was *lying*. He had to be lying.

But why would he?

Isla didn't know what to say. What to ask.

Because Lukas was very alive—in a sense—when she'd last seen him. When she'd pressed her hands to the bleeding wounds at his side that she'd inflicted herself with her own claws.

Her *own* claws.

She killed him.

Goddess, she'd killed him.

She was going to be sick.

She had to get out.

Out, out, out.

Shakily, she rose from her seat, nearly tipping over her water as she put it on the table. "I'm sorry. Would you excuse me for a second?"

The Alpha sipped from his whiskey. "I think we're done, actually." He lifted his glass to her, smiling. "Congratulations again, Warrior."

Isla barely heard his words as she turned and gathered her bag as quickly as possible, not caring if it rattled and shook. Ravona was already waiting outside for her.

"Can you show me to the restroom, please?" Isla asked, barely able to choke out the words.

Then everything moved in a blur as she was escorted to the facilities, through the hall, and through another mahogany door that felt cool on her clammy skin as she pushed through it.

Her knees screamed in pain as she crashed to the floor in front of the sole toilet in the lavatory, not caring where she tossed her bag, and rid herself of whatever was in her stomach. Over and over until all that was left were dry heaves and shallow breaths. Tears stung her sunburned cheeks as she sobbed as quietly as she could over the porcelain, gripping onto it so tightly, that her knuckles turned a matching white to keep from falling over.

She killed him.

He was dead, and it was all her fault.

His voice rang in her head, that clear look in his eyes was all she could see.

She killed him.

She heaved again. And again.

Until she could no longer hold on and simply fell back against the wall beside her.

And then she let herself sob for a few more breaths—in and out, in and out—before she steeled herself, wiped her tears as if nothing had happened, and allowed Ravona to walk her out of the Pack Hall.

CHAPTER 20

Isla was somewhere on the outskirts of the city, but she wasn't sure where. All that mattered was she was away from everyone, everything. That it was only her and this ravine, the flowing water rushing below her swinging feet high above it as she sat at the edge of a cliffside.

She'd killed Lukas.

As the words went through her mind like a shot for the umpteenth time, she didn't put her face in her hands. She didn't cry. She'd run out of tears now. Been wrung dry of any feeling but numbness. But maybe that was good. It was a relief from the despair, the pain, the all-consuming guilt that had her close to passing out as she sobbed and nearly hyperventilated against the heat and dust around her.

Imperial Alpha Cassius knew she'd been with Lukas. He had to have. The way he'd looked at her, spoken to her…he knew it wasn't injuries from the Hunt, he knew she'd been the one who'd done it. Maybe the whole conversation was supposed to build into an expression of gratitude for the loose end she'd gotten out of the way. She'd done him a favor.

Goddess…

Isla's hand went to her mouth. She was going to be sick again.

The sound of approaching footsteps didn't make her jump. Didn't make her turn. She didn't have the energy to anyway, even if she *hadn't* known who was approaching.

Adrien and Sebastian made no effort to mask themselves, and as if they could sense how upset she was, moved upon her cautiously. The

Pack Hall's courtyard had been empty when she'd stepped back into the suffocating air outside, and she'd been grateful for it. She couldn't face them. Tell them what she'd done.

Murderer.

She grimaced.

She was. She was. She—

"Lukas is alive."

Adrien's words were completely lost on her at first. Just sounds amongst the rush of the water. But then they became clearer as she played them again.

And again.

And again.

Lukas is alive.

She lifted her head and blinked at the landscape, letting the sentence run a few more times before she spun around to face him. "What?"

This had to be a hallucination, a dream. She *had* passed out beneath the beating sun. It was a foreign poison on the blade that had strange side effects. Because there was no way—*no way*—that Isla was hearing what she thought she was.

But Adrien paused at her side and said it again.

"He's not dead. My father only told you that he was."

"What?" she repeated herself, but Adrien didn't. He stayed silent and allowed the words to sink in.

Lukas is...alive?

Isla was *really* going to throw up now—the relief, doubt, and anger churning through the numbness, beyond the despair, that made her nauseous. She didn't know how much more of this she could take. The up and down, back and forth.

The tears were returning, and Isla glanced down at the water. "He lied to me?"

It hadn't been a direct question, simply a realization. And with it spoken aloud, the anger began festering until it usurped all other emotion so much that she swore she'd shift right here.

She jumped to her feet, sitting making her feel trapped and suffocated all over again. Her fingers were balled so tightly in her fists that her nails pierced the skin of her palms. Adrien stood a few inches above her as she squared herself to him, a little closer in size to her than if it were Kai. "Why would he do that? Why would he let me think that I— that I *killed* him?"

She almost wished her friend was lying, then she wouldn't have the traitorous thought of ripping through the *Alpha's* side running through her head, but Adrien wouldn't make this up. Not this.

The Heir's jaw was tight, and Isla saw even Sebastian was wearing something akin to the look of murder he'd brandished upon seeing her injured on the examination table.

"He wants you to stop looking. Stop getting involved. Pushing things," Adrien said, and there was a hint of shame in his eyes. "He wants it all to go away."

"He told you that?" When had Adrien spoken with his father?

"In so many words."

Isla couldn't breathe again, but this time, it was in rage.

She had to step away. Could feel her wolf restless beneath the surface of her skin, ready to lash out, but still stuck, somehow. Her eyes were focused on the ground beneath her as she paced a few feet.

"He sat there and looked me in the eye and let me believe that I'd *killed* someone?" She thought her teeth would shatter from how tightly she'd clenched them. "He was going to let me torture myself for the rest of my life—*for what*? Did he think I'd call the reporters? Tell them what happened? I wouldn't have said anything." She looked up at Adrien who remained in his spot, whose expression hadn't changed. Who hadn't fought anything she'd said. "He doesn't trust me." Not a question, a statement, and again, one her friend neither confirmed nor denied. Isla shook her head, face twitching as she fought between scowling and sobbing. Lukas was *alive*. "That's cruel."

There was no response.

The three remained in a tense silence as Isla continued her movements against the backdrop of the setting sun. As she continued her tirade beneath her breath. As she fought to hold herself back from storming the Pack Hall. Tore through every memory she'd reminisced upon. Every subtle detail of recent events she'd reminded herself to go through.

She knew the Alpha could be ruthless, that he had a job and owed her nothing, but to let her believe something like this...

All to keep Lukas a secret and prevent inciting panic?

"Did you get rid of the dagger?"

At Adrien's words, Isla snapped her head up, then subtly glanced at her bag that was close to his feet. "It's somewhere safe, yes."

A line feathered in Adrien's cheek, and he nodded in acceptance before taking a few steps towards the black fabric coated in dust.

"Wait!" Isla called, and Adrien halted.

His features were hard when he turned to her. So much so, that he looked more like his father than he ever had in his life. "What's going on, Isla? You've been so off since you came out of the Wilds, and I thought it was all from the Hunt, from Lukas going missing, but it's not just that. It never has been."

Isla bit down on her tongue.

She wanted to tell them everything. About Lukas, the Ares Pass. About Kai. But she couldn't. She'd promised. "It's nothing."

Adrien shook his head. "No. No, it's not."

She sighed. "I…I can't tell you."

"Why?" Sebastian had taken a few steps towards her, the two closing in.

"Because I can't. Not yet."

"The Alpha of Deimos couldn't stop asking about you at the feast," Adrien started after some hesitation, and at the mention of Kai, Isla whirled around to face him. "He saved you during the Hunt, visited you when we were with you in your room. You didn't bump into him before you came to the Gate. You were *with* him. Somewhere." His voice had been charged with understanding, rung with epiphany, as he encroached on her further, and Isla felt her chest tighten. "I thought he was just looking at you to get in Io's graces, make a statement in his new position, I didn't know—but it's more than that, and I should have been able to figure it out from the way he looked at you. Because I've seen it before." He stopped a few inches away and said without a hint of uncertainty, "Because he's your mate."

Sebastian laughed.

Isla felt like the ground had just caved in, and Sebastian laughed. But he was the *only one* laughing, and he seemed to realize that fact quickly.

His eyes darted between his best friend and his sister—now engaged in a silent standoff—his jubilant features gradually falling into those of shock. "Wait, you're serious?" His eyes were wide as he put himself in Isla's view. "You found your mate?"

Isla barely spared her brother a second glance, holding Adrien's stare instead. She didn't know what she was trying to read from it, or what she wanted to convey with her own. Part of her wanted him to elaborate—to learn *how* Kai had looked at her that should've been a dead giveaway to him—but she knew from his later words, it would only dredge up horrible memories for the Heir. Memories of the day his chosen mate's fated one had shown up to challenge Adrien for her claim.

So instead, Isla focused on what the rest of her wanted, what it felt.

The slightest bit of relief to have one of her secrets out in the open, but also fear, anger, guilt, and defiance. Maybe too much to handle after the emotional drainage she'd already gone through.

"So, what if he is?" she said softly, stepping away, only to gasp as Sebastian roughly manhandled her collar—as only a brother would—and pulled it back to check her neck.

"Did he mark you?" His voice was a mix of overprotectiveness, surprise, and maybe…excitement as he inspected the skin.

"Get away." Isla swatted at him, adjusting her clothes. "He didn't."

Sebastian moved back, a breath of disbelief from his mouth. "Why didn't you say anything?"

"Because…" Isla trailed off, directing her eyes anywhere but at them. Just the rocks, the granules of dirt, the cool water flowing down the ravine. Even with the sense of inevitability that had hung above the truth being revealed at some point, she hadn't prepared what to say. "Because it doesn't matter," she eventually settled for. "We aren't doing anything. We aren't accepting the bond."

"You rejected him?" Sebastian again, spoken quick as a whip.

"No." Isla wrapped her arms around herself, feeling the stickiness of the sweat percolating on her skin. "And he didn't reject me. We're just forgetting we ever met and moving on."

Simply saying it all out loud made her feel just as crazy as the night they'd started their grand scheme in the garden.

"Does it work that way?"

Sebastian again, and Isla found herself toeing at a rock protruding from the russet-tinted earth. "It has to." And at his follow-up question of *why*, she met his eyes. "Because it's what we want."

The "we" felt different off her tongue this time.

We.

They were a *"we"*, an *"our"*. Their bond—a little universe drawn between their souls—vast and endless and mystical and wondrous and theirs. Only theirs. No council or otherworldly force would decide for them what they did with it. If they wanted to live their lives separately, they would. And if they'd decided they had wanted to tread through existence and eternity together—

"Why keep the dagger?"

Now Adrien spoke up after spending some time in observational silence.

Isla turned to look at the Heir, his eyes more golden than green in the early forays of dusk, and still barely readable. But his words—not at all about Kai or her forsaken bond—clued her in enough on where his head was. What he had in mind was either not worth saying in his eyes, or so bad he didn't want her to hear it.

She sighed, perfectly fine with his disposition for now, but knew *something* was coming, if not for the slightest flare of his nostrils, but because she *knew* he couldn't be silent. Not about something like this. She fought away the nagging feeling of guilt and focused.

Now how much should she share? The bond was out there, but how much further down the rabbit hole would she bring them? Where would she even *start*?

"Lukas knew who I was when I went to see him," she began, moving closer to her bag, debating internally on whether she wanted to brandish the marker and explain—eventually. "I don't know if he remembered me, or if someone told him who I was, but they gave him that dagger to get himself free. And then gave him these ultimatums regarding whether he killed me or took me 'somewhere'. I want to make sure there's nothing I can figure out from it before I let it get buried with everything else."

The boys had gone entirely still as she spoke, barely catching on her latter dig. And even without ties or tethers or connections, she could sense the rage simmering beneath the surface. Worse than it had been in the infirmary when they thought she'd just been attacked.

"Where?" Adrien asked, eyes narrow and voice rasped.

"We didn't get that far," Isla said, curling her fists—though not out of anger. She felt the phantom warmth of Lukas's blood on her hands again, the feeling, the memory making her shudder. *He's alive.*

"Who would bring that to him? Who got it in? We canvased. He was guarded non-stop." Something that struck as shame lingered in Sebastian's tone like he couldn't believe that they'd allowed her to get in that position, that they'd let that happen to her. "Who would want you dead?"

The big question.

"He mentioned a nurse who'd come in to see him." Isla felt the weight lift from her shoulders bit by bit with every word she spilled. But there were limits. There had to be limits. "A second one we hadn't accounted for and the infirmary probably didn't know about either. He never said if it was a man or woman, but he mentioned a *'he'* when he had the dagger on me."

As she'd spoken, her eyes had flitted back and forth between them but remained mostly on Sebastian, hesitant to look Adrien in the eye. But when she did dare pass her gaze over the Heir, she had to double back. There was a gnawing in her gut, a little voice in her head that clued her in on what the shifty look on his face meant, and as if the words had been whispered in her ear by that tiny thing for her to relay, she asked carefully, "Where is he now?"

"Heading to Valkeric."

There was no remorse in her friend's voice. It was mostly flat. Could've been considered indifferent if it weren't for the aggravation that still lingered. Isla wished she knew exactly what was bothering him most. What she'd said about Lukas or—

Focus.

"What else do you know?"

"Just that whatever his story is, it doesn't add up or make sense. I was only able to grab your father right before I had to get to the caravan and didn't have time to convince him to give me more information."

She hadn't even seen her father before they departed.

Her eyes passed over him again, calculating, noting there was no release of that contemplative, unsettled expression. If anything, his brows had drawn in further, breathing became deeper as if he were trying to calm himself, hold himself back.

Isla braced herself with her own inhale, a sneaking suspicion of what was to come.

"What else?" She inclined her head to him. "You look like you want to say something else. What is it?"

"Why?"

She knew what he meant. The period of feigned apathy was over, but still, it felt like he was repressing something. Her next exhale had started out shaky, but she steadied herself. Their choice—this was *their* choice, and she would stand by it.

But besides that it was what she and Kai desired, what they'd decided, she added, "I can't be a warrior and the Luna of Deimos."

"That's it?"

Isla jerked her head back at the words spoken, yet again, brusque.

That's it.

That's it.

"Is that not good enough?" she asked, and Adrien didn't answer. At least, not fast enough to prevent her from becoming defensive, despite her earlier thoughts of not needing to explain herself. "How about that I don't want a mate at all?"

"Then reject him," was all he said.

One word, two words, and now three. Forget *"that's it"* for her reasoning. That was *all* he had to say?

"That wouldn't benefit either of us," she told him, trying to mind her temper. "He can't afford to be weakened right now, and neither can I. It's not worth it."

That seemed to break something in Adrien, cracked some of his callous shell, but it didn't shatter. Her friend still clung to that restraint, even as his eyes darkened. "And this is your solution? This is going to help? 'Forgetting' and 'moving on'?"

More words, all spoken in a manner that seemed to show off a glimmer of the pain he'd endured over the past year.

Guilt rushed through her like a tidal wave again. "Yes."

Adrien chuckled, but not with warmth. It was incredulity. Both she and Sebastian watched him go pensive as they danced around the topic that they, even as close as they were, barely breached. Corinne's name hadn't even been uttered aloud between them for over a year, yet the ghost of her presence hovered again amongst the trio—like it was the four of them, like old times.

"Goddess above, Isla," Adrien finally said, pacing a few steps. "I know you don't like being told what to do. But this…"

"You think *that's* all this is? Me not liking being *told what to do*?"

"What else would it be? He's your *mate*." Adrien looked away from her. There was so much more he wanted to say, she could see it clearly now. That it was there—not what it was—but she was fine if it remained hidden. If he knew well enough to keep it tempered, if he said it, she might strangle him.

"Did you not see what happens when you don't accept a fated bond?" he pushed. "Were you even *around* for the past year?"

"For every second." Her inhale and exhale were haggard again, and her tone was ice-cold. "I watched my two best friends fall apart because of a bond. You and Cora almost *died*. And she lost everything. Her sanity, her home, *you*. To be with *him*. And for what?" Isla hadn't even bothered mentioning nearly losing her father. Cora was enough. She shouldn't have brought it up anyway because now she felt ashamed.

Who was she to talk about this? After not understanding—after not *believing* Corinne—when her friend had claimed she couldn't fight off the feelings and connections to her destined mate, though still while loving Adrien. After becoming such a horrible, *horrible* friend to her when she needed Isla's support because Isla was terrified one wrong move would make her lose both Adrien and Cora.

Her beautiful, radiant, powerful best friend had gone from being the future "Queen of Queens" to a scorned exile, suffering the whole way while the man she loved and the man she was meant for battled over her in one of the very rare times destiny and choice collided.

All because of Fate. The wicked goddess who had wound such a cruel, wondrous marvel. A rare, extraordinary double-edged sword.

Isla looked down at her hand, angry, but also feeling pathetic for being so dense, for falling into the trap again. With every look Kai had given her, every handsome smile, phantom touch, tender word, and jabbing taunt, he was the deity's unwitting accomplice. It had Isla buying into all that romanticism around the fated again, and even if only in brief moments, it was too much.

"She lost everything all because of this stupid *thing*," she began hoarsely. "That drives us mad or *kills us* when we don't respect it. That pulls and tugs and blinds us with how *beautiful* it sounds and how *amazing* it feels to have one person in the world who's 'yours', but it's just a connection to someone no more than a stranger—who could very well be the most awful person on the planet—that we let hold our *lives* in its hands. That we let torture us from the minute we come of age and society, even interpretations of our *Code* tell us that's all we're meant for."

She was rambling. Rambling and ranting, but she couldn't stop. Didn't want to. This was the release she needed from the emptiness, from the bitterness she still felt over the nothing she'd found on the other side of the bond. She was angry, so incredibly angry, but most of it was with herself. How could she let herself feel abandoned again, let herself feel alone? This was their choice. *Her* choice.

"This *thing* that expects me…" Isla paused, choking on the words, feeling pieces of her fracture. "That *expects me* to completely upend my life. To give up everything I've worked for. To renounce my membership to my pack, my *home*. To leave my family, my friends, and move to this place where I'll have *no one*. Nothing. Where I'm *stuck* for the rest of my life with a man who I don't love—who I don't *know*—and who doesn't know or love me either. With people who probably don't want me there anyway, who would *hate* having me there. Where I'm a mockery in a role I'm nowhere near qualified for." Her chest felt heavy, the corner of her eyes stinging, but she kept her voice as even as she could. And when the first break of tears stung her cheeks again, she wiped them quickly.

"He didn't ask for this," she finished. "For *me* to be the one. If there's that much cost—that much *risk* with a bond, with a kingdom—Kai's better off getting to choose someone. Someone he needs and deserves— that his people do—after all the shit they've gone through."

"And what about you?"

At Adrien's immediate response, Isla lifted her head, surprised to see a gleam of their own shock and worry on both the boys' faces for all she'd just laid bare. It was the most, she realized, she'd ever poured out in a manner so raw to anyone. She was so used to wearing a mask, throwing on her facade, and having her guard up.

She blinked back another wash of tears—the final cascade—at the question. What about *her*? She had her plan. Be a warrior and when the time was right, choose a man to settle with, and start a family.

Isla wouldn't let the image of *Kai* being that one materialize in her head, all an illusion purported by the bond. She beat it away swiftly, then visualized ripping whatever remnants of the tether remained within, that tainted her mind, and chucking them off the cliffside.

It wouldn't be him. It couldn't be him. And that was okay.

"I'll be fine without him too," she said.

And hated that she felt like a liar.

∽

Isla had been in her apartment for all of a few hours—enough time to stow away the book, marker, and dagger, sit in a bath until the water ran cold, and then, when the sky completely succumbed to darkness, decide to get herself dressed up to head to the bar in the heart of Market Square to blow off some steam.

The man she'd found to help her do so—a swaggering, muscly, dark-haired, lower member of the Imperial Guard who she'd watched sweep the floor with his comrades at pool from afar before he'd noticed and approached her—was named…something.

His name was *something*, and she couldn't remember it for the life of her as they fumbled their way up to her apartment door.

He kissed her hard, his tongue parting her mouth, his hands greedy as they roamed her body. She welcomed him, even if she had some tender spots from her injuries. Even if it felt so…wrong.

Because she wanted it to be Kai. His hands, his mouth, his touch.

It pissed her off how she couldn't just *throw away* the bond. How no matter how much she needed this, to let herself get lost in booze and sex for just one night, he found her.

Isla hadn't lingered by the ravine for much longer after her declarations to the boys. In fact, it had only been a few heartbeats before she hoisted her bag onto her shoulder and stalked off, leaving them—still stunned—with the simple parting words of "you can't tell anyone." They didn't follow, knowing it best to leave her be.

It was pure adrenaline that had powered her through the territory, across the city. Adrenaline that had dipped steeply the minute she'd reached her apartment door. She practically collapsed into the alcove at the entrance once she'd gotten her shaking fingers to turn her key, and after that, she'd remained on the creaky wooden floor for Goddess knew how long, enduring a maddening cycle of silent crying and cursing. She'd finally gotten a grip of herself when she'd heard movement down the hall that she figured was her neighbor, and from then, she'd decided *that was it*.

So, she'd picked herself up, gone through her motions—her stashing, her bath, her dressing—and now she was here, tangled with a man she hoped to the Goddess was decent in bed.

She was going to forget Kai. She would. She had to.

And it started with...this...person.

Goddess, what the hell was his name?

When they eventually made it to her landing, the man tried to hoist her off her feet, but she stopped him, peeling away to reach for the keys in her pocket. But as soon as she extracted them and brought her hand to his face to pull him back in, she stumbled.

Her door was already ajar.

Her heart leaped into her throat, and without a second thought, she moved into action, pushing the man further behind her, slowly. A sneer crossed her likely swollen lips as she moved forward, inclining her head to catch a scent, hear a sound—but there was nothing. Eyes fixed on the white wood, bearing an askew *thirty-four*, she bent to her shoe—all slow and careful—and retrieved her tucked scalpel.

Behind her, the man made a noise of both confusion and concern. "Did you always have that?"

Isla raised a hand for him to be quiet.

Inch by inch by inch.

Who could it be? Lukas somehow escaping Valkeric? His benefactor coming to finish the job?

Step, step, step.

Isla vexed the squeaky entryway as she guided it open with her foot, and the creaking floor once again betrayed her arrival as she broke the threshold. But no one appeared upon the noise. No lost souls or secret killers.

Things had been moved, she noticed, mostly within the small kitchenette. Her cupboards and fridge left open, a bag and bowl of chips left on the counter. With a quirked eyebrow, Isla tiptoed over to the lot, fighting her urge to tidy everything.

She jolted at the sound of a flushing toilet and whipped around to face the bathroom door. Her scalpel was up and ready as her heart ratcheted up a few paces.

But the bracing for battle was all for naught, as exiting the washroom was her brother.

Relief and rage swirled in Isla's gut, and she almost chucked the small blade at him anyway.

"Sebastian, what the hell?" she roared, dropping her weapon to the side.

Her brother flashed a grin, greeting her with her beloved nickname before directing his eyes to the astonished guard who hadn't drifted too far from the apartment's entrance. "Who's this?"

Isla wouldn't have told him even if she knew.

Obviously, there had to have been a reason for Sebastian to just show up—or rather, *break in*—to her home. His own place was a good hour's walk away on the other side of the city in the more luxurious townhouses, so he'd gone through the hassle of getting here. But she didn't care. This was humiliating, absolutely humiliating.

She jabbed a finger towards the door. "Get out."

Sebastian strolled over to the counter to what was *his* bowl of food. The open cabinets and disarray should've flagged her off immediately as to who had come in.

He pulled a chip from his bowl. "We have to talk."

Isla's eyes narrowed to slits, but she'd entertain him. "About what?"

Sebastian hesitated, gaze flicking over to the flabbergasted man lingering by her doorframe. When he moved back to Isla, he began an explanation—through broken words and hand movements. It was entirely vague and nonsensical, and entirely something she didn't have the time or patience for.

She pointed to the door again. "Get out."

"It's about your mate."

Isla's body went stiff.

"You're mated?"

She spun to the guard to find his face, previously flushed, had paled substantially. The fear was valid. Touching someone's *actual* mate the way he'd been all over her was nearly unheard of. Even Cora's *true* mate had known better than to try anything with Cora while she and Adrien were still bound. There wouldn't have been any second-guessing on the Heir's part—he would've likely killed him on the spot —and that would've opened a whole new catastrophe.

"No, I'm not."

The guard let out an unmissable sigh of relief before he shifted awkwardly on his feet. "Do you, uh, want me to wait outside?"

He still wanted to stick around. That was a good sign…or he was just a man. Okay to wait for *however long* as long as he ended up in her bed.

It was tempting. The thought of Sebastian leaving and them picking up right where they left off…but she wasn't sure if it was her brother's presence or the verbal reminder of Kai, but she wasn't necessarily in the mood anymore.

"No," she said, taking a few steps towards him. "I'm sorry. I don't know how long we'll be."

The guard's eyebrows rose, not seeming to expect that answer. He opened his mouth like he'd protest, or make another proposal, but then he closed it and relegated to a nod. Something like defeat and disappointment flashed in his eyes.

Isla trailed him to the exit as he let himself out and then worked on each of her locks—the chain above, then the knob. Her head remained hung low as she closed her eyes and sighed a breath.

"Poor bastard."

Isla whirled around to her brother with murder in her eyes. "*You* bastard." She reached for the first thing she could find—one of her slippers—and launched it across the room. Sebastian caught it effortlessly, and Isla let out an aggravated growl. "You scared the shit out of me! Why are you here? You could've called!"

Sebastian threw her footwear to the side. "I did, and you never picked up."

"So, you *broke* into my apartment?"

"You just told me that someone tried to have you killed," he retorted as if that was answer enough. He grabbed another chip from his bowl and pointed to her closed door. "Alpha Kai could tear that guy apart."

He probably would've, even if they weren't formally mated—if how he'd reacted at the feast was any indication.

"Kai would never know that he was here," she muttered, moving to kick off her heeled boots. "How did you even get in?"

Sebastian swung around the counter with his bowl under one arm. "A magician never reveals his secrets."

"You're a con artist, not a magician."

Feeling it her right—as it was *her food* he was eating—Isla walked up and snatched the bowl from him, glowering as she popped a chip in her mouth. But as she went to eat another, she caught something out of the corner of her eye and froze. The cover of the small vent beside her sink wasn't quite the way she'd left it, one of the screws not done as tightly.

"You didn't," she seethed before shoving the bowl back into Sebastian's arms and storming to the bathroom.

She made quick work of unscrewing each piece—done so by hand very recently, she realized—and was greeted by a confirmation of her suspicions. "Where are they?" she yelled from her spot on the floor, and then exited the washroom in fury.

Sebastian had since moved to the living area and had an arm outstretched to the couch. Isla was by his side in seconds and gaped at the marker, book, and dagger perched in a neat line upon her cushions.

There were so many things she wanted to scream at him—most of them profanities—but she settled for, "How?"

"You've had the same type of hiding place since you were eight. You would think after we moved out, you'd change it up," Sebastian jeered, receiving another glare.

Suddenly, he bent to the dagger, and Isla lurched forward. "What are you doing?"

Sebastian said nothing as he picked the weapon up and ran his fingers over the blade. No flinching. No recoil. "I don't think anything's on it anymore."

"What?"

She *had* washed it—thoroughly—in order to remove all the traces of blood, but she hadn't dared try to touch it after that, especially not with her bare hands. She hadn't even taken the time to truly examine it. But she did now as she cautiously took the dagger from her brother's grasp and gripped the hilt firmly in her own hand. She felt the ridges of it along her palm—a near-perfect fit—and tested the weight in her hold.

Isla brought it closer to her face. Her reflection in the silvery metal was kissed by flecks of gold, dotting like faint stars on the blade, but appearing as freckles on her nose and across her cheeks. She noticed something like crystal weaving beneath her fingertips that she'd overlooked before.

There were *many more* fine details she'd missed, every pass of her eyes revealing something new. It was a beautifully crafted piece of weaponry.

Even if it had been used to try to kill her.

Holding her breath, Isla brought a finger to its sharp edge, and indeed, it did not burn. She even went further, applying a bit more force—just on the edge of piercing her skin—but there was no pain. No reaction from her wolf. She flicked her finger the rest of the way, and the metal seemed to sing, eliciting a hypnotizing hum under the movement of her passing touch.

Every part of her being relaxed.

"So, what is all of this?"

Isla snapped her eyes up to meet Sebastian's, dropping her hand with the dagger to her side. Casting a glance over the book and the marker, she pursed her lips.

She could tell him. She really could. But something—*something*—told her *no*. Told her to *wait*.

"My things," she answered simply.

Sebastian looked doubtful. "From where?"

"You already broke into my apartment and rifled through my stuff; we need to have some boundaries. You don't need to know everything." She turned on her heel to head back to the kitchen. "You said you wanted to talk to me about Kai."

Goddess, did it feel odd speaking so freely of him with someone else. Not trying to cover anything up with formalities and titles.

As she stopped to get a chip out of the bowl left on the counter again, Sebastian nodded towards her side. "Are you going to put the knife down?"

Isla looked at the blade still gripped tightly between her fingers. She hadn't even realized she was still holding it. It whispered through the air as she lifted it, catching her reflection in pseudo-starlight again, before she placed it on the table beside her. But to make a point, she didn't leave it far and shot Sebastian a look of challenge.

Sebastian snorted but didn't make any type of "Warrior Princess" remark as she'd expected. Instead, his face turned serious. "Does Dad know about you and the alpha?"

Isla bit into her chip and answered once she swallowed. "No. No one else knows except for you guys and Kai's beta."

"The beta knows?"

"Yes, and it has to stay that way. I meant it when I said you can't tell anyone," she warned, reaching back into the bowl. "Why are you asking?"

Sebastian took a few steps forward. "That's where I was during everything with the Gate when Lukas emerged. Why I wasn't around. Dad wanted me to tail the Alpha or Beta of Deimos, whoever I could find—which was the beta for a little while until I lost him."

Isla had ceased bringing the snack to her mouth mid-motion, her eyes narrowing. "Why?"

Sebastian shrugged his shoulders. "He doesn't trust them." As her perplexed look persisted, he meandered his way to the kitchen. "Deimos has always been a mess to deal with, but Alpha Kyran…" He trailed off, seemingly choosing his words more carefully than she thought he ever had in his life. "From how I've heard Dad and other Council members complain, he was a different kind of bastard." Before Isla could ask *how*, he continued, though the account diverged, "You and Lukas are the only two people who had to face multiple bak during the Hunt. The *only ones*. Fourteen hunters descended, and the Wilds is massive. You were either in the wrong place at the wrong time or targeted in there."

Isla had never thought of that—how *no one* else had claimed to encounter multiple beasts. She replayed Sebastian's words. Wrong place, wrong time…or targeted.

That latter option rang loudest.

"Where does Deimos fit into this?" she questioned.

Now Sebastian *really* took his time in crafting his answer. "If the alpha…if *Kai* had felt like avenging his father, he could've somehow drawn the bak to you with food or blood or—"

"Why would hurting me be avenging his father?"

"I guess we denied a lot of his proposals or something. I don't know what they were for. Dad won't tell me, and Alpha Cassius won't tell Adrien."

"Adrien didn't go to the meetings? I thought he always got to attend the forums with other alphas?"

"They were *private* audiences. Not open forums. Alpha Kyran requested four of them with the Imperial Alpha within the past year. Alpha Cassius figured three was enough."

"He denied the fourth?" Isla couldn't even believe the Imperial Alpha had entertained him for three.

"A month before he died." Sebastian let the words sit a while—as if leaving the air for respectful silence for the fallen—before he added, "If the former alpha went with unspoken grievances, if we wouldn't listen, killing you is one way to get our attention…or saving you." Another pause. "But if the alpha's your mate, it disproves that theory."

Does it? Isla thought, but then immediately brushed it away.

If Sebastian had brought this up before they'd gone on the Hunt—right after she and Kai had just met—she may have said no, it didn't disprove anything. She *did* have a vague idea of how hard Deimos had been to deal with. Knew they'd withheld information and lied to Io in the past. So easily had she questioned a product of their pack a family-slaying killer. Her own *mate* for Goddess's sake.

But she didn't feel that way anymore. At least, not about Kai. His survival was twined with hers. Talk about leverage.

Isla had to sit down as she broke down each of Sebastian's words, but he interrupted her thoughts with a question. "How did he know where to find you?"

"The bond," she stated warily, absentmindedly tracing her fingers over the hilt of the dagger. "He knew when I started fighting my first bak and stayed back to track me. To make sure I was okay—and then, I wasn't."

"It's that strong?"

Isla looked up to find her brother's eyes filled with curiosity, and it dawned on her. Adrien had his chosen bond, she'd now found her fated, but Sebastian had never known what any connection felt like. She wondered if he even cared. He seemed invested as she spoke shallowly about how the bond and feelings came and went. How they were most potent when the emotions were strong enough in any sort of way. She purposely neglected to mention how much they'd wanted to jump each other upon first meeting.

"It was all involuntary," she finished explaining, gazing at her hand. "Or most of it was."

Sebastian pulled out a chair and sat beside her, beyond the counter's corner. "Can you feel it now?" His tone had been edged in concern, surely prompted by her earlier meltdown. Another embarrassment today. Noting the absence of a particular member of their usual party, she held back her question as to where Adrien was.

"No," she responded, nearly as soft as the sound of her finger gliding over the cool metal of the blade.

"And that's okay." Not a question, but a statement. Though unsure. *Yes.*

"It's what we want."

Sebastian leaned back in his seat with a loud sigh—overdramatic and exaggerated—as if he were trying to lighten the mood. "For the record, if you *had* gone through with it—or if you did change your mind—he has my blessing."

Isla peered up at him, unsure if she wanted to laugh or scowl. "One, I don't *need* your blessing, and two, *he* gets your seal of approval?"

Sebastian snorted. "You think I want to go against Fate and the guy who killed four bak—three of them to keep them away from you? Unlike you, I know when to step back." He took a hold of the bowl of chips and pulled the whole lot towards him. "Plus, saying my sister's a luna sounds a lot more badass than saying she's a warrior."

CHAPTER 21

The two weeks leading up to Isla's lumerosi ceremony trickled by slowly—filled with cold-sweat-inducing nightmares that led to sleepless nights, days at Io's training center used by guard and warrior alike, and some intermittent periods spent at the local library.

For somewhere as large as the Imperial City, the selection of books on languages and linguistics—even books that stretched far back in history—were scarce. Many of the chronicles didn't even expand beyond Io, into the tales of the other territories, and Isla swore if it weren't for the fact she'd already possessed the knowledge, it would be easy to assume the existence of the Pack of Phobos was nothing but a continental hallucination. Still, even with the limited selection, she'd leave the building—a good twenty-minute walk away from home—with heaps of titles in her hands, some not related to narratives of the past. With how much she still had to recover from her injuries, reading had become a sort of new hobby.

She gobbled down fiction, escaping her thoughts with riveting tales of heroes and villains, love and betrayal. She engaged with some guides to "tap into her inner goddess", pages and pages full of breathing exercises, stretches, and poses that pulled and moved her body in ways she hadn't known possible. She wasn't sure if it was those actions, time, or the physical work she'd been doing at the training center, but she was finally getting a handle on her wolf again. Finally able to complete her shift, but unfit to hold it for more than a few minutes.

She'd take any progress though, especially while her research and attempts to decode what the book and marker said were going nowhere. Absolutely nowhere.

But even with the times of stress, Isla never passed another man through her apartment door. She'd gone to the bars some nights—batted her eyes, flirted, even made out with two upstanding suitors in the restroom and back alley—but she couldn't bring herself to go beyond the kisses or touching.

That little piece of her, that tiny piece of Kai that still latched onto her soul like a leech, like it had imprinted itself there in permanent ink, kept drawing her away. The number of times she'd cursed him to the moon was pathetic...

∽

Although the warriors fell under the Imperial Alpha's jurisdiction, the program's base resided in Ganymede. Set on the eastern border, it was Morai's largest kingdom solely by its mostly uninhabitable landmass. The Warrior's Village, as the area was called, didn't necessarily abide by its name. Easily, it could've been one of the largest regions within Ganymede's borders, attributed mainly to the amphitheater located further eastward by the continent's coast. Before the decimation—before the bak, the Hunt, the Wall—warriors had been deemed through duels and trials in that coliseum, filled to the brim with spectators, facing both each other and monsters that were described in ways Isla was convinced were exaggerated. Beasts other than the bak still dwelled amongst their lands, needing to be controlled, but none so terrifying.

She marveled at the large double doors of the entrance to the gallery as she approached them, the wood inscribed with the symbols of all the packs—Phobos included. Eleven markings set in a circle, Io at the top and slightly larger than the rest. Isla couldn't help but run a finger along it as she passed through the entryway, feeling pride swell and crash like a wave. She'd been too short to reach the symbol when she visited the base for a field trip as a child on the arm of her mother and she first fell in love with the idea of what she'd become. Something her mother had never gotten the chance to be for the sake of her children.

The festivities that had been planned for the late afternoon—into the evening and then night—had been a lot of mingling and drinking, some speeches then a meal, more speeches, and then finally, just before the moon reached its peak, the releasing of the successful warrior class to the temple where the Elders would bestow what they'd earned. The act of receiving lumerosi was intense, painful, but for all it represented, what it meant, Isla would take it. She'd endured it before, and she could handle it again.

Unlike at the feast where she'd socialized *beyond* her heart's content, as Isla looped through the gallery's sectors, she mostly kept to herself. Her glass of white wine was gripped firmly in her hand as she meandered through the showcases. She'd come to the ceremony alone—something else that differed from the dinner before the Hunt—telling Adrien and Sebastian that she would rather they stay in Io and not miss any important intel rather than fuss around a party with her. And she hadn't even *needed* to convince her father as he'd left Io again on some "important business".

It all worked for the best. The last thing she wanted was *any of them* coming face to face with Kai. Who she realized, to her horror, had earned his right to the warrior mark as much as she had and could very well appear here.

But she hadn't seen—or felt—him yet. Thank the Goddess...

Still, she frequently canvassed the area, stepping back into corners for the best vantage to scour the floor. It likely looked suspicious, but she was beyond caring.

No pulls. No reactions from her wolf. No sweeps of slightly curled dark hair. No catching of storm-cloud eyes. Just Elders, former warriors, the current class, and—

"There's the new recruit."

Upon the sudden voice from beside her, Isla, more on edge than she'd realized, practically jumped out of her skin, nearly coating her navy cocktail dress in wine. Heart hammering, she twisted to meet a familiar rugged face that she hadn't seen since a few weeks prior. She blinked at him for a few moments, trying to get her bearings before she forced a grin and the sweetest tone she could. "General Eli."

The general's eyes danced with amusement. "I apologize. I didn't mean to startle you. I forgot how skittish recruits can be right after the Hunt."

Isla held onto her smile like her life depended on it, remembering well the last time she'd been in Eli's presence. She had an odd, almost comical feeling that if Kai *was* in fact here in the gallery, he'd surely emerge from the woodwork now.

"I didn't have a chance to congratulate you after your victory," Eli said, swirling his drink—which smelled like bourbon—in his hand. "I'd already departed for the base, but I heard you were a marvel."

"I'm not quite too sure about a *marvel*," Isla demurred, genuine in her hesitance to his flattery.

"I am," he countered. "You've been on my radar since the high general sent me to scope the rising talent. He told me to watch out for you."

"The high general spoke of me?"

"The daughter of the Imperial Beta," Eli boasted. "He told me you could be promising, and you haven't disappointed."

Isla battled to keep her features from falling into a grimace. There it was again. All accomplishment and strength relegated to something that wasn't even a *title*, simply an association.

"Have you seen your display?" Upon the shaking of Isla's head, Eli smoothly slipped a hand behind her back to guide her in the proper direction. So much like the feast, but here, there were no possessive tugs of intangible tethers from her mate. "Let's go relish in your glory."

Relish in her glory.

The words had sounded decent enough in principle, incredible even, but as Isla found herself staring up at the large fabric banner flowing on a phantom wind towards the back of the room by the podium for the speeches, all she felt was sick.

There was too much for her to focus on. Her name—being deemed "second"—embroidered just below Kai's. The reminder of the two bak she'd killed. The fact that Lukas's name—even though he'd emerged, even though he'd slayed a beast—was nowhere in sight.

"Is this supposed to display the entire class of trainees that had descended?" she choked out, trying to sound impassive.

"I'm not too sure." Eli paused, his eyes raking over the names with intent. "Have you seen the Alpha of Deimos here?"

Isla straightened, and she suddenly became very aware of the wine in her hand. She gulped down some of the sweet liquid, feeling a slight tingle in her throat. "I haven't."

There was the smallest uptick of the general's lips that fell promptly. "Four bak. Insanely impressive—but maybe a bit much, don't you think?"

Isla pursed her lips, always finding herself so keen on the tones used when her mate was spoken of. It had happened with Adrien, then the Imperial Alpha, and now again. The urge to defend Kai—his actions, who he was—rose quickly.

"He did it to—" She cut herself off, remembering that no one knew about what really happened behind the Wall.

"Prove a point?" Eli thankfully suggested in the pause. "You two lock in some friendly competition?"

"Something like that," she offered falsely.

The general nodded, looking back up at the names. "Well, I'm going to need that fire." He turned, a smirk forming at the sight of Isla's raised brows. Like he'd wanted to build anticipation, had been preparing something.

Isla, feeling like there was a secret script she was meant to follow, asked, "What do you mean?"

Eli cleared his throat. "Warriors are being deployed along the midland borders of Deimos, Rhea, and Charon to aid in rogue eradication efforts. I'll be heading the squadron in Deimos, and as a general, I get to pick my own unit." He paused, letting Isla fill in some gaps. Gaps that quickly made the wine sour in her stomach. "I've asked the high general if he'd allow you to join me in the field. Given you're a new recruit—and it's almost unheard of—he had to reach higher up and was able to get clearance from the Imperial Alpha based on your recent showing."

"You—you want me to join you in the field...in Deimos?"

This couldn't be real. She was drunk or...something. Somehow, half a glass of wine had been too much.

"Some things may need to be on an observational basis," he acknowledged, a smile now threatening to stretch as wide as his face. Isla had no doubt he was completely misinterpreting her shock. "But it's a great opportunity not many or *any* new recruit will ever be granted, and it will look great on your ledger."

He wasn't wrong. She *hated* that he wasn't wrong. About any of it. New warriors, especially now with the times of peace, could only dream of getting time out in action. Most of the first couple of years were spent in even more training and patrols with the guard. But *this*? Eradicating rogues? Helping people, protecting and serving the continent as she'd always wanted...

But why couldn't it have been anywhere else?

She feigned humility. "Oh, I could never."

"Why not? You've earned it." Eli gestured up to the banner, and she looked at it again. Her name, just below Kai's.

Goddess, they'd be within the same borders again. Possibly find themselves face to face again.

At the thought, something stirred in her. Something *bad*. Something feral and claiming that wanted him back and had been awoken in the presence of the opportunity to get to him again.

Isla masked her groan with a sigh and battled that beast back into its dark, dank corner. "I can't go with you to Deimos."

"And what's wrong with Deimos?"

The words hadn't come from Eli.

Isla whipped around to where the voice had crooned from and found herself confronted by a woman making her way over. When she stopped before them, Isla took her in.

She stood just a bit taller than Isla herself, and her silken black hair must've been long, given how large her tightly-wound top knot was as it sat on her head like a crown—a crown it felt like she deserved. Her brown skin was practically glowing in the sunbeams spilling from the skylights above, and it drew Isla's attention to the black ink that seemed to stretch from her collarbone beneath the neckline of her ebony dress, over her shoulder, and to her back.

"Ameera," Eli greeted, but not much could be done to mask the bitterness in his tone.

The woman, Ameera, had her eyes honed in on Isla, sizing her up like prey before she turned smoothly to face the general. "Eli." She grinned, but even in its softness, it held something biting.

Eli's matched it. "Funny seeing you here, I don't recall you being at the feast." There was a smugness to his voice that gave Isla the nudge that she may not have received the invitation.

"I had other obligations," Ameera cooed, almost mockingly. "But I couldn't pass up an opportunity to check out the new blood."

"Your alpha did well," Eli remarked, again with the touch of something caustic. "Beat them all."

Her alpha?

"You're of Deimos?"

Isla's outburst earned Ameera's attention again.

"Not everyone who becomes a warrior has goals of 'ascending' into the Imperial Pack." Ameera cast another long look up and down Isla. "I don't believe we've met."

Isla was convinced Ameera could cut down entire battlefields with her stare alone, but she wouldn't cower beneath it.

Pushing her shoulders back, she stood a bit taller and stuck out a hand. "Isla. I'm the new blood."

Ameera looked at the appendage for a few moments before grabbing Isla's forearm in the greeting.

"She was second to your alpha." It was Eli who bragged from beside her, gesturing upwards to the banner before the call of his name drew his attention away.

One of Ameera's perfectly sculpted brows rose. "Was she now?" But she never looked up to observe the display as the two women pulled away from each other. Her eyes never left Isla's, in fact, even when Eli excused himself and walked off.

Just them now, the air seemed to shift. Became tenser. As if a curtain had been raised.

Isla didn't know the reason but refused to be the one to break form. She'd hold Ameera's gaze as long as she needed to.

Ameera, seemingly realizing what she was doing, chuckled. "You are certainly not what I expected." She ended the stalemate carelessly by looking down at the clear liquid in her glass.

"And what were you expecting exactly?" Isla asked.

"The warrior capable of killing two bak," she said. "Imagine my surprise when all I've seen for the past hour is General Social Climber's latest obsession skulking around like a nervous, lonely, little mouse and playing the part perfectly to his face."

The words took Isla aback. "Excuse me?"

Ameera continued as if she hadn't spoken at all, "You're going to go down as greater than most of the triumphant in these ranks for what you achieved in there, as if they weren't already prepared to chew you up and spit you out for training to be here in the first place. And now you're granted your first mission before you even bear your mark when they haven't even left their own pack borders?" She snickered. "I suppose being the Imperial Beta's daughter has its perks."

Isla wasn't sure which part boiled her more: the mention, yet again, of her parentage, that damned tone that seemed to be a Deimos custom, or the subtle, assuming look Ameera had cast in the direction Eli had departed.

Isla wasn't dense, she knew the general's manner around her wasn't what was expected between a commander and their subordinate, both at the feast and here today. But maybe a small piece of her had hoped it had stemmed from a genuine interest in *her*…but "General Social Climber"?

"Look, I don't know who the hell you think you are to pass any sort of judgment on me after *an hour* but believe me, I've *earned* my right to be here," Isla snapped, sending Ameera's eyes blazing with delight as if drawing out any grit had been her goal. "I'm more than just some Beta's daughter."

"And so am I." As Isla's face fell out of her scowl, Ameera added, "It seems we have that in common."

It didn't take long for Isla to put the pieces together, for her heart to drop to her shoes, and for her eyes to practically bulge from her skull. A beta's daughter from Deimos?

"You—you're Ezekiel's daughter?"

At either Isla's faltering or the mention of the beta's name, Ameera's face became more crestfallen. "Warrior General Ameera of Deimos," she introduced, not confirming or denying Isla's claim.

That part didn't matter anymore, though.

I don't know who the hell you think you are to judge…

Isla forced her arm to remain at her side before she smacked her own forehead.

Goddess, this girl was a general? A *general*? She couldn't have been more than a couple of years Isla's senior.

"Good luck on your mission, new blood," Ameera said, the most genuinely gleeful Isla had heard her. "I guess I'll be seeing you soon."

Soon—in Deimos.

The rogues in Deimos.

Eli's offer.

Isla shook her head to right herself. "I—I never said I was going." It only registered now that Ameera had overheard her and Eli's whole exchange, had been listening.

"And why not?" Ameera asked with a challenging lift of her brows. She allowed Isla to stew in her silence for a few heartbeats before she loosened a breath. "I mean, I know you don't want to be our luna and all, but is it so horrible to help defend us?"

It felt like Isla had been punched in the stomach.

"What did you just say?" Ameera didn't repeat herself, only grinned, and Isla was glad for it. She didn't want it spoken aloud here again.

Suddenly, a hand brushed against her shoulder.

Isla whirled around to find Eli had rejoined their party. She hoped to the Goddess he hadn't heard anything.

The male general took in their two expressions—Isla's hard as stone and Ameera's smug as could be. "Did I miss something?"

"No," Ameera answered. "Isla was just telling me how excited she is to get out in the field."

Eli's face seemed to brighten, and Isla wasn't sure which of her commanding officers she wanted to dump her wine on.

"I'll leave you two to talk strategy." Ameera took a step forward and tilted her head down to Isla. "I'm looking forward to seeing you in Deimos, Warrior," she offered and then leaned in ever so slightly just before she walked away, her voice so soft—only for her—and flecked with a taunt. "Or would you prefer *queen*?"

CHAPTER 22

Isla had taken up Eli on his offer, and on her final night before departing for Deimos, there had been a party in her honor.

It was a small gathering including her family, Adrien, the Imperial Luna—and Alpha—some of her instructors, fellow trainees of Io, and their mates. For it, they'd all gone out to a nice restaurant on the *Golden Avenue*, a strip of the finest shops and eateries in the Imperial City. In all of Io, really. It was a nice cool down for Isla, a moment to catch her breath and be with those she loved after the whirlwind that had been the past few weeks.

Unlike the lull leading up to her lumerosi ceremony, once Isla had received her warrior mark and was initiated into the ranks as an active member, she barely had time to even tie her shoes.

She'd attended more meetings than she ever had in her life—from those pertaining to actual battle strategy to those speaking of how she was supposed to behave as a "pack outsider" and "guest" while in another territory. She'd been fitted for her uniform, armor, and other sets of day clothes—shirts and jackets and pants—all bearing the same embroidered crest. She'd selected her weapon of choice and watched her sword be forged—even helping hammer down some of the molten metal—before being whisked off to her next to-do.

It was overwhelming at times but exciting, so incredibly exciting. And it also proved to be a great distraction from the frustrations of her dead-end research, the still persistent nightmares, and the sheer aggravation over everything that had happened at the gallery. Over Ameera's words. Over her knowledge of things.

After the female general had made her final taunt, Eli—or General Social Climber—had managed to distract Isla just long enough for Ameera to become the wind that blew through the open glass doors at the back of the room. No matter where Isla had turned, no matter where she stalked, she couldn't find that crown of black hair anywhere.

Since then, Isla had gone through the feelings of being naked and exposed. She'd gone through all the anger of one of her greatest secrets being known by a woman she'd known for all of five sentences. And she'd gone through all the questions as to how she'd found out.

There were only two viable options, given that she hadn't been at the feast or in Callisto: option one, Ameera's own father, but Ezekiel seemed adamant to keep Isla's existence under wraps. Which left Kai... but he had never mentioned his beta's daughter *once*.

And that made her wonder if it had been intentional.

Ameera and Kai were around the same age, with Kai maybe a year older. If they'd grown up as close as she and Adrien had, if, unlike she and Adrien, things had become more than platonic, then maybe Ameera was his...

No.

No, Isla wouldn't bring up the theory again.

"I remember when she beat the shit out of Vlad from year five because he'd taken that Cobaker kid's lunch. He went home with a broken nose."

Isla snapped her eyes up from her half-eaten plate of chicken to Sebastian cackling across the table from her. He had one of his arms slung around the back of the chair of his "plus-one" for the night—a woman named Wren who worked at one of the city's boutiques. She almost seemed too sweet for him.

Sebastian had been telling a story about her, and Isla smiled, fond of the memory. "All you asshats did was watch, and Cobaker needed help. Vlad was eating him alive. His left hook was horrendous." Then again, they were eleven.

"And right hook and jab," Adrien offered from beside her, and Isla felt herself glow inside just to hear his voice. They hadn't technically talked about Kai—or Cora—at all since the ravine. And maybe avoidance wasn't the best practice, but she was just happy to have her friend. "And his fighting stance was pretty shit, too."

"He couldn't shift either," Sebastian added.

Isla sipped her water. "I rest my case."

"Warrior Princess since the beginning," her brother said.

"I'd say Warrior Queen now. I mean, look at you," Wren quipped, gesturing to the people gathered for her achievement. But the only reaction she elicited was a choke between Adrien and Isla and a mischievous grin from her date for the night.

Sebastian stroked his chin. "You know, that does have a better ring to it."

Isla kicked him hard under the table, and Sebastian howled, but before any other blows could be dealt, there was the sound of the clinking of silverware against a glass. All heads were directed towards the head of the table, and Isla's eyes widened in fear as none other but her father began rising to his feet.

Since he'd finally returned home earlier last week, he hadn't been very forthcoming with his location. Isla knew better than to question him about anything. Not about Lukas. Not about being distrustful of Deimos. And not about if he'd known about the Imperial Alpha's plan to allow Isla to believe herself a killer.

Isla had refused to look at the man—who was supposed to be someone she trusted as her leader, as her family's greatest ally—the entire night. She wasn't sure if she'd be able to keep off her scowl, if she could restrain herself from saying something. She wondered if Alpha Cassius knew that she was aware of the truth. If he'd expected to tell Adrien that Lukas wasn't dead and have his son carry on with the fabrication.

"I'll keep this short," her father said, his already gravelly voice just that much more rasped with emotion. He looked to Isla. "And I won't *embarrass* you, my daughter, I promise."

Isla sank lower in her seat as she became the center of attention. "Oh, Goddess…"

The reaction garnered a collective laugh from those at the long banquet table.

"When Cassius told me he'd gotten a call from the high general about approving you for duty," her father began. "I'd asked him to confirm he denied it. And when he told me he didn't, that he'd given you the okay, I was ready to wring his neck."

Another chorus of chuckles, though a bit more uncertain with the pass at the Alpha only the Beta would get away with.

"I see more and more of your mother in you every day. She was a fighter and never what anyone expected her to be—she was better. And you have gone down the same path of showing me, showing everyone, that you're meant for more, that you *are* more than we could ever imagine. A warrior today, a warrior *general* tomorrow, and who knows where you'll go beyond that."

As tears stung at the corner of her eyes and a tight feeling lingered in her chest, Isla felt Sebastian's gaze fall upon her at their father's last words. She'd kick him again if others weren't watching her too.

Her father cleared his throat. "I know she is just as proud of you as I am. As we all are. And it makes me feel better sending you off knowing that she's watching over you."

Isla bit hard on the inside of her cheek and hurriedly brushed away a tear. Seeing his daughter breaking seemed to be taking a toll on the Beta who failed at masking a sniffle. Sensing the impending waterworks and probably sparing the table a show, Alpha Cassius stood up and placed a hand on his longtime friend's shoulder. He lifted his glass.

"To Warrior Isla of Io," he proclaimed, glancing over everyone before focusing on Isla.

That look alone seemed to dry up her tears. Dulled the pride she'd felt hearing her new title. Made something inside her harden.

She couldn't help but catch the emphasis he'd left on the name of their pack. Almost like a reminder. A challenge to her precision during their meeting over a month ago now.

She was a warrior—she was working to help others on the continent —but *Io* was her home. Where her greatest allegiance lay.

Swallowing hard, she steeled herself and without breaking his gaze, lifted her glass to him and took her sip. Not in acceptance, but acknowledgment.

～

"We'll be reaching the borders of Ifera soon."

Isla directed her gaze from out of the window to Eli as he stood in the aisle of their transport vehicle addressing the members of the squadron. She felt her heart thrum at the words.

Ifera. Deimos. They were almost there.

"It should be a couple more hours until we reach Mavec after that. Likely well after dusk."

Her heart jumped again.

"We'll be lodging there until we arrange our assignments on the southeastern borders by Abalys. I'll have a meeting with the Commander of the Guard and beta tomorrow morning while all of you get to know the rest of the order that hasn't been dispatched yet. There's a lot going on in this pack, but remember our objective is the rogues. While some here may be grateful for our help—and they should be—others may think we're overstepping and want us out before we even enter. Don't give them any reason to call for our removal."

Isla nodded before trailing her eyes over the rest of the members of the team. One member, in particular, was her focus.

So she'd learned, Eli was an idiot. A brilliant strategist and a great leader—but a stupid, stupid man.

Because *not only* was he bringing Isla to the home of her fated mate —a powerful alpha who she was undoubtedly attracted to and likely would have slept with if it hadn't meant being bound to him for eternity —but he had also recruited for this team of his Isla's ex-boyfriend.

Yes, her ex.

The one she'd nearly chosen.

Even as Isla stared at the back of Callan's head from her seat, she still couldn't believe the egomaniac of a bastard had managed to convince Eli of his worth at the feast. No doubt it was through wondrous stories of triumph that she was sure were laden with exaggeration, but even still, here he was. She would never tell him she was just the smallest bit grateful for his presence. At least to have something familiar.

Amidst Eli's selected group made up entirely of males—two of which were twice her age—Isla was a pariah. The air of them didn't necessarily have the "chew you up and spit you out" quality to it that Ameera had mentioned—summarizing experiences Isla had already been privy to since the beginning of her training years—but they certainly weren't falling over themselves to include her or to simply be friendly.

Suddenly, the van lurched to a halt, nearly sending Eli down the aisle and rattling the tower of trunks full of their belongings tied down to the roof.

The general whipped around and barked out a *"Warrior"* to their driver, a member of their squadron—Lavan, a Warrior of Mimas.

Lavan had lifted his hand off the vehicle's gearshift and pointed outside. "I can't move, General."

Isla, like the other members of their team—Callan, Emil, and Fitch— slowly rose in her seat to train her eyes out the window. She held back her gasp. They were surrounded. By wolves. But not just any wolves.

They were wolves of Deimos's guard.

Holy shit.

They'd crossed the border.

She was in Deimos.

The words of her realization surely hit her much more powerfully than the scenery did. She wasn't sure what she'd be expecting, but it was certainly *more* than this.

Isla had drawn such a picture in her head of Deimos. This foreign land she'd never fit into. But its border was just a border. If anything, the greatest difference from any other she'd crossed was the armada of wolves they'd come upon. Even more seemed to lurk in the shadows as Isla caught the faintest glow of eyes amongst the trees. Had things always been this way here? Or was the guard presence heightened due to the recent tragedies? Whatever the decision had been, it was Kai's.

After taking their time to circle the vehicle, one of the wolves lifted their head to howl, and Isla watched and listened as a chorus of them followed. Their calls seemed to reverberate the woods, and the world, shaking the creatures dwelling in the trees from their hiding. It went on for miles. How many were out here?

"Some welcome party," Fitch commented, settling back down into his seat, continuing to gnaw on the plethora of snacks he'd brought for the excursion. Isla had contemplated asking him for some at one point, but the man was unusually territorial over his food.

As the howls came to an end in a soft hum that seemed to linger in the back of Isla's skull, the pack surrounding them dispersed. Three figures emerged from the brush. Isla squinted to get a good look through the shadows of the trees and was able to discern two of them were guards, thanks to their uniforms. A man and woman clad in a simple, thin black tunic, the open fabric tied at their waists with cloth belts. A glint caught off them from the silver stitching of Deimos's insignia. They could shift. There was no way they'd be out on patrol weaponless and in such flimsy protection, otherwise.

Leading the two was a man clad in attire much more modest, but it wasn't another variation of the guard apparel. He tugged at the lapels of his jacket as he came to a stop a few feet from their vehicle's door. There were no words spoken. They simply waited.

Eli's face was drawn in confusion. "What is this?"

Adjusting his own attire—running his own fingers over the deep charcoal of their day sets—he moved down the aisle to greet the soldiers.

Isla could barely hear what they were saying from her spot, even after she pressed her ear to the window.

Not too long after, Eli's hand shot up as he waved them over. "Off! Bring your papers!"

Her papers?

Her features scrunching in confusion, Isla glanced down to the bag at her side before quickly surveying the others. Her papers were in this bag, yes, but so were the book, marker, and dagger. There was no chance she'd leave them at home through the duration of her tenure in Deimos, and there was no way she'd risk losing them if her trunk of belongings had fallen off the roof. It was once the others had gotten their papers that she quickly rifled around for her own. Thankfully, she'd stored the envelope containing all the documents she'd needed somewhere easy to find.

It had been a mess of things required for her to enter Deimos in a capacity beyond a typical "visitor". From her birth documents and current identification to certificates of her warrior status and a confirmation signed by both the Imperial Alpha and Kai that stated the conditions of her time here. She was permitted to stay within Deimos's borders for the span of the warrior's assignment, but at the end, she was required by law to return to Io.

As the five members of the warrior unit, other than Eli, lined up as instructed, the apparent leader of the trio stalked along them. "I'm Delta Sol," he introduced, not a lick of anything hospitable in his tone.

A delta on border patrol? Typically, deltas were—

"I serve on Alpha Kai's council," Sol continued, placing his hands behind his back as he came to a halt at Emil at the end of the line opposite Isla. "And I've been tasked with confirming your crossing through our borders."

As a round of questioning looks was shared amongst the warrior men of the group, Isla pursed her lips and took Sol in. The first member of Kai's—apparently untrustworthy—council that she'd been confronted with. There seemed to be a real lack of joy in the upper echelons of Deimos. From their betas, beta's children, down to their delta council members.

Screening those who crossed over pack borders like this wasn't common practice. Especially not in the meticulous way Sol had been doing so. As he made his way down the line of warriors, examining and questioning the details of each of their files and confirming against a ledger held by the female guard, Isla had initially wanted to listen in to know each thing he would ask, but she couldn't now. Not when she'd become so distracted by the male guard who was trying his damnedest not to stare at her. Or *to* stare at her. Every flick of his eyes in her direction ended with him looking away. She was ready for him every time.

"Name?"

Isla snapped to attention finding the question wasn't directed at her, but at Callan who stood beside her—notably a good foot away. She'd be next.

As her ex ran through all his answers, Isla forced her gaze to the ground and responded mentally with her own. Name, homeland, her parents, date of birth...mate.

"Welcome to the trenches," Sol commented at Callan's conclusion, handing him back his papers. The delta had spent just a little bit longer sizing him up before stepping over to Isla. She underwent the same scrutiny, though unlike Callan's, which had been drawn from where Sol learned where he'd hailed from, the delta didn't know who she was yet. "You're a pretty little thing."

At the delta's words, the male guard behind him appeared to cringe. Isla glared at the older man and handed him her documents.

Sol's eyes had been set on the sheets for a few seconds before he jerked his head to Eli. "*Two* Imperial Pack members, and the Imperial Beta's child." His voice had been full of exasperated disbelief. "Are you here to aid us or investigate us?"

Investigate?

"Your alpha had the opportunity to object to anyone I'd proposed for my unit," Eli countered. "If anything, the Beta's daughter was endorsed. She and your alpha had gone into the Hunt together. She was his second. He knows what an asset she is."

And there it was again.

"Isla of Io," Isla said, drawing all attention back to her. She'd made sure to put emphasis on her *name*, and for her next pieces of information, she'd reeled her tone back. "Daughter of Imperial Beta Malakai and Apolla of Io. Born twelve days after the Autumn Equinox in the Imperial City of Io...and I don't have a mate." She cast her eyes to the male guard who'd been fixated on her again. When she'd returned to Sol, he was staring her down but silent, allowing her to go on. "I completed the Hunt two months ago, I killed two bak, I'm a new warrior recruit, and I'm here to help. *We're* here to help. That's it."

The quiet that followed her words had persisted for far too long. Isla felt like she'd been under the inspection of even the trees. She waited for some type of remark, filled with something snarky or a hidden insult, but it never came. From anyone.

Sol handed back her papers before turning to Eli. "You're to be escorted into the city the rest of the way."

"I don't think that's necessary," the general said.

"Alpha's orders," Sol said. "Rhydian and Thyra will guide you."

Eli had paused as if prepared to protest, but then straightened. He turned to the warriors and ordered them all back onto the vehicle. As Isla moved to the back of the line, she overheard Sol speaking to the two guards.

"Trail them to Mavec then be back here by midnight roll call."

"Is that even possible?" Thyra asked.

"That's insane," Rhydian commented.

"So is the alpha making me drag my ass out here to flag warriors," Sol snapped. "Midnight. Run."

Isla just managed to turn and catch a glimpse of the end of their shifts as they came down on all fours. Two massive wolves in their places, their thin uniforms left forgotten on the ground.

"Isn't an escort a good thing?" Callan asked, falling back into his seat.

The rest of them made their way back to their spots, as Lavan geared the vehicle up again.

A pensive look had remained stagnant on Eli's face. "Not when it's out of distrust."

And he said nothing else.

Something about the act of having been checked up on had really gotten to him, or maybe something had been said when she couldn't quite hear through the closed window. Whatever it was, it had Eli keeping to himself. Throughout the rest of the trek through Ifera—which seemed to be endless throes of thick, lush forests and rolling green hills—he hadn't turned to Isla once, not even bringing up his earlier proposal to get drinks when they arrived. Rather, he flipped through his endless maps and books on Deimos and the rogue lands beyond it.

Out her window, Isla continued catching sight of Rhydian. The guard had been tasked with *flanking* the car, or at least it seemed that way from how Thyra had speared the excursion. But he just kept ending up at her side. She was just about ready to shift in this cabin just to ask him what his deal was.

"Damn." She heard someone in the vehicle say, and she faced forward to find what they were gaping at.

Mountains, much higher than those of Io, made of rock so dark that they'd be lost if not for the snowy caps and patches along their surface. From the angle the vehicle was driving in, they seemed to go on endlessly, acting as their own wall or barrier. Isla marveled at them for a few too-long moments before her face fell in horror.

They weren't stopping.

The mountains were looming larger and larger, their shadow

blocking them from even the moon, and yet they continued barreling forward. Heading straight towards the unforgiving surface of one.

Panic gripped Isla's heart as she noticed Thyra and Rhydian had peeled away. Nowhere in sight. Had they escorted them to a head-on crash? Had Lavan passed out at the wheel?

Before a scream could rip from her throat, it felt like her stomach bottomed out, and they were quickly entrenched in darkness. It was as if the world had been swallowed up, save small flecks of luminescent crystal in the tunnel walls and faint domes of light that Isla couldn't tell the source of. They were in a tunnel within the mountain, or rather, with how steep the decline was that they were driving along, a little beneath it. She hadn't been able to see the passageway from where she'd been sitting, especially in the dark.

A stillness overtook the caravan as they took in what was around them. No one spoke, but Isla knew what they all were thinking. This was *not* the entrance they'd prepared for in their briefings. But Eli didn't appear bothered as the midnight road seemed to go on forever. *Down* forever. She was convinced they'd accidentally found the straits down to hell. But then, finally, there was a lift. And they chugged higher. And higher. And higher. And then light spilled through. And—

Isla swore she must've died in the tunnel because what she beheld felt like a dream.

Each of the warriors let out some sort of astonished noise—a whistle here, a mutter of profanity there.

Isla wasn't sure where to look.

If the Goddess had taken part in forging a city—with the way the mountains cradled the landscape, like a pair of hands in an offer to the world, and with how moonlight seemed to kiss every inch of the streets —it had to be Mavec. Isla was convinced. None of the photos she'd seen in books and papers, all blacks and whites and grays, did the city justice.

Because they didn't capture the faintest glow of crystals, also apparent here as in the tunnel, splattered amongst the roadways and cobblestone sidewalks like fallen stars. They didn't catch the warm and inviting lights emitting from the endless storefronts and shops and restaurants. Didn't capture the rich smells of food and spices and pastries. They didn't capture people—all the people, *so many* people— dressed to the nines and flocking somewhere Isla suddenly wanted to be if it meant being as happy as they seemed. Maybe Ezekiel, Ameera, and Sol were anomalies.

Isla trailed her eyes upwards, finding Mavec was built over hills like those of Ifera, the gentle rises not covered in endless grass but more stone and sprawling homes and city houses. All of it eventually led to what was the crown city's biggest jewel—the Pack Hall. There wasn't a point from the streets where one couldn't see the building which almost looked to absorb the lunar glow, especially through the massive stained-glass window in the center of its largest tower. It could've easily been the moon itself with how, from below, it was as if the hall dwelled amongst the night sky. She could only imagine the view from up there.

Kai's view.

This was his home. His kingdom, his pack. The place that had made him who he was.

Beautiful and suffocating, he'd described it as.

Isla only saw the first.

∼

The hotel that the warriors would be staying at for the next week sat a little further up and away from the ruckus of the lower part of the city. Fortunately, the building had been set in a way that Isla could still see the soft crystal glow of the city like a sea of stars beside an actual body of water she hadn't noticed flowing out.

"The river will take you to Abalys," the woman at the front desk—Davina, as she'd previously been introduced—was explaining as she got together all Isla needed to get into her room. "We call it the town on the water."

Abalys.

Kai had mentioned Abalys. Particularly where *not* to get involved in Abalys.

At the thought of her mate, Isla glanced to the open window far off at the edge of the hotel lobby. Through it, she could see the western end of the Pack Hall. It seemed like some sort of light was on. For the first time in a long while, she brought one hand to the other and ran her thumb over her palm. She felt nothing being here. At least, nothing to do with the bond. If anything, the city seemed to be beckoning her down to explore it.

"And here you go." Davina placed a stack onto the counter, calling back Isla's attention. "Your room number, key, some maps and brochures, my own personal recommendations, and some light reading."

Light reading.

Isla snickered at the newspaper Davina had placed on the table that bore her mate's face on the cover. *Alpha of a New Age*, the title of the editorial read. *How Alpha Kai Plans to Honor Father's Legacy and Build One of His Own.*

Isla had absentmindedly raised her hand to run over the paper's surface when Davina's words brought her to her senses.

"He's a handsome one, isn't he?" the woman cooed, flipping her long hair, the color of brass that matched the dots splashed over her cheeks, over her shoulder. "I swear every unmated girl in this pack is tripping over themselves to get in his eye-line and catch his attention. Maybe get that magic spark."

Isla snorted and ignored the inkling of possessiveness—or what she refused to call jealousy—that had begun rearing its head. Magic spark...

"I wouldn't call it a spark. It's more like an inferno," she offered offhandedly.

Davina cocked her head. "You're mated?"

Oops.

"Oh, uh, no," Isla said. "I—I'd just heard that's what it's like."

Davina laughed; it was bright and melodic. It seemed to suit her well. "Well, that seems about right." She pulled down the neckline of her dress to show a mating ring—a beautiful stone of emerald—dangling off a metal chain. "Spark just sounds nicer than 'I was ready to bone you in the middle of a bar and not care who was watching'."

Isla couldn't keep in her own laughter, understanding her perfectly. She glanced over at Kai's picture again, feeling the phantom rush of their first meeting on the terrace. Would that even happen again if they came face to face?

"Can I help you with anything else, Isla?" Davina's eyes held a sparkle as she said her name, and Isla started feeling a nagging that something was off. Not bad—but that she wasn't getting the whole picture.

Much like Rhydian, Davina's look wasn't filled with any sort of ill or questionable intent. She realized now, for the both of them, it also hadn't *only* been with intrigue. There was also recognition.

∼

Isla looked up at the sign hanging from the structure before her, displaying a simple, hard-to-misunderstand name, The Bookshoppe. It was exactly as Davina had said. Very literal and to the point.

Before she'd collected her things and rushed out of the lobby, Isla had cautiously asked the woman behind the desk where she could find a library around Mavec. With the lull in time that she finally had, and given that she was sure sleep would still be hard to come by, she figured now was as good a time as any to continue her research. Deimos was the closest one could get to Phobos without re-entering the Wilds. They *had* to have something here.

Apparently, the most robust library that Deimos had to offer was in Ifera near its university, however, according to Davina, whoever Jonah was that worked here in this shop was better than any of the knowledge she could glean in that place. The store hadn't been a long walk from the hotel. Part of Isla had wished it had been a bit deeper into the city, but maybe it was a blessing as she'd since changed into her night clothes, a plain shirt and pants which didn't give off her identity as a warrior but certainly didn't help her blend in with Mavec's lavish night crowd.

As Isla pushed open the wooden door of the shop, a ringing bell sounded above her.

She muttered a *wow* under her breath as she stepped inside. Though it wasn't the books that took her breath away, even if the sheer amount of them and the way the shelves had been configured was impressive—some carved it seemed directly into walls and support columns. Instead, it was the other décor that had caught her eye.

She trained her gaze along the testaments to the continent's feats of innovation, models of the first cars invented around the time of her birth, the recently developed planes, radio bobbles, and odds and ends. They all hung from the ceiling or were perched on countertops and shelves.

Isla lifted her eyes to the second floor the shop carried to, stopping in her tracks when a man appeared at the railing of the mezzanine. Shadows cast on his dark skin as the lights fell behind him.

"Hi," Isla greeted after a tense quiet, lifting a hand and taking another step inside. "Are you Jonah?"

"Depends who's asking," the man said gently from his spot.

"Davina sent me here from the hotel. She said you could help me find some books."

The man made his way down a spiral staircase that had nearly blended into the bookshelves and crossed the room to Isla. "For her?" For some reason, he appeared both amused and concerned.

"For me, actually." Isla reached out a hand, flashing him a smile. "I'm Isla."

Something in his eyes flickered, the brown flecked with amber, warm and smooth as honey…and so damn familiar. Not only because he was giving her that *look* again. The same as Rhydian, the same as Davina.

"Isla," he said her name as if testing it on his tongue before grabbing her hand. A normal handshake, no warrior greeting. She couldn't remember the last time she'd exchanged one.

"And you *are* Jonah?" she asked as they pulled away.

Jonah nodded with a chuckle before waving her to follow him through the stacks—but not before giving the entrance a leery glance, scouring as though awaiting someone to come through it. "What can I help you with?"

Isla gave the doorway her own quick glimpse before following him. Turning a corner into the shelves, she found herself lost in an ocean of pages. There were sections *dedicated* to the other packs of Morai. A section about the rest of the world. "Anything related to languages or linguistics or—if you have anything about Phobos, besides literature on the Wilds."

One of Jonah's eyebrows rose at the latter half of her request. "I can help with the languages, but most of what our pack had on Phobos was destroyed centuries ago." He spoke as if she should've already known.

Isla's face screwed in confusion. "Destroyed?"

But she didn't have a chance to question him further on it or really give it much thought at all as something deep and repressed began to stir in her. All her senses honed to one spot, and she turned in the direction of the door beyond the stacks before the bell of the entrance had even called out an incoming patron.

"Just give me a second," Jonah said, but Isla put out a hand to stop him from walking away.

Instead, *she* moved forward, back through the way they'd entered until she found herself in open space again. Found herself face to face with a tall, cloaked figure standing by the front door. She knew who it was before the customer even lowered the hood of his jacket, and Isla's heart stopped at the sight of dark hair and storm-colored eyes that she'd come to know fairly well.

"Kai."

The voice hadn't even sounded like her own, but at it, Kai's lips parted in a relieved grin—a grin that had both melted and infuriated her more times than she'd like to admit. She could've sworn her whole body, down to her foundations, down to her wolf, sighed—just as he had—as if to say *finally*.

"Isla."

Hearing him speak had ignited something in her, though not quite the overwhelming urge for him to strip her down and take her against the bookshelves—though that feeling *did* linger. Even now, from one simple look, she could feel the bond stoking back to life, resurfacing and ready to punish her for trying to neglect it.

Isla suddenly felt Jonah's presence behind her and heard him let out a resigned, defeated breath. "You two better not fuck on my floor."

CHAPTER 23

A little over one month.
She and Kai had made it only a little over a *month* before they'd found themselves together again. Isla would laugh if she wasn't so bewildered by it.

She'd known a reunion could happen—that it likely *would* happen—when she agreed to come to Deimos. Figured she'd spot him from a distance, maybe in a crowd or a gathering somewhere down the line. There would be a moment, an acknowledgment, and then they'd part, continuing with their lives.

Like they'd planned.

But this? She'd been within Deimos's borders for no more than *five* Goddess-forsaken hours—maybe even less than that.

And yet, here she was. And there he was.

"Damn mates."

She barely heard Jonah grumble and paid little mind to him as he moved past her to go to the counter on the other side of the room.

She felt shameful for glancing to the floor if only to picture, for a moment, what he'd warned against.

Mates.

It took Isla, in her daze, a while to register exactly what Jonah had said. But eventually, the words sunk in—further and further, deeper and deeper—until they hit her full force.

With wide eyes, she looked between him and Kai, just in time to catch the two exchanging a glance. A knowing glance. A glance between acquaintances. Between…friends?

But before she could jump to question, Kai's attention was on her again. Intent and arresting.

Something familiar blazed behind his eyes, and it pulled at that wretched part of her. The part of her that craved. That skittered through her body and torched her skin in a maddening way that she remembered well. In a way that only *he* could soothe, that only *he* could touch and kiss and fuck away. Not a man she pulled into the bathroom or back alley of some bar. Not some random suitor she dragged to her apartment. Only him. And he knew it—how badly she wanted him, for the most dizzying of seconds. And maybe she'd been so blinded by her own desire the first time they'd met, or now she was more in tune with him than she'd realized, but she could feel it from him too.

And it just made things worse.

"I'm not kidding," Jonah reiterated as he sorted through some books. "I'm sure the binding of an alpha and luna is a beautiful, momentous event, but I want no part in it."

Isla managed to tear her eyes away from Kai to look towards the shop owner again, hearing the words—her "destined" title—enough to jar her from whatever fantasies had been blooming.

"You two know each other?"

Silence fell.

It didn't seem like that hard of a question, but Jonah looked at Kai. And then Isla had to.

Sensing her impending irritation, her mate let out a sigh before gesturing between them. "Isla. Jonah. My…well, you could call him my brother."

"Pleasure," Jonah said before going back to his work.

Brother.

Isla knew what Kai had meant, but still, a dumbfounded expression cast across her face. She tried to wrap her head around how she'd ended up here, feeling horrified that she'd been with Kai's "brother" for the past few minutes and had no idea. All the while, he knew exactly who she was the second she introduced herself.

She folded her arms across her chest, very aware that she was about to be a hypocrite. "You told people. We promised to keep this a secret, and you *told* people."

Kai took a few gentle steps forward.

Isla retreated the same amount.

He flashed a deadpan look, and she raised her brows, urging him to explain.

"They're not just 'people'," he said.

"They?" she echoed. "Who are *they*?"

Almost on cue, the bell above the shop door chimed—high and sweet—as it was pushed open. Through it, strolled a familiar small, full-figured woman. Davina froze a step into the shop, taking in the sight before her—Isla and Kai in some sort of stand-off, and Jonah left to bear witness.

"Hello," she drawled, letting her russet hair free from beneath the hood of her cloak. Her greeting was followed by thick seconds of quiet. All too long. "Right," she muttered before taking cautious steps over to the counter. "This seems like something I'm not meant to be a part of anymore, so I'm just going to go into the back and get a drink. Care to join me, Jonie?"

Jonah didn't speak. Only dropped everything and eagerly followed.

Isla watched as the two descended behind the shelves, not missing their whispered exchange.

"You weren't supposed to send her here."

"I didn't think she'd go out tonight."

She kept her head turned, even when they'd disappeared. She could feel Kai's eyes boring into the side of it, could hear as he moved in closer again. Could feel it.

"Isla."

She didn't turn.

"*Isla*."

Her name was said slower. Deeper. Softer. And from closer. Much closer. A manipulation.

Isla spun around slowly, a grimace prepped and ready on her face. She wouldn't let it falter as he was merely a foot away. As she clocked just the slightest bit of warmth exchanged from the proximity of their bodies, as she caught a hint of that scent she couldn't bring herself to wash out of that damn gown.

She stepped back. "Do not."

"You're trying to make me believe *you* didn't tell anyone? The Imperial Heir? *Your* brother?"

Isla clenched her teeth. There was no point in lying. "They figured it out themselves. I didn't tell them voluntarily."

The corners of Kai's lips ticked upwards. "Why? Were you losing it without me?"

"No, you arrogant ass, because *you* couldn't stay away from me for more than a few hours."

"Can you blame me?"

Her glower persisted.

Kai sighed. "If it helps, they figured it out too."

Isla's features softened, if only slightly. Whoever this "they" was—Jonah and Davina, she was sure of—she'd never met them beforehand. They weren't at the feast. They weren't at the infirmary. They hadn't seen the *look* that Adrien had mentioned. Hadn't found them together frequently.

"How?" The question spilled from her mouth before she could stop it.

Kai hesitated.

"I was different when I came back."

And that was all he said. All he *would* say, judging by the pensive, solemn look that had threatened his face. And Isla didn't know if it was the bond, but she knew not to push for more explanation.

Not for that anyway.

She relaxed her arms. "How did you know I was here?"

"I went to the hotel—where you were *supposed* to be—but when Davina rang up to your room, you weren't there. Then she mentioned she'd told you about Jonah's." Kai let loose a chuckle. "I should've known you'd run off at the first chance you had."

So, he'd always planned to see her again.

A sudden strangled ring of the bell above the door—so opposing to Davina's—caused them to jump apart as the entrance to the shop burst open. A chill swept up Isla's spine, but she blamed it on the air that had rushed through. Her eyebrows shot up as she found herself staring at the face of the person who'd been haunting her mind since they'd met weeks ago.

Ameera, hair done up again in that crown of a bun, pointed at Kai. The alpha cursed under his breath.

"You son of a bitch." Ameera pressed forward with her finger still up in the air until she was inches away from Kai. She pushed the digit into his chest. "Why would you send grumpy ass to my post? *I* was supposed to be the one to check the warriors at the border with Rhydian. That was the plan."

Isla blinked, wondering if *all of this* was some elaborate hallucination.

Kai and Ameera *did* know each other, apparently. But this didn't seem like an exchange between lovers, or even former ones.

"Because I told you not to go to Ganymede." Kai brushed her hand away, continuing before the wide-eyed Ameera could ask where he'd gotten the information. "General Eli was wondering in what capacity you'd be helping with the rogues. If you'd need to be considered part of his team and under his command as a warrior. He mentioned he'd just seen you at the warrior base"—Kai nodded to Isla—"for the ceremonies."

When Ameera finally averted her attention, Isla found herself too stunned to be as angry as she imagined she'd be upon encountering the female general again.

The beta's daughter hummed. "So nice of you to decide to help out, new blood."

"Meera," Kai warned.

But Isla ignored it.

She tilted her chin to the general, matching the intensity of her stare. "Not what you expected?"

Ameera flashed her feline grin. "It's what I was hoping for."

Isla bit down on her tongue. There were so many things she'd pictured saying to her, but they all felt pointless now. "You could've told me that he told you."

"And where's the fun in that?" Ameera said. "I wanted to see what I had to work with."

Before Isla could ask what she meant, there was the sound of a closing door, shuffling footsteps, and then laughter before Jonah and Davina re-appeared from behind the bookshelves. Jonah was holding a decanter of brown liquor and some glasses while Davina matched with her bottle of wine.

Ameera moved away from Isla and Kai, further into the room. "Thank you both for telling me Isla was here. I had to find out from my father during the *worst* family dinner I've ever had."

Ezekiel.

Ameera gestured to the liquor in Jonah's arms. "I need half of that."

As she watched the exchange, Isla had never felt like such a fish out of water. An outsider to this pack, and an outsider to what seemed to be a tight-knit group of friends. She knew nothing much of them beyond their names, and yet it felt like they could read her like a book, standing there, staring, with Kai at her back.

As if he could sense her becoming overwhelmed and uneasy, Kai craned his head down. She could faintly feel his breath as he asked, "Do you want me to walk you back?"

Isla turned to look up at him, taking note of how close their faces were. Becoming aware of the twisting and winding. Aware of the comfort. Aware that of all the unknown she'd just walked into, he was the most certain thing she had.

And maybe it was *that* which had her nodding without very much thought and saying, "Okay."

Kai's brows lifted a fraction of an inch before he smiled softly and nodded. He rose, and Isla found herself missing the closeness. "I have to head back to the hall," he announced to the room, earning noises reminiscent of groans. "I'm going to walk Isla back."

"And so it begins." Ameera sighed overdramatically, reaching over to clink glasses with Jonah. "It's just you and me, buddy." They both followed the exchange by drinking their whiskey to the dregs. As Jonah poured them another, Ameera jerked her chin towards Kai. "When will you be unchained from that place so we can go down to Abalys and stop hanging out here? Or actually *see you* more than once a week." She added the last part in a murmur.

"I like it here," Davina said, finding a spot on one of the plush armchairs set up by the shelves. "It's cozy, and it doesn't smell like a sewer."

As an argument began to ensue over the odors of Abalys, Kai turned and waved Isla to follow. He pulled the shop door open quietly, so as not to cut in or draw attention, and held it open for her to pass through.

The beautiful streets of Mavec greeted Isla with moon-touched stone and a cold slap on the face. She sucked in a sharp breath and let it out, watching the faintest cloud materialize before her mouth. It hadn't been this chilly when she'd left the hotel. She circled her arms around her body to warm her exposed skin.

"It can get pretty cold here at night, even during the summer months," Kai said while removing his jacket. An action completely at odds with his sentence.

But it made sense when he held it open to her.

Isla blinked at it for a few seconds—a *no, thank you* sitting on the tip of her tongue—but as if goading her to take it, another ice-laced wind swept by. Self-preservation trumped pride and doubt as she stepped over and very carefully stuck her arm through one of the sleeves. As she and Kai went to work the other, they both moved in a way so methodical, so unusual, they couldn't help but laugh. She'd never admit how nice it felt to laugh with him again.

Isla drowned in his clothing, the black fabric limp on her frame. The apparel was accustomed to the broadness of Kai's shoulders, and the muscles of his arms. But she was perfectly fine with it, how the sleeves extended past her fingertips and the hem ended at her mid-thigh, rather than her hips. It was warm…and it smelled like him.

"Thanks," she said.

And then the two began walking.

At first, they moved in silence, side by side, but at their safe distance. Isla shoved her hands in the coat's pockets and closed her eyes for a moment, taking in the softest of sounds. The faintest hint of music, of laughter and joy, from people down in what she would consider the heart of the city.

But mostly, she focused on the easiness of their footsteps, finding herself calmed by each rhythmic hit of their shoes on the cobblestone walkway. Completely in-sync. Her breathing slowed, and her shoulders relaxed from a tightness she hadn't realized they had.

And then, in the quiet, the disbelief hit her full force again.

She was with Kai. In Deimos.

"I'm sorry."

Kai's apology caused her to snap her eyes wide open. She averted her gaze to him. "For what?"

"That isn't how I wanted you to meet them," he said. "At least, formally. They can be…a lot. But they're family."

Isla smiled softly, feeling warmth bloom in her chest. He'd wanted her to meet the people he was closest to. "It's fine. Adrien and my brother can be the same way," she dismissed. "Are they the only '*they*' that know about us?"

"The only other person is Rhydian."

"The guard?"

Kai hummed in affirmation. "My other 'brother'. Jonah's twin and Davina's mate. I owe him for tonight—and Thyra. I'm sure Sol was pissed I sent him out there and took it out on them."

Isla snickered, remembering the delta's demands for an impossible return from the guards. "He wasn't thrilled."

Kai laughed. "Great…you can trust him if you ever need anything here, but don't ever tell him you're my mate. If he knew *that's* why he was at the borders…" Kai's smile grew. "He used to train me, Rhydian, and Jonah while we were preparing for the guard. Ameera too before she went into the warrior program, and before he became a delta. He'd bash my skull in, but he'd do it because he cared."

Isla's face contorted into a grin a mix of confusion, concern, and slight amusement. "Right." But then she went over the first part of Kai's words, and her lips fell. "Who else can I trust?"

"Ezekiel," Kai answered almost immediately, and Isla worked to fight off her scowl. "I told him that if he tried to shove you in a safe house, I have no problem with you kicking his ass. Or I would—but I felt like you'd enjoy it more." Isla's beam returned, and Kai chuckled again. "And you say I don't know you."

Isla rolled her eyes before asking with some levity, "Anyone else?"

Though, any mirth of hers dissipated when Kai's face went serious.

"I'm still working on that," he said, his voice a soft rumble. He paused. "And I think you could help me."

Isla's steps slowed enough to ruin their rhythm. "What do you mean?"

Kai's throat bobbed as he darted his eyes around them. Isla mirrored the action, and it dawned on her that she'd blindly followed him down a different path. One that veered away from that which she'd taken from the hotel to the shop earlier. With this, there was no chance of encountering anyone, cutting along a dirt road through sparse forest.

"In a couple of days," Kai began before she could question the detour, "we're having a banquet for a retiring council member. General Eli was added to the guest list, and I made sure he was allowed a plus-one. There's no doubt in my mind that he's going to ask you."

Isla averted her eyes from the surroundings and back to him. Was this all about Eli? "I would never go with him."

"You have to."

"Why?"

"Because I trust you, and you're of Io." Kai shoved his hands in his pockets, a muscle fluttering beneath his cheek. "I need you to work that charm of yours. Be the woman I saw from across the room at the feast. I need you to tell me everything you hear, everyone you talk to. What they say, how they say it. If they came up to *you* or if you sought them out."

"What are you looking for?"

"I'll know when I hear it."

Isla opened and closed her mouth, unsure what to say. She caught sight of the backside of the hotel up ahead. As quickly as she could, she attempted to break down what Kai was asking of her. "When Sol had found out that Callan and I were of Io, he asked if we were here to aid you or investigate you, but apparently, I'm here to aid in *your* investigations?"

"I suppose."

"Is that why you approved me, then?" Isla asked. "Why you endorsed me being here. So I could be your spy?"

A little hurt crept into her voice, and it made Kai slow until he came to a stop. Isla followed suit. They were a few yards away from the hotel's backdoor. He turned and gradually closed the distance between them until all that was left were inches.

"I approved you because you deserve to be here," he said. "I'm not going to deny you what you've worked for just because I have to work harder to not think about you all the time and to keep my hands to myself."

Isla bit down hard on the inside of her cheek, not wanting to address or show a reaction to the tease. "I didn't bring any type of formal wear, and I don't think I can show up to a banquet in my armor or warrior gear."

"I'll take care of it." Kai moved in just one step closer. Another, and they'd be against each other. "I need you, Isla."

The statement shouldn't have made her shiver, shouldn't have had her mind running through the other situations in which she'd want to hear it from his mouth. But it did. Thankfully, she was able to quell anything before it started.

Swallowing hard, she ran her eyes along his face. He appeared older now than he had when she'd last seen him, a tiredness to his eyes and a shadow of stubble dusting over his jaw and cheeks. Another month spent adjusting to a role he'd never prepared for and could never have a reprieve from.

Even with how assured he'd sounded, there was something pleading in his gaze. He needed her.

He needed her.

Taking a breath, Isla squared her shoulders to him and said, "You have me."

~

Kai had been right.

Before the sun had even crept fully over the mountains surrounding Mavec, before its beams could cast a gleam along the river, Eli had asked Isla to the banquet.

He'd fallen upon her in the hotel lobby just as she'd been returning from grabbing a sunrise breakfast alone at the café nearby, a recommendation from Davina. The way the general had framed the invitation, she would be accompanying him as his protégé. His second. It was all to observe how one would interact in their position within the setting. Navigating political conversation, easing minds, and maybe tempers, especially in times of uncertainty and strife.

It would've been an honor if she wasn't *so* aware of his ulterior motives. If she hadn't caught his reflection in one of the windows as she'd walked away, his eyes honed on her lower half. Still, even if his objective at times had been to woo her, he seemed shocked when she'd been so gleefully responsive, flashing him a wide smile, thanking him, and saying that she'd love to attend. She'd played the "role", as Ameera called it, perfectly, and just as Kai would want. Eager and bright-eyed, ready to schmooze and flatter.

She hadn't seen her mate or heard from him since they'd parted last night, with a *goodnight, Alpha,* and *goodnight, Warrior* that she replayed endlessly through her head as she walked up to her hotel room. She'd still been wearing his jacket, she realized. He hadn't asked her to give it back. Maybe because he liked the fact that his scent was all over her, even when she'd taken it off.

Only after an hour of scrubbing her body head to toe in the shower —while trying her damned hardest to keep her fingers from drifting *anywhere else* as lecherous thoughts of him, particularly him running *his* hands over her body, made their return—did she feel like she'd removed every trace of him.

Though a leery look she'd received from Callan as the warriors boarded their vehicle that morning made her paranoid that she hadn't.

As instructed, while Eli went to meet Beta Ezekiel and the lead commander of the entire Deimos guard, the rest of the unit went on to spend the morning and early afternoon touring the guard's main campus and getting to know the remaining order that hadn't been sent to deal with the rogues yet. The strategy was to have the warriors—being the most elite fighters and strategists the continent had to offer, according to their rank—working alongside the guard battalions to drive their nefarious brethren from parts of southern Abalys.

Isla knew the two fighter classes were meant to mix, get along, and build rapport, but she didn't have much hope for that happening. As Eli had said, it seemed they didn't want the warriors involved at all.

The campus sat at the base of one of the mountains. It was the furthest of the various peaks, deceptively so, as it took them nearly an hour of winding roads and hills and valleys to get there. It was like Io's guard headquarters—dormitories and training rings, a reference center and dining quarters, medic buildings, and a horde of new, young recruits running drills over the landscape. Some of them looked as if they'd pass out. Isla was sure they'd been going since sunrise.

When a break from the touring came at lunch, Isla was late getting to the mess hall. She'd gotten "lost", "separated from the group", and conveniently found herself amongst the books and maps of the camp's collection.

There had been *nothing* on Phobos.

Nothing on any language but the Common and the native dialect of Deimos that was now obsolete.

Both used the same uniform alphabet. Nothing like the symbols of the message, the marker, or the book.

She would have to go back to The Bookshoppe and see what Jonah had to offer her—before she'd been *distracted* by their surprise guest—even though she wasn't sure how she'd interact with the shop owner now that she knew *he* knew. Wasn't sure what their relationship was—if there *was* any type of "relationship" between them. She was simply destined to be with his "brother". The same went for all of Kai's closest companions.

Including Rhydian, who she spotted before her in the long line waiting to get his food.

The guard looked different from his twin, brawnier and more muscular compared to Jonah's sinewy stature. Rhydian's hair was longer too, the tight curls coiling a bit higher on his head. They shared the same dark skin though, and similar amber and honey flecked eyes. Eyes that were warm and inviting, and urged her forward.

After some strategic maneuvering, she was able to get beside him in one of the lines. He was distracted by a conversation with a man on his other side, glancing sidelong at him as he heaped some chicken onto his plate. Isla set her tray down to slide along the metal bar, her mouth watering as she waited and eyed the options for her meal. They'd gone through three serving stations, him leaving the utensil for her every time—but never acknowledging her—before he'd ended his exchange.

After clearing her throat, she leaned over and asked, "So, what's good here?"

Rhydian didn't turn. He picked up the serving spoon for the vegetables, a smirk threatening his mouth. "Uh, not the—" The guard looked over and then did a double-take, cutting himself off when he realized who he was talking to. His wide eyes lingered for a moment before he looked forward again. Then stepped to the side.

A smile played on Isla's lips. "Oh, come on, I don't bite."

Rhydian furrowed his brows at the quip as if he hadn't expected it, and smiled. "My brother may be disappointed then."

It was just quiet enough for her to hear, and her jerk-back reaction had his grin growing.

"Don't get the beans," he advised. Then continued down the way.

With Kai back on her mind, they didn't interact again until they were at the final station, lined with desserts. Most had forgone the sweets—with the hard day of drills continuing from the afternoon into evening—but Rhydian put a handful of cookies on his plate. When Isla took one off the tray for herself, Rhydian laughed. She wasn't sure why but either way, she laughed with him.

As her amusement faded into soft breaths, she realized that they were distant from others. There had been a question plaguing her mind since last night. Why not ask?

"Did he really make you go to the border to check on me? To escort us—me—into Mavec?" She wouldn't speak Kai's name aloud, but Rhydian knew what she meant. "And then the hotel the warriors were sent to—specifically the one *Davina* works at?"

His brows lifted at the mention of his mate. "I was on duty," he tried to reason.

"But at *that* border?"

"He wanted to make sure you got into the city safely," Rhydian explained. "He's protective—of all of us, really—but with *you*…" He flashed her a knowing look. "I get the feeling."

Isla smiled softly, recalling Davina and her mating ring. "How long have you been together?"

Rhydian's features brightened. "Next month makes a year."

Only a year? That was quick to form a chosen bond.

"You're fated?"

"Never thought the day would come," Rhydian chuckled. "It wasn't the plan, but she changed my life."

The last sentence resonated in a way Isla wasn't expecting.

Eventually, Isla followed him to the table with his squadmates.

"Shouldn't you be with *them*?" he'd asked, nodding towards the group of warriors sitting alone at the table away from the rest of the order.

Neither Emil, Lavan, Fitch, or Callan had displayed *any* hesitation in her absence. All four of them, donning their warrior gear as she did, had already made their way down the long service line, acquired their heaps of food, and began digging in before she'd even stepped foot in the hall. Her being lost didn't mean a damn thing. They were probably hoping she never returned.

"We're meant to mingle," she told Rhydian.

As they walked through the hall, Isla noticed the eyes that tracked her. It was because of what she was wearing, what she very *clearly* was, but there was a small part of her that wondered, that feared, that they recognized her also as what she was meant to be.

The long table they approached had several groups spread over its lengthy bench, but Rhydian had stopped in front of a trio. The band of four beside them took one glance at her before leaving.

Rhydian glowered at them, Isla did too, before the guard gestured to the three that remained. One of them was a young woman, maybe eighteen or nineteen with black hair that went to her chin, she recognized as Thyra.

"Isla, meet the members of unit 37B—Thyra, Belle, and Magnus," Rhydian presented in mock grandness.

Thyra waved sweetly, while Belle and Magnus both nodded in curt acknowledgment.

"Nice to meet you," Isla forced out before moving to take a seat across from them beside Rhydian.

"You're of Io?" Belle asked before her butt had even hit the seat.

Isla ran her tongue over her teeth. "Yes."

"She's the Imperial Beta's daughter," Thyra added as if they'd spoken of her before and couldn't believe that the brown-haired woman had forgotten it.

"So do you know the Imperial Heir?" Magnus asked, not even looking up from the food he was eating.

Isla raised a brow. "Yes?"

Why bring up Adrien?

The light-haired man bit into a piece of bread. "No offense, but what kind of alpha loses his mate? How can we expect him to—"

Without hesitation, Isla lifted her fork and pointed the sharp edge at him, effectively cutting him off. "If you're smart, you'll stop talking." There was no hint of humor in her tone.

This was why Imperial Alpha Cassius had been so adamant about Adrien and Cora staying together, keeping their bond. Because of how it reflected on the hierarchy and how it was viewed by the other packs.

As Magnus narrowed his eyes, Rhydian offered, "She just took down two bak. I give you three seconds in the ring with her."

Isla slowly lowered her utensil, giving the guard a thankful glance.

"The Hunt is overrated," Magnus argued.

Overrated? She nearly died.

"I'd like to see you last twenty-four hours in the Wilds," she challenged.

"I could go a week, but your alpha wouldn't approve me."

Her scowl softened. "Why not?"

"Because you can't have too many *warriors* born of Deimos," he sneered. "Then it may bring about the question if your pack is really the strongest on the continent."

Isla's jaw slackened. "That's not…true."

Magnus put his bread down and took hold of the sides of his tray, letting out a humorless laugh. "Of course, it's not," he said before rising from the table and walking away.

The silence that followed was so tense that Isla thought she'd suffocate.

"He's just bitter," Belle commented to break the quiet. "He was denied entry to the Hunt four years in a row before he gave up."

Even with that statement, a stillness took the table again. In it, Isla began digging into her lunch.

"Isn't our alpha going to have to take a mate at some point?"

She stopped eating, looking up at Thyra who'd had the slightest redness tinting her cheeks with the question.

While Isla became tense, Rhydian remained cool. He bit into the sandwich he'd made. "At some point."

"Shouldn't it be soon?" Belle commented brusquely. "We don't have an heir. By the time he chooses someone and a bond takes form, it could be *years*. That can't look good to other packs."

Isla felt her stomach twist.

Thyra pulled a piece of her hair behind her ear. "Unless he finds his destined mate." There was something light about her voice, hopeful.

Belle scoffed. "Yeah, right. What they'll probably do is line up every she-wolf within these borders, and he'll just take his pick. Who's going to tell him *no*? He's an alpha." She rolled her eyes before mocking, "*Or* he could fall back into old patterns. Ones that are gorgeous, vain, and *'Goddess forbid I lift a finger'*."

Thyra giggled. "You mean *Amalie*?"

"Amalie?" Isla said the name before she could stop herself. All their eyes went to her, and she shrunk slightly in her seat.

"A member of one of the wealthiest families in the pack, probably the entire continent," Thyra began. "She's the heiress to a fortune and the daughter of an alpha scion in Mimas. She and Alpha Kai had been on again, off again for *years*—before he became alpha. My sister followed all the gossip. The pack ate them up." She let out a sigh. "They always looked so great in pictures."

"In *pictures*," Belle made a point in echoing while one hand went to rub her temples. "She's *nothing* like she pretends to be when she's behind closed doors. I was on her private guard for a while, while I was still in training. I have never heard two people switch up from fighting to fucking so fast."

Isla straightened in her seat, feeling something inside her start to simmer. That was something about Kai's past she wasn't keen to hear about.

"That was literally all they did," Belle continued to complain. "Fight, fuck, fight, fuck, fight—"

"Okay, we get it." Rhydian put his hands up, and Isla felt his knee bump against hers beneath the table.

She turned to look up at him but found his eyes cast on her hand instead. She followed them to the fork in her grasp...slightly bent from the force of her thumb pressing down on it. Thankfully, neither Belle nor Thyra noticed.

Thyra lowered her voice. "They were together right before...you know. I heard she was with him when he found out."

It took Isla a while to register what the teen was alluding to, and when it did, her insides turned watery.

"*I heard* they couldn't find him for hours," Belle said. "The whole pack knew before he did."

Isla couldn't get herself to swallow.

She couldn't imagine how horrific that must've been for him. To wake up and find out half his family was gone forever, forget all the responsibility heaped on his shoulders. The thought of Kai that devastated made her sick and angry. At whom, she didn't know. But a part of her wished she'd been there, even if they hadn't known each other yet.

"It's all rumors and speculation," Rhydian said. "No one knows what really happened."

Did *he* know about what happened? About the murders, the killer?

"Well, whoever he picks, no one will live up to Luna Zahra," Belle countered. "She's a goddess amongst us all."

Thyra nodded. "Amen to that."

Isla bit down on the inside of her cheek, looking down at her tray. She felt Rhydian knock against her knee again, but she refused to turn to him. Instead, she pushed food around on her plate.

Amen to that.

∽

The last part of the day had been filled with endless drills with the warriors joining the guard. Isla stuck by Rhydian, doing her best to keep up with his long strides and endless supply of muscle mass. At points, they competed. Isla was beet-red and panting by the time dusk hit, and there had still been one more drill that involved climbing up a steep trail along the mountain that many had to drop out from.

Her body was screaming and aching when the warriors finally retreated to the hotel. They'd be doing the same thing tomorrow and the next day and the next day until it was time to head off.

As she bordered on a limp through the lobby, she heard her name called from behind her.

It was Davina, standing behind the front desk.

"I recognize that look," she greeted with a laugh as Isla approached, noting her physical discomfort and disheveled appearance. Her cheery mood did little to distract and alleviate any pain. "There's a package for you."

Isla furrowed her brows. "For me? From where?"

Davina shrugged before handing her the brown-encased parcel. Isla weighed it in her hand; it was considerably heavy.

Fear blooming in her chest—given her track record recently with unexpected events—she bid Davina goodbye before moving as fast as she could to her room.

As soon as she broke the threshold, she tossed the box onto her bed, hearing a faint rattle with it. She paused—then was happy no one could see her as she grabbed hold of her sword, even if she had what *she* considered valid reasons.

She poked the parcel with the tip of her blade. Once. Twice. Then made a clear slice along the side, peeling back the brown paper to reveal a sleek black box. Atop it was a white piece of paper, so stark against the surface.

Heart in her throat, she approached it slowly. Her fingers were trembling as she picked it up and read: ***A GIFT FOR A GIFT***.

She felt a thrumming in her chest, but terror was no longer the reason.

The corners of Isla's lips twitched up as she placed her sword on the mattress and brushed some of her hair out of her face that was coated in dry sweat. She lifted the lid from the box slowly. In it, she found the luxurious sheen of silk as dark as ink, the fabric rich and finely made. It was smooth beneath her fingertips as she ran her hands along it before hooking the two straps. They were thin, she noticed as she lifted the dress. Diving down into a plunging neckline that ended at the cinched waist, stitched with subtle corded patterns, just above where her navel would be. From the middle, it split again, a high slit, certain to leave her leg on display before it pooled onto the ground like an obsidian lagoon.

It was beautiful. Too beautiful. Too nice.

But her admiring of it was cut short when something else within the box caught her eye. Jewelry of silver and diamonds and gemstones so crimson they looked like blood. Like the sheen of an alpha's eyes…or the trademark color of Io.

All of this must've cost a fortune—but it was necessary. At least, in Kai's eyes.

It was a spectacle, *she* was. She had to be. As much attention as possible had to be on her tomorrow night.

If it weren't simply for the bared skin of her body and the daring cuts of the dress, the thin straps and the low cut back would leave her lumerosi exposed. If the lumerosi didn't draw attention or conversation, it would be the jewels. One way or another, Kai needed her to interact with as many people as she could, and get as much information as she could glean…a warrior and the alpha's spy.

With the dress still in her hands, Isla walked to her window where she could just catch one of the towers of the Pack Hall dwelling in a sea of sunset—reds, oranges, purples, and blues.

How bad could it be?

CHAPTER 24

Right when her clock hit four in the afternoon the next day—the day of the banquet—Isla received a knock on her door. She groaned, rising from the edge of her mattress where she'd been working to remove her mud-slicked shoes and hobbled over to it, her limbs barking in protest.

She'd just returned from training with the guard again and there was only a little less than two hours until she'd need to meet General Eli in the lobby. She would need every second of it—mostly to remove all the dirt that seemed to coat her like a second skin. She didn't necessarily have time for visitors.

Hand on her sword, that she always had perched by the exit—while Lukas's dagger, claimed as her own, remained hidden under her pillow—Isla opened the door, leaving the chain latched.

"Davina?"

On the opposite end of the threshold, the fiery-haired woman beamed, green eyes sparkling. Isla moved to close and unlock the entrance.

Once given full view of the warrior, Davina's features fell, screwing up as if she'd eaten something sour. "You haven't showered yet?"

Isla retreated a step, feeling self-conscious. "I just got back." She darted her eyes to the large brown leather trunk that sat at Davina's side. "What is that?"

The floral scent of Davina's perfume wafted through the room as she brushed by Isla, dragging the heavy-set box along behind her. "I told Rhydian to make sure you got back here by three."

No answer to the question, but Isla didn't bother asking again.

"Rhydian's not my commander," she told her, closing her door softly.

"Funny, he said the same thing, but I'd heard countless stories of the boys sneaking out of things before; I figured he'd get creative."

Davina heaved the trunk onto the bed, and Isla watched as it bounced on the mattress, listening to whatever was inside rattle. She bent down to untie her other shoe, not removing her eyes from the case. "What are you doing here?"

Once again, Davina failed to answer right away, instead, moving to flip the brass latch on the front of the trunk. It came undone with a click beneath her fingers before she flung it open. Isla rose to peer inside, abandoning her shoes in their spot.

She let out a soft whistle at the overabundance of cosmetics and hair accessories, seemingly for every occasion. From the soft hues of morning brunches to the dark, sultry shades of nights out and dinner gatherings.

Davina turned to Isla, placing her hands on her wide hips and proclaiming, "I'm getting you ready for the party."

Isla's mouth opened and closed as a particular silver and ruby comb caught her attention. It almost looked like a tiara. She met Davina's eyes. "You don't have to do that."

"I want to," Davina argued, pulling a few powders from the trunk and comparing them against Isla's skin. Isla wasn't sure how she could even see it beneath the dirt. "You're going to blow everyone in that room away. Especially that mate of yours."

Isla ignored the rise of wicked excitement her words had brought and instead focused on the reminder of her objectives. Why she was attending the party in the first place. "Did Kai make you do this, too?"

Davina scoffed, dropping the powders and picking up a rouge. "Kai is my alpha, but he doesn't make me *do* anything." She dropped the blusher, then went to examine Isla's fingernails, smudged with the grime that was also matted in her hair. She clicked her tongue before waving her off. "Go shower. We don't have much time, and you look like you've been living in the mud."

∽

When Isla emerged from the bathroom, wrapped in the fluffy white robe that had been left complimentarily with the various soaps and hair products, Davina was examining her dress hanging near the closet.

"This is gorgeous," she commented, running her fingers over the silk.

Isla continued scrunching her hair with a towel. "It's not mine."

She glanced over. "He gave it to you, didn't he?"

"You knew what was in the package?"

Davina smiled. "When it was Marin who dropped it off, I put the pieces together."

Yet another female name associated with her mate that she wasn't familiar with.

"Marin?"

"Kai's do-all." Davina stepped back from the gown. "He has his council, obviously. Then he has us—we're like his *personal* council—and then there's Marin." She fluffed the pillow on the chair in front of the bureau she'd converted into a makeshift vanity. "She wears many hats, the alpha's secretary being one of them—she was his father's, too. From my understanding, she keeps him sane, organized, and maintains face within the pack and outside of it."

At the description, Isla felt a pang of homesickness. "His Winslow," she said in a breathy laugh.

"His what?"

"Nothing."

Davina gestured for Isla to take a seat, and as Isla proceeded, she added, "She's a scary thing, quite honestly, and she was probably strung out because of the banquet. I was surprised she agreed to waste time running the errand herself, but Kai can be persuasive when he wants to be." She gathered Isla's hair in her hands and clipped it back out of her face. As she examined her features to determine the first line of attack, she said, "You have beautiful eyes."

Feeling heat rise to her cheeks, Isla thanked her before commenting, "My mother had the same."

Something flashed along Davina's face—something like regret—as she caught the word. *Had.*

"Very pretty," she complimented again before rising and retrieving a cream off the dresser. She nodded to the side, and Isla followed her gaze to Kai's jacket sitting by the window. "That looks familiar. Did he leave it here?" A playfulness colored her tone. Probably an attempt to lighten the mood.

"*No*," Isla countered just as sprightly. "It was cold, and he let me wear it."

"And you kept it?"

"I forgot to take it off and never had a chance to give it back."

"I'm sure he has no problem with you keeping it. He has plenty." She shook her head and snickered. "You know, I cannot believe you've gone this long without even *touching*. I mean, Kai is...he's an alpha *and* your destined mate. You have the self-control of a saint." She dabbed spots of the lotion over Isla's skin. "One look at Rhydian and I was ready—well, I already explained."

Isla recounted her and Davina's first interaction. "At a bar?"

Davina nodded, swiping over Isla's forehead. "Before I worked here at the hotel, I worked at a pub in Abalys. It was my second night on the job, and some hooligan started up a fight."

"Rhydian?"

"*Jonah*," Davina said as if she was still wrapping her mind around it. Isla was just as confused, as Jonah seemed the most mild-mannered of them. "Rhydian and Kai had gone in to break it up. Got caught in it themselves—not the best for a prince. All the while, Ameera was watching from the side. When I went in to berate them, I saw Rhydian and..." She trailed off into a dreamy sigh. "We went into the storeroom after that."

"Sounds romantic," Isla mused, trying not to grin too wide as Davina rubbed at her cheeks.

"We knocked over an entire rack of liquor. More than we could ever afford." She sounded both amused and mortified. "Thankfully, Kai took care of it as a mating gift."

The two women fell into a fit of laughter that forced Davina to break away for a moment.

Isla used to always enjoy hearing the anecdotes of how mates found each other, even if it caused the smallest resentment. It seemed the meeting—even with its increasing rarity—could happen anywhere. A crowded market, an elegant ball, a walk down the street, or a bar brawl. Somehow, the unpredictability made it feel plausible, *possible*.

She'd always wanted to have a story of her own—of choice or fate, she'd take anything. If only to be rid of the pitying look she'd receive when she confessed she had no one. And thus...Callan.

Though a bit unconventional, maybe now she did have that tale to share.

As Davina reached for a tinted powder, Isla began explaining for the first time to anyone. "We met on a terrace by the garden of Callisto's Hall. I was trying to get a break from the feast, and, I don't know, just found myself outside. He was already out there apparently, hiding in the shadows."

Davina grabbed a firm feather brush and dabbed it into the small glass jar. "It's like your body knew where to lead you."

Isla pursed her lips, remembering the pull. "I suppose."

"Crazy how the mate thing works." Davina chuckled. "I'd peddled this nonsense all the time, and I never really believed it until I felt it."

Isla couldn't stop her head from jerking, earning a soft tap to right it again. "You were the one who worked at the mate gatherings?"

Davina leaned back, a hand on her chest with mock amazement. "He told you about me?" After Isla nodded, unable to contain a smile, she continued her work. "The pay was horrendous, and I felt terrible about it. Sorry saps."

Isla's grin bittered. "Yeah, sorry saps."

The two settled into silence as Davina finished pressing the powder, then reached for a brush of a fluffier variety to dust a shimmer over Isla's cheekbones. As she did, Isla found herself closing her eyes, getting comfortable. She didn't know Davina that well, if at all besides these small stories that had been shared, but she felt understood by her in a way she hadn't been before.

Isla opened her eyes and looked at Davina through the reflection. "What happened after you were mated?"

"I pulled my skirt back down."

Isla snorted.

Davina smirked. "After my shift ended—meaning, I got fired—I went back to Rhydian's." She shrugged. "And I guess I never left his side after that."

Isla bit the inside of her cheek. It was exactly as she thought it would be. Mated and dropping life as one knew it to take on one with another. She'd leave—she'd *lose*—everything.

"Did that scare you?"

As if she'd sensed the sincerity and unease in which Isla spoke, Davina's tone had gone soft. "I think it scared both of us, but I don't think it's meant to not be *a little* terrifying. I find, the beauty of a mate is that..." She padded along Isla's cheeks with the rouge. "Even though it's scary and uncertain, it's not just *you* who's terrified and unsure. You figure it out together. All of it: the newness, having someone there to care for, to worry about. Someone to care and worry about you. Probably in a way no one else ever has." Isla caught her jaw tensing, and the memories that seemed to be flashing behind her eyes. "Yes, it's sudden and it's overwhelming, but that's just the way life is. I wouldn't want to work through it with anyone else. I can't picture my life without him there."

Isla swallowed, allowing the words to sink in, watching as Davina's eyes glossed over. Noting how she'd gotten choked up.

Realizing she'd gone a bit too serious, Davina cleared her throat, and her lips twitched into a devilish smile. "And then there's also the amazing sex. That helps with the adjustment."

Once again, they descended into hysterics.

∼

Isla wasn't sure how Kai had known, but the dress made her look like a dream. And not necessarily the whimsical kind. The smooth black fabric bunched and hugged, draped and flowed, in all the right places, accentuating every curve that seemed non-existent in her warrior garb. It brought out the best parts of her, and the jewels were dazzling. The mix of diamonds within the ruby made it seem like she was a fiery star fallen from the sky before the sun had finished setting.

Davina had been an artist and Isla her canvas. Her face had been made up in the perfect balance of sultry and sweet. Unassuming. There was a dewy look to her skin, drawn and highlighted, tinted rosy to the right shade of innocence. Charcoal lined her eyes, her lashes plumped and long, and crimson—matching the jewels around her neck, dangling from her wrist and ears—painted her lips. She'd allowed Isla's hair to dry into its natural state, letting the waves take the wild shape they wanted before she'd swept it off to the side, clipping it over, and then sliding the tiara-like comb through her tresses.

Davina sighed in satisfaction as she stepped back, admiring her work as Isla towered over her small stature in her heels. "Kai is going to be furious with me."

"Why?" Isla asked, feeling invigorated in the ensemble and conceitedly unable to stop staring at herself.

"Because you are sex on legs, and he already has a hard enough time containing himself around you."

To that, Isla scoffed, but her cheek nearly bled between her teeth as she kept from a wicked grin.

Eli's reaction when she'd met him in the lobby was another great way to boost her confidence.

"You look…wow." His eyes were wide as he took her in, and it seemed his gaze didn't know where to land. Though the ruby pendant glittering between her breasts, just covered enough by the deep V of fabric, seemed to be his favorite resting place. "Wow."

Isla glanced at Davina sitting at the concierge desk, pretending not to be watching and failing at hiding her smugness at the compliment of her efforts.

"A man of many words." Isla couldn't help but tease before nodding towards the lobby door. "Come on. We can't be late."

They had got a town car for the night, courtesy of the "alpha's estate". It was yet another way that Kai seemed to have his hand in everything, but it was much nicer than the warrior's transport van—which still hadn't returned from the guard's mountain base—so Isla couldn't complain much.

As they drove along the streets of Mavec to get to the Pack Hall, a soft hum of music cooed from the radio while Eli also made attempts at small talk. It mostly pertained to Io. Isla's life there. Her father. How often she'd find new members entering her pack. It seemed he didn't care he was becoming more and more transparent with his motivations as of late. Isla only offered him baseless answers, too distracted by the raucousness of life they passed on their route and the nagging in the back of her mind of Davina's words.

They hadn't gone down into the heart of the city, but they still had a fantastic view of it as they crossed the bridge over the river to Abalys. Isla gaped at the sights all over again, taking note of every little shop she'd like to visit, every parlor, every square. Where, maybe, she'd want Kai to take her. Or maybe Davina. If she ever got the chance for free time.

Once Eli had turned the car in a way that left the city nothing but lights in a whisper of fog, Isla faced forward to behold a new marvel.

"Not a palace, my ass," she muttered, observing Deimos's Pack Hall.

Eli leaned over, inclining his head. "What was that?"

"Nothing," she said, restraining a roll of her eyes at how much Kai had tried to downplay the structure.

As she'd already taken note of, the Hall of Deimos stretched tall, its looming presence bolstered by the incline it sat upon. A network of trolleys rested on either side of the road they tread along, the cable cars seemingly fit to hold hundreds to loft them to the heights without the need of other transportation or slaving through a strenuous walk. There were people in them, Isla was bewildered to find, but they vanished behind the coal-tinged stone wall that began raising alongside them.

With her brows furrowed, she gazed forward again.

While Io boasted pillars of marble and moonstone, shades of gold and burgundy, Deimos seemed to lend itself to workings of obsidian, silver, and sapphire. From the onyx columns baring flags of the alpha's seal to the sable lamp posts overworked by silver twinings and encasing writhing flames within clear glass orbs, everything followed the same motif. Dark, a little forbidding, and beautiful.

Eli suddenly let out a low whistle as he slowed to a stop within a line of other fine vehicles. Many of the guests here were able to afford them. This was the queue for the banquet.

"Are you serious?" Blinking, she leaned forward in her seat and craned her neck to get a better view.

There were so many people. And she could've sworn up ahead, there was the firing of flashbulbs. Reporters. All of this for a retiring delta?

"Who's supposed to be here again?" Isla asked Eli.

The general shook his head as if he too hadn't realized what he'd signed up for. "Anyone who the delta has influenced in his tenure. He's been in service for nearly fifteen years. It must've been quite a few."

Quite a few indeed. How in the Goddess's name did Kai expect her to navigate this place?

As it turned out, Isla had plenty of time to assess her game plan as she and Eli slogged up the rest of the hall's drive. Mercifully, once they'd passed beneath the ebony metal archway—a crafting of wolves lurching for a sapphire orb that Isla pondered if it was a representation of the moon—two attendants came to their aid. While one valet tended to Eli and retrieved the keys, the other assisted Isla, opening the door before taking her hand. Panic gripped her heart as she stepped out onto the stone, too overtaken by the commotion before her to feel proud as the attendant's eyes tore over her.

She knew the fanfare she witnessed at home, for the Imperial Alpha, Luna, and Adrien. For her father, and sometimes, even for Sebastian with the right crowd.

But this was on another level. She felt like a whole new breed of outsider. Everyone who held any type of standing in Deimos had to be at this party.

She scowled.

What the hell did you get me into?

Isla found her gaze drawn upwards, not to shoot a prayer to the Goddess—which maybe, she should've—but to the stained-glass window in the hall's high center. Even with the distance, she could've sworn she saw something like a speck move along the base. Outside of it. She scrunched her brows and squinted as if it would help her see any better, but as soon as she blinked, it had vanished.

"Ready?"

She felt a hand on the small of her back and looked at Eli whose face was a picture of pure political grace.

No, was her immediate thought. No, and *take me back.*

But she had a job to do here. Kai had given her a job to do here.

And as pissed off as she was, she'd do it.

Forcing a smile, she subtly side-stepped from his touch and nodded.

∽

They'd gone from one line to another. Driven under one archway to walk beneath a second. However, *this* passage sat at the base of what Isla deemed "the Front Hall". The facade.

It was what one could see clearest from the streets. What bore the massive pane of stained glass like the hypnotizing eye of a large-bellied beast which protected what lay behind it. Because once one walked beneath the second archway, they ended up in a wide-mouthed underpass that cut beneath the structure. And from there, they found themselves in a gorgeous courtyard.

She wasn't sure what parts were done up for the event and what was a mainstay for the hall. There were delicate lights through trees and endless blooms of flowers—deep purples, some nearly black, and blues much like the window eye above. There was a great fountain in the center that seemed to glow. Metal structures were strewn about that seemed to move, to have meaning. They likely held a story if she could focus enough on each of them, but all she was really drawn to was that same depiction of the two wolves and the sapphire; this one more detailed it seemed from her distance, than the one on the first arch.

"The alpha's choice," Eli quipped from his spot beside her, and Isla directed her eyes to where his had been.

A crowd was gathered beside them in their queue. Their chatter and laughter, along with the shutter of reporters' cameras, echoed within the open-ended cavern. Part of the group was the same band of people that had come up on the tram. Isla recognized someone's extravagant, seemingly out-of-place, powder-pink hat. They weren't in the line to come in. They were just standing there, watching, waiting. She'd been struggling to think of *for what*, when Eli's statement answered the question for her.

Many of the women, though not invited to the festivities, were dressed beautifully. In all types of ways. Much like Davina's trunk of cosmetics, from soft and delicate to bold, sultry, and daring.

"I swear every unmated girl in this pack is tripping over themselves to get in his eye-line and catch his attention."

The alpha's choice.

That roaring returned to her blood, much like when she'd heard Belle disclosing her past on guard for *Amalie*.

Davina's words itched at her mind again. They were here for Kai's attention. To be the woman the alpha chose to take as his mate or to be…*the one*.

That magic spark.

Isla shocked herself as she snarled and fought the urge to start waving her arms around, telling them all to go home.

Thankfully, Eli managed to break her focus with his never-ending remarks.

She felt him nudge her with his elbow. "A little excessive, don't you think?"

He'd said it as a joke. As if it wouldn't have taken her several moments to recall his comments from weeks ago. About Kai and his killing of four bak being *a bit much*.

He'd gestured to the heightened guard presence within the underpass leading to the banquet's entrance, and the fact they'd been waiting in this line for so long was for security reasons. To be checked out, inspected, and cleared by name and invitation. With so many guests—and so many gate-crashers—it was taking quite a while to get through.

"Necessary," she said, grateful for the protection Kai had.

"General."

At the voice from behind them, Isla felt the hair of her neck stand on end. She turned slowly.

"Beta Ezekiel." Eli beamed, reaching forward to shake Ezekiel's hand. Immediately, he nodded toward Isla. "I'm happy we crossed paths. This is Isla, the recruit I was telling you about."

When Ezekiel's worn eyes fell upon her, she bit down hard on her tongue, resisting her urge to snap.

The last she'd seen him, she'd threatened him, more or less. Told him that he had better hope she never ended up in Deimos to claim what was rightfully hers. That she wouldn't be here, his queen, to make him get down on his knees and bow to her. He'd called her brazen and stubborn and proud. He'd called her insolent and dim-witted. He'd said she wasn't right to sit at the helm of his pack…and he was right about some of it, but he was also rude as all hell.

Though she could easily pretend he'd just told her he was shipping her off to a safe house so she could just kick his ass right here, she flashed him a soft grin. So pure, so fake. Ameera would surely love it.

She could see it now, where the female general and her beta father shared their looks—the hair, the eyes, the arrogant scowl.

Ezekiel didn't smile back—Isla hadn't expected him to. He simply said, *"Warrior,"* before turning back to Eli. "Delta Sol would like to reconvene with you. He's on the veranda between the Western Hall and the House."

Western Hall and House.

Isla noted the names as Eli asked, "What for?"

"Wouldn't say," the beta said. "But it sounded urgent."

"Odd." Eli furrowed his brows. "I'll have to clear this line first."

Ezekiel reached into his pocket and pulled out a stamped placard. "Just give them this. They'll let you through." The general took it before his eyes shifted to Isla. Ezekiel caught on and added, "I'll escort her in."

Eli had no words of protest, eager to escape the waiting. "I'll see you inside," he told her with the smallest touch, and he was off.

As he walked away, now beside her, Ezekiel snickered. Isla wondered if Sol *truly* wanted to meet with the general at all, or if this had all been a ploy to get her alone.

"Aren't you two close," Ezekiel said to her once he turned back to face her. He'd noticed the caress.

"It's nothing like that," Isla said pointedly.

Ezekiel hummed, not offering a rebuttal. "Come with me."

She didn't want to—but she didn't really feel like waiting in the line anymore. Not as the number of women by the barricade increased. Not as she had to watch them preen themselves. See their beautiful faces. Be reminded that they all knew this pack better than she ever would.

"Hide your face," Ezekiel said as they moved along the line by some reporters and photographers that were *approved* to be at the banquet. To capture the moments.

Isla didn't want her time here immortalized, so she did so, using the lightweight black shawl Davina had offered just before they left to cover herself.

At the end of the line, the cusp of the courtyard, they approached a woman running over a list of items—written in a large notebook—with one of the guards.

"Marin," Ezekiel said.

As the name rang familiar, Isla examined Kai's secretary. She was short—shorter than Davina who was already quite petite—and her silvery hair was pulled into a tight low bun. But despite the color of her tresses, she appeared relatively young. Couldn't have been more than in her forties or fifties.

"Ezekiel," she greeted hastily, not out of crudeness, but because she seemed in a rush. She didn't bother turning until something—maybe the glint of Isla's jewelry in the underpass lights—caught her eye. She gave Isla a long once-over. "Which one is this?"

Which one?

"None of them," Ezekiel told her. "She's the guest of the warrior general. A warrior herself."

"A warrior," the secretary considered before her teal eyes traced Isla again. Long and calculating. "Bloodline?"

"She's not interested," he said flatly.

"Then what are you badgering me for?" she responded before waving them off.

Ezekiel laughed—so odd to hear—before stepping around Marin and breaking into the party. Isla was on his heels. But before she'd gotten too far, she couldn't stop herself from glancing behind to see what Marin was going through. The list seemed full of many names—female names.

She growled and distracted herself with the wonder of the courtyard again.

Waiters were fluttering about, holding trays of hors d'oeuvres and glasses of different types of drinks—wines, spirits, and cocktails. Davina had told her to have an eye out for an open bar, though. The guests—the entire overwhelming lot of them—seemed cheerful. Seemed to come from all walks of life if she looked and analyzed the fine details of their clothes.

She knew none of them.

"What did she mean by which one?" Isla asked Ezekiel once she caught up to him.

"Our alpha must take a mate," Ezekiel said, ignoring how Isla jerked a bit. "And before we jump to a mating ball, Marin wants to see if we can kick off something a bit more naturally. Less *archaic* in the face of younger, more *progressive* leadership."

That sounded all too political, but Isla got enough of the hint. There were potential brides for Kai here. Handpicked by his secretary, his do-all. The person who kept him sane, organized, and looking exactly as he should in the face of his pack.

"Can you control yourself?"

Isla opened her mouth for a snap retort before she closed it and reconsidered. "What does that mean?"

"You're bold in your stand against the Goddess, but you're also naive. You cannot change the fact that you're a wolf, and therefore, territorial over what's *yours*." His last word had a slight bite to it. "So unless you're here to *claim* it, don't interfere." He looked forward and nodded at a passerby who'd greeted him. "I told him you being here was a bad idea, but he insisted. If it were up to me, you wouldn't have even been approved."

"Good thing it's not up to you then," she said, now not taking time to think.

"Goddess above," Ezekiel cursed under his breath, but it wasn't at her.

He powered forward, and Isla debated ditching him but decided to keep up. He was insufferable but he was familiar. And apparently, she could trust him.

He rested his hand on the back of a woman's shoulders who'd been telling what seemed to be a highly entertaining story to a group of guests.

The woman turned, and Isla found herself stumbling a bit.

Upon the beta's approach, the group disbanded.

"Zahra," Ezekiel said, dropping his hold. "What are you doing out here? You're supposed to enter after Delta Atesh and before Kai."

Zahra.

This was Kai's mother.

The former luna narrowed her gaze, and Isla could see where Kai had drawn his looks from. The strikingness of his eyes, the elegant draw to his face. Zahra was every bit stunning and regal as she'd expected. But to Isla's surprise, her amber skin—just like her son's—wasn't sallow or drawn. Her deep blue-gray eyes not bloodshot from endless crying and sleepless nights. She wasn't hunched over and brittle-boned. From all she'd heard, the former Luna of Deimos was supposedly on her death bed. This woman seemed *vibrant*.

"And I *told you*, that's not my place anymore, Ezekiel."

"Zahra…"

"Beta."

"Ezekiel!"

Ezekiel turned as he was called by yet another person Isla didn't know to meet *someone else* Isla didn't know. He muttered something to Zahra—something like *don't move*—before stalking off. Isla pursed her lips at being left in the dirt and watched as the former queen shook her head and rolled her eyes. The typical actions shouldn't have stunned or amused her as much as they did.

As if she could sense Isla staring, the luna turned and met her gaze.

Isla blinked at her in awe, but Zahra looked at her flatly.

"Another one," she said.

"I'm sorry?"

Zahra sighed. "If one more person looks at me like I'm about to keel over and die, Goddess, help them." Isla felt heat flood her cheeks, and before she could nod in the respect she'd forgotten, the luna scanned her peculiarly. "Have we met?"

"No," Isla answered quicker than she meant to.

The luna did another sweep. "Are you sure?"

"No." Isla felt her nerves ratchet up. This wasn't only a luna, it was her mate's mother. A woman who'd lost nearly everything. What if she said something wrong and stupid? "I mean, yes, *no*, we haven't met, Your Majesty. I'm not from this pack…I'm of Io."

Isla winced, unsure how her pack's name would be taken.

"I no longer warrant that address," the former luna said, and Isla noted the uptick of her brows. "You're far from home."

No detectable animosity, at least.

"I'm a warrior. Here to help with the rogues along with my team." Isla brought back her smile. "Isla."

Zahra mirrored it, in a way much more refined, Isla was sure. "Well, thank you for your service to my pack and your service to my son."

At the last words, Isla choked.

The former luna paused but didn't comment on it. "Now, if you'll excuse me, that appetizer platter is calling my name." Before she departed, she added, "Run while you can."

Isla followed the former luna's eyes to the still-occupied Ezekiel.

She weighed her options—and then she did just that.

∾

Isla found Eli eventually—or he found her—and he immediately began grumbling about how Sol had no idea what he had been going on about.

The banquet technically would not be in full swing until three things occurred: all guests had arrived, the guest of honor finally made his entrance, and then finally, Kai, the alpha, entered the room and declared it should begin. Right now, it was aimless chitter-chatter, eating and drinking, and already, Isla was ready to stab herself in the eye with her tiny toothpick.

Kai's plan had been working. She drew attention—both good and bad. Sneers and smiles. Genuine questions and snide, underhanded remarks. Lecherous leers from unmated suitors. An offer to *get out of here* with one particularly inebriated man that was lucky Kai hadn't appeared yet.

But that wasn't the worst.

She had never heard so many people *brag* about themselves—and Sebastian was her brother. Callan was her ex. At least they didn't try to mask it in some false sense of humility. They knew they were pricks and embraced it.

And not only that but if she had to hear one more rosy whisper of *when will Alpha Kai be arriving* from the mouth of one more female, if she had to listen to the ambitions of *getting a dance* or *being invited to the alpha's chambers* one more time, she would turn feral.

Isla hadn't encountered this before.

She *knew* Kai was an alpha. That a person of his standing had that draw. She'd experienced it all the time, but it was easier to just call it the bond. But she'd never seen it, heard it, *felt it* in a room. All the people that wanted him. To be *with* him or to *be* him.

On the second open of the wide double doors set at the front of the room, Isla went rigid. The guests of the party clapped and cheered as Delta Atesh entered.

The next person to enter would be Kai.

Isla counted every second that passed, half-listening to the man in the group before her. Baron, the farmer turned game trader, had lived in Surles for his entire life until ten years ago when all his crops started dying, so he moved to Ifera. Delta Atesh had been sent on behalf of Alpha Kyran to pay for the profit he'd lost and to buy the land off him. Now, he was as happy as could be with his livestock and hunted deer.

Isla was glad.

Just as she was about to make an excuse to get Eli to walk away or to leave everything of her own accord, the room fell wholly quiet.

Everyone went still.

Isla felt Kai before she saw him. *Everyone* did. He did nothing to mask that "alpha aura" of his. Nothing to hide the strength and power he had above them all.

As the double doors opened again, Isla's breath caught.

She didn't know if it was that general aura, the bond, the relief, or just the genuine attraction to something beautiful, but he looked —ethereal.

And alone.

Isla felt a pang in her chest. Of sadness. Of guilt.

A luna would be at his side in typical circumstances. An heir would've walked in a few minutes before. But he stood alone.

Everyone bowed their heads.

Distracted, Isla's remained up for the slightest second. The tiny bit needed for him to find her. When they locked eyes, she dared to give him a soft smile, barely moving her mouth. He didn't return it. He didn't break his form. The stone expression of a leader. But she *did* feel something. Not an alpha's reach, but something like a caress through the bond. Just for her.

She'd be concerned over what that meant about its *strength* later.

Finally following the suit of everyone else, Isla dipped her head.

But it wasn't before noticing that there'd been someone else who'd remained lifted. A beautiful woman a few yards away, with long, sleek black hair, pulled back by a tiara much more extravagant than Isla's, with jewels of blue that matched her eyes. Her silver gown fit her generous curves like a glove. As she smiled, Isla could only surmise her as Deimos made flesh.

"Thank you all for coming," Kai said, voice loud and assured, filling the room. He'd make a grand speech later in the night after the dinner, but for now, as they all looked up, he told them, "Please, enjoy."

And then the party recommenced.

∼

Before the actual *eating* began, Kai made his rounds, greeting his guests. Isla had a faint idea of where he was in the room. Not only through the bond, but through the way the guests seemed to gravitate towards him. The party grew lopsided when he'd been off to sides and corners. Once again, she had to listen to all the plans, hear all the giggles. A dance, a kiss, finding their way into his bed.

Some had sounded so confident in their chances until they were reminded by their cohorts of a name. One that made Isla's blood boil.

Amalie.

Amalie was here. At this party. *Somewhere.*

"Are you having fun?"

Isla felt a warm hand on her back, felt the gentle brush of a thumb along her skin. She looked up at Eli whose eyes were slightly glazed over from the alcohol he'd consumed. He'd been getting a bit touchier as the night progressed. Enough so that the questions of *is this your mate* became more and more frequent.

Just as Isla was about to pull away from his touch, she felt it. A dark cloud. A sharp tug. She whirled around, enough to escape Eli's hold, and found herself face to face with Kai.

She could confidently say that she had never, *ever* been looked at the way that Kai gazed upon her then. With such intent, ferocity, and hunger. All that power, all that predatory focus honed in on her, on her body. He was stripping her down with his eyes bit by bit. She honestly thought he was about to pick her up, throw her over his shoulder, and take her out of that room. Or maybe clear off the banquet table and have her right there.

And maybe she'd let him, even if *everyone* was watching, though they were pretending not to.

They'd match with their outfits if it weren't for her crimson jewelry. His tailored black suit jacket stitched with, not identical, but similar corded patterns on its lapels. Isla was too distracted by how good he looked to ponder if he'd done it on purpose as a joke for the two of them, a way to get under her skin.

Neither of them was laughing.

Isla bit down hard on the inside of her cheek as she shuffled on her feet, heat rising in her blood, between her legs.

"Alpha!"

Eli, the dumbass when it wasn't battle strategy, none the wiser in his semi-drunken state, stepped forward with his hand outstretched.

For once, Isla was grateful.

Kai, in a snap, appeared to be the picture of coolness, but she still felt it lingering. That tug. That *hold*.

He grabbed the general's forearm. "General."

Eli pulled away and turned to Isla, expecting Kai to take hold of her arm next.

They would do no such thing, but they *would* pretend they hadn't seen each other for over a month.

"Alpha," Isla said, getting a grasp on herself and standing tall.

"Warrior," Kai echoed. He put his hands behind his back as if he had to lock them there. Away from her or to keep from punching Eli who was getting increasingly closer to her side again.

"It's nice to see you," Kai said stiffly, eyes flicking to the general periodically. He gestured to her arm that had once been swathed in heaps of bandages and donned her scars. "You seem to be healing well."

Isla smiled. "I'm back to form."

Kai returned it, excitement and relief flashing in his eyes. "You're able to shift again."

Eli's hand fell to her shoulder and, either from drunkenness or stupidity, caressed down the exposed skin of her back. "You couldn't shift?"

Kai's brows drew into a scowl, and his arms loosened.

Isla felt something shift in the room then. Felt Eli's fingers tense as he swayed and brought his other hand up to rub at his temple. "Oh." He shook his head as if to clear it.

She furrowed her brows, slipping his grip as she assessed if he was okay before looking at Kai. Her mate appeared to shake his head too, and his scowl had become a concerned and confused grimace.

But before she could question anything, a voice, sweet and seductive, emerged from the guests.

"Alpha Kai."

Isla turned and found it was the beautiful woman with the sapphire tiara and matching eyes. Deimos incarnate.

"Amalie."

Isla blamed the way Kai relaxed on the distraction from Eli. *Not* on the presence of the woman before him. Or maybe, somehow, through some odd bond transfer, all his tension had gone straight to Isla's shoulders.

She found her fingers constricting at her sides as she darted her eyes between them. They were a good-looking couple. Murmurs of excitement surrounded the exchange, a few too many pondering if Amalie was to become luna. The perfect fit given her ties to an alpha bloodline and Deimos's strong relationship with its southern neighbor.

"I forgot to mention something in our meeting earlier," Amalie said, not paying Isla any mind, though Isla *knew* she saw her. She noted how the woman's eyes had slid between the similar patterns on Isla's gown and Kai's jacket, signaling not a threat to the alpha-blooded she-wolf, but a challenge. "Do you have time after the festivities tonight to talk again?"

A meeting? After the festivities? That would be nearly midnight. Isla knew nothing good, nothing she'd want could happen during talks after midnight.

Kai glanced briefly at Isla. "I don't, but speak with Marin. She can tell you when I'm free, or you could talk to Ezekiel."

Isla tried to keep her satisfaction at bay, which wasn't hard when it was so overtaken by irritation as Amalie reached for Kai's sleeve.

"Okay." Her delicate fingers brushed over the fabric of his suit jacket. "Is this new?"

Like some kind of twisted gift from the Goddess, Isla spotted Ezekiel then, watching her intently.

Unless she was here to claim Kai as her mate, she shouldn't interfere.

She was going to if she didn't leave that room. She was going to interfere and make a scene and probably ruin everything.

So, she made a haphazard excuse that no one really cared about and walked out.

It wasn't hard to get away. Eli was *just* a bit too drunk and disoriented from whatever had happened to follow her body weaving through the crowd, and Kai, the only person who could *maybe* track her as she'd masked her scent, couldn't rush off without making it obvious. She found herself in the courtyard again and fighting a chill in the air. The shawl she had didn't do much.

Her eyes trailed over the expanse of the stone, hedges, flowers, and grass, and then over the doors of the multiple buildings. It was possible that she'd get in trouble for it, but she went for the one that caught her attention most, the fourth door of the Eastern Hall, and walked through it. From there, she found some stairs and walked up those, too. She ended in one of the suspended hallways, the one that connected the East and the North.

She could see down into the city from one of the windows here. Nearly all of it if she craned her neck enough. For a minute, she almost felt like she was home again. In Io. In her apartment window, watching the bright lights of the Imperial City gleam against its gold. Maybe she'd try calling tomorrow—Adrien, Sebastian, or her dad. She'd just need to find a long-distance service that would reach them, and then hope one of them was home to pick up.

She remained like that, staring out the window and drawing patterns over the stone's edge for nearly twenty minutes before that pull came.

Not the alpha.

Just Kai.

"You're never going to change, are you?" His voice had come from a different angle than the one she'd climbed from. He knew this hall, obviously. He must've gone a faster way. One that didn't venture through the cold courtyard.

She glanced at him and then back down at the city. "You should be thankful I left."

"And why is that?"

She rolled her eyes at his smugness. There was no point in hiding, she knew he could feel it.

"If you were ready to *kill* a man when there was *no chance* of anything happening between us, I can have feelings about someone you apparently have quite a history with and know *very* intimately."

Kai stopped a few feet away. "Who told you about Amalie?"

"It doesn't matter," she said, turning to face him now. "Why did you meet with her?" She narrowed her eyes as if daring him to utter the words *"pack business"*.

"It's really something that wouldn't interest you. Unless you care about the state of our trade with Mimas."

"I could."

She didn't.

Crossing her arms, Isla lifted herself from the window and paced a few steps away. She didn't know if she could go back there. Do this. Watch Kai dance with and entertain all of these—

"You look beautiful."

Isla froze, her heart stumbling a beat. She spun to examine his face. The words had been nearly breathless.

"Davina is a miracle worker," she joked before gesturing down to her gown, the jewels. "And you have good taste."

Kai laughed. "I really didn't think it through."

"How so?"

"All I can think when I look at you, all I can think when I'm down there, is what I would do if it weren't for the bond."

Isla felt that tether tremble, just the slightest bit. Felt a cruel rise beneath her skin. She bit down on her lip.

"Like what?"

"What?"

"What would you do if it weren't for the bond?" Her voice was as silken as the fabric upon her skin. "Tell me."

Kai's brows raised, a challenge, and Isla swore uncertainty crossed his face. They hadn't played this game in a while. It was dangerous. So, so dangerous.

But she didn't care.

It had been *so long* since she'd been taken to bed. So long since she'd been able to feel...this. The heat, the need, the want without the nagging of wrongness in the back of her mind. She'd take advantage of what lay between them. What he did to her. Just for this moment. She'd embrace the tension, the pull. Let it drag her deeper and deeper into the chasm it was. She'd worry about the consequences later.

Kai, bless the Goddess, seemed to think the same.

He took one step.

Then another.

Isla's breath hitched as she moved backward until she collided with the stone wall. The coolness on her exposed back and arms did little to put a damper on the fire torching her skin.

She watched as Kai's throat bobbed and resisted the urge to lean forward and run her lips over the column of his neck. Where *she* would make *her* mark on him. Maybe that was another reason she'd craved this. To make a point to those who would never see. A selfish, stupid point. The alpha was hers—even if he wasn't.

Kai braced his arms on either side of her head, trapping her in. He felt so much bigger than her like this, and her senses were flooded with all of him there was. She had nowhere to go. No way to escape without touching him.

Kai drew a long, considerate stare up her body, snagging between her breasts, and Isla could see as his mind worked while he devised what to say. What mattered. As if he'd thought about it frequently and didn't want to bother her with the extraneous details.

"Maybe I wouldn't take off the dress," he pondered in a gruff whisper. "Or the diamonds."

Her insides grew molten as she trailed her eyes over his face, his mouth, but she played it coy. "No?"

"No—waste of time."

Isla swallowed, and Kai clocked the movement. "So, you'd just have me like this then? Right here."

Kai shook his head, his mouth twitching up again as he leaned forward a fraction of an inch. "I'd get on my knees first—*only for you*—and see how ready you were for me. Feel it…taste it. I can already scent it off you."

Isla squeezed her thighs together, her heart slamming in her chest. The thought of his head buried between her legs. Of feeling his stubble scratching along her skin. Of his hands, his lips, his tongue…

"And then?" She struggled to keep her voice full.

"Then." Kai leaned closer, and she craned her neck. Baring it to him. "Then after I had you begging me to fuck you, I'd bring you to the window, so you could look out at what's yours while I take you from behind."

She couldn't pay mind to what his words truly alluded to—her, the queen of this kingdom. She was too wrapped in the idea of his fingers digging into her hips, fisted in her hair. Of his breath on the back of her neck, his teeth grazing her skin as he drove into her. As she tried her hardest not to cry out. Not to let anyone hear what they were doing. Again, again—

"I don't beg."

"You would."

Isla almost whined when he moved closer.

"We wouldn't go back to the ballroom after that."

"What about dinner?"

Kai smirked, and she knew where his mind had gone without him saying it.

As he continued, he mimicked that tone she'd used on him oh so long ago. Letting her savor in the words, the images they brought. "I'd want to take my time with you next. Peel off that dress and map every inch of you with my tongue. Then I'd take you again. Slower…deeper. And then again. Harder, against the wall. And then I'd have you ride me."

Isla felt her core throb with each word, slickness building between her thighs.

Everything ached. Her breasts felt heavy, pebbled, and pained against the fabric of her gown. Her knees were about to give out. Her hips arched forward—dangerously close. Waiting. Wanting. Eager.

Her self-restraint was dwindling.

Even still, she hummed a laugh. But it took nearly everything in her not to whimper. "You really want me on top, huh?"

"I can think of no better view."

Isla was desperate for any friction, rubbing her legs in a way that gave just the right pressure. But not enough. She wanted more. Needed more.

"Kai."

His name off her lips, breathless, made him shudder. Made him move in a way that Isla wondered…

She dared a look down, not moving her head, only her eyes, to find him hard and straining against his pants. Her fingers twitched, and her mouth went dry as she greedily traced the shape of him. The thought of him inside her…

"Isla."

She looked back up. His eyes were endless depths of a stormy night, and she imagined the crystal blue had vanished from hers, too.

He leaned in again, and Isla was about to scream, she could hardly stand it.

Maybe she would beg. Just for him to *touch her*, for Goddess's sake. Forget fucking her senseless. That would come later. Right now, she just wanted to feel his skin against her own, have the taste of him on her mouth.

One. More. Fraction.

He moved the closest he could ever get without throwing all their efforts away.

"I am the keeper of a burden I was never meant to bear," he began, speaking near her collarbone, sending hot breath along it and up her neck as he continued up to her ear. "But resisting you, all this time may be the truest test the Goddess has given me."

Isla couldn't breathe. Couldn't *think* about anything else.

She pressed her head to the wall and turned to look him in the eyes again. He was so close. *So* close. Her fingers constricted around the fabric of her gown. So, she wouldn't reach. Wouldn't touch…

She drove her hips backward.

No. *No.*

But, *Goddess,* he was…

Just as she was about to brashly throw caution to the wind and propel forward, abandon Kai's plans and just take *him,* right there on the floor, the sound of a closing door echoed from far down the hallway.

He pushed off the wall and stepped back, and Isla let out a soft gasp like she'd been drowning. As he focused down the corridor, she brought a hand to her chest, feeling her heart thrumming wildly beneath the ruby pendant.

"Maids," Kai said, turning back around.

"Do you think they saw us?" Isla asked. "Or…heard us?"

Oh, Goddess.

"Maybe saw us—but they don't know who you are. It will be enough for the staff to gossip, but it won't go far. No reporting for the columns."

"Okay," Isla breathed. "We should get back."

"Wait." Kai held up a hand. "Maybe we should take a walk first, and then we can debrief on what you've heard."

"Aren't they wondering where you are?"

"I told them I needed to step away for a while. No one will miss me—and no one will want to deal with me if I don't take a walk. Especially if you're still in that ballroom."

Isla coughed and smoothed her dress. Judging by how flushed they both were, by the outline of him she was trying her hardest not to look down at, and by how dazed she still was—still drunk on him, on her thoughts—a walk with some fresh air may have been a good idea.

"Where do you want to go?"

Kai shoved his hands in his pockets, pulling them outward a bit, maybe trying to get some relief. He glanced up. "I want to show you something."

CHAPTER 25

"I'm not going in there."

The declaration that fell from Isla's lips was met by the flattening of Kai's brows. The alpha leaned against the edge of the opening he'd revealed behind a thick tapestry and hidden door in one of the sitting rooms of the Front Hall. "You're a *warrior*, right?"

Isla met his with an equally deadpan expression and nodded forward. "What even is this?"

They stood before an empty...was it a hallway?

Isla could barely tell with how dark it was. Only faint crystal buried in the drab stone walls were present to light what was a shoddy path. The musty scent and slightest chill had smacked her in the face the second Kai had exposed it. She didn't know where it led, what it connected to.

They'd gone down a plethora of corridors to get to this point, turning various corners, and up two more flights of stairs. Though Kai was the alpha and could technically do whatever he wanted and not dare be questioned, they tried their hardest not to get caught. The long walk, along with the spike of adrenaline in avoiding lurking guards or working staff, provided a decent distraction from their *talk*.

Kai blew out a breath. "Do you trust me?"

"Enough that I know the quality of your life hinges on the preservation of mine."

"That's a yes." He gestured to the opening again. "After you, *my gift*."

Isla rolled her eyes at the endearment. "Why can't you go first?" Kai gestured again wordlessly, and she glowered, offering over her shoulder, "You just want to stare at my ass."

Kai didn't deny it.

With his laugh echoing behind her, Isla entered the cavern. The click of her heels and the hush of her breath reverberated off the walls as she moved forward through it. *Step, step, step.* She shivered, hearing the heavy wood of the hidden door fall back into place.

"Kai, I swear to the—"

"Just keep going, Warrior."

Grumbling, Isla lifted her hand and flipped him off.

His chuckling continued.

She could sense him trailing behind her, could hear his heavy steps until they eventually reached an opening that sat before a set of stone stairs. They were narrow, nearly a foot high, and splattered like paint with the same crystals of the wall. Isla leaned forward to find where they ended, but they were so closed in, they just seemed to spiral on and on to Goddess knew where.

She opened her mouth to protest, but then closed it.

One step, then another, then another. Up and up and up. Around and around and around.

A chorus of their breath and the hits of their shoes was all Isla could hear as they continued for what felt like an eternity on her legs, her feet, and her stability. The circles were making her unbelievably dizzy—especially when she sped up after feeling the need to prove a point following Kai's jeer of how slow she was—and eventually, she'd halted them to take off her shoes.

Her body was coated in a light sheen of sweat—and she wasn't sure how that boded for the silk of her dress—but she was grateful for the exercise. Just another way to redirect any of the leftover tension.

At last, they reached a large oak door. Steadying her breath, Isla traced her eyes along the inscriptions on its surface—the two wolves and the orb. She hesitated before running her hand over it, and then, without prompting from Kai, she pushed. The force needed was much more than she'd expected, the muscles in one arm straining enough that she used a second.

A gasp fell from her mouth as she stepped inside, but it wasn't for the furniture—a large mahogany desk, some chairs, bookshelves, an old dry bar, and easels with maps, slightly covered by cloth and dust—or for the high sloped ceiling that dissipated into blackness. It was the pool of color that would've engulfed everything if the pieces had been set further into the room. A cast of rich, deep purples and arrays of blues that seemed to ripple on the wooden floor.

The stained-glass window. The eye of the beast.

No wonder there had been so many stairs.

It only took a few patters of her footsteps for Isla to find herself bathed in the hues. She'd stopped right at the cusp of the window's shadow, taking in its glory, her eyes wide with wonder. She felt a strain as she lifted her head to catch sight of all of it.

"Goddess," Isla breathed, and she felt it. In the way the moonbeams amidst the color fed through the glass, she felt kissed by something divine. She looked around the room. "What is this place?"

She didn't turn to Kai but could hear him closing the door and moving towards her. He was so proud, reveling in her awe, she could practically feel it through their jilted bond. "My great, great, great, great..." He trailed off before simply saying, "My ancestor's study."

A study all the way up here?

"Which one?" she asked, bringing her eyes back to the window.

"Alpha Orin, I think. At least, that's what I found on some papers in the desk. They're written in our native dialect, so I can only pick out his name. I wish I'd paid more attention to those lessons in the academy." Kai walked by Isla to the window, and she found herself becoming entranced by the way his shadow danced amongst the colors. "I've been meaning to get some references in our library to figure out what it says —for my own curiosity—but I barely have the time."

"You have a library here?" she asked, excitement edging her voice.

Kai placed a hand on the glass. "Of course, we do. Not for public use, just for the alpha's estate and our council members." He ran his fingers on the metal panes of the window before pressing flatly on them. There was a click and then a whine as the glass loosened and freed. A whip of cool breeze moved through the space.

"Come on," he beckoned. "This is what I really wanted to show you."

Isla bit the inside of her lip. She wanted to tell Kai to wait. Wanted to tell him to forget whatever this was and get her down to the library. The private property of the alpha surely possessed knowledge not available in a local bookshop, right?

But the opening from the window had created a clear path for her like it was presenting whatever lay on the other side. Tempting and inviting.

Hesitantly, she walked along it, and as if she knew what was about to greet her would steal her breath away, she wouldn't look up until she'd stepped over the shallow edge of stained glass rising from the floor and onto a small stone balcony.

And when she finally let her eyes behold what was before her, she nearly fell over.

She was one with the mountains, on top of the world as she looked upon the entire city of Mavec rolling down hills to its faint glow of star-fallen streets. The river was an inky-black passage leading to tiny dots like the flicker of the eyes of beasts in the forest at its end. Surely, it was Abalys. Isla scoured for what she knew. The top of the hotel. The Bookshoppe. Any of the stores and squares she'd desired to visit. From here, she discovered game parks she'd never crossed. Some open fields. The train that shot through another mountain to get to Ifera.

She moved back and forth along the balcony, her eyes hungry to take in everything she could, barely blinking as if it all would disappear if she closed them.

She didn't know how to speak. What to say. How to say it. What to ask.

As she stammered over her words in an almost embarrassing fashion, she could sense Kai watching her. Could see him moving in her periphery to remove his suit jacket. She hadn't even realized she'd been shivering—the air even more frigid so high up—until its warmth enveloped her. She couldn't get *thank you* to even escape her mouth, only one simple word that seemed to be the only one she could use to describe this place. "Beautiful."

Kai hummed in agreement, but his eyes never left her.

She moved to the railing, a black metal that leveled off at her chest, and placed her hands upon it as she looked down. She mapped the path they'd traveled to get to the hall. Along the lamp posts, beneath the archway. All the spectators had departed now, and all the cars of the guests had been left parked and waiting to be reclaimed. Guards hung about, two of the half dozen sparring while the others watched and chortled, surely having placed bets.

"So, what do you have for me?"

Isla turned to Kai who'd since paced backwards to lean against the thick glass of the window. He'd surely been up here many times and wasn't nearly as enthralled by the view.

"Your pack tends towards intense vanity, for one," Isla said, sliding her arms into the too-long sleeves of the jacket, feeling the slick material that lined the inside, then subtly breathing in the scent of him that it held.

Kai snickered. "That's rich coming from the member of a pack that deems itself *Imperial*."

Though it had been a joke, Isla couldn't help but catch a biting undercurrent to it.

She pursed her lips but didn't comment on it. Instead, she crossed her arms. "My presence was really a hit or miss. People either wanted nothing to do with me or were courteous enough to ask questions and entertain conversations. A lot of people asked if I was the general's mate."

Her mention of retribution for the dig at Io was met by the unamused reaction she'd expected.

Kai began rolling up the sleeves of his dark dress shirt—somehow not freezing—stopping them just at his elbows. Isla's eyes honed in on the ink that cut a bit over one of his forearms that she'd never noticed before. The patterns of the tattoo didn't look like those of any lumerosi she'd seen.

"Who fell in what category?"

She flicked her gaze back to Kai's, and then began rattling off names —at least those she could remember—and then covered the rest with very vague descriptions. By the time she'd gone through each of her accounts, through every detail she picked up, big or small, she felt winded. But Kai had listened to every word, eyes focused on the ground, brows drawn, and jaw clenched. Isla had tried to mark every twitch of any muscle to glean what mattered most and what didn't, but her mate was unreadable.

Except for the fact that he *knew* what he'd wanted to hear.

"You know what you're looking for," she said. "What is it? Why am I here?"

Kai looked up and adjusted himself against the glass. He shoved his hands in his pockets, a picture of aloofness. "I just want to see how members of my pack act toward those of others. Seeing how much they're willing to say. What they say. We don't get visitors often, you know."

Isla didn't buy it.

"And how does that help you figure out who you can trust on your council?"

Kai pushed himself up. "You said it yourself, Delta Croan doesn't like my push to funnel more resources into re-evaluating the Wall. My Head of Trade wants more say in what can be distributed—even if she has all control besides the need for my approvals. If they're willing to share that around you, who knows what else they'll say?"

More bullshit.

He wouldn't have her here for spats of trade and resources. Back in Callisto, he'd wanted to keep her as far away from Deimos and its higher-ups as possible because he feared their lives at risk.

But instead of going right at him to cut out the act, part of her wanted to wrench it out of him, to catch him off-guard.

"Why do you want to look at the Wall?" she asked.

Kai leaned on the railing beside her. For a split second, a grimace crossed his face. "Because it borders my territory—more than any other on this continent—and if wards are failing, if the bak are acting strange, I need to make sure my pack is safe."

At the reminder of the bak and the great structure that caged them, Isla found her gaze drawing outward. She'd forgotten which direction Surles—the region of Deimos that harbored its border with Phobos—lay, but she narrowed her eyes at the distance as if she could see the behemoth rising from where she stood.

There was so much that she wanted to tell him. That she needed to get off her chest from her time in Callisto. About the word she'd heard, about the Ares Pass, about the marker and the book, about—

"Someone tried to have me killed," Isla blurted before she could stop herself.

Kai whipped around to face her, eyes wide and face twisted in a mix of confusion and budding rage. "Someone *what*?"

Isla took a breath, trailing her tongue over her bottom lip as she quickly ran through the best way to divulge the information. "Back in Callisto after you left, Lukas, he—"

"Lukas?" Kai stood; his fists clenched at his sides. "The hunter from Tethys?"

"Yes," she said softly in a futile attempt to ease him. "I went to see him—*after* the few hours you'd asked for—and he had a dagger with him. Someone had given it to him and told...told him to kill me. That they'd let him out if he did. It's fine now. I'm okay. I got away."

Kai paced away from her, and Isla could practically feel him on the edge of a shift. She wasn't sure if it was a consequence of what had occurred in the hall getting in the way—the bond tighter, stronger—but she felt her own body start to react.

"I felt something that day," he growled. "But I thought it was just from the bond and being away from you. I should have never left."

"You needed to be here with your pack," she said, still trying to abate him.

"I needed to be with you." He raked a hand over his hair. "Where is he now?"

Fury still tinged his voice.

"You're not going to try—"

"Isla, *where is he now?*"

She swore the faintest hint of red fought over the gray of his eyes.

"In a prison in Io," she told him, stepping towards him and finding her hand reaching out, just like in Callisto as they stood before the message. A phantom touch. A reminder. She was here. She was safe. Everything was fine.

But Kai had stepped back, his face contorting as if that had bothered him more than anything else. "Why would he be taken to Io? An attempt on another's life warrants trial within one's home pack—or the one it occurred in."

"Because he still doesn't remember anything," Isla said, trying to keep her own aggravation out of her voice so as not to feed his as she explained, "And the Imperial Alpha doesn't want anyone else knowing what happened during the Hunt. I thought you knew that."

"I do, believe me," Kai said through gritted teeth. Then he went quiet, pensive. "Who was still in Callisto when he attacked you?"

Isla swallowed and forced her shoulders to rise and fall. "My family, Adrien, some other members of my pack, other packs, nurses…I don't know. People. Why?"

"*Which* members of your pack?"

Isla blinked, something in her gut twisting. Which members of her pack…why did that matter?

She angled her head, asking slowly, "Why do you want to know?"

Kai didn't answer right away which was enough time for Isla's mind to contemplate the possibility that had been lingering just out of reach and out of sight since it had happened, not acknowledged. "You…do you think it was someone of my *pack* that tried to have me killed?" More silence. Isla scoffed and moved back. "Are you insane? That—that's my pack, that's my family. Why would they want me dead?"

But Kai didn't need to answer.

The pieces began to come together, despite how much she fought against them. Despite how she mentally clawed at the figments to destroy them before they came to be. Her chest felt tight like it was about to cave in.

Kai didn't trust his council. Thought ill of their intentions for him. Had wanted to keep her away and keep her safe—*them both* safe—for that reason.

But now she was here despite that fact. Because she deserved it, maybe, but there was something else.

She wasn't his spy. She was bait. The woman of Io, the daughter of a high-ranking member within a hierarchy that certainly had a history of questionable actions in its past. Actions that seemed far more farfetched than conspiring to kill an alpha and heir to maintain its order.

But why?

Something had changed since Kai had come back. Something that led him to believe that Io was responsible for what had happened to his father and brother. Which meant, in his eyes, her pack thought so little of her that she was an expendable means to an end.

Isla felt a sting at the corners of her eyes, and she backed away from him until she hit the railing. With only a glance, she could catch the sympathy on Kai's face like he could hear her every thought as she descended the hellish hole to her conclusions.

"Isla," he said gently, reluctantly. He hadn't wanted her to know. For her own sake or his?

She shook her head. "No."

"Isla."

"No." More forceful now. "No, you're wrong."

She heard him step forward. "Isla."

Grinding her teeth to hold back a scream, Isla lifted her head. "*Kai*." It was a mix of desperation and anger. "You have to be wrong."

Even closer. She was nearly trapped by him again, but he didn't extend his arms. He just stayed and waited, silent until he opened his mouth—and then looked away. "What is that?"

Isla spun, careful not to touch him, and followed his line of sight to the horde of vehicles barreling up the drive towards the hall.

"The gates should've been closed," Kai said, retreating from her.

As Isla turned fully to face the streets, the cars came to a screeching halt. Doors on either side, doors in the back, flew open. Out of them, poured over three dozen wolves—from those in full shifts to those baring claws and teeth and weapons in hand. Even from so high up above, their pungent stench made her stomach curdle.

"Rogues," Isla choked, and Kai said nothing.

He'd already set off back through the entryway to the room and to the stairs. Down below, Isla heard a rogue's howl and the squelching scream of a fallen guard before she followed right behind him.

Down, down, down.

They were so far away from the party. They had too long to go.

Around, around, around.

There were guards. A lot of guards. Everything would be fine. They could handle them.

Don't fall, don't fall, don't fall.

Isla felt nauseous and dizzy by the time they reached the bottom of the stairs, but she pressed forward, urged by the screams of the banquet, so loud they carried even in the dank, hidden space.

Kai was much faster than she was, and she nearly lost him a few times as they curved through the halls, riddled with cowering staff members and guards charging towards the western building. Through the windows they had shot past on their run through the connecting passages, Isla could see the courtyard in pandemonium, could practically smell the putrid odor of rogues, blood, and fear in the air.

How had they gotten into Mavec? How had they gotten all the way up to the hall?

Maybe it was the sight or scent that had struck him, but Kai had slowed enough to stick by her. And with a glance her way, she knew the plan. They'd shift the second they stepped outside and take down whoever they could.

As they broke out into the courtyard, Isla took a few moments of pause and surveyed the scene to ensure it was safe to leave herself vulnerable for those small seconds.

But it was moments too long.

Isla let out a yelp as she was pushed by a fleeing guest. She stumbled back, flailing to stay upright, waiting to meet the unforgiving ground, just about to go into a shift before she hit it.

But she couldn't.

Because she'd collided with something.

And though the surface she'd met was solid…it wasn't a wall.

Walls didn't have hands. Didn't grip tight.

One thought.

Only one thought rolled through her mind.

One word that reeled over and over and over again as her wolf writhed within her. As her blood rushed and fire erupted over her skin, through her body.

Mate.

PART III
THE BECK OF BONDS

CHAPTER 26

Isla straightened against the warmth, against planes of solid muscle. The heat gave way to a chill and then fire again as she felt the hold on her loosen and then constrict. As she felt calloused fingertips run over the skin of her hip, slipping under the slit of her dress, finding the lace lining of her underwear cutting over her thigh. Tracing it. Another hand sat at her waist, palm spanning across the rise and fall of her stomach, the exposed skin there, thumb raising to stroke just below the curve of her breast.

Kai held her like she'd vanish if he let her go, and Isla's body yielded to him. Every curve melding to every bend of his. His heart thundered against her back, through the fabric of his jacket which she still adorned until, with each passing beat, hers found the same rhythm. Intertwined and in time.

Mate, mate, mate.

"Isla." Kai's breath was hot on her neck as he dipped his head into the cradle of her shoulder.

She shuddered. His voice—desperate, aching, fighting—cut through the repetitions like a mind-numbing melody.

Mine, mine, mine.

Just as she was about to allow her head to fall back into his chest—to crane and expose the space meant just for him—clarity rang like a bell in the form of horrified screams.

Rogues.

They were surrounded by rogues.

Being attacked by rogues.

People needed help.

Isla forced herself to rise. To turn and meet Kai's eyes.

She choked down a breath.

It was as if she were seeing him for the very first time. As if, now that they'd touched—now that she knew the feeling of his body against her own—she'd met him all over again.

And he was familiar—*something* was familiar. From a time before Callisto, before the terrace and the garden.

Touch me, her body screamed as the initial rush—not wholly faded—began swelling like a wave ready to crash and wash her away. As it consumed the surroundings again, threatening to drown them out. *Touch me, touch me, touch*—

"Alpha!"

The cry came from a distance.

Both Isla and Kai—mildly dazed, chests rising and falling in the same heavy cadence—whipped around to find a man powering from the masses towards them. The movement seemed to take every bit of the older guest's energy. Isla searched his worn glassy eyes for anything she'd recognize, but there was nothing. Nothing but terror, denial, and —grief.

Broken—he seemed broken.

She listened with cracks forming in her chest as he explained how he couldn't find his wife amongst the chaos. His mate. No matter how much he called, she wouldn't call back. He couldn't feel her there. The only thing left at the end of their bond was emptiness.

Isla knew what that meant—knew the man did too—but he couldn't face it alone. Didn't want to. In his shoes, she wouldn't either.

Her gaze drifted to Kai. Through their own connection, she could sense rage and sorrow stirring within him. Though the emotions were also written clearly on his face. She wondered how much of it felt personal. Especially now. Now that they'd...

Goddess—what had just happened?

"I'll help you find her," Kai told him before turning to Isla.

Her heart wrenched.

"I'll do what I can," she said, eyes flicking between them. She didn't know if Kai wanted her to remain by his side—she didn't know if *she* wanted to remain by his side—but she knew what she needed to do in order to be the most effective. To aid more people. If she'd learned anything from Lukas and the Hunt.

She turned to shift and descend into the mayhem, but then gasped as she felt the warmth of a hand around hers.

Swallowing thickly, she spun back to Kai, sensing those golden workings of her, not caressed by, but *weaving* with those of darkness. Drawn taut and ready to be strummed and played along like an aria among them.

Mate.

She expected him to tell her no. Tell her to stay with him. For them to waste time in a spat about it. But he didn't.

A reluctance and worry shone in Kai's eyes as he told her in parting, "See if you can find my mother."

He let her go. He knew he had to. For the safety of his people in attendance, he needed her out there, doing what she was here to do: protect his pack. They had to put themselves aside, whatever lay between them aside, for all else.

Isla nodded. "I will."

And squandering no more precious seconds amidst the cruel backdrop, they both went on to shift, their fine clothes left as tattered fabric and Isla's jewelry clattering to the courtyard stone.

As she came down on her paws, shaking out her fur, senses sharp and honed in on the scent of blood—of the injured, of the dead—and the ghastly stench of rogues, Isla turned to her mate once more. Crimson eyes met hers—the soft hue of white-blue—appearing menacing and lethal, but Isla could find Kai beneath. Could feel the lingering essence of him that rang in time with her.

In a fleeting moment, he stepped to her, and Isla savored in the closeness before they headed off in separate, equally perilous directions. Their final exchange, his voice, echoed in the back of her head.

"Be careful."

"You too."

Not fully formed but nowhere near close to being broken, the bond seemed even more volatile now than it ever had before. As the distance grew between them, Isla felt the twisting slow, but it didn't stop, and yet at the same time, it continued to break away and fall apart.

She was all out of sorts—powered by adrenaline, anger, fear, but distracted and mystified by something otherworldly going on inside that she couldn't put words to. And though now was certainly *not* the time for her to be discovering the inner machinations of a soulmate, she couldn't keep her mind from drifting.

Form and break. Spin and fall. One connection, then two—but then none. Isla was both aware and unaware of where Kai stalked in relation to where she was—sensing him as the alpha, but also led by that tether to her mate.

Her mate…
Goddess.
Focus.
The rogues had targeted the ballroom.

Isla kept her muscles both tight and loose as she weaved through the bodies of the frenzied guests, clocking the wounded being dragged to safe corners to be tended to, silently praying for those unmoving on the stone to only be unconscious. Her stomach lurched at the thought of what that man was about to endure.

Focus.

Compared to those who were members of a pack, rogues bore little difference in appearance, in their human forms *and* in their shifts. It was their unkemptness that made the intruders stand out—their mangy fur, scarcely-fed bodies, or distinct scent—but they were easily lost amongst the ruckus. The guard was working two-fold to maintain order. Most stood off to the side—in the ballroom and out in the courtyard—to keep the hall entries blocked and protected, eyes scanning the chaos from their posts. If a rogue somehow got through to those many, many corridors—to the many rooms, many hiding places—then Goddess knew what could happen.

The rest of the guard amidst the crowd was split again, some guiding guests to safety while others tried to deal with the rogues. Isla, better skilled in the offensive rather than the defensive, decided she'd help the latter first.

But taking on too much would overwhelm her and lead to more getting hurt, more death. No matter how many rogues she'd taken heed of around her, she needed to deal with one at a time.

Focus.
Calm.
Move swiftly and calculate strikes.
Don't waste energy.
They're wild and untamed—like the bak, but much smaller.
Yet somehow, more unpredictable.

She went first for the shifted male encroaching on a woman—one who she'd heard doting on Kai earlier in the evening. Her red dress had been torn, surely by the rogue's claws that had also scraped the flesh of her pale legs. The injury had her stumbling, falling back to the floor. Isla moved quickly as he postured himself to lunge at her with his open maw, canines ready to embed in flesh. She met him with her body, solid and sending him back into a cocktail table. The abandoned glasses on it crashed to the ground and the fragments glittered on the marble amidst the blood that had dribbled from the woman's wound.

As soon as there was space, Isla barked at her to run. She was slow to get up, and Isla would've carried her away if the rogue hadn't risen too. She snarled as he returned to his paws, taking note of his eyes. Dim. Same with the lumerosi crossing over his chest. The glow of the moon, the Goddess, amiss. As if the deity no longer held his hand. No longer guided him. His morals, his principles.

"*Warrior bitch,*" he growled, catching the mark on her back, and then lunged again. Fast. Ready to rip her apart.

But Isla was quicker—much quicker—undercutting and clamping her jaws around his throat.

She didn't think.

Her instincts—her wolf—took over.

Isla pulled and blood sprayed, coating her tawny fur in a dark crimson.

The rogue could only let out a whimper before he was a lifeless heap on the floor.

Isla padded backwards, blinking, trying to will away the taste in her mouth—metallic and bitter—as she took in the corpse.

She'd just killed a man. Not a bak, not simply a rogue, but another *person.*

Murderer.

The rasped word slithered into her mind.

Murderer, murderer—

Another rogue caught her attention.

This one couldn't shift, not fully. He had his claws and some sort of wooden plank laden with spikes—short, but enough to cause damage, especially for the many here without wolves. The rogue didn't seem to have any target in mind, swinging the weapon as he pleased, connecting with a few guests, and sending them down screaming.

Isla's mind pivoted from the body on the floor, from the word repeating in her mind, as she bounded towards her new target. The rogue had noticed her at the last moment and swung, missing wide as she ducked and then weaved away from the next barrage of attempts.

Easy prey rose beside the rogue in one of his initially hit, injured victims. But before he could deliver a killing blow to the man who couldn't have been any older than Isla, she threw herself in the path. A yelp slipped her maw as the spike pierced her skin through her fur, drawing warm blood.

There was a sharp tug at the bond.

"*Isla!*"

Kai's voice made her pause and glance around in a way that nearly got her hit again.

"*I'm fine,*" she told Kai, and with a new surge of adrenaline, unleashed hell on the rogue, delivering the final blow in seconds. She felt the slightest ease at the other end of the tether, yet at the same time, felt it coil, felt it mold.

Kai had gone silent, but she couldn't think about it, couldn't question it.

She wouldn't look back at the second dead rogue as she allowed the fallen man and the others who'd been attacked to use her fur and body to clamber to their feet. She helped them quickly get a woman too injured to walk to some of the guards at one of the hall's doors.

Isla, smattered in blood, was greeted by swords before they'd realized what was happening. Their vengeful stares turned perplexed, and concerned, as she wasn't recognizable to them. But still, for her help, they bowed their heads in gratitude—and maybe respect.

She mirrored the action and turned.

Next.

Isla found her next target and made quick work. Helped who she needed to. Moved on.

And on. And on.

Protect, protect, protect—a single thought, a single word looped in her mind. Protect her mate, protect his people. She became a force of nature in the fray. A beast feared and sought after in the crowd. It was as if something had taken over her body. Never in her life had she ever felt so much…power.

When the ballroom had settled to a degree that the guards left their posts by the exits, Isla ventured out into the courtyard. Her stomach turned as she took in the scene, even more horrific than what lay inside. This was where most of the injured had been carried, where the dead had been taken. It was a choir of sobs of the mourning and screaming of the ailed. Isla paused as a familiar wail pricked her ears. She froze as, amidst the scattered, she found the man who'd come to her and Kai for help. He knelt before a body, a woman's limp hand clutched in his own. Behind him, stood Zahra; a woman who'd faced such a horror herself, now forced to relive it through another's experience. Her face was solemn and drawn with sympathy, but her features still held a refined quality that served as a pillar of strength in a storm.

A storm that Isla herself would need to navigate. Maybe now, whether she wanted to or not.

Kai had been nowhere.

When Isla had reached for the bond after nearly breaking down at the sights she'd beheld, it was weak. Distance was likely to blame, but it hadn't kept her from the terror. Hadn't kept her wolf from growing restless, not even calmed when the knowledge came that he had gone with the guard to handle rogues that had also taken to the city squares bordering the river into Abalys.

From what Isla had gleaned before she and Eli were asked by Ezekiel—likely aware of her prying ears—to leave the hall, the rogues had been able to sneak along the banks up to the borders of Mavec, and then somehow, bypassed the guards, obtained their vehicles, and made their way up to the banquet. How they were able to get through, how they knew about the party at all was still a mystery.

She was in her hotel room now with Davina, and the entirety of Mavec had been put on lockdown until dawn. Still, it took everything in Isla not to head out anyway. To track down Kai. Every thought of him had her insides coiling, the bond still unstable and driving her mad. This had to have been what Kai had been talking about, what he'd described in Callisto. Though the madness wasn't steeped in intense lust and desire as Isla had thought, it was simply in the unknown, in the bond's ebb and flow. Strong and weak pulls, the pondering if they meant Kai was alive or dying, the inability to contact him. The feeling of being able to do everything and nothing, to *feel* everything and then *empty*. It was making her crazy, and it had only been a few hours.

Touch wasn't permanent, their bond could still fray, but exactly how long was *this* supposed to last?

She'd pondered it as she scrubbed herself clean in the shower, marking the places, mentally, where Kai's body had met with hers. But her hands didn't roam. As much as she'd likely enjoy having him on her like that again, she was more concerned with him simply getting back to her again. Him being safe and okay.

As Isla rewound through the night, through her bloodied battles, over the lifeless stares she'd seen brought about by her own claws, she felt nausea bubble in her stomach and bile begin rising in her throat. There had only been a few heartbeats for her to jump out of the water and wrap herself in a towel before she'd fallen to her knees to empty the contents of her stomach into the toilet.

Davina, who'd been in the bedroom phoning whoever she could in the shops below to learn about what was occurring, had burst into the washroom.

And she was there through every spell until Isla was sure there was nothing left—from the banquet or before it.

Isla groaned and ran the back of her hand over her mouth in a long, harsh stroke as she loosened her grip on the porcelain.

"There you go," Davina eased, running a palm up and down Isla's towel-clad back.

Isla responded with another grunt.

This was the second time that the act of killing had brought her to her knees, vomiting. Only this time, it was real. Several times over.

Taking the life of another wolf was different from killing vicious monsters crafted by nightmares—rogue or not. It wouldn't get easier, she knew, but she'd become more tolerant. She would have to. She just had to keep reminding herself of the people she'd saved. How they'd go home to their families.

Though *they* were grateful, others—as Isla had gathered through the whispers and glowers received as she walked past—had seen her, the wolf of Io, as destructive and a means of her pack to make a political stand, an assertion of power. A show of how Deimos needed Io to handle their problems…Isla had never heard anything more absurd.

Her spine barked in the slightest pain, sore from her fighting, as she fell against the tile of the bathtub, the nausea still lingering.

Davina handed her a glass of water she'd retrieved, and Isla swished the liquid between her teeth and spit—one time, then again, and again—before accepting some mouthwash and going through that too.

Davina settled across from her against the sink.

Isla thanked her before asking, "Have you heard anything?"

Davina heaved a breath. "The guard is all over the city, but no one can really tell what's going on."

"Is Rhydian out there?"

"He was patrolling the outermost borders again. I don't know if they called him down for the search. I know Ameera went out there. She was with Jonah and met up with Kai."

At the mention of her mate, Isla's shoulders slumped and she averted her eyes.

"Feeling any better?"

Isla returned her gaze to Davina, feeling the bond like a heavy anvil on her chest. Feeling it attempt to loosen her tongue.

"We touched."

It won.

Davina's brows lifted at the words. "What?"

Isla brought her lip between her teeth, saying the words aloud somehow making the harshness of it so much clearer. "Kai and I—we touched, and…" She wedged her hands into her hair. "Goddess."

Davina couldn't contain her shock or her grin. "Should—should I be bowing to you right now?" When Isla's own disposition didn't reflect hers, her features dimmed. "What happened?"

Isla felt ridiculous as she explained what she wished hadn't been real—getting run into, pushed, and how Kai had caught her. After *months* of staying apart, of games and close calls, *that* was how it had happened?

"And then what?"

Isla could see Davina working hard to abate the amusement.

"There were rogues," she said. "And I haven't seen him since."

Silence settled between them as Davina ran Isla over with an assessing stare. "How…do you feel?"

"Raw," Isla answered, the first word to come to mind and probably the most accurate. "Vulnerable, exposed…and like the rogues are lucky that I don't go into their lands and slaughter all of them because they're the reason he isn't here. Because, for all I know, they could be the reason he—" Isla didn't want to say the word out loud.

Davina hummed, almost impressed. "And you haven't even accepted the bond yet? I'd hate to be the sorry bastard that gets between you two once that happens."

Once that happens…

"Touch isn't permanent," Isla echoed her earlier thoughts. "We still don't *have to* bond."

Surprise took over Davina's face and again, she went quiet. She was careful when she spoke next. "Is that what you want?"

A few weeks ago, Isla's answer would've been immediate.

Yes.

Yes—this was what they'd wanted. What they'd planned.

Being apart. Moving on with their separate lives without the bond wearing down on them.

But instead, Isla found her mind drifting back to Kai's touch, back to the hallway, back to the quiet moments walking back from The Bookshoppe, up on the infirmary roof, and even in Callisto's forest when Kai was saying goodbye. Those tiny pockets of peace. Of ease.

And with that on her mind, she said, "I don't know."

"Why not?" Again, soft and mindful.

Isla sighed before leaning her head against the wall beside her. "It's…complicated."

Davina offered a smile. "I'm all about complicated."

Isla, to her own surprise, returned the grin, albeit a bit more strained.

More than the bond had been wearing on her all this time. So many things that she'd needed to let out, for *years*, but had no one to turn to. She told herself that Davina, though, she said she was open to complicated, didn't need to be bogged down with Isla's troubles. No one did.

But there was something in those eager green eyes that had Isla unraveling and opening up in a way she never had to anyone, besides the moon on those painful nights a long while ago.

"I'm the daughter of one of the highest-ranking members on this continent," Isla began warily, reading Davina's face and ready to stop at the smallest sign of disinterest. It didn't gleam. "And I've watched people time and time again disregard me until they find out who my father is, what pack I hail from, *'what a great bloodline I have'*," she added the last part mockingly, to which Davina chuckled, but she never lost the intent stare. "I've been told over and over that it's all I'm good for—breeding, a pretty, little trophy on a man's arm—and for a while, I believed it. I accepted it wholeheartedly. It was a purpose for me finally, after always being lost in my brother's shadow. In my friends' shadows —the Heir and future princess."

Isla let out a cough, feeling her heart in her throat. Too much. She was saying too much. Yet still, her soul—Davina's gaze—urged her to continue.

Breathe, breathe.

"So, I went along, entertaining whoever gave me the time of day, doing whatever they asked of me, thinking maybe, just maybe, they'd think *I* was worth something. Not just to bear children or climb a social ladder, but to really *see me*…but even that person I was showing them wasn't the real me at all, just who I thought I had to be. When we turned sixteen and everyone began preparing for mating bonds—chosen or fated—the moment we turned of age at eighteen, I thought I'd found my saving grace. My mate—that 'one true great love', my other half—*they'd* get me. They had to."

Isla checked Davina again, still hanging onto every word.

A nag of shame began rising in her gut.

"So, I did whatever I could to find him. Went to every gathering imaginable, and again and again, I found no one. All I got were suitors who saw that bloodline and were so fed up with searching that they'd *'settle for me'*. And I was so blinded by my own insecurity and loneliness, that I settled too. And Callan was fine, for a while. I was okay with being with him forever. To stop torturing myself over something that would never happen, but then something just hit me, and I started falling further and further into this dark place. My rock bottom came one night out in these ash lily fields on the outskirts of the city."

Isla felt the corner of her eyelids starting to sting as a hollowness—an icy, numbing cold—she'd felt all those years ago, crept back over her bones.

"It was the night of our Yule Ball, and I was so…unhappy. I was drowning—I'd *been* drowning for months and months—and no one noticed. Maybe Callan did, but he wasn't much help, preoccupied with his warrior training. Adrien and Cora were wrapped up in their mating. Sebastian had his new position. My dad was—being the Beta. I was so drunk when I snuck out there, still holding a bottle of wine too. No doubt, I wasn't very inconspicuous, but no one bothered to follow me or came to find me. And I just remember lying in that field, sobbing and *begging*. Begging the Goddess to just show me, tell me, give me any type of sign that I wasn't doomed to feel the way I was forever. That I wouldn't be lost forever. That there was something *more* for me—maybe I'd find my person, my *true* person. And when I got nothing after a few seconds, I was ready to head off into *our* bordering rogue lands and see what fate awaited me there. I'd make it or I wouldn't. I didn't care. But then I passed out before I could do anything stupid."

Davina's eyes had glossed over. Her hand raised to brush away a tear on her cheek. It was what made Isla realize her own had fallen. She rubbed it away.

"I woke up not too long after because the stars were still out. And everything was so…still. Somewhere in that mess of lights, I just found clarity. Hope. It was like all I needed to do was stop. To forget everything and everyone else and just…be. I thought of everything I could do for *myself*, and maybe back then, there was a little part of me that thought about how I didn't want to be mated and give myself to someone as the girl that I was. The next day, I enrolled in the warrior program—like I'd always wanted to but had always been told I shouldn't, couldn't. And no matter how afraid I was, no matter how much I doubted and thought about quitting, no matter who told me that I should, I knew I couldn't look back. That I'd hate myself for stopping and looking back. I stayed with Callan for a bit after that, but when I started getting really into training, it took a toll on us. I wasn't that pretty, quiet trophy anymore, and I didn't ever want to be, so I ended things with him."

Despite the happiness that moment had brought in the past, the next part of Isla's story made her blood heat.

"I had never felt so free, but there was still the bond looming over my head. Those little moments when I wanted someone there to be with me or just to tell people about when they'd asked. But then I watched two of the strongest people I know destroyed by it, and the reason for it wasn't love. Not on the right end. The bond was all possession and power and...*selfishness*. And I realized I didn't want that as a part of my life either. I didn't need it to be happy. I was fine by myself for as long as I wanted to be. I didn't think the Goddess would ever bring me my mate anyway. I mean, fated mates are hard enough to find when you *are* trying. And then..."

Isla trailed off, long enough that Davina felt comfortable offering, "Kai."

Isla laughed bitterly. "Fate has a wicked sense of humor. My father visited Deimos countless times; even Sebastian went with him on a few trips, some after I'd been of age. If I'd gone, maybe I would've recognized him, what he was to me—what he is. But no, she had to bring him to me at the perfect time to—"

Isla froze as she felt another sporadic tug at the bond. Strong, as others had been out of the blue, but this time. *This time.*

Isla shot to her feet, not caring that her hair was wet and sticking to her back. Not caring that she was still clad in her towel. She became like the wind as she charged to her room's door and pulled the entrance open before Kai even had a chance to knock. Before Rhydian and Ameera, who flanked him, even had a chance to get in her direct eyeline.

The pause between them, staring at each other for the first time after they'd touched, was suffocating. The bond, rekindling in their proximity, overwhelming.

But reprieve came quick. Too quick. So fast that the dissipating madness of worrying where he was—the sheer relief of seeing him again—bred a new kind of insanity within her.

Insanity that had Isla taking two steps forward.

That had her rising on her toes. Had her running hands over stubble, dirt, and maybe blood-smeared skin. Had her fingers winding into soft curls.

Pure insanity that had Isla leaning up towards Kai...and kissing him.

CHAPTER 27

Kai's face was cold, his cheeks ravaged by the wind and chill of Mavec's summer night. But his mouth, his lips were warm and soft. And Isla became that feeling. Her body heating, her muscles going weak. Kai was her opposite, evident in the tenseness of every place they connected. But he took each caress of her mouth—gentle, shockingly timid, grateful—and Isla could've sworn his lips rose in a smile. Could've sworn he started kissing back.

That was enough to knock some sense into her.

Goddess, what was she doing? What had come over her? This wasn't right. Touching was bad enough for their objectives, but *this*?

Isla took in a breath. Dropped her hands. Pulled back.

She'd only made it halfway to the flats of her feet.

Kai wasted no time in moving forward to pull her back into a deep, punishing kiss. He held her tight, wrapping one strong arm around her waist, causing her towel to loosen, going askew. His other hand cupped her face, fingers at the back of her neck, tilting her head, wedging into her still-damp hair as he slanted his mouth to take more of her.

The taste of him was dizzying. The kiss, greedy and claiming—but it wasn't frantic. It was methodical, unhurried, purposeful. Heavy. And yet still, it felt…restrained. Kai was holding back, but Isla would take what she could get right now. A need, a desperation twined with something charged. A culmination of all the close encounters, all the teasing.

Release, relief—and payback.

Kai ran his tongue over the seam of her lips, and Isla opened for him, circling her arms around his middle and gripping the fabric of his shirt, feeling the hard muscles of his back beneath her fingertips. She tugged him closer. Her towel slipped again, her bare chest one move away from being clearly pressed to his.

As his hand drifted lower—from her waist to her hip, threatening to go further—a groan caught in her throat. She refused to let it out.

There was a fine line here. One that would be obliterated in a second. A moan, a mewl, a coo and he'd lose whatever discipline he was exhibiting, and experiencing whatever *that* was would dissolve hers too.

But she was better than this—they were. These urges. Their instincts. They'd proven so since the day they'd met.

That stubborn part they shared was still in there, trying to thrive. Coherence was in reach. Somewhere in these seconds that felt like a blissful eternity.

They wouldn't be bested today. Not like this. Now wasn't the time.

So, they broke apart. Slow. Breathless. Skin flushed and lips swollen.

Isla retreated a step, adjusted her towel, and tried to settle her heart as she took in her mate's form—as glorious as she imagined it would be. The taut muscles she'd felt—of his chest, his abdomen, his arms—on display in the uniform he seemed to have obtained from the guard after unshifting. The thin, black open tunic donning the silver insignia tied at his waist with a cloth belt. She could see clearly where his skin was lined with black ink, those tattoos stretching from his elbow all the way up to his shoulder, crossing over his chest and mixing with the lumerosi markings she recognized. She didn't ponder what they were this time; she was too focused on who they were on. How badly she wanted him against her again.

Her mouth was dry as she met Kai's stare, as dark as she imagined hers was, before he shot his gaze behind her.

"Oh, please don't stop on our behalf."

Isla turned, the female voice, not Davina's, having come from behind her. Amidst her and Kai's embrace, Ameera and Rhydian had entered the room. They'd also, thankfully, closed the door behind them. She didn't need to give any of her squadmates a show.

They stood on either side of Davina, each towering her height and Rhydian with an arm around his mate's shoulders. Davina had lifted her hand to interlock their fingers. All three of them were wearing some form of astonished and amused expression, and Isla noticed Rhydian and Ameera not only wore similar uniforms to Kai, but they also bore the same form of tattoos.

Heat flooded Isla's cheeks.

She wasn't a fan of *her family* knowing her romantic business, and Kai's was no exception.

She twisted back to her mate whose lips were pursed. And that smugness—that damn smugness in his eyes. The silence too. It was going to kill her.

"I'm going to put on some clothes," Isla announced and then refused to make eye contact with *anyone* as she shuffled past them to grab the garments off the bureau and headed to the bathroom.

Even behind the closed door, she could feel the bond humming between them, a pre-chorus for that symphony it had so desperately wanted to edge them towards.

Isla dropped everything by the sink and ran her hands over her face.

"Okay, what happened to the 'no touching' nonsense?" She heard Ameera, just on the edge of trying to be quiet—but not quite.

"They touched at the banquet," Davina said, a bit more successful in keeping her tone low. After a pause, she added, "Isla told me."

"You didn't think to mention that?" Ameera again, her voice raising an octave at the end. "Are you *mated?*"

"No," was all Kai answered.

His voice had become hard again, and Isla could sense what was brewing beneath his skin. She'd felt the same as she realized there were specks of dried blood on the tips of her fingers. Not Kai's from what she could scent.

Nothing could be about them now. There were rogues. People had died.

As Isla moved back to the sink to wash her hands and splash some cold water over her face, she heard their conversation continue. But it had gotten softer, nearly indiscernible over the running water.

"Where's Jonah?" Davina asked, citing the missing final member of their little family.

"Do you actually think he'd leave the shop unattended while rogues are running around?" Rhydian quipped of his twin.

"When I left, he was posted at his front door with a sword," Ameera drawled. "Maybe now, he'll finally put those years in guard training to use."

The laugh that followed was stilted.

"How bad is it?"

In response to Davina's question, the other three wolves rehashed everything Isla had already known. About the rogues traveling up the banks, their vehicles, the road to the hall, their taking to the city squares.

Isla began dressing.

"They shouldn't have even been able to get through Abalys," Ameera said. "I'm telling you, Kai. Something's off."

"I know," Kai breathed. Isla nearly didn't hear it. "The hall was a distraction."

Her eyebrows shot up.

"A distraction?" Davina invoked Isla's thoughts.

Rhydian spoke up before his mate could formally ask for elaboration. "The ones in the city weren't going around killing and wreaking havoc for the hell of it."

"They were looking for something," Ameera concluded.

"Like what?"

"Yet another thing for me to figure out," Kai grumbled. Behind her door, even if he couldn't see, Isla shook her head. What else could go wrong? "The ones we took into custody are being interrogated now, but I doubt they'll break."

"We wanted to check on you guys," Rhydian said, and Isla could hear as he placed a kiss on her cheek.

"What about the ones from the hall?" Davina inquired.

"Dead from what I've heard," Kai said, and Isla stiffened. "I went after the ones that tried to get away, and then into the lower part of the city. I trusted Isla and Ezekiel to handle them however they saw fit."

What?

Kai had trusted her to take over—and she'd gone on and slaughtered everyone she found.

"Which is completely against warrior protocol, by the way," Ameera said. "Given they haven't been sanctioned for action yet in Abalys, forget about Mavec in the Pack Hall *filled* with our most important pack members. You know you've set yourself up for a massive headache with the almighty asshole—and that's referring to the Imperial Alpha, not my father. Though he'll be a pain in your ass, too."

From her spot, Isla's eyes averted to the grate by the sink. She traced them over the metal. If one looked close enough, they'd realize the screws were loose. Sebastian would never be in her room in Deimos to give her a hard time for using the same hiding spot again. If they reached inside the vent, they'd find the book and marker, stained with Lukas's blood.

She was reminded of her and Kai's conversation from before the rogues attacked. How he thought Io was responsible for the deaths of his brother and father. How he thought someone of her pack, maybe someone she'd known, had wanted her dead.

Why—he'd never gotten to tell her.

But these things...

She knew the marker, the book, and the message from the killer tied together somehow.

And whether they connected to Io, whether they proved or disproved Kai's theories, they meant *something*. She needed to know why.

"Did you forget you're a warrior too?" Rhydian said.

"You know why I am," Ameera countered, voice the softest it had been. "But regardless, that also doesn't mean I can't think for myself and see what's really going on...as much as I hate to agree with my father. I wouldn't be surprised if all of this was—"

"Not here," Kai cut her off harshly, and it was followed by more quiet and whispers so delicate, Isla couldn't glean them for the life of her.

Pathetically, she pressed her ear to the door, curious what else they'd tried to discuss when she wasn't in their immediate presence.

"We should go," Kai said, a little louder. "I need to be at the hall."

Silence.

"Are we pretending your mate doesn't exist again?" Ameera said.

"Nothing's changed."

"The other day you two couldn't even *touch*, and you were just all over each other."

"When *we* figure out what *we* want to do with *our* bond, we'll let you know."

Sentiments Kai had held onto since they'd met.

As Isla heard the shuffling of footsteps like they were preparing to go, she grabbed the doorknob. All eyes went to her as she pulled it open.

As she had when she first met them at the bookshop, even if she'd gotten to know them each a little bit more, she felt like a fish out of water.

But even with that, Isla met Kai's eyes and said, "Let me come with you. I want to help more. It's why I'm here."

Her proposal drew looks from the others. She may have even called them impressed.

Kai's jaw tightened. "This isn't worth you getting discharged from the warriors."

"I think I can decide that for myself."

Ameera let out a cough and looked away as she smiled.

Kai wasn't nearly as amused. "You'd be sent back to Io. And I need you *here*. I need you safe."

Isla ground her teeth, understanding the full picture. Kai was lucky he was right. That she likely would be discharged for going out without being ordered to. That she would be sent back to Io. And right now, that was the last place she wanted to be. At least, until she'd gotten the full gist of his theories.

Isla folded her arms and leaned against the doorframe. "Were you going to leave without saying goodbye?"

Now Kai smiled, and every step he took in Isla's direction matched with a firm beat of her heart.

He angled himself to her in a way that had her blocked from the view of others as he always seemed to do. Shielding her however he could from the world. His world.

When he took her face in his hands, Isla was ready, already rising onto her toes. The kiss this time was sweet and simple. They knew what anything further would bring about.

And as those strings between them spun, as they weaved and wound and sang, as she relished in the comfort, Isla's mind drifted to the man, coated in the blood of his wife, who'd return to an empty home tonight. Who'd had every wondrous thread snapped. Had his soul cleaved in two.

Because of this *thing*.

That had her body sighing. That had her mind spinning. That had her feeling something she'd never experienced for a man she barely knew. The one she was meant to spend eternity with. That she would need to give up life as she knew it to be with.

But those thoughts disappeared as quick as they'd come.

When they broke apart, Isla looked up into those eyes and traced his nose down to the lazy smile on his lips, just enough that she could see that dimple in his cheek.

Her heart gave an unsteady beat, and she cleared her throat, placing her hands on his arms as she said, "Don't give me a reason to go after you. If I feel anything wrong—"

Kai chuckled, stroking her cheeks with his thumbs. "I know." He leaned down to press his forehead to hers. "Thank you."

She knew it wasn't just for staying put, but for all she'd done—for his home.

"It's why I'm here," she repeated, making a point of it.

Kai's grin grew, and she was about to kiss him again—something she was realizing she didn't want to ever stop doing, ever—when two hands suddenly clamped down on his shoulders.

Kai and Isla stepped apart, though he kept a hand on her back.

Rhydian was behind them, and Ameera already stood by the door.

"If you want to just deal with this now," he jeered, "we can give you two a few minutes."

Kai snorted. He and Rhydian were eye to eye, but the guard held just a bit more bulk.

As Rhydian had done, Kai brought his hand down on his brother's shoulder.

"I'm not you, Rhyd," Kai said, and Isla caught the innuendo, feeling Kai's fingers tighten against her back. A reassurance. A promise.

He'd surely want and would *take* more than a few minutes with her when the moment arrived.

If it ever arrived.

"Let's go, boys," Ameera sang, hand on the doorknob. "I'm not dealing with this dominant bullshit today."

Kai and Rhydian shared narrowed stares before the latter went to bid Davina farewell. Once they were as alone as they could get, Kai leaned down, lips brushing Isla's cheek as he went to her ear. "Tomorrow night after your training and whatever mess I have, I'll meet you here, and we'll…talk."

Talk.

About the bond. About what they'd do.

As he stepped back, Isla blinked up at him and then simply nodded.

"Goodnight," he said.

She was disappointed that he hadn't moved in to kiss her again. "Goodnight."

Once the three of them left—but not before Ameera could offer a shocking *"good work, new blood"*—Isla went and locked the door behind them. When she turned, she found Davina's cheeks tinting as red as her hair and looking like she was about to explode.

Isla waved a hand at her. "Go ahead."

Davina screamed and Isla winced. "What was that?" she blurted in excitement.

Fighting to keep a smile at bay, Isla folded her arms again. She spoke honestly when she answered, "I wish I could tell you."

∼

With the lockdown still in place, Davina couldn't leave the hotel and return to her and Rhydian's home in Ifera. Isla offered for her to stay the night, which Davina all-too-exuberantly agreed to. She'd scraped together a makeshift pajama set from pieces of staff uniforms she "borrowed" since the clothes Isla offered were the improper size.

They stood on either side of the bed with the room solely illuminated by moonlight.

Isla brought her cup of water up to her mouth, saying before her drink, "When are you going to stop looking at me like that?"

Davina, who *had* been staring, didn't avert her eyes. "Once I get over the fact that you're actually here." She pulled back the covers on the side of the bed closest to the window, the side Isla always left occupied so she had clear vantage and access to the door.

Isla lowered the glass with a raised eyebrow. "What does that mean?"

Davina took her place on the mattress. "I...I know you all have your gripes with the Goddess and Fate—you, Kai, even Rhydian and Jonah—but I do believe that they do good, and everything happens for a reason. That it all happens how it's meant to, in the end. Like Kai becoming alpha—which he probably doesn't want to hear, given how it happened—and him...finding you when he needs you most. And I don't mean because he needs you to rule. I have never seen him look at anyone like that, never seen him *look* like that—even when he *was* happy."

Isla started at the word "happy", at what it implied. It wasn't completely out of scope, given everything Kai had gone through, but...

She remembered seeing him before the message. Remembered seeing that facade fall and the mask crack. All the pain he kept buried.

Davina swallowed, swinging her legs around to get them under the blankets. "The day he left for that Hunt, we hadn't known what he was doing. And then when we found out, we weren't sure if he was coming back," she began weakly, and Isla felt like there was something deeper in the words. "The whole pack knew when he went behind the Wall. We kept up with it through the radio, the papers, and every day he didn't emerge...I don't think I've been that afraid in a long, long time. And I've been afraid many times in my life." Davina cleared her throat as if fighting back tears. "When we learned he made it out okay, even Ameera cried—and don't tell her I told you that. Kai came back a couple of days later and surprised us at Jonah's, which was the first flag that something was up. We barely saw him after everything happened." The side of her mouth twitched up. "He still seemed a little off, but Rhydian made some dumb joke and Kai laughed. I didn't realize how long it had been since I'd heard him do it or even seen him *smile*. That's how we knew something *had* to have happened, and he didn't care about the glory part of things. About winning whatever. It was something else. Then we figured out he met you."

Isla bit the inside of her cheek so hard it nearly bled. She drew her gaze out the window, to the lights of the hall she could see.

"I didn't want to say that to scare you or make you feel—" Davina scrunched her nose, not quite knowing where she was going with it. "I just thought you should know how grateful we are to you. You guys may decide not to do anything with your bond, but just the fact that he knows you're out there...that you exist." She shrugged. "It brought him back a bit."

Isla didn't know what to say, her chest feeling heavy. Wordlessly, she placed her drink down and got into the bed. Her back was against the headboard as she pulled up the covers.

"You were right, fated bonds *are* selfish," Davina began carefully, and Isla realized she was alluding to her earlier confession. "Because it's ourselves that we recognize in the other person, that piece they've been holding. And all we want innately is to feel whole again, to get it back. But when that changes, *if* it changes—when we really see the person on the other side...there's nothing more magical." She paused, letting the words sink in. "I wasn't always in love with Rhydian from the start. Not when we first mated, not when I moved in, not even after *plenty* of great sex."

Isla mustered a laugh despite the uneasiness. "When did it happen, then?"

Davina answered simply, "When he became my best friend."

∽

Isla narrowed her eyes up at the swaying sign of The Bookshoppe, her bag heavy on her shoulder.

Everything felt heavy and strained. Her wolf was livid. It wanted Kai. *Isla* wanted Kai—and could've easily looked like a crazy person muttering to herself on her journey here, telling it to calm down.

She'd barely slept, and it had nothing to do with Davina's snoring. In her and Kai's distance, the bond had been driving her mad again. So much so that she'd had to get out of bed and move around just to occupy her mind. Davina, being a heavy sleeper, hadn't even flinched. And so, Isla spent the entire night perched by the window, much like she would've done in her old apartment, much like she'd done in the corridor of the Pack Hall. But instead of looking out into the Imperial City or trying to catch glimpses of Mavec, she focused on what she could make of the Hall, the ghost of Kai's lips lingering over her own, and the power of Davina's words swirling around her head.

As soon as the sun had broken the horizon, Isla—who'd finally dozed off for a couple of hours on her chair—went into motion.

It was dawn. The lockdown was over.

Davina, once again, had barely stirred as Isla moved to the bathroom to gather her things before heading out the door.

There were only a few hours until the warriors would be going to the guard base for the day's training; that meant Isla only had a few hours to figure out all she could about the book and marker before she and Kai spoke later that night. When she presented the two to him, she wanted to be able to say something other than, *I have no idea what these are, but I think they're connected to the person who murdered your family.*

And so, here she was. Ready to bring in reinforcements that were apparently better than any library.

The doorknob of the shop was cold in her grip as she twisted it. Locked. She paused, waiting to see if Jonah, on high alert with the rogues, was nearby to detect the sound. Nothing.

Isla lifted her fist to pound on the wood. The opaque glass of its window shuddered.

No response.

She did it again—a little harder.

Nothing.

Maybe he wasn't here…but, then again, apparently he never really left.

"Jonah!" Isla called, throwing her closed hand at it again. "Jonah! I know you're—"

Isla jerked back as a shadow appeared on the other side of the window, darkness rippling over the glass. Next came several clicks—locks at varying heights—before the door opened to reveal disgruntled features. Isla noted Jonah's half-lidded eyes, the shadow of stubble, and his unbuttoned shirt, swaying in whatever breeze had been brought in. She rose a brow at the show of black ink over his well-muscled chest—those tattoos again. Like Kai, Rhydian, and Ameera.

"Why are you at my door at six in the morning?"

His grumbling had her eyes meeting his, the dazzling amber narrowing against the sunlight. Guilt gnawed at her. He was probably just as sleep-deprived as she was.

"*Good morning.*" Isla forced a smile, one that seemed too chipper for him to handle at this hour. She dropped it, realizing any faux sweetness wasn't going to get her anywhere with him. "I need your help."

"We open at ten."

"And I'll be in training."

"We close at eight."

Isla sighed. "Make an exception for me."

Jonah adjusted himself against the door. "My brother's mate, or my luna?"

Isla felt a grimace etching onto her face. Something about the words ringing in the way *Imperial Beta's daughter* did. "Just a person asking for your help."

Jonah eyed her before glancing at the barren streets. In the aftermath of the rogue attacks, there was an eerie stillness to them, but also something skittish. As Jonah shot a glance at the Pack Hall looming above, Isla followed suit, eyes drawn particularly to what she could see of that stained-glass window. She wondered if Kai was up there, gazing down upon his kingdom. Sunrises and sunsets from that perch must've been a beautiful thing to behold.

Upon realizing Jonah had long since ceased his roaming eye to focus on her, she started. His features unmoving, he stepped out of the way, allowing her through.

Isla clutched tightly on her bag strap, taking to the now-open space and smiling again. "Thank you."

Jonah muttered some sort of response, rubbing a heavy hand over his face.

The shop was quiet, save what seemed to be the soft hum of music from the back of the stacks, and the air smelled faintly of burning incense—jasmine and sandalwood. Isla turned to Jonah who was working at each lock on the door. Five, to be exact.

She wanted to ask him why he found them all so necessary, but instead, found herself drawn to the dark patterns on his back, visible beneath the light, almost-sheer fabric of his shirt. "What are the tattoos?"

Jonah finished the final lock and spun. He brought his eyes to his chest, clenching and releasing his fist. "A symbol of codependence."

The dry answer was all he seemed prepared to give.

While the shop owner disappeared to the back, telling Isla to give him a minute, she found herself meandering around the shelves, fiddling with books, bobbles, and machine parts. There was more reading here about Deimos than she'd ever been able to track down in Io—more on the other packs too. Books on its history, its culture, and fiction weaved by local authors. A lot of the books Jonah had were used but still in decent condition. Some had writing in them, notes in the margins, comments made by those now beyond. Isla found those to be her favorites.

She heard a door open and close, and the hum of music cut to silence. Jonah emerged from behind the shelves with two mugs in his hands, steam billowing from the tops of each. Isla could catch a rich, nutty scent wafting from them. Her mouth watered.

"I don't know if you're one of those tea people in the morning, but that's not enough for me." Jonah handed her one of the cups. "Especially when I'm wrenched from sleep at ungoddessly hours."

Isla wrapped her fingers around the mug, letting the heat leech into her skin. "The sun's up. Don't be a baby." She took in a greedy whiff. "This is perfect. Thank you."

Jonah snickered at the jab and gulped down a hefty amount of the searing beverage. "I'm assuming you didn't come here to ask about our tattoos."

Isla sipped on her drink and nearly moaned at the taste, going in for another quickly. But everything turned sour as she remembered why she was here.

She lowered her cup, moving towards the check-out counter. "No."

Her bag made a light clunking sound after it was hoisted onto it. She rifled through, Jonah appearing behind her just as she pulled out the marker, then the book. Her heart felt stuck in her throat, beating in her ears, as she placed them down on the table.

She waited for the Imperial Guard to storm the shop, for the world to tilt on its axis, for her and Jonah to burst into flames.

But when she turned to the shop owner, he was indifferent.

He scratched at the stubble sprouting along his chin. "What are these?"

Isla took in a deep breath. "That's what I need you to tell me."

Jonah looked between her and the items again, suspicion fluttering over his face. "And *where* did you get them?"

"Does it matter?"

The question caused the corner of his mouth to tick upwards. "Ominous."

"Just keeping you on your toes."

The statement riled the other side of his lips, and Jonah put his brew down, going for the book first. The second he opened it, his features fell.

Isla was quiet as he flipped, and flipped, and flipped, opting to fan through to the end. She cleared her throat. "Do you know what it is?"

Jonah snapped the book closed. "Not a clue." He ran a finger over the spine covered with dried blood, but he had no question about it.

"I'm curious though, which is a good start, but I'm also concerned." Jonah picked up the marker and examined its surface, realizing what Isla had, so went through the book again to catch the similarities in the writing. "This is why you asked me about languages."

Isla nodded. "It's none of the native tongues, and it's obviously not the Common…what are you worried about?"

"The fact you also asked me about Phobos." He cast an eye in her direction. "I can't think of the last time I've heard anyone refer to that pack, or try to look into it as anything other than the Wilds. And from personal experience, it's never good when Imperial Pack members ask questions."

Personal experience?

Before Isla had a chance to ask what that meant, there was a pounding at the door. Reflexively, she spun, arms splaying slightly as if to shield the book, marker, and Jonah from whatever it was. A pool of red haloed the glass and was cast down upon the floor by the sunlight. They both knew who it was.

"Is everyone in the mood to visit this morning?" Jonah mumbled, placing the book and marker gently on the counter. Isla shifted her bag to hide them from view, at least until Davina left.

The hotel secretary didn't cease her banging on the door, even as Jonah went through each of the locks again, calling for her to relax. When he pulled the entrance open, Davina—still clad in her pajamas, hair still mussed from bedhead—was panting, her face flushed as if she'd run here a few minutes after waking.

But as her gaze fell upon Isla, all the color drained away. "Oh, Goddess, you're here."

The words weren't spoken out of relief.

They were out of fear.

A horrible feeling settled in Isla's gut. "What's wrong?"

Davina looked at her with sorrow in her eyes as they became glassy.

Fearing the worst, Isla reached for the bond. It was there. Weaker, strange, but there.

"What happened?" Jonah asked before Isla could repeat herself.

Davina looked between them, opening and closing her mouth, shaking her head like she didn't understand. "Kai—he—he's being challenged for alpha."

"What?"

Jonah's voice was nothing but an empty echo in Isla's mind. Her body had gone rigid as she looped through the words again.

A challenge. A *challenge*.

"When did you hear this?" Jonah again.

For that, Isla was grateful. Speaking suddenly felt impossible.

"It just broke over the radio. I guess it was lofted to the Imperial Council—to the Imperial Alpha—last night while everyone was busy at the party and with the rogues. Now we're just waiting to hear if they approve it."

If they approve it. *If.*

"Why do they even get a say?" Davina's voice was shaky, out of fear, out of uncertainty about the protocol. "It's our pack."

Isla's chest tightened.

If...

"To maintain order." Jonah's face was a picture of stern calmness as if he knew he had to be the steady force between the three of them. "Who's calling for it?"

"They wouldn't say—or they didn't know yet. It's all just happening now, but...they think it could have something to do with Alpha Kyran's death. That someone's claiming they killed him," Davina said, letting loose a strained sob. "A challenge...that's a fight to the death, right? Kai either wins and stays alpha or he—"

"I need a phone."

Jonah and Davina went still. They averted their gazes to Isla, something in them recoiling—bowing.

"I have one in the back," Jonah said.

"Can it do long distance?" Isla asked, and he shook his head. "Where can I find one?"

Jonah described a call center in the lower part of the city and wasted no time in moving to write out directions for her. He didn't question anything until he handed the paper over. "Where are you calling?"

Isla was already halfway out the door, abandoning her bag, the book, and the marker on the counter.

"Home."

CHAPTER 28

Sunlight glittered off the length of the river as the city square yawned awake, but the workers of the boutiques and eateries, who would typically spend the time preparing for the morning minutiae, were nowhere to be found. Instead, Isla came upon near-empty cobblestone streets, dulled crystals in the absence of moonlight, and air so tense and solemn, she thought it would suffocate her.

She'd sprinted to the call center, so fast she'd missed a few of the turns drawn out by Jonah and had wound circles around Mavec's lower space. Her body was on autopilot; her mind lost in her mission, in its fight against panic. Kai was being challenged for alpha, and before she could let herself feel the weight of what that meant, she had to see if there was anything she could find out about what it was. *Who* it was. And if there was anything she could do.

There were three people inside the small corner store when she entered and judging by their weary appearances and poorly tucked-away makeshift beds, they'd been there all night. The woman behind the front desk gave a start as Isla stepped inside, her hand reaching reflexively to something beneath the counter.

Isla put her arms up slowly, showing she didn't mean any trouble.

As the woman's body relaxed, Isla began, "Are you—"

"*There is still no additional news regarding the challenging of Alpha Kai.*"

Isla snapped her head towards an older couple huddled in the corner of the room over a small radio broadcasting the Pack Report. The transmission was faint and grainy, but she picked up on what she could.

Reporters and journalists were already flocking the Pack Hall, even in the early hours, looking out for any member of the council, Beta Ezekiel, or Kai himself for any word or comment, but no one had emerged.

Twelve had died during the attacks last night. Among them, one of the pack's deltas.

Over fifty people had been injured in some capacity, two of which were in critical condition.

And most of all, they urged the public not to panic.

"What a disaster," the woman at the desk said softly.

But Isla couldn't pay it any heed, too focused on listening as the reporter had gone on to comment on Kai—

"I've been around to experience all three of these alpha shifts—Rainer, Kyran, and now Kai—and I'd say I certainly had my doubts, but I've liked the alpha's tenure so far. It's easy to forget our leaders are people, and he rose to the occasion in circumstances that would've broken many of us, odds against him and all. He's the youngest alpha to take the mantle in a while, sure, but he's shown promise. I've liked his proposals for the pack these past few months and how he's handled himself after the tragedies, not to mention his triumphs in the Hunt."

"That begs the question, who would be foolish enough to challenge him," another voice responded.

"We've heard the speculations."

No elaboration was made, but Isla figured she knew what was being alluded to. What Davina had said. Whoever was challenging Kai may have had something to do with his father's death.

"I have family who lives in Charon," the woman at the desk spoke again, and this time, Isla turned to her. "They went through a challenge and an alpha bloodline change maybe thirty years ago, and the pack has been in turmoil ever since. It's a complete tyranny. My cousin suspects foul play, maybe some involvement from…" Catching herself, she waved a hand. "I'm sorry, I'm rambling. What can I help you with, dear?"

Something in Isla was begging her to push the elder woman. To find out where she was going with her theories. But she'd already wasted too much time. "I need to make a call."

"That is what we do," the woman said, attempting to lighten the situation as she angled her body to a switchboard-looking device, littered with buttons and small levers, trailed by long wires along the floor. "Where can I connect you?"

"Io's Imperial City."

It felt like the entire room arrested.

The woman's features dropped, and Isla could feel two pairs of eyes searing into her back.

"We can't do that, unfortunately," the woman said, righting herself to face Isla fully again.

"Can't you call any region from here?"

"Calls into the Imperial Pack aren't permitted." The woman's own face matched Isla's perplexity, though for different reasons. "Those are the rules of the Imperials, and they have been for a very, very long time."

She spoke as though Isla should've known, but as a member of Deimos. Not as who she really was.

She wished she could've kept it that way, left her identity in the dark, but there was no time. The only other place one could make calls out of Deimos was likely the Pack Hall, and there wasn't a chance she'd make it up there, either within the window she needed or through the reporters.

"I'm from Io," Isla said, and instantly felt the room shift again. She steeled against it, that feeling of being out of place. "I need to call home."

She watched as the woman's fingers curled into fists on the counter. Another reflex. "Unfortunately, we still can't do that."

Isla let out a breath, ready to face whatever judgment would come her way. "Imperial Beta Malakai is my father. An exception will be made to whatever rule, I'm sure." For proof, she fished her identification card from her pocket—boasting her name, familial line, and the Imperial crest—and placed it on the table.

The woman's eyes widened, flickering between the card and Isla's face. She wouldn't move her hands, wouldn't touch it. The radio had been lowered, and whispers of the couple behind carried over it.

"Why is she here?"

"Imperial spies—they're trying to take over."

Isla bit down on her tongue, wanting to explain all of it. She wasn't a spy, not their enemy.

"Can you connect me?" Isla asked.

A look between the card and her face again. Reluctance, fear, and a touch of animosity took to the woman's eyes, but she agreed. Though, despite Isla's lineage, Io's Pack Hall remained off-limits, unreachable from a facility like this one.

Isla took a glance at the clock—well-past seven—and quickly ran through where everyone would be.

Sebastian was her best bet.

Isla gave the woman the number of her brother's townhouse, and after fiddling with some buttons on the switchboard, she returned with an outstretched hand. Isla counted out the money she'd brought with her, comparing it to the rates on the board, and handed it over. There was enough for ten minutes. She'd need to talk fast.

With the paper in her hands, the woman sifted through it again before pointing to the line of doors set up beside the small table with the couple. "Booth number three. When the light turns red. You have five minutes."

Isla jerked her head. "*Five*?"

"You're calling Io. The rate is higher. Take your complaints up with your alpha." Payment in possession, any warmth in the woman's persona had completely iced over. "I'll knock on your last minute."

Isla gaped, so close to protesting, matching the glower being shot her way, but then shut her mouth. She wasn't going to get anywhere with it.

The door to the room made it seem larger than it ended up being, with a stool, desk, and telephone set up that took up most of the space. Isla perched herself on the chair, sore muscles barking in protest, her eyes roving over the pen and blank pad of paper in front of her. A bulb just above the phone flashed a bright red.

Isla scrambled to pick it up and was immediately greeted by a steady ringing. Each toll with no response was like a punch to the stomach.

"Come on, Seb," she murmured under her breath, bouncing her knee and biting a nail between her teeth. She hadn't even thought to ask if her money was wasted if the person on the other line didn't pick up. Given the woman's disposition, Isla knew what she'd likely say, but this time, Isla didn't think she'd be able to play as nicely herself.

The ringing cut out. Silence followed.

Isla prepared herself for a battle, rolling up her sleeves—but then came a voice.

"*Hello*," the person drawled. "You've reached Sebastian."

Isla wasn't sure if she wanted to laugh or cry. She rested her head in her hand, a grin gracing her lips so wide that it hurt her cheeks. "Seb."

"Pudge?" She didn't think she'd ever been so excited to hear the nickname. His tone rang with excitement that heightened at her next confirmation. "Holy shit."

"That's Isla?"

Isla's breath caught at the second voice. A few moments passed before she heard it again, closer, but still distant. "You couldn't make it a week as a warrior without calling us?"

Adrien's jab had her eyes fluttering to stop them from stinging.

Isla laughed. Normally, she'd have a retort ready to go, but all she could muster was, "I guess not."

"How the fuck do I make this louder so you don't have to be on top of me?" She heard Sebastian mutter to their friend.

Heaviness took to her heart.

Her family. She hadn't realized how much she missed them. How much she missed home, familiarity, and not being looked at like a scourge.

"To what do we owe the pleasure of you remembering we exist?" Sebastian asked.

Isla's heart stammered a beat. "You—you haven't heard?"

"Heard what?" Sebastian snickered. "You're not about to tell us you're mated, are you? Because that's a lot to drop over the phone. Wait, how are you even—"

"Kai's being challenged," she cut him off, keen on the limited time and that she'd need to fill them in more than she'd anticipated. They went quiet, and each second that ticked by felt like hours. "The call for it came last night during the rogue attacks."

"What rogue attacks?" Sebastian said, tone harsher.

"Are you okay?" Adrien followed.

"It's not important," Isla said. "It's handled, but this...neither of you have heard anything about it? It hasn't broken our news yet?" They both made sounds of disagreement. "Adrien, when was the last time you spoke to your father?"

"Yesterday afternoon," he answered. "Then there were Council meetings all day."

Isla's ears perked in interest, though meetings of the Council weren't out of the norm. "You didn't go?"

"I had...things to handle, and I don't think he wanted me there anyway." Adrien paused, and then spoke carefully, having connected some information. "Are you and the alpha mated?"

Isla bit her cheek, saying lowly, "We may as well be." Before the boys could ask, she elaborated. "It's a long story, and we still have things to figure out, but, even if we aren't..." She trailed off as the thought that came to mind, selfishly, was, *I can't lose him.* "According to reports here, the challenge hasn't been approved yet. It's only been lifted to the Imperial Alpha and Council for deliberation."

"Who's calling for it?" Adrien asked.

"No one knows, or at least, it isn't public information," Isla said.

"Kai doesn't know?" Sebastian said.

"I haven't seen him since yesterday. I'm not sure, and I can't get to him. It's a frenzy here."

"You're mates. Why can't you link?"

"I haven't tried, but the bond—it's still incomplete and all over the place. I think it's too weak to do anything like that."

Adrien, who'd been quiet during the exchange, asked, "Should I tell them he's your mate? My father and the Council. Your father."

Isla swallowed, prepared to tell him *yes*. Maybe it could sway the decision. Or at least, her father's stance. Make him fight harder against the approval. But the more she thought—of the past, of the way mates had been used against challenged alphas, of Kai's suspicions—she opted for, "No. No one can know, and no one can know I called either." A hard knock rattled the door behind her, and she cursed under her breath. "I don't have much time."

"Why? Where are you?" Sebastian's tone was edged with concern.

"Just a place to make the call," she brushed off before saying, "I need you to do or say whatever you can to convince them against this. Both of you."

"I'll get in Dad's ear when he gets back today," Sebastian said.

Isla furrowed her brows. "Where is he?"

"Charon."

Sebastian found nothing in the words, but Isla's stomach hollowed. "Charon? Why is he—"

The line cut out.

∼

A lingering rage stirred in Isla's gut along with the weight of homesickness baring on her chest. The woman had purposely notified her at *thirty seconds* rather than sixty.

As she stepped back into the bright sunlight of the square from the call center, she shifted her gaze to what she could see of the Pack Hall. She wanted the world to swallow her up. Somewhere into a void where she could be alone—or to take Kai away from all of this.

She had a gnawing feeling that their *talk* about where they stood, about the bond, had been unofficially postponed…but that didn't mean she wouldn't see him.

If Kai didn't show up at her hotel, then she'd go to him. Whether he wanted her there or not, whether it meant fighting through every reporter and guard, she would be there.

He wasn't going through this alone. As long as she was around, he wasn't meant to.

Along the streets, Isla noted the guard and city workers that were assisting the owners in cleaning their shops. She wanted to offer her help, guilt rising amidst the anger and sadness, but the warriors would be departing for training within the hour, which meant she either had to catch one of the trolleys or go for another sprint.

She cast a hand above her eyes as she angled her head against the glare, searching for a sign pointing to the nearest station. But as she did, the hair on the back of her neck stood on end, and her wolf went on high alert. Though it wasn't for Kai this time, as it had been a lot recently, it *was* familiar. And she swore as she turned, she caught something moving so quick it was a shadow-like blur in her periphery.

The self-preserving part of her pleaded for her to let it go, to head to a station and not be late for training, but she let instinct guide her instead. Moving along the cobblestone until a flicker of red cropped in the corner of her eye.

Stopping a few inches from the source, Isla bent, taking it between her fingers and lifting it to the light. "What the hell?"

It was a blood-red ruby, but not just any ruby—*hers*. A piece of her jewelry that had broken off as she'd shifted last night.

For a moment, she figured a rogue must've fled with it from the hall, trying to steal it...but then, she caught another a few yards ahead. She went to it, taking it in her other hand, barely raising it to the light before there was another.

Another.

Another.

Another.

A trail.

She followed it, collecting the numerous gemstones in her pocket, her wolf silent now, before she froze where the trail ended. An alleyway.

With the angle of the sun and the height of the buildings bracketing it, it was well-shadowed, but enough light spilled through for another gleam to catch her eye.

But it wasn't of ruby.

Taking a glance around, finding no one near, Isla took a few steps forward, her focus entirely stolen by the glittering item. Like a trance.

Almost as if she knew in the back of her mind the care it needed to be handled with, Isla cupped the piece in her hand and carefully brought it to her face.

It was a diadem—*half* a diadem.

Not the tiara-like hair comb that she'd worn. Not like the piece Amalie had donned. This wasn't meant to be thrown on for parties.

Even incomplete, the broken metal was heavy in her hand—a mix of silver, flecked with gold, and baring a black crystal. Not a twin, but nearly a sister, to the dagger she had hidden in her room. The one Lukas had been given to kill her.

As she lifted it higher, allowing one of the gemstones to catch the light, she noticed something behind her in one of the crystal embellishment's reflections.

Isla whipped around and nearly dropped the treasure as a gasp filled her lungs. She hadn't realized she'd been moving away until she collided with the wall of the building at her back.

Drawn in what seemed to be fresh red paint—dark enough that it could be mistaken for blood—was the language of the book and marker. But though it reminded her of it, this wasn't anything like the message that had been left for Kai.

Because *this one* had symbols she *did* understand: the mark of Io and the mark of a warrior.

Because *this* message had been left for her.

The note for Kai had been left by a murderer, and Isla had no reason to believe that this one was any different. No reason to believe anything but the fact that the killer of her mate's brother and father not only knew exactly who she was but was here, in Deimos.

She made herself exhale, forcing her body to relax.

And then she ran, the clatter of jewels on stone sounding in her wake as they rained from her pockets at the jerky movements.

She stopped at the mouth of the alley, training her eyes over the streets.

Empty.

Pain shot from where the metal of the diadem jammed into the fleshy part of her tightening fist.

A murderer and a coward. Like whoever had sent Lukas to kill her instead of facing her themselves.

Any doubt that they were connected ebbed away.

Isla crept back into the alley, keeping close to the wall to take away an angle of surprise for anyone approaching. She looked down at the fractured crown in her hand, rifled through her pockets for the jewels of her necklace, then looked at the new trail of them on the ground and up at the dark writing on the wall.

What was the point of this? So, she drew the connection with the dagger? So, she knew they knew?

Her chest tightened.

Speculations were that Kai's challenger was tied to the death of his father. If *this* was them, then all of this could've been some kind of warning. For her…and therefore, for him.

Not fear but anger rose first in her gut. A defensiveness against an enemy she couldn't see. A protectiveness over what was hers in the wake of a threat.

Determination etching across her face, Isla tucked the diadem into the inner pocket of Kai's jacket, the heavy piece causing the fabric to skew.

Time was *still* not her friend, but she had to get this to Jonah with the book.

The guards in the square were startled by her sudden appearance beside them, but still, she managed to sweet-talk them out of a pad of paper and a pen. She'd slowed as she neared the alleyway again, ready to turn the corner and find something new. Ready for that lightning shadow. Ready for a fight.

But there was nothing amiss.

It took her as long to scribe the message as it did to realize she'd barely been breathing. The few slow inhales she made herself take had her dizzy, and the odd shapes and angles of the supposed letters had her fingers, her hands, and her wrists cramping.

As she looked at her poor copy of what was before her, Isla grimaced. Any improper curve or cut of her script could've completely changed its meaning or made it useless. But it would do. It would have to do.

And this—

Isla stepped back, observing the message again.

This had to go. No one could see it, especially not those two symbols. Ones that very clearly pointed her way.

Running to the guards again would only look suspicious, and none of the stores were open at this hour, not while cleaning still had to be done.

Isla looked at her arm then looked at the paint. It was so fresh, still wet as if it had been written mere minutes before she'd stepped foot back into the street from the call center.

Had they been here, waiting for her? Had they followed her from Jonah's? From her hotel?

She couldn't think of it. Not for her sanity or the sake of time.

Frowning, Isla brought up her sleeve—Kai's sleeve—and rubbed away as much of the writing as she could, staining the fine black fabric with red. The marks became smudged, losing some of their shapes, but they were still there. Taunting her. As if whoever had done this had taken extra care to ensure they stayed.

With a curse, Isla braced herself, bringing out her claws and pressing them to the brick. A searing pain shot up her arm and through her wolf as she dragged them over the hard surface. Over and over and over. A hiss slipped her mouth as she noticed the blood leaking from the wounds caused by the pulling at her skin, not able to heal as fast as she was inflicting them.

But she continued, pushing past the ache, building up the scratches until the remnants of the mark of her home and the mark of her title were nothing but a mix of dust and blood at her feet.

∽

Jonah hadn't been at the shop.

When Isla had arrived at its door, her legs and lungs burning after her run from the square, it was locked. He didn't answer when she knocked this time, and he didn't appear to be inside when she peered through one of the side translucent windows. But something she *did* see —or rather, what she *didn't* see was her bag, the book, and the marker.

The counter she'd left them on was bare.

She could only assume, or hope, he'd gone somewhere to investigate them. But after the way they'd left things, with his suspicious eye lingering over her before Davina had appeared, she couldn't help but fear that he'd done something else with them. Something that would make her regret bringing him into the fray.

She wouldn't let herself entertain it for long. Being distrustful of someone Kai viewed as family was the *last* thing she needed to add to her list of problems.

So, she wrote him a note with her borrowed pad of paper, saying that she'd be back in the morning—and for him to *make sure* he had that brew he'd concocted ready.

As she bent to slide the parchment into the small space beneath the door, Isla felt the hair on the back of her neck stand on end again. She snapped up, so fast she nearly became dizzy, catching what seemed to be a second figure in the window's reflection. Too dark and too far to discern through the glass—and gone by the time she turned to face it.

∼

Isla was going to kill Eli—and every other member of her squadron.

In the grand scheme of things, when she finally returned to the hotel from Jonah's, she had, at least, ten minutes to quickly get herself ready and get some food into her system. But apparently, the assholes had *left* her, departing the hotel for the guard base *thirty minutes* earlier than usual.

She didn't need to wonder if it had been done on purpose upon noticing her absence. Even if he wouldn't say it outright when they'd left for the hotel, Eli wasn't thrilled about her actions at the banquet, fighting without formal order from him. And the other men could care less if she made it to training.

Now, she was stuck in *this* hell.

Her cough tasted vaguely of blood as she careened around a tree on the trails alongside the campus—her punishment. Every fifteen-minute increment she had been late meant an extra mile on top of the usual two-mile warm-up.

She'd arrived one hour behind everyone else—thanks to the slowest driver in history who could only get her within a twenty-minute walking distance of the mountain terrain. A walking distance she *also* ran.

She didn't even want to think about what the rest of the day held, but the peaks of the mountains taunted her through the trees' canopies.

Ten miles up and ten miles down.

While the higher-ups met to discuss updated strategy pertaining to the newly emboldened rogues, the guard and warrior units were going on a long, *long* hike starting promptly when the sun reached its peak. Isla knew if she missed *that* start time, she was a dead woman. No doubt forced to hike an extra five miles herself or have an extra ten pounds added to her pack.

So, she pushed her tired and sore muscles further, faster, groaning and gritting her teeth. The trees were becoming a blur—either because she was moving so quickly or because she'd barely had a chance to eat. The food in the mess hall wasn't the best, but still, at the thought of it, her mouth watered. Everyone else was likely finished their drills, recuperating, and enjoying a warm meal.

Meanwhile, she was alone—*very* alone—in these woods.

As she tried to focus her eyes on what she passed, whatever false confidence she'd had earlier in the town square waned. Paranoia settled in. She swore there was a figure behind one tree. A message written on another. Diamonds at the foot of another.

There was a murderer after her.

One capable of taking down an alpha and his heir.

One supposedly bold enough to claim it and take on her mate.

She was vulnerable out here…a fact proven by the eerie sound of cracking branches behind her.

Isla stumbled but didn't stop.

The twigs had been snapped by a foot too heavy to belong to any creature that dwelled here.

More branches cracked louder from another direction. A few seconds later—again. Closer.

She was being followed—or chased?

Shit, shit, shit.

Forcing herself not to panic, Isla took a quick inventory of her surroundings. Some close-knit trees with low-hanging branches lay ahead on the trail's path.

Those became her target.

Timing it just right, she skidded around the bend and threw up her arms, catching onto the bark and using her core to swing up her body to perch on a limb's surface, ducking into some of the brush cover. It groaned beneath her weight, and she prayed the sound of that, and its brother she also snapped from the trunk as a makeshift weapon, didn't give away her location.

Her chest was on fire, and her strangled panting sawed through her throat. It was a struggle not to choke on the coarse air as she fought to settle her breathing.

But then came that feeling. Not the fear or the adrenaline, but that intoxicating, exhilarating relief.

Moments later, she felt something warm touch her back. But when Isla jerked and spun to her mate standing below her at the tree's base, any reprieve she'd felt trickled away. The question of "what was he doing here" was dead on her tongue.

Kai was shaking his head, concern flecking his eyes and a tenseness drawn in his face as he lifted a finger to his mouth, telling her to be quiet.

CHAPTER 29

With Kai's firm hands on her hips to slow her descent, Isla slid from her spot to the waiting ground below. The dead leaves prematurely fallen ahead of the upcoming Equinox barely whispered beneath her feet. Kai didn't remove his grip once she'd stood stable, instead, he pulled her to him, hugging her body to his and backing them a few more steps into the brush.

Though not done by means of affection, Isla still leaned into the embrace, letting her arms settle around him, listening closely to the steady drumming of Kai's heart below her ear, catching her breath and letting his scent invade her nose. It was a battle not to simply melt into him. After the morning she'd just had, with the message and the news of the challenge…

Isla lifted her head to look at Kai's face, confirming the notion that keeping her this close was more a method of shielding her than anything else. His eyes were focused on the woods beyond their cover. Whatever that second noise was, or the first. One of them had to have been Kai, and the other—

The blood-red markings on the wall flashed in Isla's mind, but the paranoia didn't manifest as horribly as it had been.

Maintaining their proximity, Isla dared to turn, cautiously stepping her feet and pressing her back to Kai's chest. Her hand came to rest on his forearm, his grip remaining loose around her middle as she surveyed the empty trail. Waiting…and waiting and waiting until something—whoever had been following her—broke into their vantage.

Kai's hold became tight when she jumped. Though it wasn't out of fear but surprise and confusion.

Callan.

She felt a growl rumble in Kai's chest, so low she wouldn't have caught it unless she was up against him like this, and cocked her head to cast a curious sidelong glance at him. Her mate didn't pay it any heed, only focused on the man who'd just paused his walk right where she'd disappeared. As the fellow warrior lifted his head to catch a scent, Isla shrunk further into Kai's embrace, letting whatever empty essence she was casting get lost in his.

There were much greater things for her to fear than her narcissistic former lover, but she didn't need him catching her with the alpha.

She counted out ten seconds, timed to the heartbeats she attempted to slow before Callan disappeared.

Isla didn't move until Kai did a few beats later. And when she faced him again, his eyes remained on the forest, tension still cutting his features, no sense of mirth in his eyes, even if she dug for it. There was too much going on in his head. Too much going on in general…and she hadn't even told him half of it yet.

She risked reaching up to touch his face, the stubble a little rougher beneath her skin as she ran her thumb over his cheek. At the touch, his eyes met hers, and the muscles beneath her fingertips relaxed. Something in the storm had cleared, a flicker of light where she could get through to him. And the clouds parted further when she got up on her toes, holding his gaze, and touched her mouth to his. The small upward tug of his lips was all she needed.

As he leaned in to deepen the kiss, she pulled away.

There were so many questions she wanted to ask, so much she wanted to do—either break down to him or drag him down into the leaves with her—but she settled for simple first. For obvious.

She kept her voice low. "What are you doing here?"

Kai's stare flickered between her eyes and her mouth, and she could practically see the battle going on in his head. Three steps forward and he could have her pressed back against a tree.

"There's a strategy meeting," he said.

Isla refrained from furrowing her brows. She knew of the meeting—not so much of Kai's attendance. He hadn't gone to the last one the day after the warriors had arrived. The one between Eli, the lead commander, and Ezekiel.

Before she could ask him another question, Kai drew his gaze away and back to the trail again. His throat bobbed as he swallowed, and the hard lines returned to his face. "What can you tell me about that warrior?"

Isla's eyes widened. "Callan?" When Kai nodded, she grimaced, flashing her teeth and shifting on her feet. "He's a...warrior from Io."

"Thank you." Kai offered a deadpan look. "I couldn't get that from the ledger I had to approve."

Isla mirrored the expression with her own. Though, she was happy for the dry remark. It felt like him.

She folded her arms, playing aloof. "What do you want to know?"

Kai lofted a brow at her demeanor as if clocking how disingenuous it was. "Do you know him?"

Too well.

"We grew up around similar circles," she said, clearing her throat, willing away any memories of their courtship. Though she was curious how her mate would react to the man who'd been in her bed—underwhelmingly so—much more than he had. "Why do you want to know?"

Kai's gaze turned suspicious, analyzing; it reminded her of Jonah. They both had silent, brooding moments. She wondered if they bonded over the fact they could glean so much about someone from what appeared to be so little.

As if proving her notions, Kai's face dawned with amusement, lips curling in smug enjoyment. Isla couldn't even appreciate seeing him smile, seeing that indent in his cheek, the full light shining in his eyes. "No..."

Somehow, he'd figured it out.

She let out an exasperated breath. "Kai."

"Him? Really? One of the infamous former flames." He pointed to the empty area. "He seems like a bit of an asshole. But then again, you said that was your type."

Isla glared, saying pointedly, "And it's *also* all I'm destined for, apparently."

"How long did it last?" Kai asked, that curiosity of his over her past rearing again. "One night fling? A few months?"

"Almost two years. I nearly chose him."

That seemed to sober Kai up.

The darkness came over his face again. And soon, so did that familiar feeling. The cloud above her, that tether, coiling along and through the bond. As invigorating as it was, being so...wanted, she didn't want Kai to lose that spark. Whatever form of peace that seemed to emerge, even at the expense of a headache.

"He's mated," she said, and Kai's attention returned to her. "He chose someone else after I ended it with him." She shrugged. "I suppose I knew there were better things out there for me."

The comment did rouse the side of his mouth, but the small grin was short-lived.

Back to quiet and brooding. Isla held in her sigh.

"What does he want with you?"

"Want with me? Nothing," Isla said. "What do you mean?"

"When I arrived, I was formally introduced to the warriors," Kai began to explain. "After I inquired where the sixth one was, the female, I was told very bluntly that you were late—apparently, you'd been *missing* this morning at departure—and were finishing running the trails outside the grounds. You were the *only one* remaining out here. He seemed surprised, and suddenly, the man who wouldn't stop talking about himself had nothing to say. When I saw him leaving the building, I knew where he was going."

As Kai had spoken, Isla could picture the situation perfectly: Callan boasting how ever he could in front of those of higher status, even if from another pack. He almost needed validation as much as she once sought.

Kai wasn't wrong. It did sound strange. But she couldn't think of what Callan would want. They hadn't spoken, *truly* spoken, since their brief interaction at the feast. She was about to ask Kai what made him care enough to follow him—if Callan had *said* something suspicious or off-putting—but then the realization hit. It wouldn't take much for distrust to manifest for Kai when it came to Callan.

Because he was of Io.

"He left Callisto after the feast," Isla told him, squashing whatever idea Kai had before he could verbalize it. A touch of nausea bubbled in her stomach at the rising of the possibility someone in her pack could turn against her. But the message was here… "I saw him board the vehicle and leave that night. He wasn't there when we emerged."

"Where did you run off to this time?"

Isla's features turned sour. It was a reminder, the most bitter kind, of the immediate danger at hand. To him.

Isla wrapped her arms around herself, saying softly, "I called home to see what I could find out about the challenge."

"You *what*?"

Isla sighed through her nose. "The Imperial Council deliberates with the Alpha about approval of challenges. A Council that includes my father. I knew I couldn't get to you to ask what was happening—and I wanted to see if I could stop it. I couldn't reach my father, so I talked to

Adrien and Sebastian. They hadn't heard yet, but they were going to see what they could do."

She had a hard time gauging Kai's reaction. Couldn't tell if she was happy that she'd tried to interfere or if he thought it had been a mistake. When he was silent for far too long, Isla filled in the gap with her own question.

"Do you know who the challenger is?" she asked. "Is it really who... killed your father?"

Isla could see the emotions written clearly now as Kai scowled. As the ire threatened to color his eyes. "No."

Isla straightened. "It isn't?"

"No," Kai repeated. "No matter how many times he says it and tries to claim it. It's just a no-name rogue trying to make something important of himself after being exiled. It's all a joke, a game. Inciting fear and riling up the pack for no reason."

"As rogues do," Isla muttered. Though a challenge seemed like *a lot* in terms of the lengths gone to cause the chaos and strife they craved. Even if she was losing that lightness to that rage brewing as he hashed it out to her, what he'd said made her hopeful. "So, you don't think they'll approve it?"

"I don't know what to expect with your alpha," Kai said, simply and honestly. The cool tone was almost unnerving as he went on, "My bloodline has ruled over Deimos, over this corner of Morai, since the Goddess still walked among us. Before the Pack of Io even existed. To even risk throwing away that history by considering it, to put my pack in a position where they'd be under a *rogue wolf*'s control...it tells me enough."

Over this corner of Morai.

Deimos. Phobos. The brothers. Kai's ancestors. Many great grandfathers and uncles down the family line. The packs took, or *had* taken, most of the western quarter of their land.

It tells me enough.

The words rang in her head again. "Enough about what?"

Before Kai could answer, a strangled cry sounded in the air. Like that of a wounded animal. But there was something different about it. Unsettling, yet beckoning.

Both Isla and Kai had turned to look in the direction in which it came. Isla's brow raised in perplexity while Kai's lay flat over narrowed eyes. In time, they swiveled their heads back to face each other. There was a moment of pause before the tension between them lightened. Kai's face fell as Isla bit her lip, holding back a devious smile.

"Don't do that," he said.

Isla inclined her head. "Do what?"

"That look is as concerning as it is arousing."

"You don't want to know what that was?"

Kai didn't answer, just loosed a heavy breath.

Isla released the hold on her lip and beamed, now taunting him, "It seems I'm rubbing off on you."

"Not nearly enough."

Banter. Banter was good. Anything to pull him from that place.

Isla stepped back from him, hands reaching for the hem of her shirt.

Kai's eyes grew wider as she pulled it over her head, leaving her in her tight camisole. "What are you doing?"

Isla dropped the piece to the ground, where she buried it in the leaves. Her fingers went to the waistband of her pants. She had to quell the part of her that thrummed as Kai watched her movements so closely, trailing down the length of her bare legs after she removed the covering. All that remained was her undergarments. "I'd like to have my clothes in one piece when I get back."

She turned away from him as she removed what remained on top, taunting him. "I can't be gone for long, and I'm much quicker shifted." She pulled her hair from its tie, letting the tresses flow free and wild down her back. The strands were gilded gold in the light that broke through the canopies, and she pulled the hair forward to just cover the peaks of her breasts. More teasing.

When she turned, donning only her underwear, she crossed her arms too. "You can either strip and come with me, Alpha, or stay here."

Kai's eyes didn't seem to know where to land—and for a moment, she wanted to ask what was going through his head now. What he'd do to her. What he *could* do now that they could touch…

The growl he let out took her from whatever thoughts and seemed to go straight to her core. He reached for the buttons of his shirt, fine and formal for a gathering of those of status, and unfastened one button, then another and another. Isla couldn't stop her own greedy eyes from taking in what the Goddess had so wickedly given to her as he removed the piece completely.

Now, she felt like a fool.

It took everything to remain rooted in her spot. To not look utterly dumbstruck as she followed the flow of his lumerosi, followed those tattoos over his arm, cutting over his shoulder, his pectoral. As she watched the rippling muscles of his torso go taut and loose with every breath. Found the way they dipped into the waistband of his pants—

Which he was now removing.

Isla forced her eyes back up to his as he left himself wholly naked before her.

She held herself back. Trying to temper the intrusive images of all the wicked things *she'd* do. Maybe, she'd beat him to her knees.

Not breaking eye contact as he slowly moved in on her, Isla removed her final garment, trying to do so as quick and level-headed as possible. She'd tossed her underwear to the side with the rest of her clothing just as Kai placed a firm hand beneath her chin to look up at him.

"You are an impossible woman," he told her.

Isla gulped, quashing that part of her so aware nothing stood between them finding release with each other but sheer will and stubbornness.

She placed a hand on his chest, fingers curling just slightly to dig her nails into the ink of that tattoo. Her gasp remained caught in her throat as she pressed her body to his, letting her breasts just graze his skin as she rose on her toes, closer to his face.

One last move, one last jab, for the upper hand, and to guarantee he would follow.

"*Yours,*" she hushed over his mouth, strained and gritty with deteriorating resolve.

But sense came forth when her wolf did, and as Kai leaned down to capture her mouth, Isla was quicker. She'd left him stumbling as she shifted and hauled ass into the trees.

∼

Kai knew the forest well. He told Isla how he'd trained with the guard, had been on it before he'd become alpha. For a little while, he guided them towards the initial direction of the sound. Through easy paths with less brush to fight through and narrow breaks of streams to leap over.

There was something incredibly freeing about them simply being able to *run*. To feel, to just be, free of everything. There were no murderers. No rogues. No secret messages. Even with the distinct hue to Kai's eyes, he didn't even have to be the alpha here.

It was just them.

But the bliss of it didn't last very long. Not when something in the air seemed to change. When Isla noticed how bare the trees were, how quiet everything was. Like all life had scattered, leaving this part of the forest abandoned. Kai noticed it too, the stillness and heaviness of what they walked upon. Even the wind wouldn't dare blow here.

And then came the scent.

Biting and familiar. Snaking down into the deepest, most buried parts of Isla's subconscious.

Despite the reservations, the innate fear lapping at her paws, they followed the smell, Kai staying a few protective steps ahead.

They came upon the narrow mouth of a cave, and Isla couldn't even register what Kai had tried to say through their link. All her senses were so overpowered, that she couldn't even think straight.

With every bone in her body, she knew, she *felt* what was coming when they broke the dark threshold of the cavern.

And yet, she was still stunned, still nearly incapacitated by terror when she found herself staring into the bright red eyes of a bak.

Goddess…

The beast was dead—but even its lifeless stare was enough to immobilize Isla where she stood. Enough to fill her mind with darkness and demons and memories of a life just before death. Her stomach hollowed out, and her chest felt heavy like the bak had been upon her again, ready to eat her alive. She thought she'd only ever have to encounter another in her nightmares.

Maybe this was one.

The creature was sprawled in a pool of its own dark blood, the ebony liquid still leaking from the deep wound at its neck. The tearing had been so vicious, so deep, that its large head was nearly clean off its body.

In her pause, Kai had since approached it, his paws becoming drenched in the sticky black tar. He snarled as he circled it as if it would awaken and endanger her, his home, his people.

But it was dead. Very, very dead.

Isla forced herself to focus, to get words through their link. *"How—how did it get here?"*

A stupid question. Kai was likely as clueless as she was.

The bak were supposed to be contained. Behind the Wall, barricaded by thick stone and protective enchantments. By wards and blood runes. By magic.

But—

"Could it have slipped through the Gate? If the wards are failing…" she offered. *"Maybe during a guard change?"*

"And then walked the lengths of that pack to our borders, through two *of our regional checkpoints before ending up here in the mountains? For them to*

even think that highly—to wait for guards to leave, to even break open the Gate…it's not possible."

"Maybe there's a break in the Wall. It's centuries-old, and with everything acting up, it no longer has that constant reinforcement or deterrent."

As they shared the thoughts, Isla realized this was all exactly as Kai had feared. He'd wanted to put resources into looking at the Wall, but he'd gotten pushback.

Because no one knew the truth.

Not one member of his council, besides Ezekiel, knew of what had occurred during the Hunt. The bak's odd behavior was a continent-wide secret, all because of Imperial Alpha Cassius and his need to keep this all buried and forgotten, hoping it would be lost to time.

Like all the hierarchy's secrets.

Like the Ares Pass.

The thought rocked through her like a shot of lightning.

The pass—a direct connection between Deimos and Phobos. Or rather, Deimos and the Wilds.

Isla tried to remember the rest of Lukas's words from a time that felt like a millennium ago now. From a time before he'd tried to murder her.

This pass goes into Mavec…a straight shot into the royal city…

"*Where's the Wall in relation to here?*" she asked Kai who'd since gone on to explore the perimeter of the cave.

Her voice, edged with eagerness, likely would've concerned him if he wasn't so focused. His movements were keen and sharp. She expected nothing less, his demeanor bordering militant. "*East,*" was all he answered.

Before she headed back out into the woods, Isla braced herself and dared to encroach on the creature. She lowered her snout, running it over its dry, gray, sparse-haired covered skin, tearing over near-impenetrable muscle. Its pungent odor flooded her senses, and the fatal wound, she realized, had been made with a blade.

Isla stepped back. She'd been so relieved it was dead, that she hadn't thought to ask why. Who had done this? Who had taken on the bak and defeated it?

Another pass over the creature. No other scents lingered. Not even a drop of wolf blood. They'd done it without getting hurt themselves.

She ventured back to the cave's mouth.

"*Isla.*"

The tug at the bond, her name in her mind, was sharp.

"*I'm just checking the woods,*" she said.

Kai took a few steps towards her. "*What if there's more?*"

More.

Goddess. She hadn't even thought of more.

But the question was just to test her.

Kai wasn't worried about there being more; the chances of multiple slipping through the cracks was too improbable. Otherwise, they wouldn't still be in the cave. He'd likely already have the entire pack on lockdown.

"Then I'll howl," she said, and she wondered if this was where a line would be drawn.

He'd let her fight against the rogues, but bak were an entirely different monster.

Isla didn't even want to picture the streets of Mavec if bak, rather than the rogues, had been unleashed upon them last night. That beautiful blue crystal would be *bathed* with blood, the river running red. It would be like the times of the past before the Wall was raised. When the beasts could so freely roam and take, destroying towns and taking the lives of entire villages before they could be stopped.

Kai's silence went on for too long, his crimson eyes darting between her and the creature on the cave floor. As if he was recalling seeing one nearly kill her months ago.

"Don't go too far," he finally told her.

Isla nodded and before she left, made sure to brush her head reassuringly against his. Simply to feel him relax, just a bit.

The forest had begun to regain some of its life. The birds had been singing again when Isla stepped back out into the sunlight, halting briefly to allow her eyes to adjust. That meant the bak had been dead long enough that the animals felt it safe to roam again. How unsettling the creatures were that they were able to clear a forest just by existing in it.

She lowered her head and sniffed, finding herself heading eastward down hills, moving downwind. So many questions ran through her mind as she stalked, not realizing how far she was drifting.

How literal was a straight shot?

Did the pass cut straight over and through Mavec's terrain? Did that mean there *was* a hole in the Wall?

What had made Lukas say where they stood back in the Wilds was the pass? The marker?

Is that what she had to look for? More markers?

Was she going crazy over nothing?

Isla froze where she stood as a new scent caught the wind, emerging from nothing and disappearing just as quickly. Because the person wanted to be found, but only by her. She spun just as Callan appeared from the thickets.

His smile was self-satisfied and grating. "You're off your path."

Isla snarled, lowering on her haunches. They wouldn't be able to communicate like this. In a perfect world, she wouldn't communicate with him at all, ever. But he'd found her again. He'd been looking for her. And she wanted answers.

She came out of her shift and folded her arms across her chest, crossing her legs to cover herself.

"It's nothing I haven't seen before," he jeered, and though he was right, she held the position. Her body was meant for her and the only person she'd wanted to share it with lately.

"Why are you following me?" she demanded.

Callan countered her question with another. One she hadn't been expecting.

"How long have you been fucking the alpha?"

Isla started. The query shouldn't have made her as uneasy or feel as exposed as it did.

"Did you think I hadn't noticed you sneaking around since the day we got in? Or that I wouldn't hear him in your room last night?"

Isla forced her face to remain neutral, even if every muscle in her body had tensed. The sheer invasiveness Callan's words alluded to seemed to edge out any aggravation at herself for being so careless in her actions, or for being so naïve to think no one would notice.

"Are you stalking me?" she bit out, her pulse thrumming violently in her ears. Even if Callan's assumptions were incorrect—sleeping together was the only thing she and Kai *hadn't* done—for some reason, it felt better than him believing the alternative.

"No," Callan said, his laugh bitter. Not jealous but sore. Over what, she wasn't sure. He was mated. He couldn't have still felt some ridiculous claim over her somehow? "I was told to look out for you. To make sure you didn't get into any trouble."

Isla furrowed her brows. "By who?"

"The Imperial Alpha. Your father," Callan rattled, mirroring her by crossing his own arms. "It seems their assumptions that you'd make a mockery of yourself—out of us—were warranted. I don't know why the general would make such a bid for you. Put his reputation on the line bringing you here. Regardless of breeding and bloodlines and getting into our pack, I'd want a better mate than someone so ready to whore herself out."

Isla could barely mask her disgust, but she couldn't let him see that the words stung. Not the unnecessary and hateful jab at the fact she wasn't the pinnacle of purity—which had told her part of this confrontation was that Callan felt he still held something on her—but the supposed fact her father thought of her so low...

Alpha Cassius having those sentiments, she'd believe, with all the resentment she still held towards him since that day he'd lied to her about Lukas. But her dad...a mockery of herself, of the pack, her family? It couldn't have been true.

"How long has it been?" Callan asked before she could retort his worthless comment. "Did you somehow keep in contact after the Hunt, or the moment we arrived, you were ready to open your legs for him?"

She'd nearly stepped forward to slap him, a scowl on her face, but her features faltered when she felt it. Felt him. Kai, through the bond. No scent. No alpha's aura. He was here, close, amongst the brush, hidden. Watching. Ready to strike if Callan tried anything funny.

Isla wondered if he'd also picked up on the eagerness in Callan's questions. A little bit of desperation behind them.

The answers she gave were important. Not just for him and that ridiculous inkling of possessiveness, but for something greater. Someone.

Isla found her fingers curling into fists.

She was being used as bait yet again. Not *by* Kai this time, but *for* Kai.

Her aggravation leaked into her voice as she spat, "My *personal* choices, especially who I sleep with, are no one's business but my own."

"Not when they reflect on the pack."

"I'm not the pack."

"Here, that's *all* we are," Callan said as he moved close enough that Isla had to crane her head. "You don't feel it every time we walk through this base? How these people look at us."

Isla bit down on the inside of her cheek, thinking *beyond* the base. Thinking of the banquet, of the call center, of the whispers and glares that trailed her like a bad smell. From the people she was destined to lead.

Her chest tightened. "They hate us."

"Because they want to *be* us."

"Only because they don't realize we're no different than them." She bared her teeth, feeling something cruel rise in her, and stepped in closer. Her next words were drawn out, cutting like knives. "And that the biggest difference to being a part of our pack is obligatory blind loyalty and the raging, unearned superiority complex of most of its members. *You* being a prime example."

Callan's stare was blazing and dangerous, but he remained quiet. He would continue to, even if it killed him. He wanted her to keep talking. She wasn't sure what he was expecting her to know or what he was hoping to find out, but if he wanted something to report back to whoever, she'd give it to him.

"I bet Alpha Cassius didn't even tell you why you're supposed to watch me. Why he doesn't trust me. It has nothing to do with me fucking the Alpha of Deimos—but if you did want to add that joke to your report, please, go ahead…do you know what really went on behind the Wall during the Hunt?" She caught the way Callan clenched and unclenched his fists, the confusion flashing in his eyes. "Do you want to know *why* I had to kill so many bak? Why—"

Isla stopped when the sound of rustling leaves came from behind her, and both she and Callan whipped around as Kai emerged from the brush. His wolf loomed large in front of them; his shadow-black fur gilded by the sun and crimson glower honed on them as he stalked closer. A few seconds later, he was himself again, and Isla noticed the faintest smears of dark blood over his body—his neck, hands, chest, and jaw.

Callan had taken a step away from her, his head lowered. Regardless of what pack they led, all alphas commanded the same respect.

There was an intimidating and regal air to Kai as he moved towards them, and somehow, the coolness he conveyed was more threatening than any snarl or outright warning. "What are you two doing so far from the main campus?"

So, he was feigning indifference towards her. Good, she supposed.

As she had, Callan remained quiet.

"I suppose it's wiser to stay silent than to lie to me." Kai chuckled humorlessly, and Isla retreated as her mate focused on her former lover. He was directly in front of him when Kai asked, "Callan, right?" But before Callan could even nod in agreement, he added, "Or is it Edriel?"

Callan froze, and Isla swore he was about to soil himself. She had no idea who that was, or what that name meant. And yet, Callan turned her way with pure fear in his eyes as if she could help.

"Don't look at her." A ferocity had slipped into Kai's voice. One that had Callan righting himself quickly, and one he barely dialed back as he continued, "You've been a busy man this week. Giving a false name is a commendable attempt, but pointless when you're being tailed. I heard that you finally made your way down the river last night. I'm quite fond of Abalys, what did you think of it?"

Isla blinked.

Kai was having *Callan* watched? And he was going around using a false identity?

Callan's method of self-preservation seemed to be submission and silence. Isla would've enjoyed it if she hadn't been so lost. If she hadn't realized, yet again, Kai was five steps ahead of her, keeping her in the dark about the true intentions behind his words and actions. In the dark about what he knew.

"What does your alpha have you here searching for?" Kai asked, head cocked as he analyzed the warrior. Almost having too much fun as the inferior wolf worked to avoid eye contact. "I hope it's important because right now, the way I'm seeing things, *you* were in Abalys the one and only night rogues were able to breach our borders and slaughter my people, which puts me within my right to deal with you how I see fit. *Kill you* if I saw you as a threat and if I could fool myself into believing you were intelligent enough to be responsible. But I have enough to deal with, and you aren't worth the headache of paperwork you dying on my land would bring."

Kai paused, enough for Callan to take the cue.

"Thank you, Alpha," he managed to say through gritted teeth.

Kai nodded and turned away from him, towards Isla. He took a heavy breath as he searched her expression—her flared nostrils, clenched teeth, and the hurt and agitation in her narrowed eyes. He knew what he'd done, and, for a moment, his face seemed apologetic.

For a moment.

"You have until dawn tomorrow to leave," Kai ordered Callan, turning his head his way but not fully. "Don't let me catch your scent within these borders a minute after, or I may have to reconsider. Am I clear?" Callan nodded, and though Kai couldn't see it, he still growled, "*Go*."

And Callan obeyed, leaving his clothes—and his pride—a tattered mess in the dirt as he shifted and darted as fast as he could through the trees.

Both Isla and Kai watched the spot where he'd disappeared until the sound of his paws hitting the ground was replaced by nothing but the warble of birds.

Isla turned back to her mate, meeting his stare with her own.

"I took care of the bak," Kai said, clocking her crossed expression. "I dragged it to a hidden part of the stream, and after you all head off and my meeting, I'll burn it. No one else should venture out this far today, and I'll consult with Ezekiel about what we do after that."

"Thanks for telling me." She was certain he'd only mentioned it because she'd seen it for herself. He couldn't hide it.

"We should head back," Kai said, voice straining to stay even.

And then, he shifted.

Isla was wide-eyed as he started to move away. But she was quick. In her shift and on top of him in seconds.

She had him on his back, her wolf above his, as she snarled in his face. *"No."*

Mirroring her look, Kai bared his teeth, sharp and lethal, but then, he pulled his wolf back.

Isla did, too.

And now, she was on her hands and knees hovering over him. But the rage she felt usurped any arousal the position could bring.

"Explain. Now," she seethed.

Kai's gaze traveled over her face, over the soft curves of her body before he met her eyes again. He sighed. "Isla…"

Her claws re-emerged, embedding in the dirt close to his head. "Don't. *Isla*. Me."

She was done with this. Being the general's prize. Being bait. Being a pawn.

Being used was bad enough, but it was made worse by letting her believe that she wasn't.

"You tell me whatever the fuck that was about right now, or Goddess help you, I will reject you right here."

Kai looked to either side of them, and Isla knew he was searching for anyone else around, listening. But Callan, as abhorrent as he was, had common sense and would never risk himself getting caught.

"All you do is lie to me. Hide things," she said, unable to keep her voice from cracking. "You've been doing it since the day I met you. You didn't tell me who you really were. You never told me you were in the Hunt. You never told me why you *really* didn't want to be with me. About the killer in the woods."

Kai's hand had lifted, skimming the skin of her thigh. Not to start anything but to soothe. "I'm trying to—"

"Protect me?" she finished for him, jerking herself from his touch. "I don't need you to just protect me. I need you to be *honest* with me, Kai. Actually tell me the truth—the entire truth—for fucking *once*."

A whirlwind of emotions flashed over his face before his jaw tensed.

"You want me to be honest? You want to know what I think? You want to know what I know, Isla?"

"*Yes*," she nearly screamed.

Then, before she could blink, Kai had flipped them over.

Now, he hovered above her, pinning her arms above her head, cradled between her legs. But again, there was no impish intent in his eyes, nothing but cold seriousness as he said—

"I know that every day, it becomes more and more apparent that my enemy is the family of the woman I love and that I'm running out of time with her."

CHAPTER 30

Isla had forgotten how to breathe, the sawing, shuddering sounds escaping her lips fading to empty noise as she beheld her mate's face.

Her mate—a man who had not yet realized what he'd said. The weight that it held.

The woman I love.

The words clanged through Isla's mind, her body, the bond.

Love.

Love.

For a moment, she wondered if he hadn't been speaking of her. Maybe another woman had held his affections?

But then Kai's features shifted.

His jaw went slack. His cold stare warmed. His eyes widened in the slightest fear. A fear she rarely saw on him.

He gave a subtle shake of his head, his fingers offering the lightest squeeze to her wrists as if to check if she was truly there. If he hadn't just imagined it.

But she was real.

And with the touch, Isla found he was real, as well.

Too real.

Love.

"Isla..."

This time, she'd let that tone of his pass.

Isla struggled to swallow, and her dry eyes burned when she finally got herself to blink. The voice that left her mouth was foreign and weak. "You…love me?"

Kai's stare had her pinned now, passing over the planes of her face with such intent, that she swore he could see through to her soul. See through to where those threads of her reached out to those of him. Twined with him. Were desperate for their work to end. For them to give it up and give in to each other.

Kai heaved a breath, and Isla was left cold and exposed as he moved to sit at her side, leaving a small distance between them as he raked his hand through his hair. As Isla rose to her knees, he'd only spared her a glance.

She watched his throat bob before he answered, finally, "I do."

More words like a shot, stealing the wind from her again.

The woman that I love…

The sentence ran rounds in her head. All of it.

The woman I…

But besides the mentioning of love, another phrase clawed its way along her skin.

And I'm running out of time with her.

Isla remained rooted in her spot and cleared her throat. "Why are we running out of time?" Though she didn't know the answer, it still felt like a foolish question.

Kai looked at her fully. "Because me falling in love with you wasn't part of our plan."

She wasn't sure that her ears would ever get used to that word from his lips, that her brain would ever stop pausing at it, but she did her best to ignore the feeling, to focus on what had framed it.

The plan.

Isla nearly cackled remembering that night in the garden. When the Hunt ended, she'd go back to Io, he'd come lead Deimos, and they would forget about each other. But after all of this, how was that even possible?

"None of this was a part of our plan," she said. "I'm here in Deimos."

"But you will be going back to Io once the warriors' assignment here is over," Kai said. "Right?"

Isla couldn't get herself to answer.

He turned away, focusing forward. Regret shone across his face. "You can't stay…and I don't think I can let you go. Not when we're like this."

Like this. Still tied to each other. Partially bound.

For some reason, panic rose in her chest. "You want to reject me?"

"No." Kai looked like the proposal was absurd. "But I know us being together will be complicated, and that in the end, you'll have to give up a lot more than I have to."

Isla managed to choke down a swallow, circling her arms around herself as she thought, remembered. Accepting the bond with Kai meant she'd likely never see home again. Barely see her family, Adrien. Twenty-one years washed away in a blink.

Some conditioned part of her felt like a traitor when she spoke next, entertaining an idea that she should've found ridiculous.

"Why do you think it was someone of Io who tried to kill me?" she forced out. "What do you know that you haven't told me?"

Kai held in a deep breath, but when he opened his mouth to speak, a distant howl cut through the air.

It was for her.

Isla glanced up at the sun through the canopies, nearly to its highest point. It was almost noon. They'd be heading up the mountain soon, with or without her, and she'd be forced to pick up the slack with extra speed and extra weight as punishments.

She didn't care. She'd take it. She'd take all of it to get through this, and finally get a grasp on what was happening.

But when she turned to Kai, he was rising to his feet, preparing to head back.

"No," she protested, and Kai offered her a hand. Isla glowered but took it. Standing on her feet before him, she narrowed her eyes further.

He sighed. "I will tell you everything, Isla, I promise." As doubt cast across her face, he took it in his hands and kissed her like it was the last time he ever would. In a way that took her breath for a third time. But she steeled herself as they broke apart, not letting how much it had incapacitated her show. "*I promise.*" He drew out each word.

Isla's mouth was still tingling from his, as she grabbed his forearms. "Why should I believe you?"

"Because I love you," Kai told her, running his thumb over her cheek. "And I know I'll lose you forever if I don't."

~

As if she hadn't already felt raw and exposed, Isla also had to weather the dirty looks of the guard members, typically shot at *all* the warriors, reserved today specifically for her and Callan. But now she had food, so maybe she could bear it.

Isla watched from her spot at one of the tables in the furthest corner of the room as Kai meandered through the mess hall, catching up with old friends from his days serving with the guard and making new ones of the recent recruits. All part of his plan to stall their departure so she had a chance to eat.

Because I love you.

The words bore heavier on Isla's heart than the pack on her shoulders as they began their trek through the mountains. Though not as heavy as all the talk of the challenge and rogues. It seemed to be the only topic anyone wanted to discuss on the stretch of the mountain. As if Isla didn't already have enough on her mind.

Ten miles up and ten miles down.

They went up sporadically in units, rather than all as one large battalion. And although she may have rathered hike alone, now without being forced to take any extra weight, she was grateful that the unit she was ordered to join was 37B. For Rhydian. Maybe Thyra. Belle was okay. But the double-edged sword lay with Magnus.

Of course, he was the most vocal about what was happening, and Isla, who'd already been struggling to keep her composure, found herself on the receiving end of one too many of his indirect snide remarks. By mile six of being forced to endure his shitty attitude, she was ready to tear his face off.

And by mile seven, when he commented that she had no right to look as upset as she appeared because everything happening in Deimos had "nothing to do with her", she almost did.

She felt the ripping at her knuckles where her claws would emerge as she stared at the back of Magnus's head when a hand came down on her shoulder. She turned, scowl still painted on, to Rhydian. The unofficial leader of their squadron.

"Take a walk," he told her, wiping some sweat off his dirt-covered brow and nodding towards a path off the trail between a few boulders.

Isla bit down on her tongue until the metallic tang of blood filled her mouth, the dark protrusions still threatening to appear.

"We're all on edge," he said a bit quieter, and from the bite in his voice, she realized all the challenge talk had bothered him as much as her. "Go cool down."

Isla huffed through her nose.

On edge was an understatement, but despite how she truly felt—back to angry, helpless, and useless in protecting her mate—she gradually relaxed her arm. And then she hoisted the weight of her pack up her shoulders and stalked off.

She was pacing in agitated circles around a flattened clearing when Rhydian appeared from around a bend several minutes later. "I said a walk, not a second hike."

His joke fell flat. Felt empty. Even he knew it, barely able to force his mouth into a decent smile.

Isla pointed to the space beyond him, growling, "I'm going to punch him in the throat."

"He deserves it. I wouldn't have stopped you if I hadn't thought fighting Magnus was beneath you. And if it didn't mean we'd have to carry his ass the rest of the way through the mountain."

Isla ceased her pacing, needing to stabilize against a tree after so much rapid movement. She wedged her hands into her hair, something that Magnus had said was eating away at her. "Can I ask you something?"

"That's a dangerous question," Rhydian said.

Isla took that as a "*yes*". "What did you think when Kai told you that I was of Io? Assuming that he did after you all figured out he'd met me."

Rhydian raised his brows. "When we found out you were of Io, or when we learned you were the Imperial Beta's daughter?" At Isla's frown, he elaborated. "We weren't mad if that's what you're wondering."

Isla ran her tongue over her teeth.

Rhydian may not have been up for a confessional—and he may not have been her first choice to vent to—but they were going to be out here for several more hours. He was the only option she had. Davina had been a great listener; maybe it was something the mated pair shared.

"Kai told me he loves me," Isla blurted out causing Rhydian's brows to shoot upwards again. "And if I don't talk to someone about it, I'm going to lose my mind, and I can't guarantee Magnus makes it off this peak alive."

Rhydian snickered. "About time he admitted it."

Isla blinked at him. "You knew?"

"I'm not Jonah, but I'm also not blind." Rhydian laughed. "Kai spent twenty minutes talking to Dane in the mess hall just now while you scoffed down food. He hates Dane. If it wasn't because he loves you, I'd be afraid he'd lost his mind."

Isla had no idea who Dane was, but that wasn't the point.

Seeing she was clearly on edge, Rhydian shuffled on his feet, asking gently with a bit of eagerness, "So, do you, uh, do you love him?"

Isla mustered a smile, forcing herself to relax. "You're the master of perception. What do you think?"

Rhydian didn't need to say anything. The wide grin on his face was enough to tell her he could tell exactly how she felt. That he could see the battle ensuing between her mind and her heart as the former preached it was a bad idea to the latter that wanted nothing more than to find Kai and tell him she loved him back.

Isla felt like a weight had been lifted off her chest but then replaced by another. "I've never felt like this before," she confessed. "And it's so much, so fast."

"I know."

He did, and Isla wondered when he'd realized he loved Davina.

"Everything is so easy with him…when it's only us. It's like nothing else matters," she said. "But everything *does* matter. Because of who he is and who I am. It'll never be *just us*. It can't be just us. And I know I'm not my pack, but convincing people that I'm not their enemy because of how they view where I come from and who my family is will probably be a battle I fight forever, that he'll have to, and there's already so much he has—"

"You think you two would be fighting alone?" Rhydian quipped. "What about us?"

Us—Kai's family. Maybe she'd have people here after all.

Isla actually mustered a laugh. "The whole way up here, I've been trying to think of how my life would be if we decided to reject each other. If we moved on, and I just went back to Io to continue as I was and never saw him again."

"And?"

"I can't do it…I don't want to."

⁓

The warriors' ride back to the hotel was uncomfortable, the silence resounding. Not only was everyone too exhausted to speak, but a thick tension lingered in the air. One that stemmed from each of them. Isla was most curious about Eli's, but he hadn't disclosed anything about what had happened in the strategy meeting to them. Apparently, there would be another one tomorrow.

Callan had refused to make eye contact with her from the base to the car and now within it. She wondered if he could feel her pointed stare at the back of his head. If he could feel it as she followed his every move off the warriors' van and into the hotel lobby. Her own unofficial mission: making sure he left. Until she saw him cross those borders, he was a wild card. Who knew what he'd try to do in the hours before he was technically trespassing on pack ground?

But as she was about to trail him to the staircase, she felt someone tap her shoulder. She spun and was greeted by a man in a hotel uniform, the same one Davina usually wore. She was nowhere to be found behind the desk.

"Are you Isla?" he asked, and when she nodded, he reached into his pocket and pulled out a key. "Here."

Isla observed the metal. It was for a room, labeled *324*. "What is this?"

"East wing. Take the lift to the top floor," was all he said, casting his eyes side to side for listening ears before shuffling away.

CHAPTER 31

The east wing of the hotel had the remnants of a remodel scattered throughout—tarps and paints, toolboxes, hammers, and screws. It was entirely abandoned, and Isla noticed that there were fewer doors in this hallway than the one in which she resided.

She'd contemplated not even going to the room, unsure what she'd be faced with when she came upon it. But she trusted a voice in her head that had her moving across the lobby to the furthest hallway opening and finding the lift there. She didn't need the numbers beside the doors to know she was getting close to her desired destination, because she felt it. Felt him.

Her cheek between her teeth and heart thrumming, Isla shoved the key into the lock of 324 and opened the entryway. She found Kai sitting directly in her eye-line, leaning forward with his elbows on his knees, in what seemed to be the living area of the grand suite. He sat upright as she stepped inside and closed the door behind her, but he didn't speak.

Isla clutched her bag strap tightly in her fist. She wouldn't drop it to the floor. "Hi."

Kai gave her a weak smile. "Hi."

"Why have the desk worker be so secretive?"

"You seem to be a prime target for being followed. I didn't want anyone to overhear and know that I was here. I technically should be back at the hall."

Isla nodded, accepting the answer. She peered around the room. Nearly three times the size of hers with pockets of living space throughout. The den, kitchenette, office space, and a bed that seemed all too inviting to her tired muscles in the corner. Clean and elegant but with a rustic feel, thanks to some of the furniture. It was just the right balance of luxurious and homey.

"This is really nice," she remarked, still not moving from her spot.

Kai looked around, considering the space. "They're trying to make it a bit more like Starlight. It's in Ifera, more conducive to those who're having lengthy stays here. I would've had you meet me there but didn't want to make you take the train." He looked her over, seeing that she'd cleaned up and showered at the base. "How was the hike?"

"Long," Isla said. "A lot of time to think."

"About?"

If she wanted him to have no secrets, she couldn't either.

"You." The word made Kai stiffen, and so did the next. "Us."

"What about us?"

Isla dropped her bag on the ground and folded her arms. She took in a deep breath, steeling herself.

It was time to leave everything on the table. No holding back.

"By accepting this bond, I leave things that I love. The people I love. My family, my friends, my home. All I've ever known and found comfort in. I lose everything that I wanted and worked so hard to become." She quieted, trying to gauge Kai's expression, but he was unreadable. "But I've been so wrapped in believing that I was doing exactly what I needed to and being who I was meant to be, so scared of what it meant to have a mate, to give myself to someone and open myself up to losing them, that I was blind to what was *actually* happening."

Another pause, long enough that Kai felt the need to ask, "What?"

"I fell in love with you."

The gentle words settled in the air between them, and now Kai couldn't seem to stop the small uptick of the corner of his mouth. Isla could sense his heartbeat pick up, feel his elation through the bond. But he must have read her demeanor, how serious she still was, and forced himself to relax.

"And maybe I was where I was," Isla continued. "*Doing* what I was, for this. To be with you. To be here, and maybe you saw me—*see me*—in a way no one else did. That no one else ever will...I'm not sure I can do it, be a queen I mean, but I'm willing to try if you want me to. I'm terrified, but if that's what I need to do to be with you, I will...but you need to be honest with me. Because it's the only way I can help you, and I refuse to spend forever in the dark when you're the one who's supposed to keep me out of it. I've been in a place like that, and I'm never going back. And I don't want you to end up there either. I told you that you have me, and I meant it, to and through eternity."

She took another steadying inhale while Kai was quiet, absorbing everything she'd laid out before him. He gestured to the chair at his side where she could sit, but Isla refused, remaining where she stood.

All of it, their future, wasn't in the clear until he told her what he'd been hiding.

"Where do you want me to start?" he asked.

"Why do you think it was someone of Io?"

"It's a long story."

"We have time," she said, even if she wasn't so sure that they did. "Start from the beginning."

Kai's throat bobbed as he swallowed. "The night my father and brother died, I was supposed to die, too."

Isla's eyes widened, but she tried her best to keep her surprise contained.

"I wasn't in Mavec. I'd been in Abalys with Amalie. I'd convinced her to go to an inn for the night..." Kai trailed off, knowing he didn't need to continue for Isla to understand. "While we were sleeping, there was this...scent, a feeling that woke me up, but Amalie didn't seem to notice. And then something hit me—not literally, but I remember feeling stuck, and like I was disconnected from my body. From my wolf. And then there was this pain in my side...everywhere...and I swore I was dying. I blacked out, and when I woke up, someone was knocking at the room door. It was Ezekiel and Sol which should've tipped me off enough that something was wrong because they can't stand each other."

Isla braced herself, knowing what came next.

"They told me what had happened, and I couldn't recite the exact words to you even if I tried, but I *do* remember finding a message carved into the nightstand. Those letters and symbols that I didn't understand and still don't. I found them again in my brother's townhouse near the bed where he'd died and couldn't find any in the House of the hall, where my parents slept. But I had the same feeling in both places, the same one I had in those woods in Callisto. They'd been killed, and I had no idea by who. No idea why *I* lived and they didn't." Shame crept into his tone. "Everything that happened after that is a blur. I remember having no time before the Blood Moon and going through the Alpha Rite to question my being brought to power. And I remember everyone crying while I had to keep it together and pretend that someone hadn't just murdered my family and was getting away with it. Then came the feast and the Hunt—and you.

"I didn't think the Imperial Alpha would approve me to enter at such short notice, especially with the risk I could die, and our hierarchy ends up a mess, but he did. Everyone kept saying I didn't have to do it, but I knew there were people who doubted me and wanted me to do it, especially in the council I'd adopted. My father and I didn't see eye to eye on a lot of things, some choices he'd made for the pack among them. And I know despite the fact he liked to put on a facade that our family was the perfect, united front—even down to me, who wasn't his heir—knowledge of my aversions made it to his closest confidants, who saw me—see me—as a threat to a system that they'd established to keep them as high on the top of our hierarchy as possible. I miss when I thought they'd end up being my biggest problem during my rule." He breathed a humorless laugh before his features fell. "When I left Deimos for the Hunt, part of me was ready to go to war when I got back, but another part, one I hated and couldn't get rid of—hoped I wouldn't make it."

Isla felt her heart clench and blinked away a sting of tears. As much as Kai had tried to sound steady, brokenness slipped into his voice.

"The night of that feast, when I realized you were there—my *mate*—I was furious. I didn't know what or who I was going to end up with. It felt like the Goddess had already fucked me over in so many ways—my father and brother were dead, my mother was dying, and here I was, bestowed a pack full of lost, confused, and scared people looking to me to guide them out of a darkness I could barely crawl through myself… and then, there you were. I had no clue who you were, what pack you were from, or why you were there, but you were with the Imperial Heir, that trainee, and the warrior.

"I knew you couldn't feel anything, which makes sense—being an alpha, things happen a bit faster—and then you went off with the Heir. I don't think I've ever felt as feral as I did then. I was ready to tear him apart for touching you, but then I got a hold of myself and left before I did anything stupid."

He had her latched on every word, and Isla replayed that night. Her conversations with Lukas, the one with Callan when Adrien had walked over. Kai had been in that room, had seen her from afar. He knew what she was before she knew him.

"So I went outside to the terrace," he continued. "Then I don't know why, but I felt the bond between us—stronger than I had but still barely there. I tried pulling at it anyway, calling to you to see if you'd answer, but nothing really happened. I was about to head back inside when the doors opened, and there you were again."

Isla felt her insides melt with the way he looked at her now, in a way no one ever had. With pure adoration.

"Beautiful," he said, almost the same way he had that night. "Absolutely beautiful. Crueler than anything I'd been dealt. Because you were a light—a beautiful, bright, fiery light—that I learned I couldn't hold on to. Not if I wanted you to stay that way."

Isla had to force herself to breathe, to remain upright, to resist the urge to just cross the room, forget the explanations, and just let him have her.

Kai's jaw clenched, and she caught the way his hands moved like he too was fighting a pull to have her close.

"I'm not going to say that I knew I loved you before I met you, or that I was in love the moment I laid eyes on you—because I didn't, and I wasn't—but I sure as hell knew that I would. One talk with you, and I knew it wouldn't take much, and it wouldn't be long before I was entirely at your mercy. Before I would do anything in my power to make you happy and keep you safe…even if it meant having you away from me."

Breathe.

"So, we made our plan and I let you go. But when I got back home, things were—"

Kai cut himself off, narrowing his eyes. Isla followed his gaze to the door, to the obscure shadow beneath it.

She ground her teeth, having a feeling of exactly who it was, trying to listen in before dawn struck. The concierge must've had loose lips and had told Callan the room number he'd directed her to. She wouldn't be surprised if the whole hotel soon knew the alpha was lurking about.

How long had he been listening?

When she looked back at Kai—unsure what they'd do about the intrusion—she found he'd since risen from the chair and was taking steps towards the door. Steps that felt all-too slow as everything crashed into her. Everything he'd said, how she felt. How completely enamored with him she was.

His hand reached out for the door handle, prepared to rip the structure off its hinges and likely kill Callan—but Isla stopped him, taking it in hers instead.

Then when he turned to face her, confusion written on his face, she grabbed his shirt and hauled her mouth to his.

CHAPTER 32

Nothing else mattered. Not right now.
Not as Kai had her body pressed against the wall. Not as his leg had settled between hers to rub so deliciously between her thighs.

She knew he wanted Callan to hear her, hear them. He thought this was another game she was initiating.

He teased the skin of her jaw, her cheek, up to her ear where he whispered, "Maybe it's best that he thinks I'm just fucking you." And then, before Isla knew it, she was up in the air with her legs wrapped around him and his mouth on hers.

Everything was a blur, and the only thing she could focus on were his lips, his hands, and every solid place they connected. On the words somehow still unspoken that she felt on his tongue as it tangled with hers. Words that she tried to convey in her own kiss.

She didn't just want the *illusion* that he'd been fucking her. She didn't want a game.

"Kai," she muttered his name against his lips, and the desperation of her tone had him pulling back. His eyes searched her face, and all she had to do was nod for him to know what she wanted. Needed.

"Really?" Kai's breathing was ragged; he was struggling against emotions, against self-control.

Isla brought her hands to his face and nodded. "I'm yours."

The words settled for a beat, and Kai blinked at her as if he still had to wrap his mind around it.

Isla smiled softly and leaned forward, brushing her mouth against his. "I love you."

And that was all else that needed to be said.

Kai gripped her harder, and Isla moaned as he dropped his head to her neck, licking and nipping his way to that spot at the crook of her collarbone where that primal part of her called out to him. His teeth grazed the spot, sharp and teasing.

She ground down against his hips, already finding him hard, and craned her neck, baring herself to him.

"Isla…"

One last chance to change her mind.

"Yes." She tightened her grip on his shirt. *Yes, yes, yes.*

Kai's canines pierced her skin, and she cried out at the pain, the ecstasy. Flames roared through her in his wake, and she couldn't breathe as they consumed her being, razing the world as she knew it to ash.

Her arms were tight around him to keep herself steady as she threw her head back against the wall to gasp down air. She swore she could feel it, the missing fragment of her soul that Kai had held, that he'd kept safe all this time, twining with her once again. *"Kai."*

He answered her call by bringing his mouth back to hers, the tang of her blood on his tongue, and his kisses were as much a claim as his mark. Isla was stripped to nothing but her senses, ravaged by the smell of him, feel of him, the taste of him.

The kisses that followed weren't deep enough. She couldn't get him close enough. Feel enough.

Kai lifted her from the wall, mouth catering to her fresh mark before he pressed her down onto the mattress of the perfectly made bed. She was drowning in him as their tongues tangled again, and all she could think of was her need to remove all barriers between them.

Isla bypassed the buttons of his shirt to go straight for the waistband of his pants. She fiddled with the button and zipper until Kai grabbed her wrists and pinned them above her head. Beneath his strength, she was powerless to move them.

He hummed his disagreement. "First, I get to have my fun."

And that was fun she wasn't opposed to as he made his way down her neck again. He took her jacket zipper between his teeth, pleased to find she had nothing but her bra underneath it, and pulled it down, down. Every move of his was marked by a kiss.

Please, she thought but wouldn't let it out. If *this* was torture, she couldn't imagine how it'd be when he got between her legs.

The sheer thought of his mouth there, of his cock, in time with when he wrapped his lips over her clothed nipple, made her whine louder than she'd intended. She'd bucked her hips towards him, desperate, but he held steady, interlacing their fingers above her.

"Hurry up." She wouldn't plead, but she urged her body forward again.

Kai lifted his head to look at her, amusement dancing with lust in his eyes.

Cold greeted her as he rose from the bed to remove his shirt, and she bit her lip as she took him in. The Goddess had blessed her ten-thousand times with him. She needed him against her again. Now.

Isla rose onto her knees, fully unzipping her jacket and tossing it off to the side. Her bra went next. Her nipples peaked against the chill that swept through, and she nearly quivered at the hungry stare Kai shot her way as she inched over to him.

She wrapped her arms around his neck, pressing her bare chest against his, knotting her fingers in his hair. Kai nodded his brows at her as she smiled at him, his own calloused fingers brushing up and down her bare waist, lowering to grab her ass.

"So impatient," he chastised but his actions, his appreciation, spoke louder as he reached between them to brush his fingers soft and teasingly over where she'd ached for him most. They lifted to drop beneath her waistband, and they both groaned as he ran his touch over the slickness there—all for him. Isla dug her nails into his shoulders, his tattoo, gasping and jerking as he flicked over her clit.

Now, she leaned down into the crook of his neck and breathed his name. He shuddered at the caress on his skin, and that carnal part of her rose again. Isla pressed her lips to the spot just above his collarbone, nipping at the skin until she finally drew her teeth.

She'd never felt as animal as she did then. Never so powerful and in control as her mate's pulse—an *alpha's* pulse—thundered beneath her lips.

"*Isla.*"

Commanding, yet desperate.

Kai leaned into her, offering, ready, his power ebbing through the room laid bare in her presence, there for her to take.

Isla traced her tongue over his skin, a final tease that had him growling and making the bond pull in a way that stole her breath.

Mine.

Isla braced herself and, running on nothing but primal instinct, bared down with her teeth and claimed her mate.

Kai cursed, arching into her as she bit deeper, the tang of his blood filling her mouth, something like a current flowing between them. His fingers dug into her sides, pulling her closer as if to merge their souls into one.

When Isla lifted her head, just inches from his, their chests heaving in the same heavy cadence, all they could do was stare at each other. Neither spoke as the threads coiled around them, burned at their feet. Entanglements of gold and shadow nearly tangible in the air. Singing. Sighing. Isla could smell the bond as it forged between them. Taste it.

It had been a few heartbeats of only their echoing breaths before both of them…laughed.

They actually laughed.

Unbridled joy shone on both of their flushed faces as the sounds flittered through the room. Because all of this, already, had felt *too good*. Too raw and real and euphoric.

And they hadn't even had sex yet.

Kai tugged Isla back to him and kissed her with a ferocity that had her melting. "I love you."

She'd never get sick of hearing him say that.

Isla embraced the warmth of his body against hers and brushed her nose against his. Then she dragged her hand lazily down his chest, scratching the skin until she reached his cock. She palmed along the hard length of him, holding in a moan that would've echoed his. "Prove it," she teased.

Kai's eyes flashed with the challenge, and he pushed her back onto the bed. She didn't even have a chance to settle before he hooked her legs and tugged her to the edge of the mattress.

And then, he knelt. *Only for her.*

Isla rested on her elbows, gazing down at her mate between her legs. The sight alone was enough to nearly send her over the edge, and without a thought, she touched herself.

Kai had clocked every movement as she rolled her nipple between her fingers and then replaced her hand with his when he rose to kiss her again. His mouth moved over her lips, her body. Her neck. Her breasts. Her stomach. Her thighs as if he couldn't do it enough.

Isla was an eager mess by the time she was finally bare before him, and she was grateful Kai didn't feel the need to tease. Well, not badly.

With her legs over his shoulders, he parted her with a single hand, then traced his tongue over her bundle of nerves, featherlight and maddening. It spurred a mix of pleasure and ache within her, sending her gasping and bowing off the bed. She wanted more, but the edge as he passed over and over and around was intoxicating. He continued until she was panting, squirming, and she took hold of his hand that had gone on to explore other parts of her skin. "More."

She heard him chuckle, and he kissed her inner thigh again before finally leaning down to draw his tongue over her core in a long, luxurious slide. He groaned as he tasted her, and Isla arched with her own whimper. Kai did it again, holding her hips in place as he dipped his tongue in her center.

Isla swore, and her knuckles turned white as she gripped the sheets with one hand and twisted the other in Kai's hair. He expertly worked her clit, her core, worshiping her with his tongue, his lips, his teeth. Once he added his fingers—driving not one, but two into her—she was gone, her hips undulating without abandon as he pumped them in and out of her. "Kai!"

Isla didn't know what he'd said next, her mind swimming as her release shone just out of reach. It was something about how beautiful she was like this, something about fucking her, something that even blurred by her daze had her coming undone on his tongue at the mere implication.

As Isla descended from her high, Kai stood and removed the last of his garments. Her mouth went dry at the sight of his cock and watched as he fisted the thick length, stroking and using the moisture already beading at the head to coat himself. "Your choice."

For a moment, Isla was too lost to understand what he meant.

She met his eyes, and he raised his brows in question.

Isla quickly ran through the fantasies she'd had since the day she'd laid eyes on him, but the one most prominent was held in the words he'd spoken to her just yesterday in the corridor of the Pack Hall.

Isla glanced to the side of the room where the desk for the office space sat so conveniently by a window where she could see part of the city through the curtains. Kai followed her gaze and grinned.

She met him there, pressing her hands to the wood before she felt her mate's body behind her. Her heart was pounding, anticipation making her legs tremble as he gave them each a tap to spread them further apart.

She tried to settle her breathing as he gripped her hip with one hand and used the other to guide himself to her center. But any bliss she'd felt when he finally nudged into her entrance had quickly turned to anger.

He'd only gone in an inch and held.

"Kai," Isla growled at him, trying to push back, aware of the emptiness she was left with.

"You know, you've been teasing me for months," he said.

Only he could turn what was supposed to be a grand moment into a game and way to torment, but his words were strained. He wanted nothing more than to drive into her. To make good on his promises.

Isla didn't have the patience to see how long he could last.

"Kai, I swear to the—" Another inch—she whined—and he retreated. "You son of a bitch."

Kai laughed and leaned down, kissing the column of her spine, her warrior mark. "What do you want, Isla?"

If he wanted to play, she would, too. She knew what his weakness was.

Her.

She pulled away and spun, pressing her body against him again. While she wrapped one arm around his neck, she brought the other down to take him in her hand, his skin warm and smooth as she stroked him gently, squeezing at the head. He cursed, and she grinned wickedly.

"I want you," Isla began, her nails a dragging tease along the underside of his shaft as she spoke near his collarbone, "to leave your mark in me."

At the implication, Kai's eyes blazed, and Isla yelped as he hooked her legs and lifted her onto the edge of the desk.

One needy thrust and he was buried in her.

She might've screamed. She wasn't sure. But *Goddess*, she was going to explode.

Kai had a hand braced on the wall behind her as he went still, allowing her time to adjust. Him time to settle. He swore at the tightness and feel of her wrapped around him before chuckling through a sigh. "Fucking finally."

He could say that again.

Isla leaned back on her palms, exposing her chest to him, which he watched the rise and fall of greedily.

"So…impatient," Isla panted, struggling to keep it together. Goddess above, he felt incredible. Perfect.

A dark, dangerous lust shone in Kai's eyes, but there was also that adoration as he tightened his hold on her and drew back nearly to the tip. And then he kissed her, meeting her tongue with his as he thrust into her again, rocking the desk against the wall.

Isla broke the embrace, throwing her head back, savoring the moment until she felt Kai grab her face. Rough but not enough to hurt. He forced her back up, to look in his eyes, not saying a word as he moved in her again, and again. Slow and deep so she could feel every inch of him.

Oh, Goddess.

Isla held his stare, just as he wanted, and bit her bottom lip so hard it nearly bled as waves of pleasure crashed over her. As Kai filled and stretched her. As she lifted her hips to meet him until she swore she'd die from how amazing it felt. From how overwhelming it was. She'd never experienced *anything* like this.

And she needed more. *More.*

Isla tightened her legs around Kai's waist and wrapped her arms around his neck, tugging at his hair as she pulled him closer, deeper, moaning his name into his mouth when she kissed him again. Kai picked up his pace, the desk against the wall a drumbeat as they built a rhythm.

Her nails dug into his shoulders. "Harder."

Kai obeyed, dropping his hand from the wall to hold her with both hands and pull her hips towards him with each thrust, sending her body buzzing as they rocked against each other.

"Fuck, Isla." Her name had never sounded so good. A mix of desperation, relief, and demand against her lips. Isla clenched around him, and Kai cursed again, fingers digging to the point she knew she'd bruise but loved it.

Suddenly, he lifted her off the desk and threw her back down onto the bed. With her legs high around him, he plunged deeper, making her cry out and reach for any part of him to hold.

Isla swore she saw stars with each pounding stroke, and the obscene sounds of his balls slapping against her, of the slide of him inside her, only spurred her on. Release built at the base of her spine. "Goddess, don't stop. Please."

Kai seemed to relish in the sight of her losing herself, letting go. Of her smiling. That little plea. He leaned down, bracing his elbows on either side of her head and pressing his mouth to hers. "You going to come for me again?"

So damn smug. He knew. He could feel it. Her spasming around him.

Goddess, she was so close.

Kai rested his forehead against hers, and she couldn't even utter a yes, only hum and nod and moan her answer. She grabbed onto what she could, the muscles of his back, his ass. And then she felt him too, growing thicker, harder, throbbing. His movements lost some of their control.

"Come with me," she forced breathlessly over his mouth, squeezing him between her legs, taking his face in her hands. "I'm yours."

"Fuck." Kai's fingers dug into the sheets, the words hitting a carnal part of him. He raised from her, and Isla watched in a haze as he unleashed himself, tracking the way his stomach muscles, glistening with a light sheen of sweat, contracted with each heavy breath, every flex of his hips. "*Isla.*"

Her name from him was her undoing.

Release tore through her, *shattered her*, and Kai kept his vicious pace until she was trembling. Until another wave crashed, and then, he tumbled too.

He fell forward, letting out a deep groan as he came, bracing himself as he spilled and spilled and spilled himself inside her. Marking her, claiming her. Isla dragged her nails down his back, breathing hard as her inner muscles worked along him, drawing out his pleasure as she rode out hers.

Then they were laughing again, grinning madly at each other as ecstasy and exhaustion racked their damp bodies. With the bond alight between them, their breathing slowed, and heartrates steadied as one.

Isla tugged Kai down until they were flush against each other, bearing his weight, his heat, reveling in their closeness and how safe she felt in his arms.

Kai lowered to kiss her neck, her mark, already healing. "I love you," he whispered against her skin.

Isla smiled up at him when he pulled back and reached to trace the lines of his face, the beads of sweat off his brow and jaw coating her fingertips. Now it felt surreal. Him. This comfort. This happiness.

"I love you," she said, staring into his eyes, a swirling stormy sea that she'd weather for the rest of time. Kai flashed her a grin, and they melded their lips in a kiss so deep that it skittered down to Isla's bones.

Hers.

His.

A promise forged in one of the greatest pleasures to endure, in time, the greatest pain.

But it would be worth it. Whatever life they had before them, together, would be worth it. If only for these small moments, of peace, of love.

When nothing else mattered—nothing else needed to—but the universe between their souls.

CHAPTER 33

CASSIUS

Bringing his scotch to his lips, Cassius observed the parchment laid flat beneath the glass plating over the wood of his desk: a map of the expanse of the world. He looked away from Cataea, the continent of the witches and crawlers and other beasts to the west, the barren lands of the banished fae beyond them, and the isles of the sea and sirens below; instead, his eyes honed in on the continent of wolves.

He trailed his gaze along the coast of the territories. From the lower pack regions of Mimas and Tethys to the eastern borders of Iapetus, Charon, and Rhea, up beyond Ganymede until he reached the ridges outlining Adrastea Bay and along the Valkeric Ranges, the formations that held his home. Io—the northern-most pack of the continent. Its head which wore the crown. The mind that controlled and guided, kept peace with reason, kept them protected from those creatures of the lands beyond, of their own.

A purpose not everyone seemed to understand or appreciate, no matter how many times throughout history it had been proven.

The highest monarch dragged his eyes down the piece until he found Morai's center, its heart. A line of an eight-pointed star denoting the city of Mavec.

He scowled.

Lifting his head, he gazed upon the chair where Deimos's former alpha had once sat—not once, not twice, but thrice—rambling about some ridiculous tax proposal in some poor excuse of a distraction. As if Cassius hadn't been aware of how Kyran and his entourage had taken a different route into the city each visit. As if he hadn't had eyes on his accompanying guard and council members who tended to wander through the streets, through the hall. Noting. Mapping.

So, he'd learned throughout their simultaneous tenures, Alpha Kyran was not a stupid man but one blinded by his own ego. Blinded by a sense of self-importance catered to by a history long forgotten and a lineage whose power had long, long faded since its rise over a millennium ago during its dawn of traitors. A time they were fortunate to have lapsed into nothing but whispers of hollow wind through the pages of books and scrolls in the catacombs beneath the Imperial City. A time that had attempted to return before the head of the beast had been severed and all traces of it eradicated.

But it wasn't enough.

Obviously, it hadn't been enough, if it could rise again, hidden so strategically, deviously within the brambles of bloodlines and birthrights. Only revealed when he thought they'd been triumphant, given a small blessing by the Goddess.

But Cassius could see it, had felt it in a warning from the ancestors as he beheld the scene at the Gate, even when the beast could not. And he knew now was the time to destroy it before it realized. Even if it meant he'd be the villain.

They'd thank him someday.

PART IV
THE RISE OF RUIN

CHAPTER 34

ISLA

Isla woke up to a kiss. Not from her mate, but one of incandescence.

Against the backdrop of soft, rhythmic breathing, she peeled open her eyes to be greeted by moonbeams spilling through the window, casting shadows along the hardwood floor, over the edges of the mattress, her body.

For a moment, she struggled to recall where she was or the reason for it. The reason for the comforting warmth at her back. For the intoxicating scent flooding her nose. For the delicious ache in her muscles.

But then she lowered her gaze, noticing the solid arm she'd been using as a pillow. Her bare breasts. Her torso.

Her breath hitched.

Everything came crashing back.

The duvet of the hotel bed had only been pulled up to her waist. It whispered against her skin as she twisted her body, careful not to disturb the man beside her. She would've been devastated if she did. If only she had something other than her memory to capture the image before her.

There was a softness, a peacefulness, to Kai's face as he slept that she'd never seen before, even in those moments she'd considered him at ease. It made her heart swell and an overwhelming sense of love flood her body.

Her mate.

Her *mate*.

For sure. Forever.

This picture was one she'd wake up to for the rest of her life.

Isla bit her bottom lip as if smiling would rouse him.

He was like a painting—the moon's glow illuminating and darkening, hardening, the features of his face, the muscles of his exposed body in a way only the most skillful artist could. As if the Goddess was aiding her sister in her taunts.

You tried to deny this. Isla practically heard Fate cackle in whatever way a deity would. *You'd pick a path other than the one I'd laid for you.* Look *at him.*

The man who'd loved her enough to let her go. Saw her, understood her enough to let her do what she'd wanted. Who knew how important it was for her to become a warrior, if only for a fraction of time. Words whispered in prayer that day in the ash lily fields. He was exactly what she'd hoped and dreamed and wanted.

See.

Isla huffed through her nose.

Annoying bitch.

Isla scooted in closer, placing her hand on Kai's chest, pressing her body against the heat of his.

As much as she wanted to stay in this room forever—this void, their void, where they could be safe—they had to return to the world out there.

Kai should've gone back to the hall hours ago, judging by the darkness outside. He had to deal with the rogues. With the challenge.

And Isla had to face her family. Had to tell them she'd never be home again—if she could even call Io home anymore.

She needed to officially resign from the warriors…to go through, she imagined, some process to become luna, and then prove herself worthy to the people of Deimos, who'd likely want nothing to do with her. And how could she forget the murderer and the bak and the messages and the marker and—

Not now.

Maybe they could remain in this chasm for a few more minutes.

Kai stirred, breath catching before it settled. His arm moved from around her back to tug her even closer, and Isla became so comfortable that she could've fallen asleep again.

She wouldn't look up at him as she absently traced the tattoo over his chest, even as Kai lifted his other arm to run a hand over his face and push the hair from his eyes.

"Good morning, beautiful."

Goddess above—his *voice*.

Lazy and deep and gravelly with sleep. Forget the endearment.

Isla squeezed her legs together, faintly remembering every wicked thing he'd done and said to her only hours before.

She cleared her throat. "It's actually quite late in the evening," she said, stopping her ministrations to lift her eyes to his. "We fell asleep."

The corner of Kai's mouth lifted as he stretched himself out on the mattress. Isla wasn't sure if he was doing it on purpose—so the blankets would slide dangerously low on his hips—or if he'd placed his hand behind his head, only to give his muscles an opportunity to flex.

His voice was still dizzyingly alluring as he prided, "I wonder why."

Isla's toes curled as the recollections hit her full force.

They'd lost their war with Fate—but she had never been so happy to lose. Never been happier to be proven so wrong. Kai had said he'd be the best sex of her life, and she'd challenged him on it.

Then he'd taken her on the desk and the bed.

Made her hold on to the headboard as he slid in behind her.

Let her take him in her mouth before she'd rode him until she'd collapsed on his chest, unsure if she could handle anymore.

And then he'd rolled her over to edge her until she swore tears pricked her eyes. Until she'd begged him—*begged* him—to let her finish. Only for him to enter her again, so they could go together.

Goddess.

Yes, she could certainly think of worse ways to be incorrect. And she would graciously take this loss and whatever ones the future held.

As she replayed the moments—remembering how much she'd enjoyed herself, how undone she'd become with him, for him—she couldn't help the feeling of butterflies in her stomach, and lower.

And she just *had* to laugh.

As the cheerful sounds left her mouth, Kai couldn't help himself either. He was running his fingers up and down her back as he shook his head. "I knew you'd be great in bed, but…fuck."

Isla lifted herself on her elbow to look down at him, teasing, "What a vocabulary."

Kai scoffed and reached a hand up to brush her face and the wild blonde waves from near her eyes. When his thumb dragged lazily over her lips, she nipped it with her teeth. He grinned. "I'm going to have my hands full with you, aren't I?"

Isla kissed the heel of his hand and lowered her head to peck his lips. "No going back now."

"Wouldn't dream of it," Kai said against her mouth before tightening his grip on her waist to pull her on top of him.

Isla braced her hands on either side of his head, dropping her widened eyes to where he was hard beneath her. "Already?"

Kai guided her hips to grind on him and appeared to brace himself as she moaned. "You have no idea what you do to me."

Isla smiled as he pulled her down to kiss her…and kiss her…and kiss her. Anywhere his lips and tongue could reach and tease. He was developing a quick mastery of her body, becoming aware of all the spots that melted and invigorated her all at once.

Her hand drifted between their bodies, taking a hold of him and teasing her slick entrance before sinking down, down. The stretch and pressure as he filled her, inch by inch, nearly had her eyes rolling back, and as they built a rhythm, smooth and slow and deep, she sighed.

She could get used to this.

Quickly. Easily. Happily.

If only everything could be this simple.

∽

"So, what happens now?" Isla called back to Kai from her spot in front of the bathroom mirror where she'd been examining the mark on her neck.

As she raked her fingers through her hair—damp after the shower they'd taken—she watched him work the buttons of his shirt. With each one he fastened, her gut twisted. With each one, reality set in.

"Tonight?" Kai asked, looking up at Isla as she entered the main room. Her wavering expression told him enough—that she meant much more than whatever the remaining hours of the day held. "By tradition and protocol, a lot of ceremonies—more for you than me, but I'll still be in witness."

Ceremonies. She could handle ceremonies.

Though the assuredness she attempted to convey wasn't the least bit convincing. "Okay."

"We can take it slow," Kai said, finishing the last button. "Everything doesn't need to happen at once."

Isla cast him a doubtful look. "They were trying to find you a wife at the banquet yesterday."

Kai crossed the room to take her in his arms. "And I found her." He combed his fingers through her hair, eliciting a soft smile. "Most of it is formalities and giving the pack something to look forward to," he explained. "I was never big on parties anyway—always found a way to escape all the galas and banquets and nonsense, much to Marin and my father's annoyance. Having you here and happy is what matters to me."

Isla's grin grew despite the nerves brought about by his words. She played with the buttons of his shirt, teasing, "It's going to be a lot of dresses."

A devious light shone in Kai's eyes as his hand slipped beneath her jacket, drawing circles over the skin of her hip. "I know."

Temptation reared its head, and Isla lifted her arms to circle them around his neck. But as she raised on her toes, a breath sounded from the hallway. It was so faint that she nearly missed it.

Kai seemed to notice too, and they broke away from each other.

"What was that?" Isla said, and Kai shrugged.

As he moved to the door, she was right behind him, fists clenched at her sides. If this had been Callan...

Kai wrenched open the door and a shrill scream rang out in response.

It had come from a nosy maid who'd been the source of the initial noise. Her hands were over her mouth, her chest heaving as she darted her gaze between the couple and the writing, left in dark paint, strewn along the wall.

The rush of volatile emotion that had gone through Kai flashed down the bond like a raging, red beacon. It slammed into Isla like a wave, melded with the fear ebbing through her body.

"What the hell?" Kai muttered, stepping into the hallway.

Isla wouldn't break the room's threshold.

Another message. *Another* message.

"A—Alpha," the woman stammered, dipping into a bow. Her eyes shifted along the ground to Kai's feet, then to Isla's. She wouldn't lift her gaze to meet theirs.

Kai advanced on her. "Did you see who did this?"

Though he'd sounded as gentle as he could, given the circumstances, the maid shrunk back. "N—n—no, this was just here. I was coming to, uh...uh, coming to clean the rooms."

Isla glanced down either side of the hall. There was no cleaning cart in sight, and even if there was, this entire wing was being renovated. There were no guests.

The maid bowed again, apologizing profusely before scurrying back to the lobby. Kai shot Isla a quick look—telling her to stay put—before he followed her, both to make sure she got there safely and to canvas the rest of the floor.

In his absence, Isla steeled herself and averted her gaze forward again. She trained her eyes over the paint. The strokes were coarse beneath her fingertips as she traced over them. It was drier than it had been down in the alleyway near the call center. Whoever had written this had done it, at least, a few hours ago.

When they'd seen the shadow beneath the doorframe?

They'd thought that it had been Callan, but what if it wasn't?

If the killer was here…*had* been here…while they were…

Isla shuddered.

Though smaller this time, the insignia of Io and the mark of the warriors were still among the mess, but something else was familiar. She froze over one etching, tilting her head.

It had a vague resemblance to the insignia of Charon.

"Isla?"

Isla jumped and spun to find Kai at her side.

As he took in the writing himself, he shook his head. "How did I not know? I can usually sense when they're…around."

Isla had been the same, at least, down in the lower part of the city.

"We were distracted," Isla said. Though, they should've been able to tell something was off when they'd come to the door. *If* it was them.

Kai's jaw tightened, and he looked back at the paint. Moments passed, and he squinted. "Wait."

Isla dropped her hand from the wall, trying to follow his eyes. "What?"

"This." Kai pointed to another symbol above her head. "It's my family's crest." He traced his fingers over the two curves and the circle in which they met. "It's simplified, but that's our wolves. The moon."

Isla stepped back, now able to see the motif she'd found throughout the pack. She hadn't noticed it in what was left earlier, but then again, she hadn't been searching for it.

She spun on her heel and rushed back into the room, calling over her shoulder, "Is Jonah still at the shop?" She went to the desk in the office area, rifling through drawers until she found a pad of paper and a pen.

"Is that a genuine question?" Kai side-stepped from his spot in the doorway to allow Isla to slip by him again. "Why do you need Jonah?"

Isla swallowed. The honesty she'd wanted from Kai went two ways.

"I got one of these earlier today."

"You what?"

"When I went to call home, in the city. There was a trail of the jewels from my necklace—the one that you gave me that broke after I shifted at the banquet—and it led to a message like this one. Like the one you'd gotten in Callisto."

Kai heaved a breath. "Why wouldn't you mention that earlier?"

"I was going to, tonight when we talked. There's a lot more too, but we need Jonah." She handed over the pad and paper. "Just copy this down and meet me up in my room. I need to grab some things."

∽

The warriors were staying on the hotel's third floor of the opposite wing, but Isla was moving so fast, it felt as if she'd gotten there in a blink. Their hallway was empty and eerily silent as she stalked through it to her room at the end of the corridor. After today's trek through the mountain, she wasn't expecting anyone to be awake.

Still, she moved quietly, running through the items of her mental "shit-I-can't-explain" checklist. The dagger, the broken diadem, her rubies, and whatever she had forged from the alleyway. They connected somehow to all of this. To each other. She just had to figure it out.

She was nearly to her door when a pull came. Not from Kai, but from *something*.

Isla faltered and turned her head, finding herself in front of Callan's door. It was cracked open a sliver, and Isla couldn't hear the snoring which she'd dealt with for the years they'd shared a bed.

Her blood ran cold when she spotted the tiniest swipe of crimson on the doorjamb.

Shit.

She wouldn't give herself time to doubt.

She pushed on the wood.

Its creaking reverberated down her bones, loud in her ears. *Too loud* in what seemed to be an empty room. Chilled night air swept by her face, a current from the open window caught by her entrance. The shadows left by the sparseness of the moon's aura made the room seem forbidding. Still, Isla took a few steps inside, risking a call of Callan's name. She received no answer. And unless he was hiding in the closet, no one was here.

For a moment, she figured he'd taken Kai's threat seriously and left.

But his belongings were still there. The trunk he'd traveled with, the bag with his gear, his sword, his armor. Papers were scattered across the bed's blanketed surface. Some crumpled and torn. And Isla caught the faintest smell of smoke wafting from the bathroom as if things had been burned. Could be the reason for the open window?

She scanned the door. Where had the blood come from?

She tugged her lip between her teeth, and against that part of her with better judgment, she kicked the entrance closed, lest no one come upon her as she approached the mattress. There was a ball in her throat as she sorted through the files. A lot of them were Callan's documents, as she had for herself. His papers to get into Deimos—which he would need to leave and get back into Io. Even the ripped sheets didn't seem to be anything unusual.

She sighed, scanning the room again and noticing more parchments placed on the bureau backed by a mirror.

Her eyes were wide as she picked up an identification card for Edriel of Charon.

Edriel.

The false name Callan had been using, according to Kai. Where had he gotten this? Why did he need it?

Isla dropped the card back on the table, and her gaze slid to the map that had been beside it, worn from being folded and rolled so many times. The geography depicted was a stretch from Deimos, out west towards Phobos, and displaying parts of Callisto and Mimas. He had lines drawn through it, areas circled throughout Deimos's four regions with question marks. All seemed to converge in one spot—a wide-cast circle encompassing the Wall.

"What does he have you looking for?" she mumbled under her breath, recalling Kai's words to Callan before he'd ordered him away. Alpha Cassius *had* put Callan on some type of mission, other than the rogues, other than observing how she behaved here.

Isla narrowed her eyes at the map. Beyond the border of the Wall, within the marred parchment depicting the Wilds, were notes that nearly got lost in the dark contrast of the scourged land.

"House. Bak. Entrance?" Isla read the words aloud, voice wavering with uncertainty. What the hell did all this mean?

She stiffened as she felt a sudden coolness at her back, and a shiver rocketed down her spine. Her heart stopped at the raspy sound, a word spoken, that echoed in her mind.

"Traitor."

The wind-like breath that she swore caressed her ear was like ice on her skin.

Isla snapped her eyes up into the mirror, a gasp ripping from her throat as she found the silhouette of a dark figure lingering in the corner of the room by the open window. She whipped around, clutching onto the bureau to brace herself. The action of fear was at odds with the snarl on her face, the glow of her eyes, and the claws at her fingertips.

And whatever—whoever—it was, had disappeared, leaving nothing in their wake but a billowing curtain and a blood-stained adornment on the mattress.

The other half of the diadem.

CHAPTER 35

Isla.
    Her name was an echo from a void. One she could sense at the end of a long stretch of ebony cord, twined with gold in an unbreakable stitch, drawing together two halves of a weaver's blanket. It was a tightrope to teeter along, a road to walk, into a darkness unknown but...comforting.

Isla.

The cord thrummed, and shadows of the abyss drew closer, snaking along the path, swallowing the glow in tendrils until they reached and threatened to envelop her entirely. Coiling. Tightening.

Isla.

She winced.

The icy binds dug in, sharp. Familiar but foreign. Overpowering as they tried to wriggle into her mind. Break in. Draw from it. Find that piece. That link like a doorway.

Isla's instinct kicked in, and she reinforced that wall, the barrier that protected the most precious parts of her. Ones she'd never had to guard while in her human form when that bridge wasn't exposed.

Isla.

The wall shattered.

Panic rose, manifesting with a worry lingering and powering the darkness. Not from her, but another.

"Isla!"

Wait.

Isla blinked back into reality, staring into the empty corner before her in the room. She brought her hand up to her head and scratched at her scalp.

She knew that voice. Loved that voice.

"Kai?"

The shadows dropped into nothing but smoke, and the bond became a patchwork of radiance once more.

The relief that flowed between them was mutual.

"Are you okay?" His voice filled her head as if he were standing right beside her, and any fear Isla had felt slowly ebbed away. *"Where are you?"*

She couldn't believe it.

They were actually doing this. Communicating through the bond. Not only with pushes and pulls but with actual words. She wasn't alone in this room. She never would be—anywhere, ever. Not as long as this road lay between them.

"I'm fine." She sent the words with a tinge of uncertainty, afraid the ability wouldn't work a second time. *"I'm in Callan's room. Three doors down from mine."* There was no response, but Kai's emotion on the other side felt stronger than it ever had, resonated much clearer. *"He's not here."*

Once again, he didn't answer, but Isla figured it wouldn't be long before her mate walked through the hotel room door.

She shook her head as if to clear it. It was *nice* having him there, but was linking with your mate supposed to feel like that? So...invasive? It hadn't been that way when they shifted.

While she waited for Kai, Isla inched back to the edge of the mattress. There was a scent coming from the blood on the diadem, but it wasn't one she recognized. It was dry and flecked onto her skin as she picked it up, just as gentle as she had its twin in the alleyway. Flakes of red fell like snow across the white of the blankets. As its other half, the crown was silver and gold and bejeweled with black crystal, sister to the dagger. It was clear where the two pieces had been severed, the metal jagged and caved in.

Isla pictured bringing the two pieces together, envisioning them whole—but that image was still incomplete. Another piece was missing. One last ornament, another large jewel perhaps, was absent from its center.

There was a creak, and Isla snapped her head in the doorway's direction. Kai peeked his head through first, and for a second, all faded and washed away. It was just him and the way she felt for him. But the moment was brief, as it needed to be.

"He isn't here," Isla reminded him quietly, catching how he'd been training his eyes across the room. When he broke the threshold inside, she motioned to close the door behind him, to which he obliged.

"Where is he?" Kai's voice was just as soft as hers. He took a glance back at the bathroom—nose twitching at the wafting of smoke—before his eyes honed on the papers strewn along the bed.

"I don't know," Isla said. "All of his stuff is still here."

"And there's blood on the door."

So he'd also noticed.

"I think it could be his. But his scent is everywhere here, and we went on a twenty-mile hike today. He could've hurt himself."

"He would heal." Kai sifted through the papers on the bed.

He was right. If it was small enough, if he'd returned to the hotel rather than be looked at by a medic, he would be virtually unscathed.

Isla held back her sigh, hating that worry rose in her chest for her boorish ex-lover.

"Look at the bureau," Isla told Kai. She cradled the crown, nearly hiding it in her clasped hands as if she felt the subconscious urge to protect it. Like it was calling her to.

Kai glanced up at her and then did as she said.

"It's a map," she added, trailing his movement. "Of here. Do you know what those lines mean? Are they roads or paths? Or anything about why those spots are circled?"

Before he picked up the map, Kai lifted the identification card for "Edriel" and cursed under his breath. The parchment crinkled as he took it in his hands and turned to her, leaning against the furniture as he read it over. "Nothing strange comes to mind. Just land, roads, shops, houses, temples."

"And they all lead to the Wall."

A muscle feathered Kai's jaw, and he shook his head. "It looks that way."

Isla spun to face him fully. "What are you thinking?"

"That I trust a bak more than I trust Alpha Cassius."

Isla gulped.

Alpha Cassius—no longer *her alpha*, as he'd used to say. Now she was only a few rungs below their high ruler in the hierarchy and even held superior to her own father.

Or at least, she would be after her coronation.

She felt her fingers tremble. She'd need to talk to him, to Sebastian, to Adrien, tell them she—

"What is that?"

Isla lifted her gaze to Kai. He focused on the piece in her hand, glinting with a singular stream of light.

"It's a diadem—or half of one," she answered.

Kai pushed off the bureau to come closer. "You found this in here?" Isla nodded. "And seeing this scared you so much that I could feel it?"

"I didn't just see this."

Whatever look had been on her face made it easy for Kai to figure out what she was alluding to. He stepped back as if to go search the room, but Isla reached out a hand to stop him. "They're gone too. I don't know where. They just vanished...or they were never there."

That sounded ridiculous.

"Maybe they went out the window," she offered.

She let him fall from her grasp as he went to the opening, looking at the three-story drop to the ground—manageable—before pulling down the frame and flipping the latch to lock it. "Why can't I sense them anymore?"

Isla shrugged. "We're wolves, we mask our scents and auras all the time."

"But every time before?"

Too many questions.

Isla rubbed her forehead, grimacing as she felt the flecks of blood scrape her skin. "I don't know. Something's obviously changed. They're getting bolder. I think they whispered in my ear."

"For the love of fuck." Kai heaved a breath and pinched the bridge of his nose. "What'd they say?"

Her lips turned further downwards, the word hitting a weak part of her. "Traitor."

Kai's brows lifted, the remark potentially feeding into his theory that Io was behind all of it. But something still didn't feel right. Isla knew there was more.

"I have the other half of this in my room," she said. "Everything else is with Jonah. It'll make more sense, and I can better explain once we have it."

Another look of surprise from her mate. "You told Jonah before you told me?"

Isla sighed. "I wanted to know more before I just started throwing theories at you. This is the person who murdered your family and tried to kill you. Me. I couldn't just..." She trailed off, looking off as her face screwed in perplexity.

Kai waved his hand in front of her. "Isla?"

"Why do all this?" She met his eyes again. "If this person is skilled enough to kill an alpha and his heir, nearly kill his scion—why toy with us? Why send Lukas to kill me at all when they could do it themselves so easily? They were at my back, and we can barely detect when they're around anymore. We only see them when they want us to." She cast her gaze back to the papers on the bed. "Why the messages? Why all the random things? Why…"

She lost herself again, squinting down at a specific torn parchment on the mattress. Its contents didn't matter, but what did were the four words staring back at her—*Warrior Callan of Io.*

Warrior. Io.

"What if they're trying to tell us something?" She thought back to the message they'd just gotten. Warrior. Io. Charon. The crest of Kai's family, which could essentially mean Deimos. She turned to Kai once more. "What if this was a warning? For us. For *me* in the alley. Trying to warn me about Callan. He's as much a warrior as I am."

Kai's face looked considerate, but doubt—serious doubt—still lingered. Understandably. It was a different approach and exactly why she'd wanted more information before she tossed things at him.

This wasn't a game. A murderer waited somewhere along this web. One who'd taken nearly everything from him and altered his life forever.

"Then what were the rest of the words and symbols? And why use things we can understand now? I didn't recognize any of this in what I'd gotten before."

"I'm not sure." A surge of adrenaline took to Isla's veins. "But Jonah has the marker and the book, maybe he's figured out how he could decipher the language."

Kai's brows furrowed. "The what and the what?"

Right.

"Let's go to my room," Isla said, waving her hand for him to follow her. "I'll explain the best I can."

∿

The crisp air Mavec offered was welcomed as Isla and Kai took to the cobblestone walkways. No longer inside in an enclosed space—with more room to run if anything appeared from the darkness and a moonlit path to guide them—was almost calming.

Almost.

They didn't trek through the hidden paths of the forest as they had nights ago, and the patter of their footsteps was more hurried than it had been then. But what Isla could see of the lower city—of the river and the rolling hills—was still as wondrous as she remembered. Fallen star streets and the patrons that occupied them, the faint sound of music —not particularly cheerful, but not morose—and boats with their bow lights cast along the water's surface and dancing amidst a smudge left by the Goddess.

It was a statement. There would be a vigil tomorrow for those hurt and killed during the attacks. And even before that, life would not stop, no matter what the rogues had done last night. They wouldn't win. The people of Deimos were resilient.

Isla tugged at the hood of her jacket—Kai's jacket—the red paint still staining the sleeve. At her side, hung a satchel, carrying the broken diadem and the dagger. The items clinked against each other with every step, and Isla swore sometimes, they sang, the sound reverberating longer than one would expect.

Kai had the papers with the messages tucked in the pockets of his own hooded garment. Ever since she'd clued him in on everything she could—and he told her why he'd figured Io was to blame—he'd been silent.

She hated that his claims had made sense, in theory. Linking back to Charon, the land that bordered them, a land Io was apparently "close with". But something was still missing. Something still felt wrong. So, until then, she curbed the sickness in her stomach and forced herself not to ponder it until they had more information.

Kai, it seemed, couldn't do so as easily.

Isla glanced up at her mate. He walked close to her side, their arms and hands occasionally brushing against each other. His focus held on the landscape before them, a pensive expression hardening his face.

Isla knew he would run himself ragged, spin himself into insanity if it meant he could protect who and what he loved.

On another brush of his skin against hers, Isla grabbed his hand and interlocked their fingers. Kai looked down at her as she wrapped her other around his upper arm. She tugged herself closer, happily accepting his warmth, and placed a kiss on his clothed shoulder before resting against it. She cocked her head and held his stare, smiling sweetly up at him. A little blissful distraction. An attempt to find a pocket of peace for them both.

"Hi," she said.

Kai's lips ticked upwards—not a beaming grin, but enough—and he leaned over to echo the greeting against the line of her hair. He kissed her forehead, before turning to look forward again. Isla knew his mind was still running faster than he could keep up with it, but his features had softened, his muscles loosened, and the bond felt less strained. She couldn't ask for much else.

Kai shoved his hand in his pocket, and for a few more steps, they walked, tangled like an actual couple on a midnight stroll.

Isla's eyes were fixated on the crystal-laden earth when she heard Kai say in a breath, "Luna Isla of Deimos." Even without looking up, Isla could feel the grin on his face growing. "It has a nice ring to it."

She took in a deep inhale of chilled air, nearly making herself cough as a shot of nerves coursed through her. "Does it now?"

Kai hummed in affirmation. "And speaking of rings." He loosened his grip on her hand, holding it delicately in the view of both their faces. "Would you want to pick yours, or do you want it to be a surprise?"

Isla hadn't thought about her mating ring. The glittering jewel she'd wear on her finger as a second outward symbol that she belonged to another—besides her mark which would fade into something more subtle in time.

She tugged her bottom lip between her teeth. She'd seen plenty of the gems. Davina wore hers around her neck—not customary, but also not unusual—and Cora's ring from Adrien had been gorgeous, taken from the Imperial vaults.

Isla cared little for extravagance but appreciated pretty things.

"You have proven to have good taste," she told him, hoping the image of her in her dress from the banquet flashed through his head too.

Judging by the nod of his brows and the indent in his cheek, it had. Kai lifted her hand to gently press his mouth to it. "Surprise it is then."

The action had sent sparks up her arm, through her body, and Isla couldn't resist the urge to pause their steps, just so she could kiss him properly. He didn't hesitate to deepen it and pull her closer, sending an *I love you* through the bond.

Thankfully, their journey had been free of passers-by, so they could enjoy the moment, their pocket of peace, just a few seconds longer.

When they eventually made it to The Bookshoppe's door, there was a faint light glowing on the other side through the opaque glass, though the sign on it clearly read CLOSED. Sounds of yelling and laughter carried into the night air.

Was Jonah not alone?

Kai looked at her and the bag before lifting his hand to the wood. He knocked on it several times in an off-beat, peculiar cadence. Three quick taps, three quicker ones, before the last hit that seemed to linger and leave stillness on the other side.

A few seconds passed, a wind sweeping across and displacing Isla's hood when darkness rippled across the window. Then came a clicking sound—just one lock this time—before the door swung open.

The scent of booze practically thwacked Isla in the face, and much of it came from Davina.

The hotel secretary's green doe-eyes, glazed over from what Isla assumed was the source of her potent scent of wine, were wide as she shifted her gaze between their two intruders. She wasn't the only one here at the shop. Jonah, Rhydian, and Ameera stood around one of the study tables, bottles of liquor in front of them. The four of them wore equal expressions of shock, though, she was sure it was for Kai's surprise visit rather than hers.

"You assholes, did you forget to invite us?" Kai heckled, pushing his hood back on his head, revealing hair still a bit mussed from Isla's hands through it. His happiness to see them practically radiated from him. She didn't even need the bond to feel it.

From any of them.

It was the first time that she'd ever seen their "family" all together.

Davina, still dazed with her eyes turning glossy, took a step back to allow them inside, and Isla followed Kai's suit, taking down her hood. He kicked the door closed behind them.

Ameera was obviously fighting to keep too wide a grin off her face. "And what did we do to deserve this honor, Your Majesty?"

At the address, Kai scoffed but before he could answer, there was a strangled sound. He barely had time to react before Davina, on the brink of tears, launched herself at him.

Isla recalled this morning, which felt eons ago now—a time when she wasn't mated, wasn't on the cusp of becoming luna—and remembered how devastated Davina had been with the news of the challenge.

The challenge—something else that couldn't be negated from the list of shit.

Davina hadn't seen Kai since the announcement, not like Rhydian and Ameera and she had. Jonah hadn't seen him either, but he remained in his spot beside Ameera. Watching. Observing as Jonah seemed to do.

Kai chuckled, wrapping his arms around the smallest of the bunch. "Hey, Davi."

He scrunched his nose, getting a full whiff of her, and lifted his eyes, directing an inquisitive stare at the rest of the group.

"Lightweight," Ameera whispered, gesturing towards the empty bottle of red wine. On her other side, Rhydian was shaking his head.

Davina nearly fell over with how fast she pulled away from Kai and whipped around. A lazy scowl crossed her face. "I may not be some super shifting wolf—" She jutted her finger in Ameera's direction. "But I have ears!"

The female general waved her off, and Isla couldn't hold back a laugh. She'd never pictured what a drunk Davina would be like.

Her sound had drawn the redhead's attention her way, and even if unwarranted, Davina jumped at her too. The difference in their heights had the smaller woman's head right at her shoulder. Isla greeted her as Kai had with her laughter persisting.

"Wait," Davina suddenly muttered against Isla's shirt. She took in a deep, exaggerated inhale before stepping back. Isla was at arm's length as she leaned back in to take in her scent again. Then she teetered back over to Kai. Another sniff.

"You smell like each other," she said suspiciously.

Isla pursed her lips, feigning innocence, and glanced up at Kai. *"Do we tell them?"*

Her mate smirked in return.

"No way." They spun forward to find Rhydian with his arms up, his smile wide and bright. "No fucking way!"

Kai's smile nearly rivaled his brother's as he shifted the neckline of his shirt to the side, revealing his mark. He attempted a dejected sigh. "She got me."

More sounds came from various directions—gasps, a holler, laughs, and some clapping. Rhydian scaled the room to them quickly, and Davina screamed, jumping at Isla again. As they hugged, laughing, Kai and Rhydian exchanged their own embrace.

And before she knew it, Isla was being lifted off the ground in the guard's arms.

"Welcome to the family," Rhydian said, the words so pleasant, also felt like a punch in the stomach. Especially when she realized a buzzed Rhydian reminded her a lot of Sebastian—when he was sober. "I hope you know Magnus is going to shit himself when you show up to training as his luna."

A cruel grin crossed her mouth. That *did* sound fun, but could she even attend training anymore?

Over Rhydian's shoulder, Isla caught Ameera and Jonah making their way over.

"And so, the dynasty begins," the general presented overdramatically. "I thought you two had *the look*."

Kai, who was enduring another hug from Davina, rose a brow. "What look?"

A WARRIOR'S FATE

"The 'finally fucked' look," Jonah said, lifting his glass to them, still standing a few feet away from the whirlwinds that were his brother and sister-in-law. "My rule still stands, you know."

"We have to celebrate!" Davina bellowed. Isla didn't have time to settle after Rhydian had set her down because his mate was already grabbing both her and Kai to pull them to the table of drinks.

Celebrate?

With her bag feeling heavier on her shoulder, Isla caught Kai's eye. She wished she didn't have to be the one to ruin the fun. *"Is there time to celebrate?"*

Kai's throat bobbed, and he shook his head.

"Can we tell all of them?" she asked.

Now, he nodded. *"I trust them more than anyone. But it has to be okay with you too."*

"Oh, great. Now this shit is going to start." Ameera pointed between them. "The secret conversations."

They certainly were convenient.

At the table, Davina dropped their arms, and Isla decided. If Kai trusted them—his family which she was now a part of—then so did she.

"We can't celebrate yet," Isla said, tightening her grip on her bag and turning to Jonah.

He lifted a brow, and she simply nodded at him. It was all he needed to understand. His features fell and his eyes went to Kai in question; his brother inclined his head, signaling he knew too.

"Okay, what's happening?" Ameera had thrown her hands up, zeroing her stare on Jonah. "Are you in on this?"

Jonah didn't answer, just gulped down the rest of his liquor and descended behind the shelves to his back room. Kai had since gone to secure every lock on the door, while Isla cleared some of the booze off the table to make room for her bag. Carefully, she removed each of the items and placed them in the wood's center. How garish the embellishments of gold and silver, crystal and gemstone, looked against its worn surface.

"What the hell? Who did you rob?" Rhydian asked, pushing around the pile of blood-red jewels and jabbing at a piece of the diadem as if it would bite him.

Nothing would surprise Isla at this point.

"Get comfortable," she told them all, gesturing to the seats that Kai was now dragging over. "And ask Jonah if he has more whiskey."

Isla hated whiskey, quite frankly, but she needed something strong. She downed a glass, the liquid burning her throat, as she waited for everyone to settle.

Like a display at a museum, the marker, the book, the dagger, the two halves of the diadem, a pile of ruby jewels, the sheets bearing the copied messages, and the map—which Kai had apparently stolen from Callan's room—sat atop the study table. The six of them circled it, staring down at it, features contorted in iterations of awe and disturbance. Kai and Isla exchanged a glance, a silent conversation about who would go first.

Kai took the lead and began with the night he was supposed to die.

That fact alone was enough to shake the room. Isla hadn't known that he'd kept it such a secret from all of them.

Despite their shock, they remained silent, letting him recount everything he remembered. Everything he'd already told Isla. About the inn of Abalys with Amalie, about the feeling—of being stuck, in pain, disconnected—and the first message.

Even if Kai attempted to appear the vision of strength, Isla felt each word breaking something in him, especially when he recounted walking through his brother's apartment, empty and eerily quiet after they'd taken his body away. She grabbed his hand beneath the table and stroked her thumb reassuringly over his skin as he explained how he'd never gotten to say a proper goodbye to his sibling before he'd been burned alongside their father.

After Kai had brought up the message in Callisto—the last piece of the puzzle he wanted to offer before Isla would jump in—Ameera put her hand up. A vein throbbed at her temple. "*You're telling me*, that you've had a psychopath after you for *months,* and you never said anything?"

Kai had no answer for her but, "Yes."

"*Yes*?" the general repeated. "Why wouldn't you tell us? We could've—"

"What?" Kai cut her off, and Isla had a feeling them going head to head like this was a common occurrence. "Could've what? Gone after them? They killed my father and Jaden. I wasn't getting you guys involved."

Ameera gritted her teeth. "That's not your call to make."

"Yes, it is."

Isla could feel guilt simmering within him, hear the nuances of it in his tone, but it wasn't because he hadn't told them. Grief twined within it.

But before she could put much thought as to why, Rhydian chimed in. "Does anyone else know about them going after you too?" He tried to keep his voice even, masking any anger he felt, but his nostrils flared.

"Ezekiel."

"You told my dad?" Ameera asked.

"He's my beta," Kai said.

Her features curled in a snarl, and she said nothing else.

"Does Amalie know?" Davina offered weakly, sipping from the water they were forcing her to drink. She was fading fast, leaning against Rhydian's shoulder, heavy-lidded. "She was sleeping right next to you."

Kai shook his head, casting a quick eye towards Isla at the mention of *his* former lover. She responded by running her fingers lazily, and dangerously, up his leg, stopping at the hinge of his hips and trailing back down. He stiffened under her touch. Her reminder and reassurance.

"Cruel," she heard in her head.

And then Kai spoke aloud, "She didn't even wake up."

"Your mother didn't either," Jonah said. "Right?"

Kai nodded, whatever exhilaration or joy he'd been feeling fading away. "She doesn't talk a lot about that night, but I know she woke up because she felt their bond snap, and then my father was dead."

Isla remembered the man at the banquet who'd lost his wife, and Zahra standing behind him. Imagined how her father must've felt. How Adrien must've. The thought of losing her connection to Kai now made her nauseous. Davina may have been pondering the same thing as she leaned into Rhydian.

"I might not have thought there was foul play if it weren't for what happened to me. There were no wounds. There was no blood. No scent of wolfsbane or even mistletoe or mountain ash. They were just—dead."

Isla felt a shudder whenever he said the word, and the guilt grew stronger.

Dead—*they* were dead. And he wasn't.

"What about magic?" Ameera said, folding her arms across her chest. "I remember the weeks before it happened, they were doing a lot in Surles, close to the Wall. Maybe he got too close or spent too much time in the wasteland. I mean, it was like they lived there. My dad was *never* at my parents' house when I'd visit."

Isla rose a brow. "What wasteland?"

"Along the Wall's border, there are patches of land where forest used to be," Kai explained. "It's almost like the Wilds, but without the bak.

Everything around there started dying about a decade ago. It never recovered, but thankfully, it never expanded either."

Isla hummed, something about it now hitting a vague place in her memory.

"Death by magic would give off a scent," Jonah said, adjusting himself to lean back in his chair. "That's why the Wilds smell so horrible. It's just a cesspool of death and destruction."

Isla frowned, her heart clenching. What a catastrophe that must've been. She couldn't imagine being there that day of the decimation, feeling the curse ripple through the earth, taking hold of the pack's inhabitants and ending their lives.

As she shook away the grisly images of how she envisioned the past and recalled the ghosts that lingered about in the Wilds, she also noticed that Jonah was eyeing her. "What?"

The shop owner nodded towards the table. "Where did you get those?"

Isla followed his eyes to the dagger and the broken diadem. She reached for the weapon and lifted it in her hand. Everyone recoiled just an inch. "Someone had given this to Lukas to kill me." She used the tip of the blade to point back at the table. "With the book."

"Lukas?" Rhydian asked.

Right, she hadn't gotten there yet.

"A hunter from Tethys," Isla said, before continuing through an explanation of how Lukas had lost his memory, "lashed out", and found himself restrained in the infirmary.

As she went on about how she'd gone to visit him and he pulled the knife on her, Kai tensed at her side.

"I should've been there."

"You needed to be here."

A suspicious look had crossed over Jonah's face, but he also seemed…perturbed.

"What's wrong?" Isla hated to have to ask.

"That crystal wedged in the blade and in the crown."

"What about it?"

He heaved a breath as if he knew what he was about to say would elicit some negative reaction.

"Crystals like that are known to be conduits for certain types of witch magic."

He'd been right.

The dagger clanked to the table as Isla took in a sharp breath, and almost all of them instinctually crept back.

Jonah hadn't moved. "If it was cursed, you'd be dead by now, believe me," he deadpanned. "I'm just making an observation. It could just be crafted jewelry and a weapon."

Davina had gone a ghostly white with a tinge of green. "How do you know it's witch crystals?"

"I don't. I just know the witches use crystals to better focus their power. It's one of many methods used in their craft."

"How do you know so much about witches, brother?" Rhydian prodded.

"Pick up a book, *brother*," Jonah countered. "Our continent isn't the only one in this realm. Our realm isn't even the only realm."

"I know that." Rhydian brushed him off before nodding at him, Kai, and Ameera. "I went to the academy same as you three."

Jonah narrowed his eyes in challenge. "Name them then."

Ameera put her hands up between the twins. "Can we focus please, the two of you?"

Isla heard Kai laugh through his nose beside her. *"If you ever wondered what things were like for me growing up,"* he said.

Before Isla could respond, Jonah looked back at her. "What about the crown? Where'd you find that?"

She opened and closed her mouth, her face paling. "The pieces were left for me—given to me—by whoever is trying to kill us."

"Oh, of course, how kind." That vein still pulsed in Ameera's forehead as she leaned forward to pick up the map. "What's this?"

"Callan had that," Kai said after having gone oddly quiet. "You were tailing him. What was he doing?"

Isla's brows shot up. Ameera had been the one following Callan around the city?

Ameera placed the map back on the table. "I told you, it looked like a lot of nothing, even when he went down to Abalys. He was just looking at things."

"What things?"

"I don't know—storefronts, waterways, trees? I was watching him, not everything around him."

"Certainly not a spymaster," Jonah muttered under his breath, earning a swat at his arm.

Beside him, Rhydian peered at the map. "And he obviously saw something—many somethings."

Ameera growled, snatching the map off the table and rising to her feet.

"Where are you going?" Davina questioned, her voice nearly a whisper as she fought sleep.

"To find the *somethings*." Ameera's voice was saccharine, though she glowered at the men of the table.

Isla perked up in her seat. "I want to go with you." Kai made a sound of confusion, and she looked at him. "I want to know what he was doing. Maybe figure out if the messages are really supposed to be warnings about him." A wary look appeared on his face. "Go to the hall and take care of the pack. I have us," she assured before he could offer himself to go too. Her fingers went up to brush his cheek. "I'll be safe, and I'll have Ameera to protect me."

"Me too," Rhydian said, nodding towards the passed-out Davina on his shoulder. Carefully, he rose, picking her up effortlessly in his arms. "She'd kill me if I brought her on a train like this."

Kai watched them disappear behind the stacks, avoiding the eye contact Isla kept fixated on him. Eventually, he let loose a breath and met her gaze. "Okay."

Isla smiled, pecking his lips and getting to her feet. Her eyes snagged on the diadem and dagger on the table. A sinking feeling lingered in her stomach. "Can you tell Jonah the rest of what I told you before you go?" Kai nodded, and she looked to the shop owner, who'd since picked up the book and one of the scribbled messages to compare. "Do you think you can figure it out?"

Jonah glanced at her and then at Kai. "Can you get me into the estate's library or any of the royal archives?"

Kai raised a brow. "How far back?"

"As far back as it goes."

His expression flattened, and they seemed to share their own unspoken communication. But before Isla could ask, she heard from behind her, "Let's go, Luna."

It felt odd responding to the call but she did, spinning to find Ameera and Rhydian—large but somehow deceptively quick and quiet —standing by the door.

Isla gave Kai one last kiss before walking to meet them. She threw back through the bond, *"You better tell me everything later."*

She heard a chuckle in her head. *"I'll see you at home."*

CHAPTER 36

From her seat on the trolley moving down into the lower city, Isla peered through the sheen of fog on the car's window and gazed up at the hall. The eye of the beast stared back down at her, with its wondrous patchwork of blues and near-black purples. Kissed by the Goddess's aura. Absorbing it.

She forced herself to think beyond the giant window, to envision what it protected. The enormous building of dark-wash stone at the back of a courtyard full of blooms akin to the colors of the stained glass. The House.

Her new home, her new life, with Kai.

I'll see you at home.

Such simple words but they ravaged her.

She wasn't sure if he'd realized what he'd said. If he'd meant for it to spin her mind into a tizzy. It was all she could think about during the torturously slow journey that the crowded cable car offered. Not having Kai at her side—a constant, comforting presence, even in those moments she'd wanted to rip his head off at the start—everything crashed into her, and somehow became more...*real*.

The most mundane and stupid things were driving her mad. Like how she'd come to Deimos with nothing but a trunk and a bag that held as much as her shoulder could bear. Nearly everything she owned here —besides Kai's jacket which she now claimed as her own—was warrior-given attire.

But that didn't matter, because there was surely an abundance of clothes for her to choose from. The queen. The luna.

But they weren't *hers*.

Not her favorite pair of slippers or her favorite sweater for those nights when she'd curl up next to her window and look upon the Imperial City. She didn't have her favorite blanket or her favorite books or that drink—warm and rich and chocolatey—that she'd always get from the vendor a few blocks from Io's training grounds on the way home. She didn't have the photos of her family that she kept around. Her and the boys. Her, Sebastian, and their parents. Her and her mother, happy as could be, during the Summer Solstice festivities in the ash lily fields. Even the several photos she kept hidden now, of her and Cora growing up through the years.

Some would call her foolish for thinking such things—and she felt it—but without Kai here, it was easier to see beyond the fairytale of the handsome, powerful man who loved her endlessly. Of the joy she'd feel every morning waking up at his side.

But she'd weather it, and she'd get over it.

Because this was what she wanted.

∼

Callan had five points circled on the map, negating the giant one that encompassed the Wall. Two in Mavec. One in Ifera. One in Abalys. And one in Surles.

Though it had been closest by distance, Ifera would've been a nightmare to get to, entailing either a wait for the train or an eerie, arduous trek down through the route the warriors had come in. Deep into those dimly lit tunnels hidden within the mountains. So Mavec was their best and easiest starting point.

The parchment Callan had wasn't the most detailed. It was simply the drawings of roads with shapes every so often to represent buildings. Not even all the businesses that comprised the square were shown. So, they began from an obvious point—the bridge that crossed over the river into Abalys.

It was behind them as they walked along its bank, hidden by a low stone wall that many sat along, either facing the water or away from it. Isla hadn't noticed the way the river came from underneath the structure, built against the face of one of Mavec's rocky hills. It flowed out of a wide-mouthed cavern cut into the stone, its opening illuminated brighter with lights alongside the landscape's natural crystal. From it spawned a hollow melody.

That was where most of the music was coming from.

"What is that?" Isla asked Rhydian, who stood at her side. They flanked Ameera, who she knew better than to bother. The general's eyes roved the map and the terrain before them with predatory intent. All the ferocity of a leader.

Rhydian turned his head, following the boats traveling beneath the bridge, heading inside. "A few things. A theater, an arena for sporting events, a club for dancing, gambling." At her surprise, he laughed. "It's deceptively large once you get in."

Isla hummed, squinting to see if she could get a better glimpse at what was inside, but it was near impossible from that angle. Mysterious and forbidding, as everything else here seemed to be.

So, she'd discovered, the city at night was as marvelous up close as it seemed from afar, and Isla walked amongst the heavens. She was sure she stuck out as she moved amongst the crowd, not for the fact she was the alpha's mate and the future queen, but because she was so taken by it all. Their everyday and commonplace were like a dream.

Filling in the melodies lost as they drew further from the cavern, singers serenaded the mingling masses on corners, strumming and rhythmically playing their instruments in tunes Isla wasn't familiar with but found herself entranced by. Wreaths of flowers were scattered along the ground, and every so often, there would be a small pillar of stone holding a flame, burning bright, and surrounded by those paying respects with whispered prayers blending into the music.

Pyres for the fallen.

As sadness gripped her heart, Isla noticed there was also more guard around. Some in uniform, and others that she recognized from their ramrod posture and intent gazes that rivaled Ameera's.

"Ooh."

Isla looked up at Rhydian, finding him focused on an eatery a few feet away. His hand was holding his stomach.

"What?" Ameera's voice was eager and sharp, ready to face an opponent, but as she followed the guard's stare, her tone flattened, "Are you serious?"

"I need more than whiskey in my stomach if we're going at this all night," Rhydian countered, already breaking from them to head inside.

Isla found her hand drifting to her own abdomen. She did, too.

The last meal she had was in the mess hall after the hike, and she'd certainly endured quite the…workout after that. Her mouth salivated as the smell of warm spices wafted up to her nose.

Several minutes later, Rhydian emerged from the shop with four pockets in his hands. Each smelled divine and was filled with seasoned meat, gooey cheese, and a variety of colored vegetables.

He'd already bitten into his own and handed one each to the two women, the last a second for himself. As he gave Ameera hers, he winked. "No onion."

The general attempted to keep a straight face as she grumbled a *thank you*, before taking a large, aggressive bite and noting that he'd set them back ten minutes.

As Isla mowed down her meal, which tasted as incredible as it smelled, she got lost in the atmosphere again. Tracking a killer, especially given the situation, shouldn't have been so…enjoyable.

"How could this place be suffocating?" she mumbled to herself, recalling Kai's words from the roof of Callisto's infirmary.

"How could what be suffocating?" Rhydian was already licking his fingers from the remnants of his first pocket and was ready to start his second.

Isla swallowed another bite. She hadn't meant for them to hear.

"When Ka—" She cut herself off. There weren't sizable crowds, but enough bodies close to be wary of curious ears. She wasn't sure how many named *Kai* were floating around Deimos but was sure who would be the most notable. "When this place was described to me, I was told that it was beautiful—which it is, incredibly so—but also that it's… suffocating." She looked around—at the people, the food in her hand, the star-flecked sky above, and the gems below. "I don't see it."

"It is when you're brought up within its conventions." Ameera drew Isla's attention her way. She, too, had finished her meal and was bunching the paper casing in her hand while she studied the map. "There's a reason that Pack Hall seems like it's a part of another world up there on that hill, and why I'm sure you had a *great* time at the banquet last night meeting the upper echelons of our pack leadership."

Isla's chewing on her next bite slowed.

She hadn't had the most pleasant time at the banquet, surrounded by the boastful lot. Those who looked at her as someone to sneer at or to fill the ear of with egotistical nonsense. Building a grandeur around themselves, a game of who stood higher than the rest. Manicured looks and manufactured personas. It was exhausting.

She didn't see or feel that here. Here, everyone was just—living. Celebrating that fact alone. For themselves and those that had been lost.

She glanced back at the hall. At the keen window-eye she couldn't miss, following and watching her everywhere she moved. The city's crown jewel. A reminder.

She spun back to Ameera and Rhydian and swallowed. "Is that why you all go to Abalys? To get away from here?"

"It was," Ameera said, slowing to a halt. "But you can't change the way things operate by running away and hiding." The words lingered as the general lifted her head to the building at which they'd stopped. "Interesting."

Isla did the same.

They were at a bar.

Rhydian scratched at the stubble sprouting from his chin. "Why is it interesting?"

"We never came over here."

Isla peered at the general. "You're sure?"

Ameera shot her a look that said, *of course, I'm sure*. She folded up the map and put it in her pocket. "Let me see what I can find inside. You two look around to see if there's anything else interesting around here."

Isla nodded, and Rhydian gave her a mock salute.

With her face a picture of determination, Ameera stalked forward and greeted the establishment's appointed security measures with a tip of her head. A vibrant voice carried through the air with the noises of a crowd and the smell of booze when they opened the door for her before the heavy wood was closed.

Now just her and Rhydian, Isla looked around. In the distance, a familiar tea shop caught her eye. She wasn't too far from where she'd been this morning. From the call center, the alleyway.

"I'm going to check this way," she told Rhydian, already beginning her steps in that direction.

The guard nodded before turning to the opposite side, and the two split off. Though they weren't apart long.

The alleyway had been a dead end. As Isla had walked, she'd alternated her stare from the crowd to the ground, searching for any more clues. Any more rubies. Any specific dark, forbidding crystal. But nothing was amiss, nothing added, and her wolf had not reacted. When she met Rhydian back in front of the club, he was holding another container of food. Something golden and crispy that smelled faintly nutty. Of course.

"Find anything?" she questioned, unable to mask her amusement. "*Other* than something to eat."

He shook his head, a smile on his lips as he offered the cup to her. She happily took one of the strips.

"No—did you?"

"No." She popped the piece in her mouth—yet something else to drool over and savor—before going in for another.

As she ate it, Rhydian gave her a deadpan look. "Do you want me to get you one?"

"No, it's fine." Isla took another.

The guard sighed. "Okay, Davi."

To that, Isla smiled.

She looked at the closed door of the bar. "She still hasn't come out?"

"Not yet. I don't know if that's a good thing or a bad thing." Isla bit the inside of her cheek, but before she could say anything, Rhydian continued. "Did you know him well?"

"Callan?" The question was purposeless. "Uh, you know, we ran in the same circles. Warriors and all."

Kai knowing their past was bad enough.

"Is he a bad guy?"

Isla gave the question some thought. "Not innately. He's a product of how we were raised and would do anything to get validation from certain people with more questionable moral compasses."

Rhydian furrowed his brows. "That's a lot of words."

Isla let loose a breath, simplifying, "He's an arrogant prick, but I don't think he's capable of things as heinous as murder or want to be the reason people end up dead."

At the mention of murder, Rhydian's expression had turned solemn. He looked to his food as if contemplating another bite, but averted his gaze away as if he couldn't stomach it.

"I didn't think they were really killed." Alpha Kyran and Jaden. Rhydian's voice was as soft as the breeze that blew by. "I can't believe he didn't tell us."

Part of Isla couldn't either, but she also understood.

"He has his reasons for why he does things." She matched his low tone and shrugged. "I'm still learning them."

"He's always tried to hold the world on his back." Rhydian met her eyes. "Even before all of this. Now the world's bigger, heavier, and he's still trying. It's going to break him."

"I won't let it," Isla said without hesitation.

The answer was enough to bring light back to Rhydian's face. His gaze traveled up and down her body. She was so small, not compared to most, but to men like him. He laughed. "He can be a stubborn bastard."

Isla matched his grin. "And so can I."

Another assessing look before he offered her more food. "I'm happy he found you."

Isla graciously took two pieces this time. "I'm happy I found him, too."

Another chuckle slipped out the guard's mouth as he joked, "It was my talk on the mountain that convinced you, right?"

But before Isla could answer, the raucous music filled the air, and the bar door opened to reveal Ameera. Her face seemed both annoyed and perplexed, and she subtly nodded for them to follow. They obeyed, dutiful soldiers that they were, and fell into step behind her.

"Well?" Rhydian leaned down over her shoulder.

Isla followed suit. "What is this place?"

Ameera lifted a hand to swat them both away, need not be suspicious, and gave a shifty glance around the area. "I don't think it's the place that matters. It's who works here." Upon the question of *who* from Rhydian, she looked to Isla. Her features shifted—as she seemed to undergo an internal debate—before she elaborated with one simple word, "Charon."

Isla rose a brow, the pack name like a swift kick to her gut. "Charon?"

Her confusion only intensified when she glanced over at Rhydian. His dark skin had turned green, and an understanding and fear shone in his eyes. "Why? What do you mean?"

Ameera removed the map from her pocket and began scanning it again. She took a sharp left turn, and they followed. "I asked the barkeep if she'd ever spoken to an Edriel. She didn't know who he was until I described him. He was a patron here a few days ago, the night the warriors got in before Kai had me tailing him. He was harassing one of the bartenders when—"

"Harassing how?" Isla asked, too fast, too shaken by the word. She'd just told Rhydian he wasn't *too* horrible.

"The only thing she heard was Charon before the tender brought him to the back to talk," Ameera said. "He hasn't been back to work since."

Isla's heart rate sped up. "Did Callan hurt him?"

"No, I think he scared him." Ameera turned, taking in Isla's persistent perplexity. "I suppose you're just as much a part of this now, and just as guilty if he proves what they've sent him here to prove."

Isla jerked back. "Guilty?"

Ameera's jaw tightened, and she glanced around once more before she began, "For the past few years, we've had an influx of new pack members—from Charon."

"Okay?"

"They weren't approved to leave Charon. They fled."

Isla blinked and was met with narrowed, urging eyes, forcing her to piece things together. "They didn't become rogues."

Ameera turned away, back to the map. They turned another corner to another bend of the river. "At first, as they needed to, by continental law…but sometimes, we forget to guard a border and they find their way here. And obtain new identities…and have a new chance at a life that doesn't utterly suck under a tyrant and his followers whose only purpose is to serve the wishes of a power-hungry egomaniac."

Lethal words that cut Isla like knives. It was so much for her to process.

Pushing the last dig at Alpha Cassius to the side and what she alluded to regarding Charon's own alpha, she broke down everything else Ameera had said.

Deimos had been breaching continental law. Technically, they'd even infringed on the Code.

Rogue wolves had always been a murky subject throughout the packs for a long, long while. For those cast out for criminal reasons, it was simpler, but for those who left their pack of their own accord, it was incredibly complicated. And dangerous.

One of the biggest of their sacred principles was unyielding loyalty to one's family, and your pack *was* your family. That rule could only be broken, with no question or bestowed approval, by an even greater covenant—the bond of fated mates.

If it weren't for the fact Isla was destined to Kai, to remain in Deimos and defect from Io, she'd need approval from Alpha Cassius and Io's Council. If they'd voted *no*, she would need to remain in her pack, or if asking to leave had pissed them off enough, she'd be cast out to live the rest of her life as a rogue. She could try to get into another region, but the repercussions of taking her in would be more than any alpha would risk. It would be a near declaration of war against the pack from which she came.

If Deimos had been doing this with people from Charon…

"How many?" Isla asked, voice hoarse.

"More than a few," Ameera answered, straightening. "For quite some time."

Isla's eyes widened.

She couldn't find fault in the benevolence. She'd want to do the same, but the danger that now loomed over the pack if Charon, if the Imperial Alpha knew…

For a second, Isla put herself in the shoes of her former alpha. Seeing

Deimos getting mixed in other pack's affairs, finding potential allies, maybe aiding in an uprising—or even worse, taking in citizens to build stronger armies for themselves.

A challenger, a potential threat to the hierarchy and Io's highest power.

As if she could see where Isla's mind was drifting, feel her panic rising, Ameera said, "The Imperial Alpha should know we're not looking for a war. We would be insane to do so, given nearly half that pack goes through the Hunt for fun to get the lumerosi, with no intention of joining the warrior ranks, and warriors have flocked there for centuries. Even if we'd give them a run for their money, in the end, we'd need some serious firepower to go against them and even have a shot at not being destroyed."

Those words weren't comforting in the slightest.

"It's only good grace," Ameera continued. "Maybe the Imperial Alpha should look harder at what's going on. If he wants that territory to fall in line for him, he should try out new leadership than the ones he put in power."

"That he what?"

Ameera heaved a breath. "You still have a lot to learn."

Of course, she did. She'd been mated to Kai and on the brink of queen for only a few hours.

Still, Isla lowered her head, words escaping her mouth softly. "Kai never told me any of this."

Or maybe he had—indirectly.

He'd mentioned Charon and Io being "close". Mentioned the easier access they would have to Deimos because of the pack's proximity. Mentioned his father doing something that would be looked down upon, that pushed some limits. But she'd been so distracted by the diadem and the dagger and the book and everything, that she didn't push *him* to further explain. To tell her about them taking in pack members. Tell her about Io putting people directly in power?

"I can only assume he didn't think it would be a problem."

Ameera was wrong.

He knew it was becoming a problem. Her family—the enemy.

But she kept that quiet, as Kai apparently wanted to.

Ameera held up the map. "But if Io knows, if they're searching for proof, it could be. It means they're seeing this as something more than it is."

Isla could barely gulp as Alpha Cassius's voice flooded her head. As she pictured him across from her all those months ago in his office.

"It's hard when people forget their place."
There was no *if*.
He knew.

~

There were fewer people on the ferry to Abalys—their next destination—than on the trolley through Mavec. Though many were out-and-about in the city, the same amount didn't seem to want to venture down the river to the region that bordered rogue territory. Isla had so desperately wanted to visit the infamous town that Kai and the rest of his family had felt so fond of, but she couldn't get herself to feel any excitement. Couldn't rid her mind of other thoughts. Of refugees, of Io and Charon, of a budding war.

With a sigh, she leaned over the edge of the boat and watched the water lick the metal sides. Nothing but inky blackness lay below the vessel, as depthless a void as the dark forest running alongside the riverbank. She squinted anyway, gazing into the abyss for answers. For tendrils of shadow she'd never be able to see.

She shouldn't have been hoping that the killer appeared. Shouldn't have been relying on them for pieces of the puzzle to help keep them afloat as more and more kept piling on them.

It was almost nauseating how much a foe—a *murderer*—was feeling more like an ally.

Somehow, they knew everything. Even from the disjointed, senseless messages, she was certain of that fact. Those words and symbols were warnings of what Callan had been doing, what he'd been sent to seek. What Io knew.

But *why*? Why tell them? Why warn them, protect them, protect *Kai*, now? A few months ago, they'd wanted him as dead as his father and brother.

And what the hell did the book, the dagger, and the diadem have to do with anything?

And *what the hell* would she do if they found themselves at war?

No. She couldn't worry about that. Wouldn't let herself. Not yet, anyway.

Isla ran her hands through her hair, close to the roots, digging near her scalp, and groaned. The sound quickly became a yawn that she choked on, the pungent aroma of river water tickling at her throat.

There was a chuckle and the sound of an over-exaggerated inhale. "Wonderful, isn't it?"

Isla looked to Rhydian as he rested beside her on the rail. "I see what Davi means when she describes it as a sewer."

"It's nature," Rhydian said, brandishing a grin. One that felt all too manufactured. He'd been off ever since the bar, and his unease made its appearance every so often with random frowns and pensive looks, much like his brothers, which he rarely lent himself to.

"Tired?" he asked her.

Isla rubbed her eyes. Small talk was welcomed. "I'm fine."

"I'm sure you haven't gotten much sleep." Another voice from behind them.

Isla turned just as Ameera approached to settle at her other side. Though, unlike her and Rhydian, the general remained forward, keeping a dubious eye on the deck and the few people on it.

Isla couldn't help but catch the slight innuendo in her tone. Deadly when she so desperately wanted to cling to any thoughts other than the horrors that her mind was spitting. She tried to will away any of the memories of her and Kai's time in the hotel that the words had spurred, but she was weak.

She gave into the phantom caress of her mate's fingers, of his mouth. Allowed his words, wicked and tender, his actions, gentle and rough, to consume her consciousness.

A shiver traveled down Isla's spine, and she suddenly became very aware—*too* aware—that he was nowhere nearby. And she wanted him. That primal part of her called for him. In a flash of heat and an almost delirium-inducing way—

"Oh, Goddess," Ameera grumbled, snapping Isla from her fantasy, though not entirely.

The warmth Isla had felt all over her body bathed her cheeks. Was it obvious where her mind had gone? "Sorry."

Ameera waved it off. "Honestly, I'm surprised he let you go. Newly-mated men are typically cranky, territorial, sex-crazed bastards." She nodded towards Rhydian. "I didn't see you for days after you and Davi got together. Jonah even had to come stay at my place to save his sanity."

Rhydian opened his mouth as if to protest her claim but promptly closed it. The smallest grin played across his mouth as if he were recalling the memories himself, and then his only response was a shrug.

If only she and Kai had the time to whisk off for days.

"The four of you are going to be insufferable when the season rolls around," Ameera grumbled, referring to the dawn of spring when *all* wolves sought another, but mated couples ended up in an absolute lust-filled frenzy. "Though I suppose we'll need an heir, and I'm sure Marin will want you two to have one as soon as possible."

The word made Isla's heart stop.

An heir.

She felt every muscle in her body tighten.

An heir. A child. A little her and Kai.

Her, a…mother.

She struggled to swallow as her heart gave an unsteady beat. As a part of her she'd calloused gave way. A deep hollowness—one she hadn't felt in years and years—began forming in her chest.

And the feeling remained there—festering, intensifying—as Ameera and Rhydian found themselves lost in conversation about sports games and gambling.

Glancing back at the water, new memories rolled through Isla's head. Memories that were vague and carried a stiffness because when Isla envisioned her mother, Apolla only appeared as clear and rigid as her poses in photos. She was the honey of her hair, the blue of her eyes, the radiance of her smile, and the tightness with which she embraced her children in each image.

Isla could no longer recall the nuances of her face, the feel of her warmth, the inflections of her voice. Did she remember what her voice sounded like at all?

It had nearly been a decade since that night she'd last tucked her into bed before her unit had gone off and no one heard from them again. No sign of anything, until the day her father felt their bond break and her mother fade away. Until she and Sebastian nearly lost him, too.

Biting down hard on the inside of her cheek, Isla refused to gaze at the sky. It would be impossible to keep it together if she even *thought* of sending up another plea. For a sign. For reassurance. For her mother, wherever she dwelled, to tell her how to do this. Any of this. Being a queen would be hard enough, but everything else? To be a good mate, to be a good mother herself?

The loud whistle of the ferry broke Isla from her thoughts. She shot her head up and tears she hadn't realized had been forming slid down her cheeks. She brushed them away hurriedly, hoping her companions hadn't noticed.

Forcing herself to find some peace, to forget, Isla instead focused on the golden aura of lamps and lanterns as they approached Abalys's docks. Even from their distance, she could tell it was nothing like Mavec. Maybe the stench *wasn't* as horrible as Davina had described, but it certainly was—acquired. Isla had no choice but to embrace it as the boat came to a halt, unable to continue forward as the town closed in on their path, narrowing the river to nothing but canals.

Only one man was waiting for them at the dock as the engine cut out, and he moored the boat before the ferry whistled once more. Isla hadn't realized how accustomed she'd become to its whirring.

The three of them were the last to get off the boat, and the sound of Isla's boots creaking on the metal stairs was quickly replaced by the thudding of her boots on wooden boards—what lay here most, as opposed to its sister city's cobblestones.

Even if Abalys was nothing like Mavec, even if it didn't have that same marvel of crystals and warm scents of spices or raucous crowds on its streets, there was enough for her to wonder at.

Despite the stories she'd been told, despite the worry she probably should've felt as Ameera tucked the necklace she'd been wearing—a simple gold chain with a pendant hanging from the end—into her shirt, there was something homey about the area. Something inviting about that golden aura and the same auspicious light that emanated from the many establishments along the boardwalk, their reflections bobbing on the water. Taverns and shops. More gambling dens and apartment buildings. From the dancing shadows in the windows, she imagined that was where all had disappeared to. She couldn't help but notice that no prayers or pyres were sent or burned here.

"So, this is Abalys," Isla said, turning to find both Rhydian and Ameera with a light in their eyes that rivaled the lantern's glow.

"This is Abalys," Rhydian echoed, his giddiness leaking into his tone. He pointed down a bend of the canal. "Jonah and I used to have an apartment down there. It was a bitch to get up to, and our neighbors sucked." He looked at Ameera and jerked his thumb in another direction. "And you were over by the western bank, right?"

"You lived down here, too?" Isla's voice had unintentionally risen in surprise.

Ameera rolled her eyes. "You sound like my parents. I had an escape, and I took it. I ended up back in Mavec anyway, but it was nice while it lasted." She pulled out the map but scanned Isla over first. She murmured, "Make sure you look like you belong here. This town will take advantage and rip you apart the second they smell they can. And everyone's on edge because of the rogues. They aren't afraid. Any perceived threat and they'll defend our home."

Isla took a deep inhale of river water and faint wood smoke. "Okay."

"Try not to smile." She reached to adjust Isla's collar, hiding her lumerosi. At Isla's questioning stare, she noted, "We don't want to draw attention." Then she turned and pressed forward.

As they moved along the boardwalk behind Ameera, Rhydian acted as Isla's tour guide, pointing out all the places they'd been to and the experiences they'd had there with quelled enthusiasm. Isla nodded tersely along the way, fighting smiles from her face, especially as Rhydian recounted meeting Davina at one of the pubs.

But it became easier to remain stoic as they encroached on the inner workings of the town, catching some patrons outside of taverns locked in heated conversations and embraces. Some were smoking and shooting dangerous looks as they twirled weapons in their hands. Even those sitting in their small boats, drinking from small flasks and paper-bag-wrapped bottles, cast leery looks their way.

Any perceived threat and they'll defend our home.

When Isla and Rhydian found themselves waiting for Ameera outside a betting hall Callan had circled, her proposal to split up and search again was met by a hard *no*. Rhydian noted that Kai would have his head if he let her wander off alone and recounted several instances, to Isla's amusement, when the two had fought growing up—from their childhoods up until they were with the guard.

"He's honorable, but he'll fight dirty when he has to," Rhydian finished.

Isla's eye was drawn to the tavern across the canal that was emanating music more boisterous than any tune she'd heard in Mavec. There was the pounding of instruments and clapping hands and the stomping of feet on wooden floors in time with a beat that seemed to increase in tempo and volume. Isla found herself enraptured by the sounds of dancing and laughter, calling to another part of her not beckoned by its dreamy royal counterpart.

She'd get Kai down here eventually, and a part of her wished she could drag Adrien and Sebastian here too. They always sought the rowdiest places in the Imperial City, so they'd probably love it.

As Rhydian began explaining Talha to her, the tavern they enjoyed and frequented most that was further down a different canal and closer to where there was more solid land, Ameera emerged from the betting hall.

All she did was nod, and they knew.

Another tie to the refugees of Charon.

This time, it was a husband and wife who worked as a dealer and waitress. They had a daughter too, who was sleeping in one of the apartments above the hall. Other than that, they offered nothing new.

"I'm surprised he didn't find more here," Ameera said, looking over the map. "This is the region that borders Charon. It's where most of them settle. It's all they can afford to settle in, besides Surles."

Once again, Rhydian's features had shifted into a frown. "So now what? Do we go to Surles? Ifera?"

"Are we just going to find the same thing?" Isla asked.

Ameera addressed neither of them, her eyes honed on the parchment. "You know what I don't get?" Before they could inquire, she pointed to a thick line of black ink. Another. Then another. "What these are? They don't even connect to the points."

"They start back in different sectors of Mavec," Rhydian noted, pointing out the haphazardly drawn ends of the lines. "But they all end at the Wall?"

The sentences had struck a chord in Isla and she sucked in a sharp breath. "Wait…"

There was no way. But—

Both Deimos-born wolves turned in her direction.

"What is it?" Ameera asked.

Desperate for another answer was what it was and Isla couldn't ignore the nagging hunch. Any line that connected Mavec to the Wall was enough for her.

But she didn't want to bring up the pass here. Not the history, not Io, not the hierarchy. "We need to go to the Wall."

She earned equally confused stares.

"Do you know how far that is from here?" Ameera said. "It would take us all night to get down there and back home. I was going to say we go back and continue in the morning."

Isla huffed, a restless feeling crawling beneath her skin. "We can run."

Rhydian spoke next. "And then run back? There's an early roll call tomorrow."

"Is there not another train or boat or bus we can take?"

"Not this late."

"So then, we find another way." Isla turned to Ameera. "I need you to trust me, and you know you're going to lie awake all night until you find out what those lines mean. Why not save yourself the misery?"

The seconds before Ameera spoke felt like hours.

"Interesting tactic," she said with the slightest amusement. "Why so eager?"

"I'll explain later."

Ameera hummed. "Alright, Luna." A look of assessment crossed her face, accompanied by a devilish twinkle in her eye. "Let's make a quick stop at Talha."

Isla raised a brow. "The tavern?"

"We don't have time for cards," Rhydian argued.

"We're not going for cards," Ameera said, shoving the map in her pocket. "We're finding another way."

∽

"For fuck's sake, Meera!"

From where she sat in the passenger seat of the new model town car, Isla looked up at Rhydian through the rearview mirror. He had his arms fully spanned to hold himself steady against the doors to either side of him. Isla wasn't sure if she wanted to laugh or yell too as Ameera careened around another line of trees that sent her slamming into her own door.

The young general wasn't a horrible driver by any means, however, her ambition surely carried through all the walks of her life. Ameera was doing everything in her power to get them to the Wall as quickly as possible, including this questionable "shortcut".

While Mavec was a city, and Abalys a river town, Surles was comprised of spread-out villages, with plenty of forest in between the areas to sneak through and speed about. As they traveled over makeshift roads and bumps, all they had to illuminate their path were the headlights of the vehicle, the canopies of the trees too tightly woven to allow the moonlight through.

That, and Isla wondered if somehow the Goddess was hiding behind another behemoth, beckoning her from the closing distance.

"Do you want to get there or not?" Ameera called over her shoulder.

"Yes, I'd like to get there—*alive*," Rhydian countered. "Are you sure that Charley doesn't care we took this?"

"Of course," Ameera drawled, not the least bit convincing. One more turn had light in their path. "He owes me, anyway."

For what, Isla never learned. They'd all been rendered silent.

Emerging from the forest, no matter what lay before her, all Isla could focus on was the presence that loomed above them. Shrouded by night. Nothing but a dark shadow that seemed to be the end of the world. Absolute oblivion.

"Hello, old friend," Ameera sighed.

Old friend.

Isla looked at the general. Somehow, she'd forgotten that to hold her position, Ameera had gone behind the structure and faced its horrors, too. She wondered if she felt the same way—like her heart was in her throat and like every inch closer to it made her want to jump out of her skin.

"Goddess, I hate this place." Rhydian wasn't looking into the distance at the Wall, but at the set-back homes they passed as the open field they'd been driving on led them to an actual road.

Judging by the frown Ameera wore as she glanced at him in the rearview mirror, Isla felt she shouldn't question this either.

Now amongst civilization, Ameera's speed had slowed down considerably, and Isla used the opportunity to take in what was around them.

As opposed to Abalys and Mavec, no one was outside, and the only available light came from the streetlamps, few and far between, or porch lights from homes that varied from tightly packed cottages to modest farmhouses. Near them, lay barns and fields with crops. She could imagine how barren land could pose a problem.

About a half-hour of driving later, the three of them reached the cusp of another forest. This time, Ameera stopped, pulling up alongside the trees. She cut off the vehicle's engine and exited, Isla and Rhydian following her lead.

For a moment, postured in the grass, Isla could barely breathe. A wind, a bit warmer than she'd dealt with in Mavec, swept by her face, carrying a scent she likened to imminent death and despair, awakening those demons locked in her mind.

She shook them away, steeling herself, as Ameera stood at her side with Rhydian.

"Weird." The general folded her arms. "Where's the guard? They should be patrolling, but I can't scent anyone."

That certainly didn't help ease Isla's nerves.

"Maybe they're masking it?" she offered.

Rhydian scratched his head. "We're not supposed to while on duty."

Ameera shrugged. "I know better than to question when things work in our favor. If they aren't here, they can't ask their own questions." She turned to Isla. "So, what are we looking for?"

Isla observed their surroundings. A quick look for any markers or trails...any bak. "Anything that looks like it would've been a path from the Wall—or Phobos—to Mavec."

Rhydian brought his finger to his mouth to lick it and lifted it in the air, pointing, "Mavec is that way."

Isla nodded in slightly amused gratitude for the direction.

"And what makes you think we'll find a path like that?" Ameera queried.

"The marker." Upon Ameera's raised brows, Isla elaborated, "The little wooden ball that was on the table with everything else. We found it when we were in the Hunt, and—"

"We?"

"Me and Lukas."

"The guy who tried to *kill* you?"

"Yes." Isla sighed. "Before *that*, he told me about an old pass that connected Deimos and Phobos to link the packs, and that marker was a point on it. If it's real, I think Callan found it somehow. But…"

"But?" Rhydian offered.

The bak.

That part still didn't add up.

How could a creature like that take a road all the way to Mavec without being seen? Unless they were about to find the perfect line of tree cover.

She'd bring it up to them if it weren't for the fact Kai hadn't. They'd agreed to tell the others about the killer, but the rogue bak had nothing to do with that. Honestly, Isla wasn't sure if she was even supposed to mention the pass.

"Nothing." She shook her head, peering into the forest and changing the subject. "Where's the wasteland?"

There was a pause while Ameera scoped her suspiciously, before she answered, "Beyond the brush, closer to the Wall's base. It cuts through another abandoned village."

"You'll know when you're there," Rhydian added. "And you'll wish you weren't."

"It's nothing compared to the real Wilds," Ameera said before ordering, "Callan couldn't have traveled far along the Wall by himself. We'll split up to cover more ground. I'll head down towards Mimas, Rhydian will go towards Callisto, and Isla can take the middle."

Rhydian was quicker to agree with the commands than Isla was, but it didn't matter. They were already stripping off their clothes to prepare to shift. Isla made quick work of hers, her blood rushing in her ears and heart hammering as she left her garments in the vehicle's cab.

"Howl if you find anything," she forced out, clawing for some confidence before they all found their wolves and split off into the trees.

CHAPTER 37

Isla wasn't sure if Ameera was right—if the Wilds were in fact worse than the wasteland—but she was certain of the way her skin crawled as she reached the precipice of the besotted earth. Certain of the way the air had changed. Gone stale. Gone still. Waiting for her next move.

The forest before this had been lush and full, and exceptionally green, given that autumn was fast approaching, but the hooting owls, cooing doves, and chattering bugs were no more. They'd faded as quickly as the sounds of Rhydian and Ameera's paws against the ground once they'd broken in opposite directions. Now, the only thing Isla had was the lick of breeze that rustled her tawny fur and tumbled through the landscape before her and a grove of gnarled trees, their bark gray and peeling in ribbons from their husks. Their limbs stretched tall and were entirely bare, on the edge of brittle. They strained against the coarse wind, peppering small twigs and leaves around their bases.

They created a path with the way they curved towards each other. Not *the* path, she was sure, but still an entrance. Isla stepped forward on it, the ground solid beneath her feet, no vapors wheezing from the surface. It wasn't horrible but...different. Enough to put her on edge and enough to have those demons scaling the walls of her mind.

Not the Wilds.

She'd been repeating the words to herself since they'd separated. Every move was an effort. Each one brought her closer to that mass of stone hidden within the shadow, looming larger and larger.

This is not *the Wilds.*

But she could still feel it.

As if it had left an imprint on her soul, as if a piece of her still lay in there, where her blood had soaked the earth, Isla felt the Wilds calling to her. Like it wanted her back. Wanted another shot at taking her life.

Focus.

The trees seemed to straighten as she passed them. The wood was alive. Aware. Too aware. Of who she was. Of what she was, where she'd been.

As she moved, Isla kept a keen eye on the shadows, ready for just about anything. This close to the Wall, and with the trajectory of everything in her life these past few months, nothing going wrong felt uncomfortably improbable.

She had to put herself in Callan's shoes—while ignoring the fact she didn't know where he was—and more than that, she had to think as Imperial Alpha Cassius would.

If this *was* the pass that Callan had been marking for him, how would that benefit Io?

A way to sneak into Deimos?

Even if they'd be able to march through Callisto without raising alarm, sending anyone through the Wilds to breach the pack's border seemed like more risk than it was worth.

Isla's stomach twisted.

They would not go to war.

They *would not* go to war.

A new mantra cycled through her head as she came upon a row of houses. The abandoned part of the village.

She paused at the end of the dirt road that connected them, taking in their exteriors. They were no larger than the other homes they'd seen on the way in. Barely any gaps lay between them. Their lights were eternally out, some windows broken. Their sidings, their doors, their fences rotted.

They were entirely ravaged by whatever had infected the expanse and a decade of neglect.

So why was it, when all had been ruined the same, one, in particular, had enraptured her?

Isla stopped before the house at the end of the road, a few yards behind it was an escape into lush forest once again. Her paws, possessing a mind of their own, traveled up its gravel walkway, stones shifting and crunching beneath her, echoing into the silence of the night, followed by the creak of the rickety wooden steps to the front door.

She called back her wolf, an action followed by instant regret as the feeling of being exposed fought whatever inclination had taken over. But she steeled against it and wrapped her hand around the rusted handle, jerking it and eliciting the harsh *scrape* of metal against metal. A soft breath passed her lips and she pushed.

The entrance whined as it opened, slowly at first, but then faster as it widened the gap, as though it hadn't been attached properly. Isla hesitated on the doorstep, using the pause to pick up any foreign sounds within the space. But there was no light, no life, from what she could tell. Another groan, from the floorboards this time, filtered through the air as she stepped inside. It was colder in here than it had been outside as if the warmth didn't want to enter or the house didn't want to let it.

Why am I here?

The thought flickered, came and went.

But almost like a response, a chill ran down her spine. Something eerie tickled her bones. Called her. Whispered, sang, in a familiar way. But from where, she didn't know.

Another step.

The foyer trickled into a living room. It had been a decade since this family had been here, and yet the furnishings didn't seem too obscure compared to the hotel or the Pack Hall.

Another step before she turned to glance outside.

Not a soul to be found. She was alone. Entirely alone. Rhydian and Ameera had to be miles away now. But she had Kai, the bond, no matter how unnervingly faint it felt out here.

Isla kicked the door closed with a shockingly loud thud that had her flinching.

"Hello," she chanced a greeting, her voice so soft that she could barely hear it through the blood rushing her veins.

No answer, but that buzz beneath her skin persisted. Her fingers twitched at her sides as she moved in further.

Squeaks echoed her footsteps as she encroached deeper into the living room, throwing out an arm to run a finger along the welcoming credenza, the worn wood, the surface riddled with dust that tickled her nose. She stuttered as she tested it between her touch and spun to look back. It had been a decade but the grime wasn't much but a fine layer. Not caked and immovable as she expected.

Her gaze traveled to the couches and chairs in the room's heart, a small table in their center, and a stone hearth brimming with charred firewood on the wall before them. Four teacups rested by the seats. One free of its saucer, one tipped over it, and all had been drained of their liquid or had evaporated into nothing but residue on the glass.

Disgusting and old—but again, not *ten years* old.

Isla circled in her spot to survey her surroundings again. There were several ways she could go from what she could see. A kitchen, a dining room, a set of stairs in one far corner, and a lonely door at another.

Expecting the door to be nothing but a closet, she went there first to get it out of the way. But as she reached for the handle, she hesitated and cocked her head. There were small symbols etched in the wood, circling the knob. Ones that were vaguely familiar. She reached out to touch them, but she had little time to contemplate anything.

Voices.

Voices were coming from outside.

Isla whirled around to face the front door just as their keepers' heavy feet clambered up the rickety steps. Their tones cleared in her head. They were men, and they were foreign to her.

Of course.

Isla swallowed, hastily running through a plan. The act of surprise was her best option if this were to go awry.

In mere seconds, she found herself on the other side of the door, closing it just as the creaking of the front one came.

And she hoped to the Goddess that they hadn't heard her gasp as she nearly tumbled down a set of steps.

What the hell?

This wasn't a closet.

Hand over her mouth, heart pounding in her chest, Isla rested against the wall and gazed down the flight of stairs that dissipated into nothingness.

What was this? A basement?

She couldn't worry about it. Not with whoever was on the other side.

Who would come out here at this time? Who would come out here at all—besides them?

Guards?

Isla pressed her ear to the door.

"Are you sure that it's here?" one asked the other, their voice as grating as sandpaper.

"That's what I heard," a warmer, more assured, almost alluring tone replied.

They were drifting further away from the door, the sounds of their feet at what she guessed was the beginning of the staircase to the second floor.

"And how do we know they aren't coming out tonight? If we're caught, then we'll be slaughtered like the rest."

"Because they're still concerned with what happened yesterday, which was the point. Now we get what we're owed."

Isla furrowed her brows, a horrible feeling in her gut as her mind ran through the words.

Were these men...

No.

No, they couldn't be.

Isla pulled her head from the door to shake it but froze. She became stone against the wall.

She was being watched.

A pair of glowing eyes peered at her from the darkness below.

Red eyes.

Her insides turned watery. She couldn't breathe, fought to blink as if it would make them go away.

But they were still there when she opened her eyes.

Not only that—they were closer.

Goddess, no.

Swallowing any sound, any panic, Isla spun to open the door, keeping one eye on the stairs, more apt to face what was on the other side than what lay below.

But as soon as she touched the metal, shockwaves coursed up her arm and through her body. She recoiled and hissed, shaking away the tingling from her fingertips.

"What the hell?" She couldn't stop the words from falling from her mouth, her breathing kickstarting in pants.

She tried again. The pain was worse, *burning* through her now. A whimper slipped out her lips, and she curled in on herself.

What is happening?

A low growl rumbled from the darkness.

Isla didn't even need to turn to know any time she'd been allotted had run out.

She didn't have any other option. She slammed her fists against the wood and screamed.

The bak's responding roar drowned her out quickly, piercing her soul and shaking the surrounding foundations. It thundered up the steps, left shuddering and straining under its weight, and Isla stiffened.

She would die here—it would *kill her*—if she didn't move now.

Her head emptied, and in that moment, something within her ignited. Markings and eyes illuminating the darkness, claws emerging from her fingertips, Isla ducked out of the way just as the bak swung its enormous paw—speared by its own long talons—for her head. There was a loud thud as it contacted the door, followed by the smell of something rotting, searing. The bak wailed and stumbled back. Isla couldn't ponder the reason for the scent, for its pain. She shoved her body into it, driving claws into hardened flesh, and sent the creature tumbling down the staircase.

The steps trembled beneath its weight as the beast tumbled down, down, forcing Isla to grip onto the railing so she wouldn't follow. It came to a stop with a loud crack, the third step weak and easily crumbling beneath the impact of its size.

Debris spread through the heavy air in a cloud.

Isla breathed.

Adrien's voice flooded her head, Sebastian's, her instructors', all talking her through the steps of the Hunt, offering their warrior advice. But they'd been *wrong* about the baks' behavior. Everyone had been wrong.

For Goddess's sake, what the hell was it doing *here*?

There was one sole fact that consistently rang true: only one of them was making it out of here alive.

Isla didn't glance back to listen if the two men were coming to open the door. Instead, she raced for the solid ground she assumed below and braced herself for the impact as she leaped over the bak and shifted mid-air. Her joints groaned as her paws met the dirty, cold stone floor.

What the—

She retched as her newly heightened senses picked up the most abhorrent odor.

She turned her head and faltered.

Thick columns of stone were built up the furthest wall, meeting at an archway in presentation of a wide-mouthed opening.

A cavern.

A…tunnel?

Inside, Isla could see the faintest glimmer of crystal embedded in its rock walls. The path seemed to go a few feet before it banked another way. In that distance, she sensed the source of that smell.

Wooden planks flew towards her as the bak rocketed from its fallen position to go for her again.

She barely had time to get out of the way of its claws or its teeth that followed. It had gone for her neck. The same fatal blow she needed to deal.

It went again. Again. From the left. The right. Faster. *Faster.*

Isla ducked and dodged and felt razors ghost across her fur.

Not much was stored down here, but she could barely move. There was nowhere for her to cover herself and *think*. With bak, strategy meant as much as strength. It was why warriors trained their minds as much as their bodies, their endurance. Training that few had gotten. Why they'd never survive.

Why this had been sealed…

The door was warded. Like the Gate. Like the Wall.

That's why the bak couldn't get out. Why she couldn't.

If the beast made it out of this basement. Into Surles. Abalys. Mavec.

If there were *more*, it would be catastrophic.

Isla glanced at the tunnel. She could chance it. Where she'd end up, she had no idea, but it would be better than the bak ending her life *here*, leaving it sitting and waiting for the men to be as foolish as she was.

Kai's face flashed in her head—the bond pulsed—but she pushed it away.

This was about Deimos, keeping its people safe.

But just as Isla was about to make her dash for the cavern, a creak cut through the bak's grunting and her own breaths.

Warm light spilled down the staircase, searching until its glow illuminated the pallor, rippling skin of the beast.

No.

Isla barked at the man, who cursed and stood dumbfounded.

Too slow.

Too Goddess-damn slow.

As if it could sense the easy prey, the bak screeched and moved so hastily, that it was a blur of shadow. It skipped the broken steps and launched itself onto the first floor of the house. All Isla heard was a horrified scream, the tearing of flesh, and an unnerving squelch before the bak roared.

Triumph.

There was a responding howl of woe, of warning. The other man.

Isla dug deep, racing to the staircase and propelling herself up and over the gaps, fumbling up the shaky incline. Some of the wooden boards, already unsteady from the bak, clattered to the ground.

The first thing she saw as she lofted onto the first floor was the lifeless stare of the slain man. He slumped against one of the chairs, crimson oozing from the large gash in his chest. Broken glass lay at his side. A vial, maybe. Whatever was inside, a darker liquid, swirled with his blood.

Isla whipped around to see his companion had shifted, his wolf's fur a dark gray. His eyes—dim and empty.

Rogues.

These men were *rogues*.

A blade glinted on the ground a few feet away from him, beside another fallen lantern. Abandoned once he'd realized exactly what he was facing.

A nightmare.

Death.

There was no time for Isla to deal with her conflicted heart. Rogues had come to destroy the city, to take lives, but right now, these men were wolves as much as she was. And there was a much bigger issue for her to deal with.

Isla lifted her head and called for Rhydian and Ameera, hoping to the Goddess they'd hear.

All attention came her way.

In the split moment, the rogue wolf met her eyes, then caught the flash of the crescent lumerosi on her fur. He took a step back, another, another before he darted out the front door, left ajar.

The fleeing had caught the bak's attention.

She needed it on her. Needed to keep it inside this house, contained. And if she couldn't kill it here, she had to, at least, get it down into the basement again.

Barely a strategy was enough for her.

She growled, reacquiring the bak's eye and letting it take a few steps towards her before she maneuvered through the living room and to the front door, slamming it closed.

The bak broke through every piece of furniture to get to her, ripping cloth, splintering wood, shattering teacups. And it all became like the Hunt again as she evaded it, going into the dining room, the kitchen. It destroyed everything in its path, like the grisly landscape of the Wilds.

A game of endurance.

This was a game of endurance, and though she'd been more sleep-deprived and undernourished during the Hunt, she knew she would die if she didn't act now.

On another pass through the living room, hiding her scent, Isla dove behind the chair where the dead rogue sat. She'd let the bak get close and launch herself at it, knock it off balance, go for its throat.

Step.

She moved closer. The bak sniffed the air, trying to discern her location.

Step.

She crept in, lowering on her haunches.

Step.

She yelped as her paw met a shard of glass and the fallen man's blood. And all she felt was an unrelenting, venomous burn.

The bond went taut. She thrashed, her wolf struggling against—

No.

This was more than she'd felt from the doorway, but it was still familiar. Too familiar. From when a blade had been pressed to her stomach over a month ago. From when the substance that laced it hampered her, consumed her.

She did all she could to remove the glass, and when it had finally been wrenched free, the wound healed quickly. As if she'd never been injured. But she still felt it working through her, through her wolf. The whimpering wasn't her own. That piece of her separated, pulled away.

Stop, she pleaded. The tether, Kai, did too.

But Isla couldn't hold her shift anymore.

As much as she grunted and fought, she ended up on her hands and knees, panting and shuddering as her wolf drifted out of reach, hidden away.

A glance back at the blood, gleaming with that liquid from the vial, almost led to her death.

She rolled away from the bak's blow that she'd caught coming from the corner of her eye. The broken furniture became her cover until she reached the blade on the floor left by the other rogue. Seconds moved like hours as she spun; she had one shot at driving it into the bak's neck. Its rough paws collided with her body, knocking her back to the ground and skewing her aim. It roared as the blade dug into its thick shoulder. Dark blood dripped onto Isla's body.

But not enough. It wasn't enough.

The bak hovered above. Its paws on her skin so heavy that she felt it tear, its piercing eyes cutting through her before its teeth would.

There would be no luxury of taunting this time.

The bond strained, and Isla called for her wolf. Her claws. A miracle from the Goddess. Anything.

She couldn't die. She could *not* die. Couldn't leave Kai.

Blood sprayed over her.

All Isla had seen was the glint of silver before her face, her body became coated in the warm, sticky liquid.

The bak sputtered, the gaping wound in its neck pouring blood, and collapsed.

Isla's heart drummed against her ribcage that she swore snapped beneath the beast's weight. She couldn't breathe. Barely think. She only knew that she *definitely* couldn't die like *this*. Suffocated.

She grunted as she forced the creature off, struggling for air when she'd found relief. For a moment, she lay there, bathed in the gore, choking, and staring up at the ceiling.

Alive. She was *alive*.

But—

Isla rose on her elbows to see what had befallen the creature and gasped.

Standing there, their own weapon in hand, was that figure.

No. More than a figure. A person. Completely cloaked in black. A hood over their head, and a mask showing nothing but their eyes.

They killed the bak.

And Isla had a vague sense it wasn't their first time.

She didn't move at first, couldn't, as she stared up at them. She thought she'd been imagining things, but like the bak, when she blinked, they remained. Barely breathing themselves.

Isla ground her teeth, and rational thought eddied away as she leaned over to wrench her knife from the bak's shoulder. She bit back against the pain and rose shakily to her feet. With the weapon in front of her face, she rasped, "Who are you?"

They didn't answer.

With an aggravated cry, Isla rushed forward. She threw her body against them, taller than her by inches, and pushed them into the wall. Their weapon clattered to the floor, and they made no reach for it.

No fight.

But Isla didn't care about the current passivity. She didn't trust it.

She pressed her blade to the neck hidden beneath swathes of dark fabric, peering into darker, lifeless eyes, as she gritted out again, emphasizing each word, "*Who are you?*"

No response.

"Answer me," she commanded, increasing the pressure, firm enough that she felt flesh shuddering from the force.

But again, nothing.

Isla let out a breath, and her hands began trembling. It was all catching up to her. She'd nearly died. Again.

Again and again, she and Kai faced death and chaos and—

Isla met their eyes.

They'd been warning her. Them. Could an ally really be the murderer?

"Did you really kill them?" she choked out.

A rise and fall of a chest, a beating heart within. They breathed. Their head lifted and fell.

A yes.

Isla swallowed. "Why not Kai?"

There was a pause.

Before she could show her temper again, the killer lifted a hand. It was so smeared in dirt and grime, so twisted and scarred as if it'd been broken over and over and not properly healed that it made Isla sick.

Distracted her enough that she allowed them to run their touch along the blade. Blood pooled on their fingertips. They dropped their hand and slightly inclined their head to Isla's left arm. Cautiously, Isla lifted it for them, and their touch was as cold as ice, as death, as they drew along the skin of her forearm, down to her hand. Warrior. Io. Charon. Deimos. A fifth symbol that she didn't recognize.

The figure dropped their arm, and Isla prepared to slit their throat as they reached into their cloak.

But from it, they pulled a jewel of deepest onyx, a perfect fit for the heart of Isla's open palm they'd placed it in.

She didn't even need to ask to know.

The last piece of the diadem.

"Why?" Isla asked, lifting her eyes to theirs.

She allowed the killer to touch her forehead, then followed their twisted fingers as they pointed to the bak—and themselves.

Isla shook her head. "What are you saying?"

They reached over and touched the symbol of Deimos on her forearm. A horrible, guttural sound came from behind the mask, and Isla heard it again, although barely comprehendible. *"Traitor."*

Isla gulped.

Deimos. Traitor.

Did that mean her—the new luna—or something else?

Straightforward answers didn't seem possible, but Isla chanced a question again. "Who are you?"

No answer.

Isla forced another query, "Why did you try to kill me?"

She could've sworn something like hurt flashed behind their eyes, and a scent began filtering through the room.

Theirs.

Familiar, but Isla couldn't pinpoint from where.

Acting on impulse, she reached for their mask to remove it, to reveal them, but their eyes flared red—*bright red*—and something sharp pressed against her stomach. They'd been concealing another dagger. Wielded it against her easily.

They could've slain her this entire time and been gone in a blink.

Isla stepped back, keeping her blade in front of her. But before she could act or ask anything else, howls rang through the air along with the sounds of breaking doors.

Rhydian and Ameera.

The killer stiffened before turning towards the open basement door.

"Wait, no!" Isla reached out but they were quick in their escape.

She barely heard the stairs beneath their feet as they descended into the darkness. To the tunnel.

Rhydian and Ameera appeared minutes later when Isla was standing at the cusp of the stairs, contemplating her next move. As they crossed the threshold with snarls brandished on their snouts, they scoped the area. Rhydian halted first, then Ameera. They shared a glance, a secret communication before both came out of their shifts. The guard's jaw was hanging open in astonishment as he looked over Isla, coated in blood. The dead rogue. The dead bak. The destroyed home.

Even Ameera seemed to wince at the sight of the beast, but she steeled her nerve to ask, "What, in the Goddess's name, did you do?"

Isla didn't have an answer. She tightened her hold on her blade and took a step down the staircase. "Come on."

CHAPTER 38

"Hold on," Rhydian voiced in protest, making Isla pause where she stood. "Seriously, what happened?"

She hissed out a breath, too shaky for her liking, making her too aware of the knot lingering in her chest, aware of how badly a part of her just wanted to crumble. In Kai's arms, preferably.

Isla took a step back onto the main floor and turned, facing every horrifying moment laced in each broken and overturned piece of furniture.

She'd nearly died. *Again*.

But she wouldn't let it overwhelm her. She pushed back against it. There was no time to waste doing so.

"Rogue," Isla began rigidly, gesturing to the dead body. "There were two, but one ran away. The bak was in the basement that I'm pretty sure is *more* than just a basement. It almost killed me, but then whoever's been going after me and Kai killed *it*...and I'm not too sure they're going after us either."

An amalgamation of fear and confusion passed over Rhydian and Ameera's faces as they surveyed the room again. Seconds trickled by like hours as they got up to speed, and Isla was about to leave them up here when Ameera spoke.

Though she fought to keep her voice even, the ghost of a vein began throbbing in the older woman's forehead. "I don't know if I want to start with *this*—" She pointed at the bak before drawing her hand back hastily, almost skittish. As if she were wary she'd somehow will it back to life. "Or that bastard getting near you again." Icy rage lingered in her voice, and Isla swore her eyes and markings nearly sparked alight.

She understood the anger, felt it simmering within herself. A piece of her had wanted nothing more than to drive that knife straight through the killer's heart and never look back.

"Where did they go?" the general inquired.

"Down there." Isla nodded to the basement. "There's a tunnel they probably escaped through. I want to check it out."

"I hope you mean so we can find the killer and drag them to the city so Kai can rip them apart like they deserve," Ameera said.

"As nice as that sounds, I want to talk to them first. I think—I think they're trying to warn us, to help us."

"Help?" Ameera was aghast. Even Rhydian went wide-eyed. "They killed Alpha Kyran and Jaden. Tried to kill Kai, kill you."

"I know. Believe me, I know. But they could've just killed me now, and they didn't. They saved me from the bak, gave me this, and—" Isla looked down at her forearm, the symbols scribbled there.

"It's probably them gloating."

"Humor me," Isla gritted out, and she wondered what had shifted in her face, her demeanor that had her opposition stepping back. That even had Rhydian raising his brows and bowing slightly. Instinctually. "I want to look at that tunnel, and you can either come with me or stay here."

For a moment, all either of them did was blink. *Technically,* Isla, still a warrior, not a crowned luna, was ranked under the general, and that nagging fear of offending a superior itched at her.

But Ameera's tone had softened as she said, "Let's go then." She scaled the room to look down into the inky darkness herself. "Dawn's going to break in a few hours, and if Kai hasn't already locked the territory down and sent out a search team for you or taken to the streets himself, he's about to."

Rhydian skirted around the bak's flung-out arm, nearly tripping over its long claw, to join them. As the three circled the stairs' edge, Isla warned, "We need to wedge something beneath the door. It's warded. If it closes, it won't let us out."

"Warded?" Ameera whipped her head around to Isla. "Like the Gate?"

"Exactly like the Gate," Isla said, her mind so concerned with all else, that she couldn't draw the reason for Ameera's paling features.

"Why would there be wards in a house?" She stepped back to observe the door, pulling it away from the wall to observe all its angles.

Quickly, she found the scratched-in symbols over the metal knob. "Wards can only be cast by witches, right? Witches who haven't been able to roam our continent for…decades, centuries? This house isn't that old."

Isla's gut twisted.

Silence fell between them again, the air becoming thick, as they retreated and dragged their eyes around the space.

"Did you look around?" Ameera questioned, the fierce determination marking her a leader on her face again. "Make sure no one else was here?"

"I mean, I didn't get far." Isla shook her head. "I was only in here for a few minutes before the rogues showed up."

Ice filled her veins.

In here…because she'd felt something calling to her.

As Ameera bolted up the stairs to ensure they were alone, and Rhydian went on to make another pass through the living room, dining room, and kitchen, Isla remained rooted to the spot. Her grip on the piece of the diadem, that she swore hummed in her palm, tightened.

"We would scent a witch, wouldn't we?" Rhydian re-entered the living room, sounding like he was trying to convince himself. Though wolves were born with some innate immunity to certain magic, facing one of the spellcasters was no easy feat. "I've never met one, but they're probably different."

Isla opened and closed her mouth, unable to form an answer before Ameera bound back down the set of stairs. "It's clear. No one's here."

Even with the news, Isla felt no relief.

∼

Rhydian remained above ground, guarding the door, the house, and the last piece of the diadem, while the two warriors descended into the darkness.

"How did the bak even get in here?" Ameera asked from behind Isla as they carefully ambled down the stairs.

"I'm not sure yet," Isla said, despite her sneaking suspicion lying a few yards away.

Once she'd reached the completely missing lower third of the flight, Isla leaped to the ground.

Ameera did the same, letting out the softest whistle. "You really did a number on the place." She knocked away a damaged board. "Do you go looking for trouble or does it find you?"

"I was trying not to *die*, so conserving this place's integrity wasn't top of my list." Isla pursed her lips, muttering, "And if you ask Kai, he'd argue the former."

"Rogues, bak, *and* an assassin," Ameera drawled, voice lowering to a whisper. Isla wondered if this small talk was a way for the general to abate any of her hesitations as they approached the tunnel's stone-crusted mouth. "And you held your own. It's a shame I won't get to serve with you in the ranks."

Isla tried to hide her frown at the reminder of the future she'd never have.

She made a hapless reach within herself for her wolf, the bond. Both of which stirred, but barely gave an answer. Her wolf, she understood, with that lingering sear in her veins. But her connection to Kai?

It had to be the distance.

If only she could tell him she was okay.

If he'd felt anything go wrong, noticed her drop away…

They came to a stop at the rubble-coated earth just before the entrance. Isla's skin crawled. Even with the beauty of the crystal embedded in its walls—all there was to illuminate the cavern—something felt off. Forbidding.

That horrible smell tickled the back of her nose and hit Ameera at the same time. She scrunched her face. "What is that?"

Isla regretted the deep inhale she'd taken. "If the bak came through this, I—I think it might lead to the Wilds."

Ameera straightened. "You think this is the path we're looking for? That Callan found?"

Isla couldn't really imagine Callan coming out here. But the map… "Maybe."

"This stone isn't natural," Ameera noted, running her hand over the smooth, grayish surface of the columns built along the mouth. She scratched at a particularly marred part of the rock. "It looks like there used to be some type of door or gate here too. This is here for a reason… but why would anyone need or *want* a path into the Wilds?"

The ridged grip of the blade's hilt bit into Isla's palm as she held it tighter.

Back in the Wilds. This could lead her straight back into the Wilds. Earthbound, eternal hell.

I have us—the words she'd sworn to Kai echoed in her head. She'd assured him, and she would. Them, and everyone else. A vulnerability like this could put the whole pack at risk.

"When we go back to the hall, we'll look into the archives and figure out who used to live here." She steeled and stepped forward. "Let's see what we can find inside. We won't go far."

Ameera nodded, and Isla noted the anxious twitch of her fingers. "Are we shifting?"

Isla gulped, squeezing the metal in her hand even harder. "I can't."

"You *can't?*"

"Something that the rogue had in a vial, I think, messed with my wolf. I've felt it before—a while ago, back in Callisto when Lukas had tried to kill me. I think the dagger had been laced with it somehow. And now, the rogue—"

"Like wolfsbane?"

"No. I've never been dosed with wolfsbane, but I think it's something different—maybe worse," Isla conceded. "I look fine, but my wolf...I just feel disconnected. The pain subsided, but something's wrong."

Ameera went rigid.

Isla lofted a brow. "What?"

She grimaced. "It kind of sounds like what Kai was saying. How he felt that night. The disconnection, the pain, but looking perfectly fine."

Isla's features fell, and her stomach bottomed out. "I—I hadn't..."

A poison. Fast-acting. Quick healing. No trace as it destroyed from the inside.

It made sense.

The overwhelming urge suddenly overcame Isla to tear her skin away and claw it out of her.

The right amount could kill an alpha and heir without drawing alarm. And they'd used it on her. Twice.

Ameera's face was drawn in puzzlement. "How did the rogue get it?"

Isla growled low in her throat and sneered, starting straight down the tunnel. The general's footsteps echoed hollowly from behind her, around her.

Bold or stupid—maybe she was both.

It was possible that Isla was taking this assassin's passivity and graciousness in *not* murdering her a bit too far.

"I don't know *exactly* where he got it," she said, hoping that around the corner, the killer was waiting. "But I know who probably does."

The path ended at a crossroads. No shadowy figures in sight. To Isla's left, the tunnel either banked down and down and down...or the right offered a continuous spiral to who knew where. Them splitting up wasn't even close to an option. They'd need to go back and gather more people before trying to really tackle something like this. The guard. Kai.

Isla inclined her head to garner Ameera's opinion on which direction they should take—

And then she saw it.

Wedged into the rock wall to the left, a couple of feet down. A tiny beacon of wood and inscriptions that haunted her dreams and nightmares, waking and asleep.

A marker.

Isla moved with little thought, inching her way along the decline to it.

"Goddess, Kai was right," she heard Ameera mumble behind her, though still, she followed.

After nearly losing her footing, Isla reached it and squinted as she observed its surface.

Different.

She didn't understand a single letter or symbol, but she'd looked at the piece they'd found in the Hunt so many times, that she could write it out from memory.

Only one of those characters was on here.

But markers, *these* markers, were from the Ares Pass, according to Lukas.

So, this was it? *This* was the pass? The grand hierarchy secret that she'd been standing on during the Hunt?

They were underground.

"What's wrong?"

Isla's brows furrowed. "If this is the way it's supposed to be, embedded in the tunnel's wall like this…" She trailed off, shaking her head. "Lukas found that marker in the middle of the Wilds just sitting in the dirt. It's not like I was looking, but it's the only one I remember passing."

Ameera could see her train of thought. "You're wondering how it got there?"

Isla hummed in affirmation.

The messages, the book, and the marker—they'd always spun around her head in unison, the mess of characters they were made of swirling with them. Two, she'd known, had the same source. One that seemed to lurk at every corner since they'd emerged from the Wilds.

But what if they'd been around before that?

What if they'd been trying to tell her something, Kai

something, *anyone* something, since *during* the Hunt. When the marker breached the surface.

Isla lifted her blade and ground her teeth as she jammed it into the rock beside the sphere. The clang and scrape of metal against stone reverberated through the pitted walls, along her bones.

"What are you doing?"

Isla answered Ameera with a grunt, too busy pushing and wrenching and prying until the ball finally came loose, a crater left in its wake, as it nearly evaded her grasp.

If Jonah could figure out one marker and the other, maybe he could figure out the distance between them. They'd know the exact location of where the first had come from.

"They're trying to tell us something," Isla said, peering at the wood between her fingers. "They've been trying to get Kai to see…something, since the night of the murders. Me to see something since I got here or since we emerged."

"Like what?"

Isla glanced down at her arm, trailing down the symbols until she reached—

Deimos.

She swallowed, the word slamming around her mind in the same cursed tone she'd heard it twice now. "Traitor."

CHAPTER 39

Somewhere in between the bustling morning of the early-rising Surles and the barren boardwalks of the turned-in Abalys, the cobblestone streets of Mavec held a modest crowd, a few rolling through the daylight minutiae. Shop owners opening their doors. Pack members indulging in breakfast. Isla's stomach growled as she passed one eatery, but it soured promptly after. Though it wasn't for the family—a father, mother, their two children happily munching and chattering away—it was the danger that lurked around them. That they didn't realize.

If that bak had gotten out...

If those tunnels ended anywhere else...

They had to get to Kai and figure out what the hell they were going to do.

Frankly, Isla wasn't positive where to start—the bak, the rogues, the pass, the warded door, the killer, the new marker, the final jewel, and scribbled symbol on her arm she had hidden in her jacket pockets. Or maybe that word that was cycling endlessly through her mind.

Traitor...

Traitor...

Traitor...

Who? What? She wanted to scream.

As they walked through the lower square to get the trolley up to the Pack Hall, Rhydian and Ameera were silent too. They *had been* since they'd left the house, combed the surrounding area for the missing rogue—only to come up empty—before getting back to the car.

They were understandably shaken by what they'd seen and all that had been divulged in just a few hours. From the fact that their best friend and brother had nearly been taken from them months ago and was *still* in potential danger to the fact that Imperial Alpha Cassius may know about Deimos's secret dealings. To the witnessing of a bak *not* beyond the Wall, but in their home. Isla received the occasional question from one or both of them, and she'd offer her own back, but mostly, they were silent.

It was all too much. They were tired and frustrated. At least Charley had begrudgingly let them clean up a little once they'd returned his car. Isla had been the messiest with dried, dark blood peeking from beneath her clothes. He'd given her a tavern maiden's uniform to throw on, and she'd accepted it. Though the dress was a bit too tight, meant for a woman with more dainty shoulders, a slimmer waist.

She tugged at the bodice as she lifted her head to the warm sunlight to gaze up at the Pack Hall. Any discomfort she'd previously felt seeing that large window had been overtaken by joy and excitement.

Home.

She was desperate for a proper bath. For Kai. A proper bath *with* Kai. A bed. Some decent sleep.

But would there even be time for any of that?

"Do you think Jonah went to the hall last night to look in the library, or is he still at the shop?" Ameera asked as they looked between the two transport options. One would take them closer to Jonah's and the other to Kai. Upon a glance at Isla's antsy form, she snickered. "I know what *you* want to do, and I'm sure it's what he wants. Are your mate senses reacting?"

Though the general had been sarcastic, Isla noted the bond, her wolf, and how much steadier they both felt. More present, finally. Yet still, there was something tense about their connection. Maybe it was just Kai. It was a safe bet that he'd been worried about her, about all of them.

"You can check in and see if Jonah's there. I'll talk to Kai," Isla said.

"He's going to lose his mind after he finds out," Rhydian said.

"He should," Ameera lowered her voice. "Especially, if whatever you're saying about a traitor is true."

"I don't know for a fact that's what it means yet," Isla said. "And—"

"Ameera!"

The call of the general's name had come from behind them all.

Isla had known the voice before they'd even whipped around.

Ameera grumbled from Isla's side as Ezekiel stalked towards them, appearing from a street that had led to the boats that carried people beneath the bridge and into the mountain. "What is he doing here?"

That was a great question.

As he got closer, Isla couldn't even wonder at the similarities between the family members. Couldn't laugh at the way a vein was present near Ezekiel's temple, just like his daughter's. Even their small exchange fell on deaf ears.

She was too distracted, too concerned with how disheveled he looked. How distraught. There was darkness beneath his eyes. Something wild yet cowering within them. Like a cornered doe. He hadn't even looked like this two nights ago after the rogues had attacked. He'd been shaken—yes, as they all had—but still had some generous composure.

Here, that seemed to hang on a thread.

Something was wrong. Something *worse* than what had happened two nights ago.

Isla's thoughts were confirmed when he glanced at her and caught sight of her mark, visible *just slightly* where her unzipped jacket left the skin exposed beneath her dress's wide neckline.

Since the day they'd met, since his first prideful, snide remark before the Gate, calling her a *dame*, Isla had dreamt about seeing the look on his face if she and Kai one day mated. When the "dim-witted", "insolent" woman became his superior. When he'd have to bow to *her*.

But there was barely a drop of anger or annoyance on his face. Barely any shock. All she could see on his face was pity.

And that was *all too nice* coming from him.

She cocked her head to take in the empty space behind him. "Where's Kai?" she asked, forcibly simple at first.

Ezekiel tensed, and Isla felt her blood ice over and boil at the same time.

He wouldn't answer. Not fast enough.

Her fists tightened at her sides, and Rhydian and Ameera seemed to pick up on the shift in her disposition. They shuffled on their feet, falling a bit behind her, as she pressed, "What happened?"

Further hesitation. "We should—"

Isla bared her teeth. "Ezekiel, what's going on?"

Upon the address, the older man blinked, and *there* was the hint of *that* irritation she'd been expecting. But it didn't last long. His throat bobbed and he shifted his gaze around, ensuring there weren't many people around them. "The call came a few hours ago." He spoke quietly, and they all absentmindedly leaned closer. "And we haven't released it to the papers yet, so let's try to remain calm..."

"*Beta,*" Isla said through gritted teeth, making him jolt. He'd been too slow. *Too slow.*

One last breath fell from his mouth before he said, "The Imperial Alpha and Council passed the challenge."

∽

Reporters surrounded the closed front gate at the bottom of the hill that led up to the hall. According to Ezekiel, there were fewer than yesterday. Isla could only imagine how crazy things would get once the news broke of the challenge.

It had passed. They'd *approved* it.

It didn't feel real. It couldn't have been.

But Kai was already in an emergency audience with his council, discussing what would happen next. What *needed* to happen in order to prepare for whatever befell him in ten days, on the night of the next full moon, when he'd step before another man, with his pack in witness, and *kill him* or be killed himself.

She felt sick to her stomach. Worse than she ever had before.

Kai had sensed when she'd been fighting the bak. He hadn't known exactly *what* she was doing but was aware that she was in trouble. To keep him in place, as the news had just broken, Ezekiel had offered himself to go find her, find them. The beta had been searching Mavec all night.

He seemed appalled that they'd gone to the other regions, especially Surles. When he asked about what they'd been doing, no one spoke. They were all distracted, confused, and only wanted to get to their friend, their family. Ezekiel originally hadn't seemed thrilled that Rhydian was going, but Isla made sure he knew the guard wasn't leaving her side.

As they got closer and closer to the behemoth until they were entrenched in nothing but shadow from its looming size, Isla focused on the sense thrumming beneath her skin. She shouldn't have called for Kai, especially if he was busy, but she wasn't thinking clearly. She needed to see him, hear him, *now.*

There was a second way into the hall that avoided the main entrances and the crowd—thankfully. A mysterious marked female entering the grounds with the beta when no one else was permitted could've led to speculation. Not much, but enough. And Ezekiel likely wanted the time to brace for whatever chaos *her*—a woman of Io, the daughter of one of their highest Council members who'd just set Deimos on a collision course—being their luna would bring.

As they traveled through a small side passage—a dank cavern disguised by greenery—Isla *and* Ameera flinched, their footsteps aware and looks over their shoulders frequent. It eventually brought them to a room, the door hidden behind a bookshelf.

Exactly how many places like this existed around here?

When they stepped out into the corridor, Isla noted their location by their orientation to the courtyard. This was the Eastern Hall. Now, where were council meetings held? Where were the alpha and luna's official seats? The thrones. They were usually around the same location. At least in Io.

Instead of asking Ezekiel, who'd likely be a complete dead end having wanting her to wait in the House, she began reaching for Kai again, sending down whatever words she could.

Where are you, where are you, where are you?

She hadn't meant for *those* frantic thoughts to travel, but they must've because she received a response and sensed his presence at the same time.

"Here."

Even without the echo lent by the barren halls, his voice reverberated through the space, through her.

Isla halted as Kai slowly rounded the corner a few feet in front of them and stopped at the end of the corridor. Her heart leaped and dropped all in one beat. Hours ago, moments existed when she didn't think she'd ever see him again. Moments, she was sure, that he shared.

They held where they stood and simply stared at one another.

He looked exhausted but was dressed well as he had to be to address his council. Isla wondered if he'd slept at all last night after they'd parted.

Kai looked her up and down, snagging on the amethyst cloth of the dress clinging to her, which she hadn't left in. But his confusion washed quickly when his gaze returned to her face.

She wished she could bottle the feeling she got every time he looked at her, the flutter in her stomach. She'd love to get drunk on it right now. Forget all of this.

The smallest breath of relief from his mouth was like a signal. Isla rushed forward, and he met her in the middle, ready when she flung herself in his arms with a force that nearly sent him backwards. She felt him tighten his hold around her waist, almost lifting her from the ground while she secured hers around his neck. His lips brushed against her skin as he buried his head into the crook of her shoulder, and she shivered. Their hearts thundered against one another. Back in time. Back in sync.

It took everything in Isla not to break down as she breathed in his scent, yielded to the comfort of him. Felt safe, truly safe, somehow, finally.

"What the hell did you get yourself into?"

The words were still muffled, distant. But she'd take it. Anything.

"It's a long story."

When she lifted her head to look at him, he wasted no time in giving her one chaste kiss before he lowered her down to her feet.

She wouldn't let him go, though, and he didn't seem keen to release her either. Isla settled, wedging into his side with one arm around his back while his remained secured around her shoulders.

Kai looked over Rhydian and Ameera, who also looked rough from being out all night. "Are you guys okay?"

They both nodded and swallowed thickly in unison.

"Are *you*?" Rhydian asked, unable to fight back his frown. Beside him, Ameera's features screwed up in her own sad scowl.

Isla felt something stir in Kai along the bond, and his body tensed. "Yeah, I'm good."

A lie—partly, at the very least.

As they cast their doubtful looks, he added, "Thank you."

Isla pondered if it was for bringing her back alive.

Ameera gestured her way. "You should thank her."

Kai furrowed his brows and met her eyes.

"*I'll explain,*" she told him, squeezing his side.

A faint grin played along his mouth before he lifted his gaze to Rhydian and Ameera again. "Jonah and Davi are in the library if you remember where that is."

"How could I forget where I suffered through all of my summer assignments in year six?" Rhydian quipped, giving levity to the heavy situation.

Isla caught the way Ezekiel had stiffened at the mention of the twins in the library. Kai had too, it seemed, from the corner of his eye.

He turned to his beta, his features unmoving. "We finished the meeting, but the council's still in chambers. You'll be briefed, and Sol will handle the debrief, then the two of you and Marin can meet me back in my office at noon. You can release the news to the pack in the meantime.

We shouldn't hold on to it too long. Better it come from us than trickle in by other means."

Ezekiel bowed his head in agreement, something odd still flickering behind his stare. "And where will you be?"

Kai loosened his hold on Isla's shoulders and reached to take her hand. "I'd like to spend some time with my luna."

∼

Kai had wanted to go "somewhere they could actually breathe", and so they had traveled up and up and up, around and around and around until they reached the study of Alpha Orin and stood in the glory of the stained-glass window. The chilled morning air, so high up, bit at Isla's face as she stepped onto the platform behind the lofted black metal railings. She hadn't caught the designs of them in the dark, how beautifully they bent and twirled, curving in a way that almost mimicked the phases of the moon.

As she stared down at the city as she had nights before, catching the way the sun glittered off the river, she heard Kai slowly guide the glass closed. The heat of his body radiated as he settled at her side and silence fell between them. Comfortable. Needed.

For a second, it all stopped. Even with the world before them, with the mountains and the water and the small dot-like people, it truly felt as if they were alone.

Isla turned her head to look at Kai in time with him as he did her. That feeling rumbled again, and she acted on her urge to lean forward to touch her mouth to his. As he deepened the kiss, as she felt the wave and warmth of the love he had for her—in a way no one else did, no one else ever would—something inside her cracked.

She let out a soft gasp, and Kai pulled back.

"Isla," he spoke with that gentleness that stripped her down to nothing.

Her chest tightened, and she struggled to let out an even breath. Another strained sound fell as she shook her head. She didn't know what to say, what to do, where to start.

For one, her family—*her family*—were a part of this. Her father was on the Council sending Kai off to fight for his life. That could take him away from his pack, his friends, his family, his mother.

From *her*.

"Isla."

Tears spilled over the cusps of her eyelids. One, then another, and another before they flowed freely down her cheeks. In seconds, Kai was on her, pulling her close again. As she hugged him, holding onto his shirt as she sobbed, everything crashed into her. Relentlessly. Blow after blow. The unending fear she'd felt in that house, for the past few months. What she'd seen. All she knew.

She hated feeling like this. Weak and helpless. But no matter how much she begged herself to get it together, she couldn't.

Kai had slowly stepped them away from the rail, and somehow, they'd ended up sitting at the base of the window, on the cold stone as he held her.

"I'm sorry." She cried into his shoulder as he stroked the back of her head, combing through her hair. "I'm so, so sorry."

"It's not your fault," Kai whispered in her ear.

"I should've told them," she said. "My father, if he knew, maybe…"

Maybe.

"I don't think it would've made a difference. Your father is the Beta, but in the end, the Imperial Alpha makes the final call." He couldn't hide the tinge of aggravation from his tone, but corrected it to gently ask, "What happened out there?"

Isla lifted her head, and she was certain she looked like a disaster. Kai swiped some of the salty tears with his thumb.

Through the sharp intakes of breath and rushing thoughts, Isla explained everything she could in the most coherent way possible. The rogues. The bak. The wards. The tunnels. The killer with the diadem. The new marker. When she finished, breathless and overwhelmed still, she braced herself for him to begin drilling her with questions, especially given the confusion, concern, and intermittent flashes of anger that had crossed his face. But she felt lighter now, after getting all of that off her chest. She could handle it.

She could handle it. She could handle it.

But his features softened, and he brushed a loose hair from in front of her puffy eyes, tucking it behind her ear. "You fought all of them?"

Isla swallowed, her voice hoarse. "I did what I could."

Kai chuckled through his nose and took a gentle hold of her face. "You're incredible."

He leaned forward and kissed her again with what felt like everything he had.

It wasn't long before Isla matched it, eventually rising on her knees and crawling into his lap, needing to be closer. Relief beat between their chests, the bond reforging with it.

As she settled atop him, Kai's hands trailed up her bare thighs beneath her skirt, and Isla felt that hunger rise between them. Not hurried. Not carnal. Something pure. Loving. She wanted to melt into him, to feel him everywhere, to not know what it meant to have space between them. Never again.

Kai broke away to drag his lips down her neck, ending with a kiss on her shoulder, her mark. "I don't deserve you," he breathed. "You shouldn't have to go through this."

As she sensed the guilt begin to ravage him, Isla lifted his face to hers. She traced along the line of his jaw. "I'm exactly where I need to be. Where I *want* to be," she told him before bringing her hands down to run over his chest and subtly moving her hips in a way that had them groaning softly. That told him exactly what she wanted next. What he did too.

She secured her legs around his hips as he rose with her in his arms. Her mouth met his again and again as he brought them inside to embrace whatever blissful time they had together with the world blown out of existence before it tried to rip them apart, and they fought like hell against it.

∽

"Kai." Isla laughed as her mate peppered kisses over her sweat-slicked shoulder. He snaked his arms around her, tugging her closer until she was leaning back against his naked chest. While one hand drew around her skin to cup her breast, the other traveled down her stomach, lower until it reached between her legs, already parting for him. She laughed again. "Horny bastard."

He only hummed in agreement.

With a content sigh, she sunk further into his embrace, getting lost in the pleasure radiating through her.

She'd needed this. *They'd* needed this. Something grounding and real and simple. Just each other. If only for the small time remaining. Until noon.

What had started on the overlook had quickly turned into a fierce, insatiable need once they'd crossed fully into the study. Isla's desire to melt was no more. She wanted to *burn*. Eventually, they'd made it down to the floor, and her dress was gone—torn apart by the man who growled about his lack of patience for laces and buttons. She'd pulled Kai up as he'd begun trailing his mouth down her body—no teasing, all she'd wanted was to feel him—and after the hasty removal of his clothes with her rushed intermittent assistance, he hovered over her.

But as she locked her legs around him, then as he positioned himself and gazed down at her, they paused.

A pulse down the bond was a reminder of all they had to lose. What it felt like they'd almost lost.

For a moment, Isla had clearly seen the storm behind Kai's eyes, going on in his mind. And she realized—

She'd thought about what it would mean to her and everyone else if he'd lost the challenge...but how did he feel?

What did it mean to *him* if he left them? If he left *her?*

Judging by the brief flash of sadness, fear, and desperation in his gaze, she'd gotten somewhat of an answer. He wouldn't vocalize it though. She knew he didn't want her to know or didn't want to address it himself.

He'd made love to her after that, held her stare the entire time as he moved in her, hitting all the spots that made her warm and dizzy. The only time he left her eyes, he was worshiping her with his mouth, telling her amidst kisses how beautiful she was, how much he loved her, how lucky he was to find her. It was nothing short of overwhelming, and she'd teared up as it all washed over her, the sheer intensity of the bond becoming near-tangible between them. He'd kissed those away too.

Now they were flushed, their hair mussed, bodies bare and thoroughly worked over as they sat on the carpet on the floor of the study, bathed in colors pouring through the window from the sunlight. And though hell lingered outside the large oak door, though it loomed above their heads, they were okay.

They *would be* okay.

Isla quivered and let out another sigh, squirming as tension built at the base of her spine. "Ameera thought it was strange that you let me go, given the way most newly mated men are. I thought you'd already gotten sick of me."

Kai chuckled, continuing his ministrations on her neck, her other breast, between her legs. "I'd fuck you every minute of every day if I could."

Isla bit back a whine.

She'd let him.

"When this is over," Kai continued. "*All over*—we're going away. Just you and me."

"Can we do that?" Her question left in a breath as he worked his fingers lower, to her core, ready for him all over again. As she moved, bucking forward, he tightened his hold, keeping her in place. She wrapped her arms around his, feeling the tense muscles, digging her nails lightly into his skin.

"For a couple of days," Kai answered her question easily. As if this were just a normal, everyday conversation. "We have Ezekiel, the council. We won't leave the pack. We just won't be in Mavec."

Isla had to moan now as he slid a finger inside her. Just one. Not deep enough. She wanted more, but this—now this was a game. Of focus. Of composure.

Her toes curled as she took a stabilizing breath, keeping her attention off how he curled it upwards. "Where would we go?"

"The Vierra."

"Where's that?"

A second finger. Isla whimpered.

Kai laughed against her skin, leaving her just a little colder as he lifted his head. "It's a small stretch of land next to Ifera. We *could* consider it one of our pack territories, but it's very small. Secluded. Gorgeous. We have a cottage there. Great for alone time."

Finally, he plunged his fingers deeper, harder, and Isla gasped. She dug her nails further into his arm, arching her back with a curse. She didn't know how much longer she could keep up her ruse. All her focus eddied to how he moved, how incredible it felt.

Distraction, distraction.

She twisted her head from where she'd thrown it back against him to gaze at his face. So, so handsome. All of him so *hers*. Claimed by the mark on his neck, the healing scratches down his back. She wanted to kiss him. Needed to. But she resisted.

More conversation.

"Maybe we can go for my birthday."

Kai lofted a brow, cocking his head and smirking. He could feel it. How close she was to coming undone. "That's soon, isn't it?"

Isla's heart was going to beat out of her chest. "A little after the Equinox."

"Did you celebrate that in Io? The Equinox."

"Yes—" She moaned again, louder. It echoed off the high ceiling. Pressure building, she bit down hard on her lip. Release shimmered just out of reach. "And no. We more celebrated the—oh, fuck—Solstices. Summer…Winter…Goddess, Kai, I'm going to…" She breathed, her eyes sliding closed as she fought it off just a little longer. Her voice strained. "But Summer was always my f—favorite."

Kai's mouth went to her ear as he muttered, "Should I keep going?"

Isla snapped her eyes open, narrowing as they met his. Enough to say that if he stopped, he'd regret it. He chuckled, keeping up the pace that had her breath laboring further and legs shaking.

"You'll find we make a big deal of the Equinox here. The *'winds of change'*. I always felt the gala was overkill, but the festival, the lanterns, those were always fun."

She couldn't hold it back anymore, but she tried, despite the fact she could feel herself tightening around his fingers, couldn't keep from moving with his thrusts, wanting more.

Kai cursed as if recalling the feeling when she'd been wrapped around him earlier. "Isla…"

Say it again. Say it again.

"A gala means a—a dress," she battled out one more time.

She could feel Kai hardened against her back. "Seems to be my weakness with you."

Isla writhed, both at the pleasure about to wash her away and what she knew would come for her next, *if* they had the time. Goddess, she hoped they did.

"When do we need to…"

She never finished her sentence.

Kai's hand left her breast to tilt up her chin, and he swallowed her cry out with a kiss so heavy, it took away what little breath she had. Her fingernails drew blood as they pierced his skin, her climax roaring through her again. She bowed off him, but he wouldn't let her get far. Stars exploding behind her closed lids, he continued to stroke her as she clenched around him.

He didn't withdraw his mouth or his fingers until she'd finished trembling, leaving her empty, sated, and yet still aching for more.

Limp against his shoulder, her body coated in a new layer of sweat, her lashes fluttered open. Her chest rose and fell rapidly, and she could feel his heart thundering against her back as he panted too. He never broke her stare as he brought his fingers, the traces of her, up to his mouth and sucked them clean.

A fire ignited within her again.

Fuck it. They had time.

In a quick movement, Isla twisted and rose to her knees. She kissed him so harshly, their teeth nearly collided before she pushed him down onto his back. Kai grinned up at her, his lip finding its way between his teeth as she straddled him, taking a hold of his length. He sucked in a breath, his eyes roaming her body, his fingers grazing the skin of her waist, her hips, her ass. As she lowered herself onto him, they both groaned.

Another moment of stillness overtook the room.

Isla leaned down, bracing her arms on either side of his head as her hair, gilded by the sunlight through the window, fell like a curtain around them. Shielding them.

She swallowed as that wrenching feeling settled in her gut. As she remembered that dark abyss waiting for them outside the door. As she sensed the bond in all its strength. Recalled what it had felt like for it to fade, even just a little.

"We're going to be okay," she panted softly, more a question than a statement, even if she'd intended for the latter. She should've said *everything*. They weren't the only ones whose lives hung in the balance. A familiar sting began in her eyes, but she willed it away.

Kai's throat bobbed, and though he'd exuded confidence, there was the smallest flicker of uncertainty in his stare. Still, he nodded, his thumbs drawing soothing circles over her skin. "We're going to be okay."

CHAPTER 40

Deimos's Pack Hall comprised three structures which didn't include the House, which loomed large at each side of the courtyard. Of them, the North Hall—the *original* Hall, adorning the stained-glass window with corridors having been walked by the Original Alpha of Deimos himself—stood the greatest.

It was where most *pack business* was taken care of—Kai had explained it to Isla as she dressed after having cleaned herself up in the small bathroom attached to Alpha Orin's study. *He'd* already done so since he had to go down to a phone in order to call for a member of the House staff to bring over some extra clothes. Isla pursed her lips at her former attire that he'd left in scattered ribbons on the floor.

What she donned now was one of his plain shirts, a deep maroon that ended mid-thigh on her frame. Another dress, only now she swam in the fabric. She'd taken a deep breath as she threw it on, warmth, woods, and spice flooding her nose. Even if it had been freshly cleaned, it somehow still smelled like him. *Home.*

As she worked on gathering her hair in a way that didn't scream what they'd just been doing for the past hour, she caught Kai eyeing her from his spot against the wall. She turned, tying half of the tresses back out of her face while the rest flowed down her back. "Can I help you with something?"

Kai took his time, trailing his gaze from her face, down the length of her bare legs, and back up. He pushed himself up, taking the few steps across the room to close the distance. When he reached her, close enough she could feel the heat of his body, he danced his fingers over her waist, two applying the most pressure, in particular. "Have I ever told you that you look *great* in red?" Another sweep up and down. "And my clothes?"

Isla bit the inside of her cheek, not allowing herself to get caught up in the gruff words, his stare, the way certain parts of her still fluttered and felt him.

Offering him a deadpan look, she placed a hand on his chest and ushered him back. "Down, boy."

As he stumbled a step, she seamlessly breezed by him to grab her jacket, the fabric weighed down by the diadem's jewel and the marker still in its pockets. She could feel his eyes boring into her back as she walked to the door, *maybe* exaggerating the sway of her hips, and his laugh echoed around them as they took down the steps. Down and around.

Back into reality.

∼

Isla had never seen such focus on Kai's face. Now, down in his office, leaning against his desk, she watched him as he rested his hands on the wood surface opposite her. He shifted his gaze between the last piece of the diadem, the newly acquired marker, and what she'd written of the fifth symbol.

He'd been silent for a while. Almost too long.

With each pace of their descent from the study, any tension that had left Isla's body had begun coiling again, and she'd decided that she would let the unease stay. Let it drive her, fuel her, along with her new mantra that everything would be okay.

For a moment, she wondered if there was a way for her to somehow use the bond to read Kai's mind. Break beyond the wall of stone protecting his thoughts, the way it felt like he'd crumbled hers when their link started working. Though *that* had been just to talk. Sneaking into his head and taking something that didn't belong to her would be a step too far, and frankly, not possible.

As his quietness persisted, she let her eyes roam the room again before gazing out the window. Spacious and more ornately decorated than she'd been expecting, Kai's office also had a view of the city. Not quite as wondrous as the one captured from the overlook, but enough. From here, the crystals of Mavec's squares and the dancing lights of the boats on the river could be seen and appreciated.

She'd noted earlier how the walls were barren but held signs—

specific demarcations on the blend of stone, dark wood paneling, and wallpaper—that at one point, there *had* been pictures. Some artworks.

If this space had always been for the Alpha of Deimos, then that meant this had previously belonged to Kai's father. Bore the images he had chosen. Been arranged in the way *he* had wanted. Certain scratches on the floor told her the furniture had been shifted, maybe an inch or two, but the bare walls never recovered.

She wouldn't mention it, not now, but something about the room felt empty. Cold in a way the hearth at the far side of the space couldn't warm.

The desk creaked, and Isla whipped her head back to Kai as he wordlessly pressed up from the wood and turned to approach the antiquated map splayed out on the wall. It displayed Deimos's four territories and what was once Phobos *before* it had been destroyed. Though the more accurate portrayal of today's world sat on his desk, this one seemed more relevant.

Unlike Deimos's four regions, Phobos, in its glory, boasted six. Here, Isla saw the entire expanse of land, the former pack stretching all the way out to the Great Ocean that separated their continent from the mainland of the witches and other creatures beyond. Deimos and Phobos together were nearly as large as Ganymede.

"We have rogues on our southeastern border," Kai finally began, his voice even-toned yet edged with irritation. "Charon further beyond that, the Imperial Alpha breathing down our necks from the north, now, the Wall in the west." He let out a heavy sigh and ran both hands through his hair. It was so much. Spinning back, he said, "We need to work backwards."

Isla adjusted herself on the desk. "Backwards."

Kai nodded. "And we need to move carefully. If everything's connected like you think it's been, when we pull one piece on the board, another moves with it, and we're back to square one, trying to figure out what the hell's going on."

He was right in that regard, and she was sick of always playing catch-up.

"Where do you want to start?" she asked.

Another breath and another glance at the map. "Other wolves, rogues or not, we can handle. Io, we can manage, but *bak* getting beyond the Wall is the biggest issue we have. We don't have those defenses. And I highly doubt, given the current climate, Alpha Cassius would be keen on sending me more warriors." He mumbled the next words, "If I could even trust them here."

Isla winced, though she got the point. She folded her arms. "He doesn't have a choice about sending warriors if they're needed. Regardless of who was to dispatch us, if we know there's a threat, anywhere on the continent, we'd want to help. I mean, I came here even though I knew the consequences."

Kai rose a brow.

She rolled her eyes. "You know what I mean."

The smallest upturn of his mouth told her he did.

Not long after, he began pacing the floor, eyes flickering from his shoes along the ornate carpet, to the dark metal chandelier hanging from the ceiling to the map. Eventually, he cursed. "I knew we should've been looking into the Wall earlier. Maybe we would've caught those tunnels. We need to figure out how far they stretch, and where they go. If Callan found them. Why he was looking." A muscle feathered in his cheek. "I never thought I'd be so grateful to a witch."

The ward on the door. Keeping the tunnel sealed and the bak in. Isla knew they'd need to figure out how that one beast got up to the guard base—hell, they needed to know when and who cast that ward—but it had to be a step at a time. Maneuvered carefully.

Though she still found herself unsure of Kai's sentiment of gratitude. "You don't think a witch could be a problem?"

"Not as much as a bak."

"How would a witch even get over here? Ameera said *that* house wasn't too old, and the witches haven't been invited here for an extensive amount of time. They'd never make it past Io's border from beyond the mountains. I mean, we were always guarded, but the prison's right there too. No one gets near it, even from our end. *Every* pack border is protected, including the coastlines. They wouldn't get in without us noticing."

"All coastlines but one," Kai corrected lowly.

It took a moment for Isla to realize which he was talking about—but it made little sense.

"You think a witch could—*would*—sail to the Wilds? The bak would eat them alive within hours, minutes of touching land," she said, before considering, "Though, they do have magic."

"It wouldn't work," Kai said, to which Isla cocked her head. "There's a reason we had to build a Wall to contain them rather than wipe them out in the way they came. The bak were birthed by magic from the decimation. Whatever that witch did couldn't be reversed, repaired, or even touched by any of the others that came to aid us and repay the debt. The only way to kill them is how we've been doing for centuries—brute force and strategy. No matter how strong our people are, they wouldn't stand a chance." A grimace cast across his face. "The only comfort I can find, as sick as it makes me, is that whoever killed my family doesn't want the bak getting out either."

Isla gnawed on her lip as she mulled over his words. She'd known some details of the decimation and was aware of the consequences and what had been done and raised as a result. But she never knew the why, how witch magic worked. At the thought, her eyes drifted to the crystal perched on Kai's desk, glittering in a stream of sunlight. She wondered what Jonah would have to say about it.

"You think that everything, all of this that we've been dealing with, is connected," Kai repeated his earlier statement, catching her attention again. At Isla's nod, he continued, "And they know *how* it's connected. They've been trying to tell us how."

She gave another dip of her head. "I think they've been trying to warn you about something since the night of the first message."

"But why warn me after nearly killing me?"

"I don't know." She gestured to the wooden ball on the table. "But I *do* know that the marker Lukas and I found belongs underground in those tunnels and that someone, something, brought it to the surface. We can't know for sure when, but if it *was them* because they knew you were in the Hunt, the tunnels are probably what they wanted you to know."

Kai paused, considering that. "But I ended up nowhere near where you and Lukas were when I was hunting. I was already heading back to the Gate when I felt you. If they had wanted me to just happen upon it, then the chances were remarkably low."

Isla sighed. That was true.

Quiet descended between them again as she pondered her thoughts.

Sebastian's voice being the one that rang clearly in her head was the last thing she'd expected.

Suddenly, she was back in her apartment after he'd broken in to talk to her—and eat her food. But besides aggravation, he'd delivered something else.

"My brother had told me they—" She stumbled. *They*—her father, Io... "They thought the two of us were in the wrong place at the wrong time—or targeted. What if it was both? Lukas and I were the only two hunters that faced multiple bak. What if they'd targeted me, left the marker there for us to find, not with the intention of me dying—though that was easily possible—but to lure you back?"

Kai reached up to scratch the shadow along his jaw. "Then that means they knew you were my mate, and that I'd come back for you." He let out a low hum before saying, "Those two hunters that I sent for you after you'd been attacked said they found you in a house."

Isla didn't want to think back to that day, especially after what she'd just faced. But the flashes of her memory reeled, and she recalled the cold floor, the searing pain, the distant questions as she fell in and out of consciousness about whether she was even still alive.

"The bak starting to work as a pack, I understand," Kai said. "Becoming more intelligent—I get that too. But they're predators, they know death, and they would never stow you away—at all, really—but *especially* if you were still alive."

Isla blinked, following where Kai led.

The pain she'd felt, like razors slicing through her side when she'd run after Lukas and hesitated for her mate—that was dealt entirely by a bak. But what happened next, in the darkness, in the cold…

"They saved me." The realization came out in a breath. And though he had left its safety… "They saved Lukas too and hid us in the house with the marker."

Kai's features were stone as he nodded in agreement, a couple of times, before he released a bitter chuckle and shook it off. "I don't want to trust them. I don't want to listen to them. What they're doing now doesn't make me forgive the past if reconciliation is what they want. But that's a personal sacrifice I'll have to make for the sake of the pack…so from here on out, we'll consider them our ally."

He studied her face to gauge her reaction. One could only be so overjoyed to align with an alpha-killer.

She flashed him the faintest smile. "And everything they've given us will point us to our enemies."

Kai's sound of agreement was cut through by the resonating chime of the grandfather clock close to his bookshelves, not nearly as barren as the walls. Isla watched the large brass pendulums sway before directing her gaze to the timekeeper's face. Both hands pointed upwards.

Noon.

Two knocks in rapid succession came from the door.

Talk about timely. It was likely Ezekiel, Sol, and Marin.

Isla went rigid.

What was she supposed to say? *Ezekiel* knew about them, but the other two had no idea. She found herself rehearsing pathetically in her head, *Hello, I'm Isla. I'm Alpha Kai's mate, which therefore means your future luna…don't ask me what pack I'm originally from. Don't ask who my father is.*

She felt a warmth at her back that spread as Kai wrapped his arms around her middle much like he had earlier. Her nerves eased as he pulled her close and leaned down to whisper, "We don't have to tell them right now. We can pick another time."

Isla twisted her head to him, scanning his face to get an idea of what he would want. But something about *her* expression, her pause had him leaning in to peck her lips, then her forehead, before he unfurled himself from her. It was enough to say they'd do it later, maybe when the challenge wasn't so fresh.

Another knock at the door.

Kai huffed and ran a hand over his forehead. "Come in."

In the few seconds it took for the entrance to open, Isla smoothed out her makeshift dress, her hair, and plastered a serene smile on her face.

But the only person on the other side was Ezekiel.

Isla frowned.

The beta stepped into the room, shifting his keen eye between them, likely noting Isla's change of clothes and catching the mix of their scents.

"Am I interrupting?"

Isla wanted to say "yes" just for the hell of it, but there was something a bit more satisfying.

"No, you can come in," she permitted him, a little smug and finding her grin again.

The one Ezekiel returned bordered a grimace.

She could hear Kai's laugh through the bond. *"Behave."*

The word had her eyebrows raising in intrigue.

"Marin and Sol?" Kai asked as Ezekiel closed the office door behind him.

"On their way," the beta said, approaching them at the desk. His gaze drifting to Isla, he began, "Will you be—"

He stumbled a step and froze.

Though it wasn't for her, but for the glare that had seemingly caught the corner of his eye.

As Ezekiel turned his head to observe the gleaming jewel of the diadem and the marker on Kai's desk, his eyes widened for just a heartbeat's time and his body gave the slightest tremble.

Isla pursed her lips.

Even Kai straightened where he stood. "Ezekiel?"

The beta righted himself, but though his posture held assured, that cornered doe look slipped back into his eyes. But it wasn't only that. She could've sworn *awareness* lingered too.

Isla braced herself for questions, especially given Ezekiel's need to know and have a hand in everything. But he acknowledged Kai and then turned to her, placing his hands behind his back in a dutiful, near-respectful manner. She wondered if it was to hide the slight shake of his fingers.

"Will you be joining us, Luna?"

It was hard for her to keep the surprise off her face.

Luna.

She didn't warrant that title. Not yet. And Ezekiel was the first person who would know that—making him the very *last* to use it.

Was this a test to see if she'd get ahead of herself? To give him something to rake her over the coals for in the royal etiquette she had yet to learn?

Isla glanced at Kai, whose own eyes had narrowed slightly. The stormy gray shifted between his beta and the items on his desk that she suddenly felt incredibly protective over.

"I won't be, unfortunately," Isla said, bringing her focus back to Ezekiel, and something about him, about the air, seemed to shift.

She pushed away any fear that she'd sound ridiculous as she asked Kai without looking, *"Do you think he knows?"*

In her periphery, she caught Kai's hands ball and release from fists. He didn't answer.

A few moments passed before his features relaxed, and his reach over the globe of the world on his desk drew both Isla and Ezekiel's undivided attention. He picked up the jewel—only the jewel—and let it linger in the sunlight before it collapsed into his closing palm.

With a sidelong glance, Isla noticed Ezekiel shift on his feet, retreating just an inch.

"Where did you get that?" he nearly blurted the question as if he'd been biting his tongue. He forced his shoulders to relax. "Is it from the vaults?"

Kai grinned curtly, daring to toss the gem up in the air before catching it. A low intensity simmered behind his eyes as he turned to Ezekiel. She sensed it then, that alpha's aura, Kai's power. A reminder.

"No," he said with a coolness Isla felt down her spine.

A turn to her was enough to end the conversation.

Partial instinct had Isla closing in on herself under Kai's gaze, but she kept her shoulders back as he closed the distance between them and took her hand. He placed the gem into her open palm before leaning down to kiss her cheek. As soon as his lips touched her skin, his voice flooded her mind, overwhelming, dark, and agitated. *"Go to Jonah in the* library, and do not stop or speak to anyone until you reach him. No staff, no council members, and if a guard asks, you're Marin's guest."

Isla blinked at the orders and realized that he'd kissed her specifically on her right to hide her face from Ezekiel. "What are you thinking?"

"That I need to work backwards further than I thought."

Isla swallowed. Did he mean consider what had happened before the first message?

There wasn't time to ask.

"What about the marker and the paper?"

"I'll bring them later."

Before Kai had completely stood upright again, he kissed her properly. He held her hand with the jewel beneath her wrapped fingers for a second longer. "I'll circle back with you at dinner. Get some rest."

Rest now seemed like a joke.

Isla played along and nodded.

Throughout their exchange, Ezekiel had been silently observing, and he may have moved a few inches closer to the desk where the marker and symbol still sat, taunting him.

Isla felt her nostrils flare, but she battled to keep her features even.

If he knew something...Had known all along...

"Beta," she bid him farewell, her voice laced with the sweetest venom.

Ezekiel bowed his head to her in return and nearly matched her tone. "Warrior."

The gem bit into her palm as she squeezed it tighter and smiled. "For now."

CHAPTER 41

Isla couldn't stop cursing under her breath. Disgracing her ancestors, and likely sending her favorite enemy, Fate, cackling again.

For one, she couldn't remember for the life of her where she'd been told the library was, and she'd been ambling the corridors of the Pack Hall for minutes and minutes too long with no direction. Staff members passed by, guards too, maybe one delta or another, but everyone seemed to live in their own worlds. A necessary defense while the real one seemed to crumble around them, beneath their very feet.

And two—she *hated* leaving Kai with Ezekiel.

As she drifted further away from where they stood in his office behind the heavy oak door, as she felt their bond dull where she knew trying to communicate with him would be hopeless, her skin crawled. She knew her mate could perfectly well take care of himself—he was the most powerful and feared wolf within this pack territory. Viewed powerful and feared in most pack territories, she supposed, after his showing in the Hunt. But she couldn't help her instinct—not only as his mate bound to him by her soul but as a person not easily swayed from protecting anyone she loved. Protecting anyone who may have needed it.

She couldn't allow herself to jump too far in her conclusions. Though Ezekiel was certainly privy to something—and he was also most certainly an asshole—did that make him a threat worth fearing, or just another item on the too-long list?

She couldn't risk being blinded. Couldn't risk a piece on their board shifting without their notice.

Everything's connected.

After a glance around a hallway's corner, Isla wriggled the diadem piece from beneath the jacket she had slung over her arms and looked down at it in her hand.

Ezekiel had recoiled when Kai had picked it up like he'd been afraid of it. But why? Because of what it was, or because he was afraid the alpha would chuck it at his head?

As much as she'd rather the latter, her gut called for the former, especially in those heart-halting moments when she swore it hummed to her. Like its missing sisters, like the dagger. There was more to them than intricately crafted weaponry and embellishments—she realized as she touched her fingers to her forehead as the killer once had. They just needed to figure out how and why.

Isla came to a halt at the beginning of one of the many long bridges constructed to connect two of the three main buildings.

Kai had mentioned the location of the library while they were up in the study—somewhere amidst his explanation of the hall's multi-faceted layout—but within the shuffle of the many rooms and histories of construction, she'd lost it. By a process of elimination, after figuring the Northern Hall was for business and the Western Hall, if she remembered correctly, mostly for entertaining guests and visitors, meant to house the galas and balls and various other crowd-wooing activities, the Eastern Hall was her best bet. She vaguely recalled claims of cultural enrichment. Close enough.

The carpet beneath her shoes whispered as she stepped into the empty passageway and took a moment to drift over to one of the many open windows feeding light onto the floor. She sighed and leaned against its stone encapsulation, embracing the pause, the split second of rest she'd allow herself. She hated feeling shameful as she closed her eyes and thought back to a simpler time. In Io—when that scorching heat during training sessions, games outside with the boys, or nights out where it melted her cosmetics were the greatest of her worries.

With the memories and the sense of homesickness, she ground her teeth.

"Isla?"

Isla started, eyes snapping open as she pushed off the stone. Her fingers splayed reflexively, but her wolf was still resistant and no claws emerged. It was safe to say her body was running on fumes and borrowed waking time.

The voice was vaguely familiar, though not clear enough, so she braced herself with a quick story and a plan to dash away. But all of it became nothing when she turned and found herself face to face with Zahra.

Isla's heartbeat ratcheted up as the former luna—Kai's mother—approached her. The older woman tilted her head, her dark hair, braided along the crown and held back by a silver comb, shining as it slid off her slim shoulder. A smile played along her lips. "It is Isla, correct?"

Isla couldn't believe that she remembered.

She righted herself, her hands going up to fix her hair, even if it was hopeless.

Zahra stopped a few feet away, hands folding within the billowing sleeves of her housecoat, emerald green and finer than anything Isla had ever worn.

Effortless and stunning and regal. As Imperial Luna Marlane was.

Embarrassment formed in the warmth creeping up Isla's neck. She tried not to look down at Kai's too-large shirt. Or compare the glow of Zahra's skin to the sallowness she imagined of her own. Or picture the dark circles she'd noticed under her eyes—maybe still a little bloodshot from crying—in the mirror.

She was in way over her head. Completely out of her league.

She was supposed to replace *this woman* in continental gatherings, in discourse with leaders of other packs?

As Zahra's face contorted in suspicion, Isla forced herself to nod, to smile. "Uh, yes, that's right. It's Isla."

Zahra's eyes drew up and down her frame. No disgust crossed her face, thankfully, but the persistent intrigue was alarming. "May I ask what you're doing here?"

"Do not stop or speak to anyone until you reach him. No staff, no council members, and if a Guard asks, you're Marin's guest."

His mother hadn't been on Kai's list, but—

In her pause, Zahra took another step closer, and Isla gulped as she caught the former ruler's nose twitch.

Goddess, did she smell of Kai?

"I'm a...I'm a guest of Marin's."

"Marin? I hadn't known that you two knew each other."

"We met at the banquet."

Zahra's brows raised. "One of her many maidens after my son's hand?"

Isla opened and closed her mouth. She could tell her. She'd certainly learn, eventually. But instead, she answered quickly. Too quickly. "Oh, no. Definitely not."

She swore she could hear Kai laughing in the back of her mind, ready with taunts of how easily he could have her putty in his hands and pursuing him with a few well-placed kisses and well-spoken words. Hell, even a look could get her.

Isla's answer had Zahra's smile growing along with a nod of concession. "May I ask now where you're headed?"

Isla couldn't think of any valid excuse but a semi-truth. "The library. Marin wanted me to retrieve a book for her."

"I didn't know our warriors also served as errand girls."

So, she remembered her position, too.

Isla bit the inside of her cheek.

Did she also remember where she was from?

"Not an errand," she said. "A favor."

Another nod, now in understanding, before Zahra moved in even closer. "I'm quite happy that I ran into you. I've been meaning to thank you for what you did during the rogue attacks."

Pride blossomed in Isla's chest, though behind her, she swore she felt the weight of the moment banging on the window. As if the ghosts lingered in the courtyard just outside it. The death, the screaming, and chaos.

Isla forced a grin as she answered as she had to Kai, "I did what I could."

"Well, it was commendable. You saved many lives. All I wanted to do and couldn't." At Isla's inquisitive stare, Zahra continued, "Without my wolf, I fear I would've been more of a hindrance than a help."

Without her wolf?

"You can't shift?" Isla attempted to abate her surprise and resist the desire to crawl in a hole for speaking so out of line. It wasn't her business.

Zahra pursed her lips. "Not anymore."

Isla swallowed. There were so many questions that she wanted to ask. "When did her ability to shift stop" was the biggest one.

Zahra gestured out the window. "I was just about to head back to the House for some lunch if you'd like to join me."

Isla's eyes widened at the offer.

Her hand went to her stomach, grumbling low in response. With all that was going on, she'd forgotten to eat. It would also be rude to refuse, but she had to get to the library, to Jonah, to the book, the original marker, the old messages. "Uh, I really should—"

Zahra pinned Isla's tongue with a narrowed stare and a lofting of a perfectly manicured brow. A look of dangerous, daring persuasion.

Isla let out a nervous laugh. "I'd love to."

∼

Two guards and two members of the House staff flanked the large double doors of the home's entrance. Isla wasn't sure if the additional protection had been commonplace, or something established after recent events. The doormen readied their grips on the thick, curved metal handles as the two women meandered up the stone walkway to its several ascending steps. They greeted their former queen with a bow of their heads. Further away, the guards did as well.

The four sets of eyes rested on Isla with wary yet curious looks before they bowed again, now in greeting, not nearly as enthusiastic.

She could've sworn amusement perked Zahra's features.

Isla stared back at them with the same level of judgment, recalling two words.

Deimos. Traitor.

She wasn't sure who she could trust.

The large wooden doors groaned as they were pried open, the reverberation enough to prepare Isla for the grandeur that awaited her, along with the scent of jasmine and hints of rose that tickled her nose. Yet, her breath was still stolen as the taps of her shoes echoed through the House's short opening archway—much like the Pack Hall's underpass—and entered the great foyer.

Her steps beside Zahra slowed until she came to a stop. The former luna carried ahead before she realized it. She turned and said something that Isla missed as she spun herself where she stood.

Between the multiple structures of the hall and this house, Kai was a dirty liar.

Not a palace, her Goddess-damn ass.

She'd give him hell for it. *After* he'd given her a tour of the place.

Their…new home.

Deimos's classic motif of black and silver and the deepest blues, which all seemed to lend themselves towards, was used to accent encompassing shades of ivory. The walls, the columns, the floors, all hues of the brightest white and near-beige. Shadowy but eye-catching artwork and onyx sculptures were perched on the walls and gleaming floors. The surface so clean, the decor's reflections along with Isla and Zahra's served as splashes of color along with the blooms of flowers, picked not from the courtyard garden but from another.

Isla's gaze traveled up the grand staircase in the House's center, its steps covered in intricately designed sable carpet that bisected as it did, carrying into the estate's two wings. After one landing, Isla caught the dark railings continuing, eventually where they'd meet another.

Her eyes drawn upwards, she squinted against the sunbeams spilling through the skylight. It made everything feel that much more spacious.

Though she had to admit, for as magnificent as it all was from this one spot, much like Kai's office, the space lacked a warmth. That coziness and sincerity that she felt from him. Like he had made no marks in it himself.

For a moment, Isla wondered if it was possible to feel *underdressed* under what was supposed to be one's own roof.

"The reigning luna typically oversees the interior design," Zahra said, as if she'd been reading her mind, and Isla snapped to attention. "It fits my tastes for now, but as Kai's moved back in—as much as he insists it's fine if I stay—I'll be moving out soon. Then he or whomever he marries will have free rein to do as they wish. Start fresh and make new memories." A somber smile spread across her lips as she trained her own storm-colored eyes over the space. "It's been far too long since these halls have heard any laughter or joy."

The catch of her voice had Isla biting down on the inside of her lip so hard she nearly drew blood. She was distracted from whatever future she'd begun picturing as the words stirred in her. A future against the backdrop of pattering little feet on marble floors.

Because in a flash, Zahra became that woman who'd lost her mate, lost her child, and was at risk of losing another. The woman who woke up every day and faced the world with that weighing on her chest, but still held tall through all of it.

"Go ahead," Zahra said quietly before turning to Isla. She dipped her head in invitation. "Ask me."

Isla blinked, contemplating again if she was being tested. If she'd be overstepping. But she still asked, just as softly, "How are you still okay?"

Zahra sighed through her nose. "Because the Goddess knew she'd have hell to pay when I got up there if she took me from Kai, too. I would never leave my son to bear this all alone, even if there's only so much I can do. Alpha is a very lonely role." She closed the distance between them to say even lower, "So I'm very happy that now he has you."

It took all of Isla's willpower not to drool as the food was placed before her on the patchwork stone table. A hearty bowl piled with grains, colorful summer vegetables, and a generous helping of spice-rubbed lamb served with a side of bread and oil and a glass of white wine.

She thanked the server, another member of House staff, and Zahra followed suit before saying, "The vegetables are from my garden." She gave a sweeping gesture to the land behind Isla, a deep mass of colors and greenery.

Isla wasn't sure what poor excuse she'd used for an intrigued response, so blinded by hunger, but whatever it was, it was enough to amuse Zahra and get her to encourage Isla to eat.

Still, Isla waited until the former luna took her first bite before she allowed hers.

They ate in silence at first, soft sounds of their chewing and drinking blending into the trilling of birds and buzz of insects tending to the grounds along with its other keepers, caring for the lawns and clipping hydrangeas along a small white picket fence. For a chance of fresh air, they'd sat for lunch beneath the pergola over the House's back terrace—extensive enough to entertain numerous guests—giving Isla the perfect view of the expansive backyard, a glimpse at Zahra's garden, and the length of a swimming pool and its accompanying house further away. A look up and in the distance, beyond the forest, gave her a view of the surrounding mountain peaks, their outlines gray-cast.

A compliment for its beauty sat on the tip of Isla's tongue, but there was something more important to be said first.

She *still* hadn't asked Zahra how she'd known about her and Kai.

By the time her initial shock had worn off, Zahra had them moving through the hallways of ivory, and Isla had become too caught in keeping up with her and distracted by what they passed. Particularly by the corridor of family photographs, which had rendered her completely speechless.

Isla counted out twenty-eight of them, and they varied in size, yet despite the abstractness, they flowed somewhat chronologically. It seemed the favorites, the key photographs, were the largest. The year of one infant, and the year that infant had become a toddler and was joined by another baby.

As Isla had traced how Kai had aged throughout the years—from an adorable newborn to the man he was now—Zahra explained, "We always take them on the Equinox. It's a time to reflect, be grateful, and there is nothing that I was more thankful for than my family." The Equinox had explained the warm hues of autumn.

Isla noted how Kai had always tended to the side of his mother, while Jaden—who

just as eye-catching as Kai—kept close to his father. She could've stood there for hours trying to break down the royal family's dynamic through their shifting expressions and body language. Because there was something with Kyran's push that they were a "loving, united family front, always" that a picture couldn't hide.

Somewhere, along the way—as the boys lost their exuberant smiles, and Zahra and Kyran drifted farther apart—they'd fractured.

After a particularly large bite of her meal, Zahra sighed, savoring it, and threw her arm over the back of the empty chair beside her. She tilted her head and shut her eyes, sunning her face. Her brown skin seemed to glow in the light.

Isla paused herself after another swallow, holding back a grimace at a slight ache in her stomach. Maybe she'd eaten too fast.

She lifted the napkin from her lap and wiped her face before finally daring, "When did you figure it out?"

Zahra's head remained lulled. "At the banquet, after we talked."

That long ago?

Isla choked and reached for her glass of wine. That meant Zahra had known the entire time in the hall as she lied straight to her face. "How? Did I—did I say something?"

Zahra laughed, lazily lifting her head. "Your bond."

"You could…sense it?"

"I sensed him—or that part of him that's been with you since your destinies were woven before your time. Call it mother's intuition." Zahra lunged for her own glass of alcohol, inspecting the way the liquid sparkled in the sunshine. She motioned towards Isla's neck. "You were not mated then. I would've noticed in that *dress* you were wearing. Chosen by him, I'm assuming, along with the jewelry from our vaults."

Isla flushed and absently reached up to graze the spot on her skin. There was a question in her words. A *why*.

How could she best describe what the past few months, the past few *years*, had been? Everything she'd felt and experienced since she'd come of age at eighteen. Even a bit before that.

"I didn't want a mate," Isla settled on. "For various reasons, and Kai respected that—among other things."

Zahra appeared amused by her vagueness, and maybe a bit prided by her son's actions—or lack thereof. He hadn't forced her into anything, something Isla had also made note of that night they'd met.

"So, what changed your mind, then?" She swirled her glass before taking a sip.

"I love him."

The answer was simple. So easy and quick and wholeheartedly honest, Isla laughed as she'd said it.

For as much as he drove her crazy and could piss her off…

"I love him," she repeated through a breath. "And I can't picture my life without him in it."

Zahra nodded her brows as if saying, *good answer*. "I've heard and I've seen that with fated connections, the love isn't guaranteed, so I'm happy it seems you two…" Her eyes drew along Isla's frame again, and Isla realized that she somehow recognized the shirt as Kai's. There were only so many assumptions one could make—given the circumstances, how she looked. In the middle of the damn day, too. "Get along."

As Isla's cheeks heated again, Zahra's laugh echoed through the yard. "Just saying, I am fully prepared to spoil my grandchildren rotten."

Isla's thoughts returned from the ferry, from the foyer, along with that gut-twisting feeling that came with the notion that she'd one day be…a mother. Not just to anyone, but to a future alpha.

Her hand drifted to her lower belly. If they were trying to prevent anything, they really hadn't been smart about it.

"We haven't really talked about it yet, but I hope we have some time first. It's a lot to adjust to already," Isla confessed, surprising herself with her own openness. But Zahra, of all people—maybe would understand. "I'd be lying if I said I wasn't scared of all of it. What comes next. I mean, as the Beta's child, I was merely a spectator growing up. Within the circle, yet far enough away that with the inner machinations and what goes on behind the curtain, I'm as good as clueless. I can play the lady, but I'm not a queen."

"No one is *born* a queen. The idea of what a luna is shifts like the seasons. Changes as easily and routinely as the moon. Over dynasties. Within years, *months* even, what's needed…it's different." Zahra's tone was soothing and assured. "You're not meant to be me, and Kai isn't meant to be Kyran. Our pack is entering a new age with you two at the helm, and the continent, the entire world is changing, too. And you'll adapt with it. You'll become exactly what it all requires when it's time." She nodded her head. "Frankly, you may be ahead of the game right now, too. A queen with a warrior's heart and skill seems necessary."

A weight on Isla's chest eased, was replaced, and she gnawed on her bottom lip.

Talk about overwhelming. Driving a new age? A changing *world?* Being what's needed. At the right time.

She hated that Ezekiel's voice, of all voices, rolled through her head. His words that had haunted her since he'd spoken them to her in the woods of Callisto.

A queen needed and a queen *deserved*...

Isla ducked her head to focus on her food. "I know I'm going to need to earn people's trust here and their respect, and I want to—earn it, I mean. I don't want them to feel stuck with me as a ruler because they have no choice. I don't want them to think I don't care or have what's best for them in mind. They deserve better than that. They should feel secure in who's leading them. Protecting them." She sighed. "And I'm sure it'll be hard, but I want to do it without completely renouncing my family or where I came from. Because as angry as I am about certain things happening, I wouldn't be who I am today without them either."

She chanced a look up at Zahra, unsure what to expect, but was relieved to see a soft smile on her face. She carefully lifted her glass to Isla in a toast. "Well, you've already earned mine."

Isla's heart swelled, and she beamed back. "Thank you."

And they returned to finish their meals.

∽

After lunch, Zahra had offered Isla something else that she'd so desperately needed: a chance to bathe and wear some proper clothes.

She'd pointed out the eastern wing, where Kai's rooms were—now also *Isla's* rooms—but Isla had been hesitant. Call her crazy or sentimental or whatever, but she hadn't wanted to go in there without him. At least, not for the first time. Zahra had understood—as she always seemed to—and instead, directed her to one of the guest suites. It was there that Isla had met one of her handmaidens, not much older than she herself was. Tall and thin, donning a plain navy apron-style dress over a white shirt, with her dark hair intricately braided into a coronet, was Maeve.

Though Isla had said the assistance wasn't necessary, both Zahra and Maeve insisted.

And after opting for a quick shower rather than a bath in order to get moving to Jonah, she'd exited the bathroom, clad in a dressing gown, to find Maeve had laid out her clothes.

She wasn't sure where the dress had come from. It was a carnation red meant to wrap around her body, cinch at the waist, and flow down to a sliver above her knees. Its neckline tastefully dropped into a V, enough to show the layers of delicate gold necklaces that had also been left out, but not reveal *too much*. Tiny white petals decorated the thin but exquisite fabric, perfect for a summer's day. Great, along with the flat, nude-colored shoes, for easy movement.

As Isla tested the cloth between her fingers, Maeve took a comb in hand. It was yet something else Isla had deemed unnecessary, telling her not to let her hinder her day, but Maeve was persistent and eager to try out a braiding style that would accent the way lighter and darker shades of gold played in Isla's hair.

So, Isla sat before a vanity as she had days ago for Davina, and tried to relax as Maeve worked the tangles from her damp tresses.

"You're mated?"

Maeve spoke softly, and Isla glanced at her and then herself, in the mirror. Her mark was clearly visible beneath the loose, white silk of her gown.

The corners of her mouth curled upwards. "I am."

Maeve's brown eyes met hers briefly. "Fated?"

"Yes, actually."

Maeve's fingers stalled at the ends of Isla's hair. "Really? You don't hear that much anymore."

"I know," Isla mused.

Maeve bit her lip, continuing her ministrations. "So, who's the lucky guy?"

Isla smiled, and though she spared his name and most of the dead-giveaway details, she was more than happy to share about the day they'd met and feed into whatever other questions Maeve asked. A spark had lit in the handmaiden's eye—one Isla was familiar with, and one she'd resented in her life. The hope that it was possible to find the person one was meant for, and the all-consuming drive to find them.

Any joy that the two women had found soured after a knock came at the door.

It was another staff member, a man, clad in a navy buttoned tunic and dark pants, and the news he shared, although Isla had been aware, seized the room. The world.

The alpha's challenge had been approved.

Maeve gasped, her fingers trembling so much that she'd dropped a strand of Isla's hair, and Isla willed her teeth not to shatter as she experienced that horrible sinking feeling all over again.

"There will be a broadcast shortly," the man said. "Alpha Kai will address the pack."

Isla perked in her seat. "Over the radio?" He nodded. "Can one be brought in?"

Another nod, and he vanished.

"Goddess," Maeve breathed, taking hold of Isla's tresses again. "I can't believe it."

Isla cast her eyes to the floor. "Tell me about it."

Once her braid had been woven, Maeve had helped her into her dress, and the man—Cesar, she'd learned—had arrived with the radio, then the broadcast began.

Ezekiel spoke first, presenting the situation, the logistics.

In ten days, on the night of the full moon, Kai would face his challenger, Brax, a wolf hailing from rogue territory.

The beta left out any explanation of Brax's claim of murdering Kyran and Jaden but supplied the new information of it being held in the arena burrowed in the mountain at the end of the river. All pack members could and were urged to attend, but he warned that the arena could reach capacity. There would be a broadcast for those who couldn't make it with live updates.

Isla's lunch turned in her stomach, and the weight of reality forced her to sit down again. She tasted blood as she bit down on her cheek to distract her from the sting of her eyes and the thoughts of having to sit and watch Kai while he—

Her grip tightened on the fabric of her skirt as her mate's voice came through the speaker.

"I wish I was addressing you all under better circumstances."

Both Maeve and Cesar seemed to hold their breath.

Her heart sank. She should've been there with him. They were somewhere in front of the hall, she assumed. Either before the gates, or they'd been opened to allow the reporters in.

As Kai continued, urging everyone not to panic, recounting the longevity of their bloodline, and the challenges all won by his ancestors in the past, she watched the hard emotion pass over Maeve and Cesar's faces. He spoke of what was being done to handle the rogues from days prior. The ones that had been captured and were being questioned, and ensured everyone that they would be safe because though it was unlikely the rogues would strike again as they had, there was an even heavier presence being placed at those borders.

A presence—resources, Isla realized—that had been taken away from around the Wall.

"We've been dealt a heavy hand these past few months," Kai finished. *"But we are resilient, and we will prevail against all else. There is*

light for us at the end of this, I promise you—and I don't just mean the lanterns of the Equinox."

His voice had lightened with the quip, and even Maeve, her eyes lined with silver, managed a chuckle. But Isla had to steel herself. Because she knew what he meant by that light, she felt it. He'd told her.

Kai called for any last questions.

Amidst the raucous roar of questions from pack reporters, Isla heard the cracking of flashbulbs.

Another voice came through the speaker. *"Is it true that this rogue Brax is claiming he is responsible for the deaths of Alpha Kyran and Alpha Heir Jaden?"*

"Yes, it's what he claims."

And it wasn't true.

A new voice. *"Continental law states that the Imperial Alpha needs to be in witness of the challenge. Will he be coming to the pack?"*

Isla went rigid, her breath hampering. *What?*

She hadn't heard that and certainly wasn't prepared for Kai's answer of—

"Yes."

CHAPTER 42

Imperial Alpha Cassius was coming to Deimos.
Isla felt one with Maeve and Cesar in their shock. One with the crowd in their uproar, faint but audible through the speakers.

How long had Kai known *that* condition and neglected to mention it?

Not only that but—

"*And a few other members of the Imperial Council as well."*

"What?" she whispered, drawing the attention of the other two in the room. She didn't care.

Was he kidding?

Isla's mind was whirring too fast for her to keep up with, so much so that she missed the final lot of questions, and only came to when the radio had become nothing but white noise. With her gaze drilled on the floor, fingers constricting and loosening, wrinkling her dress, she tried to settle her breathing.

There were a few choices for her now—

Go kill her mate if he'd known all along and not told her about their upcoming visitors.

Rush to a phone in the hall to call Adrien and Sebastian and ask if they'd heard of the approval, and if they'd find a way to Deimos, too.

Or go to Jonah, finally, to have one part of the day go as planned.

Right now, Isla craved routine. Answers. No more surprises.

So, she picked herself up off the chair, grabbed her jacket, thanked and bid Cesar farewell, and asked Maeve to guide her to the library.

She'd been correct in her assumptions that it lay within the Eastern

Hall. After traveling across the courtyard and trailing up a flight of steps, they found themselves in front of the large doors carved with Deimos's insignia and the crest of Kai's bloodline. Maeve had said that the area spanned the second and third floors, but only on this level was the main entrance, while a few concealed ones lay above, hidden within rooms.

Isla bowed her head to the handmaiden. "Thank you."

"It was my pleasure." Maeve returned the gesture. "If we don't cross paths again, Happy Equinox to you and that special mate of yours."

Isla grinned tightly.

Yes, a special one, he was.

She wished her the same merry holiday, and when the young woman disappeared, grabbed onto one of the wooden handles with two hands and pulled.

Her murmur of surprise seemed to get swallowed by the expanse of what lay before her.

She'd been impressed with The Bookshoppe's size and inventory, given what it was, but this…at least *six* of those could fit in here. And that was just her assumption from where she stood.

When Isla stepped inside, letting the door close with a loud creak and heavy thud behind her, she was not in a library. She was in a small city.

Towers of books lay at her sides as she traveled down the length of the wall next to the entrance. Volumes upon volumes, collected over what she imagined centuries or millennia of time given how ancient Deimos was. She'd need to live at least several lifetimes before she could read through half of it. Could she even retain so much information?

Longing to get lost as she had after she returned to Io from the Hunt —curled up with a good story, getting lost in new worlds—tugged at her gut, her tired mind.

Beyond the opening stacks, she heard murmurs of conversation and the faintest smooth melody, full of horns and drums and taps of piano keys.

A figure and flash of red cut through her periphery. She halted and stepped back.

Davina stared at her from the other end of the aisle. "Isla!" She rushed forward, her arms outstretched.

Isla embraced her with a bright smile as the petite woman wrapped her in a tight hug.

A good change from last night—she was awake and didn't smell like she'd bathed in wine.

"Ow, shit." Davina recoiled and reached for her head, a grimace on her face.

Maybe she still bared some traces of the events prior.

Isla chuckled. "Hangover?"

Davina groaned. "I'm never touching alcohol again."

The same words had passed Isla's lips countless nights. Not once had they been true.

She followed Davina's lead as she directed them to a common area where Jonah, Ameera, and Rhydian had spread themselves out between one of the long mahogany tables, a rung of a ladder against a shelf, and a spot on the mezzanine overlooking it all.

Ameera noticed them first.

"And she returns," she mused, pushing herself up from her wooden perch. She closed the book she'd been flipping through, leaving her finger to mark her page. "And she's changed clothes. Again."

Isla wouldn't tell her it was her *fourth,* not *third,* change in garb.

Rhydian rose from his place on the floor of the upper level and rested his arms on the railing. "Were you with Kai?"

"Only until noon," Isla said, masking any annoyance at her mate. "I left him before his meeting."

"Then where've you been?" Ameera asked.

"Zahra caught me on the way here and stole me for lunch."

"Oh, the *mother-in-law,*" Ameera teased.

"I've never met Zahra," Davina moped, though her eyes were bright, excited, as she took a seat on a small leather armchair. "Did you tell her the big news?"

"She'd figured it out, actually." Isla laughed. "Some kind of mother's intuition, she called it."

Ameera scoffed. "Don't tell my mother that's a thing. She'll travel around the pack talking to anyone, trying to find who she can marry me off to."

Jonah snickered from his place at the table, behind his tall stacks of books. They nearly shrouded him. "Goddess, help that man."

"Fuck off."

Isla turned fully to face him, finding *the* book held open to a page by the marker. The pieces of the diadem, the dagger, and her scribbled messages sat at its side. She reached for the final jewel in her jacket pocket and stepped towards him.

"Did you listen to the broadcast?"

She spun. Rhydian had descended from the mezzanine and stood beside Davina.

Lip curling, Isla nodded. "Yes."

Tight smiles graced everyone's faces, and they shared uncomfortable looks. Who would be the one to broach the subject?

It was Rhydian.

"Talk about a family reunion from hell," he offered, earning a light swat on the stomach from his mate.

Ameera shuffled back to her ladder spot, taking the open air to ask, "Will your father be coming with the Council?"

Isla swallowed. "I don't know."

"Does he know about you and Kai?" Davina asked.

Isla shook her head. "None of my family do, but my brother and Adrien."

Isla wasn't keen on the tenseness that had befallen the room with the mention of his name. The exchange, yet again, of those awkward looks.

Rhydian broke the silence for a second time. "*Imperial Heir* Adrien?"

"He's family to me," Isla said pointedly. "They're the only people that know besides you guys and"—she gestured to Ameera—"your father."

Ameera scowled.

Isla saw it as an opportunity. Shuffling on her feet, she asked, "Does he seem like he's acting…strange to you?"

"Always," Ameera snipped with a roll of her eyes. "Define strange."

Isla breathed deeply, aware of what she'd be accusing him of and very familiar with the fact familial annoyance didn't negate a sense of loyalty. "What are the chances he knows about the tunnels?"

Ameera's features dropped, and she turned to Jonah.

Isla, shocked by the action, did the same. Rhydian and Davina retreated, eager to become solely observers.

"High," Jonah answered, the amber of his eyes darkening. "It's not knowledge that's freely shared. It's a secret of this pack on its way to being lost to time, but Alpha Kyran—being the alpha—would've been aware of them."

"And they did everything together," Ameera commented begrudgingly. "He hid nothing from my father."

Isla blinked. If Alpha Kyran had known…

"But Kai's never heard of them," she said.

"Kai was a scion," Ameera countered. "He'd even tell you himself that his only role was to not fuck up so much that he marred the family's reputation."

Ironic how the entire bloodline and said reputation now rested solely on his shoulders.

"So why wouldn't anyone say something when he became alpha?" Isla inquired.

Jonah tipped his head, considering. "Sometimes, questions hold the best answers."

Isla gritted her teeth as she quickly put the pieces together.

They didn't *want* Kai to know—Ezekiel and whoever else was privy to the information. But why hide it?

And better yet, why had the killer been so adamant about making them see?

What was there to see?

No more questions. *No more* questions.

Isla crossed the room to Jonah and dropped the diadem's jewel on the table with a clunk so loud, so heavy, that it made them all start. At her back, as if they'd already dealt enough with what Jonah was working through and maybe fearing *her,* just the slightest bit, everyone returned to their own doings.

"So that's it."

The last piece.

He didn't ask how she'd gotten it. Rhydian and Ameera must've filled him in on everything.

Isla nodded towards his spread. "What have you found?"

Jonah rose from his seat and sifted a tome from the highest of his multiple stacks. The leather was worn, and the cover skin raised in places. Whatever was written was too faded for her to decipher. He opened it up to a page riddled with dark writing and symbols. Symbols she recognized—but also not at all.

"What threw me off at first was the messages." Now he pulled at one of the papers she'd sketched on. "There isn't just one thing to pull from here, but three." He traced his finger over the symbols she'd scribbled down from the alleyway, focusing on one whorl. "This isn't any type of language, but a rune—or, at least, an attempt at one."

Isla's stomach bottomed out. "A rune? Like from a witch?"

"Yes, but it's incorrect enough to tell me that whoever sketched it had no idea what they were doing."

Easily explained. "I copied it. What if I'm the one who messed it up?"

"It's more than a mistake from duplication. It's just wrong, but close enough to this—" He pointed to a symbol in the tome, several of them, and then motioned to certain glyphs copied onto the paper. "It's for protection—all of them are, in some way—but I doubt whoever left them for you is magically inclined and meant to use them."

"How do you know?"

"Because if they cast this rune with it depicted incorrectly, either they or the surrounding area would've been turned inside out." Isla went wide-eyed, trying to picture what that would look like. "Ill-practiced spell work is no joke from what I've read. Witch magic has limits, costs, and if it's not respected…it's not pleasant."

It sounded like it. Curiosity beckoned her. Maybe she'd do a bit more digging herself into those of the other continent.

But for now—

"So, they…copied it themselves?" she asked.

"Or tried to draw them from memory because they knew them or had seen them somewhere."

Isla quieted, taking in the information before gesturing back to the message. "What's the rest, then?"

Jonah pointed to the symbols also in the book she'd gotten from Lukas, on the markers. "This *is* a language, but it's old. Very old. Nearly pre-dating written record, which is odd." He paused, and Isla raised her brows, urging him to continue. "This is a journal that belonged to Alpha Aneurin."

A journal?

Though that was shock enough, the name didn't ring any bells. "And that is?"

"The final Alpha of Phobos. The one in power and killed alongside his people during the decimation." Jonah heaved a breath, placing a hand on his hip as he looked at his haul. "That took me all damn night to figure out."

Isla's gaze shifted to the open book on the table, the writing in it so crisp and clean yet it could've been scribbles for how little they understood it.

Why would the killer give Lukas an old alpha's journal? What was the message *here*?

She glanced up at Jonah. "Do you know what it says?"

"Just the *name* took me all night, and getting it was luck," Jonah grumbled, hunching and placing both of his hands back down on the table. "I don't know how I'll get what the rest of the words are. I've only found writing like this in one other place." He shuffled through his lot before picking up a folded parchment. He opened it and laid it flat on the table to reveal an ancestral chart tracing back, starting not from Kai, Kyran, or even Alpha Rainer. She wasn't sure how many generations prior it was, but that didn't matter. She couldn't understand it. It was while Jonah explained how much research and puzzling he'd done to figure out Aneurin's translation from the chart when Isla caught it.

She stepped back, jaw unhinging, before moving forward again. She squinted down at the fraying piece she noticed could've been torn. Beside the two names at the pinnacle of the lineage lay the fifth symbol.

Jonah clocked the action. "What is it?"

Isla pointed to the small marking. "What is *that*?"

Jonah's shoulders sagged. "It's a—pack insignia."

Isla furrowed her brows. She'd never seen that before but recognized the symbols of Deimos and Phobos beside the various names below it. "Which pack?"

"Ares."

Isla met Jonah's eyes. "There's no Pack of Ares."

"There *was*, before—" He gestured to the two names at the top of the tree-like figure again. Ghosts behind the foreign lettering. "It was split. Divided between the alpha's two sons after the War of Realms concluded."

The War of *Realms*?

Isla had heard pieces of those battles oh-so-long ago that had changed the tides of the world. When wolves, witches, and all other beings banded together, aided by the deities from their divine lands, against the cruel, immortal fae. What was left after the "original keepers of magic" had lost and retreated to their ethereal domain was their mortal ruins beyond the witch's western border and "other stains on the world" that everyone who'd passed on the tale didn't know the true meaning of.

Isla couldn't wrap her mind around it. Why that mattered now, millennia later.

"But I thought back before the *decimation,* the alphas were brothers, not dating all the way back to the War of Realms, and Ares…it wasn't a pack. It's a *pass between* the packs. Lukas told me—"

Jonah's eyes flashed with anger as he said lowly, "Lukas had no idea what he was talking about and had no business saying it."

Isla swallowed. Aggression was something she'd never seen from him, and that felt…personal.

The smallest bit of defiance, for that man who she still felt defensive over despite nearly having killed her, rose in her gut. "How do *you* know Ares was a pack?"

Jonah's own throat bobbed, and he schooled his face to sort through the stacks. What else did he have? "I read the right books."

An answer all too familiar.

Isla felt her nostrils flare but moved on. For now. "If Alpha Aneurin was in power during the decimation…that was the time of our native languages, if not the Common. Why would he use an ancient dialect *beyond* the ones we're even aware of to chronicle in a journal?"

"Maybe he didn't want anyone to know what he was writing," Jonah answered with a lift of his shoulders before pulling over a canvas envelope of some sort. From it, he extracted a wrinkled, discolored piece of artwork and laid it out for Isla. "What do you recognize?"

Isla gazed down at the parchment. The portrait, done from the waist up, had been crafted by what seemed to be a shaky hand. It showed a woman with moon-white hair and eyes such a dark violet, they were nearly black. Atop her head, stark against the lightness, she donned a crown. Not quite the diadem before them, but in her hands…in her folded hands over its hilt, she clutched a dagger. *The* dagger.

Eyes widening again, Isla noted the woman's extravagant clothing and other pieces of large jewelry. "Who is this?"

"No idea." Jonah flipped the page, revealing more of the old language scribbled on the back of the sheet. "But I'll see what I can piece together with these names." He nodded to the marker. "And then maybe I can figure out what that means. Ameera said you found more."

"Kai has the one I took last night," Isla said, before deducing, summarizing, for herself, "They mark points of the tunnels—which means the language makes sense if those have existed since Deimos and Phobos were *one* Ares." How could that have gone unlearned, unknown? Hidden. "The packs have *always* been linked…even though nearly everyone's forgotten."

"Always," Jonah echoed before his voice darkened. "Which begs the question—why is that important now? What's changed?"

Isla didn't have an answer. Didn't know if she wanted one.

∽

Isla felt a warm touch on her shoulder and the light brush of lips against her forehead. She jolted up from where she'd been slumped and dozing on an armchair beside the wall-scaling hearth in another area of the library, its crackling fire the only source of light and heat. She'd been fighting off sleep for hours, each time she closed her eyes for too long brought reminders of bright red stares and imminent death.

She lifted her hand to rub at her tired eyes and turned her head. A hauntingly beautiful image stood in her wake as the glow of the flames danced over Kai's face.

He stared down at her, a soft grin across his mouth, but he said nothing.

Isla lazily smiled back at him and adjusted in her seat. The book she'd been reading fell out of her lap and onto the floor.

Kai bent down and picked it up, his brows drawing together as he read. "You were reading about the witches?"

A hum passed Isla's lips as some form of answer as she sat upright and rubbed her face again. Her voice was hoarse as she asked, "What time is it?"

Kai closed the book, bringing it to his side. "Nearly midnight." He reached out a hand to her.

She took it and steadied herself after he'd helped her to her feet. Her hand went to his chest, and she felt his heart drumming beneath her fingers. "Have you been in meetings all day?"

He nodded and lowered his head to kiss her softly. "Have you eaten?"

"Not dinner."

"Me neither."

He took her hand in his and led them back through the stacks to where only Jonah sat under the illumination of a small lamp. Everyone else must've headed home while she'd dozed off.

"You've nearly been in here twenty-four hours," Kai said to his brother. "Did you eat at all or—take a break?"

Jonah gave some sort of gesture, vaguely a nod. "I'm good."

Kai sighed exasperatedly. "Try not to stay in here all night and try to eat something. Do you remember where the guest wing of the House is?"

Another nod, and another sharp breath in reply.

"I'll see you in the morning," Isla called before she and Kai ducked away.

As they moved along the wall to those large double doors, Kai muttered, "It's hard to get to him once he focuses on something."

Isla could see that much and resisted the urge to call Kai on the same behavior. She may have also exhibited it…

"If he's gone all day without being at the shop, you know he's serious," he added.

"It's a lot," Isla whispered back. "Did he tell you what he figured out?"

"The gist of it." Kai pushed on the wood, making opening the heavy doors look effortless. He didn't drop her hand when they were out in the hallway, and though they were in view of whoever they'd come to pass, Isla didn't retract. Only tightened her grip on him.

It was enough to raise the corner of his mouth before it fell sharply. "It's not surprising—being misled and lied to by the people I trust most."

Isla looked at him, brows raised, catching the insinuation. "Ezekiel."

"I didn't ask him outright—not yet," Kai said, trying to keep the hurt and anger she felt coiling through the bond off his face. "But he knows about the tunnels. I don't know why he's keeping it from me, but we'll see how the pieces fall. If he knows about that house and tries to cover it up…"

The house, the wasteland, the Wall…

Isla chewed on her lip, recalling her thoughts from something he'd mentioned during the broadcast.

She offered carefully, "You know—with the movement of the guard to account for the rogues, you're taking eyes away from the Wall."

Kai's features hardened and he kept his gaze forward. "I know."

"Do you think…"

They reached the staircase to take them down to the ground level, and Kai didn't seem to care that his voice echoed in the cavern as they descended. His tone was as cold and wrathful as death itself. "I think if the rogue attacks were in fact an inside job, whoever's responsible better hope to the Goddess that I don't survive the challenge."

Isla shivered, not for the resurfacing of the challenge, and not for the chilled air that greeted them when they stepped out into the courtyard. She took a moment to let it settle in, find the beauty in the lights in the trees, the flow of the statues, the fountain, the flowers, the stars winking at them from above. But the moon was…hidden.

Kai was tense at her side, and she knew he saw what she'd felt earlier. The chaos, the pain.

She leaned into him, curling her other hand over his upper arm reassuringly. A soft smile bloomed on his mouth, and they wordlessly turned away, heading for the House.

Kai slipped his other hand into his pocket and said after a few steps, "You changed."

Isla gazed down at her clothes. "Yes, after lunch with your mother."

"You had lunch with my mother?"

"I did," Isla said coolly, enjoying the slight tinge of fear and maybe embarrassment on his face. What hadn't he wanted her to know? "She's very kind."

He recovered and grinned. "She is." Unspoken words, more questions, flickered in his eyes, but he moved on. A few seconds later, he noted, his stare drawing over her again, "Kept the red, I see."

Isla snickered.

Unintentionally.

But with the playfulness, the innuendos, a reminder had festered that he may not have wanted. A reason that she'd been peeved with him.

Isla bit her lip, lowering her voice to croon, "You like it?"

"I mean, you look great in everything," he said, smirking. "And nothing."

Isla gave a small laugh. "Well, too bad you won't be getting me in *nothing* for a while." She let her features fall into a pointed glare when Kai gazed at her, confused. "You should've told me that my dad might be coming, asshole."

Kai grimaced. "Right." He lifted his hand from his pocket to present, "In all fairness, it wasn't confirmed to me until before the address."

"You could've mentioned the possibility," she said.

He sighed. "I'm sorry." His hand slid back into his pocket, and he cast his eyes to the ground. "Are you going to be okay?"

What a question.

"Because my father might be here? The fact Alpha Cassius will *definitely* be here? Or because I'll have to watch the man I love fight to the death in front of thousands upon thousands of people?"

Kai lifted his head, brows drawn. "How many do you think can fit in that arena?"

She gave him a deadpan look to which he chuckled. He maneuvered his arm so it was thrown around her shoulders, while hers crossed her front, their fingers still twined. "It's going to be fine." He tugged her closer and kissed her hair. "Now, what do you want to cook for dinner?"

Despite wanting to maintain her stand, Isla pressed into him.

She wasn't sure how it worked in a place such as this. When one was a *prince*, or an alpha now. Late-night eating back in her apartment was typically a bowl of chips or whatever she had on hand.

"Are we really making the chefs cook this late?"

Kai looked at her like she was crazy. "No."

Isla raised a brow, judging the look on his face. "*You're* going to cook?"

"Don't act surprised. I do pretty well."

She laughed. "I'll be the judge, I suppose."

They encroached the doors of the House, already having been pulled open after having seen Kai approaching. The guards and doormen—different from earlier—greeted him with a deep bow and greeted her with quick nods, smiles, and looks away. Turning a blind eye—as if they'd been instructed to whenever their alpha passed a woman through their door. She narrowed her eyes, though a smile played on her lips.

They breezed straight through the grand foyer and a hallway she and Zahra hadn't ventured down. "Food, then bed, then think in the morning," Kai drawled.

Bed. *Their* bed. Their room.

But—

"Oh, Goddess," Isla murmured as the realization hit. Truly what it meant. She could think all of this was hers now, but no one *knew* they were mated. She was *still* a warrior. "I haven't reported or been at the hotel all day. Where do they think I am? Where I've been? I still need to follow protocol."

"You're covered," Kai told her, as they walked past a living area and into a pristine kitchen. "I had a meeting with the lead commander and General Eli. You've been on my call for the day—you could be for a while if you want—and I'll take whatever heat for that. At this point, what can Alpha Cassius do to me? And there's no sending you back to Io." He softly pushed her against the counter before lifting her onto the marble top. He corralled her in, settling between her legs. His face, his lips, were inches from hers, his hands ghosting over her bare thighs. "You're mine now."

Isla's toes curled but she held her resolve. "But *technically*," she cooed, reaching to brush a curl from his eye and draw a line down his face. "I still have a choice if I want to spend the night."

A crooked grin crossed his mouth, a dimple appearing on his cheek. "Technically."

Isla held his stare, challenging him, for a few moments before conceding, "Try not to hog all the blankets."

He scoffed. "Try not to ice me out with your cold feet."

CHAPTER 43

The days leading up to the challenge would be busy, to say the very least.

For Isla. For Kai. For all of them.

As much as they didn't want the upcoming event to feel like they were up against a clock—against an *end*—it did. Everything had to be sorted within the remaining nine days.

Or as much of it as possible...however that was possible.

So, they'd discussed over dinner, Isla would spend her nights with Kai at the House, though they'd keep her identity as his mate a secret—for now, for safety.

Her new "role" was being a means of "protection for the alpha during these times"—or so that's what she'd explain to General Eli when she finally checked back in with him in the evening.

What she *wouldn't* mention was how her morning had gone on said "duties".

Wouldn't say how she'd woken up wrapped in strong arms and was met by soft kisses on her neck and shoulders, her mate's warmth, his hardness, against her back. How Kai's hands, his fingers, slipped beneath the second shirt she'd borrowed from him and worked over her body until she lazily, playfully demanded, masking her desperation for him to "just fuck her already". Wouldn't say how he'd laughed—that gravelly, sleepy, spine-tingling laugh that could've done her in on the spot—before chastising her mouth, mocking with a *"good morning"*, and giving her what she'd wanted. The easy, toe-curling strokes gradually evolved into a rhythm that had her wide awake, alive, and forcing her own face into a pillow to muffle her moaning.

He'd since gone back down to the kitchen to make them breakfast while she remained in bed for a few more moments, savoring her aching muscles and the heat and scent of him…everywhere.

Eventually, she forced herself to move.

Her features weren't as sunken, she noticed, as she washed her face. Though they'd risen early to sort through things before Kai's daily commitments and she'd been jarred awake a few times from those nightmares—aided by soft words and those kisses—it was the most sleep she'd gotten in days.

The most clarity she'd had in a while.

She was ready to do whatever had to be done to figure this all out.

Before heading downstairs, she shuffled over to the two sets of tall glass doors at the end of the room, each curved and dark-paned, leading out to a small terrace offering her views of the backyard and the land beyond. Their bedroom was one of three rooms in their "chambers", spaces that were simple, comfy, but lavish. More like she'd imagined for Kai than any of the other extravagant places she'd seen.

She shivered as she stepped out onto the balcony, a light wind skittering along her bare legs. Behind the fog-tipped mountains, the sun chased away twilight.

A feeling rumbled beneath her skin as she took a deep, centering breath of the chilled morning air and glanced down at her hand.

Focus. Into your belly. Let the energy flow.

Claws ripped through her skin, healing quickly, and though she hissed at the pain of shifting bone, a sigh of relief passed her lips.

Good.

More than good.

Bless the Goddess.

That feeling of disconnect from such a fundamental part of her would be hard to describe to anyone. How truly *unsettling* it was.

Where had that poison *come from*?

The killer had used it that night on Kai, Kyran, and Jaden—though hadn't killed Kai. And that rogue had it in the wasteland.

But the killer was their ally, *protecting* them, why would they allow the rogues to get a handle of it? And why, after saving Isla in the Hunt, would they give it to Lukas and weaponize him against her?

Isla exhaled sharply through her nose.

Something wasn't adding up.

It was like they couldn't decide whether they wanted to help or hurt them.

"*Do I have to drag you out of bed?*"

Isla jolted at the voice. She spun, checking if Kai was behind her, but found nothing but a small living area and their unmade bed. He must've still been downstairs in the kitchen. A decent distance away, but now that her wolf had recovered and the bond settled, communicating was going as expected.

She smiled, drawing in her claws. "*I'm coming.*"

"*Again?*"

Isla snorted. "*I hate you.*"

"*Not what I heard earlier.*"

∽

For a moment, Isla stood and watched Kai from her spot at the kitchen's entrance. She'd been quiet on her way downstairs, and he hadn't turned around yet.

He was clad in nothing but a pair of loose gray pants hanging low on his hips, giving her the perfect view of the shifting muscles and ink on his back as he made their breakfast plates. She bit her lip as her eyes drew down the planes of his skin, lower. Whatever he'd cooked smelled wonderful, as it had last night. He *had* impressed her with dinner, she would admit.

"Are you just going to stand there and watch me all day?" he asked, still not turning.

She wouldn't question how he knew she was there.

Pushing off the wall, she crossed the floor towards him. "It seems quiet around here."

Kai reached for some pepper, sprinkling it over the omelets he'd made. "Staff knew they had the morning off."

Isla moved to his side to slide her arms around him, scratching her nails teasingly over his skin. "Because they knew I stayed the night, and you needed more time to woo me with breakfast?"

Kai snickered and threw his arm over her back, tugging her close. He picked up a piece of chopped potato dusted with spices and lifted it to her mouth. "I think I'm beyond needing to *woo* you."

Isla parted her lips for it, moaning in satisfaction at the tastes that caressed her tongue.

Kai looked away and shifted on his feet at the sound. She held in a laugh. Oh, what power she had over him.

She traced her eyes over his body again—his chest, his torso, down to his waistband, and a bit below…then back up—before snagging on a particular place. She lifted a finger to the black etching of his tattoo. The curves and lines drawn heavy and light. The same, yet different, from the ones Jonah, Rhydian, and Ameera bore. "What do they mean? I asked Jonah once, and he said they were a symbol of codependence."

Kai barked a laugh. "Of course, he did." He offered her another bite. "It's an old pack practice that fell away when lumerosi became widespread—which began with Io, by the way, so thank your ancestors for one of our most painful traditions." She narrowed her eyes. "We learned about and researched it a lot at the academy, and when we finished school, we got them. It's our history, our heritage, our bond. The four of us have gone through a lot together." He paused, his throat bobbing. "A lot of pain, a lot of change, *a lot* of loss—even before this."

Isla wouldn't ask the specifics of what he meant, judging by his demeanor. If he wanted to share, he would, and if the others did, they would, too.

Kai carried their plates to the counter where their stools were still set on opposite sides from last night.

Isla slipped onto hers and smiled sweetly up at him as he placed the dish before her. "Thank you."

Kai chuckled, joking about how sex and food seemed to be the key to her manners, and leaned down to brush his mouth against hers. Isla held him there maybe a bit longer than he'd intended to stay, deepening the kiss when she felt something inside her break again.

Because that time—those nine days—hung over her head like a dark cloud. And she didn't even want to imagine there could only be nine more mornings of this with him.

Her chest was tight as Kai pulled away, face drawn in confusion, before taking his seat across from her. It had been merely a bite into their meal when he asked, "Are you okay?"

Isla swallowed her piece of omelet, nodding. She didn't want to tell him, frighten him in any way, with what *she'd* been afraid of, so she went with what their plan for breakfast chatter had been all along.

Strategy.

"Do you think the killer's being used by someone else?"

Kai nearly choked at the proposal. "Why would you think that?"

"Because their behavior isn't consistent," Isla said. "They nearly kill you, now warn you. Nearly kill me, then warn me. It's like they…broke character. Snapped."

He furrowed his brows. "By killing?"

"By *not*." Isla hesitated, pushing around the food on her plate and trying to figure out the best way to explain her theory, especially because of the topic she'd be broaching. "They killed your father and brother first and intended to kill you. Something that extreme requires planning and skill which they've proven to have." She was mindful of the way Kai shifted in his seat, the tenseness of his jaw, and what she felt on the other end of the bond. "They broke from the plan when they got to you."

"Why?" Kai asked gruffly, that guilt flickering in his eyes. "What made me any different from them?"

Isla answered as she had in his office, "I don't know."

"So why would that mean they're being used?"

She shoved another piece of egg into her mouth, fueling her for what would surely be another rabbit hole.

"After that, they left you messages, and then saved me and Lukas in the Hunt. *Then* nearly had me killed—and then went back to helping us again." She made a point of each nonsensical action.

Kai took a bite of his food, shrugging. "It's definitely weird."

"It's more than weird," Isla countered before starting carefully, "In the wasteland before Rhydian and Ameera showed up after the killer saved me from the bak, they seemed—hurt—when I asked them why they did it. Why they tried to kill me." She knew she would sound crazy, but still posed, "What if it was because they…hadn't wanted to?"

Kai dragged a hand through his bed-mussed hair. "They hadn't wanted to, but they had to?"

Despite his assessing words, he didn't look at all convinced.

Still, Isla answered, "Yes."

Kai heaved a breath. "Isla."

That *tone*.

Her back went straight. "What?"

Kai's smile was soft, though there was still a tenseness to him. "You were the same way with Lukas when he came back from behind the Wall and tried to kill that hunter. Twice. And then turned on that other Callisto guard." Now he looked as if he were choosing his words carefully. "How much you care is one of the many things I love about you—but Lukas? He tried to kill you. Had reason to. They told him that if he did it, they'd let him out, and he was going to. How can you still defend him?"

Isla dropped her fork and looked down at her hands, remembering the feeling of Lukas's blood coating her skin, recalling how it had felt to tear through his flesh. Recalling that look in his eyes that still haunted her sometimes. That sudden clearness, openness, before she thought she'd watched him die.

"Because something still doesn't feel right. With *anything*, him included. No one goes into the Wilds and leaves forgetting their entire existence." She clenched and released her fists, refusing to look up, shame coiling in her gut. "We have nine days until the challenge, and the rogues *have to be* a distraction, one that's working. We're missing something—big. And if we look at what's been given to us...I think it has to do with the house and the tunnels."

"Fuck."

Isla lifted her eyes in time with Kai dropping his own fork and wedging his hands into his hair. He lowered his head, shaking it and cursing again and again.

"What?" she asked, and he met her gaze, a low simmer behind his stare as his nostrils flared.

"I think there's a witch in the Wilds."

CHAPTER 44

"A witch in the Wilds?" Isla leaned back in her seat so far, she'd nearly toppled off. "How? They'd never survive."

"For an extended time, likely not," Kai said, his face drawn in grave seriousness. "But if they had a means of getting in and out, somewhere safe to *return to*." His teeth flashed. "Shit."

Isla knew where he meant. "The house."

"It explains the warded door."

It did, but—"Why? How? When?"

Kai sat upright. "I don't know how a witch would get here or what desire they'd have to go into the Wilds, but if there was one in there during the Hunt, if Lukas *saw them*, what better reason to get rid of his memories?"

Isla's gut twisted. "But how? I don't understand the laws of magic, but wiping memories to that extent sounds really potent, especially against us."

"Lukas can't shift, which means his susceptibility is higher than it would be for wolves like you and me."

Isla opened and closed her mouth, not knowing where to even begin —or end. "So that's what the runes are for in the messages. That's what the killer's pointing us to, warning us about. There's a witch here." She shook her head. "But the house was empty when we went. There were some signs that someone had been there, but not recently—though also definitely not ten years ago. Do you think they're...back in the Wilds? Or somewhere in the pack?"

"I'm not sure." Kai nudged his plate away as if he'd suddenly become sick. "But they're a bigger problem than I thought."

"Why?"

He met Isla's stare. "Because they can survive the Wilds, which means they've found a way to conquer the bak."

Isla couldn't even entertain the question of *how*, she'd already doubled back to what it *meant*. There had been a witch in the Wilds. A witch had cursed Lukas. Made him act as he had. He had no reason to be in Valkeric, no reason to be wiped from the realm. He should've been a warrior, been home with his family.

"We have to tell someone," she said, her rapid heartbeat leaving her breathless. "The Imperial Alpha, if he knew—"

"We can't do that."

Isla jerked back before pressing her hands into the counter. She narrowed her eyes at her mate. "Kai, he's in *prison*, and it's not even his fault. He didn't know what he was doing."

A bit of sympathy shone in his stare but still, he said, "I'm hoping Alpha Cassius doesn't declare war over refugees here building a non-existent army. If he thought we were harboring a witch, too?"

Isla's gaze was pleading as she reached across the table, taking hold of his forearm. "But you didn't *know* about the witch."

Kai's eyes dropped to her touch, and his shoulders relaxed, a sigh slipping through his mouth.

Suddenly his features shifted, and he slowly pulled away. "What if we did?"

∽

Kai had been pacing the floor of his office—back and forth, back and forth—so much, so fast, that Isla had to stop tracking him to abate her oncoming headache. Not his fault, but…everything.

Right now, she had to resist the urge to scale the entire continent to get to Valkeric. To somehow break Lukas out of their land's highest security prison. Her fingers twitched as she stared at the phone on Kai's desk certainly capable of reaching Io. Sebastian and Adrien may have been up to assist in a jailbreak.

But first things first, they needed to talk to Ezekiel. It was Kai's first meeting of the day anyway, a quick thirty-minute brief as it always had been. She wasn't sure how it would turn out, though. Kai was seeing red by the time they'd finished struggling through the rest of their breakfast. Because if Ezekiel had known about the tunnels, about the house, then he could've very well known about the witch.

The grandfather clock chimed, the hands set perfectly to the left and the sky—nine o'clock.

A knock came at the door. Right on time.

Like the flick of a switch, Kai ceased his pacing, and Isla felt his power yawning awake through the room. No efforts were made to mask it. "Come in."

The entrance creaked open to reveal Ezekiel. As yesterday, a look at Isla sitting in a chair that had been pulled beside Kai's desk prompted a disconcerting smile.

He took a step in. "Back aga—"

"Sit."

Ezekiel stuttered and looked at Kai, who'd settled against the front of his desk. He gestured to the chair before him—before them—before crossing his arms.

Isla honed in on the beta's heartbeat, the way it skipped, and listened to how his breath hitched. But he kept his shoulders back as he closed the door behind him and strode through the room.

He cast another glance her way as he sat.

"I'm not going anywhere," she said, crossing one leg over the other.

The flatness of her tone, the lack of *bite*, seemed to tell him enough. Made him stiffen.

And if there was *any power* that the bond, her connection to Kai, had offered her as luna, even if she hadn't gone through the Rite, she brought it out. Made sure he felt it.

Something flew across the room in Ezekiel's direction. His reflexes were quick, and he caught it easily. Upon a glance at what lay in his hand, his eyes flashed.

The marker. The beta swallowed and lifted his head. A careful question, "What is this?"

Isla had to hold in a laugh of disgust. Bastard. Why even *try* to hide it? He had to know that they knew.

She noticed Kai's grip on his forearms tightening—a small flicker of rage, of roiling power—but he remained quiet, assessing, allowing her to answer, "I got it out of the tunnels beneath the pack. After I found that house in the wasteland with Rhydian and Ameera."

Ezekiel jolted and spun to her, his voice harsh as he asked, "You had Ameera out there?"

"Mind your tone," Kai gritted out, still standing with that unnerving calm. Control. "Why not tell me?" He paused. "And *don't. Lie.*"

Ezekiel had been his father's best friend, was his best friend's father—but the unspoken threat in the words...

Any restraint or patience Kai had with Ezekiel, with everything, had worn *so* thin. Obligatory loyalty and respect couldn't save the beta. Couldn't save anyone.

Ezekiel swallowed and glanced down at his hand. The room had become so quiet, that Isla couldn't drown out the sound of the ticking clock or miss the faint whistle of the train shooting through the mountains to Ifera miles away. She fought the urge to tap her foot and tightened her grip on the pants Kai had given her.

The bond trembled, strained, became...unfamiliar. Dark. A coiling of shadows, of cold, at the end of that bridge. She looked to Kai who wasn't looking at her, but at Ezekiel with a stare so intense, it was as if it could see straight through him, would *rip* right through him.

The beta shifted uncomfortably in his seat, giving a subtle shake of his head with a grimace, and then he looked up.

Isla felt the tether ease as Kai gave a small start. At what, she wasn't sure. But he blinked, shaking his head, too.

"You...had a lot going on," Ezekiel began. "The Alpha Rite, the coronation, and then you were preparing for the Hunt. I planned to tell you afterwards, but while we were in Callisto, new *information* came to light."

Information, she gathered, the moment his gaze flickered her way.

"Me," Isla answered before he could elaborate. "You met me." She narrowed her eyes, trying to understand. "Why would that matter?"

"Mating bonds are complicated—they cloud our judgment, especially in the early stages—and somehow you two made it *worse*. It was a risk," Ezekiel said, that haughtiness of his slipping into his tone. "Io isn't aware of the tunnels. If they were, they would've been sealed long ago."

"Maybe they should be if it leaves the pack vulnerable," Isla argued. "If it allows *bak* to get through them."

"They've been open since this pack's founding. Bak have only been an issue recently with the Wall's wards failing."

That made sense. The wards typically repelled the beasts from the borders.

But Isla still didn't understand. "For what reason would you *want* to keep them open? Just to stroll in, every once in a while, and look at the scenery?"

Ezekiel inclined his head. "Do you know what the Wilds once was?"

Isla straightened.

Phobos.

The packs had been two sides of the same coin. Connected, prospering with each other even after separation, until one of them had been ripped away. There were roots of their people in there, wedged in that soil, tying back to those primeval times when they were once one.

"Why else?" Kai finally spoke again, sensing their volley's end. "As unfortunate as it would be, losing history doesn't make it *a* risk and reason not to mention it to me."

Another glance Isla's way by Ezekiel. "Because it's an open front. One difficult to guard, and one Io could use to their advantage."

To their advantage?

Isla scoffed, though memories of her pondering war burned in the back of her mind. "Io has no reason to attack Deimos."

Ezekiel lifted his brows, challenging. "Despite its strength and despite serving its purpose in world relations, Io is in a poor position to rule over all of Morai. The Imperial Alpha is too far away for the expanse of territory he wishes to control. He's losing touch with Tethys, Mimas, and Iapetus. Why do you think he's entertaining that general? The yappy one who fancies you."

Eli.

That would make sense. He was the son of Beta Sampson of Iapetus. Bringing him into Io through Isla—or even sending her there—would be a way to build relations, to get a foothold.

Kai snorted at the jab before saying, not questioning, "That's why they've moved in on Charon. Why they have Locke as their puppet."

Ezekiel nodded. "But Kyran and I feared that wouldn't be enough for him. That Cassius would want the head and *the heart* of the continent under his control."

Kai tensed, and his gaze snapped to the globe on his desk. Where dead at the continent's center, sat—"You think he'd try to take Mavec."

"It wouldn't be surprising if it eventually came to that," Ezekiel said, picking a piece of lint off his jacket. No look her way, but Isla felt the words directed at her. "It may already be in motion."

Her stomach bottomed out, and she couldn't fight the odd sensation of being split in two.

"Your father got wind of it before he passed. Heard the rumblings from the refugees of more frequent visits of Io's Council, particularly the Imperial Beta, to the territory. Potentially rallying troops...and he discovered something else." Ezekiel paused, looking directly at each of them before finishing, "They have witches hidden in their prison. An unwitting army."

"What?" Isla jerked back in her seat. "No, we don't."

We.

Both Kai and Ezekiel turned her way, and though she'd expected the pointed look she'd received from the beta, the one she'd gotten from her mate—the slight hurt along with the empathy—she hadn't been ready for.

She pushed them away. Shoved Io and her family away into the *other*. For right now, for this conversation, she had to. She was the future Luna of *Deimos*. Talks such as these would be had. And Io as a political opponent wasn't the one she'd grown up in and called home. Though that anger, that doubt, rumbled beneath her skin.

She glowered. "And what about the one *you're* hiding?"

The world seemed to stop moving.

They hadn't had a plan to drop the witch on Ezekiel, just that they'd ease into the question. Feel out what he knew, what he'd be willing to tell. If he'd want to hide it, even now, even after the mention of the house. Maybe he *had been* prepared to, judging by the paling of his face, the tremble that rocked his being.

But he recovered quickly, finding a scowl. "She's the one who told us. She *escaped*."

"Who is *she*?"

Kai didn't miss a beat while her mind stumbled to keep up.

She couldn't filter through the shock, the feelings of—betrayal. Io keeping witches? Planning an attack? Taking Mavec for Charon?

Maybe it was the anger at the confirmation of another secret that helped Kai push forward. To press and press for as much information and take time to break it all down and absorb it, later. Or it was a way to keep Ezekiel off-balance. Give him less time to spin a tale, a lie, in pauses.

"All we knew of her was that fact. We offered her refuge here in exchange for protection, need Io strike." Ezekiel seemed to steel himself with a breath. "And then she turned on us. Had that dog of hers kill Kyran and Jaden, go for you, and then she disappeared."

Isla stopped breathing.

Kai may have, too.

"That dog"—the killer.

Silence befell the room again.

A *witch* had been behind it all. Had been the reason—

"Why would she want us all dead?" Kai's voice cut through the silence, and Isla couldn't place the emotion within it. It was hollow, cold, and the closest she imagined she'd ever be to understanding how it had felt that day to wake up and find out his life had changed forever.

Recounting the deaths also seemed to move Ezekiel, whose eyes gleamed. "I won't pretend to understand the reasoning of a witch."

But there was something else. Something else he wouldn't say. Ezekiel was manipulative, conniving, and those words—Deimos, traitor — nagged at her.

"Who's the killer?" She chanced the words gently. "The one who did it."

His stare hardened, and his nostrils flared. "I never saw their face. I never heard them speak. I don't know who they were. She simply called them 'her sword'."

Her sword.

If that witch had been in the Wilds, then she'd need one. That was how she'd conquered the bak.

From the new quiet, came another question, "That jewel you had yesterday, where did you get it if not the vaults?"

Kai, who'd since gone to sit in the chair behind his desk, inclined his head. "Why?"

Ezekiel tightened and released his grip on the marker still in his hands, rolled it between his fingers. Fidgeting. Anxious. "She had a crown, the witch. Obsidian stone. It looked just like it."

"It was a gift for Isla."

"What did she look like?"

Both Kai and Isla had spoken simultaneously, but Isla's eager question, rather than Kai's vague brush-off, was what Ezekiel had been interested in.

With his eyes on her, she clarified, "The witch. What did she look like?"

A tug came at the bond, reining her back. Kai hadn't wanted her to push him. Hadn't wanted to reveal their hand?

"Black hair, blue eyes. Fragile and pale," Ezekiel answered, making a point of the last two words. "Like she was a ghost, maybe a prisoner for years."

Isla swallowed the bile rising in her throat and took in the facts. It *hadn't* been her that the artist had depicted. Ezekiel wouldn't look away as if he could see her thoughts coiling around her, threatening to suffocate her. Like he wanted to will them to.

"Why keep the desire for Mavec a secret?" Kai asked, drawing the attention away from her. "Mate of Io or not, you know I'd defend the city."

"I apologize; it was just too much of a risk at the time," Ezekiel conceded, lowering his head. "But now Fate has had her hand, and everything has fallen as it should." He cast a look between them. "When are you planning to share the news? I imagine the mark won't be wholly faded by the time the Imperial Alpha arrives."

"When we tell her family is for Isla to decide, and the pack will know when the challenge is over." Kai folded his hands over his desk, jerking his chin towards the door. "You can go. I'll see you in an hour for the meeting with Gamma Hersch."

Ezekiel nodded, rising to his feet. Carefully, he placed the marker on Kai's desk, then bowed. "Alpha." He turned to Isla and dipped again before drawling, "And Warrior—*for now.*"

Isla scowled, biting, "You're dismissed."

At her side, the corner of Kai's lips ticked upwards.

Once Ezekiel had gone, Isla turned fully to her mate, whose features had fallen into a grimace. He'd dulled his power and was massaging his temples. "How the fuck was that worse than I thought?"

"I know," Isla said, barely over a breath.

Kai laughed bitterly. "And he's *still* hiding something."

"How do you figure?"

"After you and I parted in Callisto, when I came back, all anyone—including Ezekiel—tried to do was convince me that Io was to blame for killing my father and Jaden. To turn me against them, against *you*…and I believed them."

Isla remembered that time at the overlook, how nauseated she'd felt at the prospect.

"But Ezekiel knew the truth the entire time," Kai finished. "That it was the witch they'd been helping who turned on them."

"He just said why he didn't tell you."

"But why try to turn me against Io so violently, so *quickly*?" Kai let the question linger for a few moments before answering for himself. "My father wasn't someone who would deign himself to assist a witch as a *precaution*. 'Need Io strike.' If he heard rumblings that something was happening, he'd want to strike first."

Isla's eyes widened, though her brows drew inward. "You—you think they had a plan to attack Io with the witch?"

Kai heaved a breath, likely catching the flash of fear in her gaze. He leaned back, looking at the ceiling as he spoke and thought aloud. "One witch wouldn't be enough. Neither would having numbers on our side, especially against the strength of Io's guard, the fact they can all pretty much shift, and with their own supposed arsenal of witches." He glanced at the map on the wall beside him. "To even entertain the idea, he'd need to feel like he had another weapon."

A weapon effective against wolves and witches alike. Brutal enough to take down feral armies but resilient enough to withstand magic.

Isla fell back in her own seat, her eyes snagging on the map. She trained her eyes over the terrain of Phobos as she had yesterday. The regions that had once been homes, the land once walked by people, brothers and sisters of Deimos, now ravaged by beasts.

What business would a witch have in there? Why go through the trouble of needing a sword, protection?

Isla felt that *sword's* icy touch on her forehead again. Relived that crooked finger shifting over to the bak and then pointing to themselves.

They'd been holding the last piece of the diadem.

A piece of the diadem, the crown, that the witch had supposedly possessed.

Isla sat up in her seat, her mind buzzing.

"What is it?" Kai asked as she had at breakfast.

She wondered if he'd felt as crazy proposing what he'd thought.

"What if—"

She stumbled. How would it even be possible? If there was a resistance…but Kyran would need a weapon, the greatest weapon, one that couldn't be destroyed. If the witch had figured out how…if she could… wield like a sword…many swords…

"What if she could control the bak?"

CHAPTER 45

"Is that even—possible?" Isla followed her own question with another, and at Kai's look of perplexity, she explained her vague reasoning steeped in desperation.

If the killer had been acting not of their own volition, on behalf of someone, someone who had a crown, *that* crown, maybe they weren't the only ones. They'd pointed to the bak, too, that night in the wasteland.

Kai tilted his head, considering, and then reiterated, "But bak can't be influenced by magic."

"Unless she found a way," Isla suggested. "Or maybe she can...talk to them?"

Because *reasoning* with bak sounded perfectly plausible.

Kai huffed a curt laugh. "I guess anything is possible at this point."

Isla lunged forward to pick up the marker left by Ezekiel and traced her fingers over its etches. "I'll talk to Jonah. I can take a closer look at the diadem, and he's the closest we have to a witch expert. I'll bring this, too. Not that he needs more to do, but maybe we can figure out where the original one came from. I'll help him out."

She looked to Kai to see if he had any objections and found him frowning. "There are council members that are keen on world matters like this. I should be able to trust relaying the information to *them*, but..." He trailed off, his jaw tight. "I don't have time to weed them out and bringing in more people is too risky." The downturn of his features held as he remained back in his seat. He folded his hands over his stomach and pondered, mindful of his words, "All the secrets that have

A WARRIOR'S FATE

been kept have been because I met you…and I have to imagine that's why Ezekiel's still hiding things. The plan is still to move in on Io."

Though her body locked up, Isla tried to keep the fear off her face. But the bond—oh, the bond gave her away.

Kai's lips were pursed, his face drawn in concern, understanding, and maybe the slightest discomfort. The family of the woman he loved —maybe not *the* enemy, but was certainly not an ally. Tricky waters he'd need to navigate forever.

Isla swallowed but found her mouth dry. The headache she'd been abating cropped up again. "How? He wouldn't do anything while they were here, would he?"

"I wouldn't let him. Anyone," Kai assured, a timbre in his voice showing he meant it. He'd do whatever he had to in order to prevent it.

Though the words didn't ease any queasiness Isla felt. The thought of the beta still had her prickling, had her wolf prowling beneath her skin. "If Ezekiel knows you wouldn't support action on Io, how do you know he won't hurt you?" Her grip on the marker tightened so much, that indents had been left in her palms.

Kai exhaled sharply through his nose, a bored expression casting across his face as though he'd already thought of it. "He could try but he needs me. Once a hit be dealt on Io, they'll hit back, and we'll be at war. And if not for strength, he needs me for pack morale. Our people will be too shaken to stand if there's another sudden change in leadership, especially given I'm the last alpha of this bloodline." His voice shuddered at the words, at the implication. The last of the original alpha's heirs—of Deimos, even of Phobos and Ares beyond it. "Which means he knows the witch isn't a threat to me, if she had been before, or else he would've said something. If I believe anything from him, it's his love for this pack, his family, and loyalty to my father."

Slightly more reassuring.

Isla began fiddling with one ridge at a curve of her chair. "Do you think he knows where she is?"

"Maybe. But we won't get much from asking again. He knows there's no coming back from this, that he'll never regain my trust, and that he'll be replaced, and—" A darkness shone in Kai's eyes, one that made Isla remember that intensity she'd seen as he'd stared down Ezekiel. One it seemed even the beta felt bearing down on him, making him squirm.

What would be done with Ezekiel after? How would he be dealt with? He'd lied to Kai, his alpha, about something as serious as *this*.

More precarious lines for Kai to walk.

He wouldn't just be cutting such a strong tie that the beta had historically maintained with his family, but he'd also be upsetting *Ameera's* life.

Kai didn't elaborate on any plans or offer any options. He only moved on to say, "I suspect he'll be moving, a lot, and doing everything he can to ensure whatever the plan is works out. So, we'll watch." Another downturn of his mouth. "And I'll need to talk to Ameera."

"You're going to have her trail him?"

He raked a hand through his hair, tugging at it so much that some of its curls loosened, curving towards his temple. "I don't want to have to, but who else is there?"

Isla gazed down as she thought. Who else *was* there?

For a moment, she found herself in Ameera's shoes, ones she also wore. The beta's daughter.

If Isla had been assigned to spy on her father and watch how he moved within Charon, what he was doing—even with any hostility she'd felt, even if she'd wanted to defend Deimos with everything she had, it was her *father*. She'd be terrified of what she'd find, what she would have to do upon an unfortunate discovery.

With another shot of desperation, Isla lifted her head. "They're—they're no longer working on the witch's accord, the killer."

She caught the way Kai flinched at the mention of the one who'd actually delivered death upon his family, as if an old wound had been re-opened now, knowing the whole truth.

She continued carefully, "She wouldn't want them warning us about her as they are, so maybe they're no longer in league together. Maybe they know, too. They could tell us."

"That's possible," Kai said, righting himself in his seat. "But it's not like we can go ask them."

And with their luck, an answer would be another riddle for them to crack. In another fresh language that they couldn't understand. Probably from the world of old gods and rulers. It was hopeless.

But trying wouldn't hurt. "I could go to the house and see if they show up."

"No."

Isla blinked at the quick refusal.

Kai sighed, his frustration mounting, draining. "Maybe if you weren't alone."

Isla bit the inside of her cheek, recalling the last time she'd been in the killer's midst. "They run from everyone else." And then it dawned on her. "They…trust me, for some reason."

A WARRIOR'S FATE

She wondered what was going through his head as he went quiet and then shook it a few moments. "No. It's too dangerous. I don't really want you to be *anywhere* alone right now. Not when things are like this."

"Hurting me also hurts you," Isla argued in favor of Ezekiel's sparing her in his plans.

She felt rage simmer at the other end of the bond, within Kai, at the thought of anyone laying a finger on her, as he maybe remembered how it had felt. Her in trouble, her in pain, when the only way he could reach her was this tether between them. When it strained and pulled, while a part of him, intentionally or not, kept her rooted to the world.

They fell into silence, and she felt Kai again, watched him drift into that place of solitude. Sparing her from all of this, what she shouldn't have had to deal with to be with him.

Without a word, she pushed up from her seat and circled the desk. Once at his side, his eyes flicking her way, she leaned down, pressing her lips to Kai's forehead, his temple, his cheek, and as a small grin bloomed on his mouth, he tugged her down to sit on his knee and she lay another on his neck.

Isla wrapped her arms around him, as he did her, and with her head leaning against his, Kai closed his eyes—and breathed. Breathed in her scent, embraced her touch, the bond coiling around him, grounding him.

Time slipped away while they sat in the quiet as he continued to think. She waited, not pushing, knowing that eventually—

"I spent my entire life telling myself I'd never be like my father," Kai began, tracing an idle circle over her thigh. "And then I became alpha, and that's all I've done. I thought adopting his council, his beta would make it easier. For me. For the pack to adjust and feel secure after so much—change. Fast change…forced change. But I've been alpha for three months—*three months*—and we've been attacked by rogues, bak are slipping through the Wall, and witches are using our territory to hide and hurt other wolves. Who hurt *you*." His circling ceased. "There were—*are*—plans for an attack that I don't even know about. I've made everyone more vulnerable than they even know."

"Your father made them vulnerable," Isla said quietly. "And Ezekiel's kept them that way, among others."

"I should've realized."

"Maybe, maybe not. But you know *now*, and what matters is how we fix it." His stare burned into hers, the *"we"* seeming to touch something inside him. "You're not doing things alone anymore. You can do your little alpha protective thing, but we're a team now."

He smiled, and his broad hand settled flat on her thigh. Leaning forward, he pressed a kiss to her jaw. "There's a lot going on with Io. It's going to be like that for a while."

Lukas's words echoed in Isla's head, along with that gutting urge to get him out. *A lot of bad blood.* She should've known since the Hunt. "I know."

"And you *want* to know," Kai tested.

He'd keep her out of things?

"Of course, I want to know."

Kai squeezed her thigh in a haste affirmation. "Okay."

Isla let out a breath and gazed down, lifting her fingers to play with the collar of his shirt, his skin, and finding a pattern of the tattoo beneath it. "Even when I lived in Io, I knew there were dark and light sides to the pack. Maybe not as *dark* as they seem to be, but there's that split everywhere." *Even here*, she thought but didn't mention. "I have great memories and not-so-great ones from my time there, and I can hold onto them, but—I just have to look at things differently now. There's Io, there's my family, and then there's what matters most." She raised her eyes to meet his, flattening her hand on his chest over his heart. "My future here. With Deimos. With you. The waters are messy, but I can get through them."

Something in Kai's eyes gleamed, and he was still as if the words had arrested him, stunned him, and then she felt him squeeze her again. As if to check if she was, in fact, there. In fact, real. He leaned up to kiss her again, tentative and restrained, given he'd pulled away a few seconds after she kissed him back.

As Kai lazily lolled his head back, smiling up at her in that way that made her want to melt into him, *down* on him, she bit her lip. "And speaking of *futures*." She began fiddling with his collar again. "We have not been careful about what could enter ours."

Kai raised his brows, and the easy smile grew as he chuckled. "*No, we have not.*" His hold on her tightened a bit as if all those *not-so-careful* moments had just tumbled through his head. Isla narrowed her eyes at him—though they'd gone through hers, too. Another laugh before his face settled into that sweet, gleaming look again. "When?"

When would they start their family…

Isla's stomach fluttered, and with him there, staring at her like that, she didn't feel any numbing fear.

"I know we'll need an heir, sooner rather than later," she said. "But a year to adjust to it all—a year of just us—sounds good."

Kai nodded, and Isla could sense and hear the way his heart had sped up. He was excited. Nervous. "Then a year it is."

He pressed another kiss to her mouth. Another. Then another. Harder. Deeper. Lower.

"Kai," she protested, though beaming, as his lips had gone to her neck. He simply laughed against her throat before nipping at it. She held her moan. "Defeating the conversation."

Kai pulled back, but not before pressing one more to her lips. "I have to go anyway." Isla slid from his lap as he rose from the chair. "And you're going to Jonah—who Goddess knows must be still in the library if he hadn't turned in to the House."

Isla nodded before glancing at the phone on Kai's desk. Her hands became anxious fists at her sides. "Can I make a call?"

"To?"

"My brother or Adrien—or likely them together, honestly." Kai's mouth opened, but words didn't escape right away. Understandable, given the climate of the prior conversation. In his hesitation, she added, "The news of the challenge has probably spread, and they know about us. They may be worried about me."

Kai closed his mouth before conceding a nod. His throat bobbed. "You know—you know you can't tell them anything, right? Not yet. Maybe not ever."

Isla didn't feel like she had a right to be offended. It was an honest question. One even she'd ask herself given how freely she was used to sharing things with them, and them, her. "Of course, I know."

Another *okay* from him, just as fast. He kissed her gently with a muttered—and then echoed—*I love you*, before he left the office.

When he was gone, Isla fell into the cushioned seat, large enough to make even Kai seem small, and dominating her with its width and high back, the top etched with a crescent-like crown above her head.

She glanced at the clock.

It was nearly ten now. They could honestly be anywhere. A training ring, the hall, or either of their homes.

Isla braced her hand on the slick exterior of the phone, her heart leaping into her throat.

She'd call them, they'd talk about the challenge, and she could offer nothing else. Maybe she could ask if they'd heard anything about Lukas? Ask what was going on at home? Or—just Io, as it was now.

She clenched her teeth.

Would sharing things with her put *them* at risk? Be some sort of treason? Now that she and Kai were *officially* mated, now that she'd be crowned the Luna of Deimos, would they distance themselves?

Isla's throat was too dry to swallow again, but shakily, she spun a number in, getting through all the arduous, necessary networks and hurdles to cross pack lines and reach Sebastian's townhouse.

Then the phone rang and rang and rang, and they didn't answer.

Isla put the receiver down and didn't try again.

∽

There was no music playing when Isla entered the library. No other sounds but the ruffle of turning pages and faint mumbling of a *singular* person.

Jonah had been moving when she turned the corner of the stacks into the common area. She noted that his pile of books had grown substantially, and he was *also* still in the clothes he'd worn yesterday.

Kai had been right. He hadn't left.

"As much as I appreciate it personally, you will need to stop at some point," she called to him, adjusting the box settled under her arm. *And change. And bathe.*

Jonah glanced at her—no surprise in his features since he'd heard the door—before returning to the tome before him.

Isla sighed. "Who's taking care of the shop while you're here?"

"I'm not the only one who works there," Jonah said.

Isla slipped the box on the sliver of space on the table, left after she'd nudged a book over, to his annoyance. She popped open the lid to reveal it was full of pastries she'd gone back to the House and grabbed before coming here.

Jonah's nose twitched, and he glanced up at the food. Then back to the book. "You know we shouldn't eat in here."

Isla flashed him a blank look, even if he wasn't looking. "You're welcome."

She could've sworn the corner of his lips raised in some semblance of a smile. "Luna now and making your own rules."

"What's the point if I can't?" she mused before taking the stack of napkins from her pockets. She plucked one from the top before grabbing one pastry and placing it on it to present to him. "Eat. As your queen, I demand you don't die in my library."

Jonah laughed and stopped what he was doing. He stood up straight, twinging a bit, likely from being hunched over for so long. On cue with his reach for the treat, his stomach growled, making Isla smirk. He snickered and said before his bite, "As you wish, Your Majesty."

Isla rolled her eyes. "Have you even gone to the bathroom?"

"There's one on the second floor." Jonah jutted his chin upwards, and Isla followed his eyes to the mezzanine.

She hummed before turning back and ripping off a piece of pastry for herself. "Anything new?" She popped it in her mouth and took in the spread, eyes sliding to the artwork of that woman on the far end of the table, the diadem beside it. Her chewing slowed, and swallowing was difficult. "Anything about *her*?"

Jonah clocked the reaction. "I haven't gotten anywhere with that, but *maybe* the journal." After downing his pastry in three impressive bites, he shuffled through some documents. "Most of the knowledge of Phobos, for the public, was destroyed but—"

"How?" Isla cut him off. Her stomach twisted, having a hunch of what the answer may be.

Jonah ceased his movement and straightened again. "There are no *confirmations*—those who had done it were quick and eerily effective —but there is a strong chance that it was Io."

Of course.

Isla didn't have the energy to ask why. Didn't think her mind could handle the *why*. Maybe never wanted to know, at all.

So, she urged him to continue as he was.

Jonah eyed her cautiously, but then began again. "Knowledge of Phobos was destroyed, but I could piece some things together from texts of Deimos chronicling the same timeframe before the decimation. I figured out what the dates were of the entries and mapped them to these fragments here. Colliding with Io seems to be a popular pastime."

At Isla's heaved breath, he added, "Though it's not just Io, it's other packs, too. We tend to ally with the more southern territories, further from Io's reach in the north. From the language in these speeches, from what I can translate of our native dialect, it seems like some territory war. Io had the strength—a lot of warriors deemed from those coliseum trials and battles. And they had bigger numbers, too, even with Ganymede, since Io's population was surging once they'd recovered from the eruption. Deimos, Phobos, the allies in Mimas and Tethys were outmatched and outnumbered. But Aneurin..." He pointed to a line of text in Deimos's native tongue that Isla had no hope of translating. "Apparently, Aneurin had a weapon. A great one. Big enough that he had *personally* come to Deimos and traveled to those other packs to assure them of their victory, and even persuaded Iapetus *and* Rhea to join the fight."

"A convincing guy," Isla said.

"Indeed," Jonah said through a breath. "I bet that Aneurin's writing about whatever the weapon is, and he doesn't want anyone to know about it."

Isla leaned against the table, eyes trailing across the pieces. A weapon sounded *very* familiar. "But what could it be?" she whispered, more to herself. "There were no bak then."

"Bak?"

She flicked her gaze up to Jonah. "Would it be possible for a witch to control the bak?" He raised his brows, and she *somewhat* elaborated, "I could try to explain it all to you, but it's a lot—and I may need alcohol to do it. But in short, a witch is to blame for most of this. Kyran and Jaden's deaths included. Would it be possible for her to control them?"

Jonah flattened his mouth but didn't ask questions. "It's…unlikely. The bak were created by some pretty powerful magic."

"I know, Kai told me. It's why we have the Wall, and all of them aren't dead."

"It's difficult to alter a dead witch's curse, not to mention one that potent. It would only work if this witch you're talking about is *stronger* than she had been."

A shiver crawled up Isla's spine. "*Stronger* than the witch that decimated Phobos?"

That had destroyed all that land and *murdered* all those people.

Jonah nodded, fear even flickering in his eyes.

It couldn't match hers, though, writhing in her gut, scraping at her bones. Because all she could think about was Io. If Alpha Kyran had unleashed a weapon such as that on it. Those streets, the ones she'd grown up on, gilded in gold, bathed in blood blending with the burgundy drapery. Red stone dust valleys caked in darker crimson. Her family—

Isla flinched.

Luna of Deimos or not, as a person, as a wolf, unleashing that kind of hell and destruction on any of their kind, *any* kind…*that* was unthinkable.

She swallowed hard and shifted down the table to the artwork and the diadem, the dagger buried under some papers.

"The witch had this or something like this," she told Jonah, who inclined his head, asking how she knew. Isla hesitated, debating if this, all of this, had been safe to share. But Jonah was Kai's family, and he'd said she could trust him. "Ezekiel, he lied. He knew about the tunnels and he knows about this witch."

Jonah's eyes blew wide, likely thinking and worrying as she had. For Kai. "Is she…"

"Kai doesn't think she's a threat right now—and he's dealing with Ezekiel."

Jonah's features twisted into a scowl. "That guy is a dick." Blunt and to the point.

Isla snorted. "You don't say."

"He never liked me and Rhydian. Neither did Kyran, frankly," Jonah said, surprising her with his openness, maybe even shocking himself. He rubbed his face harshly like he'd been sleep-deprived and hadn't meant for the words to come out. His explanation of why was to the point of his insult, "Our father wasn't a good man."

Isla knew not to press, only replied softly, "Seems to be a trend I'm finding." Her gaze returned to the diadem, her voice still soft. One confession in answer to another. "My father isn't a bad guy. At least, I don't think he is…I never thought he was."

Jonah didn't press either.

Isla shifted the papers away from the dagger to take it in, and her fingers caressed the metal. A coolness eddied through her body, and she took a breath. That was…new. She brushed it again and dared to pick it up, her grip constricting over the hilt. She gazed at her reflection in the metal, speckled with gold. The weapon hummed as she twisted and angled it through the air, and its three sisters, the diadem pieces, sang to her, too. So delicate, so soft and lilting, yet jilted and hurt. Drawing her to lift them, to care for them as well.

She put the dagger down, not rushed but careful.

Jonah had been watching her closely.

"You said if these were cursed, if they were—influenced by some sort of magic—I would've already been dead." He nodded, intrigue crossing his face. "What if I'm not because it's broken?"

"The crown?"

"I mean, we never stopped to wonder why *a crown* was in pieces. Who broke it? Why?"

Jonah took a couple of steps forward, peering at the items. "I suppose it's possible. But if it's also *her* diadem—judging by her clothes, by the wear on this, she's old. That's old. For that magic to linger, to persist after being broken, it would've come from a potent source, a deep well of power."

"Could it be the witch that destroyed Phobos?"

"I don't see why we'd have an image of her around here."

So imbued by another deep source of power, then.

Isla turned on a heel to head for the pile of books on witches and their continent that she'd left on a small desk that hadn't been shelved yet.

"What are you doing?" Jonah called after her.

Heaving the tomes into her arms, she brought them back to the table. "Getting books."

"You're staying?"

Isla raised her brows in challenge. "Would there be an issue if I was?"

Jonah mustered another grin, plucked out another pastry, and sat down. "Of course not, Your Majesty."

∽

Somehow, the days leading up to the challenge were more strenuous than Isla's days leading up to her warrior debut here in Deimos. So much happening, so many movements, she didn't know which way was up or down. Though they were more aware of the pieces on the board now, there were some additional ones needed to be kept track of. A lot of pieces they were waiting to watch make their move and react, and a lot of bases they had to ensure were covered.

While protocol forced Kai to endure meeting after meeting—even *more* than he'd experienced transitioning to alpha—as well as preparations and training to ensure he was in *fighting* shape, Isla fluttered from place to place, becoming a general of sorts in a different manner. Never alone, she worked with those they trusted, which were Jonah, Davina, Ameera, Rhydian, and Unit 37B.

Jonah continued focusing his work on the journal. Given the mention of an ancient weapon, his curiosity had been piqued. And since it held the same language as the markers, it was their best shot at figuring out what was where within the tunnels. When Isla was with him, she alternated between looking into witches and looking into the poisons of the world. What worked on wolves, *how* they worked. Nothing seemed to be the one that had been used against them.

Efforts on the rogue front, down at the southeastern border, had been amplified, and Rhydian, along with the warriors, aside from Isla, patrolled frequently. But the rogues didn't move, barely even a whisper as if they were waiting to emerge the day of the challenge. Isla had asked Kai if any of them had the right to *be* at the battle—as it was another rogue fighting—but he'd said that didn't matter. They wouldn't be permitted in. *No one* had been permitted in, including refugees from Charon.

For those that were already within Deimos's borders, Isla went to their homes with Davina who she'd learned was a refugee of Charon herself.

"I made it into Deimos about a year before I met Rhydian," she'd said, fighting back tears as she finally told Isla her story in the darkness of the House's den, a fire roaring before them.

She divulged the information in bits and pieces, but emotion would overcome her before she got too detailed. Isla learned of how Charon's economy had been a slow collapse over the last decades, leading up to the point where no one had any money, everything going to pay high taxes to fund pack leadership's questionable endeavors. Davina told her of how outside the kingdom's heavily guarded capital, Ayr, where most finances were funneled to, the streets were falling apart, the crime rate high, death not uncommon due to that or disease.

Davina could barely speak of her parents, mostly because she barely knew them. Imprisoned when she was young, forcing her to live with her neighbors and their cruel children, they never came back for her as they'd promised once they'd been released.

It was when she was sobbing that she shared the day she'd overheard at the rundown marketplace that Deimos would take refugees in if they were able to make it through the rogue lands to its borders. How she'd been frightened until *something* had happened that made it clear she'd rather die than live another day there.

And so, a few days after her twenty-third birthday, along with another woman she'd met on the edge of Charon's pack territory, Davina had left. And all Isla would let her explain then, as panic had clearly racked Davina's paling form while Isla tried to soothe her, was that she'd made it into Abalys *alone* weeks later—weak, starving, and traumatized.

Then she worked to make a life for herself here…and then she met her mate. The handsome member of Deimos's guard who would go on to love and protect her in a way no one ever had, and how no one else ever would.

Isla hadn't let Davina see the anger that had festered within her. She waited until the secretary had gone before the emotions took over, and she fought the urge to go into Charon and rip Alpha Locke to shreds. Imperial Alpha Cassius, too, if he was taking part in this.

And her father…

Isla checked in with Ameera sparingly.

Though the general had put on a brave face, one of a leader of the highest order, the news of her father's actions, his secret, had rattled her. Him lying to Kai—she took it as a betrayal to her, too.

The two warrior women rarely crossed paths that week, only when Ameera found Kai in those perfect moments when Ezekiel had been at the hall and Kai on a break, when he and Isla would take a moment to just *be* with each other for a few seconds. And though she could've stayed, Isla took it as her cue to go. There was something else she could do, and Kai would've told her later, anyway.

Though, Ezekiel, frankly, hadn't been doing much out of the ordinary—keeping Ameera occupied, of course, when Isla would've been happy to have her by her side.

Without her, Isla and Rhydian had taken it upon themselves to scout where the tunnels fed into Deimos. Jonah couldn't find any type of map of them, and Callan's didn't offer much. It seemed he'd been guessing their locations.

Reassuring was the fact that even if the Wall's wards were breaking down, since the Hunt—since the witch, *possibly*—the bak weren't moving in packs. At least, not close by. Most of them remained in their favored areas away from the Wall, the ones in the tunnel by the guard base, as well as the wasteland were anomalies.

Still, Isla was asked—basically told—never to go to the house alone, even if she'd figured that was her best chance at contacting the killer.

And hence—Unit 37B.

One of the few units assigned to patrol the Wall's borders. And they served nothing more.

Magnus, the obnoxious asshole, had no idea he may have been on the brink of achieving his warrior dreams.

In the trips Isla had taken down into Surles with the unit along with Rhydian, she'd learned the male guard was quite a fan of her mate. Frequently spouting how Kai would destroy his rogue opponent and show Imperial Alpha Cassius in the process that Deimos wasn't a pack to be messed with.

Because Kai's victory was "*his*" victory.

Now she understood the morale he'd been talking about.

But of course, Magnus couldn't let go of the fact Isla was of Io—at least, to *his* knowledge—and she contemplated on many instances going into the backseat of their vehicle, as Rhydian drove them, and chucking him out into the streets.

It was on one of their later nights on patrol that she found herself at her wit's end, and whipped around to face him, wedged between Thyra and Belle on their ride back to Mavec a couple of hours before dusk.

"Do you want to know the truth?" she'd seethed, lowering the neckline of her warrior uniform, flashing her mark. "I'm Alpha Kai's mate, and I swear to the Goddess if you don't stop talking *right now*, the first thing I'm going to do when I'm crowned luna is…"

She'd trailed off once she realized she had a gaping audience and heard Rhydian laugh beside her.

There hadn't been doubt in their eyes, something about her, her demeanor, they knew she meant it.

Belle had cursed in disbelief, Thyra had nearly cried, and Magnus had paled, turned green, opened a window, and paled again. Then he'd been blissfully silent for the rest of the ride and went statue stiff every time she passed him for days on later.

But unfortunately, those prior hours of suffering had been for nothing. The killer never showed up. Never left another clue. Not as, on intermittent nights, Isla perched herself in one of the broken chairs of the house and waited. She wasn't dumb enough to venture into the tunnels alone. Not desperate enough, but close.

Close enough that on the rare occasions where she and Kai could be together, he asked her a few times to be sure that she hadn't done anything rash.

She cherished those moments with him and found it cruel that these days, when sometimes it felt like their time together was running out, they were too busy to see each other. Most nights, they met in their bed, each too tired to do anything but share a kiss and pass out. Other nights, pleasure, release, and relief from the day's stresses were found quickly, *and then* sleep would take them.

There had been *one day* that Isla had seen him while awake for quite a few hours. When she'd gone to visit him while he'd been working out, he beckoned her down from the mezzanine overlooking the training fields to join him. Half-nude and sweaty, their running of drills and their sparring with practice swords—which Isla stood by she'd been victorious in, a greater master in the intricacies of weapons' handling while he edged her out in brute strength and ferocity—hadn't lasted long…

But Isla was grateful for the busyness. Grateful that she barely had time to think.

Because in those free moments, her mind drifted to Io. To the threat ahead. To her father. To Sebastian and Adrien.

She'd finally spoken with them but only briefly. Only to tell them that she was okay, everything would *be* okay, and that they should remain in Io.

She didn't tell them she didn't want them in Deimos. Didn't tell them the risk was too great. That she barely trusted anyone or their intentions, and she wouldn't be able to live with herself if anything ever happened to them.

And after that, after she'd hung up the phone—overwhelmed and a *touch* lonely in the silence of Kai's office, curled in that large, regal chair—she'd cried. For a life she knew she'd need to let go, for the people she may have had to, too.

Then she picked herself up and went back to work.

∾

Three days.

Only *three days* remained until the full moon. Until the challenge.

It had been yet another hectic twenty-four hours being here and there, everywhere and nowhere. But tonight. Tonight, three days out, they'd take a small break. A breather to gather in Jonah's bookshop as a family and not speak at all of what loomed ahead. Just drink and laugh and be with each other—if that were possible.

Isla's muscles were stiff as she settled into the armchair, a freshly poured glass of wine between her fingers. Davina, to her surprise, was firm in her stance of not consuming alcohol, holding a cup of water at her side.

The redhead surveyed the room. "Where are Ameera and Rhydian?"

"You don't know where he is?" Isla asked.

Davina ran a hand over her braid. "I—I thought he'd be back from the rogue borders hours ago."

Worry flashed in her eyes, and Isla wondered if she did as Isla frequently had with Kai in their distance, assessing the bond, making sure Rhydian was sound on the other side.

"I asked them to run an errand for me." Kai stepped forward from where he'd been talking with Jonah. He sipped from his whiskey, and Isla grimaced when he looked at her, practically feeling the burning in her own throat. He only winked and drained the rest of the glass.

He didn't elaborate on what the job had been, and though they had met him with curious stares, Jonah and Davina didn't ask. Likely figured it was alpha business. But if *that* were the case.

"*What errand?*" Isla asked Kai through the bond. He'd been in a playful mood all day, and she'd attributed those high spirits to the upcoming gathering. But this...

Kai poured more whiskey, not looking at her as the corner of his lips ticked upwards. *"I'll tell you later."*

"Why later?"

He didn't answer. Never had a chance to as a knock came at the shop's door.

Davina let out a sigh of relief, a hand on her chest. "There he is." She traipsed over to the door to turn each of the locks. Only three of the five engaged today.

Isla downed the rest of her wine and rose to her feet to get herself another.

But when she'd gotten upright as the entrance opened and a chilled Mavec summer wind swept through, carrying Rhydian and Ameera —*and guests*—she nearly fell over.

Because standing in the doorway—in The Bookshoppe, in Deimos, grinning at her like they'd gotten away with a robbery—were Adrien and Sebastian.

CHAPTER 46

Isla wondered if the noise that had escaped her lips sounded as pained as it felt in her throat. Something between a choke and a gasp, bolstered by the dryness of the wine and driven by some melding of fear and excitement. Elation and anger.

For a moment, she thought her mind had been playing tricks on her. That it had been pulled in so many directions this past week that the *here and now* was becoming muddied with memories of the past. She took in the two men who both appeared just as she remembered, but though it had only been a few weeks, it had felt like a lifetime had passed since they'd been together.

Maybe because it had been just that—a different life.

She couldn't get her feet to move.

What the hell were they doing here? She'd told them to *stay home*.

"Are you drunk already?" Sebastian shattered the silence and tension she hadn't realized was rising. It earned snickers and clipped laughs from around the room, but no one dared to speak a word. Either feeding off her reaction or being shocked themselves by the visitors.

Isla opened and closed her mouth. "Am I…"

A piece of the reality she'd been missing was finally clicking into place.

Sebastian had said those words.

Sebastian, her brother.

Goddess above, they were here.

Abandoning her glass on the table, in a movement so quick, Kai had to stop it from falling off, Isla bound forward. Rhydian, Davina, and Ameera only had a few seconds to clear the path.

Both Adrien and Sebastian let out a cough as she rammed into them, going up on her toes to throw one arm around each of their necks, pulling them down to her. They both smelled of fuel and metal and wood smoke, from a car, maybe an inn. But most importantly, they smelled of Io. Of the salty air of the Barit Sea, of warm sand, of rocky plains, with subtle hints of ash lily that she always felt permeated the air.

It awakened something in her, a part that had been dulled but still craved. That missed.

Missed that heat and those perfect summer nights as the humid air cooled to something temperate, the warm breeze rolling past, rustling her hair as the three of them sat on a cliffside, watching as the sun cast oranges and yellows and reds amidst fading blues over the distant horizon. Nights she cherished, even in their simplicity.

She could hear them laughing, could feel their loose grips on her, each with a hand on her back.

Adrien was the one who spoke first. "Glad to see you missed us, too." Relief slipped into his voice, and it felt as if he'd looked at Sebastian and shrugged.

Her brother's shoulders rose and fell, communication she couldn't see, before he patted her back. "It's been weird without your nagging all the time."

Isla, whose eyes had slid closed during the embrace, snapped them open to glare at the side of each of their heads. When she unfurled herself and stepped back, she found they were, in fact, relieved by her positive reaction.

Idiots.

She held back her glower, just long enough for them to settle, before she shoved them both—hard. "Why do neither of you ever fucking listen to me?"

"And there's Isla," Adrien muttered, rubbing his arm.

Sebastian scoffed, rolling his shoulder. "Yeah, hello to you, too, Pudge."

"Pudge?" She heard Rhydian question from behind her. He, along with Davina and Ameera had moved to the other side of the room, dividing it evenly between the wolves born of the north and central packs.

"He has many names for her," Kai replied, voice dancing with an amusement that should've tipped her off, but she was too focused on her family before her to think.

"Why are you here?" She continued to glower between the boys, despite the excitement blooming in her chest. Worry for them usurped it.

"I can't visit my sister?"

"Not when she tells you not to." She pointed her glare at Sebastian. "How—how did you even get beyond the borders?"

Her brother jutted his chin. "Called in a favor with the brother-in-law."

His brother-in-law?

Isla tilted her head, the words sounding so foreign before they clicked.

A warmth spread through her, a fluttering at the fact Kai was becoming a part of *her* family.

But then it clicked again.

Isla whipped around and found her mate smiling wryly, standing a few inches closer than everyone else. Either because he'd stepped forward or they'd shrunk back. Behind him, Ameera was pouring a sizable glass of liquor.

One night before bed, half-asleep, Kai had asked her how the talks with her family had gone, and she'd told him she assured the boys that she was okay and that they didn't need to come for the challenge. That seemed to surprise him enough to crack his eyes open a bit wider, and upon the slight catch of her voice as she explained further, he pulled her close. She confessed that she'd wanted them there but couldn't risk it. Any of it. Their safety in Deimos or their safety in Io for fraternizing with her.

Yet, here they were.

"You did this?" Isla asked.

Kai opened his mouth, ready to defend himself, and then closed it. "He is unnervingly convincing." He tipped his glass towards Sebastian. "I couldn't say no."

Isla blinked. Though it felt like there was much more unsaid she could push him for, the situation he presented sounded so bizarre it distracted her. She could barely picture it without wanting to laugh. Sebastian phoning Kai, maybe in the middle of the day, maybe cutting through a meeting, after convincing several operators that he had dire news to deliver to the Alpha of Deimos. Only for Kai to pause whatever he was doing to pick up, to entertain her brother's nonsense, and then scheme a way to get him here. Both of them, here.

As if he could feel the emotions battling within her, Kai's voice became a caress in her mind. *"I wouldn't have let them in if I didn't think they'd be safe, no matter how much they asked. I promise I won't let anything happen to them."*

"Well, it *is* family night."

Everyone's eyes went to Davina who'd stepped forward. She was the unofficial organizer of the night, ensuring that each day leading up to this, everyone knew the gathering was about having fun and forgetting about everything. There was to be no talk of the challenge or Ares or Phobos or rogues. She'd already confiscated Jonah's research and shoved it beneath the counter.

This was a night to simply be with each other—a night Isla desperately needed—and though there were three men in this room that she was ready to kill, they were arguably the three who cared for her most and her, them. She'd let them have it, but for now—

Isla turned back to Adrien and Sebastian, both tensing.

"You are both dumbasses," she said before going on her toes and throwing her arms around them again. "And I did miss you."

They both let out sighs of relief, and she sensed Kai relax, too.

She sent back through the bond, *"I'm not done with you yet."*

A laugh echoed in her head.

"I figured."

The following round of formal introductions was more awkward than she'd expected. Sebastian had gone over easily, earning waves and quiet *hellos*, but presenting Adrien as solely her best friend, family, too—something *other* than the Heir to the position held highest above them all—had earned blank stares and exchanged glances.

Rhydian was the one who asked, "Are we supposed to bow?"

Isla looked back at Adrien as he lifted a hand. "No, I'm just here as a friend. For Isla." He gestured towards Kai. "For you."

Isla rose a brow as Kai and Adrien met each other's stares and held like they were having their own form of secret communication. It hadn't dawned on her how similar they were, how frequently they were drawn to converse with each other. Sat together at the feast all those months ago—when her mate had first asked the Heir about who she was—and speaking again at the Gate. There was mutual respect and understanding between them, the only people in this room born of alpha blood with a heap of expectation on their shoulders.

It was that respect, Isla figured, that had Kai bowing his head anyway, albeit shallowly. At his side, the other four of his family did the same.

Isla finished presenting everyone else to the boys, ending with Rhydian and then Ameera who'd picked them up at the borders.

At the general's assumed second introduction, Sebastian chuckled. "We've met."

Isla wasn't sure what had happened on their trip into the city, but fire lit in Ameera's eyes as she downed her heftily filled glass of liquor and replied smoothly, "So we have."

Isla's brows shot up. All of them appeared taken aback, except for Rhydian.

Were they—flirting?

"What the hell was that?"

Isla looked at Kai, whose brows were drawn in confusion. She shrugged at him. *"I have no idea."*

"Wait, are you two doing the mate thing?" Sebastian's voice made her jump.

Before she could answer with a jab for him to mind his business, Ameera declared, "Well, no more tonight!" She picked up the decanter again while pointing a finger between both Isla and Kai. "We are making this a no-mate-to-mate-secret-communication zone. No mind-flirting or mind-fucking or whatever you two do. Make things obvious so I can see myself far away. I'm not dealing with it."

Isla cringed, and she heard Adrien taunt quietly behind her, "Mind what?"

"Shut up," she mumbled back.

"Looks like someone needs to get laid," Jonah mused beneath his breath after a low whistle, but loud enough for Ameera, who had since turned to gesture a warning at Rhydian and Davina, to hear. Needless to say, on her next spin, her fist made contact with his shoulder.

And at that moment—as Isla *also* caught the way Sebastian's eyebrows rose at the statement and heard Adrien murmur for him to *relax* since they'd only been there for *two Goddess-forsaken hours*—she felt an even deeper understanding with the female general.

By fate or by choice, since they were children, their lives were forever entwined with their respective idiots for male companions who, somehow, they wouldn't trade for anyone else.

And true to form—

Sebastian stepped forward, and Isla resisted the urge to grab him before he said anything stupid to incite Ameera's annoyance any further.

Her brother's eyes roved over the spread of alcohol. "So, this is the party, huh?"

Isla tensed as Ameera whirled back on him and stilled. She took all of it in—him, the booze, the family—and something shocking flashed behind her eyes.

Sheer frustration and hurt. Not *at them*, and not an entire brokenness, but a fracturing Isla had seen too frequently with her lately. Always during those times when she would bid Ameera goodbye so the general could discuss Ezekiel's movements with Kai. Tonight, while she was certain her parents were having their "date night" together, had been her only reprieve.

"You want a party?" Ameera countered, that look disappearing as quickly as it had shown up, though there was still an edge to her voice. She held Sebastian's eyes but addressed the room, "Let's go to Abalys."

At the mention of the region, Kai, Rhydian, and Jonah appeared to perk up, smiles sliding across their faces. Even Isla felt the corners of her mouth ticking upwards.

"Abalys?" Davina's nose scrunched as if she could already scent the river town.

Ameera hummed in affirmation, breaking eye contact with the Imperial Beta's eldest and finishing her second drink. "Kai's challenge is in three days, and I've just had one of the worst weeks of my life. I want to go out, I want to get drunk, I want to play cards, and maybe—" She cast a glare at Jonah. "Maybe I'll get laid, who knows."

Sebastian pointed. "I don't know what this place is, but I'm in."

Ameera snickered. "Of course, you are."

Discussions on whether the trip would be smart or safe were had in haste, and it wasn't long before all of them agreed that a night out, like old times, was truly what they needed. Adrien and Sebastian had to simply not broadcast who they were. Lay low.

Isla hoped to the Goddess that was possible.

As everyone began grabbing their coats, sneaking alcohol beneath the fabric, and shuffling towards the shop's door, Kai came to Isla's side and set her jacket on her shoulders.

She held him back as he moved to walk with her and called to the rest of the group, who'd nearly all exited, "We'll meet you outside in a minute."

"Well, I should've expected that," Kai muttered before taking a few steps back to sit on the table, settling in for whatever she had to say.

"My rule stands!" she heard Jonah yell from the street.

"What rule?"

Isla winced, hoping Sebastian never got the answer.

Adrien, too, who she also realized had been exceptionally quiet.

Though her brother typically overpowered any conversation, the Imperial Heir didn't tend to shy away within a group.

The final one to exit, Adrien paused in the doorway, one hand on the handle. He turned to look at her and Kai, mouth moving like he was about to say something before he shut it. "See you outside," he eventually offered, before closing the door.

Weird, Isla thought before becoming very aware of the eyes boring into her back.

Her brows flattened as she spun slowly—so, so slowly—to find Kai flashing her one of those disarming grins. Her deadpan look didn't waver.

He reached out to take her hands, his touch warm and inviting, as he pulled her close. "Have I ever told you," he began, his voice as languid as the movement he made to wrap his arms around her waist and bring her to settle in a spot between his legs, "how beautiful you are?"

Isla held her scowl, though her heart skipped at the feeling of his fingers dancing over a small sliver of skin he'd begun tracing beneath the hem of her shirt. "Not going to work." She placed her hands on his forearms, loosening a heavy breath. "You should've told me."

"It was a surprise."

"This isn't something you surprise me with. I told you I didn't want them here. That I didn't think it was safe."

"I won't let anything happen to them," Kai assured, continuing his ministrations on her skin. "And they were just going to end up here anyway. Alpha Cassius wasn't keen on his only Heir being here, but Adrien knew he could sneak away for a few days. They called me with a plan, not to ask permission."

Not surprising on the Imperial Alpha's part. Isla didn't bother querying how Adrien felt he could "sneak away".

"You're the alpha," she argued. "They need your permission."

"Not when the goal, if all else fails, is getting arrested here for trespassing."

Get arrested and thrown in a Deimos prison. That was one way to do it.

"You can't be serious," Isla said to which Kai nodded. "How are they so Goddess-damn stupid?"

"They love you. I can't say I'd go to any lesser lengths in the circumstances."

"But I told them I didn't need them here."

"Maybe you don't, but maybe *they* do." Kai swallowed, hesitating. "Maybe I do."

At her questioning expression, he removed one of his hands from her back to brush a hair from her face. He focused on it, the way he tucked it behind her ear and drew his fingers down her neck, avoiding her eyes as he confessed gently, "This entire week, meeting after meeting, has been about preparing for the worst-case scenario. What we can line up to make any transitions easier in case I…" Another hard gulp, but Isla felt the unspoken words like a punch in the stomach.

In case he died.

"And I realized I hadn't been taking care of the most important part of my life." He met her eyes now, his stare shadowed. "If anything happens to me…if anything happens, I want you to be okay. I need to know that you could be. That you have people here."

Isla's heart leaped into her throat, her chest left hollow. She felt like she'd suffocate on it. In a blink, she became the man kneeling before the body of his dead wife in the courtyard after the rogue attacks, her limp hand in his, Zahra at his back, the only form of comfort as he dwelled in the deepest darkness he'd ever come to know. The greatest, most maddening silence and emptiness all wolves were cursed to one day endure.

Three days.

There were only three days before that could become her reality. And as strong as she'd try to be, she knew it would shatter her, and she'd need the boys, need anyone, to get her through that moment. When their future could be snuffed out as quickly and easily as a candle.

"Oh."

It was the only word Isla could manage. So soft and cracked, it was barely audible. She willed her tears to remain at bay. Nothing had happened yet. No.

No.

Nothing *would*.

There was even a gleam in Kai's gaze as he brought both of his hands to her face, echoing her thoughts. "It's going to be fine. Just think of it as my own peace of mind. Theirs, too."

Despite the words, Isla still felt like her chest had caved in. Her limbs were shaky as panic still slithered beneath her skin. "Okay."

Kai leaned forward to press his mouth to hers, and the action made Isla feel worse before it did better. A further reminder of what there was to lose.

He pulled back and, noticing the tear that had slid down her cheek, swiped it away with his thumb. "We're going to be okay," he reassured her, forcing a smile that didn't reach his eyes.

Isla nodded, and then closed the distance between them again, kissing him deeply before she retreated to wrap her arms around his neck and lean into him.

He held her in silence, tight to his body, as she buried her face in the crook of his shoulder. She wasn't sure how long they remained like that—her listening to the sounds of his breathing, feeling his heartbeat against her chest, lulling with the way he rubbed his hands soothingly up and down her back—but eventually, he began pressing his lips to her neck.

Kai worked his way up her skin, back to her mouth, before kissing her one last time.

"Come on. No more challenge talk," he said, letting amusement adorn his tone, shine in his eyes. "Let's go get drunk, I'll show you how to play cards, and maybe," Another kiss. "Maybe we'll get laid."

Isla snorted and took a breath, albeit shakily, to pull herself together. To find comfort in the present, in their little games.

"If you're lucky," she teased, her hands dropping to trail down his chest. "I'm not sure about your chances. You still should've told me."

"Make me pay for it, then."

Isla raised her brows at the dare, lightly tugging on her lip with her teeth as she lowered her hands to run over his thighs. Close to certain precious parts—but not close enough. "You're going to regret saying that."

Kai tensed beneath her touch but laughed. "I'll deal with the consequences."

The kiss they shared this time—with Kai's tongue a sweeping tease along the seam of her lips—made Isla feel molten inside, made her skin feel too tight over her body and her clothes become too much. A kiss that blew the rest of the world, all other existence, away. That usually led to…

"Kai," Isla moaned his name over his mouth, the soft sound a weakness of his he'd stupidly divulged to her.

He tightened his hold on her waist, just as she'd expected and wanted, and timed perfectly with a pounding knock at the shop's door. Isla pulled away from him—as she'd initially planned to begin this night of teasing and *making him pay*"—while Kai grumbled.

"Screw on your own time!" Ameera yelled so loud they could hear it through the door. "Let's go!"

A WARRIOR'S FATE

"Almost done!" Isla shouted back before turning to Kai, whose eyes were narrowed at her.

"Cruel."

"You asked for it," she taunted before her tone became serious again. "I don't think she's okay."

Kai knew who she was talking about and gazed at the shut door. He raked a hand through his hair. "I know, but Ameera will say something when she needs someone. That's how she is. If we push too early, she shuts down and shuts out."

"And if we push too late?"

"We haven't let that happen," Kai said. His brows drew together in perplexity. "Is he really going to try to sleep with her?"

Sebastian.

"I can almost guarantee an attempt will be made."

Kai blanched. "Good luck to him, then. I know I promised I'd keep them safe from many things, but I'm not sure I can assure protection against Ameera."

As Kai rose, Isla took his hand and shrugged. "Well, one woman's going to have to teach him."

∼

Isla sighed and tucked further into Kai's warmth as the group splayed across the benches of the ferry to Abalys. The action wasn't necessary, the brine-tinged winds around the river not as chilled as the hilly city they'd departed, but she'd never turn down the opportunity.

She tried her hardest not to focus on the way Ameera and Sebastian were sitting before her, alongside Adrien, her brother's arm thrown behind the general, laying casually on the bench's back. But not touching her. Isla knew Ameera was aware of it, and she didn't seem to protest or recoil.

The seating of the vessel only catered to three persons at a time, maybe four, but given the size of the men, all muscle-bound and long-limbed, they couldn't get it to work comfortably. So, the eight had split off. Jonah, Rhydian, and Davina in the frontmost row, Adrien, Sebastian, and Ameera in the row behind, and Isla and Kai taking the back. It made it difficult for them to engage in the conversation being had—with Sebastian enrapturing the group in a tale of their youth, leaving out Io's name, while allowing Adrien to add in some commentary—but Isla was fine with it. Seeing them, hearing them, especially getting along well with the rest of the group, was enough for her.

Plus, it helped that their distance and the darkness had also made it easy for her to run her hand *absentmindedly* along Kai's thigh without watchful eyes. Made it so that Ameera couldn't see her occasional glances at her mate's face, which at times made it obvious what wicked things she was pondering mind-to-mind to him for when they got home.

On a particular contemplation—one that involved her making him wait at the foot of their bed while she took care of herself, with a rule that he could only watch—Kai adjusted in his seat, letting out an airy chuckle and throwing his head back in a way that had even more lewd thoughts whirring through her head. She bit down hard on her lip, catching the faint scarring of where her teeth had left a mark on him. Entirely hers, he was.

She could feel the desire coiling in her lower belly. It had been a while since they'd had sex that wasn't rushed or half-asleep. If *she* wanted to make it until the end of the night, to taunt him until they made it back to their bedroom, then she needed to stop.

As if sensing the rise between them now, Ameera turned slightly, narrowing her eyes to which Isla returned an innocent smile.

And then she distracted herself, moving her hand lower to rest on Kai's knee and looking out into the trees that lined the distant forest.

She tensed.

Nothing like the fear of seeing a pair of red eyes emerge from the darkness to kill one's libido.

Kai had either felt her tighten up or sensed the shift in her demeanor because he asked, casual but alert, "*Do you see something?*"

"*No.*" Isla faced forward again.

She knew that tonight was supposed to be free of talk of the challenge and all their other problems, but she couldn't shake them away entirely.

They hadn't been able to track down any other tunnel openings within the pack, Callan's map seeming to highlight a *theory* rather than actual locations when it came to its drawn lines.

If only he was around when she *wanted* to speak to him. But she hadn't seen him since that day in the forest when Kai threatened him to leave Deimos. It didn't appear to be a concern to anyone else. Never brought up by Eli or any of the other guards or warriors. Their silence made her warier than him still being here. She would imagine him leaving his post would've been an issue.

She thought back to that night in his room. The blood on the doorframe, on the piece of the diadem, the killer lurking in the shadows.

Where had *they* been this whole week?

It had felt like every minute, Isla was looking over her shoulder for them to appear, and now they were simply—silent.

Had she pushed them too far that night in the wasteland after reaching to unveil them? Were they *regretting* helping? Were they assisting the witch again? Had the witch *got* to them? Angry over what they'd done—or hadn't done. Not killing Kai that night.

Isla heaved a deep breath, trying to wrap her mind around how she could possibly be afraid for a monster.

∽

Isla and Kai, with their hoods thrown over their heads, had moved with her arm looped through his as the group strode down Abalys's wooden streets to Talha. Tonight, they'd decided, they wouldn't hide. Not any more than Kai would as the alpha out in public courting a woman for the night.

Mavec was the homestead of the key pack gossips, the ones that would deconstruct everything about her once it officially broke that the alpha had found his fated and a new luna was on her way. The ones that would either vilify her or…not be *so* horrible.

But in Abalys, the rule was what happened here, remained here. Kai had done many things—things he wouldn't disclose to Isla, brushing it off as him being young and stupid—that had never left these docks.

Specifically, hadn't left Talha.

It wasn't the first time Isla had been to the tavern the group favored, but it was the first time she'd gone inside to see it full and in its glory. The heat thwacked her in the face first, the expansive open floor packed with patrons, some flittering between the bar, their seats, or the dance floor near a raised platform where musicians were performing, or the corner where a few billiards tables had been set up. The smells were something to adjust to. Overwhelmingly of bitter ale and pungent spirits, body odor and the faintest hint of smoke, as if the hearth had been burning earlier. At least something smelled decent cooking in a kitchen somewhere.

The noise Sebastian had made sounded as if he'd died and gone off into eternity.

And from his spot behind her, a surprised Adrien muttered, *Goddess*, almost simultaneously with a patron in front of them.

Kai had dropped his hood, Isla realized, and she was happy she'd unfurled herself from him before they'd walked in. She wasn't sure if she would've been able to handle the attention.

The awareness of his presence was like a drop of water in an ocean, rippling across and defying all sense in the way it calmed the untamable.

Everyone, *everything*, came to a halt.

No music. No speaking. No eating. No drinking.

For a split second, it was only the sounds of everyone's breathing and heavy heartbeats.

Then came whispers, questions of if it were all some illusion.

And finally, the raucousness resumed.

Greetings were boisterous and plenty for *all of them* by the tavern's regulars, but mostly Kai.

Though the men and women of various ages offered him the respect he was owed as their leader, they also spoke with him as a friend they hadn't seen in a while. Some apologized for his losses, some shared their own. Shared their triumphs, new mates, new babies, new businesses. It had brought that light to his face that appeared too rarely. Like when he'd been talking to the guard members back at the base. A life he'd had and loved and missed. One that he'd never have again.

He didn't let her get lost as the conversations continued—it almost felt like a haphazard line had been forming to have an audience with him. While everyone else broke off further in the establishment to get drinks, Adrien and Sebastian included, she felt Kai, through the bond, tug her to stay.

She obliged and began removing her jacket, the action enough movement to bring attention her way.

One gentleman, a mug of ale in his hand, his dark hair peppered with gray, unabashedly roamed his eyes over her. "And who's this pretty thing?"

Isla felt another tug at the bond, only this one seemed much like the night of the feast when Eli had shown an interest in her. Maybe she should've worn a sign to show that she'd already gotten her mate riled up for the night and that all should proceed with caution.

Kai turned, helping her remove her garment the rest of the way. His tone was calm but lethal. "This *pretty thing* could probably kick your ass into next week before I had a chance to, Raglan."

Isla snickered, observing the man, Raglan, herself—the way he stood, how he stiffened, how he shifted on his feet. Even without his mildly intoxicated state, she probably could.

"A friend?" A woman had questioned from beside them with some suggestion, maybe annoyance, her eyes seeming to linger on Kai.

Isla smiled tightly at her before meeting her mate's gaze. The taunting raise of his brows answered any wondering she had of if he had felt the same possessive pull from her.

She rolled her eyes, not wanting to feed his ego, and spun back to answer, "A very good one."

∽

Isla had only heard one person mention the challenge. As if it hadn't just been Davina's rule, but *everyone's* to forget it was happening.

The music of the tavern was a steady drumming in her ears as she perched herself beside the redhead, leaning back against Talha's bar, watching as Sebastian and Ameera engaged in a game of pool.

Her brother cursed as the general sunk another one of her striped balls into a corner pocket, more exaggerated than necessary. They were garnering a small audience. Despite their promise to lay low, Sebastian already had a hustle on his mind from the moment he'd heard the tavern's description. Ameera was to make him appear as a weak opponent, and then they'd split the cut of what he won as he took on other competitors.

Isla told him that if he was chased out of here, she wasn't saving him. Adrien agreed he wasn't either, but she didn't think it would get to that point. Despite being obnoxious, her brother wasn't stupid. Far from that. Isla knew he'd find victory in a way that wouldn't make it obvious to people that they were being swindled. Find the perfect amount of give and take, the fine line where skill could hide behind the illusion of luck. It was a horrible misuse of his abilities, of how perceptive and cunning he was. A born and bred warrior like most men in Io.

Isla was surprised Ameera had gone along with the charade, opting to remain up above at the gaming table while Kai, Adrien, Rhydian, and Jonah had gone below to where the card games were held—Isla had been there briefly before they'd gone into a mysterious den with more *serious* competition at Charley's table.

The general appeared to be genuinely enjoying herself, not just because she had to play up her victories. Isla didn't care what happened between the pair at the end of the night, she was just happy to see Ameera in good spirits. Though she had noticed, even after their initial flirtations back at the shop, both of their eyes seemed to run the crowd for other pursuits.

Eventually, as the night drew on and the alcohol took to Isla's bloodstream, leaving her head buzzing, *want* echoed along with it.

Her body heated.

She sent a simple, innocent *"Hello"* through the bond.

It was met by an unsure and amused reply from her mate. *"Hello?"*

"How are you doing?"

She could practically hear Kai laugh. *"I'm about to win this hand. Can I help you with something?"*

It was the perfect opening.

"Actually…" Isla drawled before continuing her toying from earlier. Explaining how she felt and what she wanted, now. Painting him a picture the best she could with her words.

It wasn't long before she swore she was in that room, hearing Kai tell Charley that he was ready to cash out.

She felt him before he appeared from within the crowd. Davina squeaked and scooted out of the way, Isla jumping herself as she found her body corralled on her barstool. And then Kai's mouth was on hers, the kiss hot, deep, claiming, and frustrated.

He wedged his hand into her hair, pulling gently from the roots to angle her head and sweep his tongue past her lips to caress hers. She didn't mind the taste of whiskey much anymore.

Somehow, the embrace felt endless but so brief. Too brief.

She was breathless as he broke away and went to her ear.

"You have no idea what you're in for later," he whispered, his breath hot on her already searing skin. "If I didn't want this whole place knowing how sexy you sound when I'm inside you, I'd take you in the back."

Isla didn't know what to say, didn't know what to do with her hands, her body. She'd arched off the bar as he spoke, her breasts grazing his chest. Enough friction—but not enough at all—to leave her thrumming with need.

"I can be quiet," she sent, not able to get her mouth to move, every part of her aching to feel him.

His low chuckle reverberated through her, and his lips grazed her ear. "I don't want you to."

The following kiss he placed on her temple was gentle, very at odds with how she imagined things would go later.

She swallowed hard, crossing her legs tightly as Kai took a seat on the other side of her and ordered food and drinks, not just for them, but for everyone in the tavern.

Isla couldn't even manage to be impressed.

Her eyes went to the floor, her entire being on fire. She refused to gaze at Sebastian and Ameera but eventually glanced at Davina. The secretary's eyes were wide and her cheeks stained as red as her hair. Whether it was for the actions or words she'd overheard, Isla shot her an apologetic look.

Suddenly, Rhydian appeared, followed by Jonah and Adrien.

The foremost kissed his mate on her rosy cheek, and his brows furrowed as he pulled away. "Are you okay?"

Davina gulped and looked Rhydian over, the inside of her lip between her teeth. She nodded briskly, humming her *yes*.

Rhydian still appeared doubtful, and Isla recognized the look as Davina spoke to him mind-to-mind. Recognized the spark in his eyes and the smirk that he failed to hide as he nodded, and they attempted to appear as normal.

Apparently, she and Kai weren't the only ones breaking Ameera's rules.

But maybe the general had been smart because Isla still felt wired and she wasn't sure what—aside from a *very* cold bath or Kai making good on his word right here, right now—would make the feeling go away.

As Adrien stood before her and met her eyes, he caught on to her flustered state. His gaze flickered to Kai's turned back before he raised his brows at her.

"Shut up," Isla snapped under her breath before a smile could grace his mouth.

Adrien put his hands up. "Hey, I didn't—"

He cut himself off as a finger tapped him twice on the shoulder.

The Heir spun, giving Isla a full view of a young woman. Her chestnut hair flowed long over her shoulders, and her bright green eyes shone behind fluttering lashes.

"Dance with me?" she asked Adrien, barring any other pleasantries.

Both he and Isla wore equal expressions of shock at the general question and the boldness.

Adrien opened and closed his mouth, surprising Isla further. He wasn't typically one to stammer or hesitate, especially with female attention, but then again, he'd been acting strange since they'd got here.

With each second that passed, Isla could see the woman's demeanor shifting, eyes dimming, smile fading. She'd been there before. Felt the sting of flat-out rejection, or the even more painful attempt at working around it, prolonging the inevitable heartbreak and brutal blow to her self-esteem.

Isla looked up at her friend, catching uncertainty in his eyes battling with the fact he seemed to find the woman attractive. He'd entertained a few after Cora—she knew that for a fact after some visits to his home—but he'd been cautious. As the Heir, everyone's eyes in Io were on him. His people, the Council, his father…but he didn't have to be the crowned prince here. This woman didn't seem to know who he was or care enough to ask his name.

Tonight was supposed to be about fun. About letting go, relaxing. For all of them. Maybe Isla could give him a little push.

Literally.

"He'd love to." Isla nudged him forward, and Adrien tripped just enough that he had to brace his hand on the woman's arm. Something behind her stare flashed, and she shivered before her eyes flicked briefly between Isla and then Kai.

"Sorry," Adrien apologized, stealing her attention.

Isla waved him off, though a part of her twisted became unsettled. "Have fun."

Adrien gave her one more look over his shoulder as the woman dragged him away, too far into the crowd and the noise for Isla to hear who she'd introduced herself as.

"Are you playing matchmaker?" Kai asked as the bartender brought over their drinks. He turned and rested his arm on the wood behind her, then began fielding waves and shouts of thanks from patrons whose orders were being taken.

"No," Isla said, grabbing her glass. "I just think he should get to enjoy himself after…everything."

"I thought he'd be different," Davina said quietly.

"Yeah, he's not bad," Rhydian said, not nearly as soft, gulping from his ale.

"I expected him to be worse," Jonah added bluntly. "Both of them."

"I heard that!" Sebastian's voice came from the pool table, and the group turned as he pointed at the shop owner and then tapped his chest. "And I appreciate it."

Jonah lifted his glass.

Isla scoffed and rolled her eyes, garnering her brother's attention. His gaze traveled between her and her mate. "Don't think I didn't see you two." He grumbled before going back to his game. "Gross. And I'm going to be stuck in the same fucking house."

Isla had forgotten that they'd be their guests for the next few days.

"Maybe you will have to be quiet."

Isla was about to agree with Kai when she caught Sebastian glance up at Ameera, his brows lifted in question and interest. Another place for him to spend the night?

The general sunk the final black ball into her called pocket and won the game. "Not going to happen."

A chorus of snickers followed, along with a challenging, doubtful look from Sebastian. Though Isla's laughter faded as her eyes drifted over to Adrien in the distance. His silhouette that she could find in any crowd.

Any grin she'd been wearing faltered.

She knew her friend. Had known him since before she could speak, could walk. And she could tell, in a manner as easy as breathing, when he was off.

There was something—*something*—stiffening his muscles and darkening his eyes and forcing his smile.

She needed to figure out what.

CHAPTER 47

"You're staring."

Isla averted her gaze away from Adrien to Kai, who was reaching for the food on the bar top. "Should I be afraid that you're jealous?"

She gave him a flat look. "No." Though it was a struggle not to turn her head for another glance.

Sighing, she leaned her elbow on the wood and rested her chin in her hand. She tapped her foot anxiously to the beat of the music against the leg of her stool.

Kai offered her the greasy chip he'd picked up, and she opened her mouth for it. As she chewed, his eyes drifted down to watch the movement closely. They rose when the corner of her lips did, and when he met her amused stare, a silent tell that he wasn't subtle, he laughed. But it didn't feel like it was at her.

Isla finished her bite. "What?"

Kai took hold of his drink and forced himself to look down at it. Away from her. "Nothing."

But that smile on his face—joyous but edged with nerves—it wasn't just nothing.

If she was anyone else, she may have called the alpha smitten.

And with the way her stomach fluttered and heart gave an unsteady beat, she would say she was, too.

Isla didn't care that people were watching, that she and Kai had agreed to keep the rest of the romantic gestures to a minimum—for the sake of their sanity and to temper rumors. Maybe it was the alcohol or

Fate pushing at her back, but she leaned forward. Kai moved, too. Her lips met his in a kiss, soft and sweet and soothing. Simple.

A promise. An always. Until they reached eternity and carried through it.

They didn't say anything as they sat back in their seats, aloud or through the bond. They didn't look out to the rest of the tavern. They ignored the whispers, the gasps, the questions. Not inquiring if they were fated—that was still too farfetched—but if the alpha had found someone who he'd want to take as his queen. Their queen.

Isla took in a deep breath and tried to force her shoulders back. To sit tall and proud and regal as she'd seen Zahra. As she'd seen Imperial Luna Marlane. Seen Kai. Seen Adrien.

But it was unfamiliar territory. Not a battlefield or ballroom where she could hide amongst comrades or a crowd. The phantom crown she bore now left her open and exposed, and she didn't know how to navigate the path it presented.

Her heart leaped into a gallop, her breathing just a bit shallower…

And then there was a chip in front of her face.

Isla met Kai's eyes, his raised brows.

The food was his offer. A distraction. Along with the silent words, *"You're fine."*

She took both the encouragement and the food.

As she chewed, she couldn't hold back the urge to glance over at her friend again. Kai didn't try to stop her.

Adrien had danced with that woman for a few songs, and now the pair had retired to have their drinks on Kai's tab alone at a small table by the unlit fireplace. Isla wished she could hear what they were saying. Wished she knew this woman's name. Who she was at all.

What was Adrien telling her that was making her laugh so hard? What had her occasionally brushing her hand over his arm, his leg, picking *something* Isla couldn't see out of his hair?

"Isla."

Now Kai butt in through a laugh.

Isla realized her features were screwed up tight, and she lacked any sense of subtlety.

Facing Kai again, she took a chip from the plate. "I'm…protective."

"Oh, are you?"

Isla glared at him.

Kai only smiled. "I thought you wanted him to *enjoy himself?*"

"I do."

"So, what's wrong?"

Isla sighed. "I don't—where's he going?"

She hadn't been able to resist another look and now caught Adrien standing, excusing himself, and beginning to meander through the crowd. When he reached the tavern's exit, he didn't bother glancing back before he went outside.

Isla looked at his companion who hadn't budged an inch. She only sat, sipping on her drink. Whatever Adrien's reasoning for going, one of them wasn't them "getting out of there".

Isla's feet were on the ground in an instant, and Kai's hand was on her arm just as fast. He appeared as confused as she did, and maybe a bit disturbed.

How far did Kai's trust go exactly when it came to Io's Heir?

"I don't want you going after him alone," Kai said.

"If I can't see him right away, I'll get you."

A look of doubt came her way.

"I will," she affirmed.

Kai was still wary, but he dropped his hand. From the way he maneuvered in his seat, Isla knew he was going to find a reason to wait by the door, find someone over there to talk to until she came back inside.

And *she* was protective.

Without any other words, brushing off the stares directed her way, Isla made the same movements to weave through the bodies and out the tavern's door.

Coming from the crowded bar floor, the air outside seemed colder. She wished she'd grabbed her jacket, if not for its warmth but the hood. *Don't attract any attention.*

Adrien wasn't anywhere immediately in sight.

Isla wrapped her arms around herself and shivered. With the tavern's door closed, its rowdy noises muffled, her steps were loud as she transitioned over from grass and stone to the boardwalk.

"Isla."

"I'm fine," she said, and then turned her head, closed her eyes. She focused on scent, on sound. Parsed out the hollow noise of boats rocking against wooden beams, the raucous sounds of the other businesses, the nighttime birds and bugs, and a whirring she didn't know the source of. Through the scent of brine and smoke, she attempted to find the one she'd likened once to home.

She opened her eyes and went right.

Panic swelled in her chest when she couldn't find Adrien for a short but substantial time. She'd gone a decent distance from Talha. It was when Kai's voice came again, him likely feeling her pull away, that she finally located her friend, leaning at the boardwalk's railing beneath a street lantern, looking down into the murky water. The lamp gilded him in gold.

"*I found him,*" Isla told Kai, offering him another vote of reassurance that she was okay before he went silent.

Isla didn't keep her steps quiet as she approached Adrien, and she didn't make any true attempt at masking her scent, but the Heir didn't bother turning. Not even when she settled at his side.

"Did we not give you ground rules?" She tilted her head to catch his eyes. "No going out alone."

"I didn't go far," Adrien said. Still no look. He remained focused on the water.

Isla followed suit and kept her arms folded over the railing. "I don't care. I'd kill you if you let anything happen to you." Adrien furrowed his brows which she answered with, "I said what I said. Why'd you come out here? Your new friend—*who I don't know the name of*—not doing it for you?"

Adrien caught the hint. "Her name is Dhalia."

"Dhalia," Isla tested it on her tongue. "That's cute."

Adrien agreed and snickered. "She asks a lot of questions I can't answer. And I've been here before, but the most I can offer as a lie as to where I 'live' is Mavec on a hill."

Isla hummed before presenting with exaggerated confidence, "*Well,* there are also apartments here along the banks or some farmhouses over in Surles. Ifera has a lot of open fields. It may rival Mavec with some of its hills."

She quit her drawling as Deimos's worst tour guide when Adrien's lips ticked up, and he finally looked at her. "Impressive."

"I know this place like the back of my hand," she joked before softly relenting the truth. "I have a lot to learn."

"Apparently." Adrien laughed, though the joyous sound faded too fast. His gaze went forward again, and the only sounds became the boats, birds, and bugs until— "Do you think Fate did it on purpose? Mated you to him."

Isla glanced at the moon. "I don't know why Fate does anything... but I'm happy she did."

"So much for not wanting a mate," he heckled.

Isla shrugged. "Yeah, he's okay. I'll keep him."

There was barely anything behind Adrien's chuckle this time, and Isla couldn't help but cringe as it dawned on her. Could this have been weird for him? Was *that* why he was acting so off? Seeing her and Kai, how happy they were…

A fated bond had ruined Adrien's life, had taken the woman he loved. And though he'd let Corinne go so she had a chance at being okay, maybe being happy with her destined mate who'd claimed her, Isla wasn't sure if deep down, Adrien hoped that Cora would miss him. That her forced fated bond wouldn't be as fulfilling as the long love Isla had seen them share since they were younger.

"Are you okay?" she asked, preparing to speak of her old friend. "You've been off all night. Since you got here."

Adrien didn't respond, no agreement, no denial.

Isla sighed. "You can talk to me."

"I don't think I can."

"Why?"

He turned to her, and there was something about the graveness of his face that tipped her off.

This wasn't about Cora. This was bigger. Political. And he had realized the same thing that she had. That he was the future Alpha of Io, and she would be the Luna of Deimos. They were on opposing sides.

Isla's blood chilled. "Adrien?"

What did he know? What *had he* known?

Seconds went by too slow before the Heir said, "I spoke to my father ahead of the vote, right before they went in the chambers that night. He hadn't been happy about my opposition—at all." Adrien winced at the recollection of the memory. "I was surprised he'd called the meeting so late, but the moment your father got back from Charon, they went in, and a part of me wondered if it was so you and me and Sebastian couldn't get to your dad."

Isla's nails dug into her palms. "So, he knows about me and Kai." It was a confirmed suspicion.

Adrien nodded, nostrils flaring. "And he figured you told me about it which is probably why he's been shutting me out since the Hunt…but something's been going on, even before that. He really started changing after Cora while I was gone."

Gone?

"Where'd you go?"

Adrien stiffened as if he hadn't meant to mention that part.

And in his hesitation, Isla affirmed, "I'm still your friend. Talk to me, please."

Another heaved breath fell from his mouth, and he glanced around them to ensure no one was near. He leaned in closer, but still, his voice was so soft, she could barely hear it. "After we broke the bond, I wasn't recovering fast enough. So, I went to a healer—a witch."

Isla jerked back, her eyes wide. "You were healed by a witch?"

Though a whisper, she'd spoken too loud for his liking, given his warning look.

It made sense.

Broken bonds destroyed even the strongest wolves. To get back to where he was now, to where he had to be to eventually lead as Alpha, Adrien may have needed a miracle. Magic. But if anyone found out...

What Kyran had been doing, what Cassius had been doing, *harboring* witches, working with them, that was dangerous. But Adrien being healed, *enhanced* in some way with magic, that broke continental law, maybe even their sacred Code.

"Does your father know?" Isla asked.

"He arranged it." There was a harshness to his voice that told her he knew the implications. "I don't know how. They dislike us as much as we aren't fond of them. But the healer lives in a small village that's part of their territory on our continent, right on the other side of the Valkeric Mountains, away from their mainland. Not many there to see or sense me. I'm assuming he paid her handsomely, but I didn't ask."

Paid her or threatened her, Isla thought.

Cassius must've been desperate. Adrien was his sole Heir, and if he couldn't handle going through the Alpha Rite when the time came, his legacy would end.

"Is that where he thinks you are now, then? You told Kai you could sneak away for a few days. Does your father think you're in their territory to be healed again?"

"In part."

"Why in part?"

Adrien went quiet for a moment. "When a witch crosses our borders, the treaty drafted between us states that they can be dealt with as we see fit. Over the past decade or so, there has been an influx of them in the mountains. Maybe spying, maybe planning to do something to us, I don't know, but they were caught and put in Valkeric."

Isla had to force her face into a look of shock.

Adrien continued, "They're still there, and...I think my father's been bargaining terms with them for their release."

The fear that cast across her features wasn't so fabricated. "What terms?"

"Work on Io's guard. Defend our outer and inner borders."

"Why would he want to keep witches on the inner borders?"

"Can you tell me?"

"No," she answered without thought, but then remembered what Sebastian had said.

Io had been suspicious of Kyran since those meetings he'd called with Cassius. They didn't trust him and his intentions. Cassius may have been planning to strike at Deimos and take Mavec—he also may have not—but if he suspected Kyran was planning something, then he'd be on the defensive.

It was another thought of hers confirmed when Adrien mentioned, "He's bringing one here when he comes for the challenge under the guise of a guard. There's an enchantment they can use that can keep them hidden from us until they use their magic again. She'd only be for his protection. Used if…something happened." Isla let out an astonished breath, and Adrien added, "Can you blame him?"

She bit down on the inside of her cheek.

As much contempt as she held for the Imperial Alpha right now—and as angry as Adrien may have been with him after approving the challenge, after all that had occurred with Cora—she understood the hurt and nerves in her friend's voice, on his face. Cassius was still his father.

"How can we trust that it's just protection?" she asked gently.

"Because I convinced him, at least, to not take one of his untested recruits. He thinks that I'm also making a deal right now with the healer's daughter."

"And that is?"

"Raana." Something shifted in his face when he said her name. Became…softer. "You can trust her."

"She's a witch?"

"Yes."

"I'm not really in the business of trusting witches."

"Then trust me."

There was the smallest piece of her that took those words with hesitation, and she hated it. "You know her well? Raana?"

Another test on her mouth, and another change to Adrien's face.

The question, the repetition of the witch's name, seemed to spark something behind his eyes. Had the corner of his mouth threatening to lift before he pressed his lips together tightly. He looked off into the distance, down the river, and Isla caught the way he clenched and unclenched his fists as if wanting a touch that wasn't there. "Pretty well."

It was a reaction Isla had seen from him before.

She had to keep her jaw from falling open. "You slept with her?" Her whisper was loud enough that she shouldn't have even bothered.

Adrien faced her again. "Is sex all you can think about right now?"

"Adrien."

"It was one time. It never happened again."

Though it was said as a brush-off, Isla didn't miss it. The way his eyes dimmed, and every part of him tensed again.

"Good," she said carefully, guilt gnawing at her gut. "You're the *Prince of All Wolves*. The last thing you, of all people, need is to be screwing around with a witch. More than you apparently already have."

Adrien gave her quip a flat look, the expected reaction, and then settled against the railing again.

He looked up at the night sky and the jewels that adorned it, shining bright in the low lights of the town. His eyes slid from the moon to the stars, where the witches saw their deities, marked in the heavens by constellations. "I know."

Isla frowned and didn't want to address any more of what she was seeing—how resigned he sounded, the smallest hint of longing in his stare.

Shame and doubt coiled within her.

After all this time, wondering if Adrien would ever find another, a witch capturing his attention was the last thing she'd expected. Part of her itched with fear that this healer's daughter had found a way to manipulate his feelings, was using him. But there was a clearness to his face that told her something real lurked beneath. Something that meant trouble.

She wanted to, would, support him in most things, but there was no way this could end well. At least, he knew that, too.

She changed the subject, for his sake and hers.

She picked at a splinter on the railing. "What did my dad vote?"

"I'm not sure," Adrien said with the same mindfulness she'd used. "I know it wasn't unanimous, but I'm not sure who was against it… does it matter? I'm sure he doesn't know."

Isla clenched her teeth, pushing against the wood so hard it cracked away. There was a hollowness in her chest. "If my dad thinks a rogue wolf is better suited to lead a pack than its current alpha, especially this one after all they've gone through, after all they've suffered…I'm happy he doesn't know about me and Kai. At least now, I'm getting to see what kind of person he is."

And now she wanted to change the topic again before she got into anything about Charon.

"And why am I being left out of this?"

Perfectly timed, Isla turned along with Adrien to find Sebastian strutting towards them.

"What happened to your game?" Adrien was quick to respond, so quick it seemed he wanted everything that they'd just spoken about to be washed away.

Did Sebastian know about the healer and this *Raana*? He and Adrien were basically brothers, a future Alpha and Beta. They weren't keen on keeping secrets from each other.

"I just got my ass handed to me again, so I stormed out," Sebastian answered. "But not before flashing how much money I still had to lose."

Isla rolled her eyes, knowing that everything was going to plan for him. "You're incorrigible."

Sebastian guffawed before putting a hand on her shoulder. "My dear sister, I'm—"

A scream tore through the air.

CHAPTER 48

Eyes and markings flaring, Isla, Sebastian, and Adrien turned in the sound's direction. Raw and pained and followed by so much *silence* that they didn't hesitate.

They ran.

Isla called for Kai, but he was already outside Talha by the time they reached the tavern. In his wake, the rest of the group filed out of the building. There was no question of where the noise had come from. A fear-drenched scent beckoned them from the distant darkness.

They took off for it—all of them—and all Isla knew was the rush of blood in her ears, the thundering of her heart, the pounding of their footsteps, and such a keen awareness of where everyone was, where Kai was, the boys. Her wolf was ready to tear out of her skin.

They came to a skidding halt at an alleyway solely lit by the lamp across the boardwalk.

"Dhalia?"

It was Adrien who'd spoken; the name said in a breath.

The woman he'd spent the night talking with, wooing, was sprawled on the ground where the wood met tar, arms out and legs bent. For a moment, Isla panicked, thinking the halo of hair around her head was blood.

Dhalia's chest rose and fell in a shallow cadence. She was breathing but barely.

Isla was the first to drop to her knees at the woman's side as everyone else caught up and gathered at the alley's mouth. She heard Davina take a sharp breath, heard Rhydian curse.

Reaching out, Isla touched Dhalia's shoulders, hoping she could carefully jostle her awake. "Dha—"

Isla gasped.

Dhalia's head whipped around, and her eyes snapped open. Dark. Not the ones Isla remembered.

She tried to recoil, but Dhalia took hold of her arm, the grip so tight Isla couldn't wrench away. There was a sharp pain in her head, a sudden ringing in her ears.

"Murderess child."

A chill took over Isla's body, starting from that place on her skin. It burrowed so deep that it imprinted on her bones, stilled her wolf.

The words had come from Dhalia's lips, but it wasn't her voice. Not the sweet, innocent one Isla remembered asking the Imperial Heir for a dance. This one was ancient and edged with lethality in its ease. Female. Still female.

Isla tried to move again, but Dhalia's grip tightened. Why wasn't anyone helping her? She opened her mouth to call for Kai.

"Warrior heart," Dhalia cut in, taunting. Chastising. "You should've fought harder. You will lose everything in this war, and he is the reason. He is *always* the reason."

Icy spiders crawled underneath Isla's skin, cast webs over her mind, and skittered along mental walls. But they avoided one thing, one dark and forbidding thing.

"Kai!"

No response. Nothing.

Isla shifted to turn to him, to anyone, when Dhalia's nails dug into her skin, keeping her still.

She bit down on her cry. What was happening? "What do you want?"

A cruel smile slid across Dhalia's pretty mouth. "I've wanted to talk to you for a very long time, little thief."

"What?" Isla trailed her gaze over Dhalia's form, fully aware she'd never met her before in her life. But when she returned to her eyes. Those *eyes*. Dark. Violet. Not hers, but…familiar, still.

This couldn't have been her, the same glittery-eyed girl that had approached them in the tavern. Was this some kind of waking nightmare? Magic? A curse? The witch?

Isla shuddered.

"Who are you?" she asked, reaching for the bond but hitting what felt like a wall.

A labored but even breath passed Dhalia's lips. As if she'd been straining. As if she were working against Isla to make sure she couldn't get to Kai, to that tether. She gave no answer.

Isla didn't care. She needed this to stop. Whatever this was.

Why wasn't anyone helping?

"Kai!" Isla pushed and clawed and dug through ice and shadow to find that familiar darkness. She tried to calm her racing heart, warm herself. "What do you want?"

There was a pull at the bond, and an overwhelming sensation she'd felt once before. When she and Kai had first used their connection to communicate. She winced at the strangest feeling of breaking she didn't understand before trying to turn.

But Dhalia snarled and dug her nails deeper.

"They'll try to stop him," she warned. "They're trying to, and they'll fail. They always fail."

"Stop who?" Isla pressed, trying to reach her other arm back to find Kai, but she was stiff.

"It's the fate we've been dealt. A burden we must carry. It can only be us," Dhalia said. "It's only ever been us."

Her hold eased, but now, Isla was curious amidst the terror. "What do you—"

Isla gasped, collapsing forward and narrowly missing falling onto Dhalia's frame.

Warmth eddied through her trembling body from the firm hold on her shoulders. She turned her head and nearly sobbed when she could not only move but also found Kai's face—his handsome, beautiful face—there, inches from hers.

He'd gone down to the ground with her, knee to knee. One of his hands went to her cheek as his eyes, tinged the slightest hue of crimson, furiously darted over her features. She felt him everywhere. His power, his presence. On her body, tugging at every thread of the bond. "What the hell was that?"

Isla put her hand over his, happy to have the touch, barely able to catch her breath. Immediate answers eluded her. Both because she had no idea, and her mind was still fuzzy and jumbled, trying to recover.

"What is wrong with you two?"

They both turned to look at Ameera, at everyone. They were concerned, as they had been for Dhalia, but there was no outright fear. Not the same fear that Isla and Kai were feeling.

"What was…" Isla trailed off, turning her head and losing Kai's touch to see Dhalia still unconscious, laying with her head turned away as if she'd never moved at all. "What?"

She didn't have time to protest as Adrien bent to Dhalia's side. He lightly jostled her, and as Dhalia sputtered a cough, groaning, Isla tensed. Kai secured his arms around her as she sunk further into his embrace.

Dhalia slowly peeled open her eyes to reveal a dulled green.

"Thank the Goddess," Adrien mumbled, sliding his hands underneath Dhalia's arms, behind her back, to help her sluggishly move into a sitting position. "You're okay."

"What happened?" Isla asked.

"You were out of it," Kai said. *"It was only a couple of seconds, but the bond...something was wrong."*

A couple of seconds?

"What happened?" Kai echoed the question.

Isla swallowed. *"I don't know."*

Dhalia's words—her warnings—swirled in Isla's head as she watched the now coherent woman sit up.

"Thank you," Dhalia said, soft and unsure, with a tilt of her head. Her voice was her own. "Do I, um, do I know you?"

Adrien jerked back, and a collective noise of shock filtered throughout the group as Dhalia loosened herself from his hold. Her eyes scanned the rest of them in a hurried sweep. "Do I know any of you?" She struggled back to the alley wall, crawling on her hands, pushing with her feet. Leaning against the brick, she curled her legs to her chest. "Where am I?"

Nausea bubbled in Isla's stomach, and she held onto Kai tighter. He pulled her in close, and Adrien cast his eyes their way. They were all remembering the same thing.

Lukas.

Not again. Not again.

Isla wriggled from Kai, and despite the tug at the bond, she inched forward. This was Dhalia, not whoever, *whatever*, she'd spoken to...somehow.

"You're in Abalys," she said, easy and tentative, even though her stomach was in knots.

"I am?" Dhalia looked around. So, she remembered something. "Where?"

"By the western bank of the Eyre Canal," Kai said.

Dhalia turned his way, and her eyes went so wide that Isla could see the whites around the green. "You—you're Alpha Kai."

"I am." Kai offered a soft smile and moved in even closer than Isla. He was the only person here Dhalia recognized. "And you are?"

She swallowed and relaxed her shoulders. "Daisy."

Isla whipped around to Adrien, whose eyes were wide as if saying, *"I swear, she said her name was Dhalia."*

Dhalia—no, Daisy—wasn't paying attention to him. She only focused on Kai, bowing her head. "I'm sorry, Alpha." She sobbed into her hands and shook her head. "I don't know—I don't remember how I got here."

Kai closed the space between them, stopping about a foot away. Enough distance, but enough closeness for security. Another side to an alpha. Along with the dominance and the power, there was also the comfort they offered that earned even more trust from their people.

"What do you remember?" Kai asked.

Daisy wiped a tear that had been sliding down her cheek. "I—I was at the shops in the marketplace, looking for a dress for the Equinox, and there was this woman on the street selling this jewelry, and it looked beautiful, so I tried some on. And—and I don't remember. It's just...dark."

*I remember darkness. Everything being dark, and I don't know anything but the darkness before the darkness—*Lukas's words that had nagged Isla since he'd said them. Gaps in memory, loss in memory brought about because he'd been cursed.

"Did it look something like this?"

They all spun to Jonah at the mouth of the alley. In his hands, he held a fallen stick from one of the few trees planted along the boardwalk. At the end of it swung a necklace, the delicate gold chain ending in a circular pendant. It hung loose, wrapped at one side with a link in its chain broken. Isla was too far away to see what was etched on it but couldn't help but notice how quickly Jonah dropped it away from watchful eyes.

"Yes, that's the one," Daisy said, but Isla barely heard it.

Her eyes darted across everyone as she counted. *One, two, three, four...Adrien, Kai...*

She shot to her feet, her heart in her throat. "Where's my brother?"

CHAPTER 49

Isla had felt such fear like this quite a few times in her life. Too many times in the most recent years of it. And in every instance, she swore the sensation of her stomach bottoming out got worse.

"Did you see him walk away?" she asked no one in particular as she stormed past them onto the boardwalk.

She scouted for her brother's tall frame, his golden hair. Nowhere. The walkway was empty. "Seb!"

No response.

Adrien was at her side. Ameera not too far behind.

Kai, still with the frightened Daisy, tried to ease her mind. *"Maybe he went back to the tavern."*

Maybe. But that wouldn't have made sense.

Isla took a few more steps down the wood, and then it hit her. That scent. The one she couldn't quite place. One she'd been seeking for over a week now, and one she maybe shouldn't have let her guard down for.

"No."

She took off in a sprint, her name called in question aloud and through the bond, but Isla only had it in her to respond to Kai, giving him one word, one identifier before she tuned him out. Heavy footsteps came from behind her, but she wasn't sure who followed.

She sought Sebastian's scent, his aura, listened for his voice. Her mind went to the worst, and it cycled through the prospect of the pain of loss over and over until her claws emerged and her body thrummed with power. If something had happened to him. If something—

Isla stopped.

There, on the other side of the canal, at the end of the dock where the water opened to the more expansive river, was Sebastian.

She ran and tackled him with a hug that had him collapsing into the rail, and thankfully, that image of a happy family of four, becoming three, becoming two blew away on a brine-kissed wind.

"What are you doing over here?" she asked him, holding back any berating words she had in mind.

Sebastian, however, barely uttered a word. Even his touch on her back, as he wrapped a loose arm around her, was weak. He glanced down at her once, and the look in his eyes was distant yet focused, somehow. He lifted his head to train his gaze along the waterways and the surrounding buildings.

Isla stepped back from him, her stomach coiling again. It was Adrien, Rhydian, and Ameera who'd followed her. Kai probably couldn't leave Daisy's side without the fear she'd completely break.

"Seb?" Adrien chanced the call to his friend, moving to Isla's side.

He turned to them, appearing dazed. "Do you smell that?"

Isla's brows shot up. He noticed it, too.

"Smell what?" Adrien asked.

Sebastian shook his head, his features drawn in a grimace as he stared into the darkness. "I thought I saw something."

Not an answer.

"Like what?" Isla asked, even though she knew what he'd seen. A cloaked figure there one moment, then gone again like a shadow in the presence of light. If what had happened with Daisy had been some sort of magic, there was one easy to assume was the source. And wherever the essence of that source went, the killer seemed to dwell in its wake. Helping them. Keeping them safe. They must've gotten that necklace off Daisy.

"Someone watching us. It was too dark and they were too fast. I couldn't see their face." His throat bobbed. "But then the smell..."

Isla felt Adrien glance down at her, concern etched on his face. If he'd known the witches well, he may have had his theories, drawn the connections, between what happened with Lukas and what he'd witnessed just now.

"What about it?" Ameera asked.

Sebastian turned to her, and it seemed to dawn on him that he was in the presence of others. He rubbed a hand over his face. "Nothing—too much beer and too much running." He powered past them all to go back to the alley. "I need a drink."

They all shared a glance at the contradiction.

Adrien was the first one at his heels, then Rhydian. Ameera hung back, going to Isla's side as she canvased the area and breathed in deep that fading scent.

"Is he okay?" the general asked, thrown by the shameless man's sudden shift in demeanor.

It wasn't strange, though. Not to Isla. When pushed to the right—or wrong—point, Sebastian's laid-back facade melted away. But that didn't negate how concerning it could be, especially when it happened so rarely.

"He's fine," Isla said, more from hope than assurance.

∼

Isla could feel Adrien's eyes sliding between her and Sebastian's forms, likely unsure which one of his friends to be concerned about most. Both Imperial Beta's children were silent as they, along with the Heir, Jonah, and Davina, walked to the ferry back to Mavec.

The night of fun and forgetting had officially unceremoniously ended.

Isla alternated her gaze between her brother, the buildings they passed, and the ground as her mind tore through thoughts at a rapid pace. She couldn't settle on one thing, and to make matters worse, she was worried about Kai. He, Rhydian, and Ameera were bringing Daisy back to her home by the region's southern borders. Close to rogue territory.

Isla had wanted to go with him, but it was safer for Adrien and Sebastian if she got them back to the House.

It was obvious from what Daisy described, at least to them, that somehow magic had been involved in the gaps in her memory. That necklace she'd put on had been spelled in some way, and the woman on the street who'd given it to her may have been the witch they were looking for. The same witch who'd killed the Alpha and Heir of Deimos. The same witch who'd been imprisoned by Imperial Alpha Cassius, and apparently, escaped.

You will lose everything in this war, and he is the reason.

The words played back in her head.

What war? The one she feared impending with Io? And who was *he*?

They're trying to stop him...trying, but they'll fail. They always fail...it can only be us. It's only ever been us.

Isla looked off, those horrifying moments looping over and over. She wanted to write them all off as a hallucination, even if all of it had seemed so real. That chill. That breaking.

She was the only one who'd seen them. Who'd gazed into the dark, depthless eyes and heard that voice. Kai had only known something was happening because he'd felt it—her terror and something even more horrible keeping her from him.

When Adrien focused his efforts on raising Sebastian's spirits, Isla fell back from where she'd been at Davina's side to Jonah a little behind them. The shop owner had been just as quiet as she and her brother, but that was wholly expected. She imagined Kai was the same way right now, trying to break it all down. He seemed off when they'd parted ways.

Isla wished that she and Jonah could speak mind to mind too, but thankfully, they seemed to have an uncanny way of communicating without words. She met his questioning stare, hardened hers, and then glanced down at the side of his jacket.

Jonah looked at Adrien and Sebastian a few feet ahead before reaching inside his pocket to remove a cloth napkin he'd stolen from the tavern. Folded within it, a precaution taken in case there was any lingering enchantment on the piece, was the pendant. He unfolded the fabric to reveal its surface.

Now Isla understood why he'd hidden it. Etched into the burnished gold was a symbol she recognized. She quelled any audible reaction and lifted her eyes to Jonah's.

It was the symbol of Ares.

Jonah flipped the necklace in his hand. On the other side, more words were scribed into the metal. All of them in that ancient language.

Isla steeled herself, pushing past the shock she felt there was no more time for, to think.

This piece was all too specific to spell and give at a marketplace. Too in line with everything else. It was chosen with purpose.

She reeled through what had happened with Daisy again, recalling specifically what had happened to her eyes. Isla had recognized those eyes somehow, and now she knew why. It was the artwork of the woman holding the dagger.

She'd called Isla a thief.

Forcing herself to remain calm, Isla faced forward again. The sereneness of her features did nothing to portray the frenzy her mind had become as she wondered if she'd truly just spoken to the violet-eyed woman from the picture.

"Isla…Isla, you're going to leave a hole in the floor."

Isla ceased her pacing through the sitting room to look at Adrien, who was playing cards with Davina and Sebastian. She let out a breath. "Shouldn't they be back by now?"

Daisy didn't live *too far* from where they'd been, and they weren't planning to look around for long. She figured she'd wait at the House for Kai to return before joining Jonah back in the library.

"It's been a few hours," Davina said, calmer than Isla had expected. Though Isla could see her fingers trembling around her cards. "Sometimes the ferry gets delayed. It's why they used to have their own boat before they capsized it."

Isla vaguely remembered hearing that tale of the drunken idiots who'd nearly drowned.

Adrien and Sebastian looked at Davina for an explanation, but she didn't give it.

"You need to relax," Adrien said, earning a glower from his friend. He weathered it easily. "We brought you that chocolate you like from home." At the last word, he grimaced and didn't seem sure how to correct himself.

It didn't matter because Isla was already at the bags that they'd brought her with some of her things. Another secret arrangement Kai had made with them. Though it had meant that Sebastian had broken into her apartment…again.

She unzipped the smallest of the three bags first, figuring it would be a good place to store food, but when she shifted the flap to reveal its contents, her chest tightened.

It was all her pictures. The ones she kept on mantles and tables and in albums.

"Goddess," she said beneath her breath, picking up one of the frames.

"What?" Davina asked.

Isla looked up, feeling a slight sting at the corners of her eyes. "All of my photos. My family and stuff."

Davina placed her cards face down on the table and shot up to her feet. "Oh, I want to see!"

She was at Isla's side in an instant and, deeming their game at a standstill, Adrien and Sebastian rose too. Pointless, though, because Isla brought the bag to them, anyway. Taking a seat on the floor before the end of the coffee table that was spared from their playing, Isla removed each picture, frame by frame, and laid them out on the glass. While Davina wondered, she offered small explanations for each. But on one, she paused, not wanting to let go of the frame right away. She bit down hard on her lip before silently placing the picture down.

Davina lifted it with the same gentleness as if she already knew the care it required. "Is this your mother?"

Isla tried to force a smile as she nodded and gazed upon the image of her wrapped in her mother's arms while Sebastian hung over her back. All three of them caught in a fit of laughter. Immortalized in the long-forgotten happiness.

"We were nine and twelve here," Isla offered, hoping no one noticed the way her voice cracked. She looked up at Sebastian for confirmation, but there was a darkness to his face that made her hesitate. His armor was still cracked from earlier, and this—what she was certain was responsible for that iron forging long ago—didn't help.

Her eyes flickered to Adrien, whose features had also become crestfallen.

Isla turned back and found Davina studying the photo. "What happened to her?"

The way Davina's eyes widened made Isla think she hadn't meant to ask aloud. She handed the photo back and wouldn't meet anyone's gaze as if she wanted the query to fade into nothing.

"It was a couple of weeks before my birthday," Sebastian said, making Isla go stiff. "It was just a quick trip down to the southern territories with a task force to check in on them for the Imperial Alpha. She promised me she'd be back in time."

Isla's stomach turned as she added in his pause, "They usually checked in at every pack they passed through, and they made it to Mimas like they were supposed to...but then they were never heard from again."

"And no one really bothered looking either."

"They sent people," Isla countered Sebastian quietly.

"Barely. It was just Dad and whoever he could muster to track them down. She shouldn't have had to go in the first place, no matter how important Dad says it was. She retired from all that work for the pack, and Alpha Cassius knew that. He shouldn't have—" Sebastian cut himself off with a grunt. "I can't do this again."

Isla sighed, knowing there was nothing she could say to him. Nothing to make it easier.

Ten years later and what happened to their mother—along with what had and hadn't happened after she'd left them—haunted her brother more than he'd ever like to admit. Even if he'd only been fourteen when she disappeared, sixteen when their father felt their bond break, he felt responsible. Like he should've done, could've done, more to find her before it had been too late.

The sound of a heavy door opening and closing came from the front room, followed by that familiar tugging inside her.

Not long after, Kai and Rhydian, sans Ameera, entered the sitting room.

Isla abandoned her photos and met her mate at the entryway. Kai greeted her with open arms, a kiss on her hair, and an embrace too tight and too long for Isla to suspect anything but something wrong. She lifted her head to gaze at his face. "What happened?"

His eyes traced over her features before he kissed her forehead again, and they broke away from each other.

"No signs of the woman Daisy saw or the stand she was selling from," Rhydian said, parting from Davina's embrace.

"Where's Ameera?" she asked, earning a sidelong glance from Sebastian that Isla didn't miss.

"She went to check on Ezekiel," Kai answered.

"Your beta?" It was Adrien who'd questioned it. He'd done so carefully, likely feeling what Isla had with Kai's disposition. Higher ranking in the hierarchy or not, better not to push an alpha in his pack. Never mind his own home.

Kai nodded in confirmation along with, "Her father."

And he left it at that.

Everything was left at that as a tension already lingering from the photographs bolstered in the room. Unspoken words sat on everyone's tongues, and Isla had a feeling each person had something different to say or question.

Eventually, Rhydian broke the silence, throwing an arm around Davina, "Ready to head home, my love?"

"You can stay here," Kai said, his tone unnervingly impassive. "We have plenty of room."

Rhydian and Davina looked between each other, more in concern for their friend than anything, before agreeing to take the offer.

Kai turned on his heel. "I'm going to bed," he said and stalked out of the room. Not even a goodnight.

Isla furrowed her brows and looked between where he'd disappeared and where everyone else stood.

"He's been like that since you all left. You know how he gets." Rhydian shrugged. "But I can't figure out exactly what it is, though."

Isla nodded as if accepting the challenge and looked at the boys. "You remember where your rooms are, right?"

They both gave sounds of agreement, and wasting no more time, Isla spun to follow her mate.

Kai had been quick and was already undressing in their bedroom when she opened the door. He tossed his shirt to the side and turned to face her.

"Are you o—"

Isla never got to finish the question. Kai's mouth was on hers, and she was up in the air before she even had the chance.

He kicked the door closed behind them while her legs wrapped instinctually around his waist, her fingers knotting in his hair as he carried her over to their bed and laid her down on the mattress. He pressed his hips into her as he brought his body weight down, drawing the softest moans that he smothered with a kiss. Her shirt disappeared in one swift movement, and he braced his arms on either side of her head.

Isla could feel her mind swimming as she became lost in the feeling of his bare skin against hers, his warmth, the solidness he was. She wanted him to wash the night away. Wanted to get lost in this ecstasy, in his touch—that had gone to her breasts, tauntingly tracing along the hem of her undergarments, making her greedily bow into him—but she couldn't. Because he clearly wanted the same.

She recognized these kisses of his. The ones that were heavy, weighted down by thoughts he'd rather ease the burden of with intimacy before they were shared.

"Kai," she whispered as he trailed his lips down her neck to her chest, where his tongue teased as his fingers once had, while his free hand worked lower, lower. She groaned, feeling her stomach tighten, parts of her begging to feel him there next.

"Isla," he muttered back against her skin, his mouth now making its way down, too. His fingers brushed that sensitive spot between her legs, making her whimper and arch for more. She felt him smile against her stomach, his fingers hooking into her waistband to remove her pants.

Isla ground her teeth.

Goddess, she didn't want to stop, but—

"Kai."

Kai lifted his head at the tone; his eyes darkened with lust and hunger that nearly had her saying, *forget it*. Whatever he had in mind would be hard and fast and deliciously brutal, enough to have her forgetting her own name along with the night, but they couldn't.

She steadied her heavy breathing, her hand going to brush his cheek. "What's going on?"

His muscle pulsed beneath her fingertips as a million emotions flashed behind his eyes. And then Isla was left cold as he rolled off her to lay flat on the bed. She didn't let her gaze linger on the clear outline of what she'd turned down.

Kai ran his hands over his face, pushing back his hair, before he folded them on his stomach. His gaze focused on the ceiling. He was silent.

Isla sat up, leaning on her elbow. "What's wrong?"

"I…" Kai began, his voice gruff. He winced. "I don't feel right."

Isla's eyes tore over him for any evidence of injury. "What do you mean?"

"It's just this feeling," Kai answered quickly in a way Isla figured was meant to abate her worry.

But it only made her question more.

She inched closer. "What kind of feeling?"

He breathed deeply, slowly in and out as if preparing himself. "It's always been there, but it's got…worse. Since I became alpha. Since I went through the Rite. And somehow, even worse recently…I can't describe it."

Isla blinked. "Can you try?"

Kai turned his head to look at her, a pained and almost frightened look on his face. Not for anything it seemed but for her judgment. It was a different kind of vulnerability.

He averted his gaze back up.

"Power," he said, and Isla felt a chill down her body. "Out of nowhere. That I don't understand and can barely control—if I'm even the one controlling it. I just get pushed to this tipping point, a triggering point, and suddenly, I just…"

"Just?"

"Feel."

"Feel what?"

"Everything." Kai's jaw clenched. "From whoever I'm…I don't know, focused on." He shook his head. "But it doesn't stop there."

Isla resisted the urge to reach out and touch him, feeling like if she did, whatever door had been opened, that had him sharing this, would close. And frankly, she didn't understand what he was talking about.

All she could do was ask the questions that felt right to ask. "How do you know?"

"Because a part of me wants to push further, knows that I can, but that's when I realize what I'm doing and try to hold back. I felt it with Ezekiel the other day," Kai confessed, and Isla's mind reeled back to when the beta had been sitting across from Kai, under his scrutiny, stirring in his seat. The way he'd shaken his head, the same way...

"It happened with that general at the gala—and I feel it sometimes with you, or felt it with you when the bond wasn't fully there or working. It had been so weak, and you were so new to me that I thought it was just part of us being mates. But just now..." He looked at her again. "I heard something or someone, and it wasn't you. It felt like I got to it —that voice I think you were hearing—*through you*. And it didn't feel like it was because of the bond. It was something else. And I know you felt it. Me."

Isla opened her mouth to speak, but nothing came out. That breaking she'd felt...

As if he could sense her unease, Kai's features fell in shame, and he turned his head.

Isla frowned. "Why—why didn't you tell me earlier?"

"What was I supposed to say? I'm freaking out because I feel like I'm getting into people's heads?" he said humorlessly. "I don't know what's happening to me. And I've looked into it, I know it's not an *alpha* thing—and I'm afraid I'm going to hurt someone because of it."

The silence that followed the statement settled in the room, settled in between them, like a thick, dark cloud. Isla didn't know what to say and wasn't sure what to do with the kernel of fear that had been planted in her chest. Not *of* him, but *for* him. It certainly didn't sound normal.

Kai suddenly sat up and moved to put distance between them, but Isla reached to grab his arm. She leaned up to take his face in her hands and press her lips against his, long and slow, before pulling him back down on top of her.

When they broke away, Kai trailed his eyes over her face and down her body. "I don't want to hurt you, Isla. I—I can't..."

Isla shushed him, bringing him back to her mouth and cutting him off with another kiss. And though her heart thudded with an all-new emotion, she ushered him to touch her again. "You could never hurt me."

CHAPTER 50

The night before the challenge, it rained. Thunder and lightning crashed, whipping wind through the trees and casting waves across the river as if the Goddess knew Isla would need the extra comfort. Need to listen to the sounds. Need to feel the cool drops on her skin when she took a moment to step outside.

No one had wanted to make the notion of the challenge a big deal, especially on the eve of it, so nothing occurred out of the ordinary. The group didn't gather for any special dinner or big event. Isla and Kai simply ate with Adrien, Sebastian...and Zahra.

It had been difficult to keep secrets from the former luna when she stayed in a wing of the House, and as it turned out, she knew the Imperial Heir. Or, at least, recognized him, stating he looked like his father. Thankfully, being given the reason for the two Io-born wolves' intrusion, she found as much amusement as she could, given the circumstances, and agreed to a vow of secrecy. How she managed to be so poised and lively even in the wake of her son's fight and the way she weathered all hard times and loss, would be something Isla forever wondered at.

After dinner, Isla and Kai had turned in early to prepare for the tumultuous next day, but they weren't tired, too on edge. So, rather than go to bed—or jump directly to *other activities*—they found themselves on the floor of their room next to the hearth with a bottle of wine beside them. Lightning occasionally lit up the space, adding to the glow of the roaring fire, the only other source of light. The moment had been so peaceful, so perfect, Isla thought she'd fallen into a dream.

With Kai's arms wrapped around her as she leaned back against his chest, they spoke of the future, but only *their* future. No challenge, no strange and worrying feelings. No royal protocol, no pack traditions. They spoke simply of what they wanted to try making for dinner in a few days, when they'd want to formally marry, then endured a fight over names for the children they'd have someday, with Isla reminding him that the title *alpha heir* had to flow nicely with the girls' names they were proposing too.

When nearly the entire bottle had disappeared, most barriers had as well, and the sound of thunder and lightning and crackling embers was joined by the breathless chorus of their names, while the bond, their covenant burned between them.

And as Kai drifted off with her head on his chest, his heartbeat and eased breathing like a lullaby, Isla remained awake, watching until the flickering flame dulled to cinders.

You will lose everything...

She bit down on her cheek and shook away "Daisy's" words, that mysterious warning, and sidled her bare body closer to Kai's. He'd heard it and hadn't known what it meant either. But they'd deal with it later. After tomorrow.

Isla trailed her eyes over the planes of his face and watched as his features tensed and relaxed as if he was having some sort of nightmare.

He was sleeping, at least. He needed all the rest he could get, and maybe she did too.

Isla dropped her gaze and closed her eyes, focusing on the sounds of his heart and breathing to lull her to sleep.

She wouldn't lose this. Wouldn't lose him, and she'd fight like hell to make sure of it.

~

Mavec's streets had been thrumming with the masses as Isla and Kai, along with Ezekiel, Marin, and Sol descended into the lower city. Citizens from all the pack regions gathered, hoping to get a chance to witness the challenge or, at least, wanting to be in the area for it. With the way they cheered when they realized Kai was in the town car carrying them through, Isla figured they wanted to support their alpha, too.

The raucous crowds didn't stop, only grew, when they'd eventually reached the stretch that led to the loading docks for the boats that sailed into the open mouth of the rocky hillside to the subterranean city where the arena lay.

As Isla exited the car after Sol and before Kai, she adjusted the cloak around her shoulders. It was a dark and airy fabric stitched in intricate patterns of sapphire and silver. It belonged to Zahra and was nowhere near functional to fight in, but Marin insisted she wear it to cover her warrior uniform. Though the status wasn't something to be ashamed of, it would be best for her to keep as low a profile as possible.

The alpha's do-all was now very aware that Isla was Kai's mate, and she had been less than pleased with her leader that he'd: one, left her to spend the months since Isla and Kai had met scouring the entire pack, wasting "precious hours of her life" to find him a wife. And two, gave her no warning but this morning of what Isla was, and thus gave her no time to prepare for what was essentially their first public appearance together. Though unofficial.

They didn't mention Abalys.

Isla took a shallow breath at that certain public and cast a hand over her eyes to shield herself from the incessant snapping of flashbulbs. Along with them came the chittering of reporters' voices. At least she'd let Maeve take the time to braid her hair if she were to be immortalized in this moment forever. She felt her body tighten up under the attention.

To distract herself, she glanced at Ezekiel and Sol, another member of the group now aware of their bond, as they stood a few feet away from each other, refusing to make eye contact. From that, and the way they'd spent the car ride barely interacting but with glares and clipped responses to initially brushed-off questions, she'd learned that Kai hadn't been lying. They *did* hate each other.

Points for Sol in Isla's book because somehow, her hand always found a home on the hilt of her blade strapped to her leg whenever the beta opened his mouth. Ezekiel had been useless to them these past ten days. Ameera hadn't been able to gather anything from his movements like he knew they'd follow.

He'd be gone soon, though. Kai would appoint someone new as soon as this mess was over.

Step by step—this day would go step by step, and then they could move on from it.

She felt a brush against her back and turned to find Kai behind her. *"You okay?"*

She could've easily asked him the same thing.

The question had been shared between them all too often the past few days, the past few hours. It was easier to forget the challenge when they weren't going through these motions for it, but the moment they awoke to the sunlight spilling through their bedroom window, reality set in.

She nodded, giving him a smile, and then heard the click of a tongue.

Marin was glowering between them.

Though Kai laughed, Isla would be lying if she said the secretary didn't frighten her, just a bit.

As they moved through the crowd surrounded by a heavy circle of guard as an escort, Isla scanned the horde for the people she knew, even though she was aware they weren't there. Adrien and Sebastian were back at the House with everyone else who'd come over in the morning, except for Jonah who'd basically been living in the library. Decoding the necklace and that woman had become one of his priorities. They'd come down to the city in a few hours, once Kai had finished most of the *official* business that would need to take place.

"The bastard's in there!" Isla cringed as someone shouted. She knew who they meant.

One of those orders of official business—talking with Imperial Alpha Cassius.

The boat they were meant to travel on bore Kai's family crest on its side, made specifically to transport the royal entourage up and down the river. Alpha Kyran had used it mostly, whenever he'd, according to Kai, deigned himself to visit Abalys, made official trips to Mimas or Tethys where it traveled by to feed into the sea, or be in attendance for some performances or sporting events held in the underground space.

They filed onto the deck one by one, and as they settled by the bow, Isla couldn't help but notice the way Kai's eyes lingered on everything that they were about to depart—the people, the cloudy sky, and the smallest sliver of the Pack Hall on its high perch as if it were the last time he'd ever see it.

Isla's chest hollowed, and the boat lurched as they began sailing forward. Now away from many of the prying eyes, she brushed the back of her hand against the back of his. Kai got the hint and didn't flinch or look her way, only loosely entwined his fingers with hers.

∼

The area surrounding the arena was a magnificent show of stonework with the mouth of the entrance into the coliseum boasting structures carved into the rock depicting images of wolves and nature, pack history and leaders along with a grand piece showcasing the three sisters who ruled over them all. Isla nearly snapped her neck trying to observe them for as long as possible until they were out of sight as they passed through the archway into the stadium. Fire-lit torches lined their tunnel path.

Ominous, she thought, lifting her fingers to unfasten her cloak and drop it into Marin's arms. Now down here, she had to maintain an all-new appearance. Not the future Luna of Deimos but the Warrior of Io.

She clenched her fists at her sides to stop her fingers from shaking. Her father was here. *Her father* was here—and she still hadn't decided whether she wanted to tell him about her and Kai before or after the challenge was over, if she could find him at all.

It was hard to be too concerned about that, though, with the essence of familiar power emanating from a place she couldn't see, and the rise of the same aura from the man now a few steps ahead of her, tied to her. A calling, a warning before two forces of nature collided. Everyone must've felt it, given the slightest stutter in their steps before pressing forward with greater purpose. Isla could practically taste the hostility on her tongue and fought to keep her features even. To not think of the animosity between the pack she once called home, and where she belonged now.

A few more turns and a small flight of steps later, Isla felt her feet scuffling on a mixture of rough and smooth stone, heard the echoing of their footsteps, and squinted at a sudden brightness as the passageways opened to a grander space. She tried not to look directly up into the enormous skylight carved into the coliseum's ceiling. It seemed to amplify the sun's heat and glow, then carry it down to them as they moved across the platform. As she gazed around the arena, the same manner of images as the entrance carved over each section holding rows and rows of seats, she wondered if it did the same for the moon.

A low growl at her back drew Isla's attention, but the guard wasn't directing it at her.

No, it was for what lay before them.

Stood there in between a horde of guard, a feral smile on his face as the sun cast perfectly upon him, was Imperial Alpha Cassius.

CHAPTER 51

Isla kept her hands at her sides and fought every instinct she had to reach for her blade or draw her claws.

She counted forty members of the Imperial Guard. Forty. Meant to cover Imperial Alpha Cassius as well as three other members of his Council who flanked him. She was too distracted to recall their names. Too irritated by the looks they all had on their faces, so much like the one Callan wore. Not one that everyone in Io possessed.

Isla wondered if Cassius had chosen his protection with purpose. Brought all the guard with that skewed sense of superiority who'd do whatever he said, no matter how horrible, without thought or question.

This was the closest she'd felt to being on a battlefield.

As they drew nearer to the opposing group, it was as if the ground beneath her feet trembled. Not just from Kai and Cassius—who were still restraining the true extent of their power—but everyone else. It was overwhelming how no one in the stadium made the effort to mask their auras. Not the guard at her back, not the guard before her.

Not her, either.

But maybe she should've, given the way stares flickered in her direction, seeking the rising essence's source while she lingered a few feet back from the front line amidst the Deimos soldiers. Confusion had risen on both sides. The power was not of an alpha, but stronger than one should've been for a common wolf.

But she wasn't a common wolf. Not anymore, even without having gone through the Rite to make her Kai's equal. Even if the rich amethyst of a queen hadn't colored her wolf's eyes. She felt it. The surging in her blood, prickling on her skin like during the rogue attacks at the banquet. A power of her own writhing in her gut, working alongside the beast she held within her.

Luna…

Luna…

Luna…

"Alpha Kai." Alpha Cassius's voice echoed within the space as he took a single step forward, his guard following suit, to meet the wolves of Deimos in the dead center of the arena.

After a narrowed look from Marin and a caress along the bond as if Kai were trying to soothe her, Isla reined in her power. She looked down at her feet, noticing she was standing on a large inscription of the full moon. Spanning out left and right were its preceding and subsequent phases.

Kai shocked her as he smiled at Cassius, not as feral as the Imperial Alpha had but with that lethal coolness he'd exuded since they'd met in Callisto. "Imperial Alpha." He gave a deep bow of his head, and Isla clenched her teeth as Cassius's eyes ran over him, sizing him up.

When Kai straightened, the Imperial Alpha lowered—his bow just as deep, to Isla's surprise—and as he rose, his hand went up with him. He extended it towards his peer, and Kai's brows raised at the Alpha's gesture. Once it dawned, he fought a frown and reached forward.

A warrior's embrace.

The action wasn't commonly exchanged between two alphas, even those who'd both successfully completed the warrior rite as they had. It was as if Cassius wanted to make a point. Wanted to remind Kai that whatever had occurred in the Hunt, whatever had earned him that warrior status—a status he did not wear on his skin as Isla did but would be immortalized in every tome and history book—no matter how many bak he'd killed, Cassius had put him in this arena today. He'd been the decider on him fighting for his life.

It would always come down to him.

Isla growled under her breath. *"Prick,"* she remarked down the bond, and Kai's soft returning laugh, though not visible on his face, helped ease her aggravation.

Not enough, clearly.

As though Cassius could sense it, sense her, he dropped Kai's arm and moved sideways to put her in eyeshot. She hated the way he looked at her, so falsely gleeful, so predatory. "There's a familiar face."

It was the spark to a flame. Not within her, but within her mate. A flaring of Kai's power had eyes going his way, and *she swore* Cassius stepped back, just a hair. Could've sworn his features faltered. Sworn she tasted his fear on her tongue.

It was the opening something cruel in her had been seeking, and despite the third warning look she was now receiving from Marin today, she stepped forward. And forward. And forward. Her fists were clenched behind her back.

Imperial Alpha Cassius was in *her* home. Standing before *her* mate. He'd lied to her back in Io. Wanted her to believe herself a murderer. He probably knew what was wrong with Lukas all along and had him imprisoned regardless to keep his secrets safe.

Isla didn't balk or break the Alpha's stare until she was at Kai's side. And after a shallow bow, she fixed her gaze on his again, her shoulders back, her head high. "Imperial Alpha."

Her voice hadn't even sounded her own. If Kai's was laced with ice, then she breathed fire. She felt the guard behind her stand at attention and clocked every twitching muscle of Io's battalion. Mostly men. No weapons on hand. All of them could shift. Where was the witch he'd brought? Raana.

"*I like this side of you,*" Kai said, something like pride ebbing between them. "*Alluring as it is terrifying.*"

Cassius's eyes narrowed. "Isla, what have I told you? You're family. No need for formality."

The drop of her name, his words rippled through both sides, sending them whispering.

She ignored it. "In the presence of others, I feel it is necessary. Better to set an example than boast as the exception."

The Alpha pursed his lips as if impressed by her philosophy, though still countered, "It seems General Eli didn't share the same sentiments when it came to you." He turned to Kai. "I'm surprised you could convince him to let you have her. He's quite fond of our Isla. As it seems you are."

Kai may have appeared coolheaded, but Isla could feel his temper flare. Felt him reach an edge and knew that one more comment or ill glance directed her way would lead to a full-scale war on this stone.

She could see Cassius's game. The line he was drawing between the two factions, using her as his tool. She hadn't wanted to renounce where she'd come from to be respected as queen, but from what she was hearing from everyone around her—with every word he spoke, pulling her to Io's side—he was making it seem near-impossible not to.

The sounds of several approaching footsteps drew everyone's attention to a space on the far side of the arena. From a tunnel's mouth emerged fifteen more maroon and gold-clad soldiers and leading the group was Imperial Beta Malakai.

Isla's heart leaped into her throat, not caring to wonder where they'd been. Shock washed over the battle of contempt and elation within her to see his face.

It had only been a few weeks, but he looked…tired. In stark contrast to the dark circles beneath them, Malakai's eyes lit up when they fell upon his daughter.

Through the bond, Isla felt Kai tense, but it wasn't for anger or defensiveness. He was nervous, and it seemed like it was for no other fact than he was meeting her father.

The Beta picked up his pace, steps ahead of his men, and Isla could only release a breath and accept his open arms when he damned all protocol to blow by everyone and go right to her. His body like a bear's; he'd always given such great hugs. Perfected for those moments when he tried to pick up the pieces—uplift his children—after their mother had gone. But they had become less frequent as they got older, as something drew him—or maybe drew them—away.

Isla's feet were suddenly off the ground, and Malakai squeezed her tighter. "My little warrior." The pride in his voice nearly broke her.

"Dad, you have to put me down," Isla grumbled but couldn't hold back a smile. "You're embarrassing me."

Malakai let out a staccato sound of apology and obliged, but not before giving her one last squeeze. He nodded to everyone on Io and Deimos's sides before bowing deeper to both alphas. He focused on Kai in particular. "Apologies, Alpha."

Isla couldn't miss the conflicting emotions on Kai's face. "It's fine. I understand. Your daughter is," Kai glanced down at her, "one-of-a-kind."

"She is," Malakai said. "I wish we were here under different circumstances."

"As do I."

Malakai looked to Isla. "What are you doing here? Shouldn't you be with the warriors?"

So, he really *was* uninformed. About many things.

"I've been on Alpha Kai's guard because of the…circumstances," she said, resisting the urge to glare at Cassius. He was playing her father a fool.

Malakai glanced back at his alpha and best friend, his brows furrowed. Cassius's features remained impassive, and he looked beyond him to Kai. He inclined his head. "I'm sure you have much to get to. May Fate be in your favor, Alpha."

Walking away. Cassius didn't want to breach the conversation. Didn't want Malakai to know.

"It seems she has been so far," Kai said, and Isla knew Cassius had caught the hint that many others had missed.

As the two sides split away, Isla found herself rooted, watching her father's form recede.

Did she want him to know what she was feeling? The way her heart couldn't settle. How she couldn't hear the word *tomorrow* without feeling nauseous. It wouldn't have made a difference. He couldn't stop the challenge. Cassius knew everything and had no qualms. He'd been treating her father more like his foot soldier, it seemed, than his second-in-command.

"Dad."

Isla called his name before she could stop herself, and Malakai turned around. She balled her hands into fists. Behind him, Cassius and the guard who'd gotten a few feet ahead had frozen where they stood, and Isla felt a rise in power from him, a warning that was answered by another that rose at her back.

She and her father were in the middle.

Isla swallowed, concern usurping any desire to lash out. "Never mind."

～

"Is it weird that we're having a fight to the death in a place like this?" Rhydian's question, those particular chosen words, had earned a few sidelong glares from those around him. He was perched on one of the many chairs meant for the athletes or performers who frequented the space to prepare or unwind before and after their events.

"This arena was originally used for battles like this. Not alpha challenges but duels," Jonah offered his twin, not lifting his eyes from the two books in his lap. Neither of them was the journal. One was text in the native language, and the other he kept to translate what he couldn't understand.

"Why are you doing that here?" Ameera muttered to him with a subtle glance up at Adrien and Sebastian.

Jonah wouldn't look up at her either. "Because I've almost figured this out."

The woman's name and Aneurin's ramblings. For a moment, Isla thought she'd be able to handle helping him. That doing so would distract her from what was to occur in a mere hour or even less.

The challenge would begin when the moon was at its peak, and even if she couldn't see it, she could feel its aura now, more than ever. Could sense the deities hovering. The Goddess and Fate watched while Eternity, Aeterna—the third sister—waited eagerly for the new soul she'd guide through to the afterlife.

There must've been something done to the room to make the noise of the crowd seem louder. Something to make participants eager to get out there and bask in their glory. But with each passing second, the amplified sound only made her feel sicker.

There was the warmth of a hand on her back as if he could sense it. Adrien. She hadn't told him she didn't see Raana, and he didn't ask. Sebastian sat on her other side. They left her little room on the couch, or maybe it just felt that way, the walls closing in as reality did.

"Where is he now?" Davina asked, voice quivering.

Isla couldn't bring herself to look at her. It was foolish, but the way she'd been clinging onto Rhydian for stability and support made everything worse.

Ameera answered, "Being prayed over, probably."

Because they wouldn't be able to reach him for his last breath to mutter the invocation for safe passage into the next life.

Isla could feel something stirring in her from whatever he was going through with the Elders. The challenging of an alpha was as much a spiritual endeavor as it was physical and political. It was why it took place beneath the full moon, like the Alpha and Luna Rites.

By now, Kai would've stripped and been painted with the proper runes. Would've been given the ceremonial robes that he'd remove before shifting, and as whatever Elder or priestess prayed and hummed over him, he'd be taking in the pungent odor of jasmine incense. It was always jasmine when they reached out to the Goddess. While she received her lumerosi and when Adrien and Cora had broken their bond. Though they weren't the classical magic users, something within the rituals and traditions of wolves drew from the ethereal.

Isla squeezed her eyes shut. Goddess, this needed to be over.

"Has anyone seen him? Brax?" Ameera said the name with such disgust. "They kept him covered while they brought him in from the rogue lands."

Sebastian stirred at Isla's side. "I did."

She whipped around to face him, snapping, "Is that where you disappeared to? You gave me a heart attack."

"I took a little walk around. Scoped the terrain," Sebastian brushed her off before meeting Ameera's eyes and then everyone else's. "He looks exactly as you'd expect a man who's been a rogue for twenty years to look. Rough. Covered in scars. He's a big guy. If you told me he'd survived the Hunt, I'd believe it."

Isla bit the inside of her cheek as her stomach turned. She'd been briefed on Brax's history, and the fact he had been a warrior did nothing to ease her spirits. Nor did the reason he'd been exiled before he'd received his lumerosi or joined the ranks. He'd killed two men during a bar brawl—unshifted—following his time in the Wilds when he'd returned to his home pack of Rhea.

Sebastian nudged her with a shoulder. "But Kai's the alpha who killed four bak. I'd put my money on him."

Isla narrowed her eyes. "You haven't put any bets on this, right?"

"I have limits, Pudge," Sebastian said, sounding offended.

"I'm sorry," Isla groaned before jumping to her feet. "If I keep sitting here, I'm going to lose my mind."

But before she could start pacing, the door of the room opened. The smell of smoky jasmine filtered through the air, and everyone stilled, holding their breath, staring at Kai in the doorway.

His hair was wet, glistening with some type of oil, and pushed back like he'd run his fingers through it, though some pieces curled back around his forehead. He donned black silks, much like those of the Hunt, and beneath them, Isla could see a glimpse of black paint on his skin. The moon phases, like the arena's stone floor, across his chest.

Kai cast his eyes between them all, closing the entrance behind him. "Don't look at me like I'm a ghost already."

No one thought it was funny.

He sighed and ran his hands through his hair again. "I have to go. So, you might want to go to your seats."

No one moved.

Several seconds of quiet passed before Rhydian rose. His eyes were glassy, as were all of theirs, and he moved to hug his brother. "This is so fucked."

Kai had his arms around him and squeezed his shoulder in agreement but said nothing.

Ameera wiped her eyes, going to Kai next. "Rip him apart," she commanded through gritted teeth.

Jonah had abandoned his books. "What she said."

Davina had barely been coherent, and after Sebastian and Adrien went forward to offer him the shake of a hand and a pat on the shoulder, all that was left was Isla.

She and Kai simply stared at each other as the rest of the group waited by the door, not sure if they should watch or look away or leave. She didn't think she could open her mouth and speak without her voice cracking, and once that happened…

She didn't want to cry. Not here. Not now. Not yet.

Kai held out a hand. "Do you want to walk with me? By tradition, as my luna, you would be at my side until I stepped in anyway, but you can taper off before anyone sees you. It'll just be the rest of the procession."

It was a simple decision for Isla to make.

When they all exited and everyone else went left to go to their seats, Isla and Kai, her arm looped through his, went right. There was a stretch of passageways that meandered from the underbelly of the arena up to the main floor, where they'd been before. It struck Isla how similar they felt to the tunnels they'd found beneath the house in the wasteland, and every so often, she'd catch a glimmer of unharvested crystal in the walls. The crowd was getting louder now. She could hear them clearer with each step, and she battled for every even breath.

They took maybe longer than they should've to get to their destination. Kai explained that he'd spoken with his mother, and that the priestess who'd been praying over him knew he'd been mated. She could feel it, feel Isla, a steady presence threaded through him.

"She said you must've been strong-willed. I said it was more like stubborn."

Isla bumped him with her hip while he laughed. But all joy faded to nothing as they turned a corner and found themselves before a group of guards. All of them sketched a bow—for him—then their eyes shifted in her direction. Some of them she recognized as members they'd walked with before.

"Lead the way," Kai told them while Isla remained at his side. She held onto him tighter.

The crowd was impossibly loud now. So much like the city, making Isla dial back her senses. She focused on Kai's presence, his scent, the bond, and the feel of his skin against hers. Drank in every piece of him she could.

One more turned corner, and they would be on the long stretch that fed into the arena. The light from the stadium spilled through the tunnel's mouth and cast back to them, a yawning glow that had soldiers' shadows dancing on the wall.

Isla had glimpsed the hollow path before Kai came to a stop, holding her back.

"Give us a moment," Kai said to the guard, and without question, they obeyed; their growing shadows showing their distance.

Isla focused on the darkness, wholly still and clinging to Kai's arm. She didn't want to look up. Didn't want to acknowledge him or any of this. She wanted to wake up. Needed to wake up right now, wrapped in his arms, her head on his chest. All of this having been a nightmare.

"Isla."

"No."

Her voice cracked, and she felt wetness trail down her cheek.

Kai spun her around and took her face in his hands, forcing her to look up at him.

Her lip quivered as she mapped every feature, her breathing shallow. "I don't want to say goodbye."

Kai stroked her skin with his thumb, flicking away her tear. "When have we ever said goodbye?"

Isla lofted onto her toes, bringing her mouth to his with a force that sent him backwards. He held her so tightly, it was as if he thought she'd vanish.

Nothing much else was needed after the kiss. No emotional last-minute confessions. No last-chance declarations. Only three simple words muttered against her lips, and then again as Kai pressed his forehead to hers. "I love you."

It took every bit of her to remain upright. "I love you."

As Kai walked away, Isla felt a new kind of cold. She hurriedly wiped her tears and schooled her face before a guard approached from the other side of the wall, meant to get her safely to where her friends were sitting. Isla wasn't sure if she even wanted to watch.

The separateness of the shadows morphed into a pool of darkness as they drew further away, closer to the light, and Isla could feel Kai's emotions shifting. Raw and volatile.

"*Shut me out,*" he told her, but she didn't know if she could.

Within the arena, they'd be close enough to communicate, which meant their perception of each other's feelings, each other's pain, would be amplified. He didn't want her sensing anything he was going through, and she didn't want to distract him with how she felt either.

So, as she turned her back and walked away with the guard, Renoir, at her side, as they meandered through the same passageways to get to the stone staircases up to the spectators' wings, she tried to build a wall.

To cut herself off from him, but not before uttering those three little words one last time.

They were almost at the room they'd been waiting in when she felt it. When she smelled it.

Isla reached for her knife, and with a swiftness she didn't know she had, stopped short and spun, lunging at the person who'd been silently stalking them through the darkness.

She pressed her blade to the killer's cloth-covered throat, seething, "What are you doing here?"

An ally or not, they were the last thing she wanted to deal with right now.

They didn't flinch, but she felt them swallow. "We need to go," was the only thing they said.

CHAPTER 52

G*o?* Isla pressed the blade a touch firmer. "Go where?"

The killer didn't answer, only glanced at Renoir who was stalking closer, his claws drawn at his side.

"Wait," Isla commanded, but the slight movement was enough opportunity for the killer to push against her. She stumbled back, and they easily slipped away.

Then they ran.

Isla blinked, taking a moment of pause to gather if this were, in fact, a nightmare. "For the love of fuck."

She broke out into a sprint, Renoir not far behind her.

The killer was fast—she'd always known that—but in chasing them, she learned just how swiftly and agilely they moved. Shifting would've given her a better chance at catching them, but Kai would know, would detect that kind of rise from her, even shut out from each other. He was in the arena now, the gates closed, leading ceremonies beginning. If he felt her feeling threatened, if he attempted to step out, it wouldn't be law, it would be the *Code* he'd have enforced upon him.

A forfeit from an alpha warranted not just the stripping of a title, but the losing of one's honor and a sentence of—

She shuddered at the thought. Only one wolf who'd just stepped onto that stone was living to see another day off it. There were no loopholes. No exceptions.

The killer had taken a path she hadn't gone at all with Kai in their aimlessness. Inclines and descents. Darker and deeper into the unknown. The roar of the crowd—that had become a wave of cheers and boos—faded farther away.

Isla dug within herself, forcing her human legs to pump faster, but she was losing ground, and her wolf was barking at her to let it out. But just as she was about to damn all to hell and power into a shift on her next step, the killer stopped. They stood before a weather-worn statue, which they hurriedly pushed out of the way to reveal a small fissure in the rock wall. They squeezed through it just as Isla reached for them.

She cursed, and Renoir's protest fell on prideful and deaf ears as Isla followed into the small space.

She didn't let up to marvel at the crystals that illuminated the cavern. Instead, she went right to the killer and with a cry that could've shaken the surrounding mountains, gripped their bony shoulders and hurled them against the rock wall. Their cloak, its hood, jostled as their back met the hard surface. They drew a blade and met hers with it.

Steel on steel, their weapons reflected the blue-white gems and the hardened look in both sets of eyes. With the movement, the killer's hood had fallen a little off their face, revealing gaunt features that Isla could see more clearly now. Their eyes were dark and sunk into their sockets. They didn't bear the bright red flare they had when Isla had lunged at them, and their skin was peppered with scars. One particularly gruesome one slashed from their temple down into the scarf they were using to cover the lower part of their face.

Isla lifted her gaze to the top of their hood, pushed back enough to reveal their hairline and the smallest wisp of dirty hair. Maybe a burnished gold if it weren't for the mud caked on it. She didn't harp on it long, and instead, brought her eyes back to theirs.

Renoir was catching up, claws and teeth drawn, eyes shining. His power radiated through the tunnel walls. Before Isla could even press the killer with any question, they spoke in a rasped tone, "I'm sorry."

Isla tensed, and her claws tore through her skin. She wanted to look around to see if she'd stupidly fallen into a trap, but she didn't want to remove her eyes, in case *that* was the diversion.

Thankfully, Renoir had taken to the canvassing.

"What?" Isla pressed, mentally assessing the next move she could make. Drive her claws in their side, sweep their legs, let up on her dagger's hold just enough to catch them off-balance?

More rasped breathing and sounds, as if they were trying to work out the words, struggling for each syllable. "I am sorry."

They brought down their weapon. Isla didn't drop hers.

She barely let up as she processed the words, the grief and remorse behind them. Not for right now, but—

Isla blinked. "Kyran and Jaden," she said, and the killer winced. Isla lowered her weapon, and her voice softened. "You didn't want to do it."

As the killer shook their head, a confirmation of an action, Renoir growled. "What?"

The killer tightened their hold on their blade as the guard lunged with no thought. Isla wedged herself between them, stopping him with a hand on his chest. His wild gaze fell on hers, and she drew her wolf just enough that her eyes and lumerosi glowed. "Stand down."

Renoir, albeit hesitantly, obeyed, ducking his head and stepping back.

Isla turned to the killer, who hadn't moved. Hadn't run away. "Was she controlling you with magic? Were you cursed like Lukas?"

"Yes—and no," they rasped before letting out a hard breath. "Would've been mercy."

Mercy?

"Were you threatened?"

"No."

Isla's brows drew together. She asked next, "Why did she want them dead?"

"Don't know."

It had only been four months—but this wasn't a case of not remembering. This was not knowing at all. They hadn't *wanted* to do it, but they hadn't done it to prevent anything. There was no threat.

Isla looked them over, putting the pieces together quickly. The broken hands, the scars, how skittish they seemed.

Nausea bubbled in her stomach. "She tortured you."

They visibly recoiled, and the words settled between them. They festered and thickened, unanswered, before the killer finally answered, "Very...very long time." Their voice cracked, and for a moment, Isla wondered if it had a feminine quality beneath the grating, fractured tone. She'd never heard them speak so much. Never used so many words.

"How did you get away?"

Their grip on their blade tightened, but Isla didn't feel threatened. "Remembered."

Before Isla could ask if that's why they hadn't killed Kai, because they *remembered,* something rumbled from deeper within the tunnels. They all exchanged glances before the killer ran towards the sound. Isla followed. The stone walls she steadied herself against were cold and slick beneath her fingertips as she shimmied through the narrowing and widening path. Rainwater from the storm trickled down from above, weathering the rock.

This hadn't been a *true* tunnel, not like the one they eventually stared down into.

Peering over the killer's shoulder, Isla examined the crossroads. Four paths—north, south, east, west, she'd call them—with markers and large wooden poles wedged into the walls. Each had similar and differing symbols—symbols known by those who lived in Ares—and what was emerging from the western pathway…

Isla put a hand over her mouth and instinctually threw her hand over Renoir's before he could utter a sound.

Three bak, their thick, heavy claws scraping along the tunnel floor, their harsh, labored breaths echoing off the walls, continued through to the east.

When they'd disappeared, Isla looked down at the killer, who hadn't been alarmed at all.

That's what all of this had been for. They'd known.

"Are you serious?" she whispered, barely over a breath. "Why didn't you say it was bak?"

"Only three. We are three," was their response.

Simple. Confident.

So, they were supposed to kill them.

Isla turned to Renoir, whose eyes had since dimmed. His claws and teeth had retracted while his body trembled. The guard was white as a ghost, gaping at the space the beasts had once been.

Three seemed more like *two*.

Renoir warbled, "Were—were those…"

"Yes."

He swallowed thickly. "How–how did they get here? They should be behind the Wall."

"Yes, they should." Isla looked at the killer. "You know these tunnels. Where are they going? Is there an opening somewhere?"

"An opening." They gathered themselves, their words. "At the base or into the arena. No longer closed."

No longer closed. So, someone had opened them, and it wasn't this narrow path. But the *who* could be figured out later.

Isla straightened. "The arena?"

Upon their nod, she began removing her uniform, and wouldn't field Renoir's questions about why she was doing so. If the bak got into the arena, or onto any pack ground, it would be a disaster. Any blood spilled before they were taken down would be too much.

"Renoir." Isla turned, removing her tunic. "I want you to go back to the arena and tell Warrior General Ameera and Rhydian exactly what you saw. Don't let anyone else hear." The last thing they needed was to incite panic.

"Alpha Kai wouldn't want me to leave you," he said, fear of a new kind in his voice. Given the way he bowed again, she knew he'd figured what she was, *who* she was to his alpha.

Isla's heart clenched. She didn't want to think of Kai or what lay above. Didn't want to glimpse over that wall she'd built.

Removing her pants, Isla let the fear of never seeing her mate again ebb away before it could arrest her and have her crumbling. "Alpha Kai will understand."

"I–"

"*Renoir.*"

The guard stood straight.

"Go get Ameera and Rhydian. Tell no one else. Now."

He moved without another word, and Isla wasted no more time. She shifted. The sounds of her snapping and cracking, groaning and knitting briefly filled the cavern. Enough so that she knew a bak's keen ears would detect it. They'd be coming back soon.

Stretching out her wolf's limbs was hopeless as her new larger form took up most of the space, but she shook out her fur, let the power and strength and peace overrun her body before the ferocity did.

There was a tap at her mental wall.

Oh no.

Another tap—then a pounding.

Bracing herself, she brought the barrier down.

"*Isla.*"

She nearly broke hearing his voice, edged with panic. Over her or—

In an instant, she felt Kai shift too.

Any opening ceremonies and formalities must've ended. The fight was about to start.

"*Kai.*"

"*Where are you?*" His tone was a growl.

If she told him he'd try to leave, he'd worry more. It would distract him, and she couldn't describe it if she tried. Rhydian and Ameera would get here if worst came to worst. It would all be okay.

"They're coming," the killer muttered, tightening their hold on their blade.

Isla tried to keep herself as calm as possible. *"It's just a run,"* she said. *"I—I couldn't sit in there."* Horrible. She should've been in there to support him. *"I love you."*

Something changed within the bond before she could say anything else. Overwhelming and powerful, it nearly stole her breath away.

It had started.

He was fighting.

He would walk out alive or die right there. She may never see him again. Never hear him. Never—

The hurried scrape of nails against stone cut her panicked thoughts off, and Isla slammed that mental door closed and launched herself from the passageway's mouth.

The bak weren't expecting them at all or from above. With the element of surprise, both Isla and the killer made quick work of two of them, a clean deep slice from their blade and a ferocious tearing from Isla's maw. Black blood sprayed, splattering on her fur, among the crystal, and then became a steady flow down the rock. But as she spat out the acrid flesh of the first beast she'd killed, Isla saw, to her horror, that they'd gained a friend.

Two more stood before them.

You only said three! She wanted to scream at the killer but knew they'd never hear. And there was no time to be upset about anything.

Quick, quick, quick.

Isla had faced the beasts more times than many by now, and though it was still a challenge, she was growing used to the rapid thinking, the movements. How they always swept down with their claws, never up. How they rooted themselves to lunge for their attacks. How they couldn't see past a certain point in their vision. Their weaknesses.

While Isla's wolf was large, they were even grander, and the crossroads had limited space for the four of them all to fit. So, Isla lunged, forcing her bak to fall back into its companion, leading to enough of a slip that she found her opening.

She leaped for the monster's throat, sending it toppling back, making it ram into the other, pushing it to the side.

A mistake.

A horrible mistake, she realized while tearing through her bak's neck.

Because behind her, she heard a cry, a roar, a clank of metal, and a thud.

She whipped around from the dead beast beneath her and found the killer clutching their side, their hand soaked in dark blood. Not of a bak but their own. There was a slice through their side, revealing pale skin beneath, scarred and welted.

They were on the ground, and the bak was closing in on them. It was also injured, bleeding from a wound where its thick neck and front shoulder met. Not deep enough to kill.

Isla only had a few seconds to act, bounding forward to get the bak just as it lunged to feast. It may have been vengeance or pride that had her maintaining a hold on the beast's neck, allowing it to think it had a chance, before she let its blood run like a river with the others. Growling, she pulled, and it fell in a heap atop one of its brethren.

Isla stopped and listened down each path, pushing through the adrenaline and rush in her ears, past the scent of gore and death, for any other sounds, any scents. But there was nothing but trickling blood and water, heavy breathing, and the faintest crow of a crowd.

They were still fighting. Was that good or bad? She wouldn't let herself be concerned by it. Wouldn't peek through that door or check the bond.

Isla spun, just as the killer fought to sit up against the wall.

And with their movement. *With their movement—*

The hood of their cloak fell, their scarf tugging away.

And Isla was staring at the pained, paling, bruised, and scarred face of her mother.

CHAPTER 53

Isla stumbled back a step—another, another—until she lost her footing over the slung-out arm of a dead bak and fell into the opposite wall. It was shock or some conscious desire that had her falling out of her shift, her hands and knees meeting the cold, blood-covered stone.

She could barely make a coherent thought. This wasn't possible. Her mother was dead. Her father had felt her die, their bond break.

She had to be hallucinating. Delirious and traumatized and exhausted. Maybe the witch had made this woman look like her somehow.

Shame mixed with the pain on the killer's battered face, and Isla knew. This was real. It was her.

Her lip trembled. "Mom."

"I'm sorry," her mother said again, the words easier off her tongue a third time. Now Isla could see how jagged her teeth had become, cracked in places. Broken.

A very, very long time…

Isla's entire chest caved in as ten years of lost time weighed down on it. Ten years that her mother was *alive*, tortured—and they'd stopped looking.

Before guilt could ravage her, Isla noted the blood. So much blood. Too much.

"No." Isla crawled over, not caring how the stone cut up her skin. She would heal, but her mother wasn't. Not fast enough.

She reached for the wound, pressing on it with two hands atop

Apolla's. Her skin was cold, but it wasn't the first time Isla had felt its chill. Her mother had touched her before. Back in the house. She'd drawn on her arm, touched her head, pointed to the bak, herself.

The blood continued to leak beneath their hold. "Why isn't it stopping?" Isla asked, voice wavering. "Why won't you heal?"

"Need more time," Apolla said between wheezes. "Healing is weaker now...the witch."

Rage coiled in Isla's gut, along with the shock they were actually speaking. Even if she'd been here all along, it felt like the last time they'd conversed was in her childhood bedroom before she'd gone to sleep the night her mother left.

Isla ground her teeth. "She did this to you."

"Makes it easier for her. So I forget." Isla nearly missed the free hand that came up to graze her cheek, the twisted, icy fingers covered in blood. Apolla wiped away tears Isla hadn't realized were falling. "But I remembered you...I saw you...in him." Her breathing became heavier, her eyes glossing over. "And it broke enough."

The spell, or whatever it had been.

"Kai," Isla breathed.

Apolla's gaze hardened. "He's in trouble."

Isla started, the movement of her hands making her mother wince. She apologized before asking, "What?"

"She wants him," Apolla said, just over a whisper. "She needs him to break it."

"Break what?"

Apolla gave a sudden cry, and Isla's hand slipped as her mother struggled to keep her own in place. Her skin became an impossibly paler shade.

She wasn't healing fast enough.

Isla met Apolla's eyes, no longer the blue they shared, but that dark hue. She'd been changed by whatever the witch had done.

"What do I do?" Isla said through a choked breath, and in an instant, she'd become a child again, looking to her mother for help. She suddenly became all too aware of the scent of blood and death, the past and the imminent. She took stock of the wound, of their surroundings. If she could get her above to a healer...but if she moved her too much, she'd hurt more. Lose too much blood. "I—I can't move you." She was shaking. She couldn't get her hands to stop damn shaking.

Or was that her mother? She was getting colder. Weaker.

Focus.

Apolla's eyes were closing.

"Mom." Isla's voice was frantic. "Mom!"

Apolla slumped against the rock wall, eyes shut, but Isla forced herself to remain calm, to hone in on her heart. The beat was steady but sluggish. She checked the wound beneath her bloodied hands. It was healing. But slowly. Too slow.

Isla looked around. The path they'd come in was a way up, but even getting her through the tunnels here would be difficult. She'd need to shift. She wouldn't be strong enough, fast enough in her human form to carry her while she was unconscious.

And she needed help. *Now.* Quickly.

Isla leaped back into their smaller passage, found her wolf, and ran.

Her blood was screaming in her ears as she moved as fast as her paws would take her. She alternated between her wolf and human forms with expert precision as the pass's mouth narrowed and widened. All thought had eddied away besides the ten years lost, and so much rage that she could scream. They hadn't found her. They'd stopped looking. And she'd been alive. Sebastian and her father were right there above them. When they found out…

Isla had been so lost in thought and had the scent of acrid blood so stained on her senses that she missed the metallic stench of one more familiar. Her paws had trekked through something warm and wet and sticky before they collided with something firm. She regained her footing and glanced down.

Renoir.

Horrified, she studied the guard bled out on the ground, deep gashes in his stomach.

From claws.

Isla turned. There was a larger pool of blood further down, trailing up to where she stood. Where he'd died.

He'd tried to get out. To get away. From what? From who?

All she felt was a sharpness and a searing pain before she got the answer.

CHAPTER 54

Isla was watching Kai.
It took a moment for her to register it through the ringing in her ears and the initial fuzziness in her vision, but she was staring down into the arena, illuminated by the moon and raging firelight, filled with its spectators all focused on the center stone. She lifted onto her elbow where she'd been laying on her side and touched her hand to the rock in front of her, outlining one of the few small windows peering in. Along the phases of the moon, deep red painted the floor as two wolves circled each other. One gray with lightless eyes, and the other flaring crimson with a coat of shadow black; both matted with blood.

Isla gasped as the gray one lunged, sharp canines bared as it went for the throat of his opponent.

"Kai." Her throat was raw. She spoke as if he could hear her.

There was a harsh tugging at the bond, a slamming against that mental wall, as Kai maneuvered out of Brax's way. Then they became a blur as they battled, a melee of claws and teeth. Equal in size, equally quick. That shouldn't have been happening. This fight shouldn't have been going this long. Brax was a rogue. Kai was an *alpha*.

Something must've been wrong. Something he was trying to tell her.

Isla dropped the barrier between them, but when she felt an overwhelming wave of the raw, volatile power, she couldn't hear him. Not clearly. He was muffled and distant.

"You were missing a good fight."

Isla whipped around at the voice and blinked into the darkness of where she was. It was a small, unused spectator's room—private, likely for those of status to celebrate after events. All the furniture, tables and chairs, were covered in canvas tarps and dust. A figure stood in an opposite corner of the room, shrouded until her eyes adjusted. A male of sinewy build stepped towards her, and Isla caught the glint of a blade against the little bits of light streaming through.

She jumped to her feet, blood rushing to her head, legs unsteady. The man was masking his scent but from the look of his disheveled appearance—

Rogue.

Isla reached for her wolf but found it cowering. Her eyes widened.

The distance, the pulling away, the bond…

The rogue ran at her, and Isla couldn't dwell. His teeth were bared but no claws, no light to his eyes, just his weapon. He favored his right side. Isla waited until the last moment and side-stepped. She swept out his legs and knocked the blade from his hands, claiming it as her own. There was no hesitation as she drove the knife into his gut and used his keeling over to slit his throat deep enough that he'd never recover. He clutched at his neck, gurgling and crumbling onto the floor.

Isla's hands were shaking, her breathing shallow as she wiped his blood from her skin, mixed with that of another.

She went stiff and spun again.

"Mom," she whispered into the dark, taking in the surroundings again.

How did she get here?

There was an exit in the far corner. She made a step to take it.

"A wolf's pride is something to behold."

She stopped at the coo, an unnervingly melodic tone, and from the exit emerged two more figures. One, she assumed was another rogue from his teeth, claws, and lightless eyes, and the other—a woman. She'd had the hood of her emerald green cloak over her head, but she dropped it to reveal pale skin and ink-dark hair. Her eyes were a bright blue, brighter than Isla's, more pure ice. Cold in a way that made Isla's skin crawl nearly as much as her wide smile did.

"I told him he wouldn't be able to kill you," the woman trilled, and then Isla noticed what she was hanging from her neck and perched on rings adorned on three of her fingers. Dark crystals. "But they're so eager to prove themselves."

Isla gulped and urged her hands to steady, keeping her ire concealed for just a second longer.

Think. Don't just react. "You're—"

"*You're,*" the woman interrupted, plucking something from her cloak, her fingers delicate. Perfect. "Someone I didn't expect to be such a thorn in my side, little mutt."

Isla snarled, seeing her mother's battered face, and saw red. She tightened her grip on her weapon, begging her wolf to come out.

This was her. The witch who'd been behind it all.

"You took my mother from me," she gritted.

The witch tutted. "Your mother left you." She examined her nails, the gems of her rings flickering. "She should've never come after me. None of them should've. It could've all been avoided."

Isla had been so ensnared by the words, what they meant—that her mother hadn't left to explore the southern territories but to capture Cassius's escaped witch—she wasn't ready for the witch's rogue companion to catch her with something sharp.

Isla cried out, knees wobbling as the burning of poison lanced her veins. The rogue used her weakness to take hold of her, his strength too much as he pulled her arms back at odd angles.

She couldn't manage it all. Him, the poison, her wailing wolf, the bond. Kai kept tugging at her, and she tried to scream, to tell him to shut her out and focus, but it was all becoming a blur. A thick fog settled over the bridge between them. As the poison worked through and dizziness overtook her, Isla slowly lifted her head.

She had to think. She needed to get out of this.

"You tortured her," she panted, voice breaking as she thought of her mother bleeding, dying, *alone.*

"Tortured," the witch said in breath. "I spared her from half the hell they put me and my sisters through in that prison."

Isla ignored her, attempting to wrench free only to be dealt another jab. Turning her head, she didn't catch the gleaming of a blade, but a cylinder filled with dark liquid and a crude needle at the end. Isla didn't need to wonder what that amount in her system could do. She knew it would kill her.

Wickedness glinted in the witch's eyes as if she fed off Isla's pain, the terror she couldn't mask. "And it was the only way to get through to her, to help her…*understand.* You wolves can be quite hard to get to sometimes."

Their immunity to magic. She'd needed to break down her mother's defenses. That's how the control could work on her.

But she'd broken her parents' bond. That shouldn't have been possible.

"We thought she was dead," Isla said, praying the rogue didn't take the flexing of her fingers as a reason to stab her again, though she was testing for her claws. Nothing.

"The blood of those beasts makes for a powerful elixir," the witch said. "Enough to kill that mongrel under your skin while leaving you whole, *just enough* that you're still useful."

Isla blinked sluggishly, eyes casting to the side in search of the dark liquid. "It's bak blood."

"In part." Pride shone in the witch's voice. "My own personal concoction. Stronger than any bane I've come across." Her gaze flickered to the rogue, and Isla felt that sharpness at her side again. A demonstration.

The man's hand over her mouth muted her scream. Every part of her was on fire, inside and out, her skin only cooled by tears and sweat. If this was what Kyran and Jaden had been given to kill them, then that one dose must've taken them instantly. There was no way to weather this quietly.

Isla felt the bond pulling. Taut, *straining* like it could…like it could snap. Her wolf pulled farther away. Panic rose in her chest.

She needed to get away. The witch was going to kill her.

Think, damnit.

"You all locked them away like some feral abominations, slaughter them like they're nothing. For sport, for *glory*. Your own brethren. While you preach family and loyalty." She put a hand on her chest, stating with a hint of sorrow. "It wouldn't be the first time a wolf was bastardized by magic."

Isla had tuned out her ramblings, focusing instead on the fight, the crowd. It was still happening. Why was it taking so long?

"At least that alpha believed the same as me—that the beasts should be embraced, utilized—for a little while, at least." The witch's words regained Isla's attention, and the spellcaster knew it. "We worked well together. He was kind—as he could be, the bastard—gave me somewhere to hide, sent food, supplies. For *years* we made our plan, and then when it was finally time to move, he had second thoughts. I don't appreciate being lied to. Unfortunate for his son, but his beta seems to be coming around." Isla flinched as the witch touched her head and brushed hair from her face. "We could all work together, you know. We have similar interests."

Isla wished she had enough energy to spit at her. It was building back slowly, her wolf whimpering but returning to focus. If she waited for the poison to wear a bit more, maybe she'd have a chance. One clean shot at the witch's throat.

"No," Isla choked out.

"No? Don't we all want the King dead?"

Cassius.

"I—I don't want him—"

The witch stepped away, and Isla didn't waste energy on more words.

"More," she said, and Isla braced herself as the rogue administered another fraction of poison, right on cue, with no hesitation like a dutiful servant. His hand went over her mouth for the screaming, and he moved her around like a ragdoll. His hold tightened, and Isla realized everything about him was rigid. He obeyed the witch's every command with the least bit of reaction.

As the witch looked through the spaces, down into the arena, Isla's vision became spotty, her heartbeat so loud in her ears, a sluggish drum.

She was dying.

"Such a shame. So pointless." The witch hissed as if she'd witnessed a bad blow, and Isla felt the pulling get worse, more desperate. Seeking.

Kai wasn't only getting tired but distracted. By her. He could feel her fading away, could tell something was wrong. He couldn't find her, but he fought. Held onto the tether and wouldn't let it, let her drift into nothing.

If he didn't stop, *he* was going to die.

Isla could sense the rise of dread within the crowd. She didn't want to look; she didn't want to know why. Her bottom lip quivered.

The witch turned, her lips pursing. "Oh, you don't look so well." She folded her arms. "I don't want you dead, by the way. Same as him; it would be wasted potential. I just want to see what he's capable of; if it's really true. Brax's enchantment should wear down soon if the alpha doesn't become sick of holding himself back before then." She took slow steps back towards Isla, and her hand went to her face, cupping her chin, pinching her cheeks between sharp nails. "If you're anything like your mother, you'll serve me well. Hard to break but worth it." She inspected her, eyes drifting up to the crown of Isla's head, glimmering with greed. "And if the stars are to be trusted, I'll need you for something else."

Rage powered Isla through her words. "I'm...going...to kill you."

The witch grinned, amusement dancing in her eyes. "I'm going to have fun with you."

Isla knew she'd reached the peak of whatever power she'd muster, and one last time, her wolf emerged. She freed herself from the rogue's hold, and her claws tore through flesh with a vengeance.

The witch screamed as blood flowed down her face from the long scratches crossing over her features, what remained of her eye, her torn lip. And Isla could do nothing but fall to the ground in a heap at her feet. The witch's blood rained down on her skin as she battled her body to move, but she couldn't. She was so exhausted that even the sharpness of the needle, the burning pain from the poison were simply signs she was still alive.

"Get her up!" the witch roared, and Isla was lifted violently.

The liquid flowed through every bend and curve of her body, and her wolf thrashed and shuddered and whimpered. It fought and fought, as the bond twisted and tugged until the beast went wholly still.

And one last pull from Kai—hard and pleading and desperate—was the last thing Isla felt before everything went dark.

CHAPTER 55

KAI

It was too quiet.

Everything was somehow so *loud*—but too quiet.

Head aching, pulse thrumming, Kai looked up at the bloodied man before him.

A pool of crimson lay around Brax's limp body, oozing from his eyes, nose, mouth, ears, and the deep gashes in his skull made by the rogue's own claws. Like he'd fallen from his shift and just gone—mad.

"Isla."

To his call, Kai heard nothing back. He felt nothing there. Just cold and darkness. Just *him*.

The gates were opening, the crowd who could get to the floor rushing towards him in a wave of flailing arms and cheering. But—

She'd been fading away, and he'd felt it before. Too many damn times. Something was wrong, and it was all he could do to hold her and keep her there. Keep her *here*. With him.

"Isla."

He didn't know what happened–or rather, *how* it happened. He knew what he did.

He pushed. Let himself into that void festering inside him.

It had been beckoning to him for months, this power. A taunt, a haunting that all his problems would be solved if he embraced it. Used it. A gift it was, it told him. And he needed the fight to be over. Needed to *find her*.

So, he gave in.

"Isla!"

People were behind him—talking at him, gawking at him, beholding Brax's body with curious and disdainful stares and confused words. There was a hand on his back, and Kai whirled with a snarl that made Ezekiel stumble. Made everyone stumble. Made them cower. Made them bow.

The power writhed in his gut, rising, calling him to use it again.

The beta had lied. For months. Was still hiding things. Had to know what he was doing to Kai, to his own daughter. What he was risking for the pack.

Kai could end it here, he knew. He could end *a lot* here. If he got his hands on Cassius...

But—

Get out. Get out. Get out.

Those had been Brax's pleas that he couldn't speak—because Kai had taken them away.

The rogue had been rendered silent to all but primal screams as he thrashed, clawing at himself to rid his mind of whatever was inside. Whatever had snuck in through barriers and shields and tore him to ruin.

Kai didn't know how he did it, but he'd broken him. And if he didn't pull back now, he wouldn't just shatter Ezekiel or Cassius. He felt like he'd shatter the world.

Rhydian and Ameera emerged from the crowd. Davina, Jonah, eventually her brother, but no Isla.

It's just a run.

No. She wasn't there. He couldn't feel her.

Kai lifted his head and howled.

And everything stopped.

CHAPTER 56

KAI

Barely anyone knew who Isla was, but that hadn't stopped Kai from ordering every Goddess-damn person in the arena, everyone in the city and over the radio who could hear, to look for her. It wasn't long before the truth spread. That the female warrior they were so frantically searching for was the alpha's mate—his fated, their queen. He didn't mention that he'd felt something off with their bond, but it was obvious by his demeanor that something had happened. Something bad.

The city was on lockdown, Ezekiel was watched by the guard, and Kai was alone as he sought Isla's scent. Renoir's too. All his family had scattered, either scouring within the arena or somewhere outside. Even her father had tracked Kai down for confirmation, and all it had taken was one look at him for the Imperial Beta to run off searching, too.

Every moment that ticked by, every turn without a trace was too much.

She couldn't be—

No. Kai wouldn't even entertain the thought, even with the void. Maybe this was what made those who lost their mates fall into madness. This pit that grew with every breath, every heartbeat, taken in a world bare of that connection. A world he wanted no part of—a duller world, quieter, colder.

He should've had protection for her, should've sent her with more guards. Maybe they should've told people, the whole pack—but that could've put her more at risk. Right?

He could think about the what if's later, *after* he found her, okay and alive.

As he was about to exit the arena and head into the city, the Imperial Heir, his wolf's eyes the hue of a flame, cut into Kai's path.

Before he could growl at Adrien to move, a panting woman dressed in a uniform of the Imperial Guard came up behind him. Her tanned cheeks were flushed red, and her dark spirally hair was flying in all directions. She'd been running for a while it seemed, trying to keep up with Adrien's wolf.

"She can help," he said, giving Kai an answer to the question he hadn't spoken.

This was Cassius's witch; the one Isla had told him the Imperial Alpha was bringing.

What was her name? Raana?

Despite Adrien's claim, Kai couldn't hold back a snarl. He was done with witches. Done with magic.

The Heir returned the gesture with equal ferocity, crossing a paw in front of the witch, shielding her enough to make Kai let up from the shock. Isla hadn't directly said it, but he figured from her words that the Heir had a fondness for the woman. But he didn't expect this.

Though not thin, she was small, at least by their standards, barely reaching the top of the Heir's shoulder and disappearing behind his body. Kai couldn't scent anything off with her. From that enchantment. The witch hadn't used any of her magic and broken it.

"Adrien," she whispered with a harshness Kai was surprised the Heir let pass. She had an accent to her tone. Adrien didn't remove his eyes from Kai as he stepped back, exposing her completely. Raana was bold or knew nothing of protocol when she looked Kai dead in the eye. "Let me help." Kai inclined his head. "I think I can find her, but I need to go somewhere where no one will…" She trailed off, and he knew what she meant.

Maybe he could accept magic this one last time.

He racked his brain for a spot where scent wouldn't carry, and then led them to one path he and Isla had trekked. Where his mate had remarked there was the stronger brine of the river water, where the air had become thick with the brackish scent, the ground muddy. It was an abandoned section of the arena's underbelly. With Raana throwing an arm over her nose as they descended further into it, he knew he'd made the right choice.

It became dark quickly, only faint, intermittent crystal light and wall lamps for their path, and though Kai knew she could barely see, Raana didn't protest.

When they stopped at a section with some brighter light that was a decent distance from the masses, she looked at him. "I need you in your human form," she said, and then caught onto his question before he asked. "Even when you're human, it's not easy to do anything to a wolf. Like this, it would be hopeless."

Kai would only let himself think about it briefly. Too much time had gone by already.

His arms and legs were unfamiliar to him after he shifted back, worse than they had been after the Hunt. He felt an all-new kind of off-kilter without Isla there now, and he'd been so distracted by his own dizziness, he nearly missed the new flush over Raana's face. The blush only intensified after a glance back at the Heir, now also on his two feet.

She shook her head, muttering something to some spirits, before stepping towards Kai with an outstretched hand, palm facing him. "May I?"

Kai didn't know what she was planning but nodded. Her cold touch went to his chest, over his heart. "What are you doing?"

Raana met his eyes, hers a dark rich brown. "You two are a part of each other. I'm using you to find the piece you're missing. That she has."

Hope in the form of Isla's light he held sparked. "It will work?"

"It should. If she's still—"

"Don't say it."

Raana took a long breath and then closed her eyes. Kai glanced at Adrien, who was watching closely, before doing the same.

He felt something like small pinpricks over his skin, spanning from that spot where the witch's hand lay. Spreading and retreating. Spreading, retreating. She was mumbling something under her breath in a language he didn't understand.

"You need to relax," she interrupted her chant. "I can't get through."

Kai's eyes snapped open. "Relax?"

Raana's remained closed, her brows pinched in focus as if she had a hold she didn't want to lose. "Think of something else. Go somewhere else. Think of her."

Think of her—he'd done nothing *but that* for months.

Kai swallowed before shutting his eyes again. He forced his shoulders to ease, and he focused on that light again, traced it back to the memories it held.

"*The moon. Beautiful.*"
"*Yes, it is.*"
"*Are you from Callisto?*"
"*No...Io.*"

The feeling of magic spread further over his body. From his chest, over his shoulders, down his back, up his neck, but a piece of him fought against it. Only a piece. But the other...

"*You did not mesmerize me.*"
"*The pounding of your heart says otherwise.*"

The other part of him, the void, seemed to like the magic and called him to embrace it.

To take it.

Kai battled that piece away, focusing on Isla. Only Isla.

"*I wasn't sure what to expect when I realized my mate was at that dinner, but you definitely weren't it.*"
"*Sorry to disappoint you.*"
"*You didn't.*"

Not at all.

She'd woken him up that night on the terrace like a new morning—a new beginning—and stoked a flame, encouraged it to burn, just enough, when it was ready to simply go out. Finally, with her, he could breathe. He felt hopeful. Saw a future.

"*I was blind to what was actually happening.*"
"*What?*"
"*I fell in love with you.*"

Words he never thought he'd hear her say. He had hoped, *hoped* that she could love him, hoped that she'd stay, but he never thought she would.

Kai pictured Isla sitting beside him at the tavern's bar. When he realized he fell more and more in love with her every second they spent together. Remembered the image of her. Not the tear-stained face he'd walked away from, but the one from last night. That glowed in the firelight as she smiled at him, as she moved on him. Pressed against his chest, her heat enveloping, *her* enveloping all his senses. When all he knew was a base need and the desire to worship her with everything he had, everything he was. Beautiful and powerful and yet, soft. Her skin, her curves, her lips. Her.

That void beckoned again, that well of power, as Kai's mind became clouded by shadows, and he suddenly felt like he was—everywhere. The light, her light, glowed and expanded out like a traced line through walls and barriers. He didn't push back against any of the magic. He pulled at it greedily as the void grew and all became clearer, as shadow swirled and eventually parted to—

Isla.

Only her face, her closed eyes. There was blood.

Kai nearly fell over when Raana ripped her hand away, them both panting. She braced herself against the wall, brushing off Adrien's assist, and looked Kai up and down with wide eyes. Though she didn't speak. Because she didn't know what to say or because Kai had interrupted before she could. "Was that real? Where was that? Where is she?"

"I don't know where that is, but I think I can get you close," Raana said with hesitance, fear.

His fists were clenched at his sides, his wolf an unsteady presence beneath his skin. Suffering, angry, and ready to do whatever was needed to get Isla back.

"How?"

"I'll need you to let down your defenses. Entirely. You need to completely yield to me."

Kai ground his teeth, nostrils flaring as if that were the craziest thing he'd ever heard.

"I *cannot* have you fight me on this," she said. "So, if you want to get to her fast *and* alive, you need to trust me."

Kai looked to Adrien, who nodded like he'd gone through whatever the reason was for Raana's outstretched hand. He'd yielded to the witch and seemed fine—and he would never jeopardize Isla. This was Kai's only chance.

So, he took Raana's hand, but watched her this time, even when her eyes had closed. Kisses of cold traveled up his body, and he glanced down to find darkness like its own entity surrounding him. Cloaking him.

"You need to yield," Raana said firmly, her voice straining. The grip she had on him tightened, and instinct howled for him to rip away, to figure another method of finding Isla, but this was it.

Kai let go, embraced whatever was happening, and everything dropped out from under him. All he knew was the feeling he likened to being underwater and a swirling obsidian sea of nothing and everything, everywhere. Of bone-chilling cold, but comfort. Familiar.

And it was only a blink.

Kai was unsteady on his feet when they met cold stones. His mind spun as he coughed and observed crystals embedded in walls and wooden markers. It took little for him to deduce from what he'd been told that they were in the tunnels beneath the pack. Kai wouldn't bother asking Raana how she did it. He didn't care. Not now.

Raana had said she could get him close, and Isla wasn't here in front of him. The tunnel spanned in two directions.

Bringing his wolf to the surface to hone his senses, he listened to the crowd moving above them, frantic footsteps and yelling. There was the moving of metal, like a gate. They were beneath the arena. This was where Isla had been.

He sought her scent, tried to find that thread of light, a shred of their bond, but it was nothing but a flickering ember. What had happened to her?

But then—there. A familiar scent, a rise of roses but twined with something metallic, putrid.

He ran left.

Raana made some kind of sound before her footsteps echoed behind him. They faded into nothing. Even without his wolf, he was faster.

And then he found her.

"Isla!"

Both relief and disbelief washed over him before dread and grief overtook them.

Kai skidded to a stop at her body on the tunnel's stone floor. Her skin was pallor, covered in slow healing scrapes and bruises and caked in blood. Not her own. Not one he recognized. It was a mixture of drying crimson and then something even darker. Like bak.

The smell.

It *was* bak.

They'd been down here. She'd fought them.

Why the fuck didn't she say anything?

Why was that even a question—he knew the reason.

Kai dropped to his knees, not recognizing the black cloak wrapped around her. She was entirely bare beneath. He pulled her head up into his lap, finding her heavier than he'd expected as he cradled her. She was completely out, and her skin when he went to touch her cheek was freezing.

"Isla." His voice was just above a whisper but echoed through the cavern.

This was a nightmare.

He put a hand over her chest, even though he could hear it—her heart was beating but barely. The same sluggish cadence of her breathing.

"Isla," he chanced again, brushing blood-crusted hair from her face.

He needed her to open her eyes, needed to hear her voice. "Isla, wake up." He dug deep for that light again, that thread, but it was dimming, nearly gone. *Fuck.* "Come on, I'm not doing this without you."

He lifted his head, taking in what was around them. He had no idea where they were, how to get her out.

He heard footsteps and panting, followed by, "Oh no."

Kai turned to Raana, and with the movement came the jostling of tears he hadn't realized were forming. "Can you get us out of here?"

Raana frowned. "I can barely travel with one person. I could never do both of you."

"Then take her."

"It's not an easy trek, I can't guarantee she'll survive it."

"What *can* you do?" Kai snapped, and Isla's breath caught, becoming shallower. He lowered his head in an apology. "She's dying." The word gutted him. "And there's nothing I can do. And I can't…I can't lose her. *None of us* can lose her, so if there's something you can do. A spell or a potion or whatever, I need you to do it. Take whatever you need from me. Any of my power, all of it. Just save her."

Kai's chest felt heavy, his breath hampering as if he could feel Aeterna over his shoulder, ready not to take him away as he'd wondered this morning, but for her. And he decided at that moment, he'd fight even death and eternity to get her back. Whatever that power was inside him shuddered at the thought.

"My mother's a healer," Raana began quietly, and Kai turned to her again. "And I know…something, but my magic is different. I don't know if it'll work. If I'll hurt her or hurt you."

Hurt him?

He didn't ask. He didn't care. "Please."

Raana gave a firm nod and went to kneel at Isla's other side. "Whatever you do, whatever you feel, don't let her go. Focus on that piece of her. You're her anchor. If she starts to pull away—just—just tell me." She hesitated before removing the ring from her finger. A hiss passed her lips, and Kai felt something in the air shift, a new scent emerging, and energy beating and twining with the world around them.

As she steeled herself, he inspected the metal. Iron.

The pieces came together oddly hard and fast, and he lifted his head, examining Raana's face, her ears—round, not pointed. But…

"You're fae."

He didn't know why he was so certain.

Raana stiffened and met his eyes briefly. There was something different about hers now, brighter. She looked down. "Half. My father's fae, my mother's a witch." She reiterated, "So my magic is different."

As if witches couldn't have gotten worse.

Alpha Cassius couldn't have known, even he wouldn't have been reckless enough to tangle with the fae. There was a reason they'd been locked out of the mortal plane, their continent now left to ruin. How did Raana even exist?

As if she could see Kai's train of thought, feel the weight of history, Raana drew her hands back. Hurt crossed her face. "Do you still want me to—"

"Do it."

There was no other option. Isla would die.

Raana nodded before tying back her hair. She pulled at the chain around her neck, settling a smooth crystal, opalescent, over her chest. As she clutched it tightly in her hand, she muttered something in that foreign tongue, and then her eyes closed as her palms hovered an inch from Isla's body. "I'm starting. *Don't* let go."

There was a near-pleading part of her voice that also said, *don't let me kill her.*

The air cooled and pulsed around them, and Kai took hold of Isla's hand. As Raana murmured, darkness seemed to gather, encroaching on them, circling them. The shadows responded to her, danced with her, and Kai's thoughts briefly wandered to the scarce amount he'd ever learned of the forsaken fae courts.

His heart was a steady drumming, calling Isla's to beat in time, and he tightened his hold on her as he pulled at whatever shred of their bond was left, what he could forge.

For a moment, he thought he felt a warmth, that glimmer of light, but the air became sharp. The light fell away.

"Shit."

Kai snapped his head up. Raana still had her eyes closed, still focusing. Sweat beaded on her brow. "What happened?" he asked.

"Don't let her go," she gritted. The shadows began pulling up Isla's body, her lower half disappearing in time with when Raana's hands, her forearms, starting from the tips of her fingers, became piercing white light that morphed into the darkest black at her elbows. Kai squinted as the air became hollow. He had a sinking feeling that Raana hadn't wanted to push this far as she flickered between becoming something else entirely. Darkness like webs crawled up her skin, consuming her. This wasn't the magic of witches. This was something greater.

And that part of him, that power, responded to it. Rose not to fight but to acknowledge, to greet. Kai blinked at her before feeling a pull.

He looked down, and through the darkness, Isla's cuts healed and her skin warmed. Yet still, she was fading. Something was happening that he couldn't see.

"Stop," he said, reaching out to Raana. Her skin was so cold it burned, and the touch sent a chill down to what felt like his soul. He threw a wall up to it, to fight it away. "You need to stop."

He was about to lunge at her when everything fell. Darkness collapsed and evaporated like a cloud of smoke, tendrils snaking away but not far as if waiting for when she was ready to call upon them again. Raana blanched, falling forward and bracing herself on her hands as sweat poured from her face, mixing with what seemed to be tears. She shuddered, swallowing hard as if to keep down bile. She met Kai's concerned stare. "I can't go anymore," she panted and flicked her gaze to Isla. For Kai to check, to see.

He looked down, brushing his hand over her cheek. There was color to her face, and her heartbeat was slow but becoming faster. Faster.

"Isla," he called, not broken but hopeful. And though she did not answer—

She opened her eyes.

CHAPTER 57

ISLA

The first thing Isla registered was pain.

Though not the burning she'd known before everything faded but a soreness. Like her body had been through hell and reworked over. Her mind was swimming in a sea of attempted understanding as she peeled open her eyes, and then she was floating in an ambient blue. Everything was blurry for a moment, and each one of her senses felt dulled. For a moment.

All awareness of her surroundings came at her hard and fast. The craggy, rock-lined passageways with crystals in the walls, the chill in the air, the warmth she was resting on—and the someone who was holding her hand.

She turned her head, wincing, and her eyes fell onto a handsome face backlit by crystal blue. A face she thought she'd never see again.

This was a hallucination. It had to be. The witch's first method of torment, how she'd break her.

Isla's heart clenched but she wouldn't cry. Wouldn't give her the satisfaction. But she couldn't stop herself from chancing the word, his name. "Kai." Her mouth was dry, her throat still raw and she braced for another dose of poison. For the image of the man she loved to fade into mist.

But his touch on her cheek as he brushed it felt so real. The smell of him, the sense of him in a distant way she'd felt before they'd mated, felt right.

There was a line of silver along the bottom of Kai's eyes, the same storm clouds, and the way the corners of his mouth moved revealed the slight dimples she knew.

If this *was* a trick or an illusion meant to rip away from her and break her apart, she'd accept it. She'd live in this joy that sparked in her chest. This fantasy where she had him.

"A run," he said, his voice guttural like he really had been crying.

"Really?"

Isla's heart stopped. Could this be happening?

She released a breath, afraid to make any sudden movements, but she couldn't fight the tears. "You won?"

His throat bobbed and he nodded. She noticed the blood on his skin over where many cuts had healed. Blood that belonged to him and Brax, and there on his neck, the faint lines of her mark. All of this—too hard to replicate if it hadn't been true.

"Kai," she sobbed his name this time as if she were still trapped and needed help. Needed him to prove it to release her from this prison she'd put herself in.

"Isla," he said, and the floodgates opened, tears flowing down her cheeks as he pulled her up higher and hugged her to him.

Isla was shaking, shuddering with sobs as she wrapped her arms around him. She pulled herself even further into the embrace with as much strength as she could muster, burying her face into his neck, breathing his scent, timing his heartbeat. And despite everything she'd endured, it felt like nothing in the world could touch her.

"You're okay." She felt his lips against her skin as he whispered and kissed it. "We're okay." She pulled back to look at him, finding wetness on his cheeks, too. She wiped it away and felt him lean into her touch as he repeated, "We're okay."

She closed the distance between them, and the kiss was the last piece she needed to ground her in the fact that this was real. That she was with Kai, that somehow, she'd…gotten away.

That question fell briefly to the back of her mind as she relished in the comfort, in his touch. But something was still off, missing or dimmed between them. Missing within her.

Isla broke the kiss, her breathing heavy as she pressed her forehead to his and said, "The bond–it's–I can't…you're not there."

Kai squeezed her tighter. "I know."

He didn't ask why, not yet. Likely afraid to push her.

Isla reached inside herself for another piece but found stillness. More tears threatened to fall. "My wolf is gone."

Kai's jaw tightened beneath her fingertips, and he pulled back only slightly to better view her face. "What?"

Isla braced herself and looked around them. If this was real, if Kai had her....

"Did you kill her? The witch?" She pulled herself from his grip, and when she turned to settle her back against him, not keen to entirely leave his hold, she found they weren't alone.

A woman was kneeling beside the far side of the cave wall, her skin flushed and hair messy. She donned a familiar uniform of maroon and gold. Isla pressed into Kai whose arms had circled her waist. "Who are you?"

The woman offered a tight but pained smile. "Raana."

Isla's brows lifted. "Adrien's witch."

She laughed but cringed at what must've been a tinge of pain. Isla resonated with the feeling. Every movement of hers still ached. "Is that what he calls me?" Raana attempted to joke.

"She healed you." Kai's breath was warm against her skin, and Isla snapped her head around to look at him, eyes wild. Seeming to understand her concern with the implications, he said, "You were dying. There was no other way."

Isla's mouth felt like sandpaper as she swallowed. She knew immediately that no one could ever find out.

"Where's the witch?" she asked, and Kai's brows drew in confusion. "She had me. The one who had your brother and father killed. She was here, and—" Isla fought to stand, dread sweeping through her. "We have to help my mother."

"Your mother?" Kai wouldn't let her get up. He took her face in his hands and forced her to look into his eyes. He scanned her features before giving a glance at Raana. Questioning and threatening as if asking, *what did you do?* When he returned to Isla's face, he spoke gently, "Isla, your mother's dead."

Isla shook her head so furiously it hurt and wrenched out of his grip. "She isn't. She's the one who…" She didn't know how to say it—or did but didn't want to. "She killed them."

It wasn't hard to understand what she meant.

Kai's eyes widened, and Isla didn't know if she should've been grateful not to have such a keen awareness of what he was feeling. "What?"

She brought her hand to his face, his features crestfallen as he shook his head, and Isla *knew* he was refusing to believe that the person who'd taken his family, who'd ruined his life, who he hated with every part of him was the mother of the woman he loved.

Guilt roiled in her gut. "I'm sorry," she said, and her voice became a small plea. "She didn't know what she was doing. The witch had complete control of her."

Kai said nothing, only blinked and looked away, jaw tensing. Isla didn't know what she could do. There was no way to make it easier, no words she could say. She remained there until Kai met her gaze again, his eyes frighteningly dark. "Where is she now?"

Isla fought every instinct in herself to jump up and run these tunnels to track her down. "I don't know." She settled just a bit longer to let him adjust as she explained, "There were bak down here. We fought them together, but one got her and she was bleeding, badly. When I went for help, the witch got me. She killed Renoir, or her rogue did. His body's somewhere towards the end of the tunnel wherever we were. She did something to Brax, so he'd have a better chance fighting you."

All Kai seemed to be able to do was listen and then sigh a curse. All of *this* had occurred while he was fighting. He pinched the bridge of his nose and ran his hand over his hair. "Well, that makes sense."

Isla inclined her head, recalling something of the witch's words in her haze. *I want to see what he's capable of.* "How did you beat him?"

Kai cleared his throat, his shoulders rising and falling. "I just—did. He got tired, I guess."

Isla narrowed her eyes, knowing he wasn't being entirely truthful. "The poison she uses, it kills our wolves. That's how it works. It breaks our bonds."

"Our magic can't break your bonds." A voice came from behind her. Isla turned to find Raana looking less sick than she had. "I mean, maybe, what do you call them, chosen? Because those are fabricated, but true bonds like yours are a deity's power. We can't counter the gods —even though some of us think we can."

Her features fell as she spoke, and Isla was surprised she knew so much about wolves and their bonds.

"So, the bond will come back?" She felt her face light up.

"It will probably heal as your wolf does," Raana said. "It's not dead, but it's very, very hurt. I couldn't do anything to it without risking you losing it all together or—changing it. You. I suspect it will recover on its own in time."

Isla's favorite phrase. Recover in time.

Kai's loosened grip gave her the opportunity to find her footing. Her limbs felt unfamiliar beneath her, trembling and weak, but strong in new ways. She was about to say they needed to go when her fingers brushed against the fabric on her skin.

Fabric.

She hadn't been wearing anything before.

The piece was heavy on her body, rigid with dried blood, and there was a tear on the side. This was the cloak her mother had been wearing.

Had she given this to her? Was she okay?

"Where are we?" Isla spun so fast that she fell, kept only on her feet by Kai who'd risen to stand beside her.

He appeared a bit dazed as if still trying to process, but made sure to catch her eyes. "Hey, Warrior Princess, you just nearly died. You need to slow down."

She sighed. "We have to find Renoir. We can't leave him down here."

"Of course not." Kai's hand brushed her waist like he couldn't stop himself from touching her. To make sure she was really there. For a brief second, he looked away from her. "What, uh, what do you want to do about your mother?"

Isla couldn't miss the conflicted look in his eyes, and she had a horrible feeling this would be a battle for a while.

She looked at the cloak she was wearing and remembered the shame that had painted her mother's face. All along, she'd been evading the witch and never revealed herself to Isla, to anyone. She'd wanted to remain hidden.

And maybe there was a selfish part of her that wanted to *keep* her hidden, too. To keep her safe.

She answered truthfully, "I don't know."

∽

Finding their way out of the tunnels had been a nightmare, but when they finally breached the surface into the arena, Kai located the first guard he could and called off a search. Apparently, he'd had the whole pack scattered and looking for her.

So, their secret was out.

And soon, it was joined by more.

Because when he explained where Renoir's body was located, he also explained the tunnels as he brought the rest of the guard that had gathered to it. He issued a new search for the witch, for the rogue that Isla had given a vague description of but refrained from mentioning the identified murderer of their late alpha.

They didn't mask their scents when they finally settled back in the room they'd been waiting in before the fight, cleaning up and claiming new clothes. They knew that the news would spread that Isla had been found, so they waited.

She'd only just hidden away her mother's cloak after changing into a tunic and pants she'd found when the door of the room was nearly broken down. More faces she never thought she'd glimpse again flooded the room.

Isla was the first target for the onslaught of embraces. Even *Jonah* hugged her. Ameera, too. Davina was a mess of joyous cries. One second, she was lifted by Rhydian, the next, her brother who she embraced with guilt in her heart for what she now knew. She cast a quick look at Raana and Kai as she hugged him, both sworn to absolute secrecy, for now. She didn't know how she'd tell him but knew the second she did, he wouldn't rest until he found Apolla and brought her home, whether she wanted to be tracked down or not.

"If you died, I would've killed you," Adrien said, circling his arms around her.

Isla leaned into his chest, snickering, before noticing his attention had also drifted elsewhere to where Raana stood in the room's corner.

The witch pretended she wasn't paying attention to him, but Isla had been there before. Raana made the mistake of turning for a better glimpse at Adrien and accidentally met his eyes. She looked down, suddenly very interested in her shoes as she mumbled something under her breath. Adrien laughed, something sparking behind his eyes, and Isla bit the inside of her cheek.

The last person he'd ever looked at like that was Cora—which meant he was in trouble. More than she'd initially thought.

So, she'd learned on their trek back, Raana wasn't only a witch but also bore the blood of fae. And putting aside her own fears and confusion, amidst the gratefulness, over what that meant for her healed self, Isla was concerned for her friend. This woman he held a fondness for may as well have been a bak. The pack, all the wolves of the continent, would view her the same way.

The amount of trust that Raana must've had in him, magic on her side or not, was great if she'd been willing to risk herself like this. To come here. To surround herself with predators that would've shredded her apart the moment they broke the surface if she hadn't recast the enchantment meant to mask her from them.

Maybe she'd be useful in tracking down the other one.

Adrien left Isla, crossing the floor, and she watched closely as he and Raana spoke.

"Thank you," he said to her.

Raana shrugged as if feigning it wasn't a big deal. "Now, we're even."

Adrien grinned again, but it fell promptly. "We should get back to my father. He's already on the boat to go back into the city. Now that the lockdown's lifted, he wants to leave immediately."

Isla glanced at Kai, also listening, his features drawn in a scowl. No meeting, no parting words, no congratulations, she assumed. If she could hear him through the bond, she imagined he'd been thinking, *good riddance.*

"We?" Raana asked. "I thought you didn't want him to know you were here."

"It'll just be a few long lectures and painstaking visits from Winslow," Adrien said. "I promised you'd get home safely."

Everyone else's behavior was just as awkward and unsure now while Raana and Adrien said their goodbyes as when they'd met the Heir and her brother. Though they didn't know Raana was a witch, only thought she was of Io.

Isla let her arms linger around her friend for a few seconds longer than necessary, and he held her tighter. By the time they saw each other next, she'd likely be the Luna of Deimos, and they'd officially be on different sides.

But before they could go, there was a knock at the door, and silence descended upon the room.

Ameera was closest to the entrance as if guarding it, and pulled it open to reveal Imperial Beta Malakai.

He looked at no one else, not his runaway son, the Heir, or the other bewildered gazes. All he focused on was his daughter, tears lining his eyes.

"You're okay," he said, and for a moment, Isla forgot everything else. She forgot about the challenge vote and Io's agenda.

Isla rushed for her father, and as he hugged her, she could feel him shaking like he was fighting back tears. She let a few of hers fall, and when he looked up at the nearby Sebastian and didn't get angry, but beckoned him over, a couple more broke through. The weight of the body missing felt heavier now than it ever had, and Isla might've cried harder for it. For the words she just couldn't speak.

Malakai stepped back from them and bowed his head to Kai. "I'm sorry. If I had known…I would've pushed harder."

"Pushed harder?" Isla was wiping her face with her sleeve. "You said no?"

Malakai wasn't allowed to say what he'd voted, but with the slight tip of his head, Isla knew. He let out a grunt as she nearly tackled him with another hug, and now his body shook with a chuckle.

"I need to go," he said as Isla broke from him, and his eyes went to Kai again as the alpha shuffled closer. Isla took the few steps needed to stand at his side and looped her arm around his, then took his hand in hers. Malakai gave a tight smile and his voice was strained. "You have her?"

Kai's grip on her hand tightened. "Always."

Malakai swallowed hard, failing to subtly wipe his face, and bowed to them both. He turned to his son.

"I think I'm going to stay for a bit," Sebastian said before glancing at his sister and brother-in-law. "If that's okay with your majesties."

Isla furrowed her brows. "Why do you want to?"

"Give my baby sister some support, destroy anyone who opposes you, and I hear this Equinox thing's pretty fun," he drawled.

Of course, overprotective, and of course, a party. She wouldn't want him any other way.

"You're still not coming over," Ameera muttered from close by.

Sebastian put out a hand to signal he was aware of that but grinned like he knew it was only a matter of time. He said to their father, "I just want to be sure I won't be declared a rogue by not coming home."

Everyone seemed to grimace at the word.

Malakai said, "I'll make sure you're cleared." And he and Isla exchanged one last embrace before he, Adrien, and Raana left.

"So, what now?" Rhydian asked. "You won. It's over. The Imperial Alpha left with his tail between his legs. What's next?"

"You're probably wanted everywhere," Ameera said, then gestured between them. "Both of you."

Kai wrapped an arm around Isla's shoulders while hers went around his back. He looked down at her smiling at him and leaned down to kiss her forehead. "Yeah, well, it's late." He lifted his head and trailed his gaze along his family. "I want to go home."

CHAPTER 58

Isla and Kai were on the roof of the House, a landing of flattened stone amidst the sloping that Kai had apparently escaped to many times as a child. The perch offered a perfect view of the night sky, much like the overlook before the hall's window, but rather than feeling alone on top of the world, they were alone and hidden within it. What Isla had to behold in the cloudless sky was starlight and endless, uninterrupted darkness where mountains lay. The moon had disappeared somewhere behind them, bathing the city.

Though they'd gone through the motions of preparing for bed—cleaning and putting on their nightclothes—after their tumultuous exit from the arena, sleeping wasn't close to a possibility. And rather than go where they could bump into anyone when all they wanted was to be with each other, Kai proposed another one of his old hiding places.

As soon as he had laid down on the blanket they'd taken, Isla collapsed onto him. He let out an exaggerated grunt at the weight.

She murmured, "prick," and the only response to his answering grin was to bring her mouth to his. Something she thought she'd never be able to do again.

The kiss heated quickly as she felt his arms tighten around her waist and his tongue trace along her bottom lip, coaxing her to open for him. She did so happily, and his hands wandered beneath her nightgown and robe of thin red silk, mapping her skin and the parts of her body he knew very well. An assurance that she was here, every part of her. She was alive. He was alive. They were both okay.

But those moments when they thought they'd lost each other

couldn't be forgotten. Both of them nearly dying couldn't be forgotten. They could chase them away, though. With this. These grounding touches and reminders.

Alive. Alive. Alive.

Before long, Isla was on her back, humming in response to Kai's praises for what she'd done to protect the city, their people while his lips teased her neck, her breasts. She moaned softly as his fingers worked between her thighs, drawing out pleasure and drawing away sense as she unraveled, his name a whisper to the stars. But it wasn't enough, not even close, and though earlier they'd felt too tired for sex, she needed him now.

They didn't waste time removing all their clothes, and their kisses were furious as he positioned himself and she wrapped her legs around him. All thought eddied to the gradual pressure and feel of him until there was no space between their bodies. Isla's fingers tightened around the muscles of his arms as they both sighed, grateful and relieved, and Kai stilled, taking her in beneath him.

Even without the bond, without its pulling and twisting and thrumming, that connection she felt to him was still there. The love she had for him was still there, stronger than it ever had been.

Kai had become everything—he *was* everything—to her.

Her best friend, her lover. With her unknowingly in her past, now forever her present, her future. Someone who would hold her when she fell apart. Who would fight and fight for her until he had nothing left. Being fated to him, having the bond, that was extra. She would've fallen for him a million times over without it.

And as Kai smoothly drew out before driving back into her, smothering her gasp with a dizzying kiss…as he echoed each deep thrust with a murmured sweet nothing onto her skin…as she met him with her hips stroke for stroke, greedy and desperate for more of him, harder, faster, their bodies still completely in sync, she knew he felt the same.

But the darkness couldn't be staved for long.

As they settled, coming down from their highs with her head on his chest as he held her tight, reality crept back in, the euphoria fading.

Isla's mind wouldn't turn off and couldn't be distracted by the languid patterns Kai drew over her skin. Random bouts of fear at what dwelled in the surrounding shadows had her heart skipping. Pondering where her mother was and hoping she was okay, thinking of all she'd gone through, had it breaking.

It still didn't feel real.

The challenge was over. Kai had won but with the witch out there, with the quickness that Alpha Cassius had left, it only felt like the beginning of something so much worse.

Swallowing down panic and the threat of tears, Isla gazed at Kai's face, noting the way his brows were furrowed as he studied the sky, as if scouring it for an answer. He couldn't escape anything either. There was a lot for him to be thinking about, too much, but Isla tried to figure out what was bothering him most.

After they'd exited the arena and had come upon the crowd, Kai's initial desire to go home had dwindled—Isla's too—as they realized just how many people they had to look after, to protect. All the danger they might be in. Even if the guard had been notified of the witch, the tunnels, and the potential for rogues within the territory, and had been dispersed accordingly, they wanted to oversee it all. To make sure no path was left unfollowed or stone unturned, which received heavy pushback from everyone who knew and cared about them.

Rhydian had called them stubborn, workaholic bastards and told them an alpha and luna were no good dead from exhaustion—not the best choice of words, again. He remained out with the guard units, guiding their search along with Ameera, eager herself for a distraction, it seemed, as Kai had ordered Ezekiel be taken into custody.

Sol would oversee his questioning, find out everything the old beta knew of the witch, and starting tomorrow, Kai would begin anew. Decide on his new second-in-command, turnover his council, and first thing in the morning, Isla would endure her first lessons with Marin in preparation to be the luna at his side.

When early afternoon came, they would make their first official address together, and judging by the way reporters and their flashing cameras followed them through the city to their car—honed on her, shouting questions *her* way—they were all eager to pry Isla apart.

But there was something they'd shouted, unrelated, that now nagged her, too.

She chanced an old question to her mate. "What happened to Brax?"

Kai tensed, glanced at her once, and then back at the sky. "I don't know."

Earlier, he'd said the rogue had just "gotten tired" and she assumed that meant Kai had taken the chance with his sluggish movements to kill him.

But according to reporters, that wasn't the case.

Apparently, the rogue had just lost his mind. Completely broke down on the stone and clawed himself to death. A downfall so horrible to watch that people had to look away. Some thought the pressure of the fight had become too much for him to take, or he truly didn't want to become alpha. Isla wondered if it had something to do with the witch's wearing enchantment, but that pondering didn't last long the more she observed Kai.

Isla sat up, and the act of her pulling away from him made him frown. "What happened?"

A look, a mix of fear and pain and confusion, crossed his features. He wouldn't turn to face her. "You were dying, and I didn't know what else to do."

Isla swallowed, feeling her heart beat faster in her chest. "What happened?"

Kai appeared to gather his thoughts by counting each of the stars. "You know how they teach us to mind-link after we learn to shift?" Isla nodded, though she knew teaching methods differed between instructors, between packs. She'd been taught to go about it like seeking a doorway that only existed and was left open as wolves. They could shut each other out if they wanted. "It was like that, but...I could go further. I *went* further." Kai adjusted in his spot, but he didn't sit up. He placed his hands on his stomach, remaining focused on the sky, and with every following word he spoke, sounded more troubled. "It moved so fast. I wasn't in the arena anymore. Just in this mess of his...thoughts, his feelings, and these moments, like pictures, like...memories, I don't know... but he couldn't get me out. I could see everything—places he'd been, people he knew, had interacted with, and now, when I think about it, maybe I saw that witch. Maybe I should've stayed. But you were dying, and I needed to find you. I needed the fight to be over. So, I..."

Isla did her best to mask that she was shaking. If anything, she'd blame it on the cold that had settled in the air, *not* on the fact that this scared her. Only because she didn't understand. Because she questioned reality again. "You what?"

Kai grimaced, closing his eyes as if he were reliving the moment before he snapped them open. "I let the power guide me, and I tore it all apart. I tore *him* apart—from the inside." The words were so quiet like he hadn't wanted to speak them.

Even without the bond there, she could *see* how he felt. It practically radiated from him. Disturbed and shattered. He grew distant. Isla wished she had something encouraging to say, but she was still trying to wrap her mind around it. When the silence between them became too long, too much, she reached out and brushed his face.

Kai barely reacted to the gesture. His eyes, which had become glassy, remained upwards. "I have never heard anyone scream like that, *felt* anything so horrible, and I know he was a rogue, and he was trying to kill me, and in the end, I won, but I feel sick. And I can't stop thinking about it." He clenched his teeth. "It's not normal, it's not right, I can't explain why I can do it...and you know what the worst part is?" A pause. He opened and closed his mouth, shook his head, unsure what he wanted to say or how to say it. "I don't know if I can stop myself from doing it again."

Isla had never seen him so broken, so bare, so vulnerable. So *terrified*. And of himself.

She leaned down and kissed his temple before hugging him so tightly that her muscles strained, just as they had when she'd embraced him in the tunnels. Again, she was fearful he'd fade away, only this time, not into an illusion.

"It's getting worse," Kai said through a hard breath. He slid an arm around her, accepting her warmth. "Something's wrong with me."

"No," Isla said firmly. "Nothing's wrong with you. It's just different." She lifted herself to look at his face again. "Do you think you should talk to someone?"

Finally, he met her eyes, and something about seeing her face made him relax. "Like who?"

"A healer or one of the priestesses? An Elder?"

"No," Kai breathed, his gaze going to the stars again. Isla was about to pry for what he was thinking when he said, "While Raana was healing you, or even when she was helping me find you, I swear her magic called to me. To whatever this is."

Isla blinked. "You think it's magic?"

"I don't know what to think, but I'm not a witch. It's just this —*thing*," he said. "But I don't want anyone to know. Not until I figure it out."

"*We'll* figure it out," Isla pressed, and when he met her eyes again, she smiled. "You could never hurt me. You will never scare me. I'm with you until the end and wherever we drift after, and if you have a problem with that, then talk to Fate because she's why you can apparently *never* get rid of me."

Kai hummed a small chuckle, his fingers tracing small circles over her skin. He brought his lips to her forehead in a gentle, grateful kiss before leaning his head back on the blanket again. "I suppose there are far worse fates than being destined to someone who doesn't know how to stay on her side of the bed."

Isla narrowed her eyes, holding back her retort as she climbed fully on top of him, smothering his large frame the best she could with her

A WARRIOR'S FATE

body, trapping him. A silent affirmation she wasn't going anywhere. "Or being fated to someone who'd be better off living in an eternal winter of Tethys with how cold he keeps the damn place."

A wider grin crossed his mouth as he studied her face and brushed back her hair, mussed from their lovemaking. "What was it you promised? With me to and through eternity?"

Isla nodded, remembering when she'd first told him she loved him what felt like a lifetime ago. She laid a kiss on his jaw. "To and through eternity."

ACKNOWLEDGMENTS

End of book one—four words I never thought I'd write for two different reasons.

One, because I wrote a book…like what? And two, because apparently, I've started a series. Oops.

When I started writing *A Warrior's Fate*—or rather, *The Alpha and the Warrior*—back in January 2021, I didn't know where I was heading. The idea stemmed from a fantasy novel I've always wanted to write but just couldn't find the right pieces to put together.

At first, in this former idea, Isla had still been Sebastian's little sister but was only the "female best friend" of a different main character. And it was like she *demanded* to be more. So I took her, and my setting of Morai, and began to craft a short "exploratory piece" to see what could happen. To see what I could learn about Isla and what I could discover in my "land of wolves". Then came her stubbornness and her drive, and then came Kai. Then their bond and his backstory, his family, the expansion of Deimos, the history…and suddenly, I had a four-book series plan.

Naturally, I was terrified to put the story out there. The only other book I've ever written and completed before was a serialized young adult romance in my teens. This was my first attempt at writing older characters, writing in the third person, building a world, a magic system, and creating a plot as complex as this one. There's quite a journey ahead of us here, if you couldn't tell.

But I made the leap and began posting the first chapters of *The Alpha and the Warrior* online. Fast forward a little over a year and a half later, and not only has that first draft been viewed over six hundred thousand times, but it has led me to find some of the most wonderful readers and fellow writers who have become dear friends of mine. If I listed you all by name, this would be pages longer, and I've subjected you to so many already. Just know if it weren't for you, this book wouldn't be in your hands right now.

So thank you, thank you, *thank you* to everyone I've met through the Inkitt community and the members of my *Alpha and Warrior* family who've supported me through all of this. From #TeamNoSleep chapter updates at 3 am to a published novel—who would've thought?

To my family and friends who have been wondering what the heck I've been working on day in and day out—one day, I'll tell you this book's title, and when that day comes, I'll also tell you not to read it or to "just pay attention to the plot". Thank you for putting up with me being distracted and sleepy a lot of the time.

To Jamie, who *has known* about this book from its little beginnings and is Sebastian's number one fan, thank you for listening to me ramble about plot ideas non-stop. You've been putting up with it since we were in eighth grade writing fanfiction and *finally*, I've written and finished something! One day, I will convince you to co-write a book with me, but until that day comes, I'll probably continue throwing plot ideas at you. Apologies in advance.

To Kirsty, probably Kai's number one fan, who's read this 217k word behemoth four times in I think two months and put up with my countless messages and questions. Thank you, thank you. I will never throw a book this long at you to edit again…I type this with my fingers crossed behind my back, but also with a lot of hope in my heart.

And finally, to you, the reader holding this right now, thank you for giving this book a chance. Whether you've been here from the beginning or joined us along the way, I hope you enjoyed following the start of Isla and Kai's journey as much as I loved writing it, and I hope you'll stick around for their next adventure.

Until book two!

- Melissa ♥

THE JOURNEY CONTINUES...

A QUEEN'S SHADOW

A WOLVES OF MORAI NOVEL

COMING 2023

TO BEST KEEP UP TO DATE WITH SERIES NEWS, FIND ME ON SOCIAL MEDIA OR VISIT MY WEBSITE.
WWW.MELISSAKIERANAUTHOR.COM

Melissa Kieran

Melissa Kieran is a Massachusetts native, who fell in love with storytelling and fantasy at a young age. Though, she began her author journey writing young adult romance when she was fifteen on serialized fiction sites where her stories have amassed over six million combined story views. Her fantasy debut, *A Warrior's Fate*, is her first attempt at the genre and the first book she's written in this "adult" chapter of her life.

When she isn't writing or dreaming up new stories, you'll probably find her searching for some sunlight, doing something "sciencey" (she has her degree in biology), or binge-watching a show she's likely already seen twice…or five times. She loves connecting with her readers, so don't be afraid to say hello on social media!

- facebook.com/melissakieran.author
- instagram.com/melissakieran.author
- tiktok.com/@melissakieran.author
- goodreads.com/melissakieranauthor

Printed in Great Britain
by Amazon